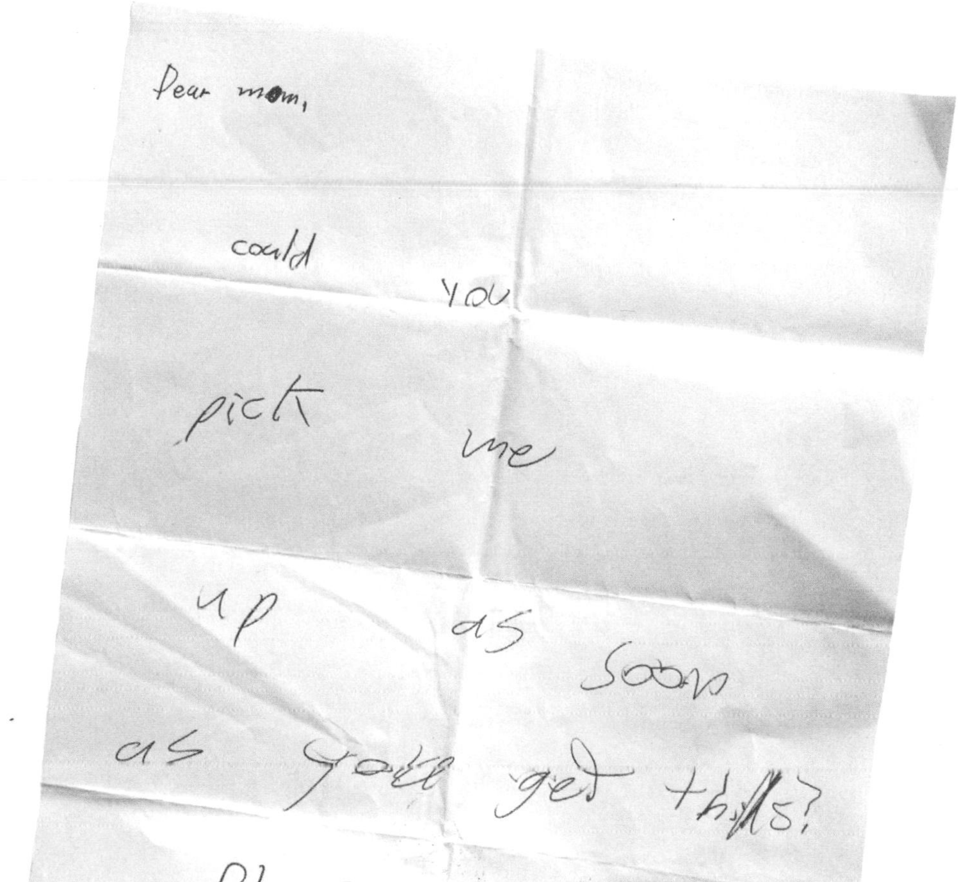
Dear mom,

could you

pick me

up as soon

as you get this?

PLEASE!

I'm desperate

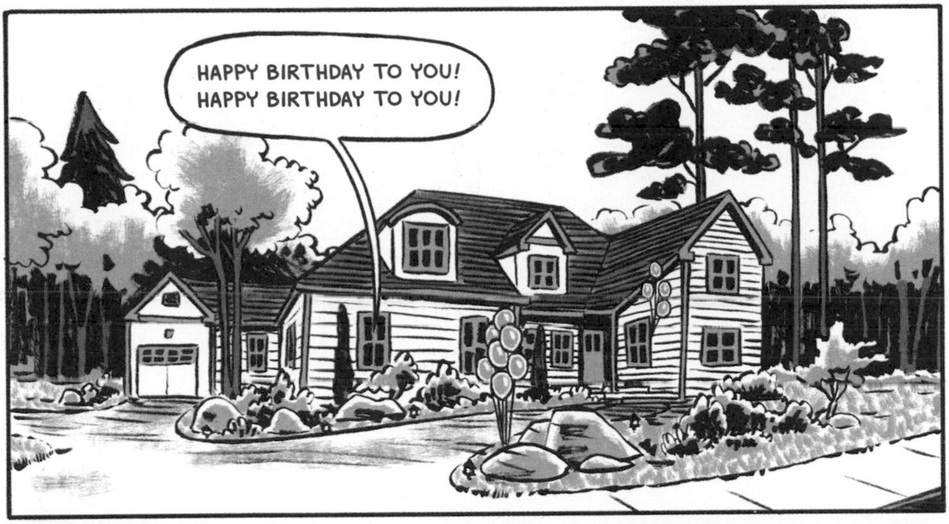
HAPPY BIRTHDAY TO YOU!
HAPPY BIRTHDAY TO YOU!

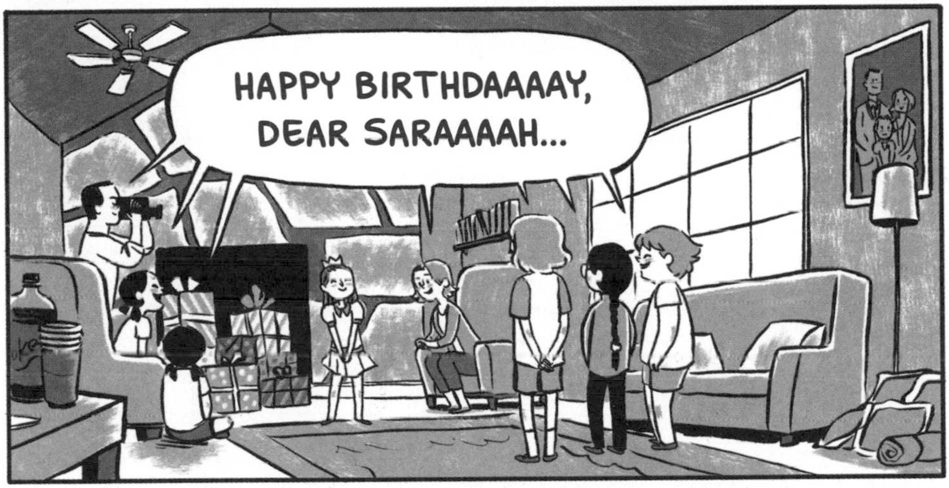
HAPPY BIRTHDAAAAY,
DEAR SARAAAAH...

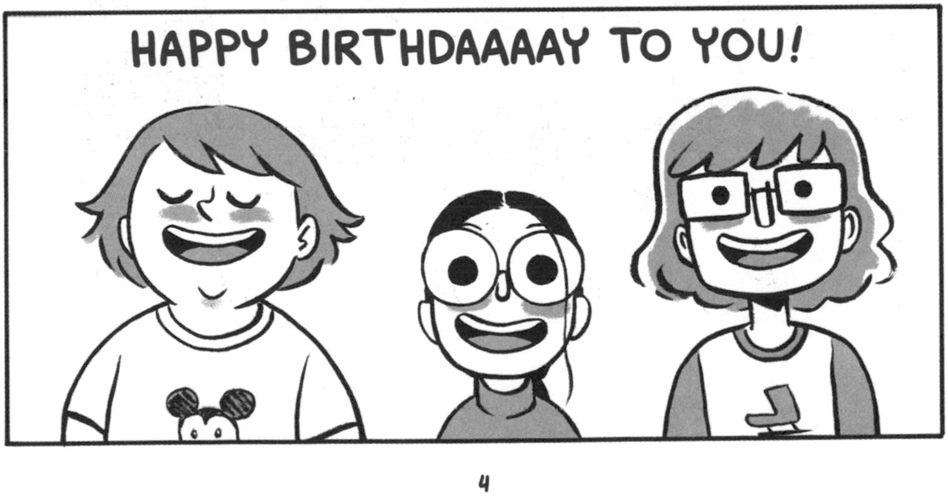
HAPPY BIRTHDAAAAY TO YOU!

BE PREPARED

VERA BROSGOL

COLOR BY
ALEC LONGSTRETH

First Second
NEW YORK

SARAH HOFFMAN ALWAYS HAD THE BEST BIRTHDAY PARTIES.

I THINK I HAD THE RECIPE DOWN.

CARVEL ICE-CREAM CAKE. VERY IMPORTANT.

cookie

vanilla

chocolate

PIZZA HUT PIZZA. STUFFED CRUST A MUST.

earrings

GIFT BAG FULL OF HIGH-QUALITY PARTY FAVORS.

AND MOST IMPORTANT, IT ABSOLUTELY *HAD* TO BE A SLEEPOVER.

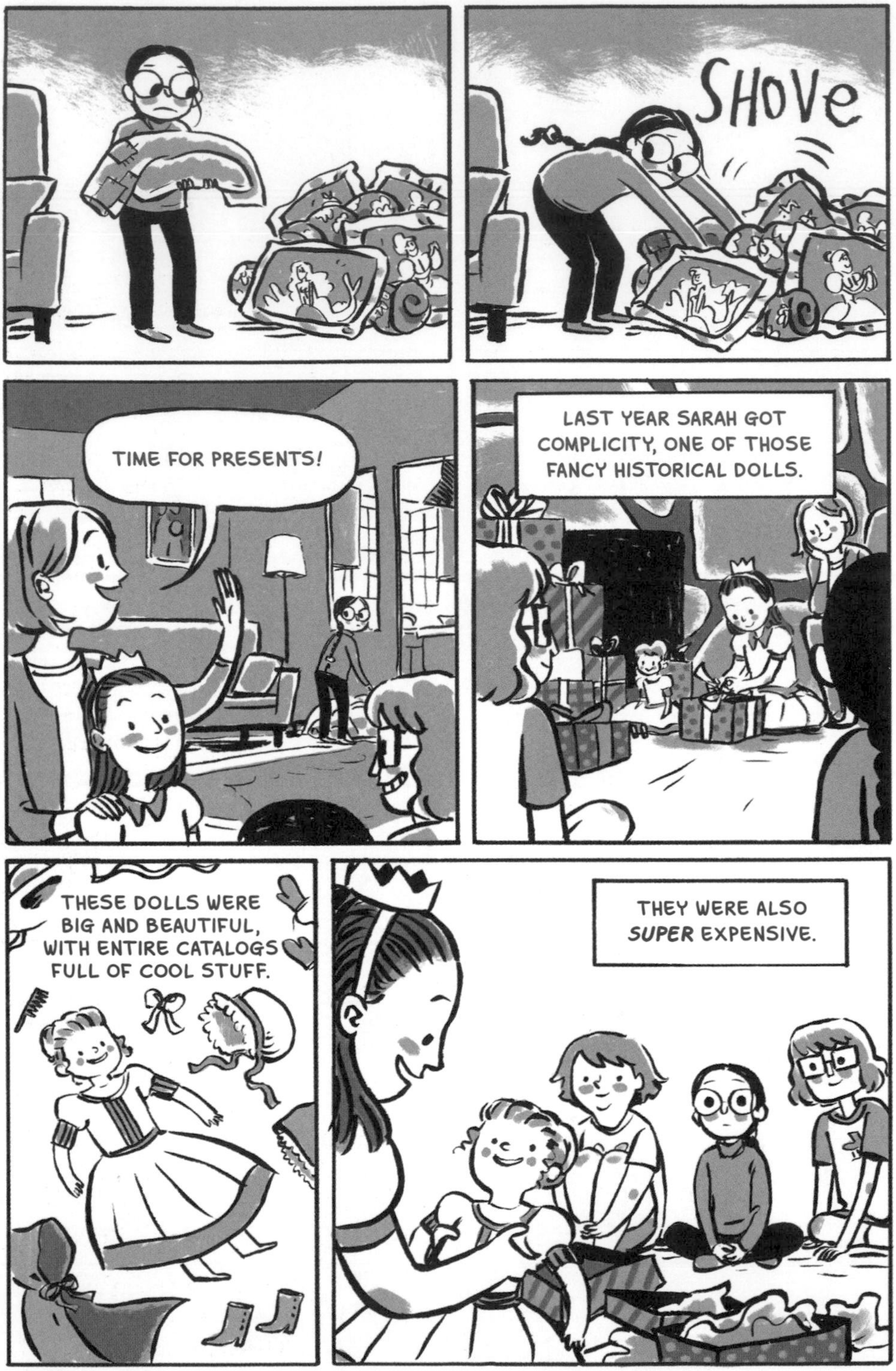
SHOVE
TIME FOR PRESENTS!
LAST YEAR SARAH GOT COMPLICITY, ONE OF THOSE FANCY HISTORICAL DOLLS.
THESE DOLLS WERE BIG AND BEAUTIFUL, WITH ENTIRE CATALOGS FULL OF COOL STUFF.
THEY WERE ALSO *SUPER* EXPENSIVE.

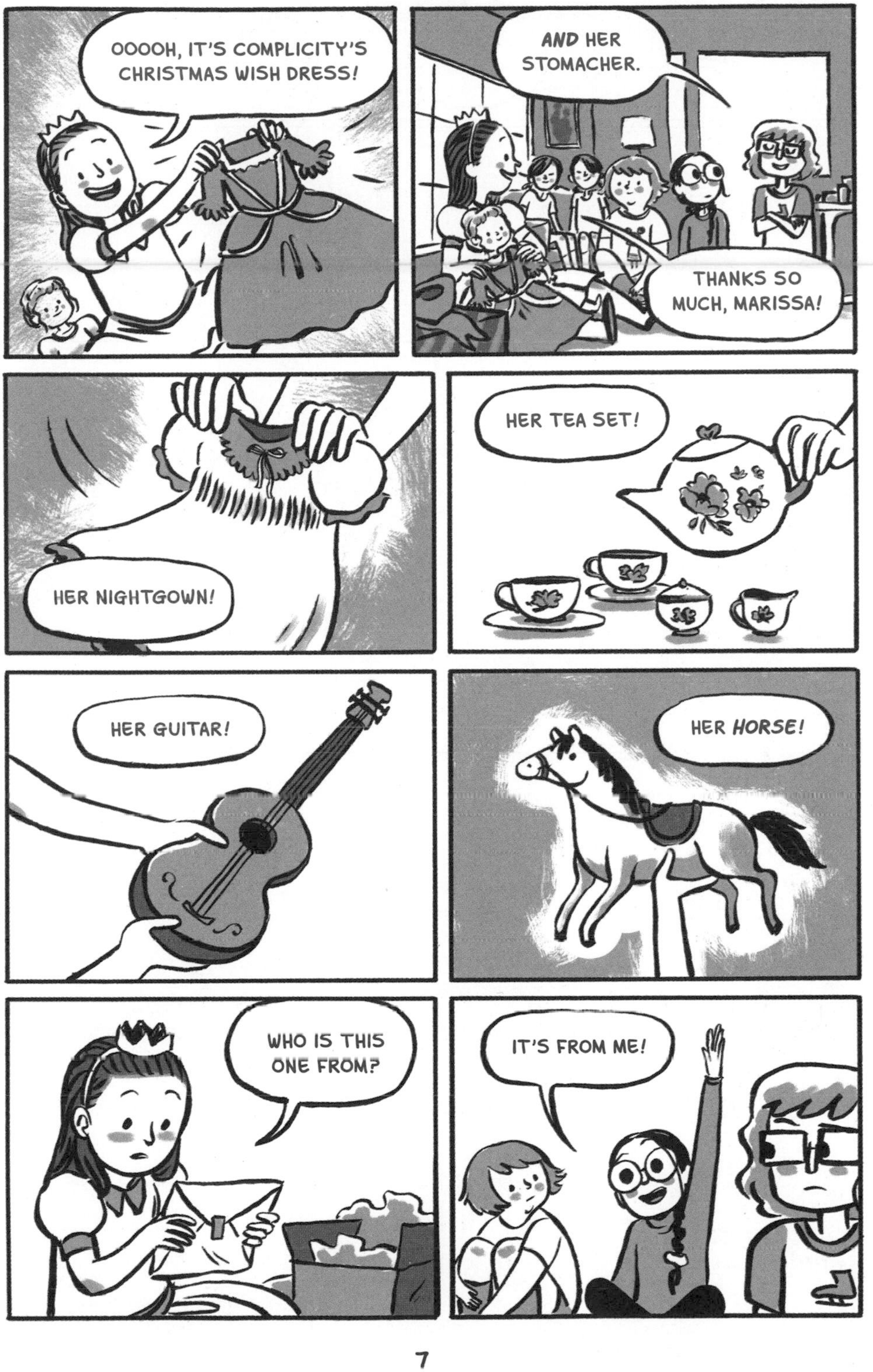
OOOOH, IT'S COMPLICITY'S CHRISTMAS WISH DRESS!
AND HER STOMACHER.
THANKS SO MUCH, MARISSA!
HER NIGHTGOWN!
HER TEA SET!
HER GUITAR!
HER HORSE!
WHO IS THIS ONE FROM?
IT'S FROM ME!

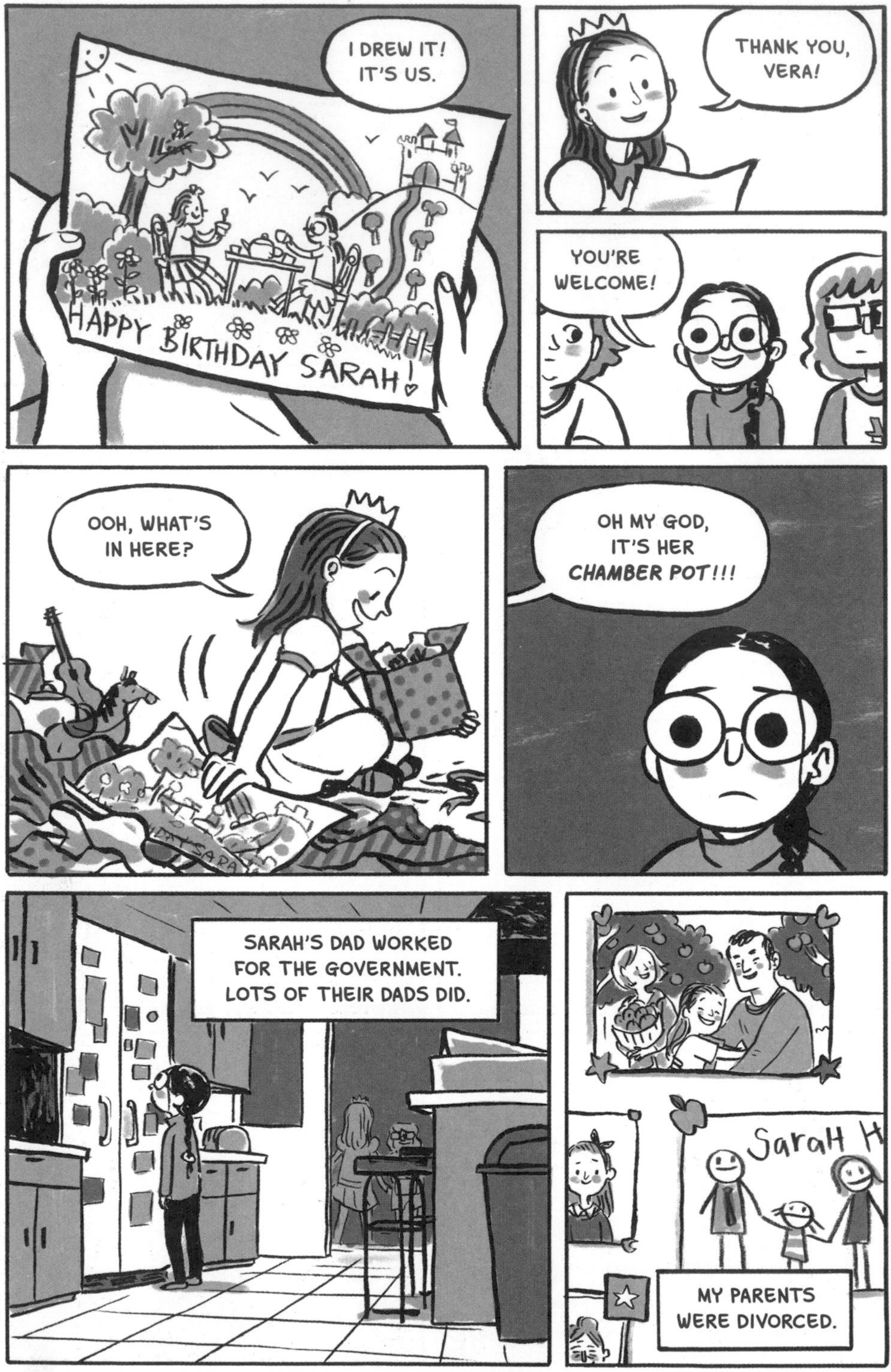
I DREW IT! IT'S US.
HAPPY BIRTHDAY SARAH!
THANK YOU, VERA!
YOU'RE WELCOME!
OOH, WHAT'S IN HERE?
OH MY GOD, IT'S HER CHAMBER POT!!!
SARAH'S DAD WORKED FOR THE GOVERNMENT. LOTS OF THEIR DADS DID.
Sarah H
MY PARENTS WERE DIVORCED.

I HADN'T SEEN MY DAD IN A FEW YEARS, BUT WHATEVER HE WAS DOING, HE WASN'T SENDING US ANY MONEY.

...HAHAHAHA!

OH, MELLY, THANK YOU SO MUCH FOR SAVING MY HORSE!

NO PROBLEM, COMPLICITY!

I COULDN'T LET HITLER GET AWAY WITH HIS EVIL SCHEME TO RUIN THE CHRISTMAS PARTY!

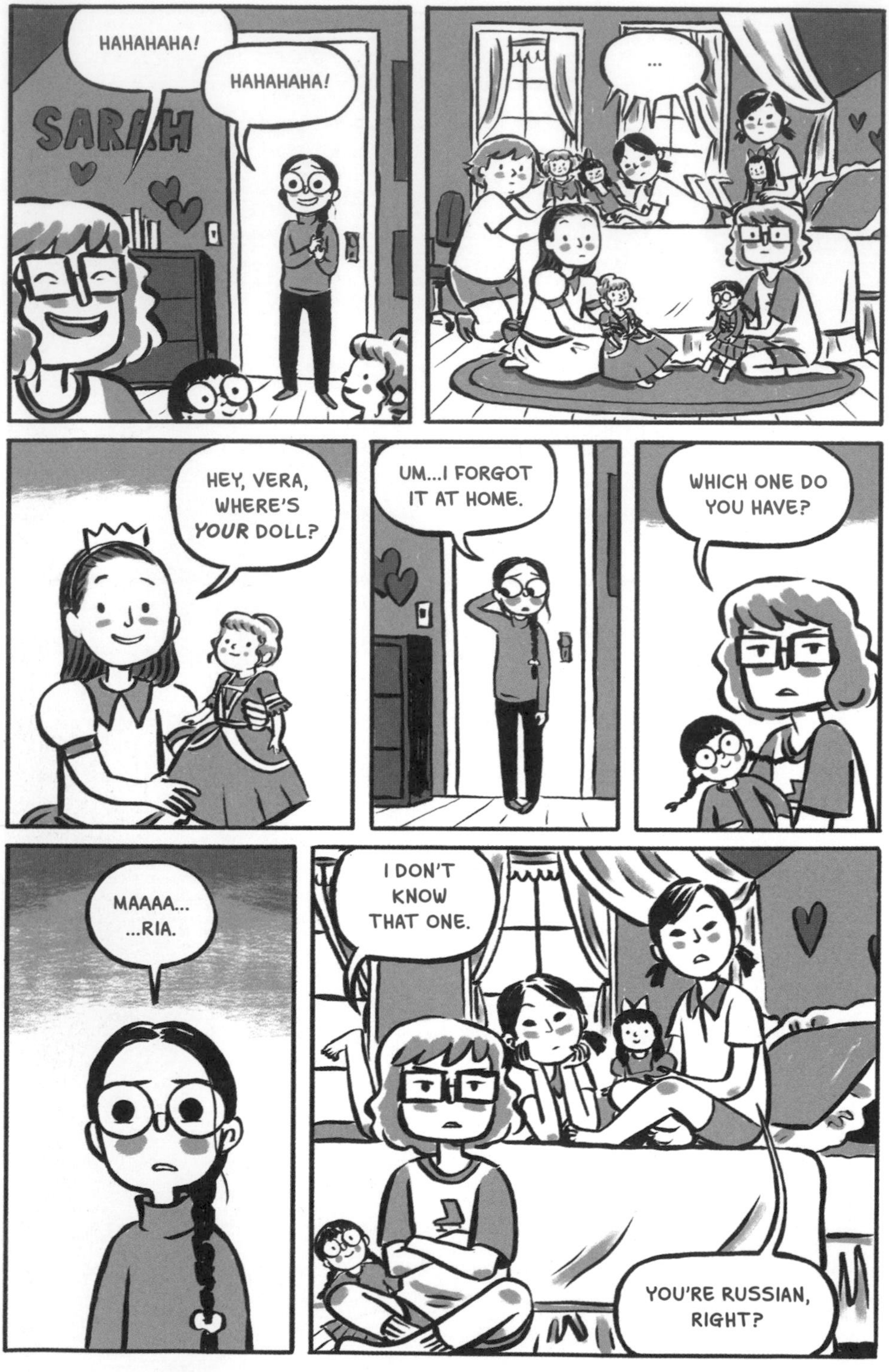
HAHAHAHA!
HAHAHAHA!
SARAH
...
HEY, VERA, WHERE'S *YOUR* DOLL?
UM...I FORGOT IT AT HOME.
WHICH ONE DO YOU HAVE?
MAAAA... ...RIA.
I DON'T KNOW THAT ONE.
YOU'RE RUSSIAN, RIGHT?

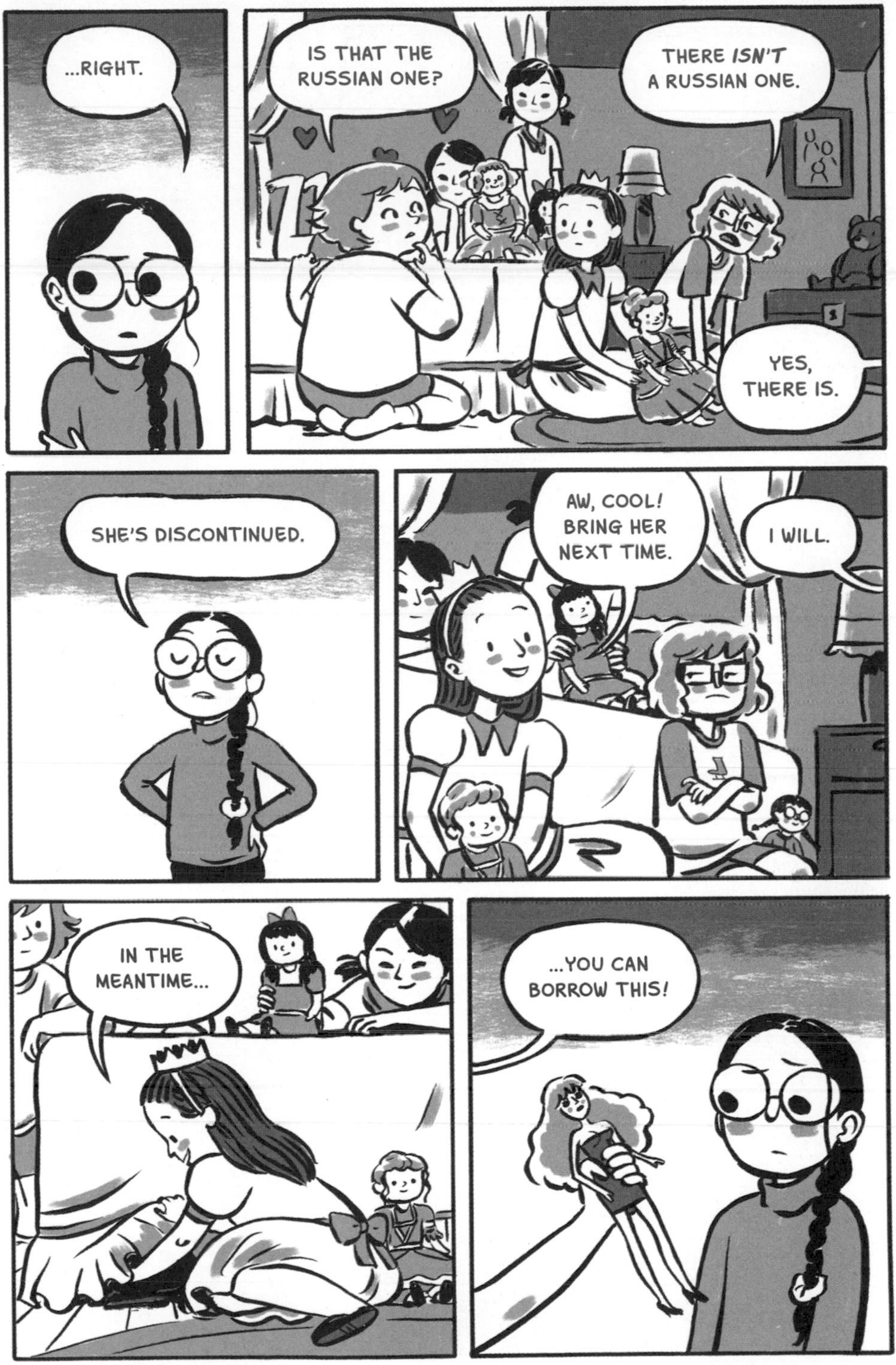
...RIGHT.
IS THAT THE RUSSIAN ONE?
THERE *ISN'T* A RUSSIAN ONE.
YES, THERE IS.
SHE'S DISCONTINUED.
AW, COOL! BRING HER NEXT TIME.
I WILL.
IN THE MEANTIME...
...YOU CAN BORROW THIS!

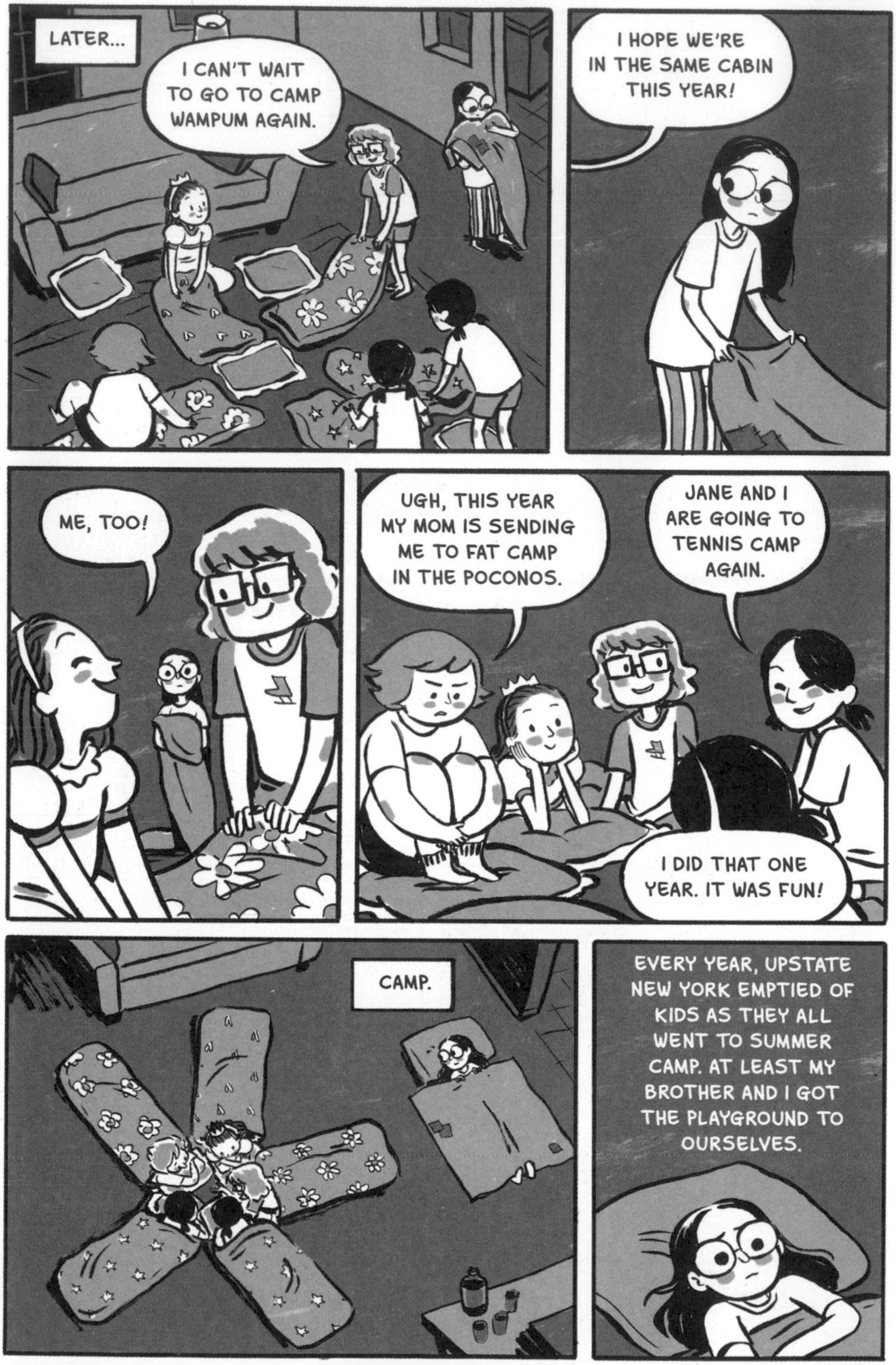
LATER...
I CAN'T WAIT TO GO TO CAMP WAMPUM AGAIN.
I HOPE WE'RE IN THE SAME CABIN THIS YEAR!
ME, TOO!
UGH, THIS YEAR MY MOM IS SENDING ME TO FAT CAMP IN THE POCONOS.
JANE AND I ARE GOING TO TENNIS CAMP AGAIN.
I DID THAT ONE YEAR. IT WAS FUN!
CAMP.
EVERY YEAR, UPSTATE NEW YORK EMPTIED OF KIDS AS THEY ALL WENT TO SUMMER CAMP. AT LEAST MY BROTHER AND I GOT THE PLAYGROUND TO OURSELVES.

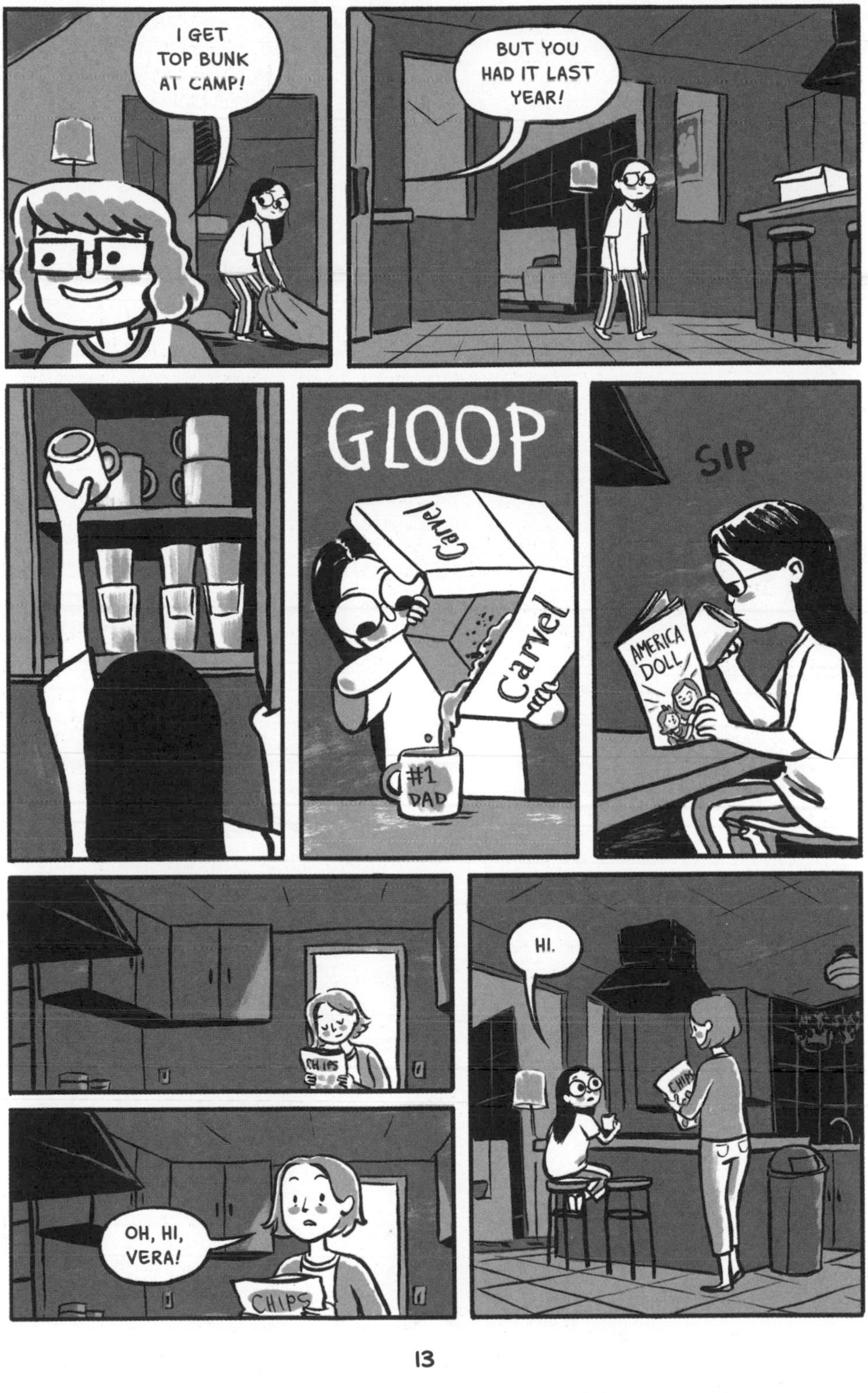
I GET TOP BUNK AT CAMP!
BUT YOU HAD IT LAST YEAR!
GLOOP
Carvel
Carvel
#1 DAD
SIP
AMERICA DOLL
CHIPS
OH, HI, VERA!
CHIPS
HI.
CHIPS

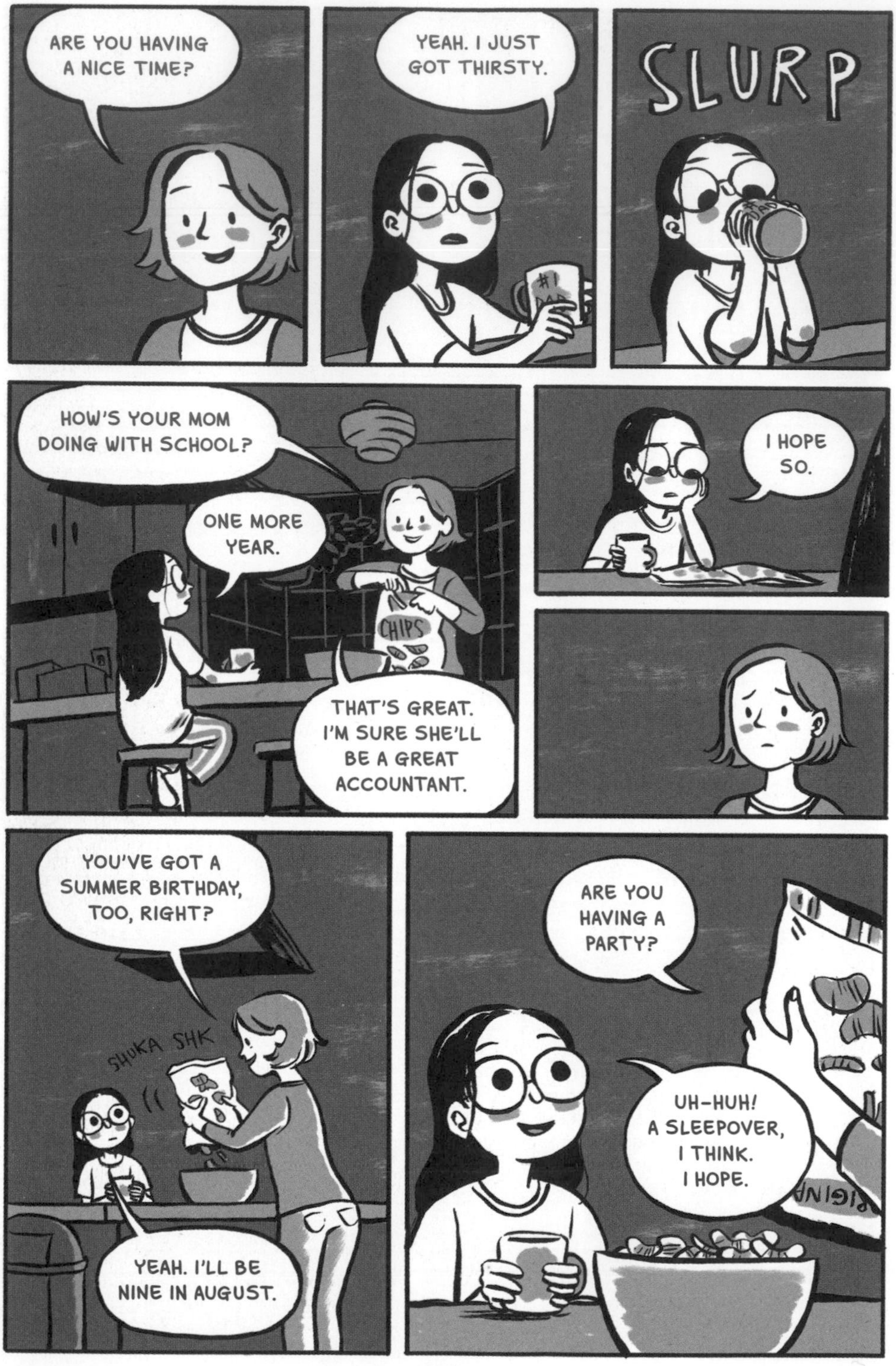
ARE YOU HAVING A NICE TIME?
YEAH. I JUST GOT THIRSTY.
#1 DAD
SLURP
#1 DAD
HOW'S YOUR MOM DOING WITH SCHOOL?
ONE MORE YEAR.
CHIPS
THAT'S GREAT. I'M SURE SHE'LL BE A GREAT ACCOUNTANT.
I HOPE SO.
YOU'VE GOT A SUMMER BIRTHDAY, TOO, RIGHT?
SHUKA SHK
YEAH. I'LL BE NINE IN AUGUST.
ARE YOU HAVING A PARTY?
UH-HUH! A SLEEPOVER, I THINK. I HOPE.

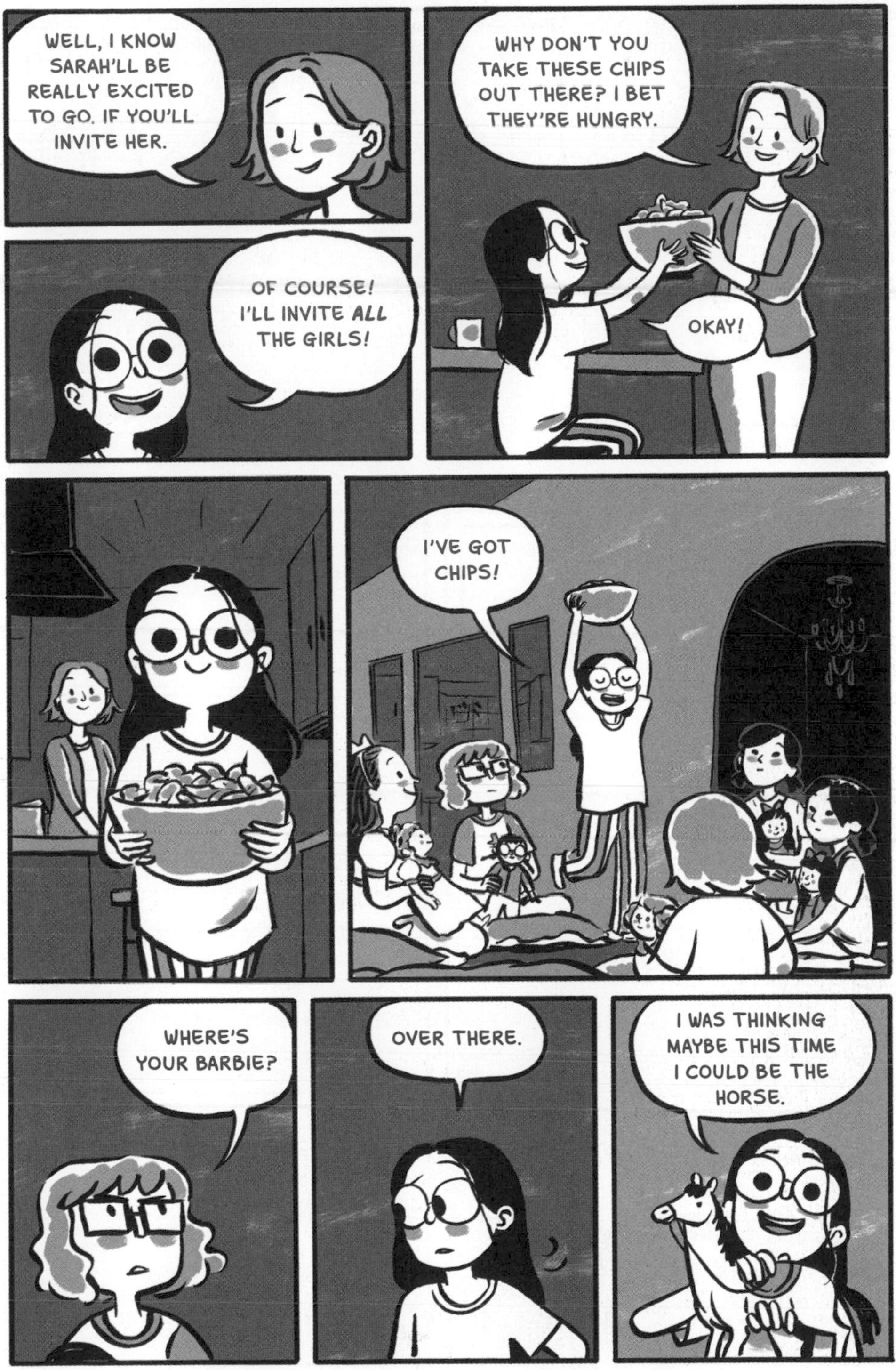
WELL, I KNOW SARAH'LL BE REALLY EXCITED TO GO. IF YOU'LL INVITE HER.
WHY DON'T YOU TAKE THESE CHIPS OUT THERE? I BET THEY'RE HUNGRY.
OF COURSE! I'LL INVITE ALL THE GIRLS!
OKAY!
I'VE GOT CHIPS!
WHERE'S YOUR BARBIE?
OVER THERE.
I WAS THINKING MAYBE THIS TIME I COULD BE THE HORSE.

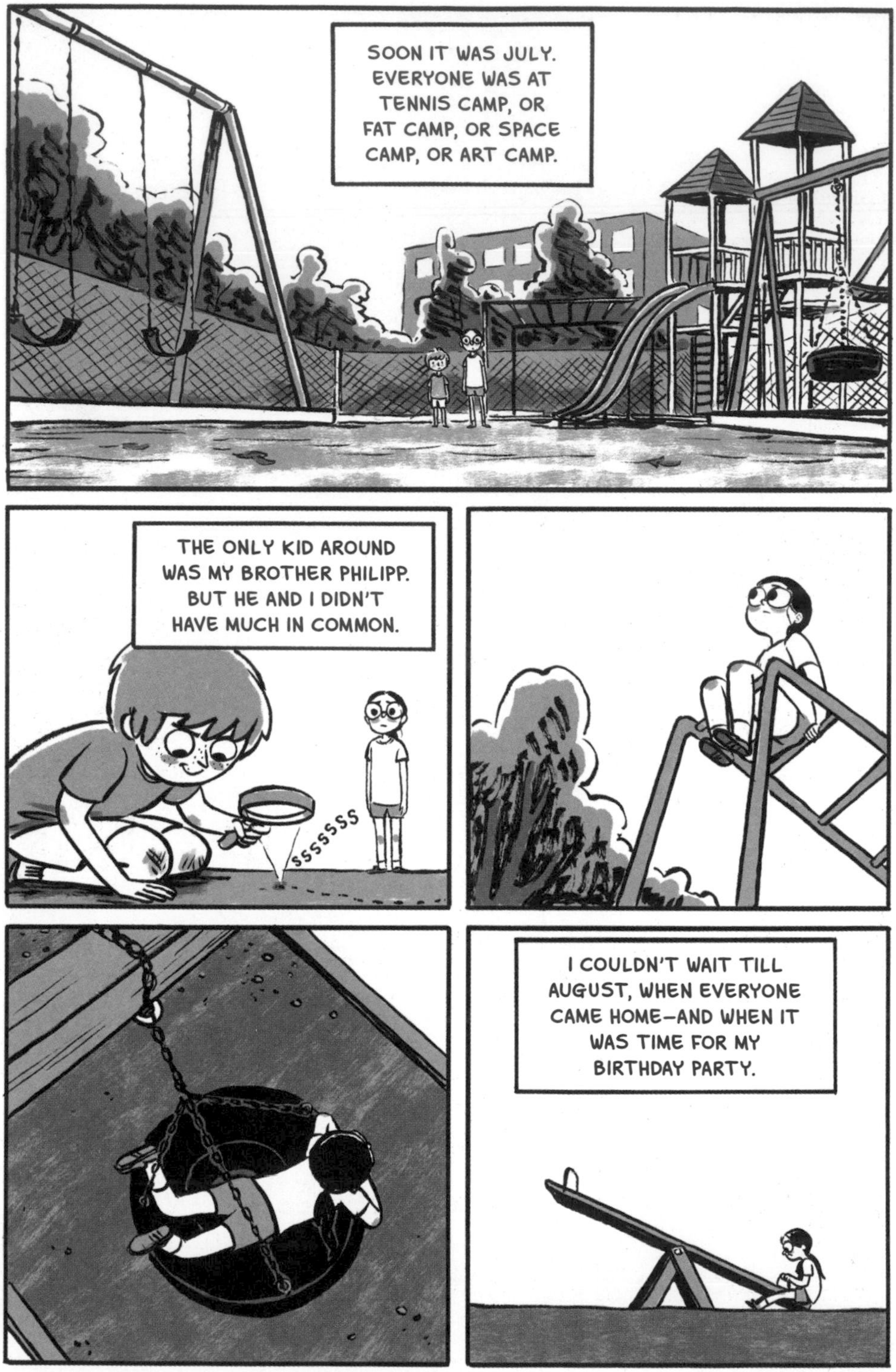
SOON IT WAS JULY. EVERYONE WAS AT TENNIS CAMP, OR FAT CAMP, OR SPACE CAMP, OR ART CAMP.
THE ONLY KID AROUND WAS MY BROTHER PHILIPP. BUT HE AND I DIDN'T HAVE MUCH IN COMMON.
SSSSSSS
I COULDN'T WAIT TILL AUGUST, WHEN EVERYONE CAME HOME—AND WHEN IT WAS TIME FOR MY BIRTHDAY PARTY.

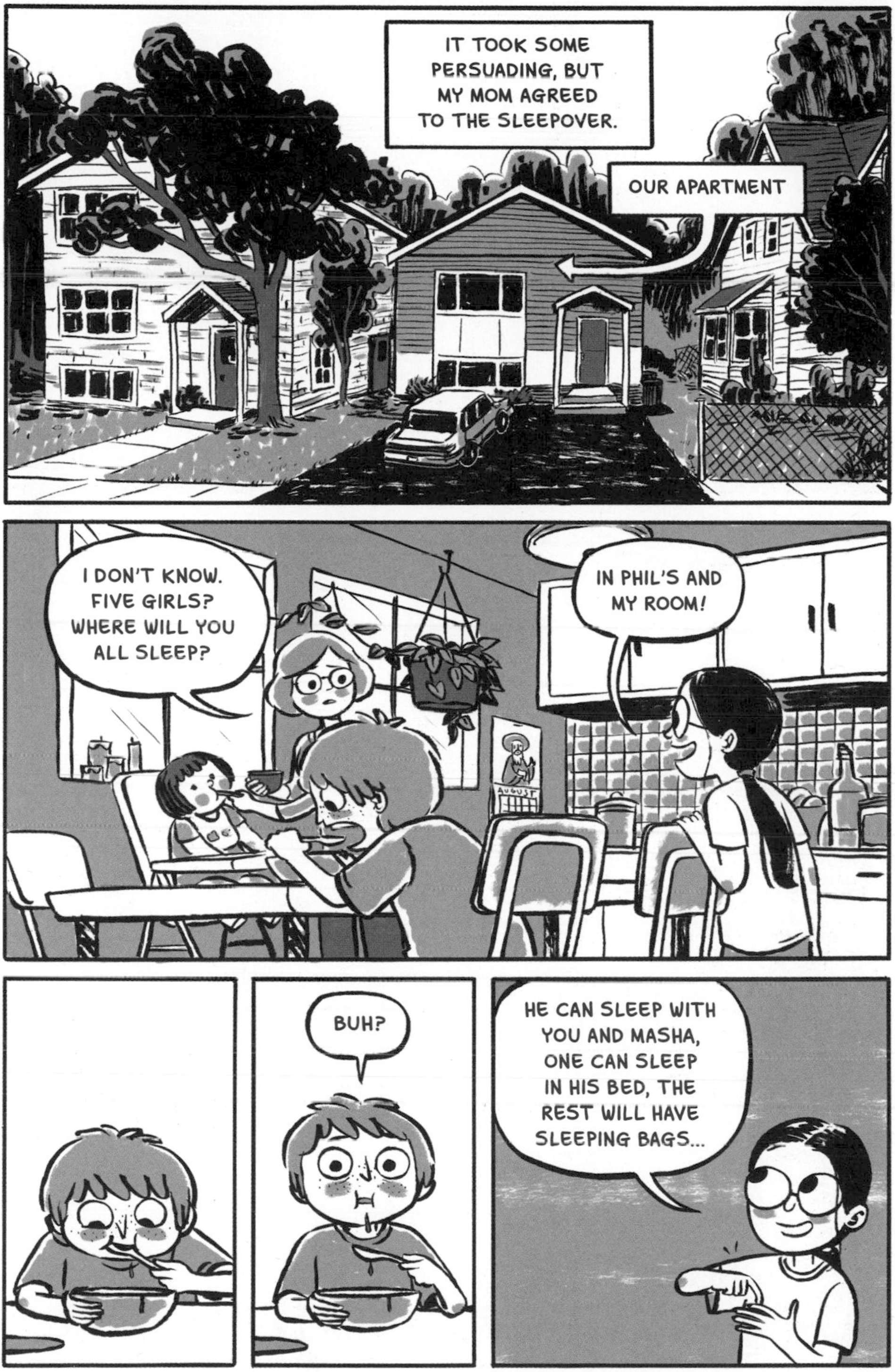
IT TOOK SOME PERSUADING, BUT MY MOM AGREED TO THE SLEEPOVER.
OUR APARTMENT
I DON'T KNOW. FIVE GIRLS? WHERE WILL YOU ALL SLEEP?
IN PHIL'S AND MY ROOM!
AUGUST
BUH?
HE CAN SLEEP WITH YOU AND MASHA, ONE CAN SLEEP IN HIS BED, THE REST WILL HAVE SLEEPING BAGS...

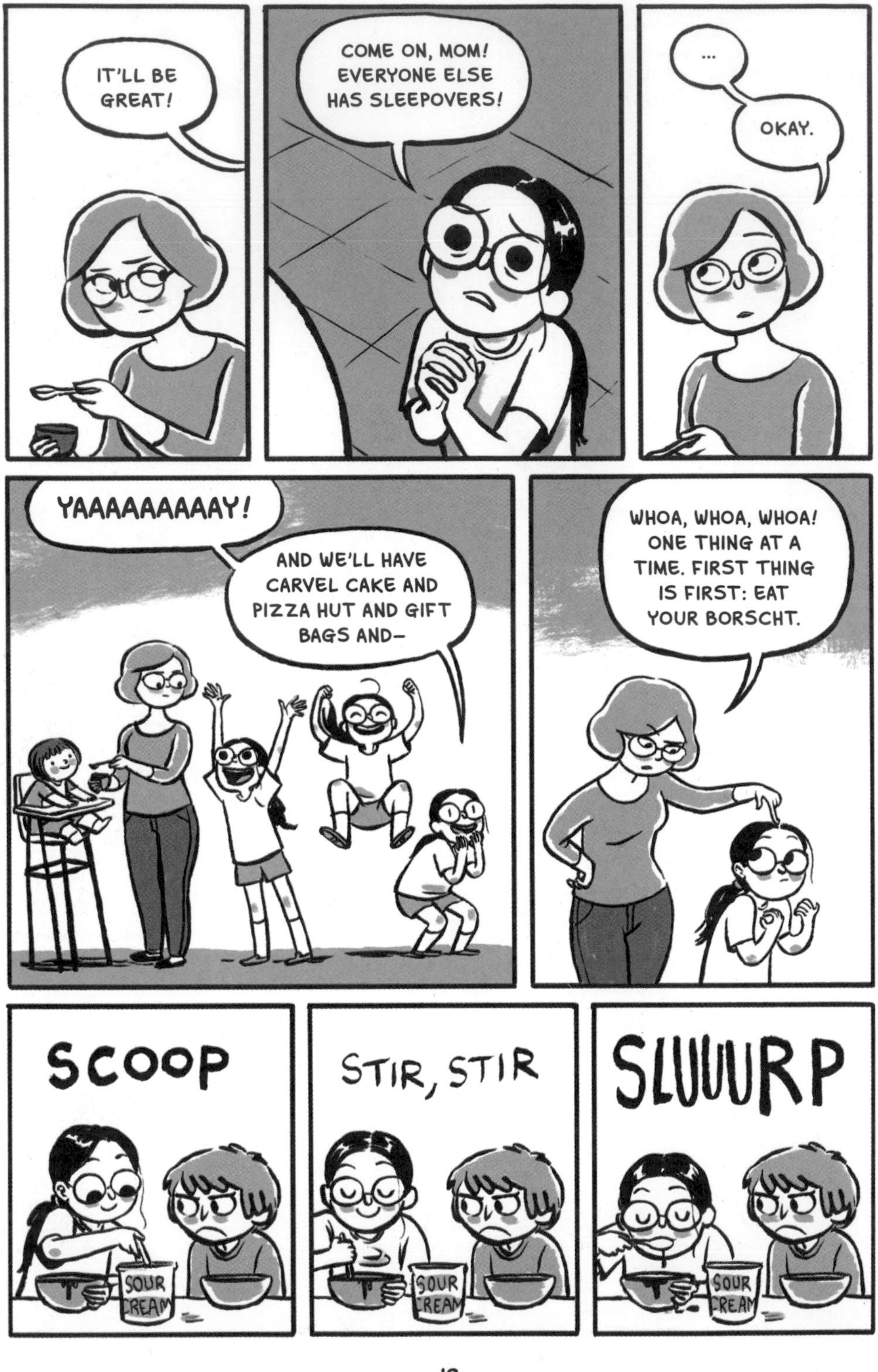
IT'LL BE GREAT!
COME ON, MOM! EVERYONE ELSE HAS SLEEPOVERS!
...
OKAY.
YAAAAAAAAAY!
AND WE'LL HAVE CARVEL CAKE AND PIZZA HUT AND GIFT BAGS AND—
WHOA, WHOA, WHOA! ONE THING AT A TIME. FIRST THING IS FIRST: EAT YOUR BORSCHT.
SCOOP
SOUR CREAM
STIR, STIR
SOUR CREAM
SLUUURP
SOUR CREAM

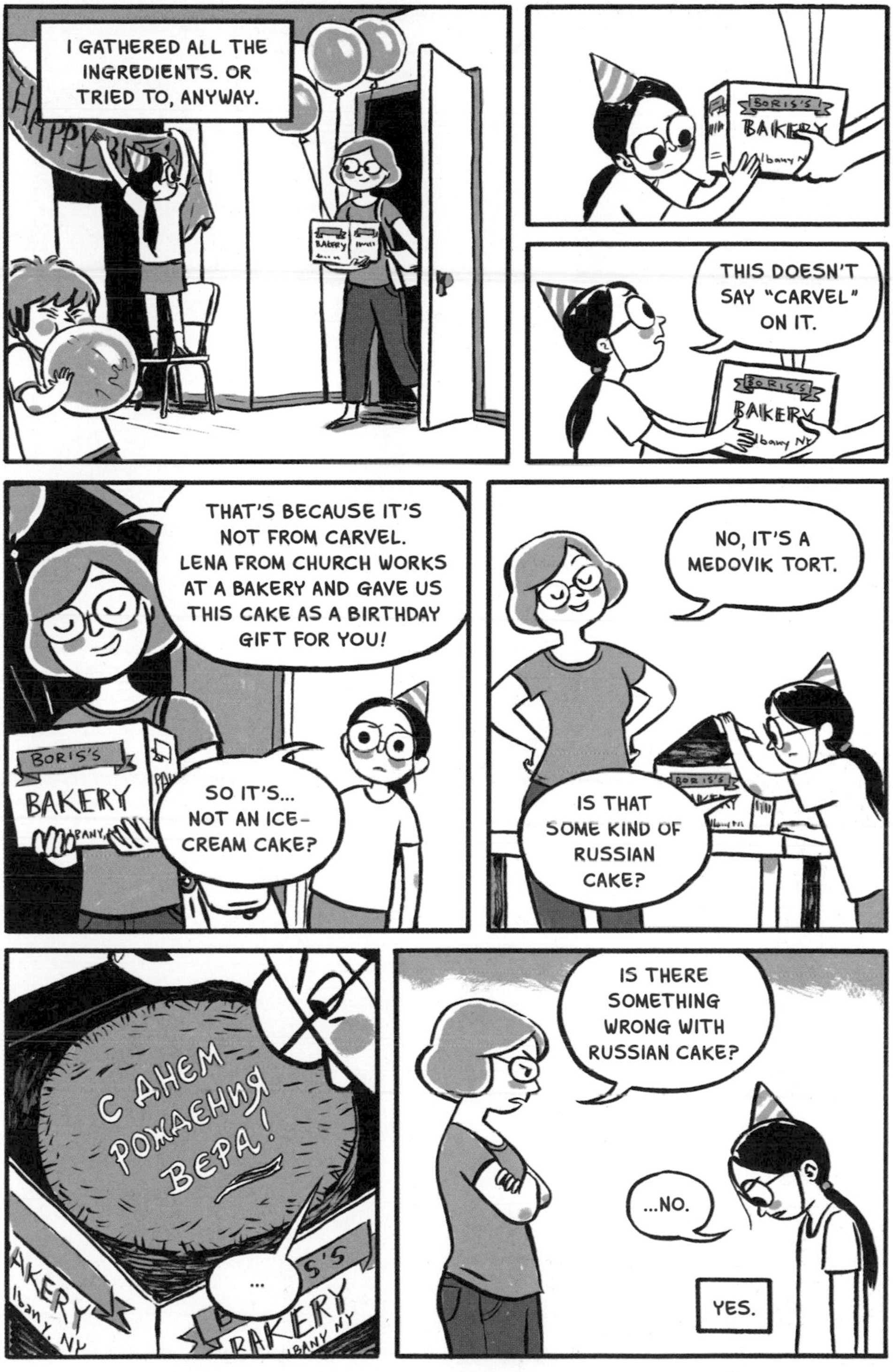
I GATHERED ALL THE INGREDIENTS. OR TRIED TO, ANYWAY.
BORIS'S BAKERY
THIS DOESN'T SAY "CARVEL" ON IT.
THAT'S BECAUSE IT'S NOT FROM CARVEL. LENA FROM CHURCH WORKS AT A BAKERY AND GAVE US THIS CAKE AS A BIRTHDAY GIFT FOR YOU!
SO IT'S... NOT AN ICE-CREAM CAKE?
NO, IT'S A MEDOVIK TORT.
IS THAT SOME KIND OF RUSSIAN CAKE?
С ДНЕМ РОЖДЕНИЯ ВЕРА!
...
IS THERE SOMETHING WRONG WITH RUSSIAN CAKE?
...NO.
YES.

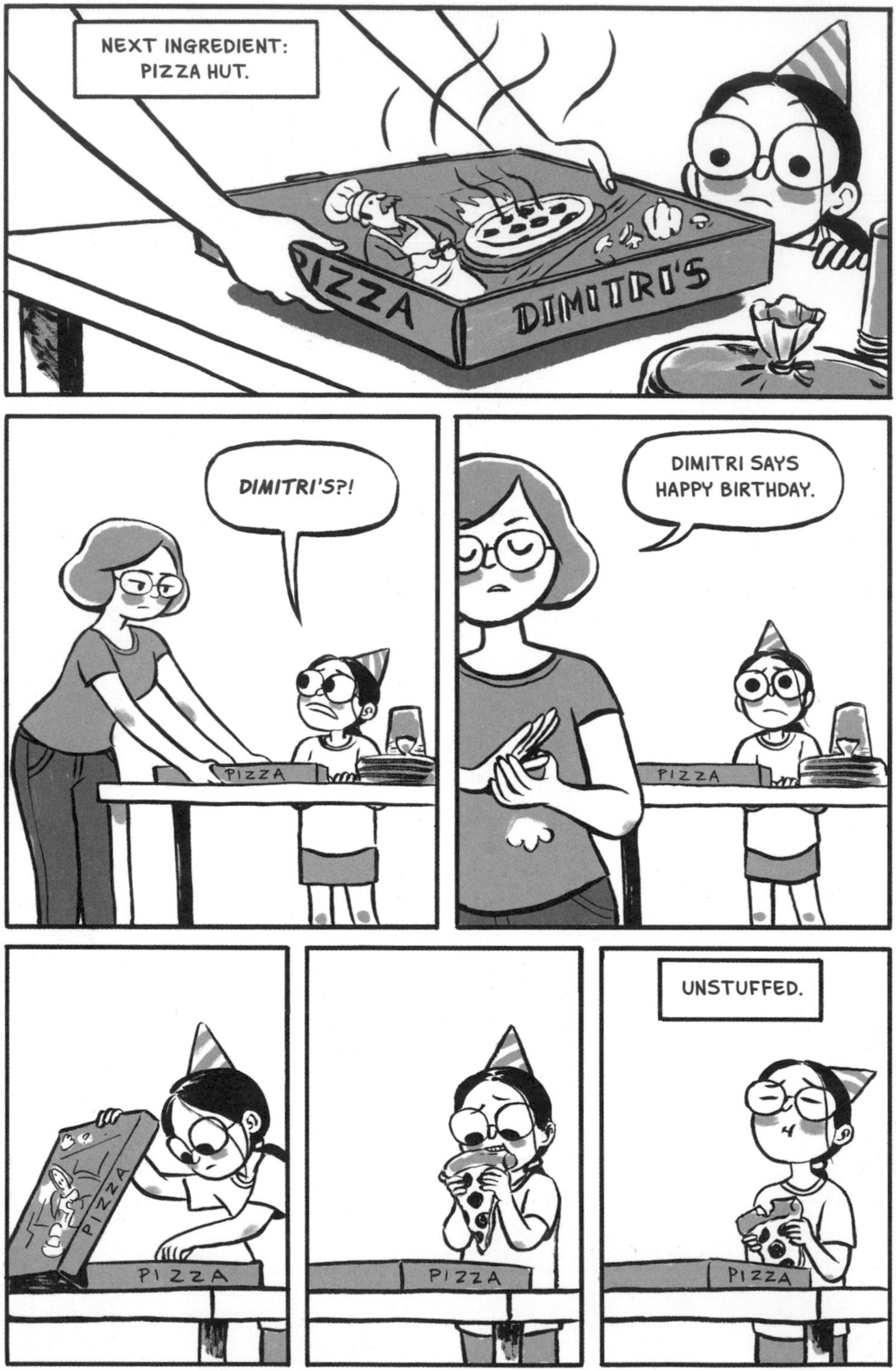
NEXT INGREDIENT:
PIZZA HUT.
PIZZA
DIMITRI'S
DIMITRI'S?!
DIMITRI SAYS
HAPPY BIRTHDAY.
PIZZA
PIZZA
PIZZA
PIZZA
PIZZA
UNSTUFFED.
PIZZA

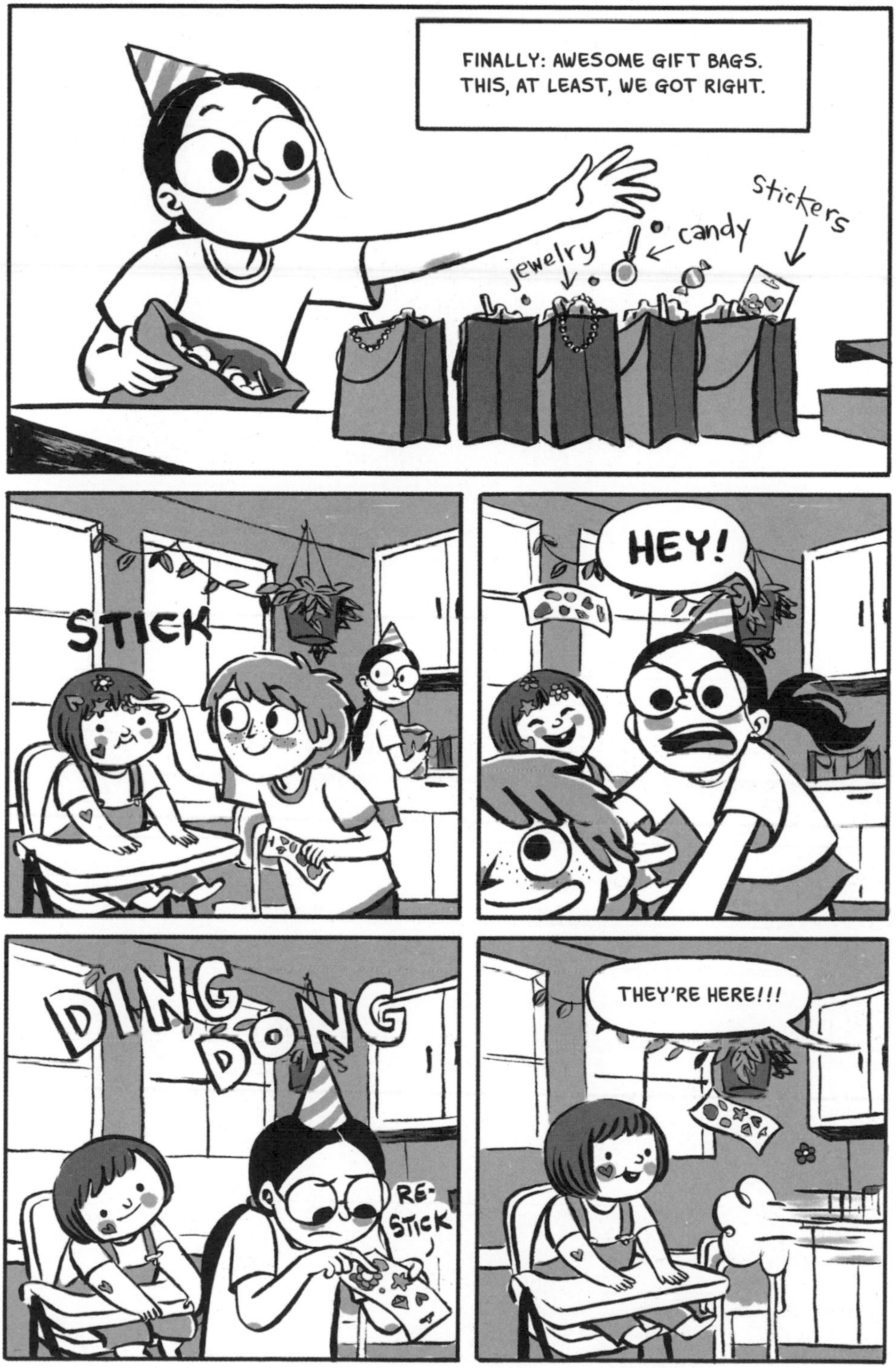
FINALLY: AWESOME GIFT BAGS.
THIS, AT LEAST, WE GOT RIGHT.
jewelry
candy
stickers
STICK
HEY!
DING DONG
DING DONG
RE-STICK
THEY'RE HERE!!!

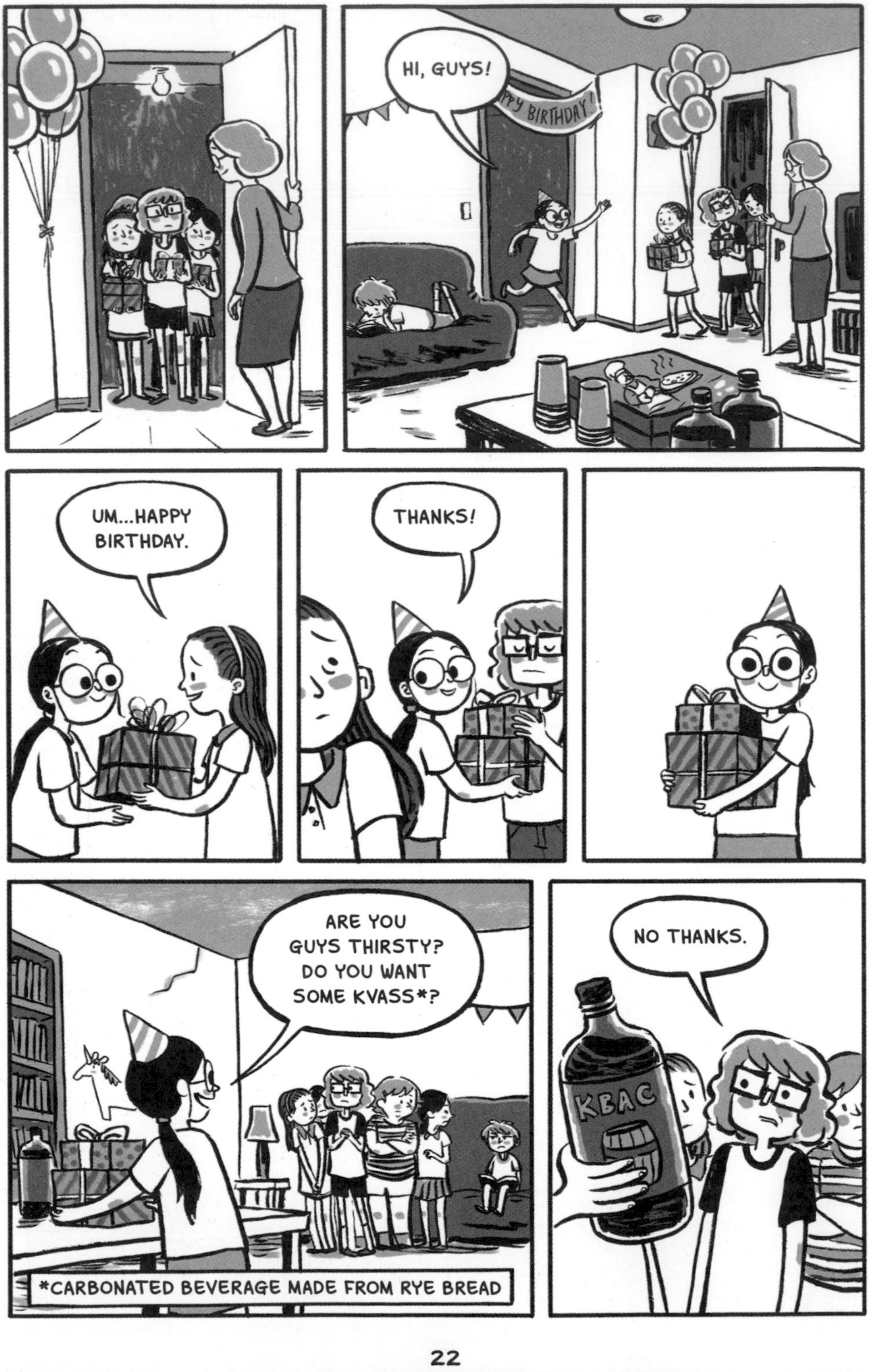
HI, GUYS!
HAPPY BIRTHDAY!
UM...HAPPY BIRTHDAY.
THANKS!
ARE YOU GUYS THIRSTY? DO YOU WANT SOME KVASS*?
*CARBONATED BEVERAGE MADE FROM RYE BREAD
NO THANKS.
KBAC

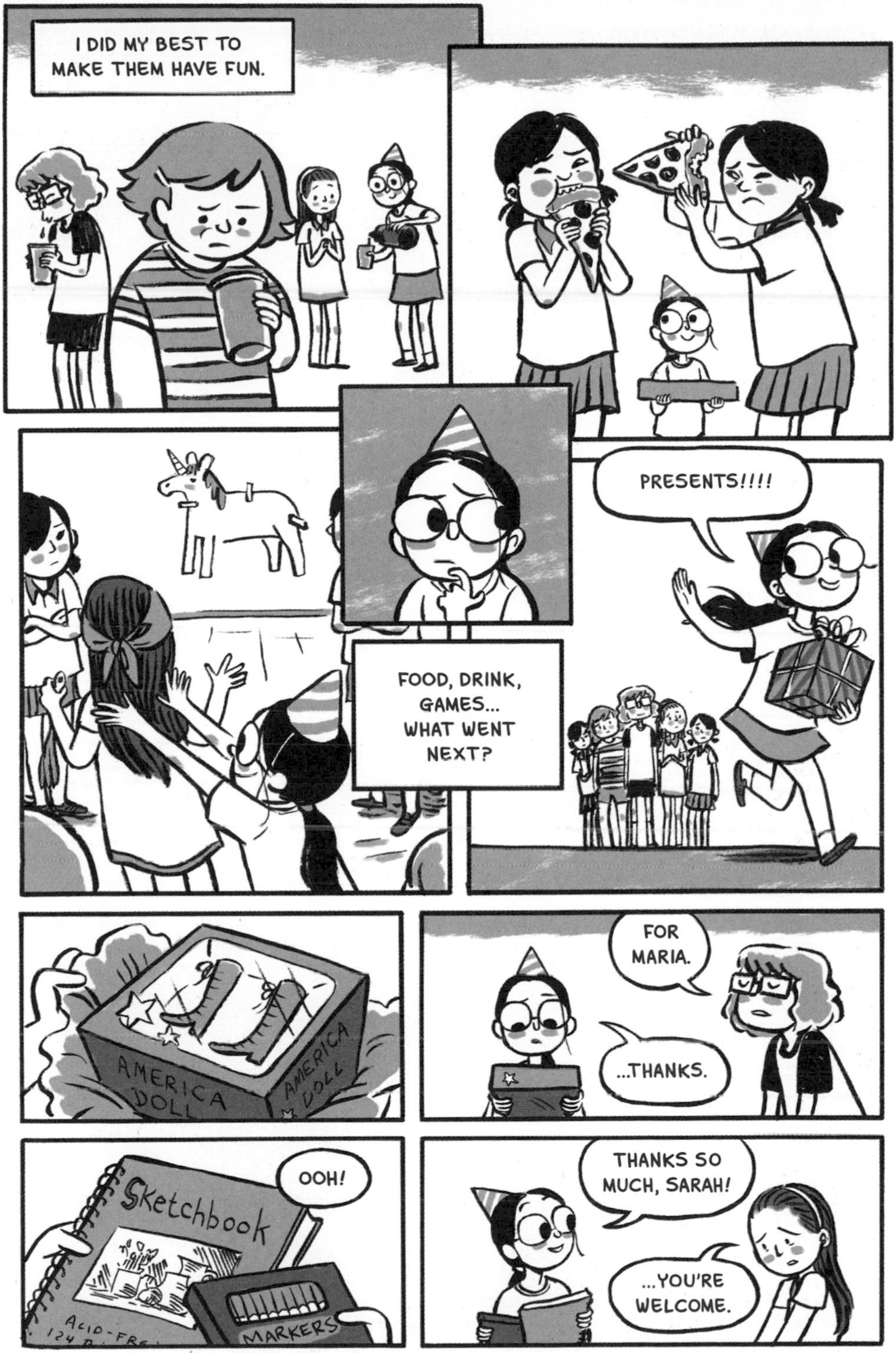
I DID MY BEST TO MAKE THEM HAVE FUN.
FOOD, DRINK, GAMES... WHAT WENT NEXT?
PRESENTS!!!!
AMERICA DOLL
AMERICA DOLL
FOR MARIA.
...THANKS.
Sketchbook
MARKERS
OOH!
THANKS SO MUCH, SARAH!
...YOU'RE WELCOME.

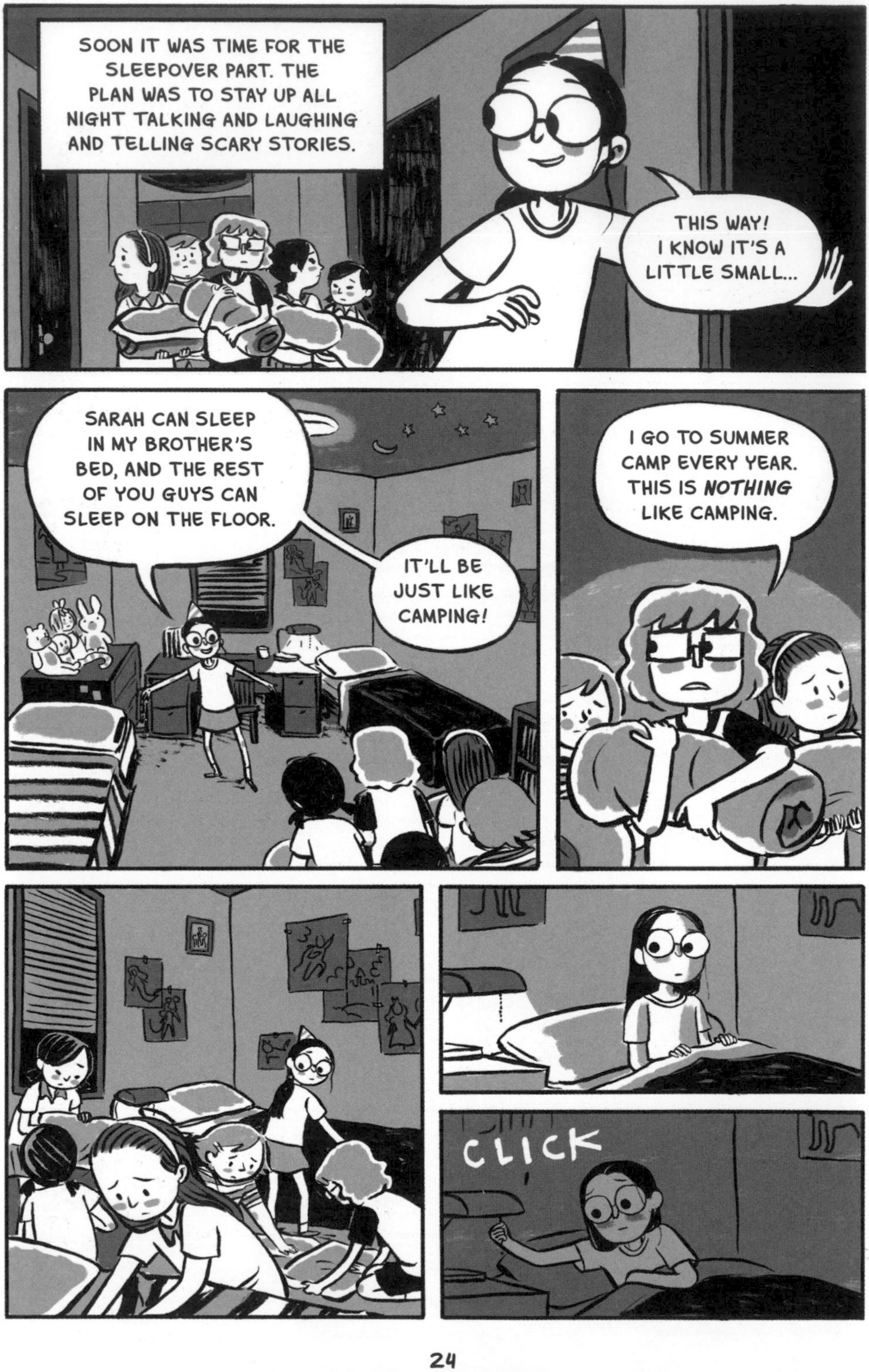
SOON IT WAS TIME FOR THE SLEEPOVER PART. THE PLAN WAS TO STAY UP ALL NIGHT TALKING AND LAUGHING AND TELLING SCARY STORIES.
THIS WAY! I KNOW IT'S A LITTLE SMALL...
SARAH CAN SLEEP IN MY BROTHER'S BED, AND THE REST OF YOU GUYS CAN SLEEP ON THE FLOOR.
IT'LL BE JUST LIKE CAMPING!
I GO TO SUMMER CAMP EVERY YEAR. THIS IS *NOTHING* LIKE CAMPING.
CLICK

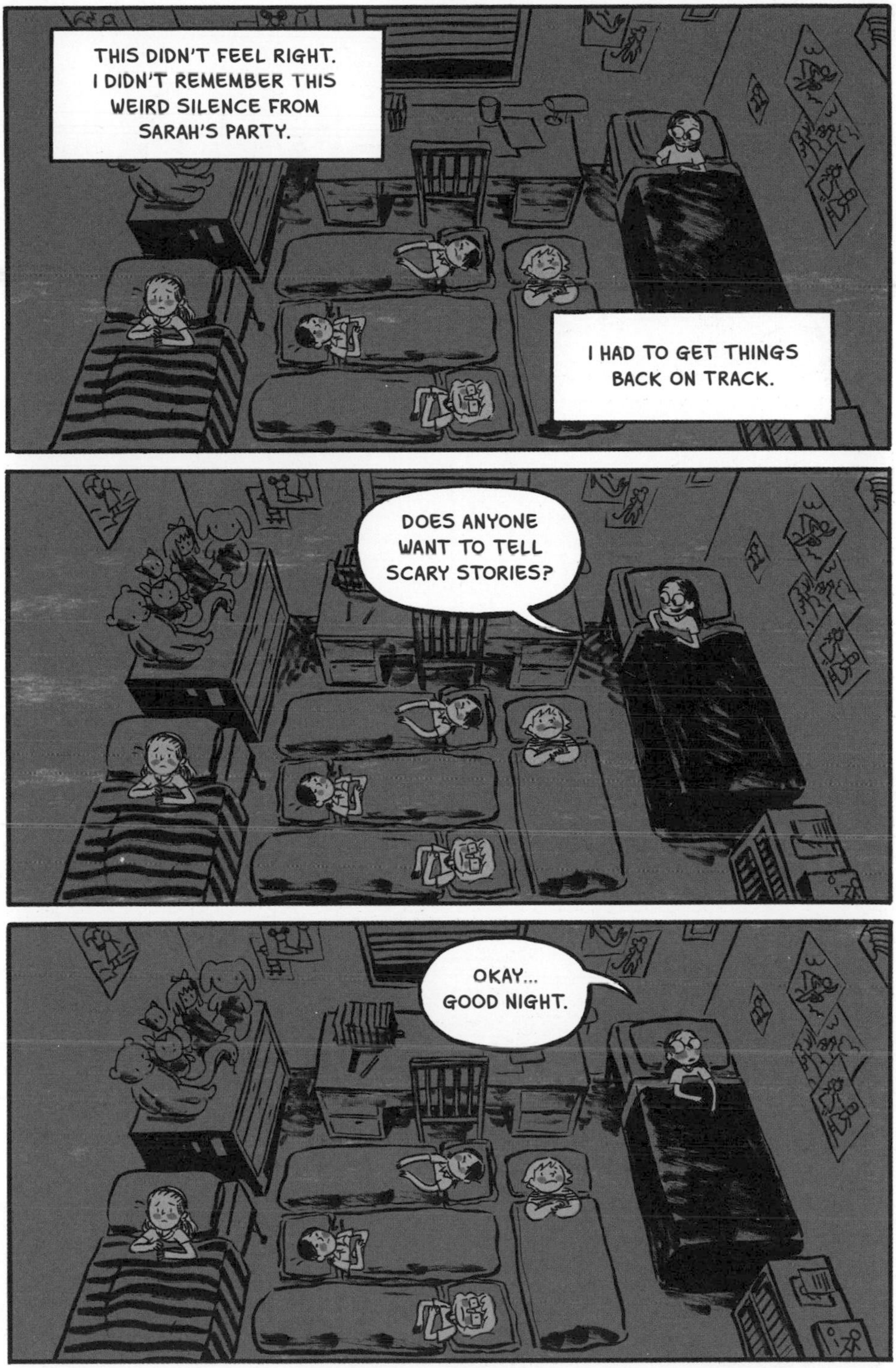
THIS DIDN'T FEEL RIGHT. I DIDN'T REMEMBER THIS WEIRD SILENCE FROM SARAH'S PARTY.
I HAD TO GET THINGS BACK ON TRACK.
DOES ANYONE WANT TO TELL SCARY STORIES?
OKAY... GOOD NIGHT.

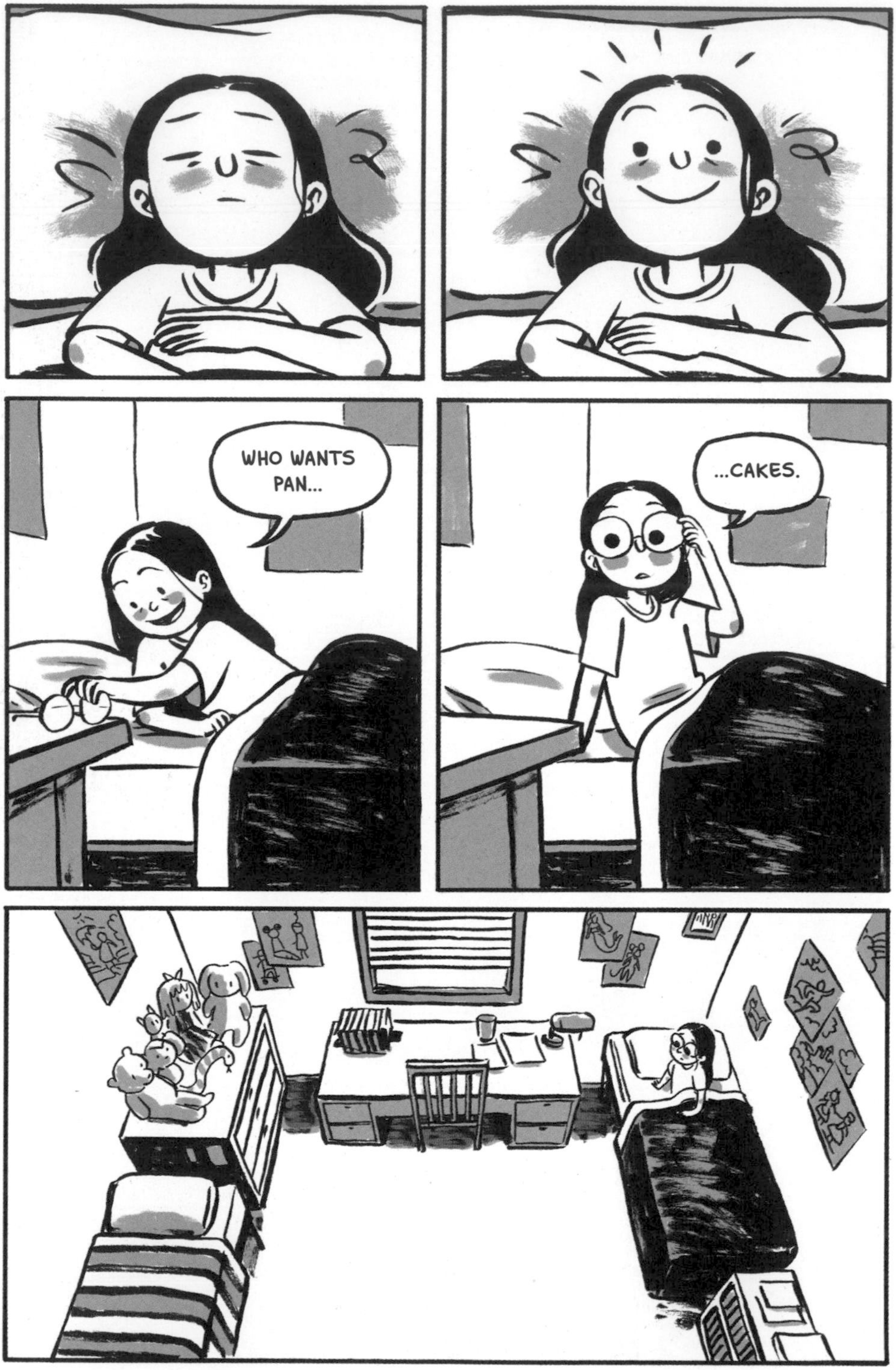
WHO WANTS PAN...
...CAKES.

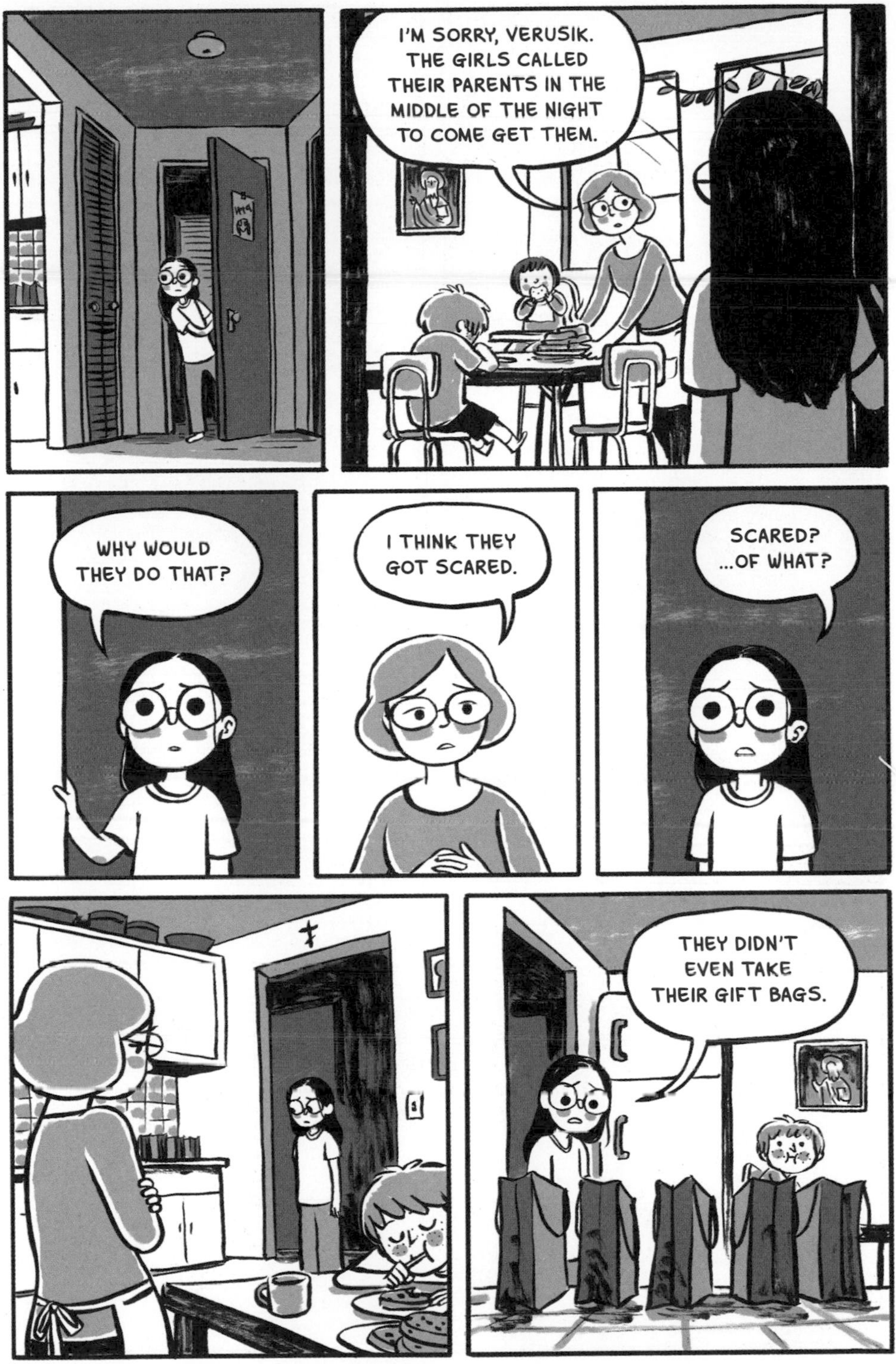
I'M SORRY, VERUSIK. THE GIRLS CALLED THEIR PARENTS IN THE MIDDLE OF THE NIGHT TO COME GET THEM.
WHY WOULD THEY DO THAT?
I THINK THEY GOT SCARED.
SCARED? ...OF WHAT?
THEY DIDN'T EVEN TAKE THEIR GIFT BAGS.

THE NEXT DAY, SARAH APOLOGIZED.

I'M PRETTY SURE HER MOM MADE HER DO IT.

I KNEW THE PARTY WASN'T RIGHT. CLOSE, BUT NOT RIGHT.

IT WAS TOO POOR. IT WAS TOO RUSSIAN. IT WAS TOO DIFFERENT.

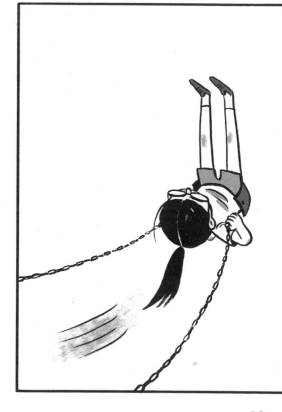
I WAS NEVER GOING TO FIT IN WITH THE AMERICAN KIDS.

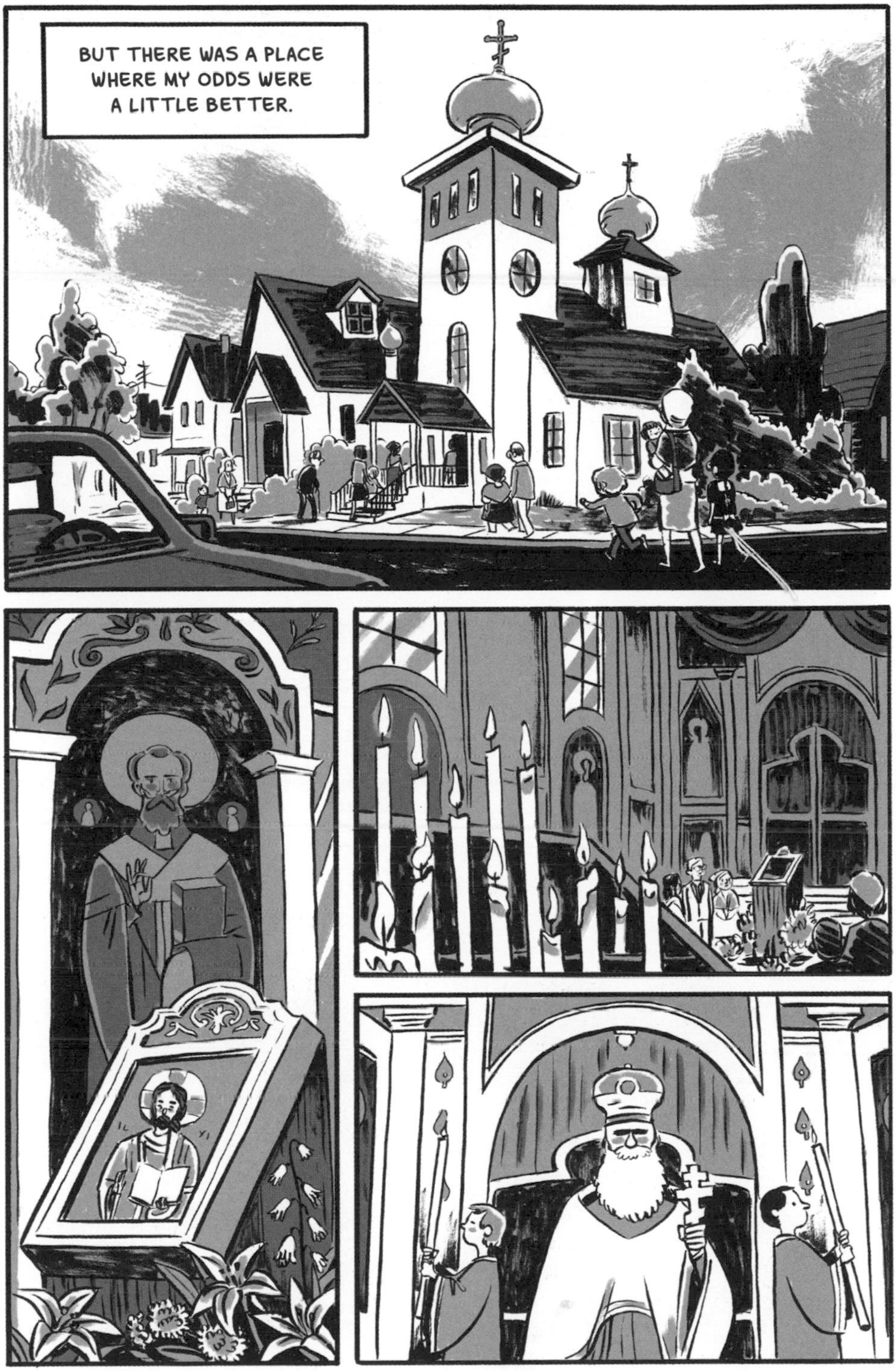
BUT THERE WAS A PLACE WHERE MY ODDS WERE A LITTLE BETTER.

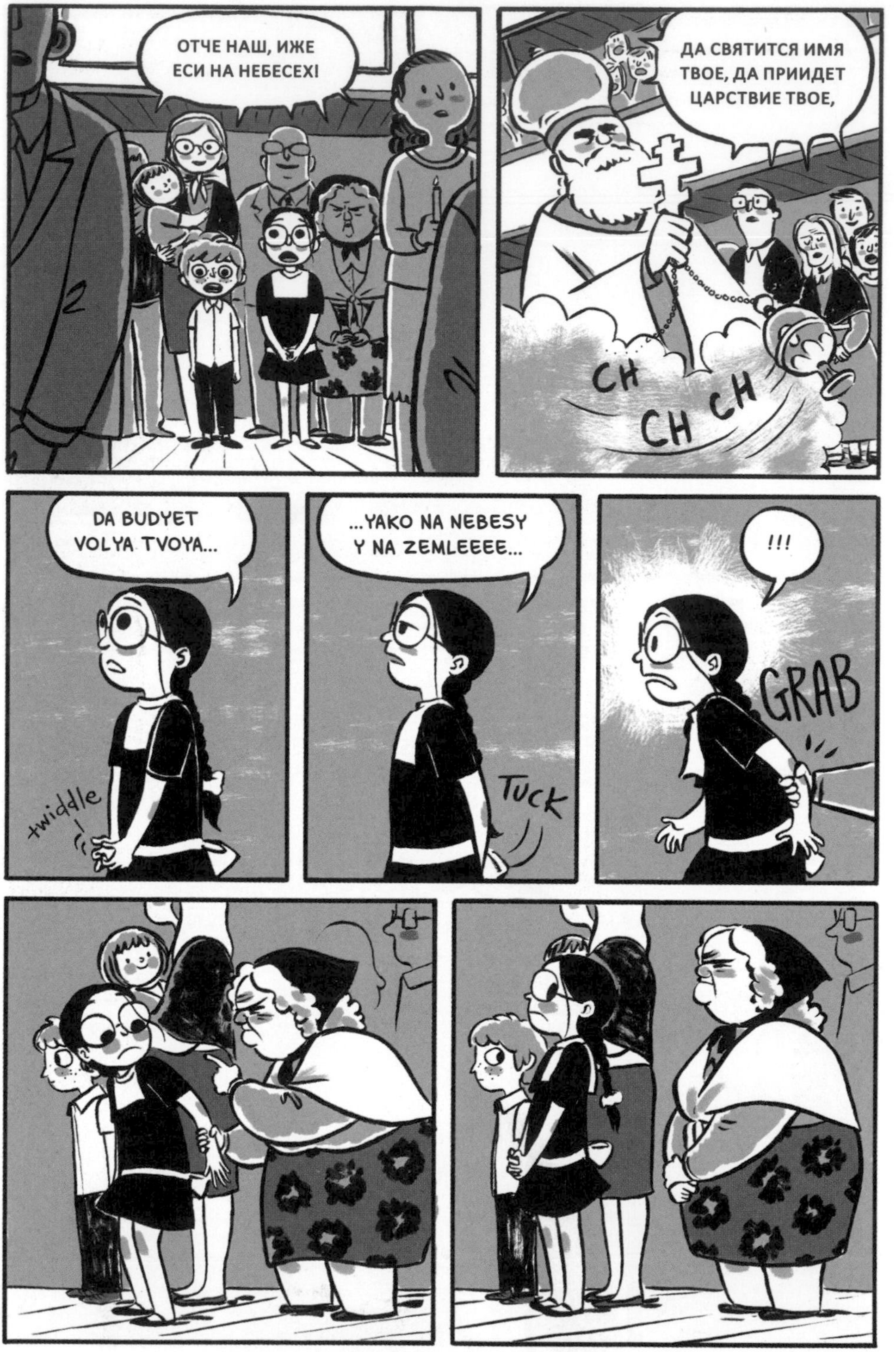
ОТЧЕ НАШ, ИЖЕ ЕСИ НА НЕБЕСЕХ!
ДА СВЯТИТСЯ ИМЯ ТВОЕ, ДА ПРИИДЕТ ЦАРСТВИЕ ТВОЕ,
CH
CH CH
DA BUDYET VOLYA TVOYA...
twiddle
...YAKO NA NEBESY Y NA ZEMLEEEE...
TUCK
!!!
GRAB

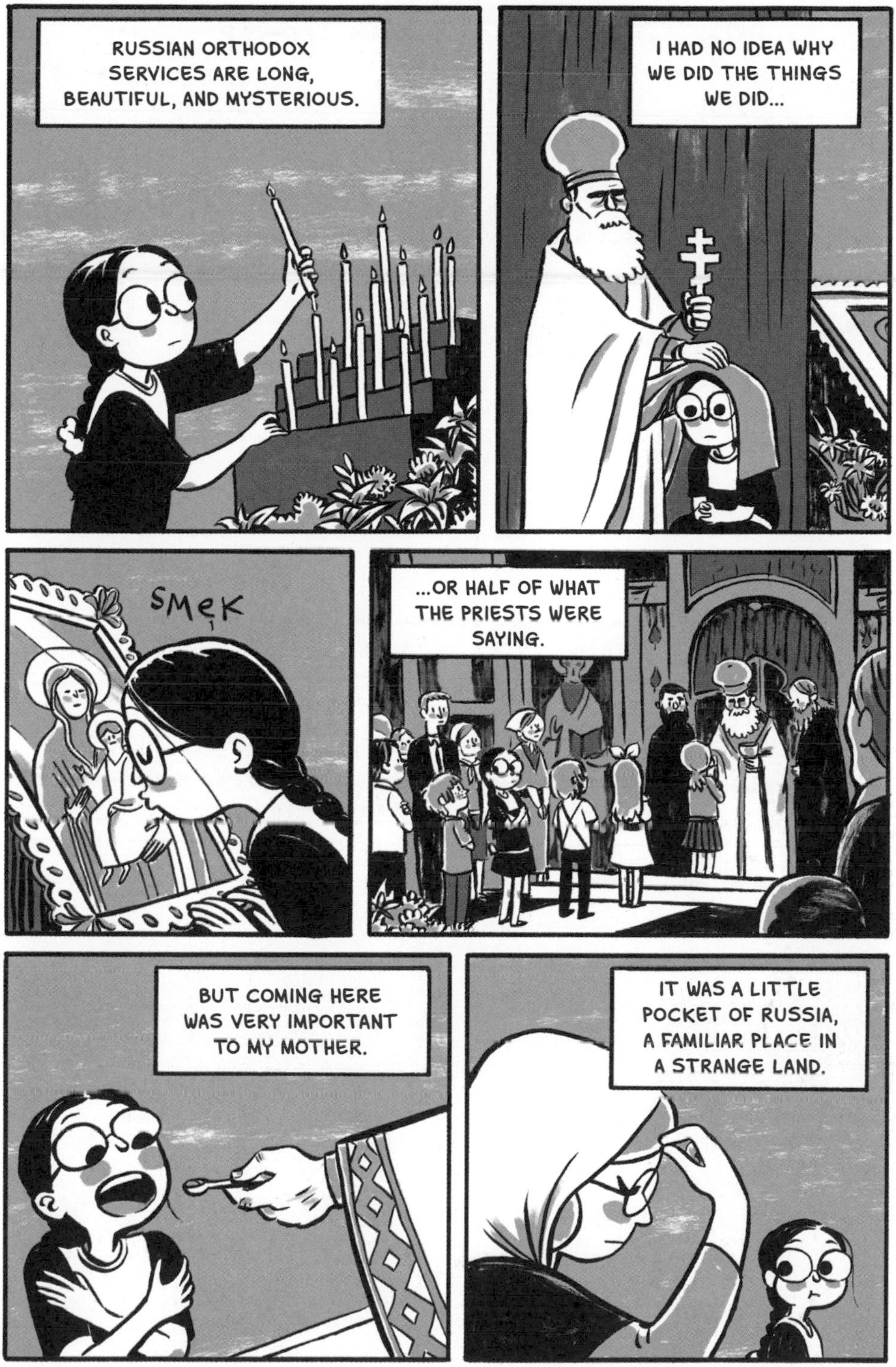
RUSSIAN ORTHODOX SERVICES ARE LONG, BEAUTIFUL, AND MYSTERIOUS.
I HAD NO IDEA WHY WE DID THE THINGS WE DID...
SMEK
...OR HALF OF WHAT THE PRIESTS WERE SAYING.
BUT COMING HERE WAS VERY IMPORTANT TO MY MOTHER.
IT WAS A LITTLE POCKET OF RUSSIA, A FAMILIAR PLACE IN A STRANGE LAND.

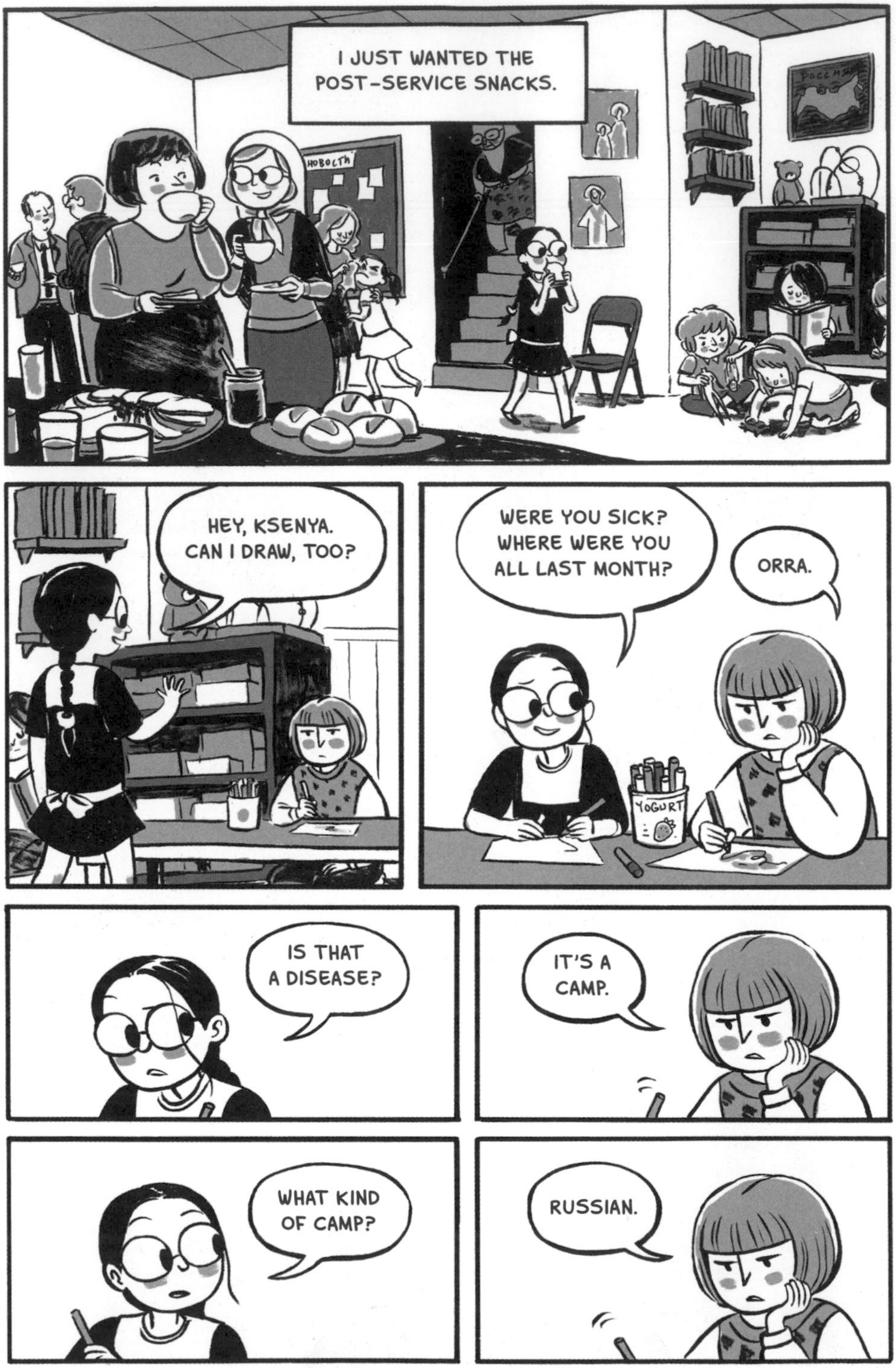
I JUST WANTED THE POST-SERVICE SNACKS.
HEY, KSENYA. CAN I DRAW, TOO?
WERE YOU SICK? WHERE WERE YOU ALL LAST MONTH?
ORRA.
IS THAT A DISEASE?
IT'S A CAMP.
WHAT KIND OF CAMP?
RUSSIAN.

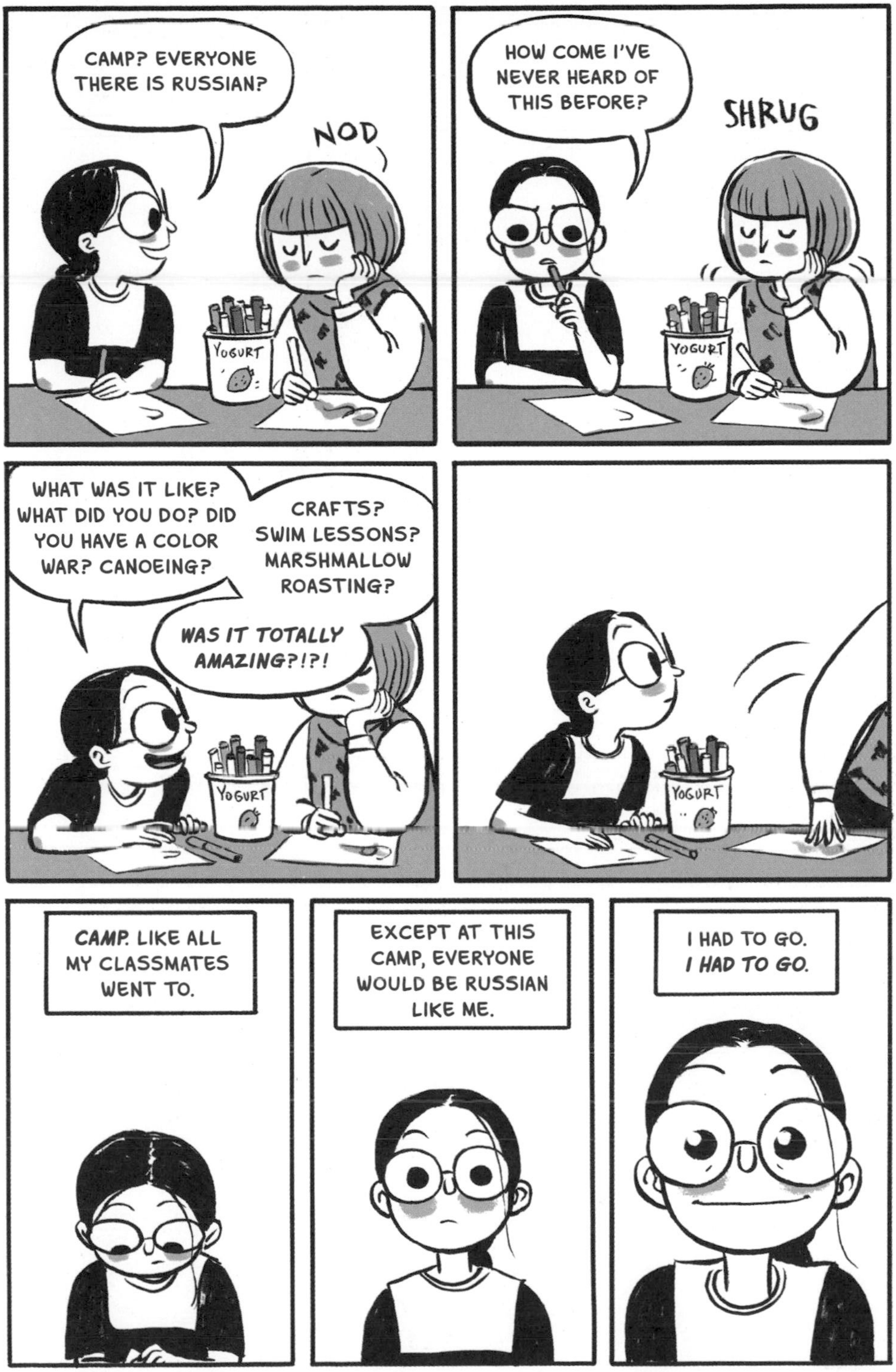
CAMP? EVERYONE THERE IS RUSSIAN?
NOD
HOW COME I'VE NEVER HEARD OF THIS BEFORE?
SHRUG
WHAT WAS IT LIKE? WHAT DID YOU DO? DID YOU HAVE A COLOR WAR? CANOEING?
CRAFTS? SWIM LESSONS? MARSHMALLOW ROASTING?
WAS IT TOTALLY AMAZING?!?!
CAMP. LIKE ALL MY CLASSMATES WENT TO.
EXCEPT AT THIS CAMP, EVERYONE WOULD BE RUSSIAN LIKE ME.
I HAD TO GO. I HAD TO GO.

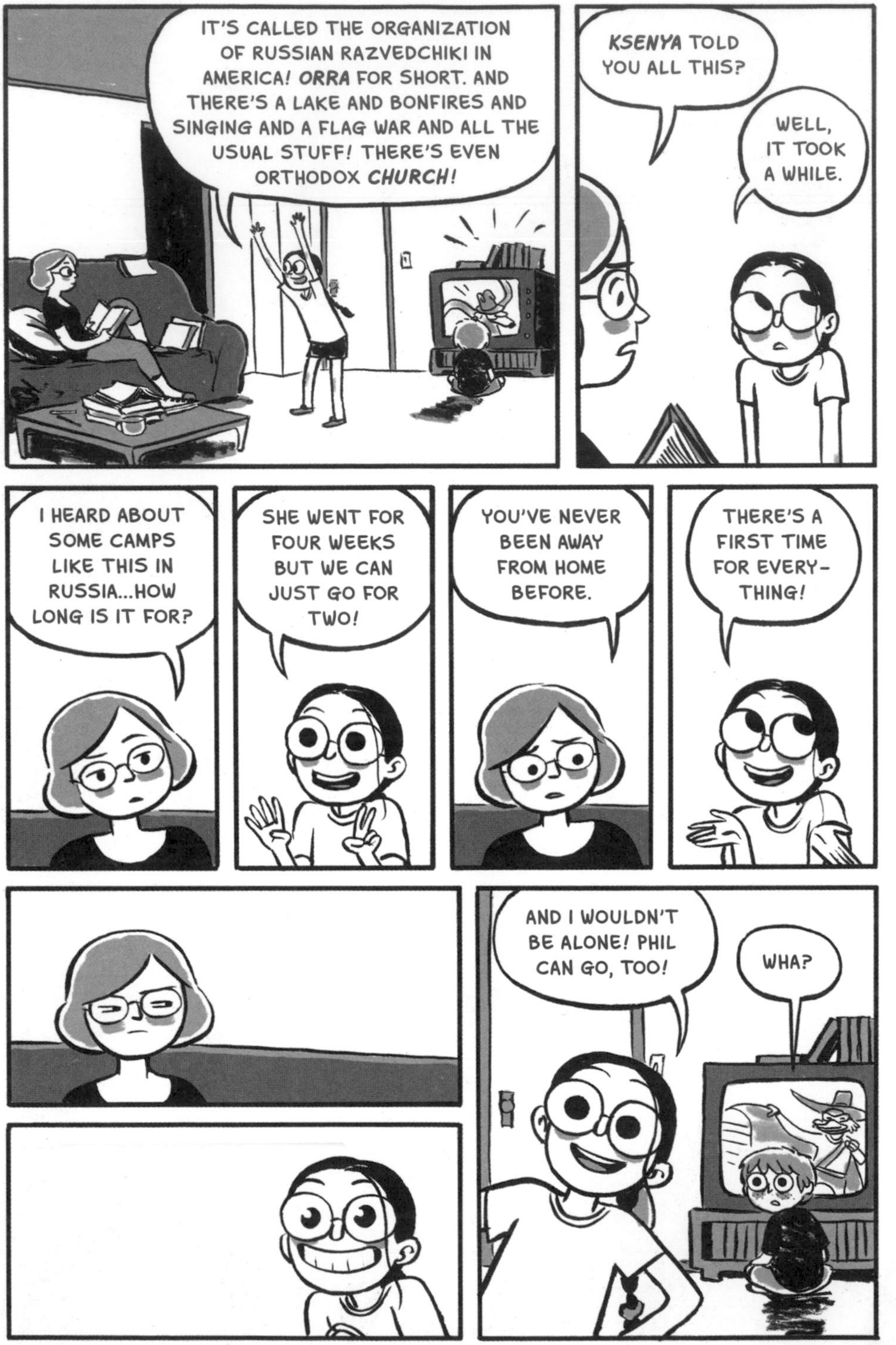
IT'S CALLED THE ORGANIZATION OF RUSSIAN RAZVEDCHIKI IN AMERICA! ORRA FOR SHORT. AND THERE'S A LAKE AND BONFIRES AND SINGING AND A FLAG WAR AND ALL THE USUAL STUFF! THERE'S EVEN ORTHODOX CHURCH!
KSENYA TOLD YOU ALL THIS?
WELL, IT TOOK A WHILE.
I HEARD ABOUT SOME CAMPS LIKE THIS IN RUSSIA...HOW LONG IS IT FOR?
SHE WENT FOR FOUR WEEKS BUT WE CAN JUST GO FOR TWO!
YOU'VE NEVER BEEN AWAY FROM HOME BEFORE.
THERE'S A FIRST TIME FOR EVERY-THING!
AND I WOULDN'T BE ALONE! PHIL CAN GO, TOO!
WHA?

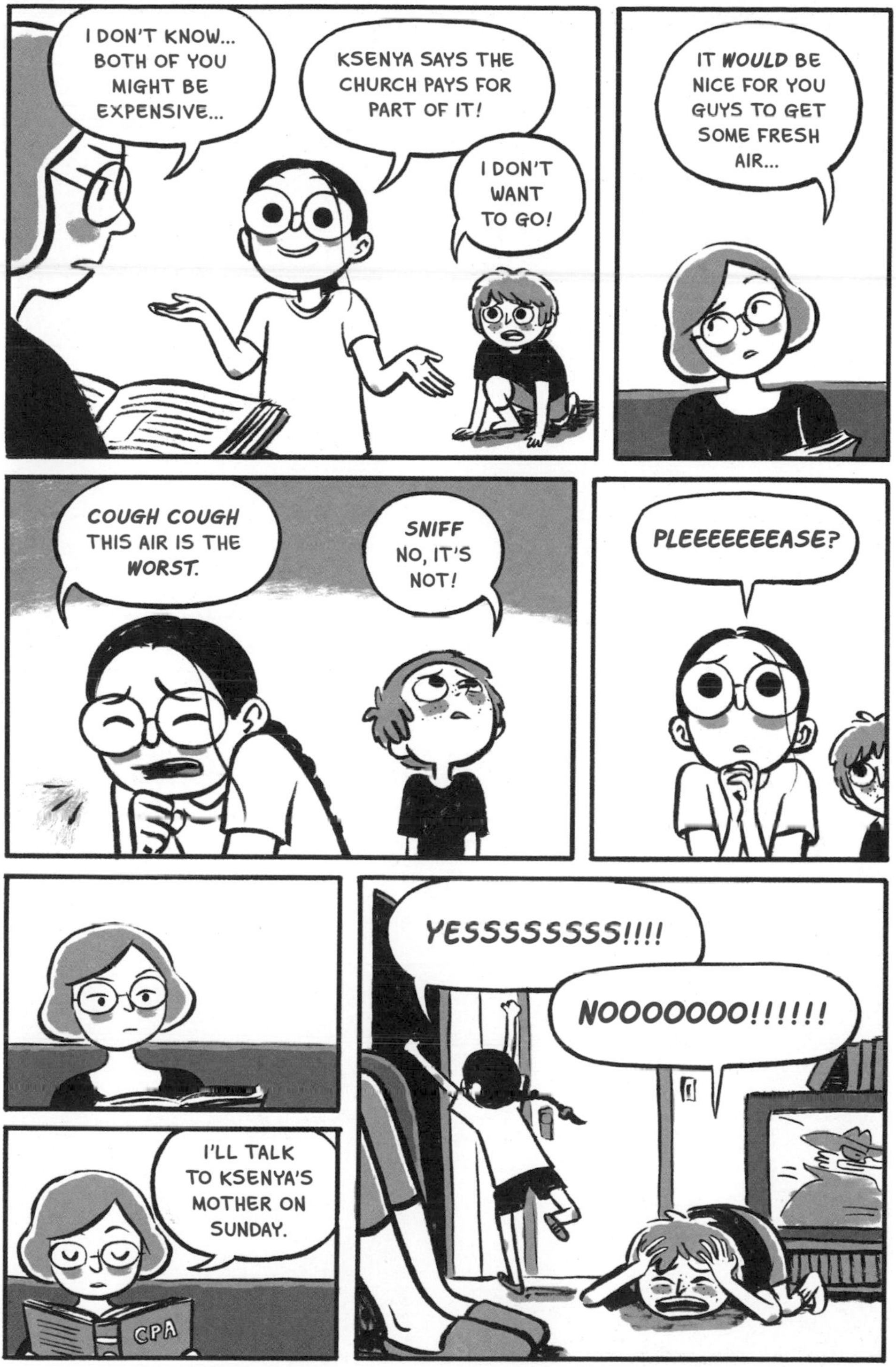
I DON'T KNOW... BOTH OF YOU MIGHT BE EXPENSIVE...
KSENYA SAYS THE CHURCH PAYS FOR PART OF IT!
I DON'T WANT TO GO!
IT WOULD BE NICE FOR YOU GUYS TO GET SOME FRESH AIR...
COUGH COUGH THIS AIR IS THE WORST.
SNIFF NO, IT'S NOT!
PLEEEEEEEASE?
I'LL TALK TO KSENYA'S MOTHER ON SUNDAY.
CPA
YESSSSSSSS!!!!
NOOOOOOO!!!!!!

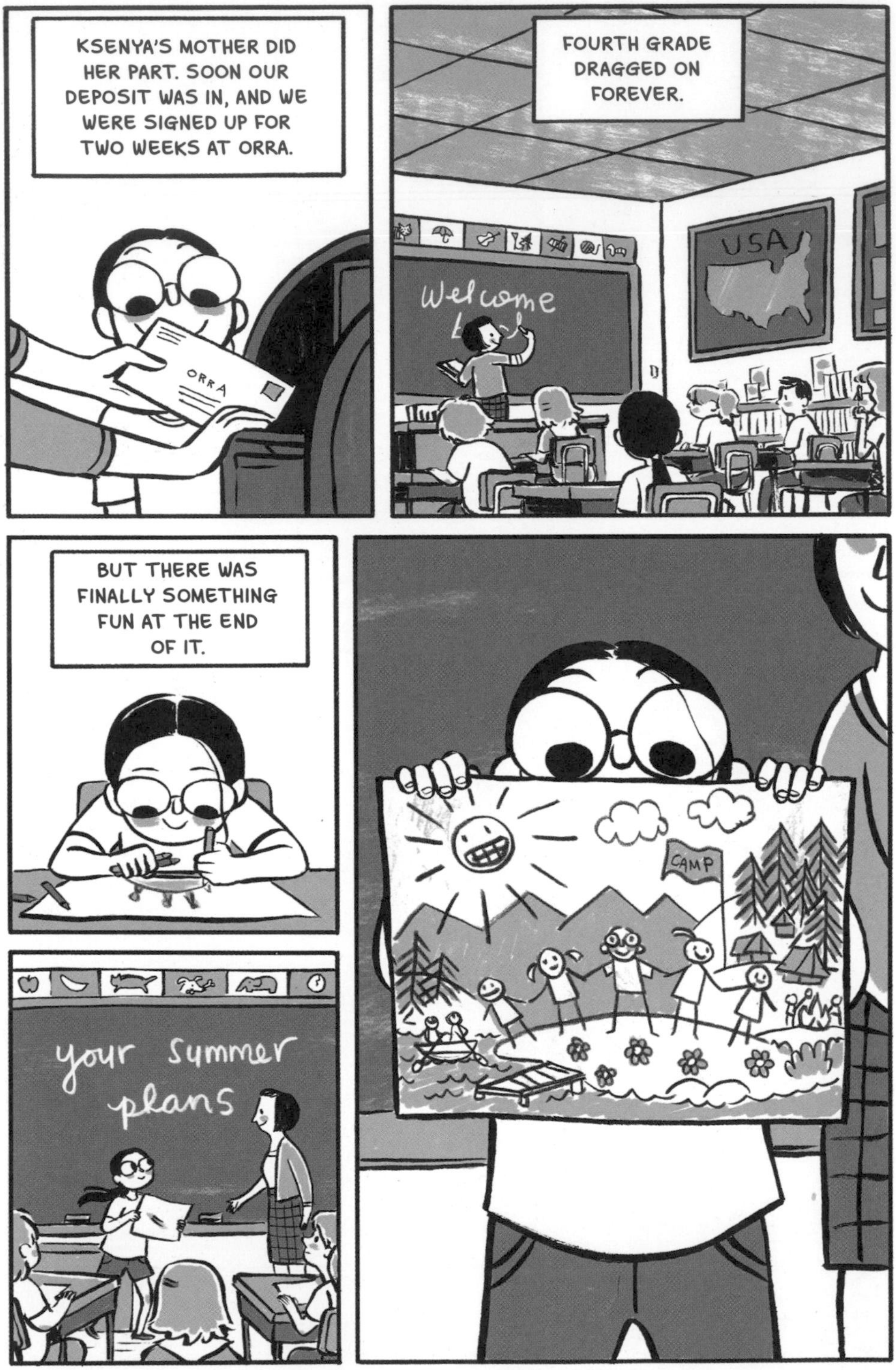
KSENYA'S MOTHER DID HER PART. SOON OUR DEPOSIT WAS IN, AND WE WERE SIGNED UP FOR TWO WEEKS AT ORRA.
ORRA
FOURTH GRADE DRAGGED ON FOREVER.
USA
Welcome
BUT THERE WAS FINALLY SOMETHING FUN AT THE END OF IT.
CAMP
your summer plans

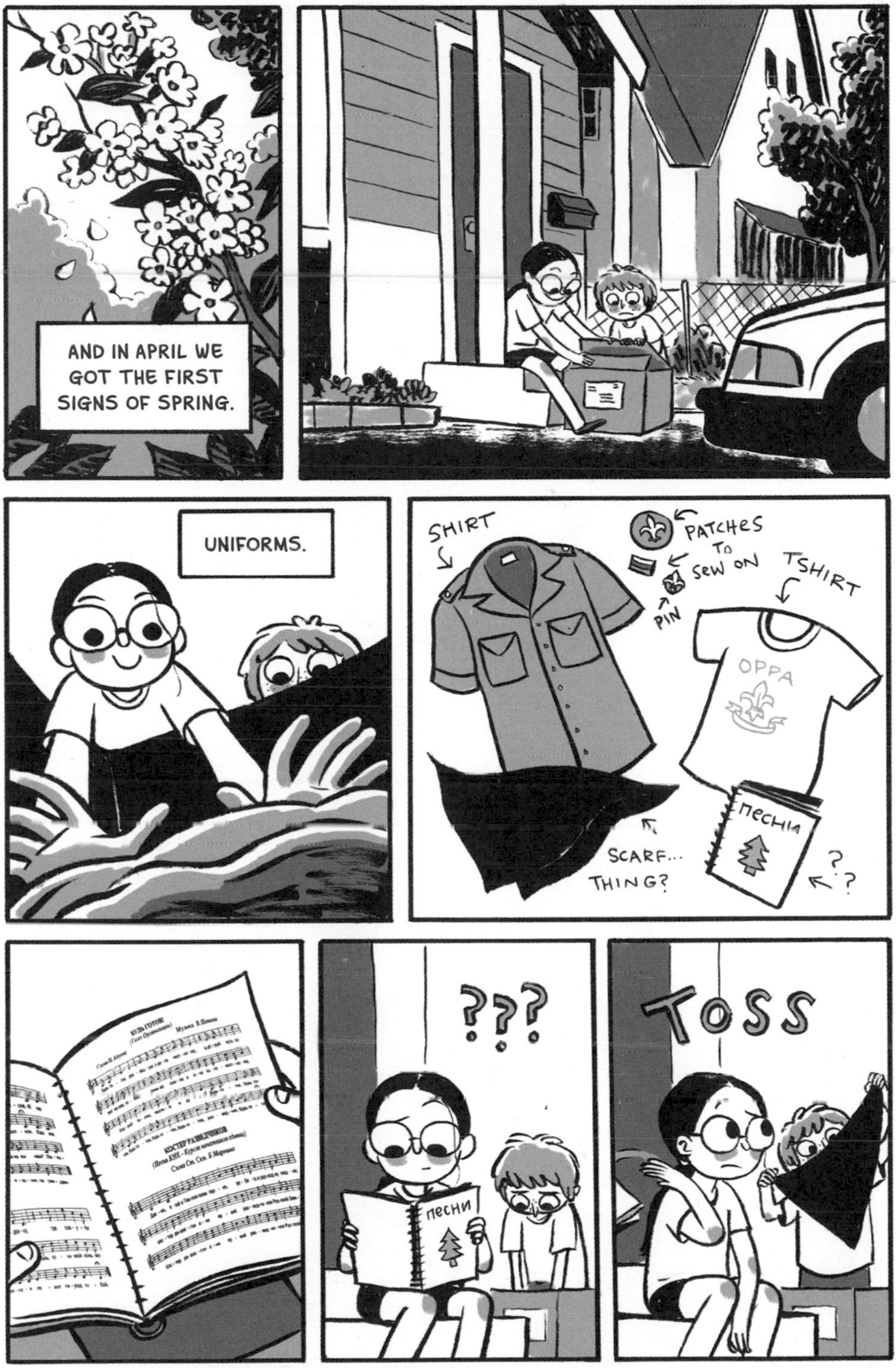
AND IN APRIL WE GOT THE FIRST SIGNS OF SPRING.
UNIFORMS.
SHIRT
PATCHES TO SEW ON
PIN
TSHIRT
OPPA
ПЕСНИ
SCARF... THING?
??
???
ПЕСНИ
TOSS

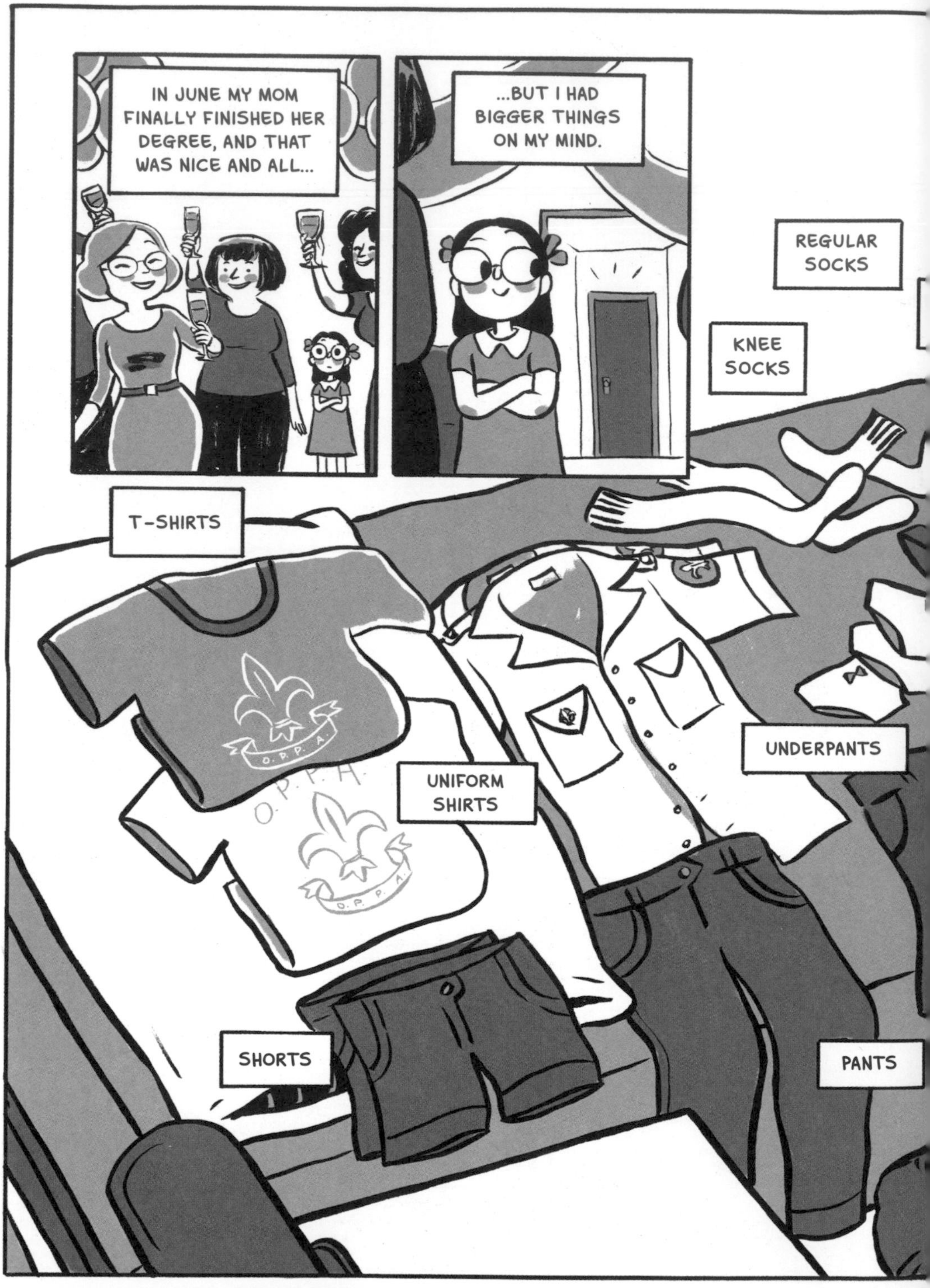
IN JUNE MY MOM FINALLY FINISHED HER DEGREE, AND THAT WAS NICE AND ALL...
...BUT I HAD BIGGER THINGS ON MY MIND.
REGULAR SOCKS
KNEE SOCKS
T-SHIRTS
O.P.P.A.
O.P.P.A.
O.P.P.A.
UNIFORM SHIRTS
UNDERPANTS
SHORTS
PANTS

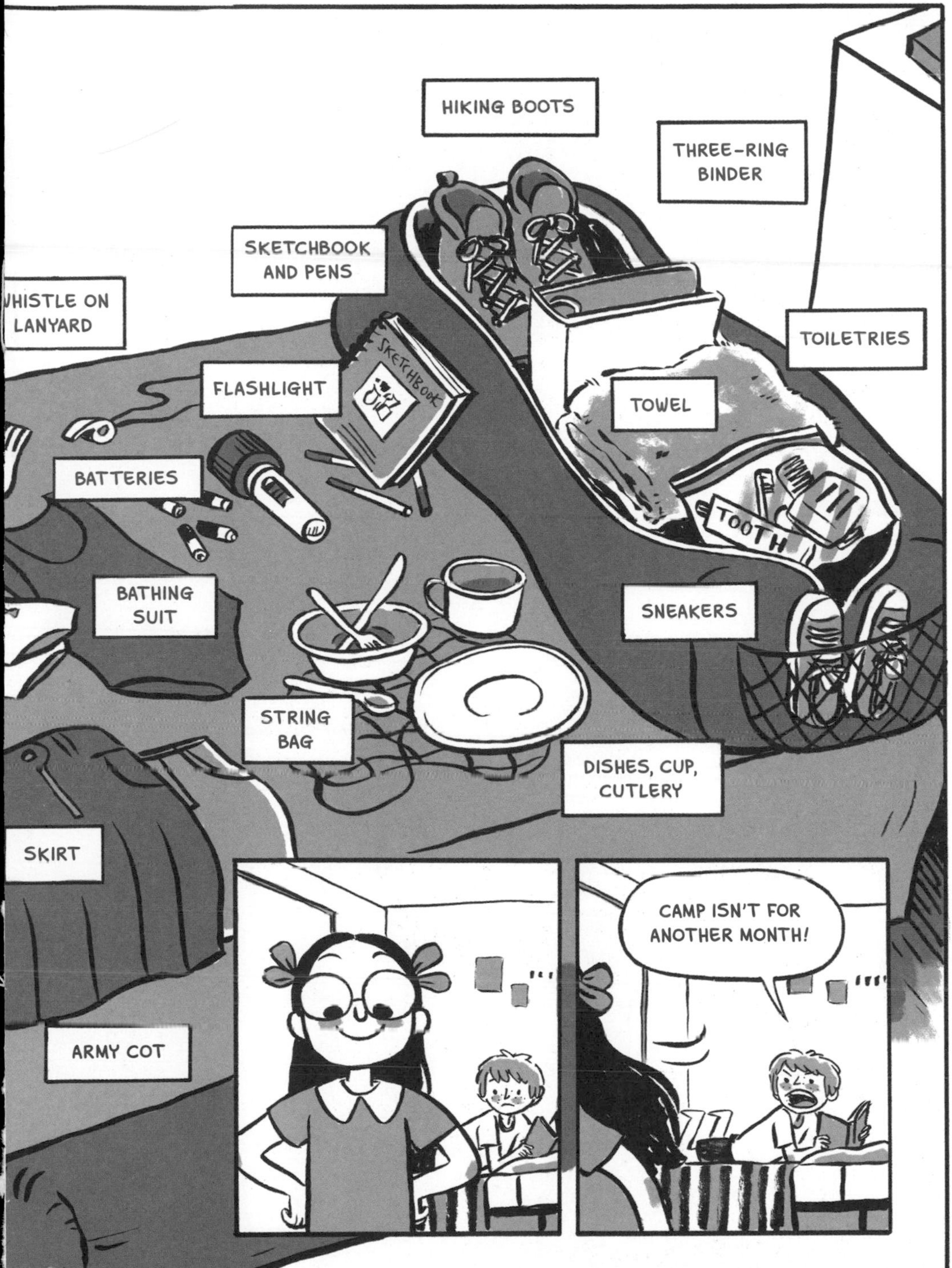
HIKING BOOTS
THREE-RING BINDER
SKETCHBOOK AND PENS
WHISTLE ON LANYARD
TOILETRIES
FLASHLIGHT
TOWEL
BATTERIES
TOOTH
BATHING SUIT
SNEAKERS
STRING BAG
DISHES, CUP, CUTLERY
SKIRT
ARMY COT
CAMP ISN'T FOR ANOTHER MONTH!

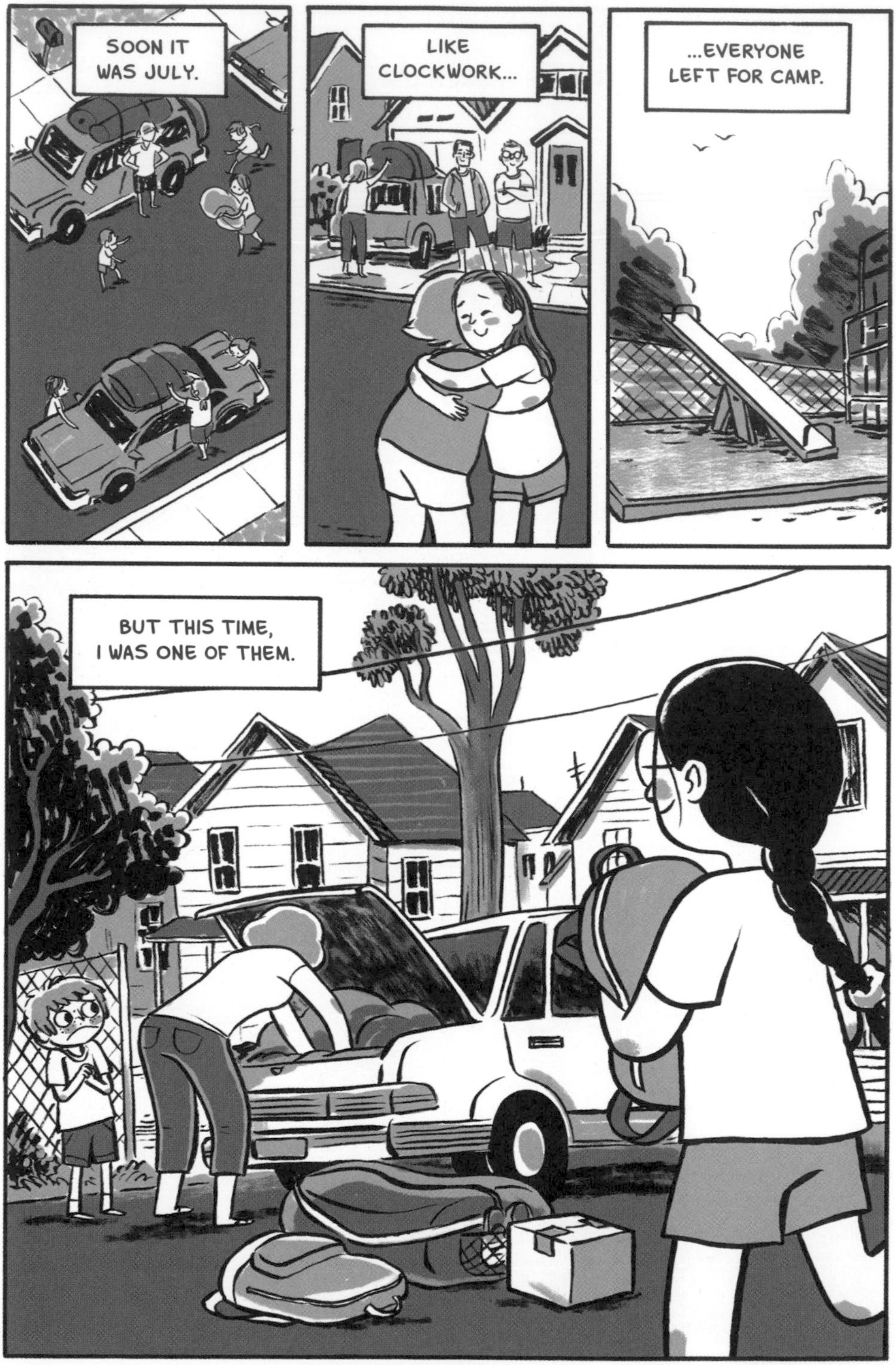
SOON IT WAS JULY.
LIKE CLOCKWORK...
...EVERYONE LEFT FOR CAMP.
BUT THIS TIME, I WAS ONE OF THEM.

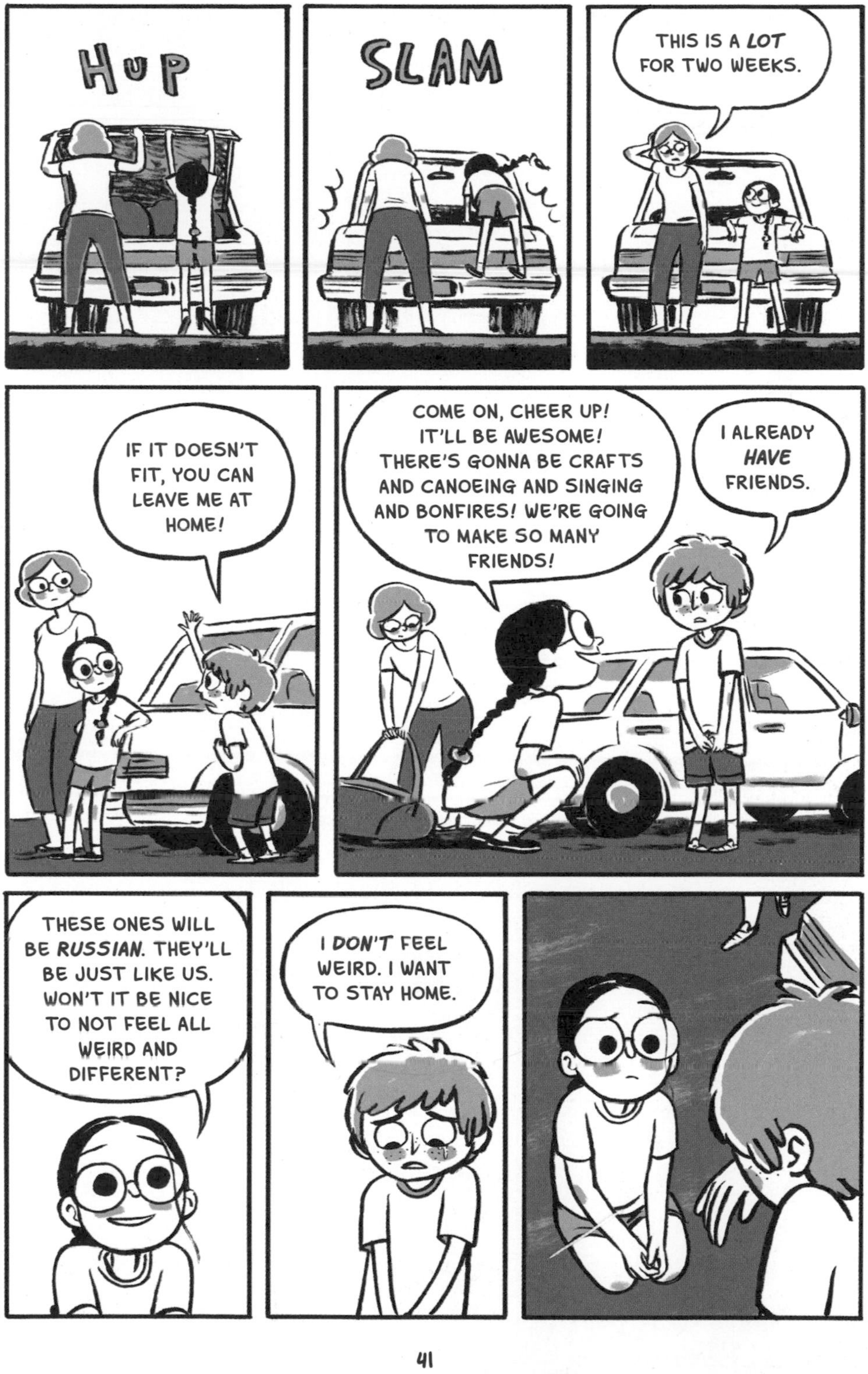
HUP
SLAM
THIS IS A *LOT* FOR TWO WEEKS.
IF IT DOESN'T FIT, YOU CAN LEAVE ME AT HOME!
COME ON, CHEER UP! IT'LL BE AWESOME! THERE'S GONNA BE CRAFTS AND CANOEING AND SINGING AND BONFIRES! WE'RE GOING TO MAKE SO MANY FRIENDS!
I ALREADY *HAVE* FRIENDS.
THESE ONES WILL BE *RUSSIAN*. THEY'LL BE JUST LIKE US. WON'T IT BE NICE TO NOT FEEL ALL WEIRD AND DIFFERENT?
I *DON'T* FEEL WEIRD. I WANT TO STAY HOME.

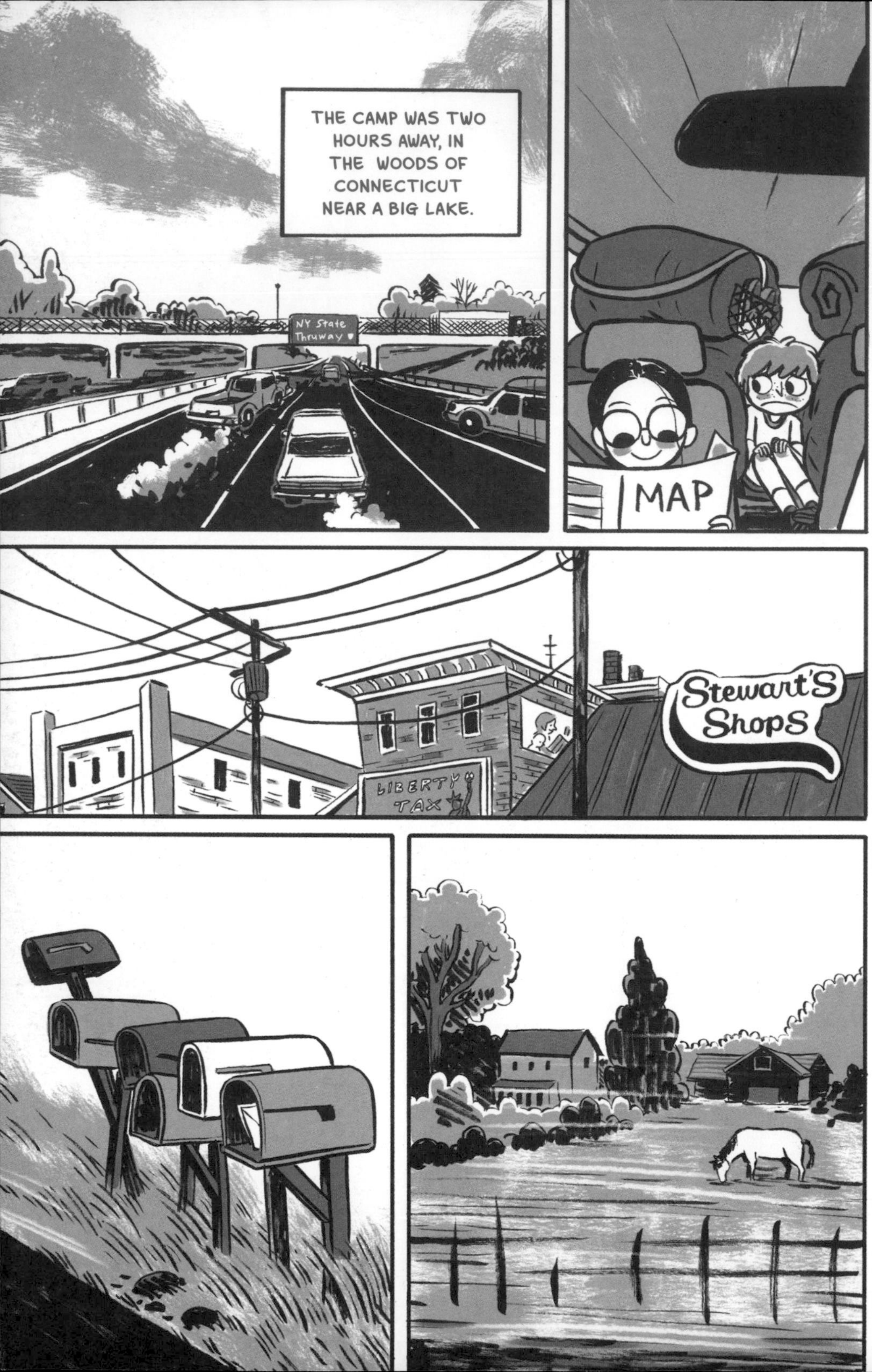
THE CAMP WAS TWO HOURS AWAY, IN THE WOODS OF CONNECTICUT NEAR A BIG LAKE.
NY State Thruway
MAP
LIBERTY TAX
Stewart's Shops

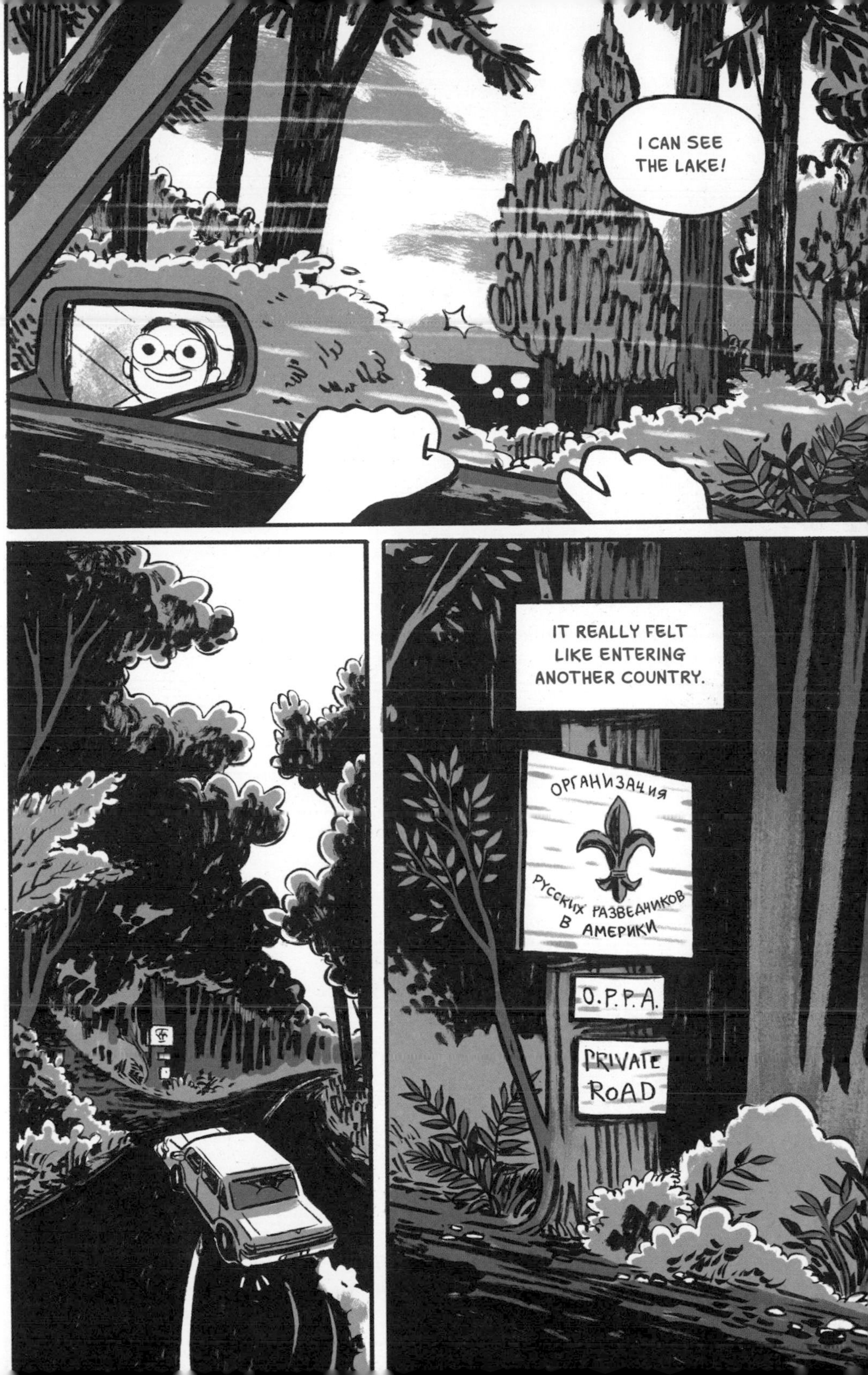
I CAN SEE THE LAKE!
IT REALLY FELT LIKE ENTERING ANOTHER COUNTRY.
ОРГАНИЗАЦИЯ РУССКИХ РАЗВЕДЧИКОВ В АМЕРИКИ
O.P.P.A.
PRIVATE ROAD

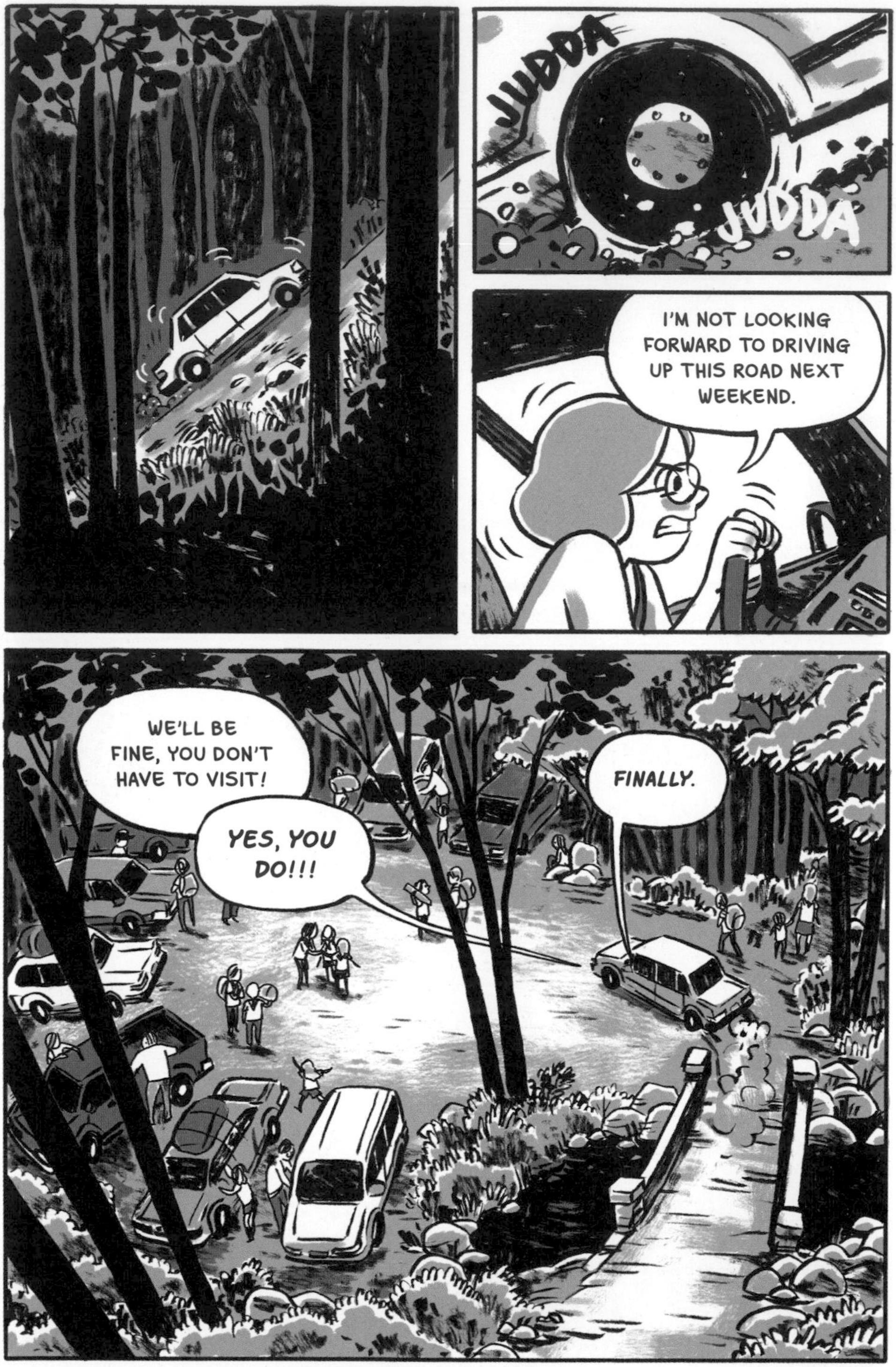
JUDDA
JUDDA
I'M NOT LOOKING FORWARD TO DRIVING UP THIS ROAD NEXT WEEKEND.
WE'LL BE FINE, YOU DON'T HAVE TO VISIT!
YES, YOU DO!!!
FINALLY.

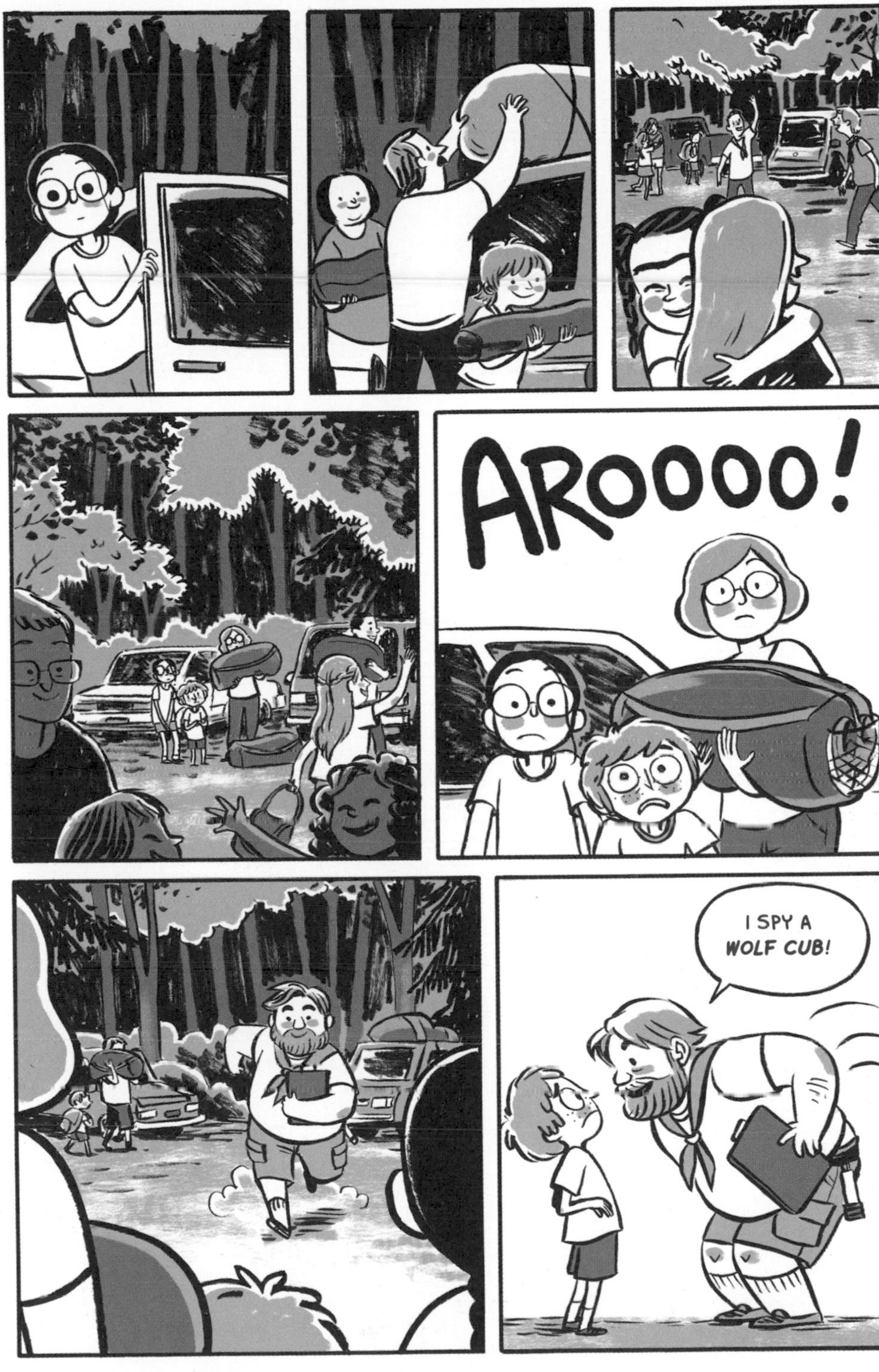
AROOOO!
I SPY A WOLF CUB!

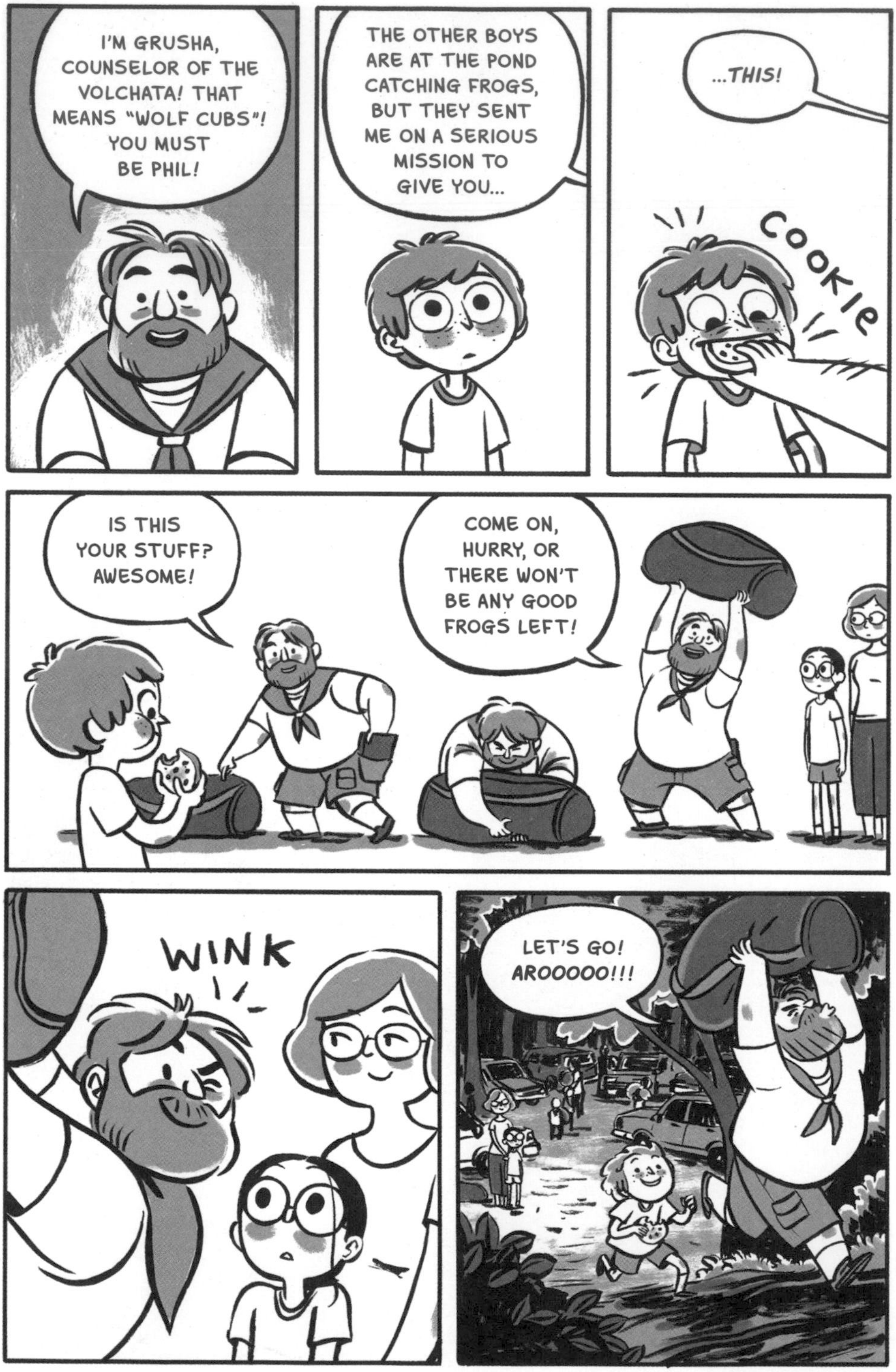
I'M GRUSHA, COUNSELOR OF THE VOLCHATA! THAT MEANS "WOLF CUBS"! YOU MUST BE PHIL!
THE OTHER BOYS ARE AT THE POND CATCHING FROGS, BUT THEY SENT ME ON A SERIOUS MISSION TO GIVE YOU...
...THIS!
COOKIE
IS THIS YOUR STUFF? AWESOME!
COME ON, HURRY, OR THERE WON'T BE ANY GOOD FROGS LEFT!
WINK
LET'S GO! AROOOOO!!!

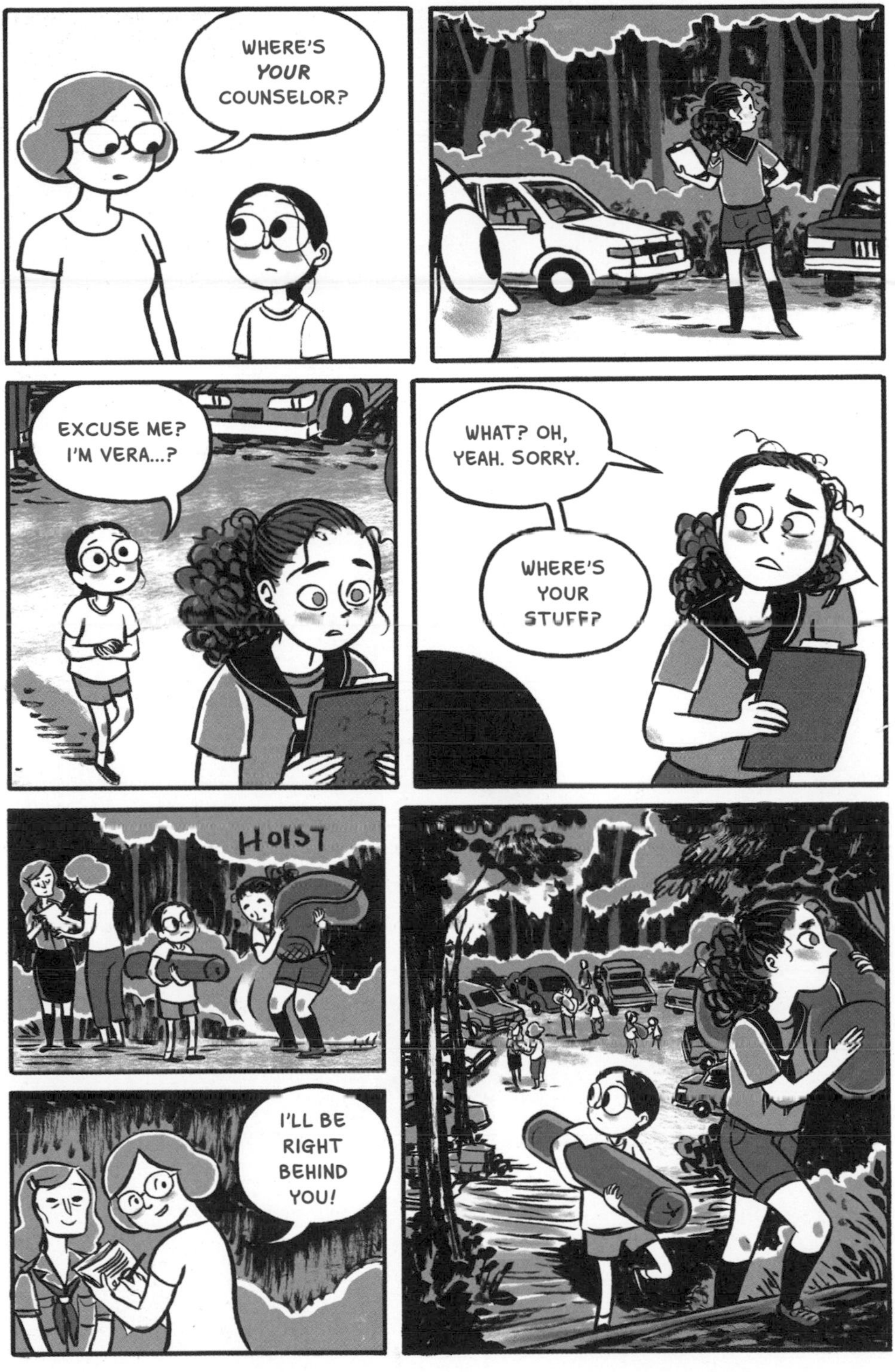

WHERE'S *YOUR* COUNSELOR?
EXCUSE ME? I'M VERA...?
WHAT? OH, YEAH. SORRY.
WHERE'S YOUR STUFF?
HOIST
I'LL BE RIGHT BEHIND YOU!

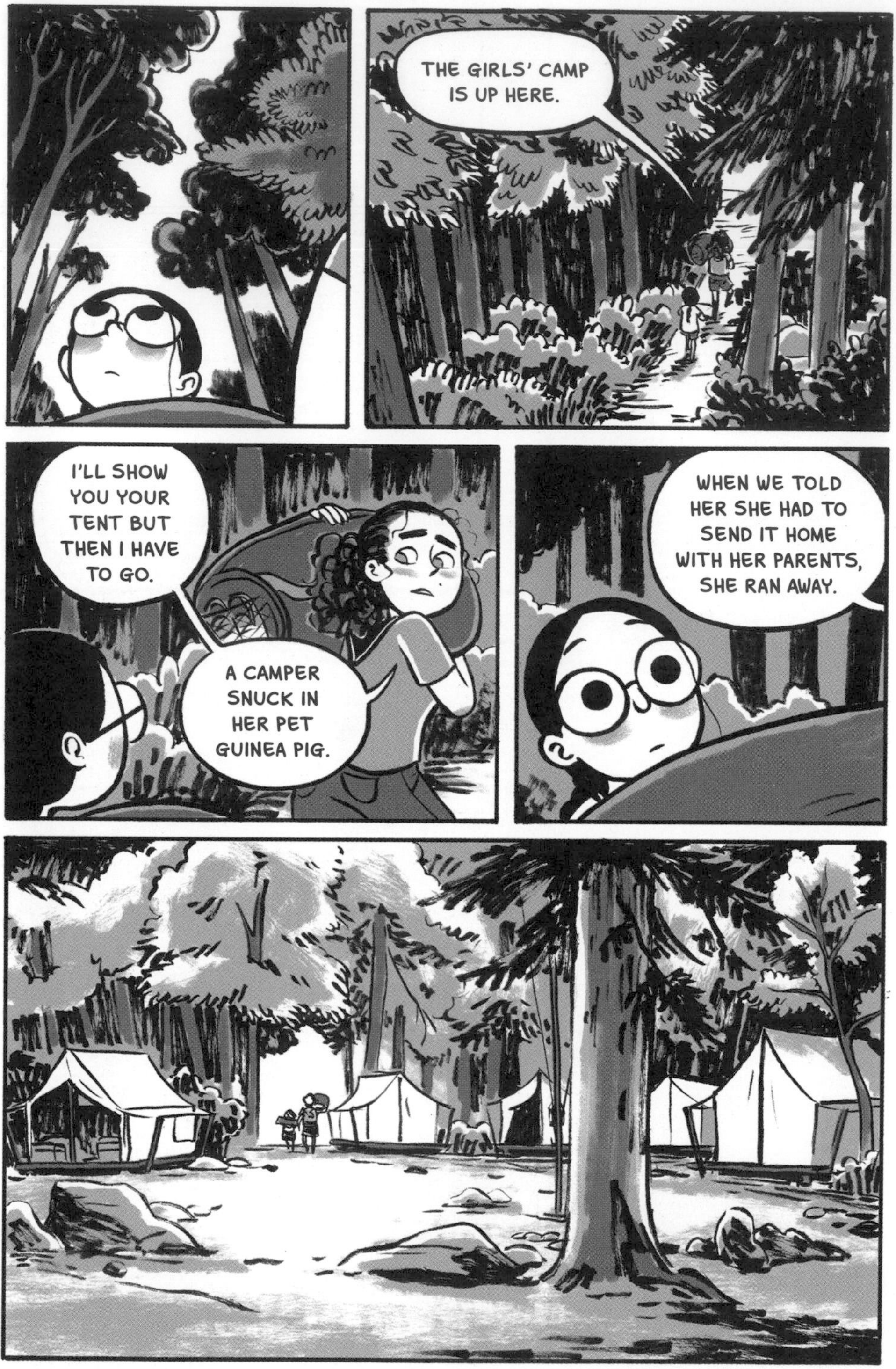
THE GIRLS' CAMP IS UP HERE.
I'LL SHOW YOU YOUR TENT BUT THEN I HAVE TO GO.
A CAMPER SNUCK IN HER PET GUINEA PIG.
WHEN WE TOLD HER SHE HAD TO SEND IT HOME WITH HER PARENTS, SHE RAN AWAY.

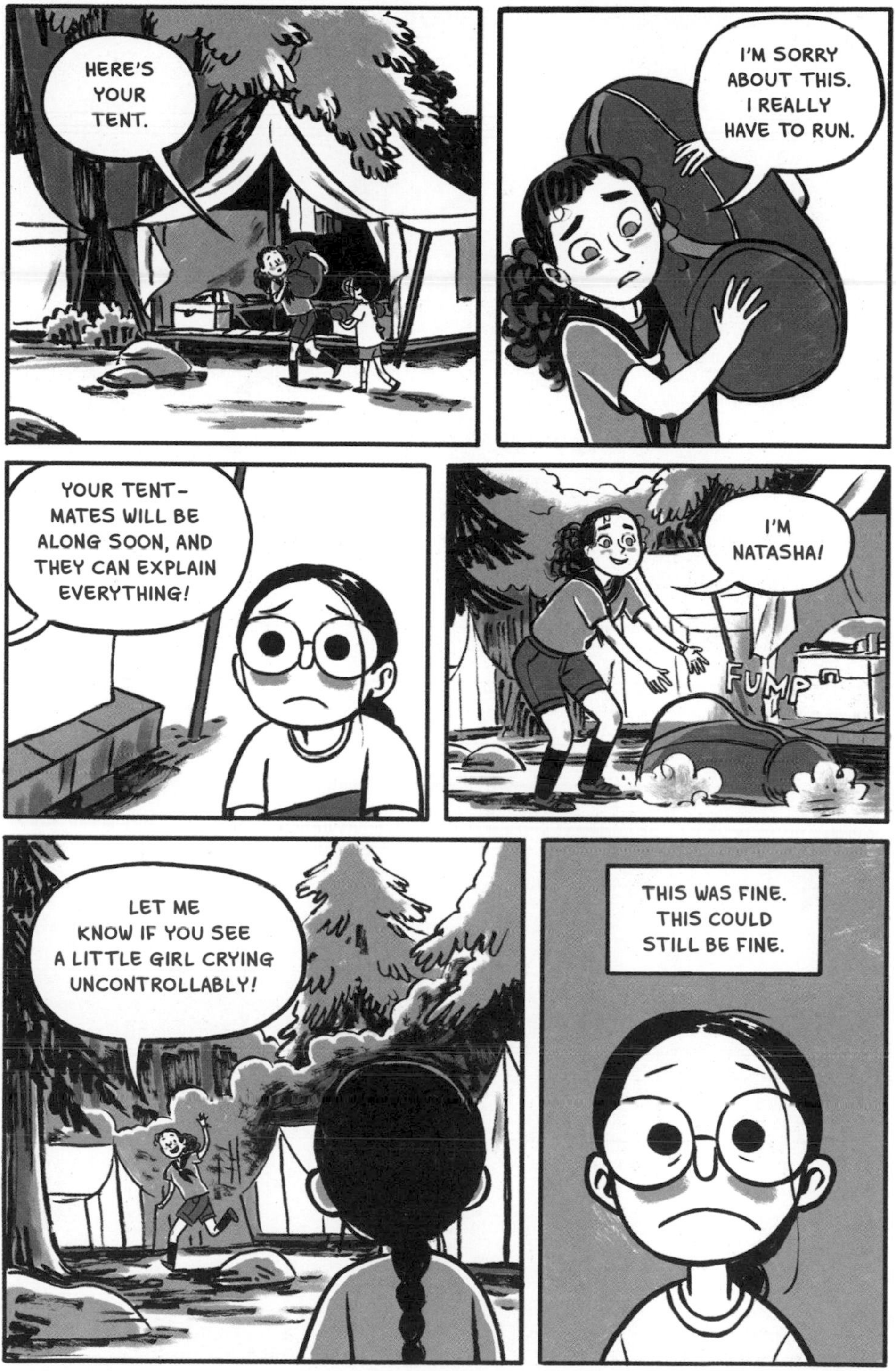
HERE'S YOUR TENT.
I'M SORRY ABOUT THIS. I REALLY HAVE TO RUN.
YOUR TENT-MATES WILL BE ALONG SOON, AND THEY CAN EXPLAIN EVERYTHING!
I'M NATASHA!
FUMP
LET ME KNOW IF YOU SEE A LITTLE GIRL CRYING UNCONTROLLABLY!
THIS WAS FINE. THIS COULD STILL BE FINE.

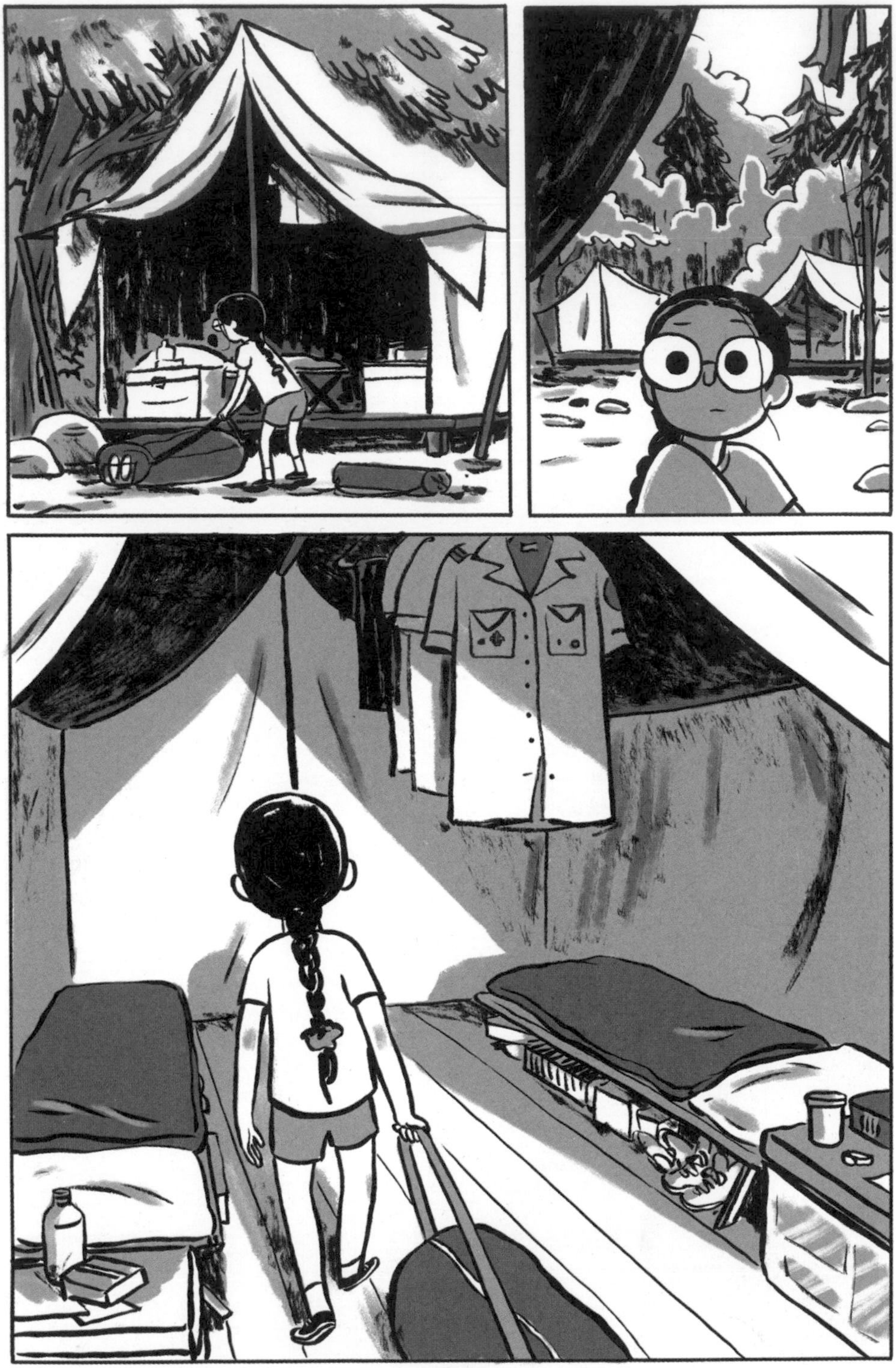

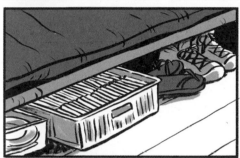

WHAT ARE YOU DOING.

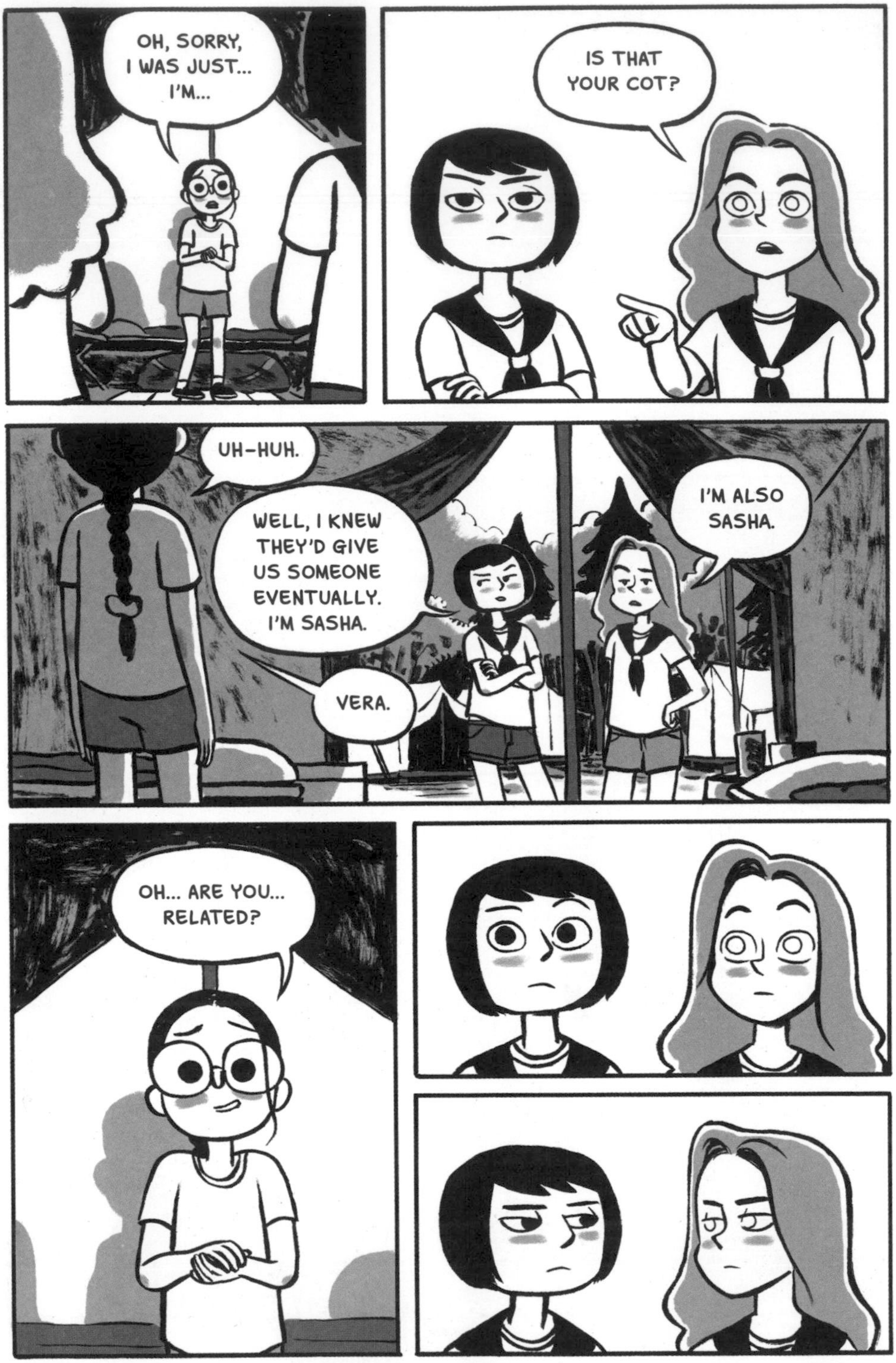
OH, SORRY, I WAS JUST... I'M...
IS THAT YOUR COT?
UH-HUH.
WELL, I KNEW THEY'D GIVE US SOMEONE EVENTUALLY. I'M SASHA.
I'M ALSO SASHA.
VERA.
OH... ARE YOU... RELATED?

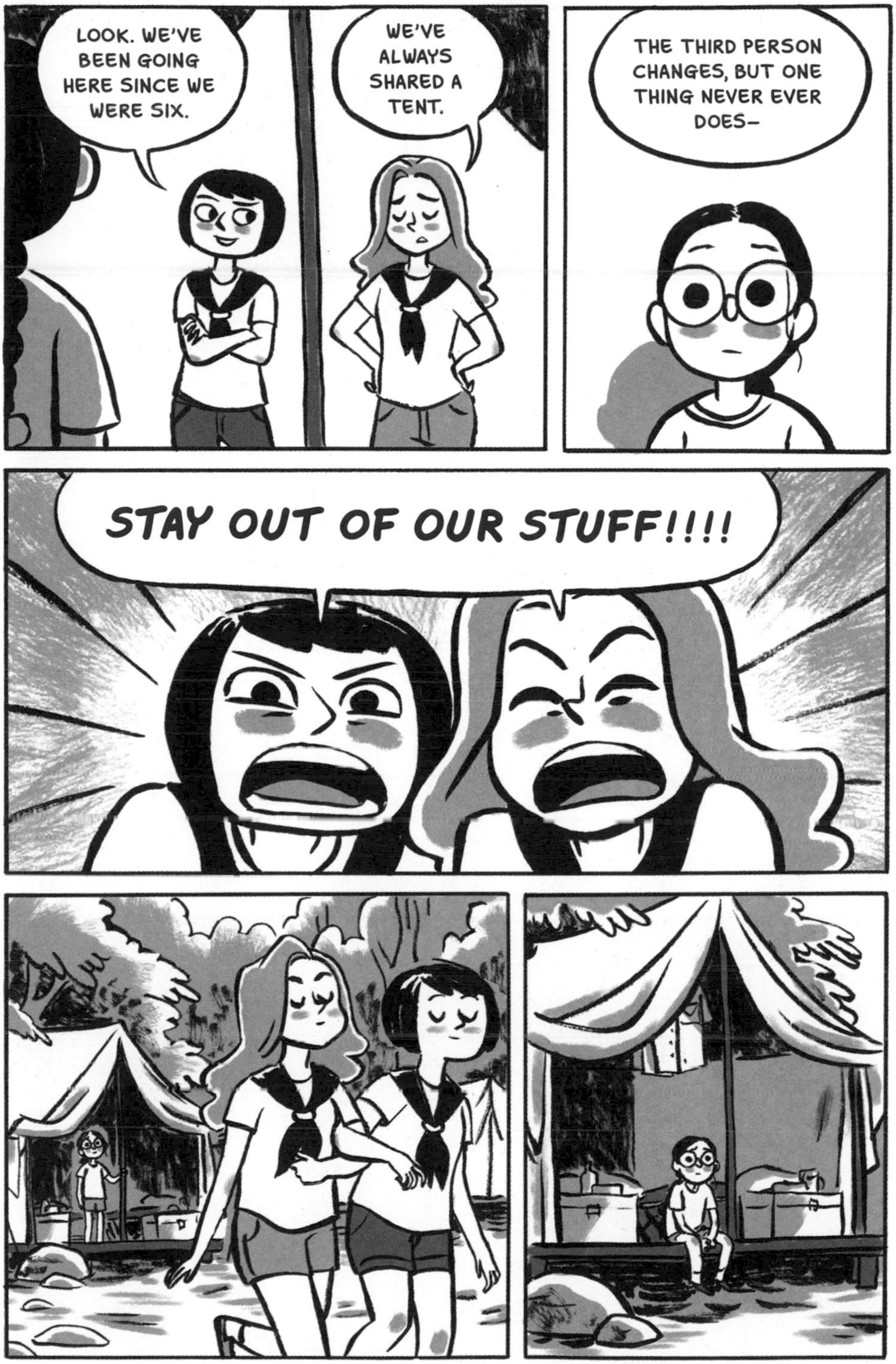
LOOK. WE'VE BEEN GOING HERE SINCE WE WERE SIX.
WE'VE ALWAYS SHARED A TENT.
THE THIRD PERSON CHANGES, BUT ONE THING NEVER EVER DOES–
STAY OUT OF OUR STUFF!!!!

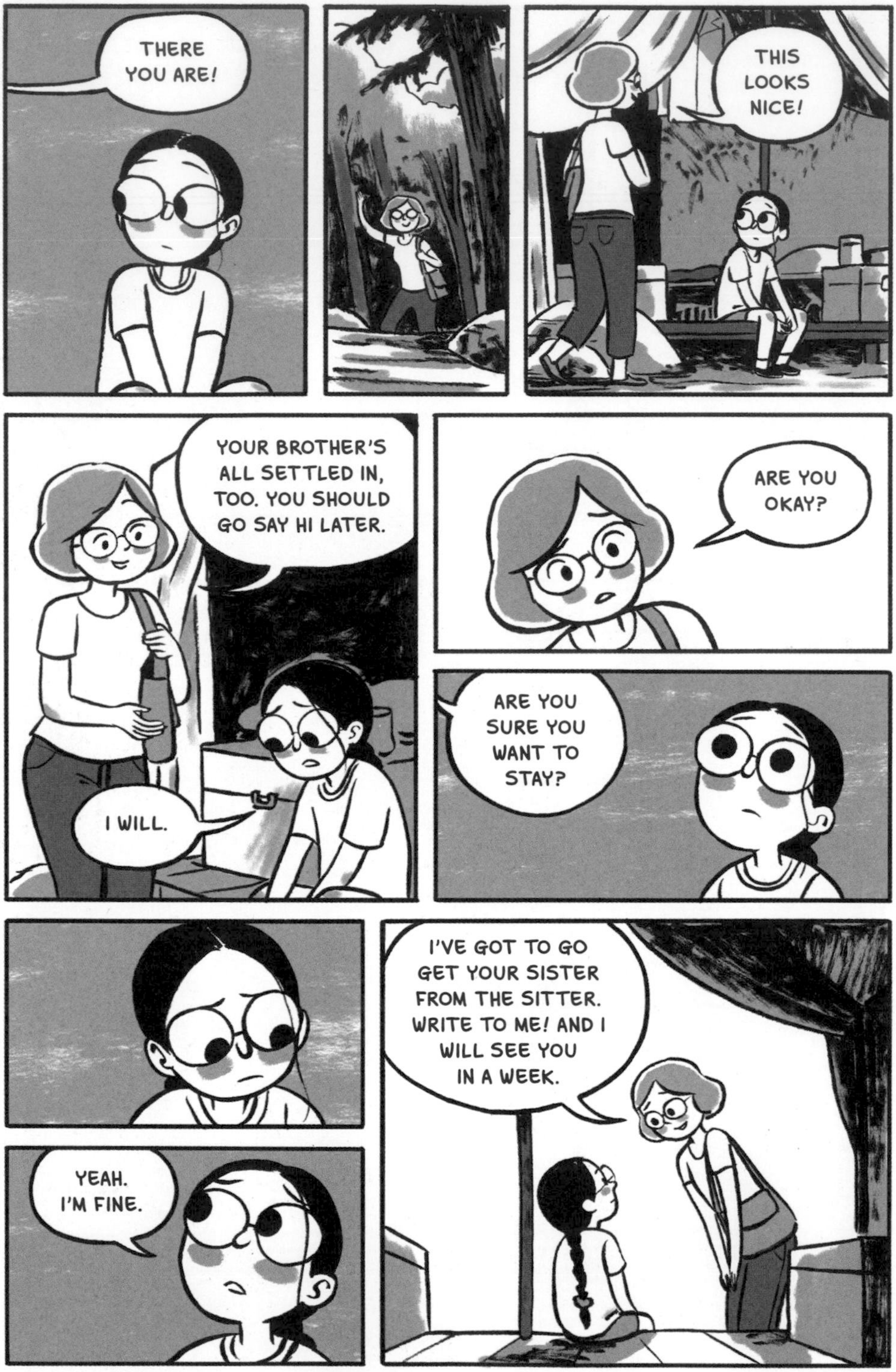
THERE YOU ARE!
THIS LOOKS NICE!
YOUR BROTHER'S ALL SETTLED IN, TOO. YOU SHOULD GO SAY HI LATER.
I WILL.
ARE YOU OKAY?
ARE YOU SURE YOU WANT TO STAY?
YEAH. I'M FINE.
I'VE GOT TO GO GET YOUR SISTER FROM THE SITTER. WRITE TO ME! AND I WILL SEE YOU IN A WEEK.

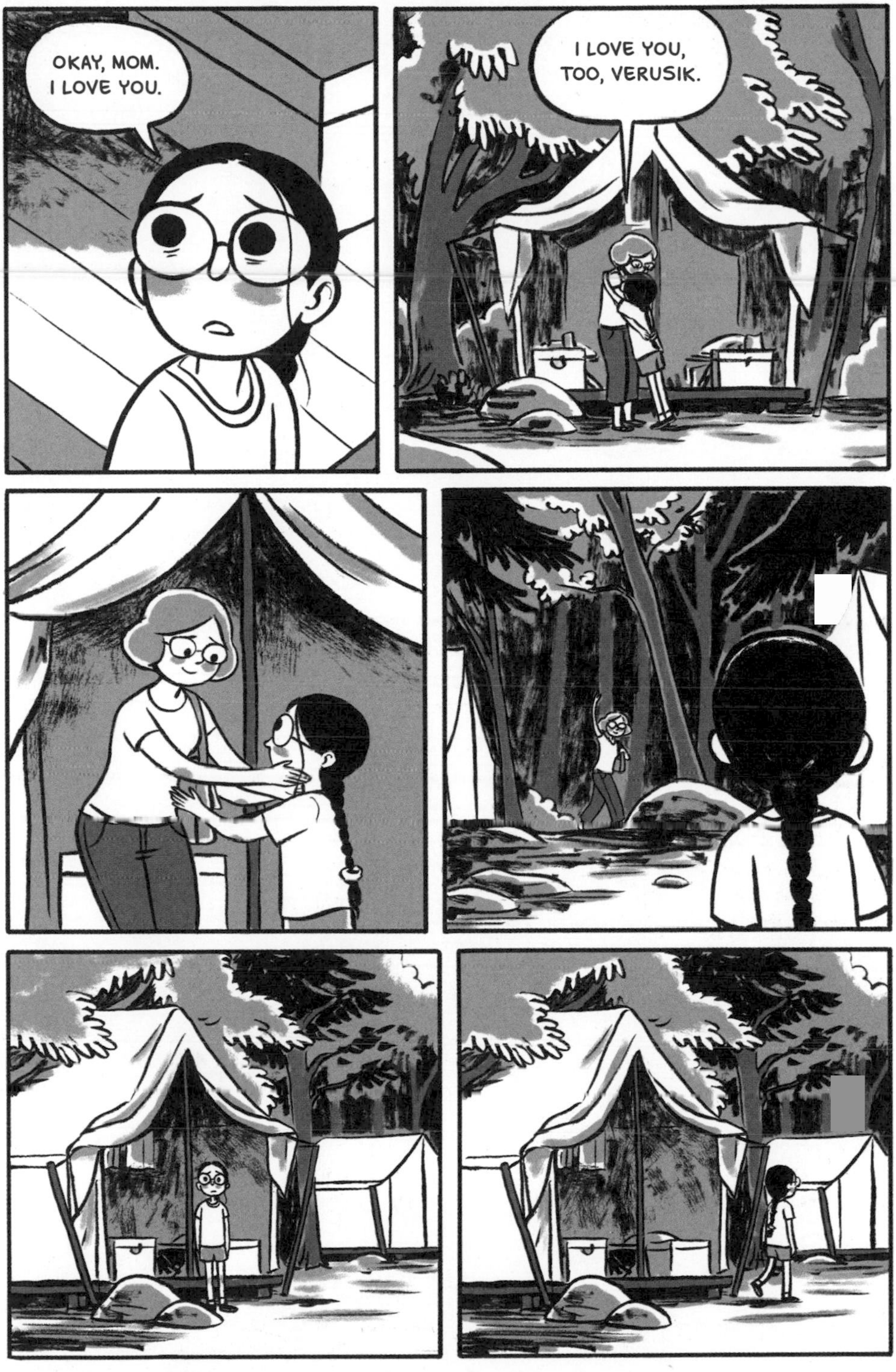
OKAY, MOM.
I LOVE YOU.
I LOVE YOU,
TOO, VERUSIK.

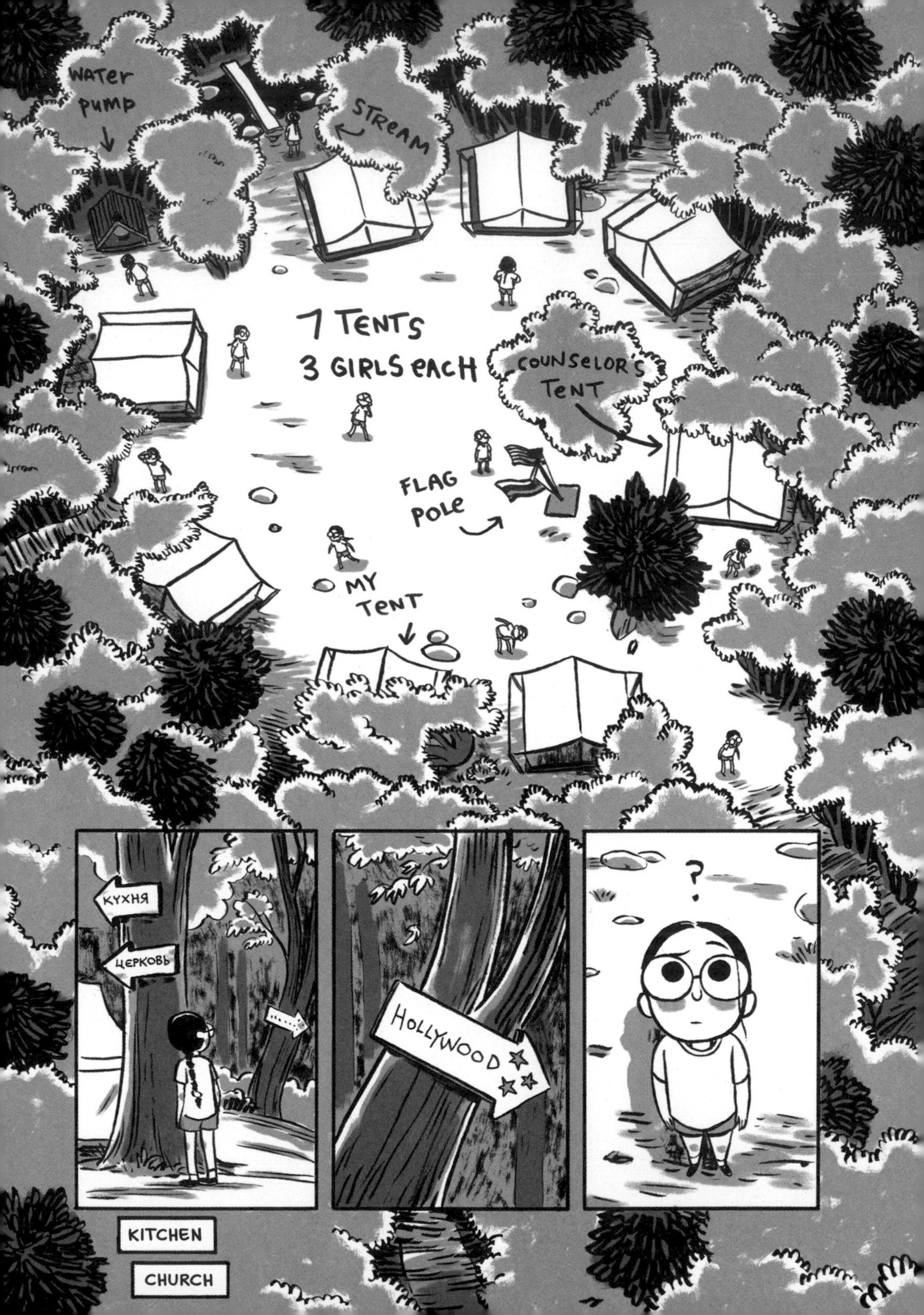

Water pump
Stream
7 Tents
3 girls each
Counselor's Tent
Flag Pole
My Tent
КУХНЯ
ЦЕРКОВЬ
HOLLYWOOD
?
KITCHEN
CHURCH

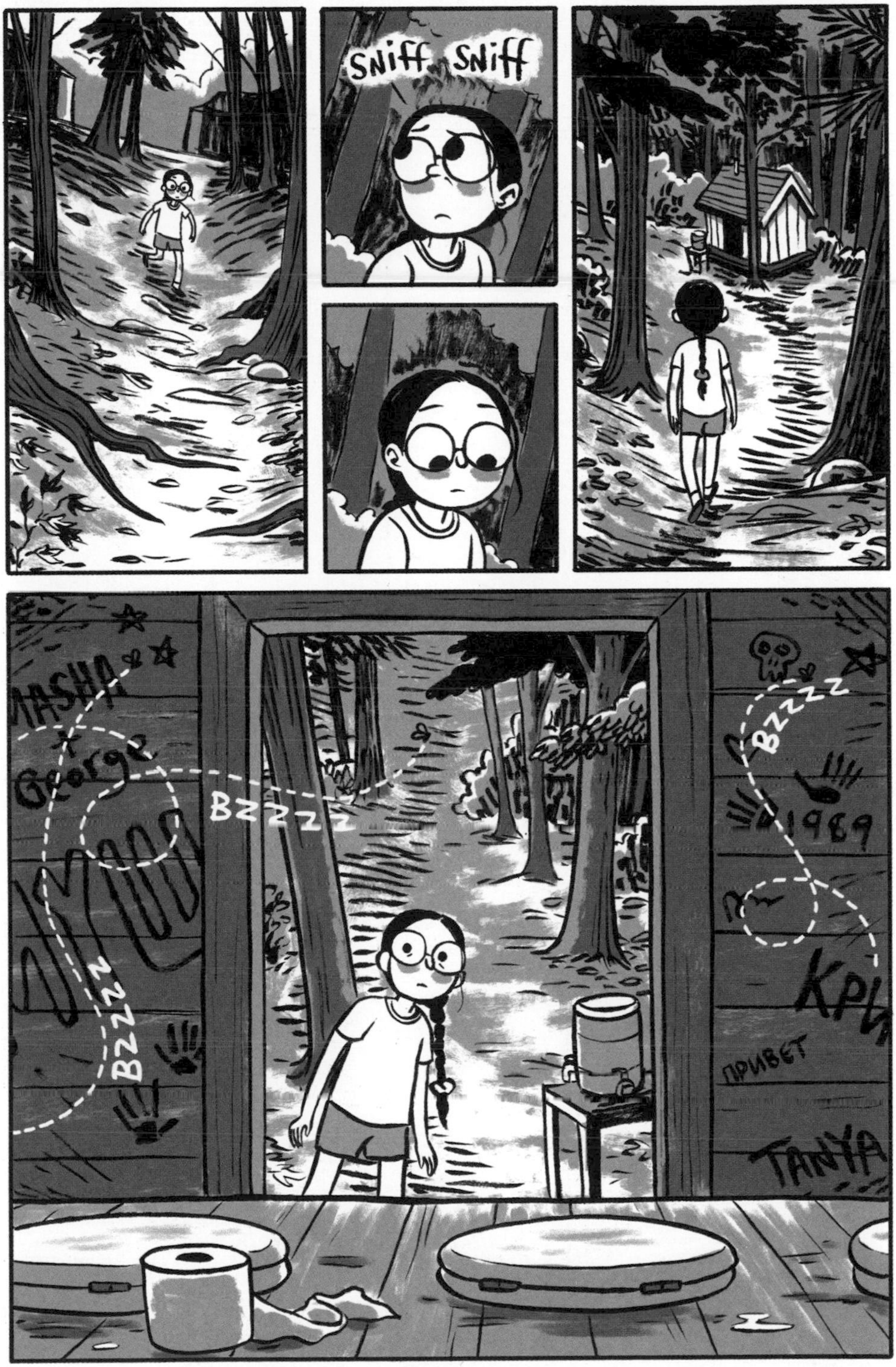
SNIFF SNIFF
MASHA
George
BZZZZZ
BZZZZZ
BZZZZ
1989
KPИ
ПРИВЕТ
TANYA

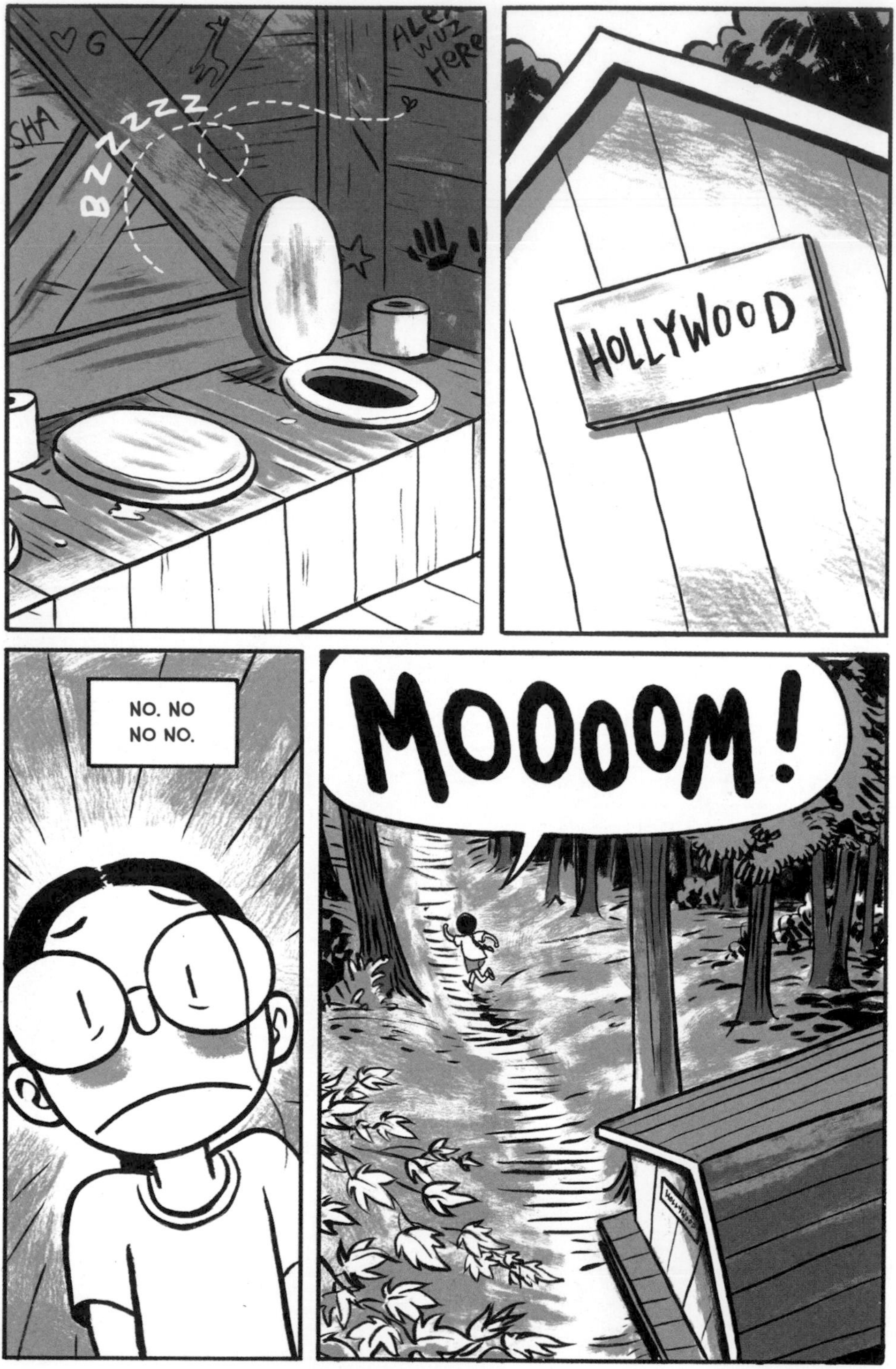
G
SHA
WUZ HERE
BZZZZZZ
HOLLYWOOD
NO. NO
NO NO.
MOOOOM!

Huff Huff Huff

BUT IT WAS TOO LATE.

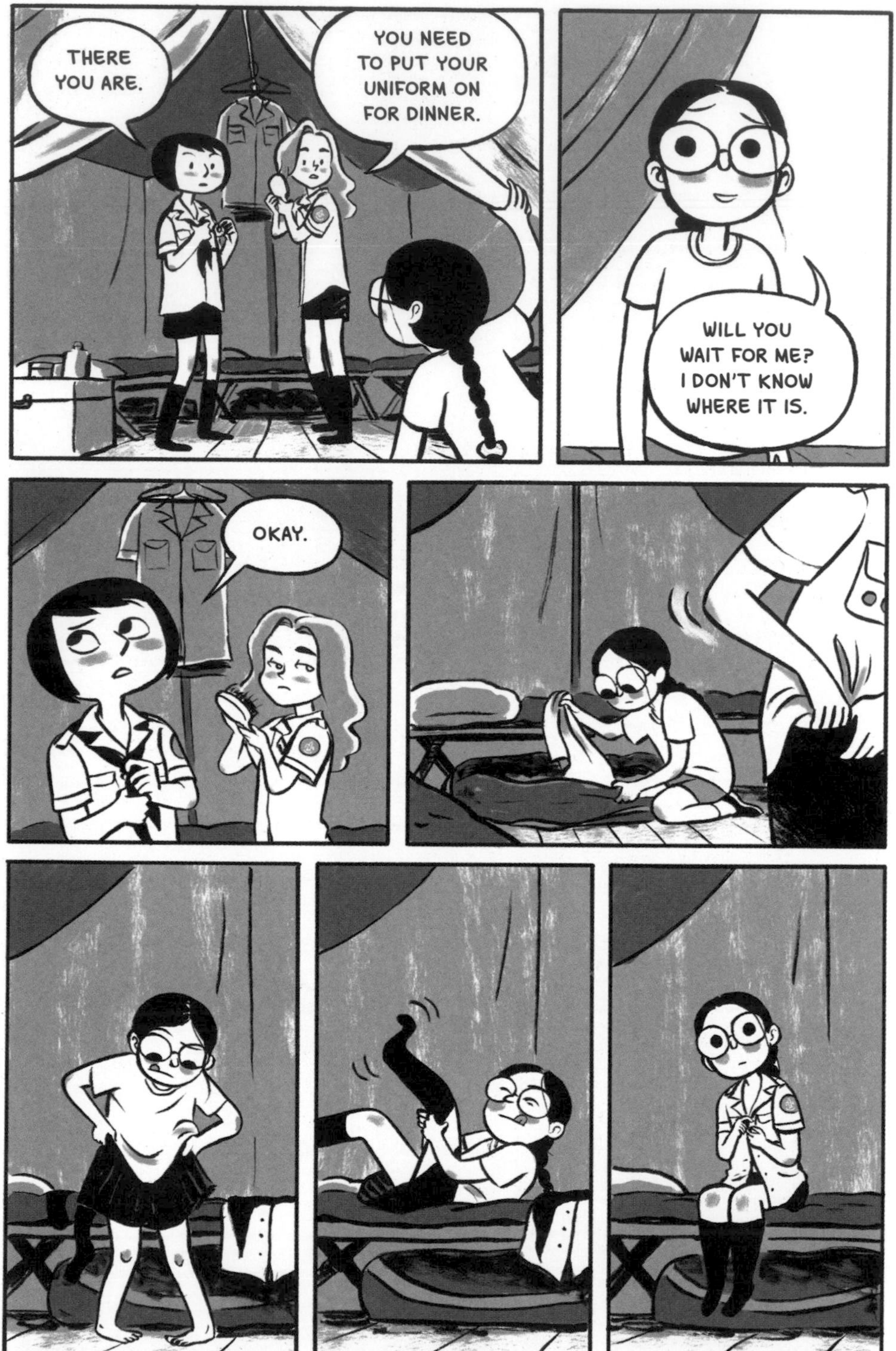
THERE YOU ARE.
YOU NEED TO PUT YOUR UNIFORM ON FOR DINNER.
WILL YOU WAIT FOR ME? I DON'T KNOW WHERE IT IS.
OKAY.

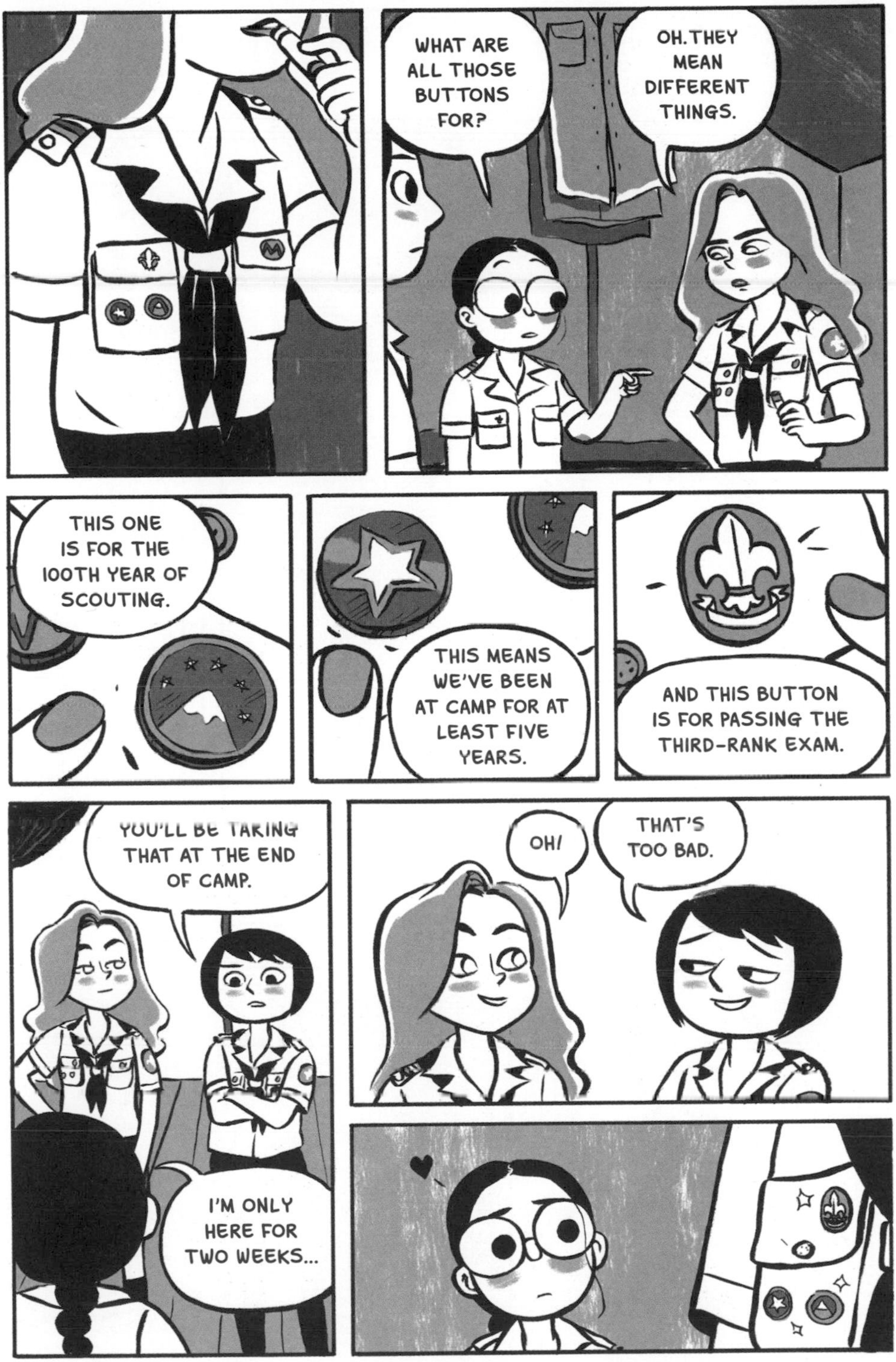
WHAT ARE ALL THOSE BUTTONS FOR?
OH. THEY MEAN DIFFERENT THINGS.
THIS ONE IS FOR THE 100TH YEAR OF SCOUTING.
THIS MEANS WE'VE BEEN AT CAMP FOR AT LEAST FIVE YEARS.
AND THIS BUTTON IS FOR PASSING THE THIRD-RANK EXAM.
YOU'LL BE TAKING THAT AT THE END OF CAMP.
I'M ONLY HERE FOR TWO WEEKS...
OH!
THAT'S TOO BAD.

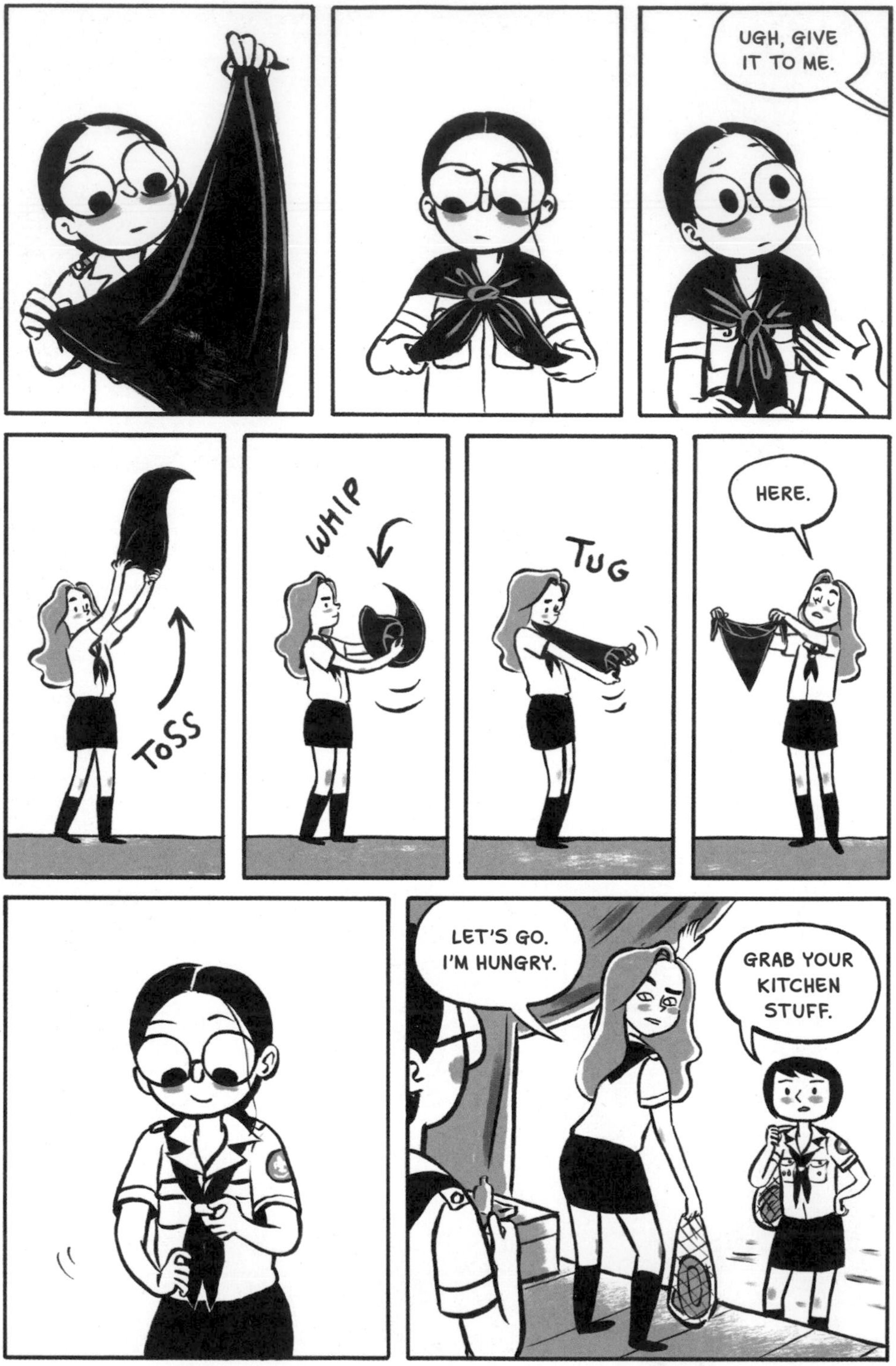
UGH, GIVE IT TO ME.
TOSS
WHIP
TUG
HERE.
LET'S GO. I'M HUNGRY.
GRAB YOUR KITCHEN STUFF.

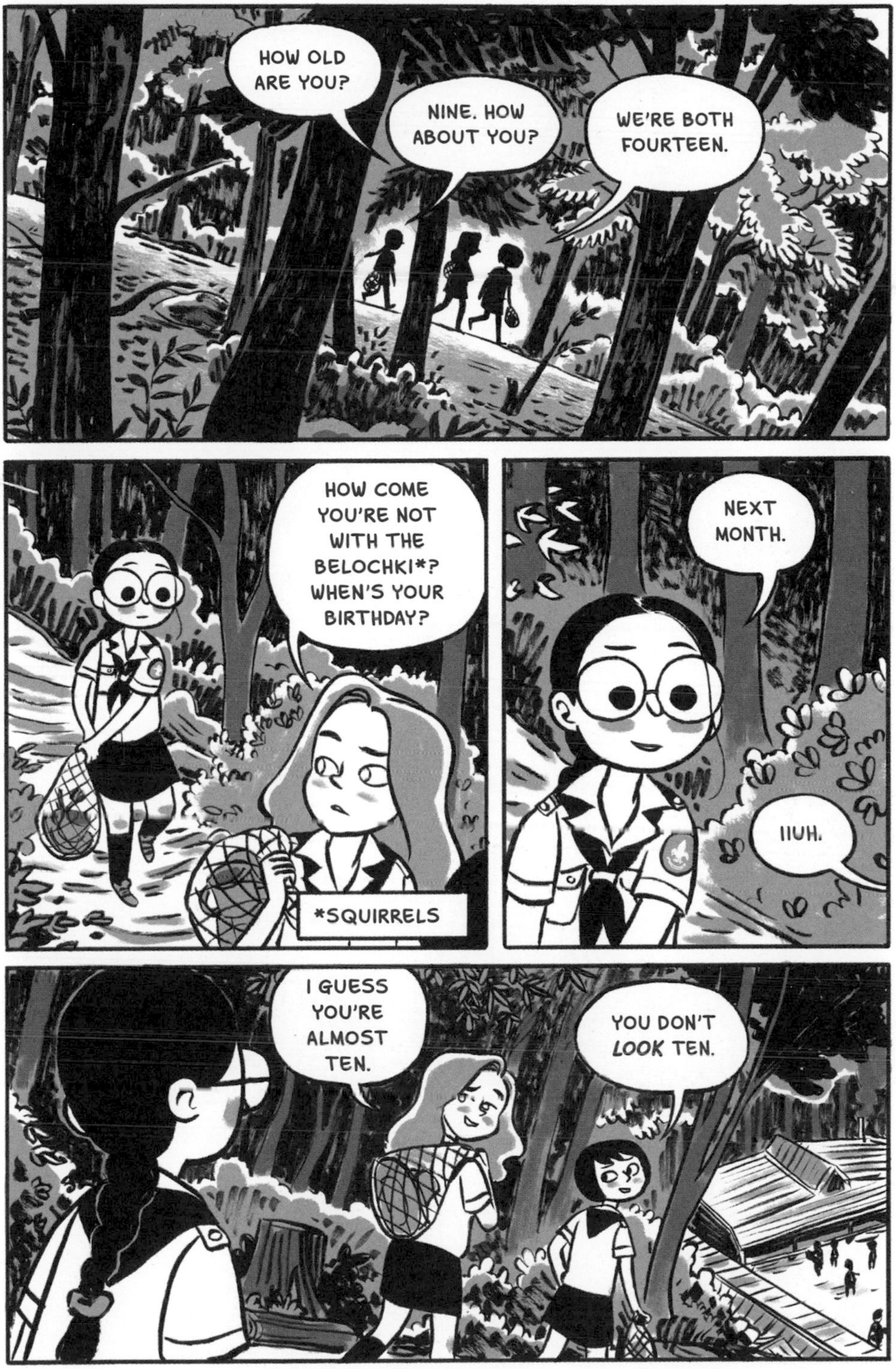
HOW OLD ARE YOU?
NINE. HOW ABOUT YOU?
WE'RE BOTH FOURTEEN.
HOW COME YOU'RE NOT WITH THE BELOCHKI*? WHEN'S YOUR BIRTHDAY?
*SQUIRRELS
NEXT MONTH.
IIUH.
I GUESS YOU'RE ALMOST TEN.
YOU DON'T *LOOK* TEN.

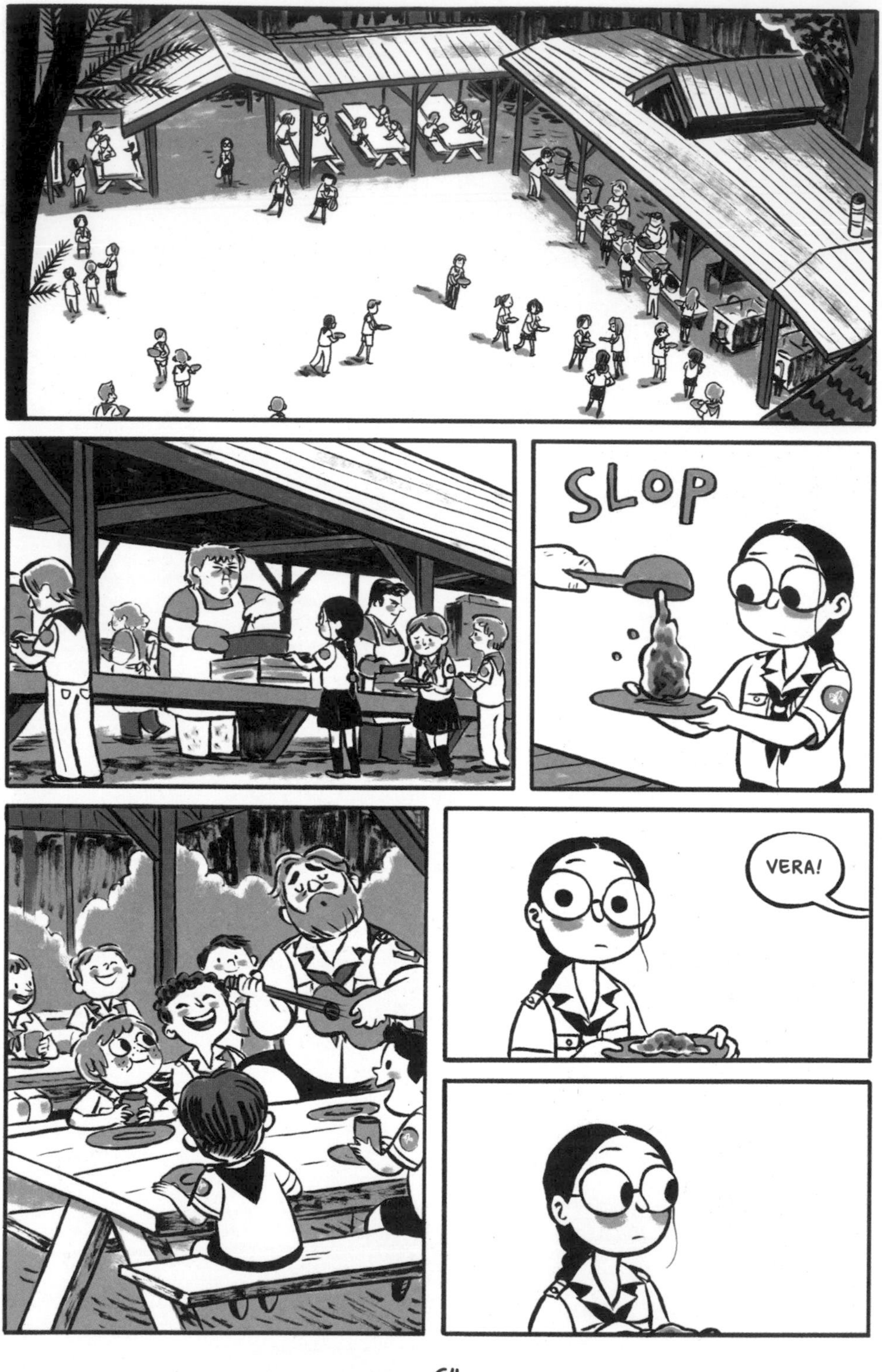
SLOP
VERA!

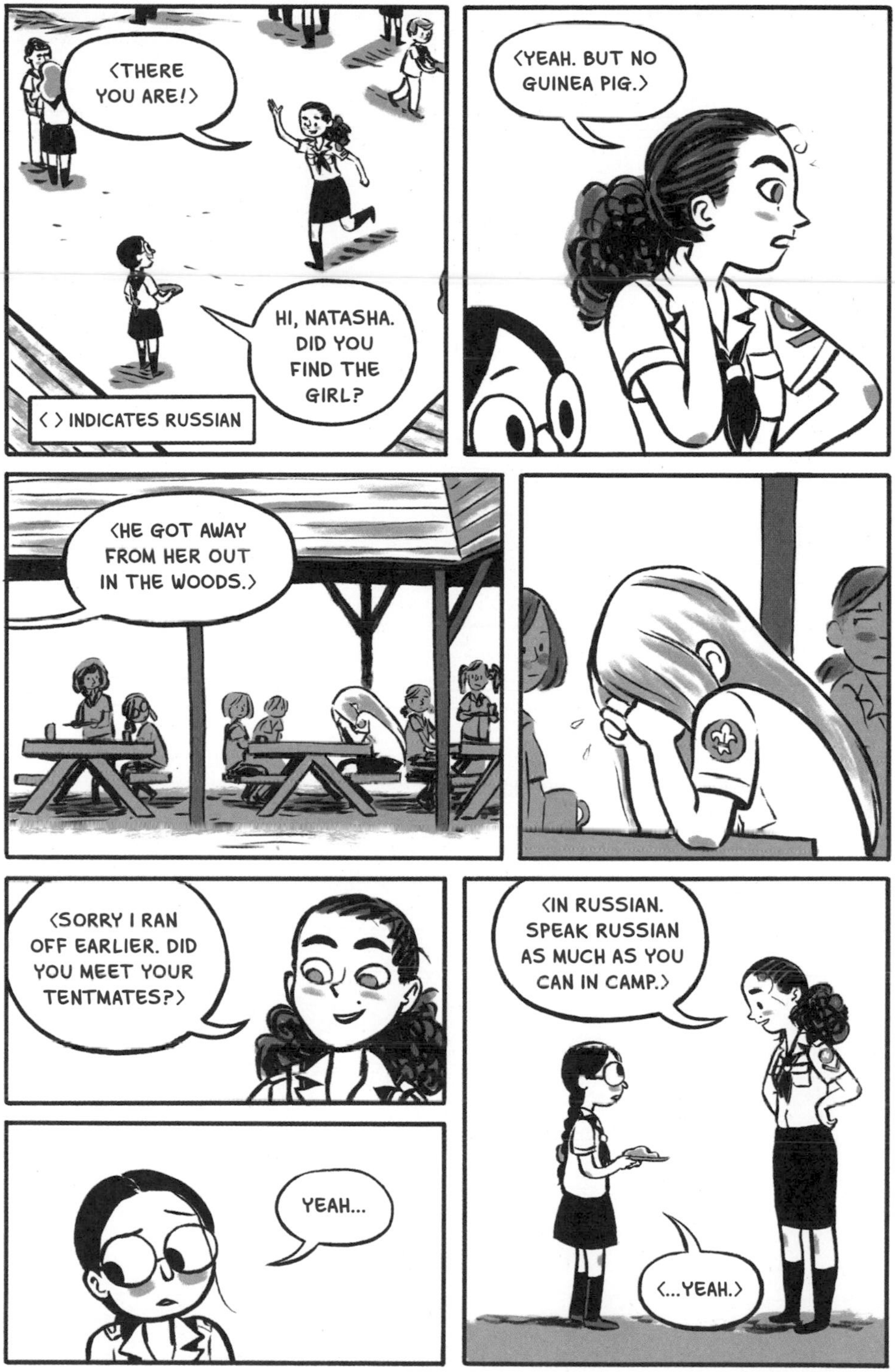
<THERE YOU ARE!>
HI, NATASHA. DID YOU FIND THE GIRL?
< > INDICATES RUSSIAN
<YEAH. BUT NO GUINEA PIG.>
<HE GOT AWAY FROM HER OUT IN THE WOODS.>
<SORRY I RAN OFF EARLIER. DID YOU MEET YOUR TENTMATES?>
YEAH...
<IN RUSSIAN. SPEAK RUSSIAN AS MUCH AS YOU CAN IN CAMP.>
<...YEAH.>

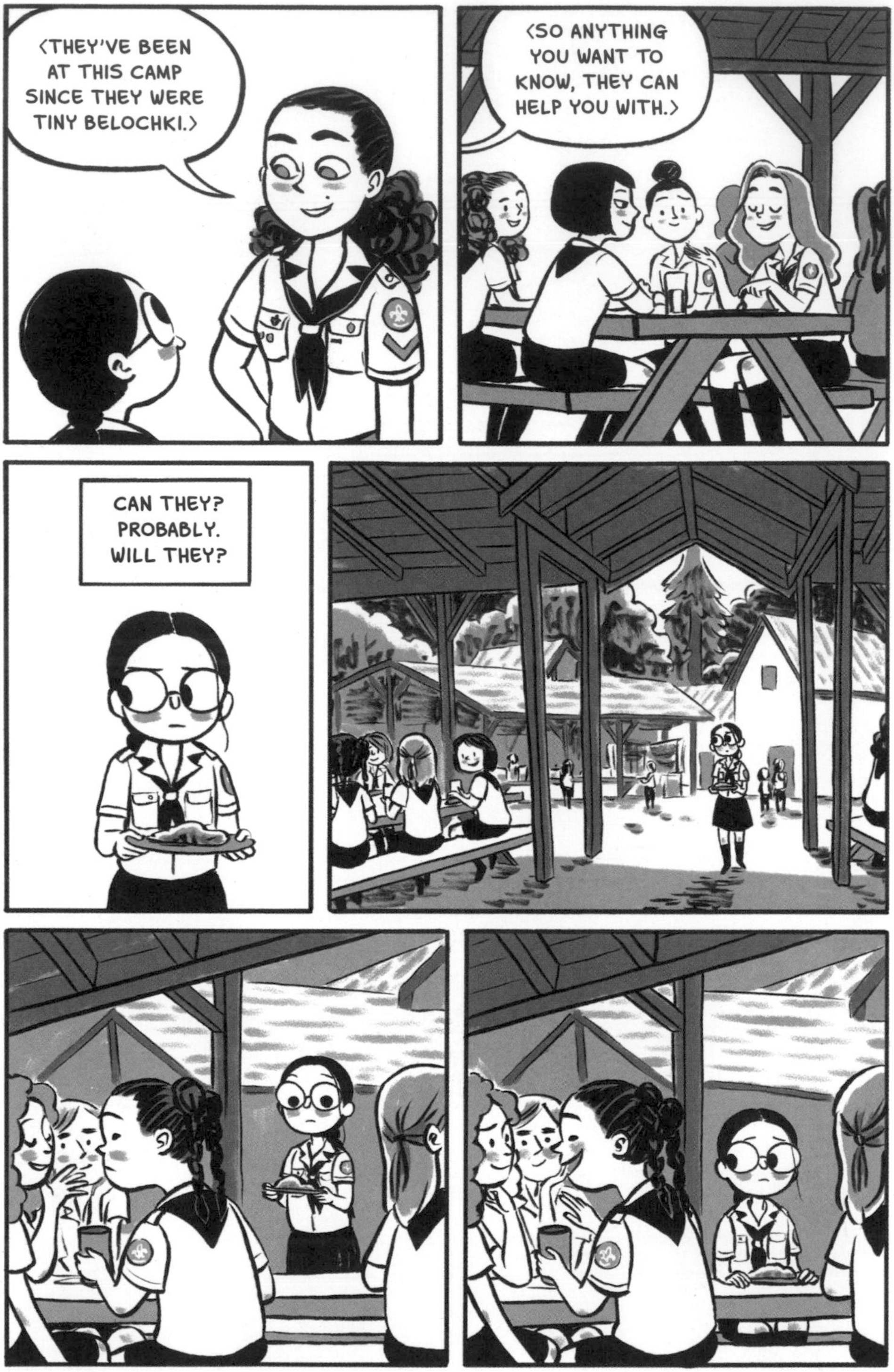

<THEY'VE BEEN AT THIS CAMP SINCE THEY WERE TINY BELOCHKI.>
<SO ANYTHING YOU WANT TO KNOW, THEY CAN HELP YOU WITH.>
CAN THEY? PROBABLY. WILL THEY?

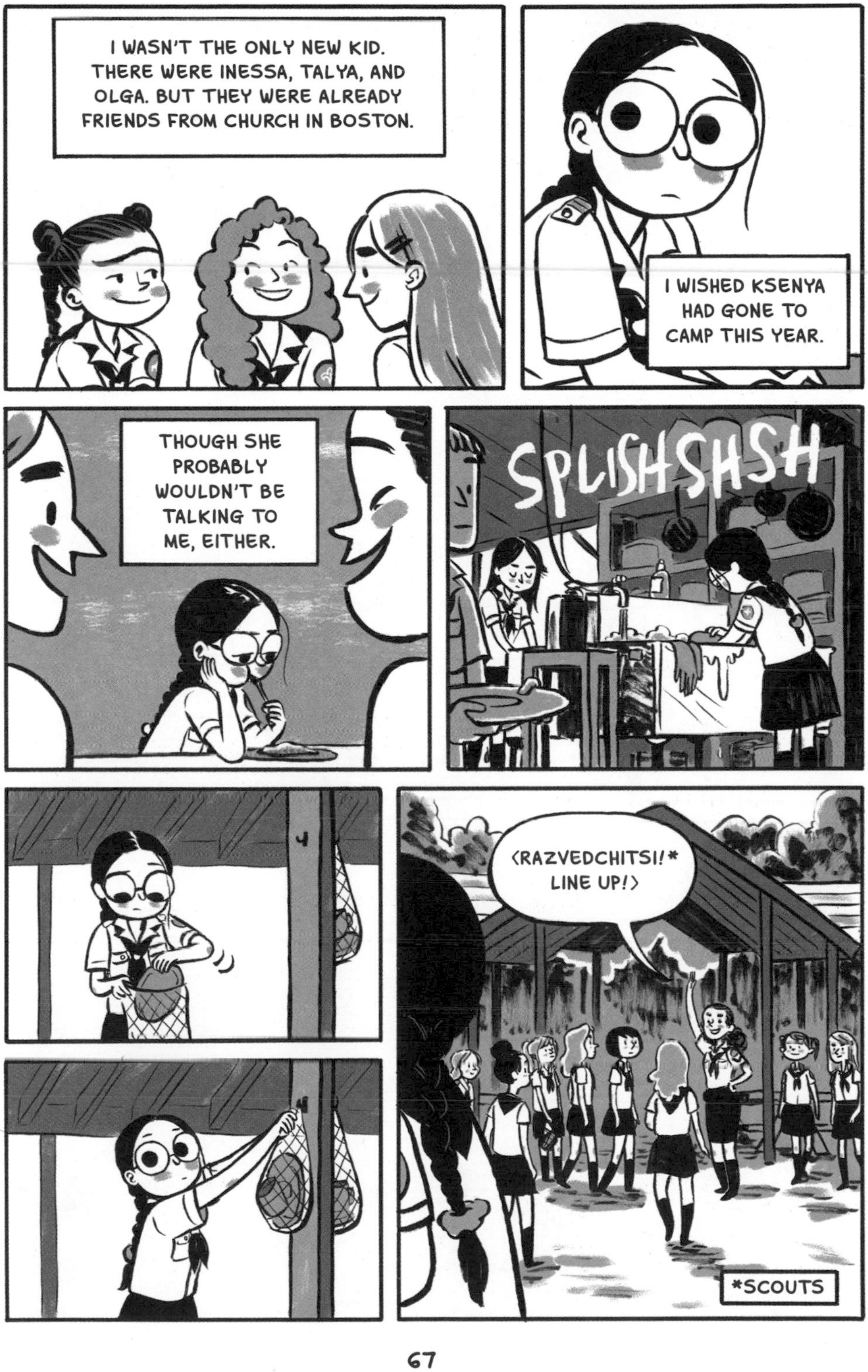
I WASN'T THE ONLY NEW KID. THERE WERE INESSA, TALYA, AND OLGA. BUT THEY WERE ALREADY FRIENDS FROM CHURCH IN BOSTON.
I WISHED KSENYA HAD GONE TO CAMP THIS YEAR.
THOUGH SHE PROBABLY WOULDN'T BE TALKING TO ME, EITHER.
SPLISHSHSH
‹RAZVEDCHITSI!* LINE UP!›
*SCOUTS

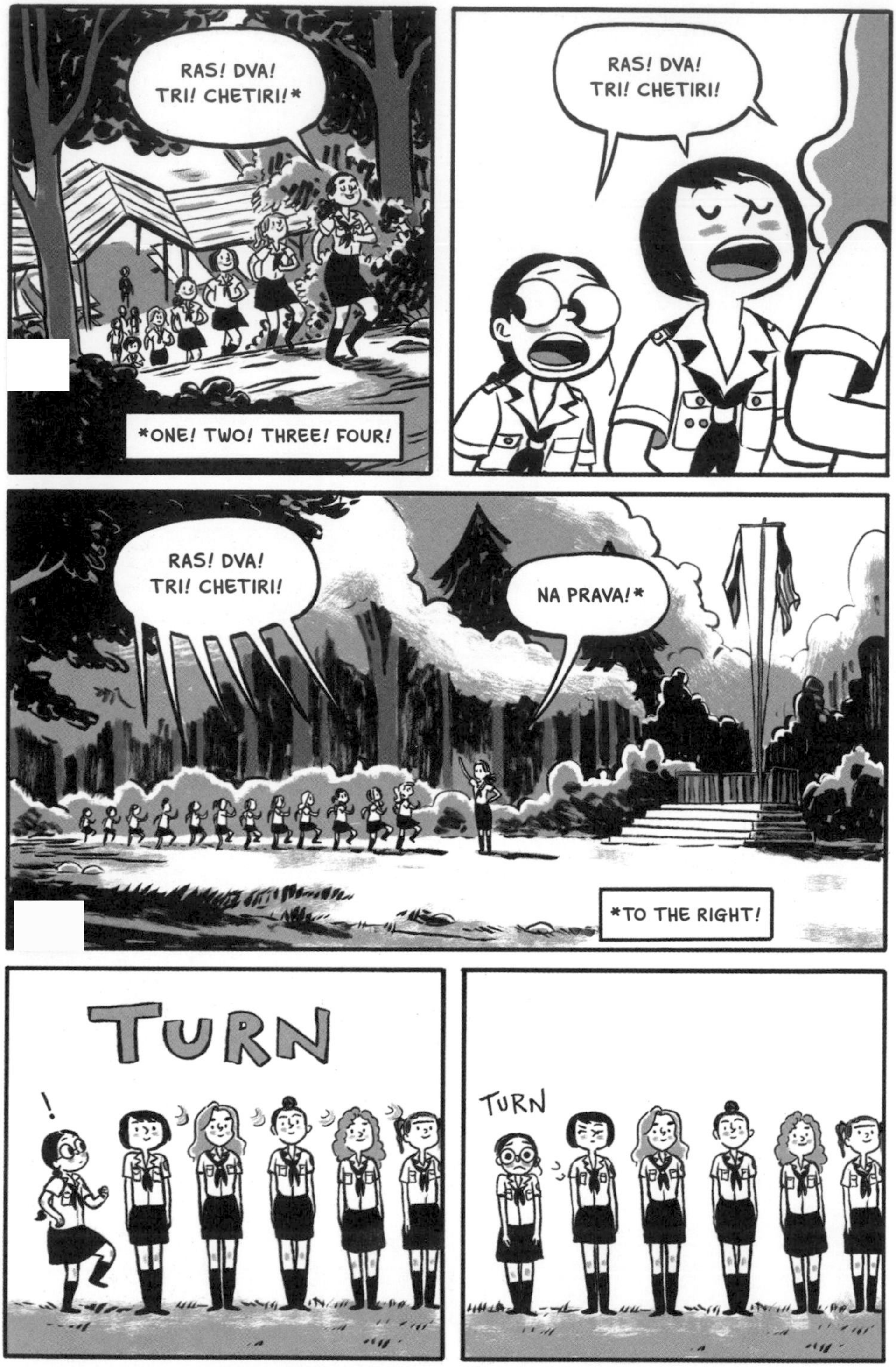
RAS! DVA! TRI! CHETIRI!*
*ONE! TWO! THREE! FOUR!
RAS! DVA! TRI! CHETIRI!
RAS! DVA! TRI! CHETIRI!
NA PRAVA!*
*TO THE RIGHT!
TURN
!
TURN

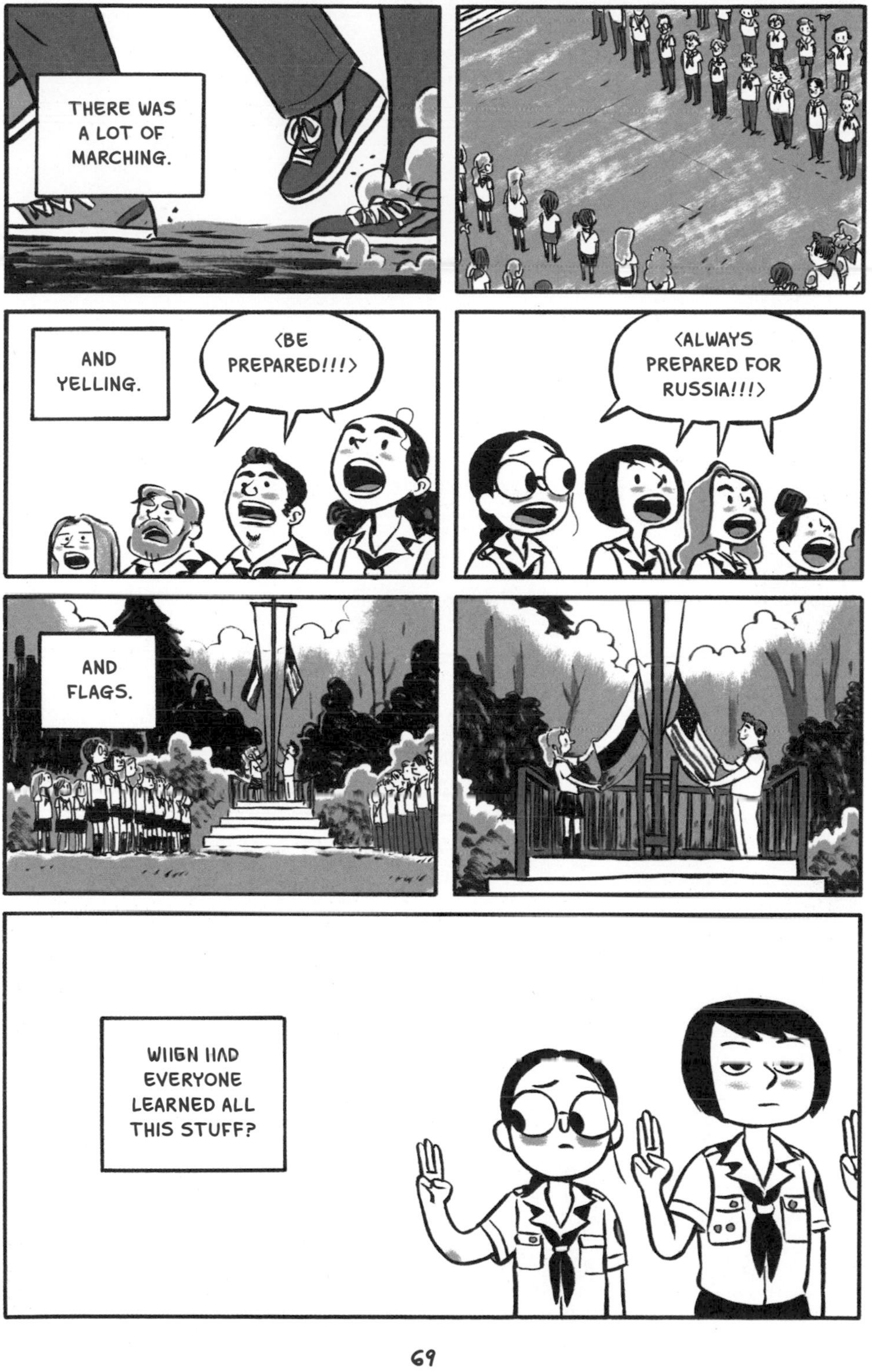
THERE WAS A LOT OF MARCHING.
AND YELLING.
<BE PREPARED!!!>
<ALWAYS PREPARED FOR RUSSIA!!!>
AND FLAGS.
WHEN HAD EVERYONE LEARNED ALL THIS STUFF?

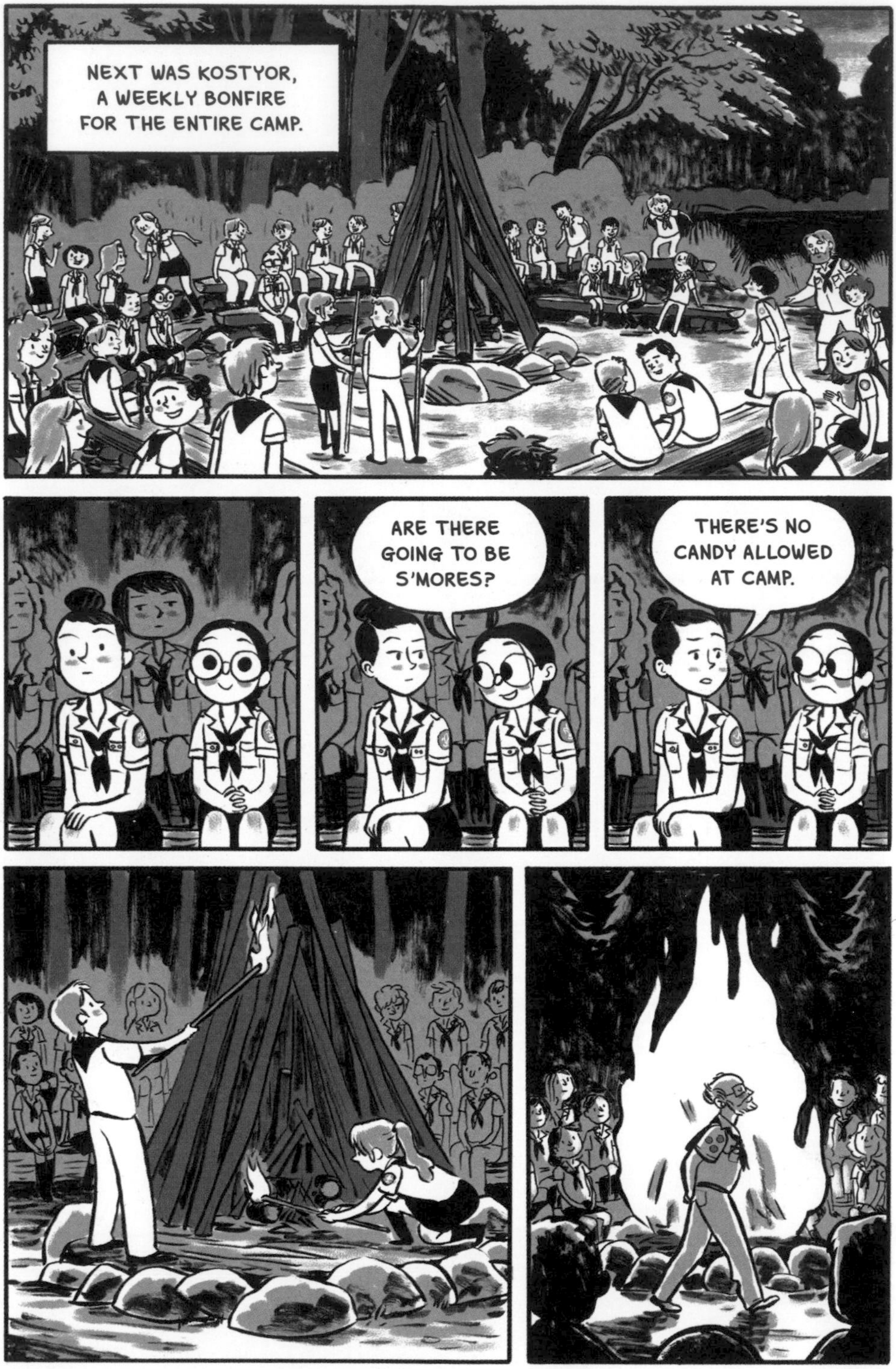
NEXT WAS KOSTYOR, A WEEKLY BONFIRE FOR THE ENTIRE CAMP.
ARE THERE GOING TO BE S'MORES?
THERE'S NO CANDY ALLOWED AT CAMP.

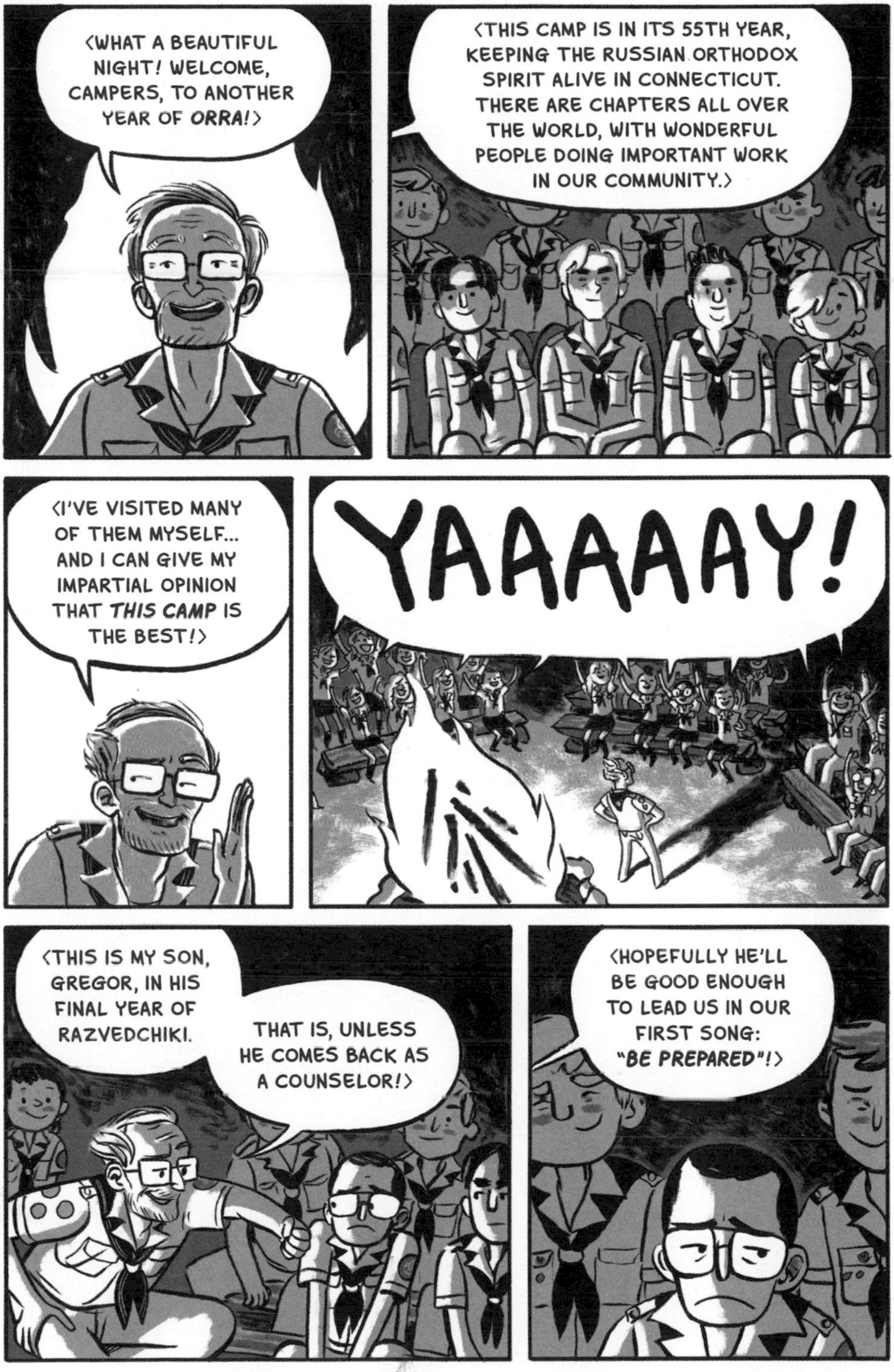

<WHAT A BEAUTIFUL NIGHT! WELCOME, CAMPERS, TO ANOTHER YEAR OF ORRA!>
<THIS CAMP IS IN ITS 55TH YEAR, KEEPING THE RUSSIAN ORTHODOX SPIRIT ALIVE IN CONNECTICUT. THERE ARE CHAPTERS ALL OVER THE WORLD, WITH WONDERFUL PEOPLE DOING IMPORTANT WORK IN OUR COMMUNITY.>
<I'VE VISITED MANY OF THEM MYSELF... AND I CAN GIVE MY IMPARTIAL OPINION THAT THIS CAMP IS THE BEST!>
YAAAAAY!
<THIS IS MY SON, GREGOR, IN HIS FINAL YEAR OF RAZVEDCHIKI.
THAT IS, UNLESS HE COMES BACK AS A COUNSELOR!>
<HOPEFULLY HE'LL BE GOOD ENOUGH TO LEAD US IN OUR FIRST SONG: "BE PREPARED"!>

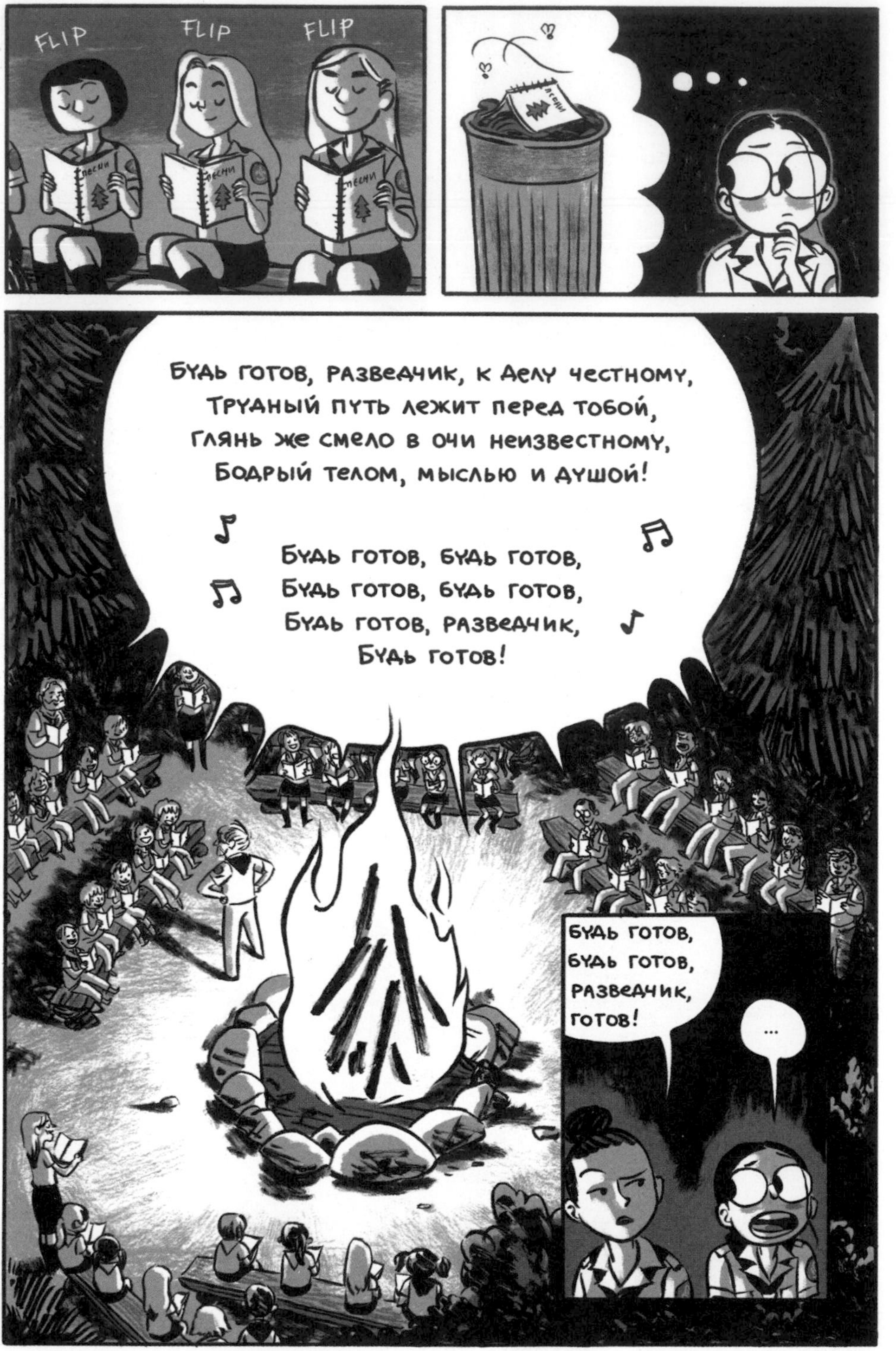
FLIP
FLIP
FLIP
песни
песни
песни
Будь готов, разведчик, к делу честному,
Трудный путь лежит перед тобой,
Глянь же смело в очи неизвестному,
Бодрый телом, мыслью и душой!
Будь готов, будь готов,
Будь готов, будь готов,
Будь готов, разведчик,
Будь готов!
Будь готов,
будь готов,
разведчик,
готов!
...

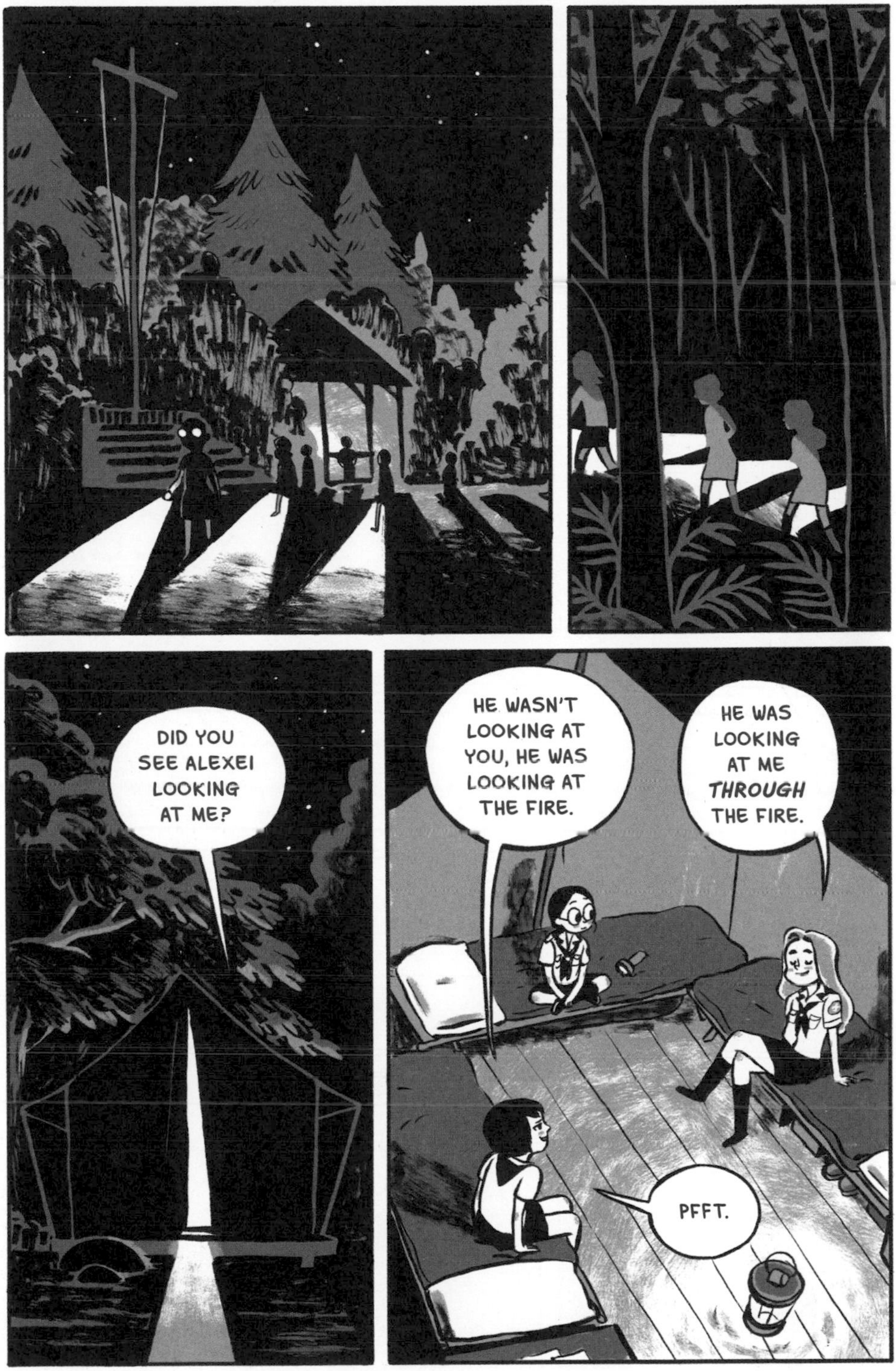
DID YOU SEE ALEXEI LOOKING AT ME?
HE WASN'T LOOKING AT YOU, HE WAS LOOKING AT THE FIRE.
HE WAS LOOKING AT ME *THROUGH* THE FIRE.
PFFT.

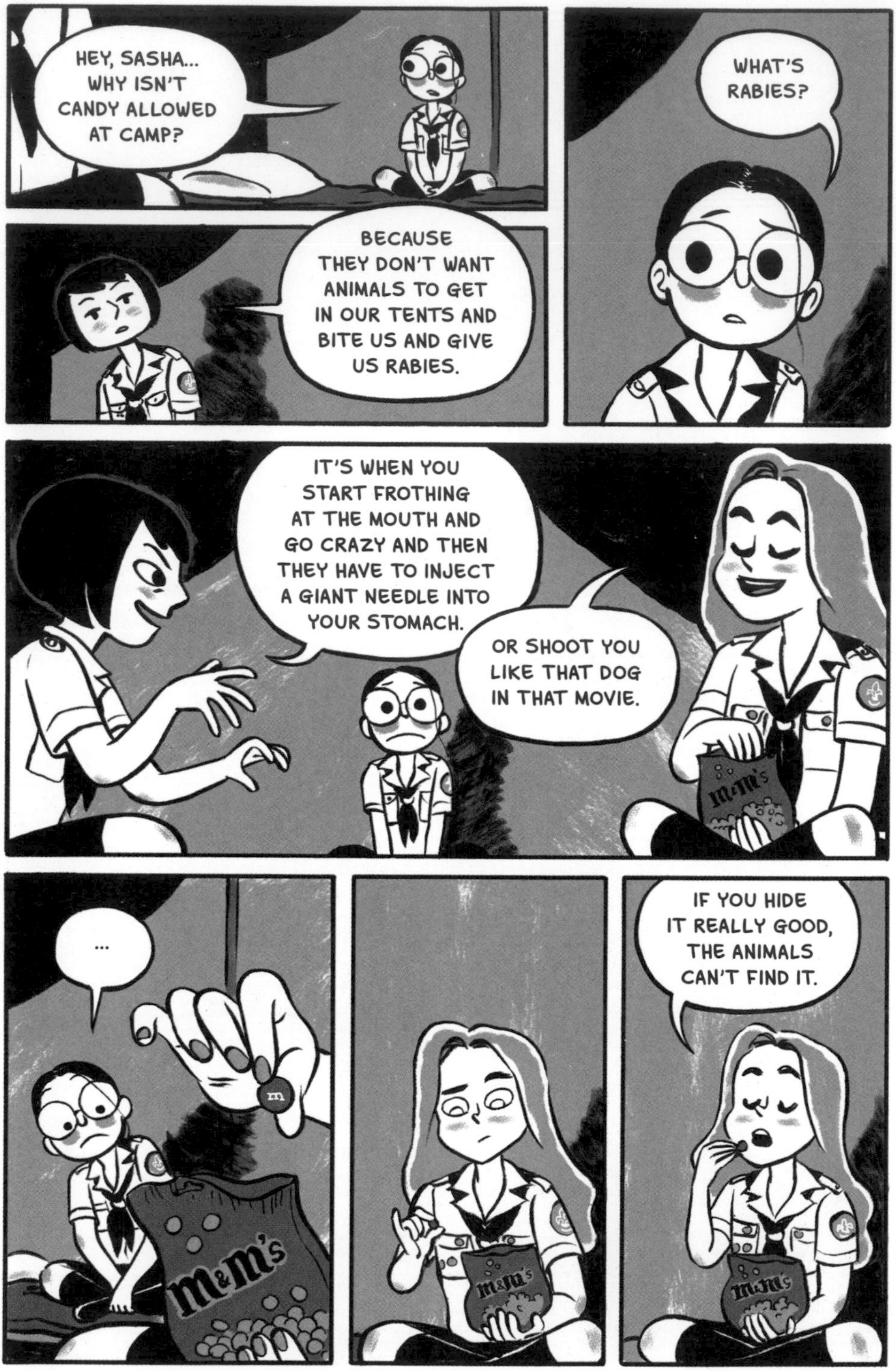
HEY, SASHA... WHY ISN'T CANDY ALLOWED AT CAMP?
WHAT'S RABIES?
BECAUSE THEY DON'T WANT ANIMALS TO GET IN OUR TENTS AND BITE US AND GIVE US RABIES.
IT'S WHEN YOU START FROTHING AT THE MOUTH AND GO CRAZY AND THEN THEY HAVE TO INJECT A GIANT NEEDLE INTO YOUR STOMACH.
OR SHOOT YOU LIKE THAT DOG IN THAT MOVIE.
M&M's
...
M&M's
M&M's
IF YOU HIDE IT REALLY GOOD, THE ANIMALS CAN'T FIND IT.
M&M's

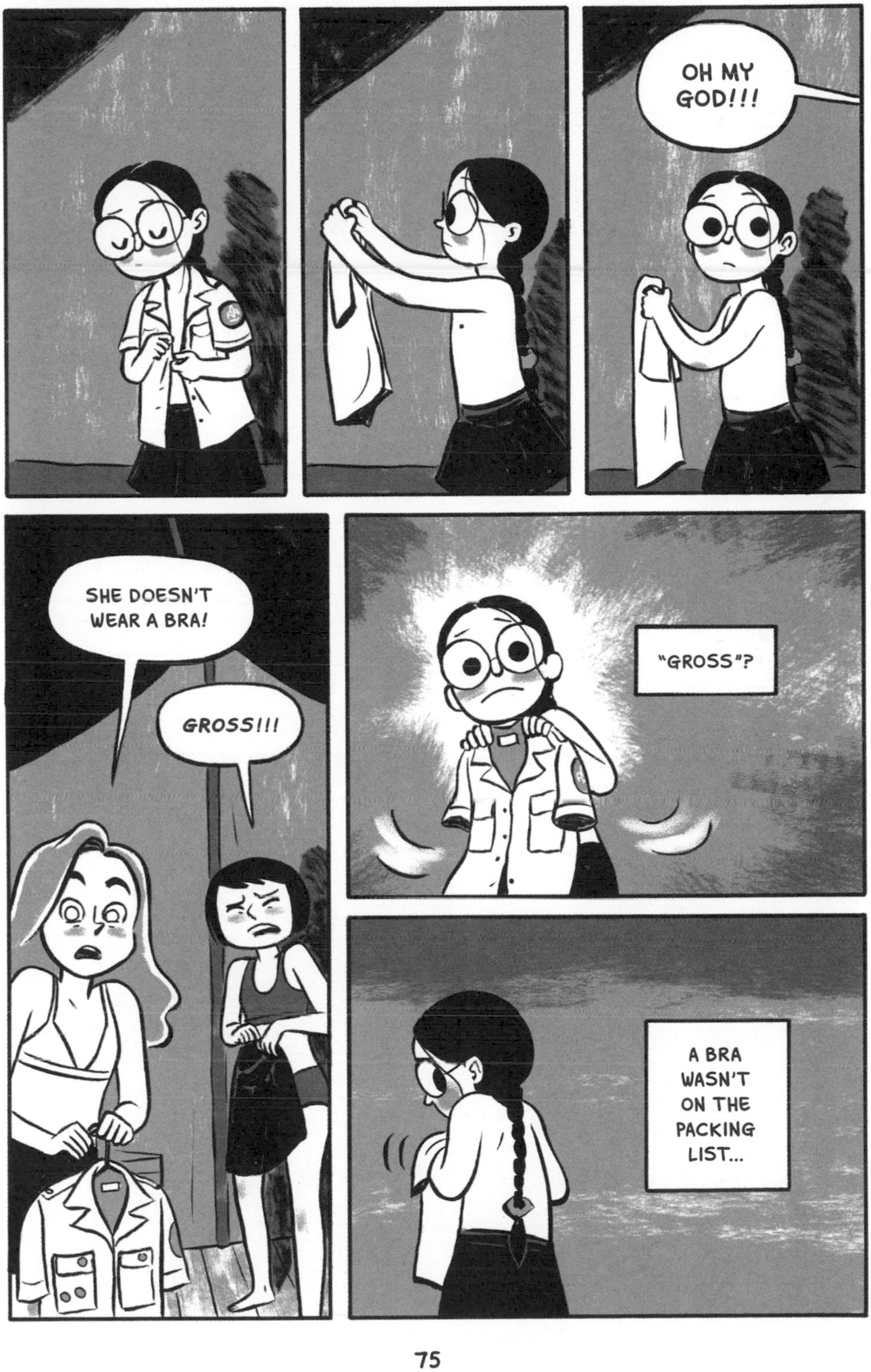
OH MY GOD!!!
SHE DOESN'T WEAR A BRA!
GROSS!!!
"GROSS"?
A BRA WASN'T ON THE PACKING LIST...

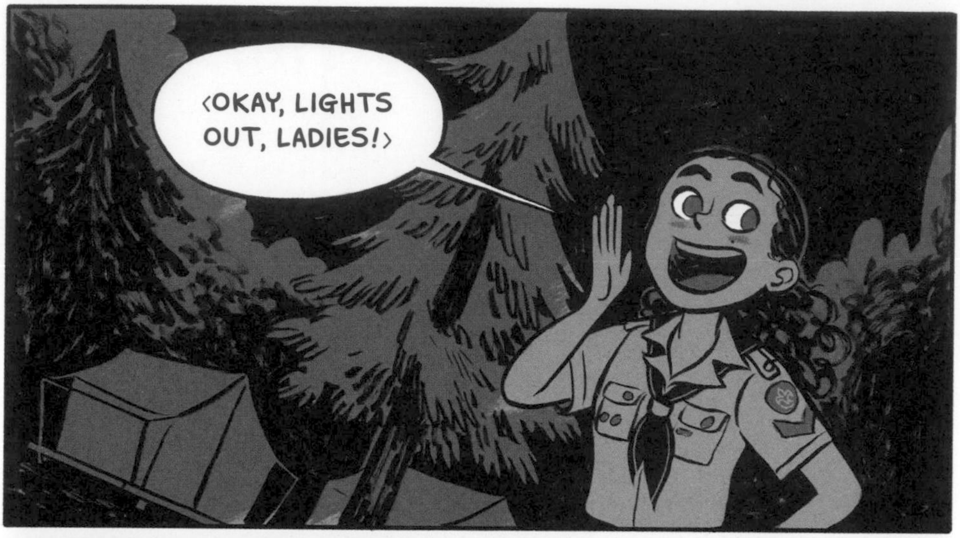
‹OKAY, LIGHTS OUT, LADIES!›

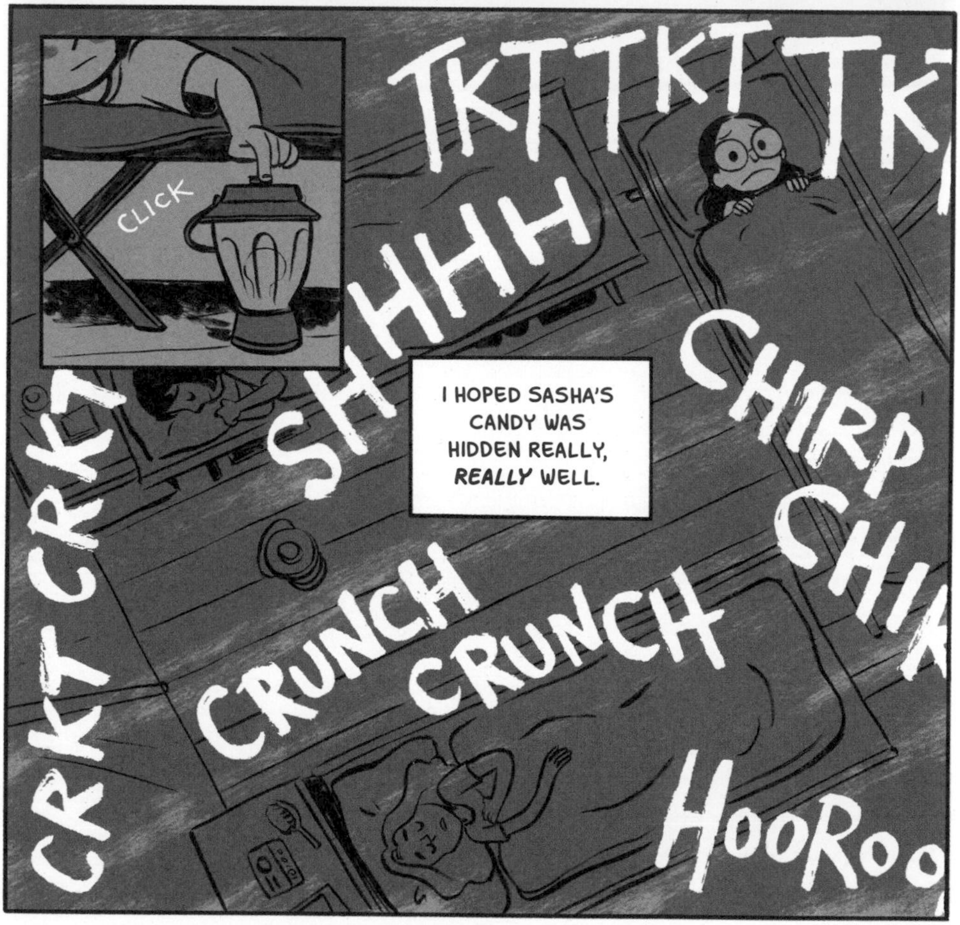
CLICK
TKTTKTTKT
SHHHH
CRKT CRKT CRKT
I HOPED SASHA'S CANDY WAS HIDDEN REALLY, *REALLY* WELL.
CHIRP CHIR
CRUNCH CRUNCH
HOOROO

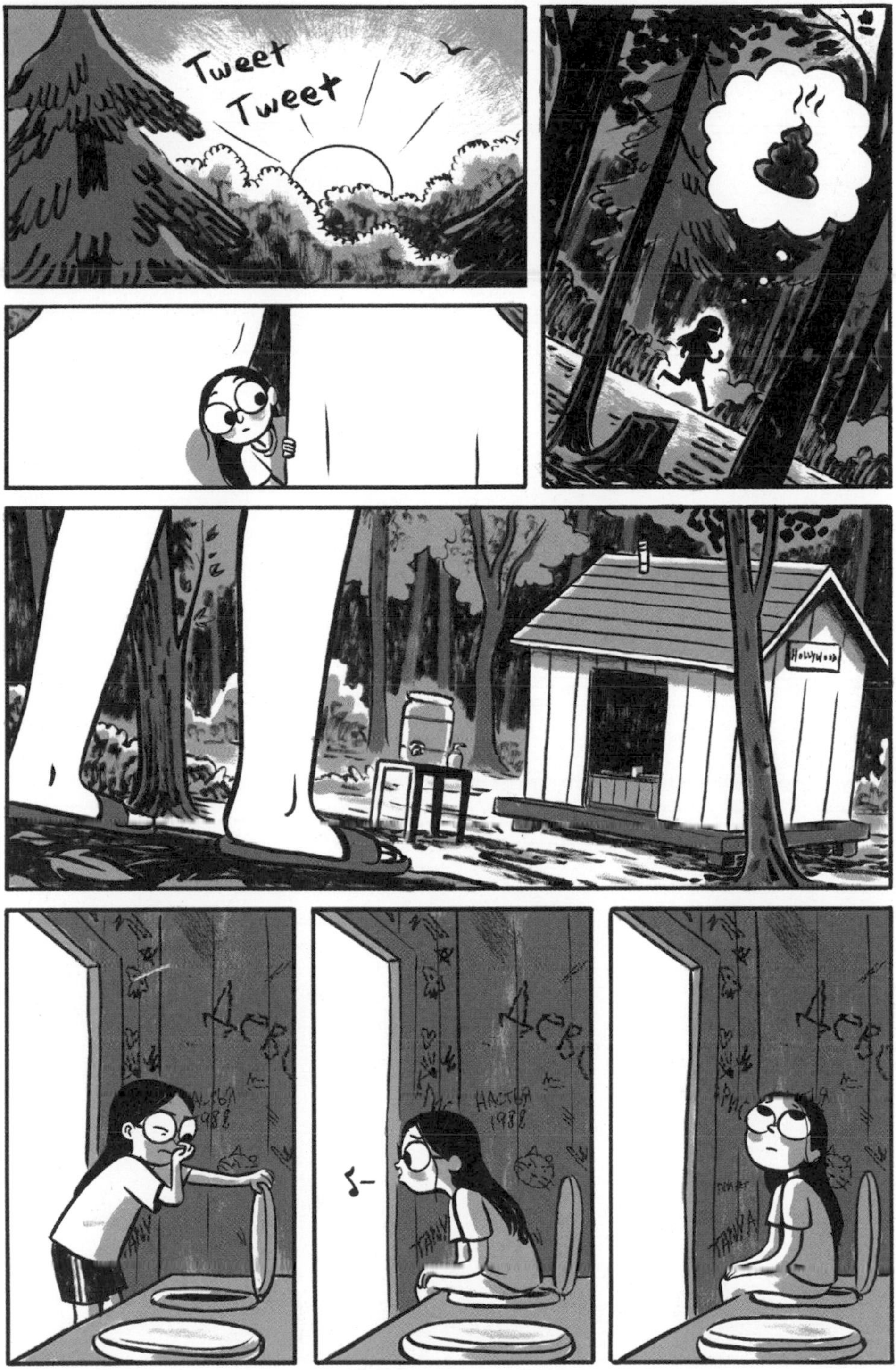
Tweet
Tweet

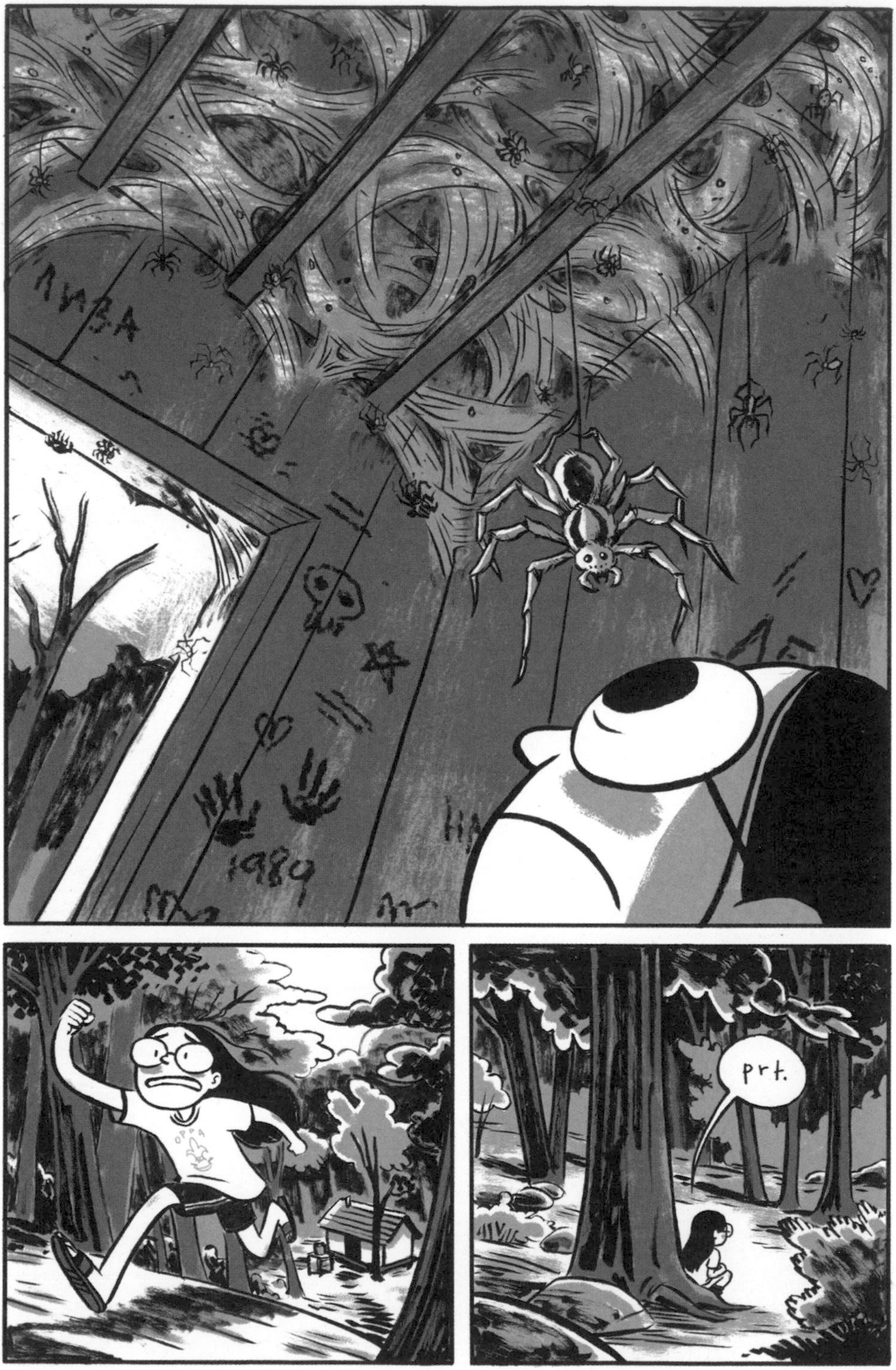
1989
prt.

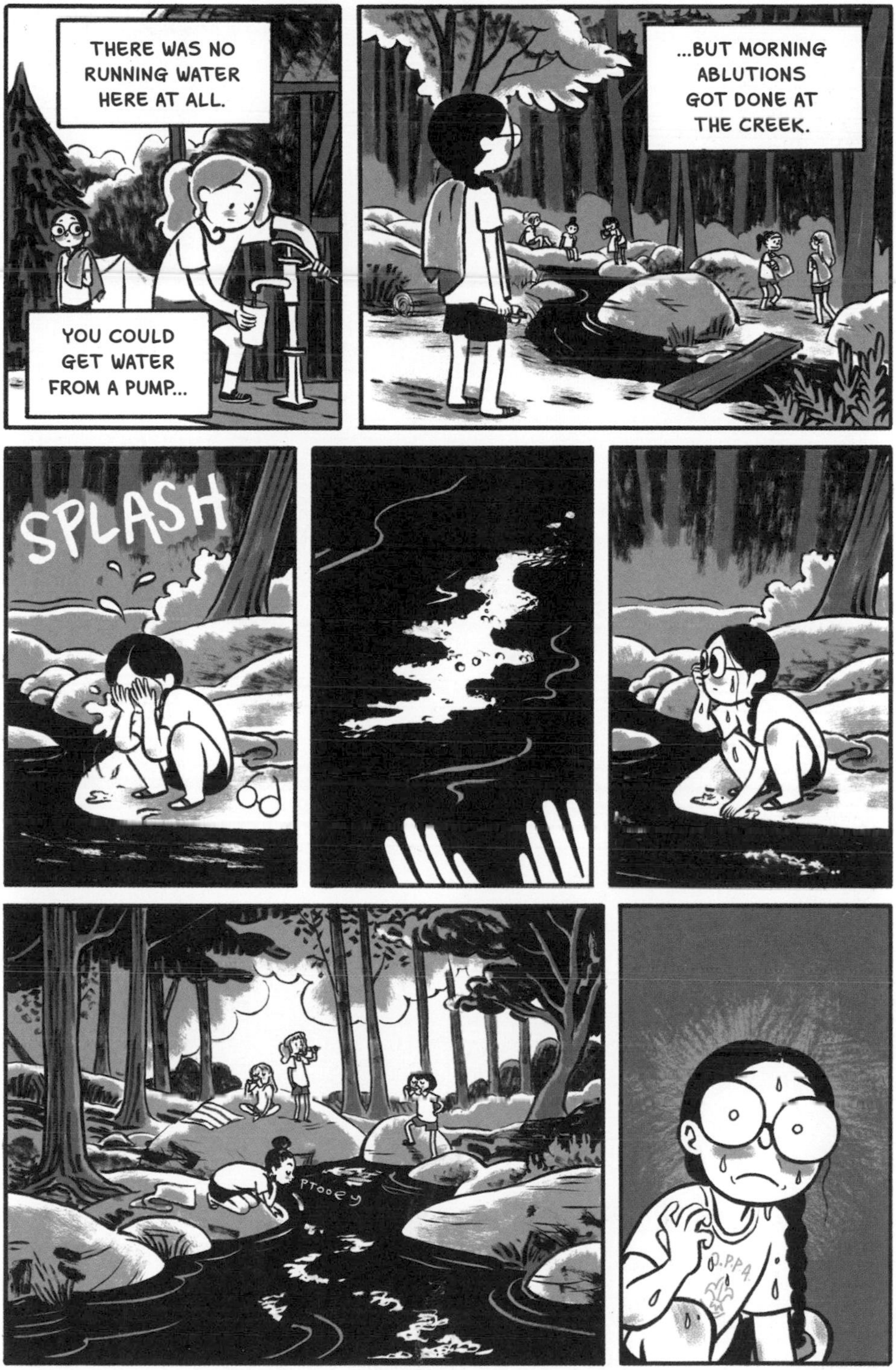
THERE WAS NO RUNNING WATER HERE AT ALL.
YOU COULD GET WATER FROM A PUMP...
...BUT MORNING ABLUTIONS GOT DONE AT THE CREEK.
SPLASH
PTOOEY
O.P.P.A

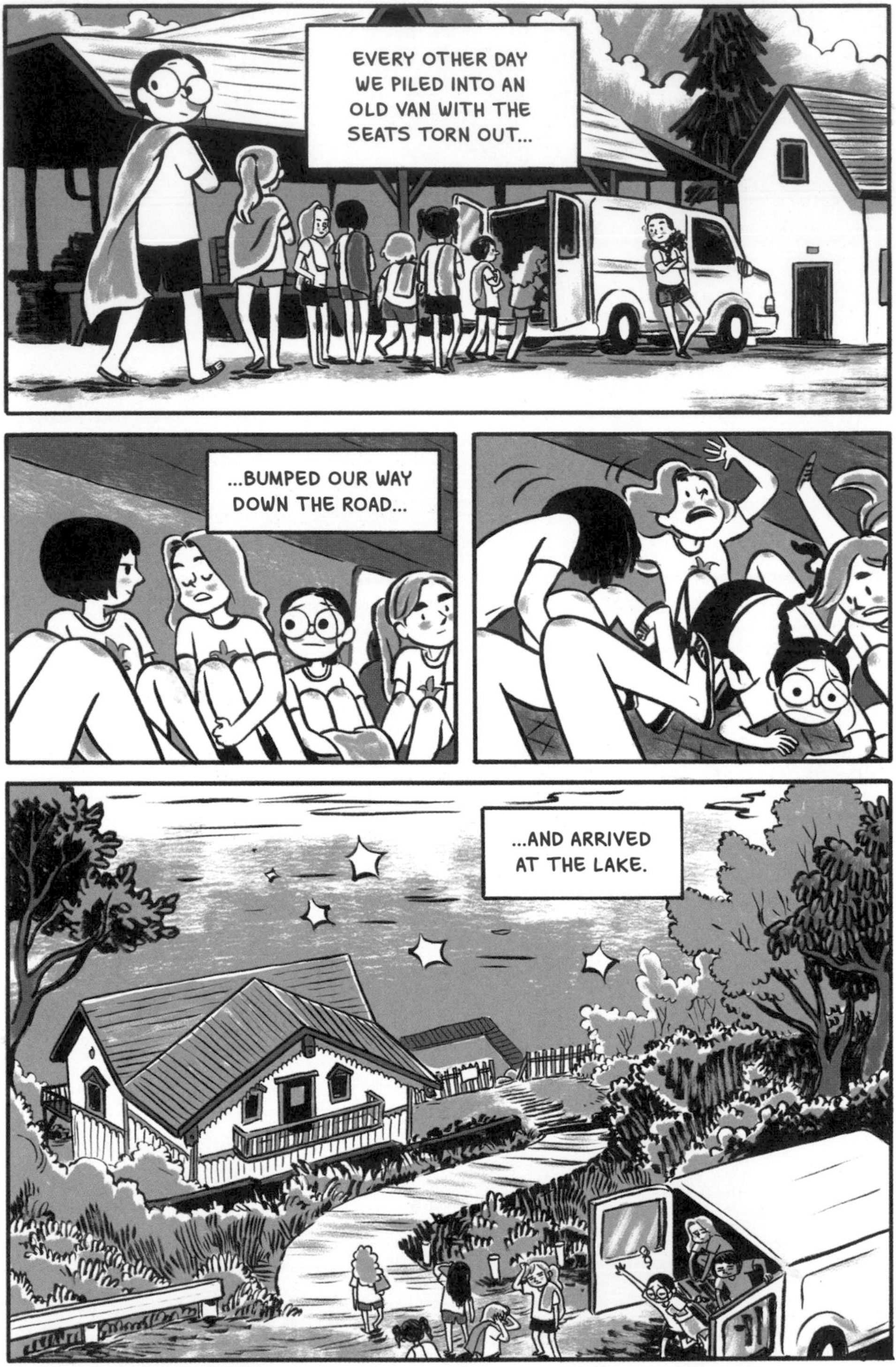
EVERY OTHER DAY WE PILED INTO AN OLD VAN WITH THE SEATS TORN OUT...
...BUMPED OUR WAY DOWN THE ROAD...
...AND ARRIVED AT THE LAKE.

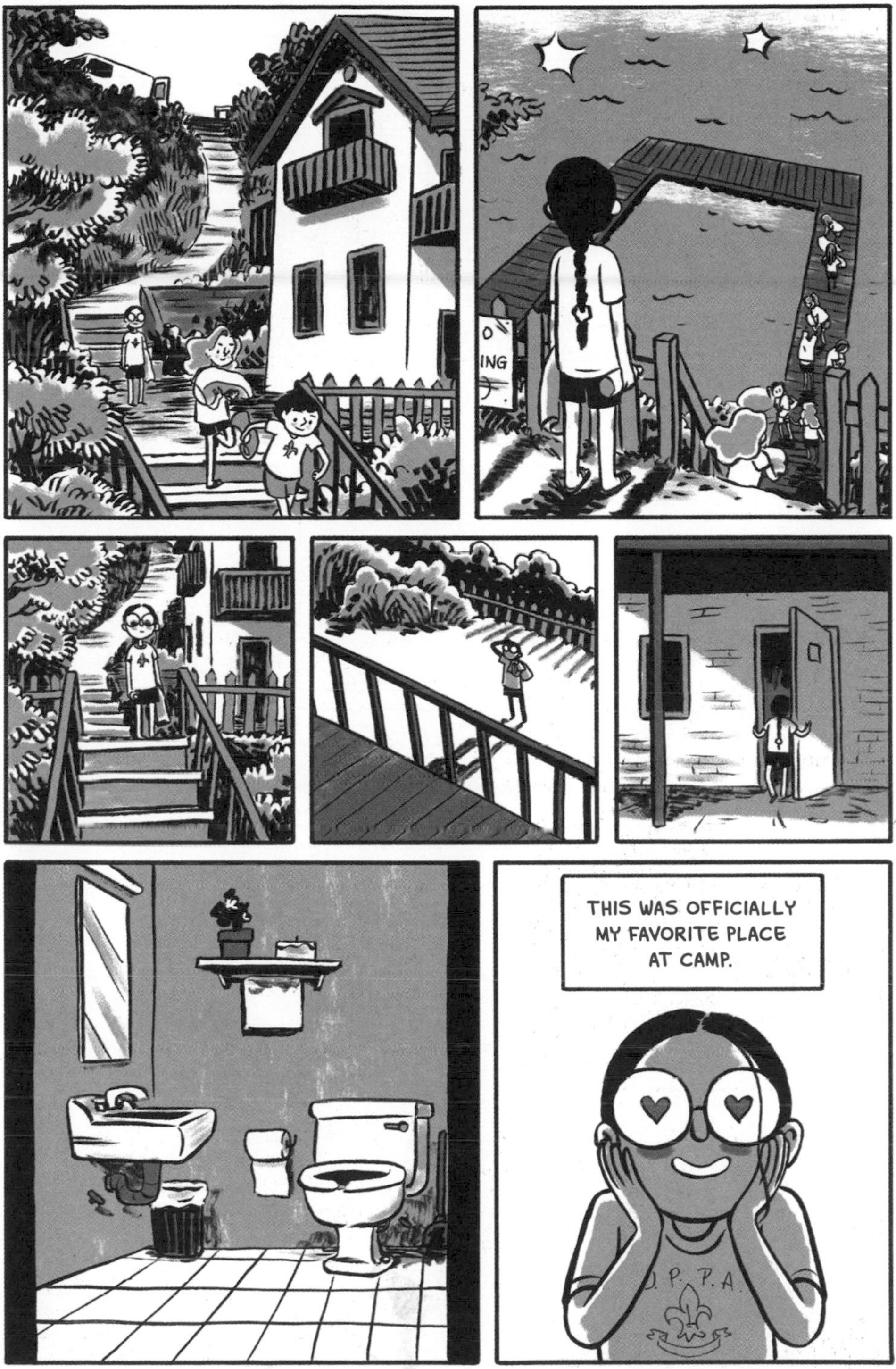
THIS WAS OFFICIALLY MY FAVORITE PLACE AT CAMP.

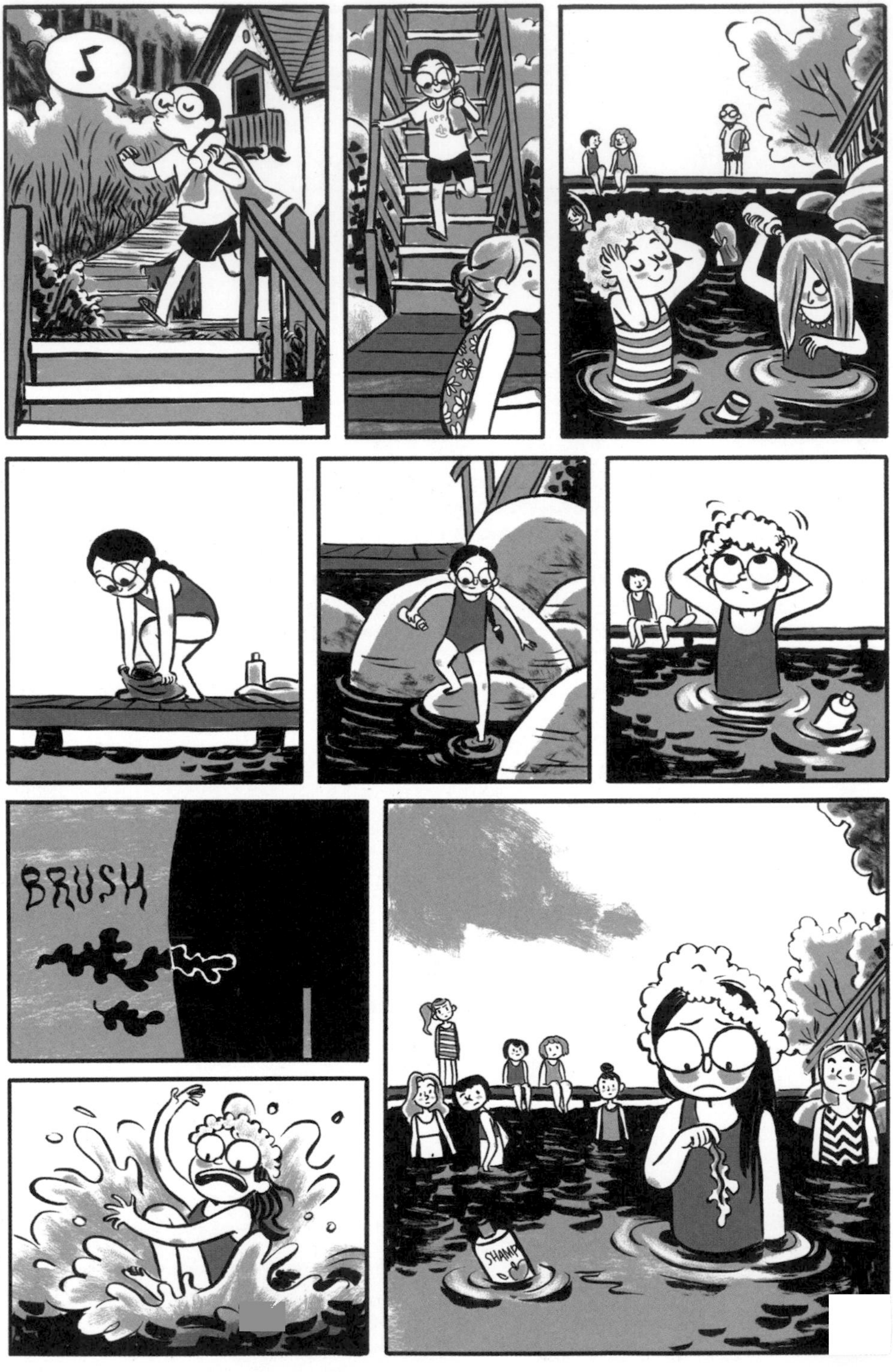
BRUSH
SHAMP

NOW THAT WE WERE MARGINALLY CLEANER, IT WAS TIME TO GO BACK TO CAMP. EVERY DAY WE HAD TWO HOURS OF CLASS— RUSSIAN HISTORY OR SCOUTCRAFT.

SASHA SAID THERE WAS A TEST AT THE END OF THE FOUR WEEKS, BUT I WOULD BE GONE BY THEN. SO HOW COME I HAD TO GO TO THE CLASSES?

⟨ALL RIGHT, CAMPERS! FOR OUR FIRST LESSON, WE'RE GOING TO LEARN ABOUT THE ANIMALS THAT LIVE AROUND HERE.

CAN I HAVE A VOLUNTEER?⟩

WHIP

OKAY, I ADMIT IT, I'M A NERD.

⟨EXCELLENT! WOULD YOU PLEASE READ THE FIRST PARAGRAPH?⟩

UH-OH.

ЖИВАЯ ПРИРОДА

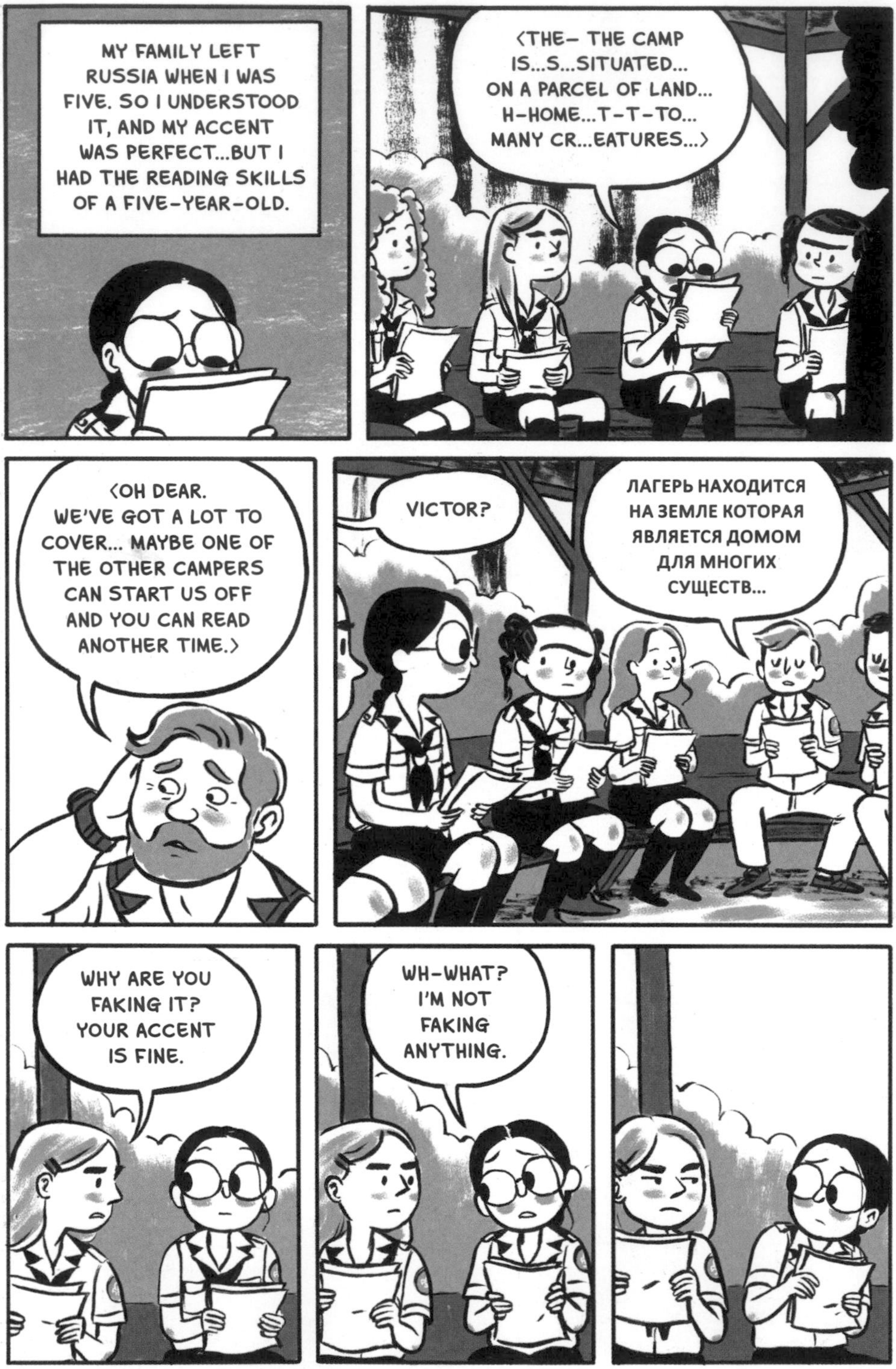
MY FAMILY LEFT RUSSIA WHEN I WAS FIVE. SO I UNDERSTOOD IT, AND MY ACCENT WAS PERFECT...BUT I HAD THE READING SKILLS OF A FIVE-YEAR-OLD.
<THE– THE CAMP IS...S...SITUATED... ON A PARCEL OF LAND... H–HOME...T–T–TO... MANY CR...EATURES...>
<OH DEAR. WE'VE GOT A LOT TO COVER... MAYBE ONE OF THE OTHER CAMPERS CAN START US OFF AND YOU CAN READ ANOTHER TIME.>
VICTOR?
ЛАГЕРЬ НАХОДИТСЯ НА ЗЕМЛЕ КОТОРАЯ ЯВЛЯЕТСЯ ДОМОМ ДЛЯ МНОГИХ СУЩЕСТВ...
WHY ARE YOU FAKING IT? YOUR ACCENT IS FINE.
WH–WHAT? I'M NOT FAKING ANYTHING.

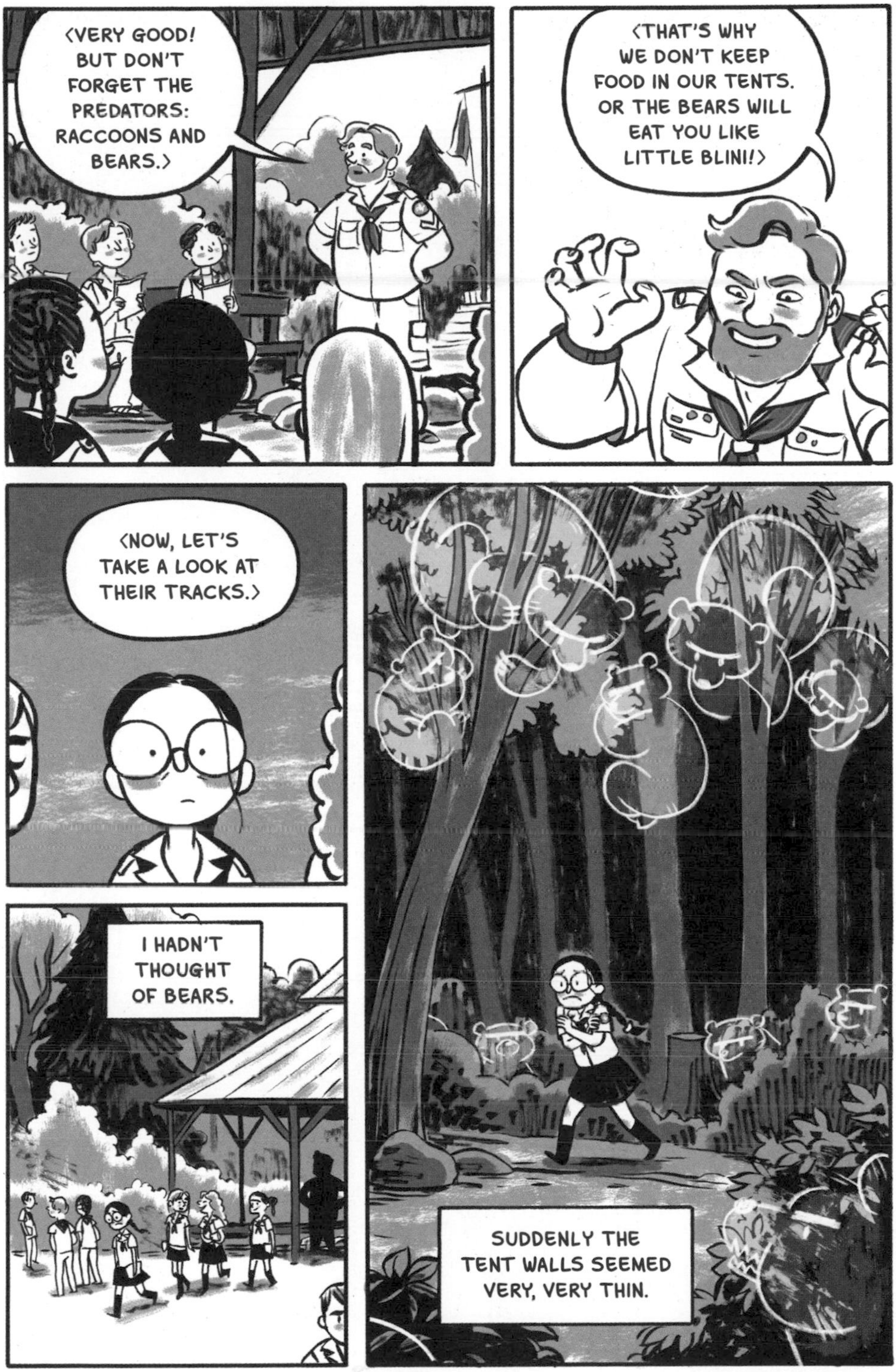

<VERY GOOD! BUT DON'T FORGET THE PREDATORS: RACCOONS AND BEARS.>
<THAT'S WHY WE DON'T KEEP FOOD IN OUR TENTS. OR THE BEARS WILL EAT YOU LIKE LITTLE BLINI!>
<NOW, LET'S TAKE A LOOK AT THEIR TRACKS.>
I HADN'T THOUGHT OF BEARS.
SUDDENLY THE TENT WALLS SEEMED VERY, VERY THIN.

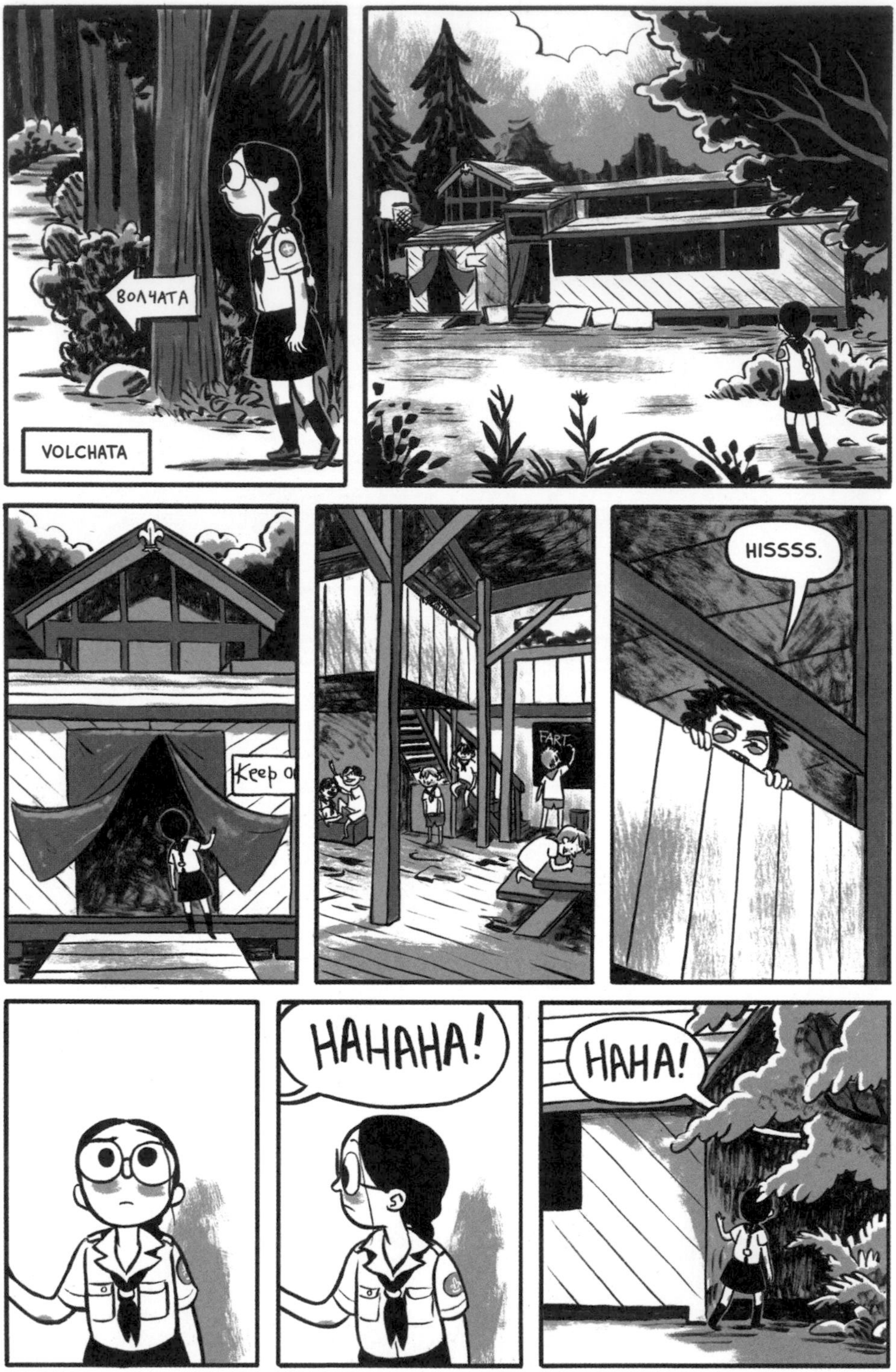
ВОЛЧАТА
VOLCHATA
Keep o
FART.
HISSSS.
HAHAHA!
HAHA!

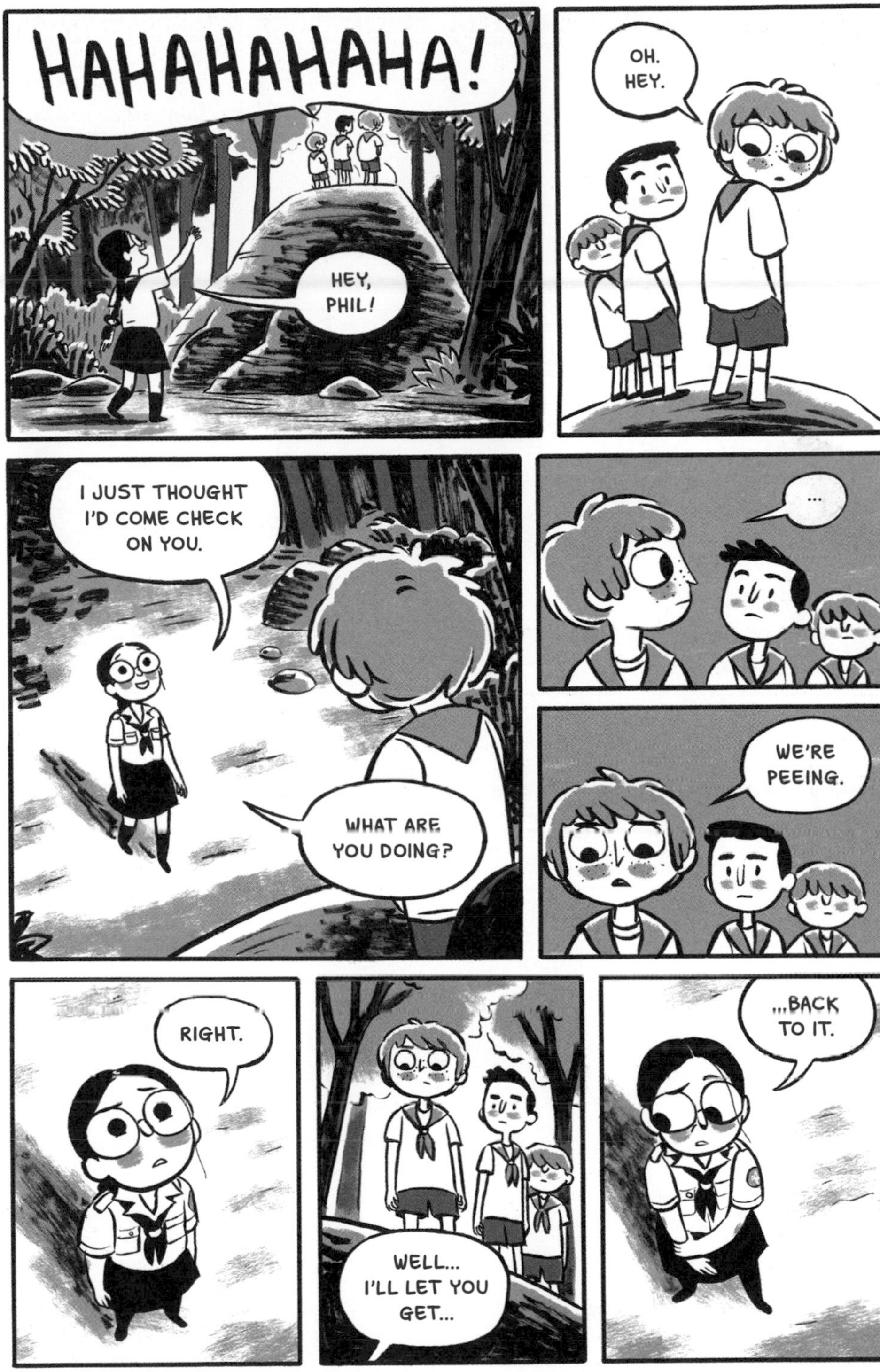
HAHAHAHAHA!
HEY, PHIL!
OH. HEY.
I JUST THOUGHT I'D COME CHECK ON YOU.
WHAT ARE YOU DOING?
...
WE'RE PEEING.
RIGHT.
WELL... I'LL LET YOU GET...
...BACK TO IT.

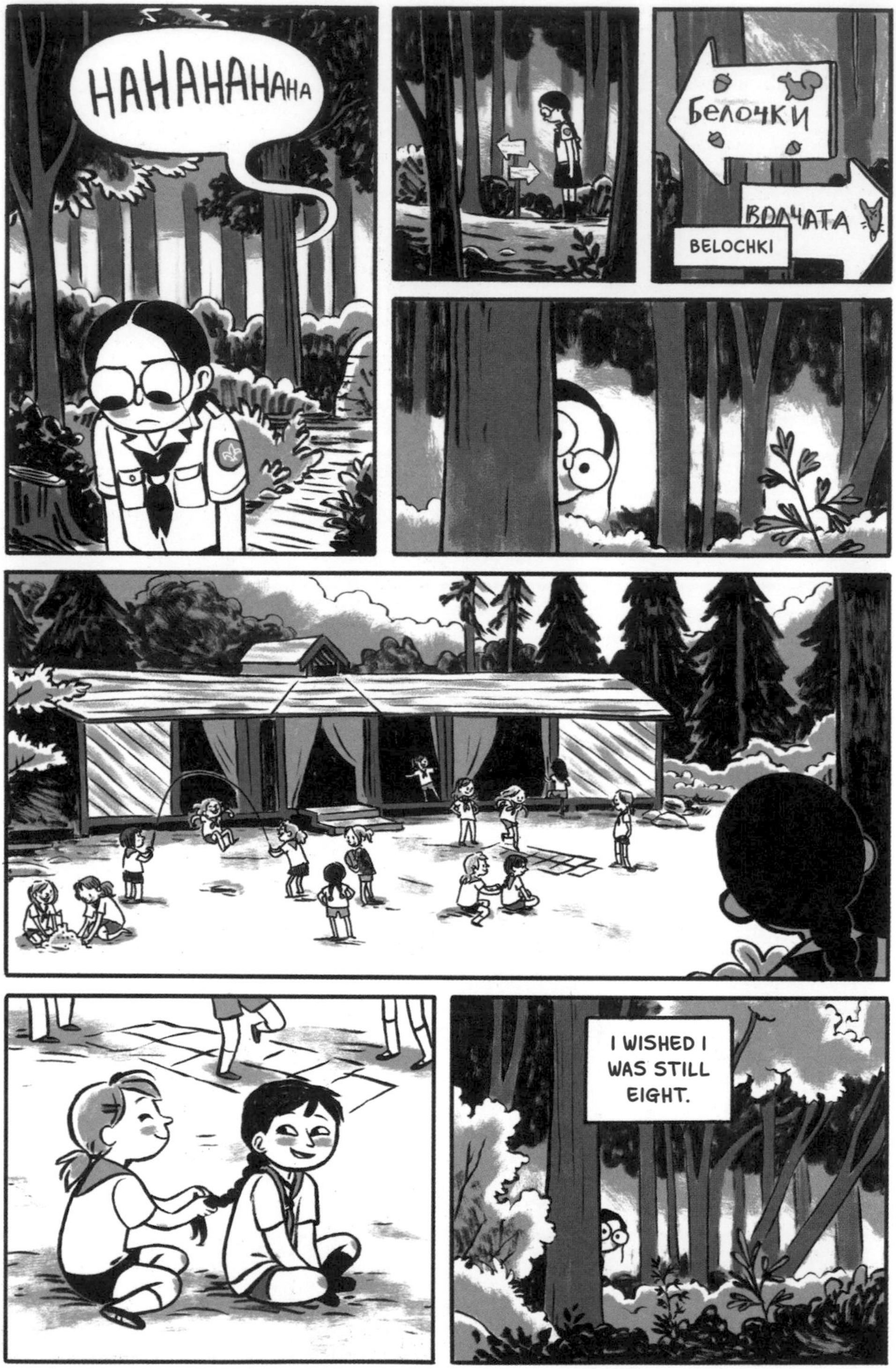
HAHAHAHAHAHA
Белочки
ВОЛЧАТА
BELOCHKI
I WISHED I WAS STILL EIGHT.

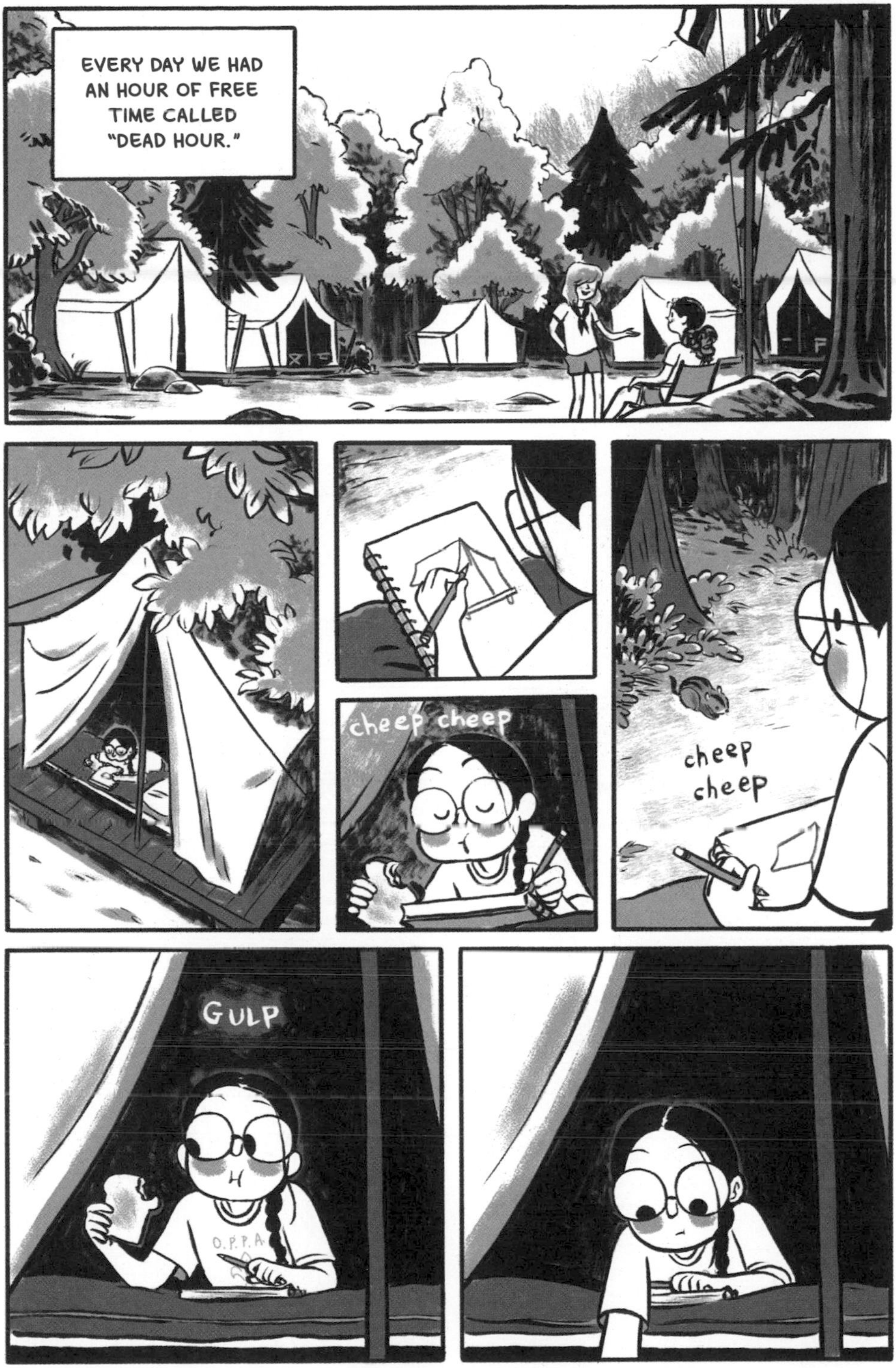
EVERY DAY WE HAD AN HOUR OF FREE TIME CALLED "DEAD HOUR."
cheep cheep
cheep cheep
GULP

PET

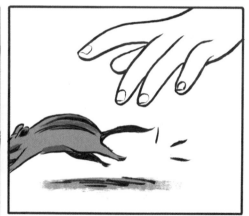

I NEEDED TO
GET MORE FOOD.

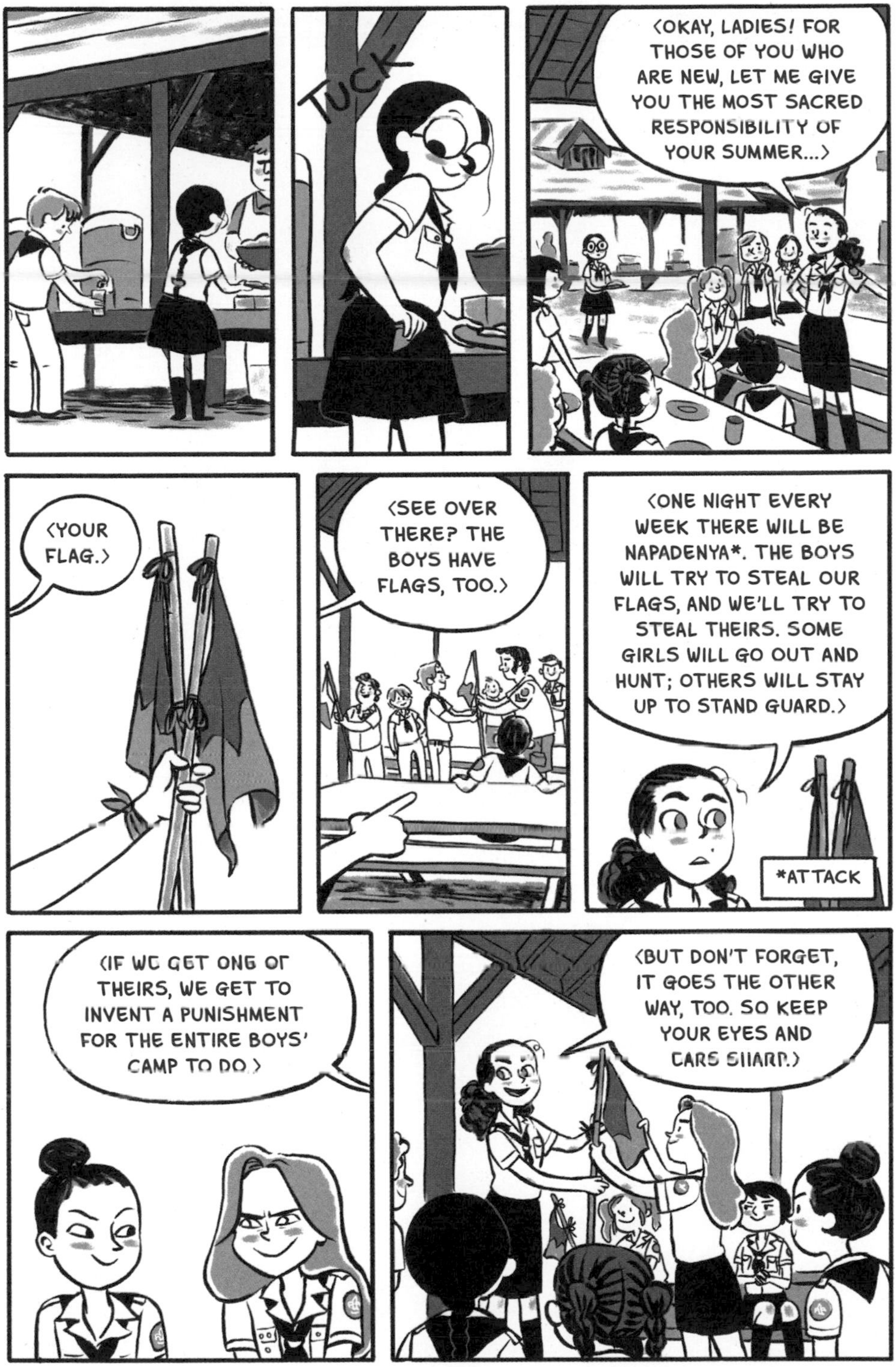
TUCK
<OKAY, LADIES! FOR THOSE OF YOU WHO ARE NEW, LET ME GIVE YOU THE MOST SACRED RESPONSIBILITY OF YOUR SUMMER...>
<YOUR FLAG.>
<SEE OVER THERE? THE BOYS HAVE FLAGS, TOO.>
<ONE NIGHT EVERY WEEK THERE WILL BE NAPADENYA*. THE BOYS WILL TRY TO STEAL OUR FLAGS, AND WE'LL TRY TO STEAL THEIRS. SOME GIRLS WILL GO OUT AND HUNT; OTHERS WILL STAY UP TO STAND GUARD.>
*ATTACK
<IF WE GET ONE OF THEIRS, WE GET TO INVENT A PUNISHMENT FOR THE ENTIRE BOYS' CAMP TO DO.>
<BUT DON'T FORGET, IT GOES THE OTHER WAY, TOO. SO KEEP YOUR EYES AND EARS SHARP.>

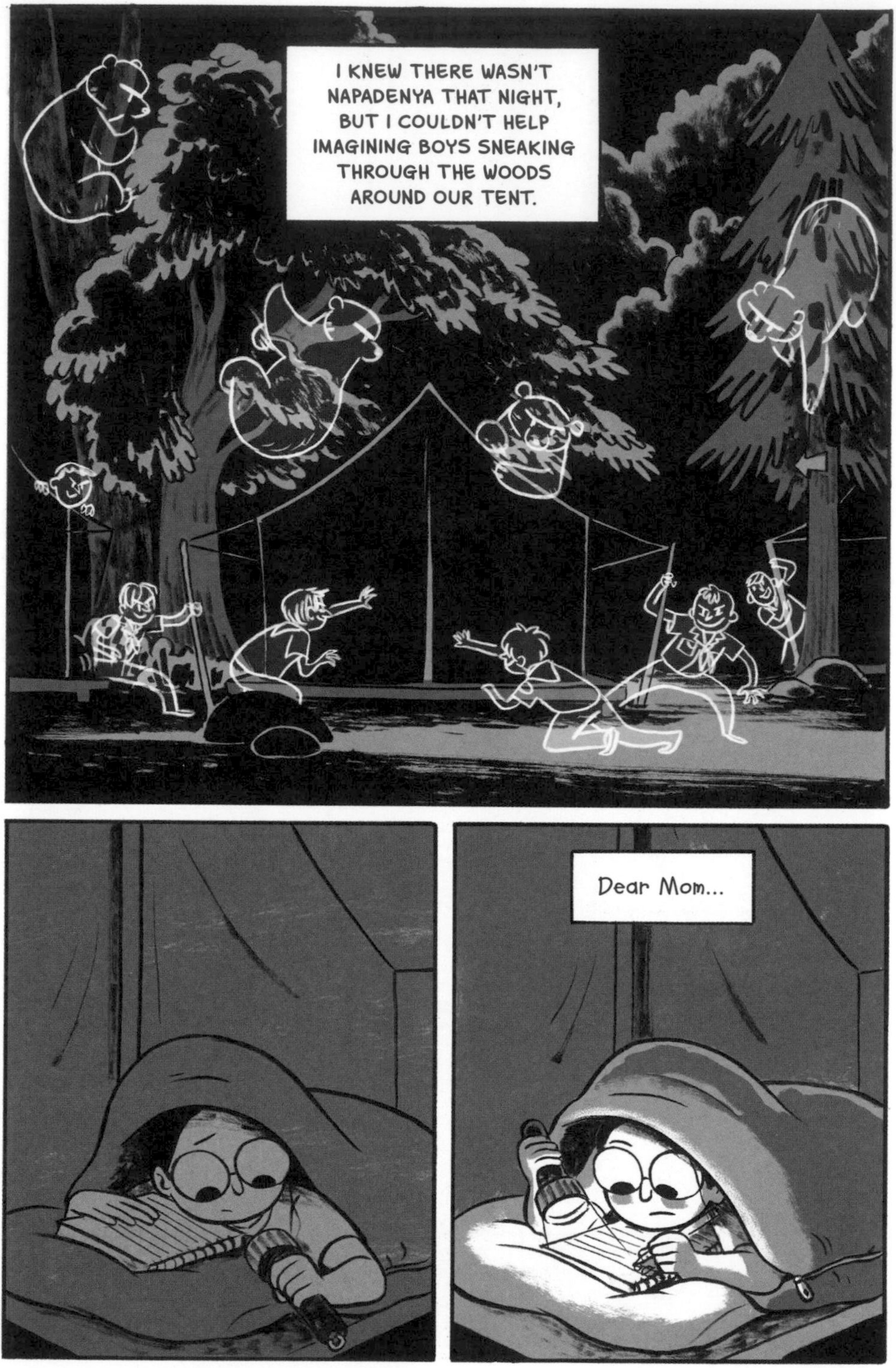
I KNEW THERE WASN'T NAPADENYA THAT NIGHT, BUT I COULDN'T HELP IMAGINING BOYS SNEAKING THROUGH THE WOODS AROUND OUR TENT.
Dear Mom...

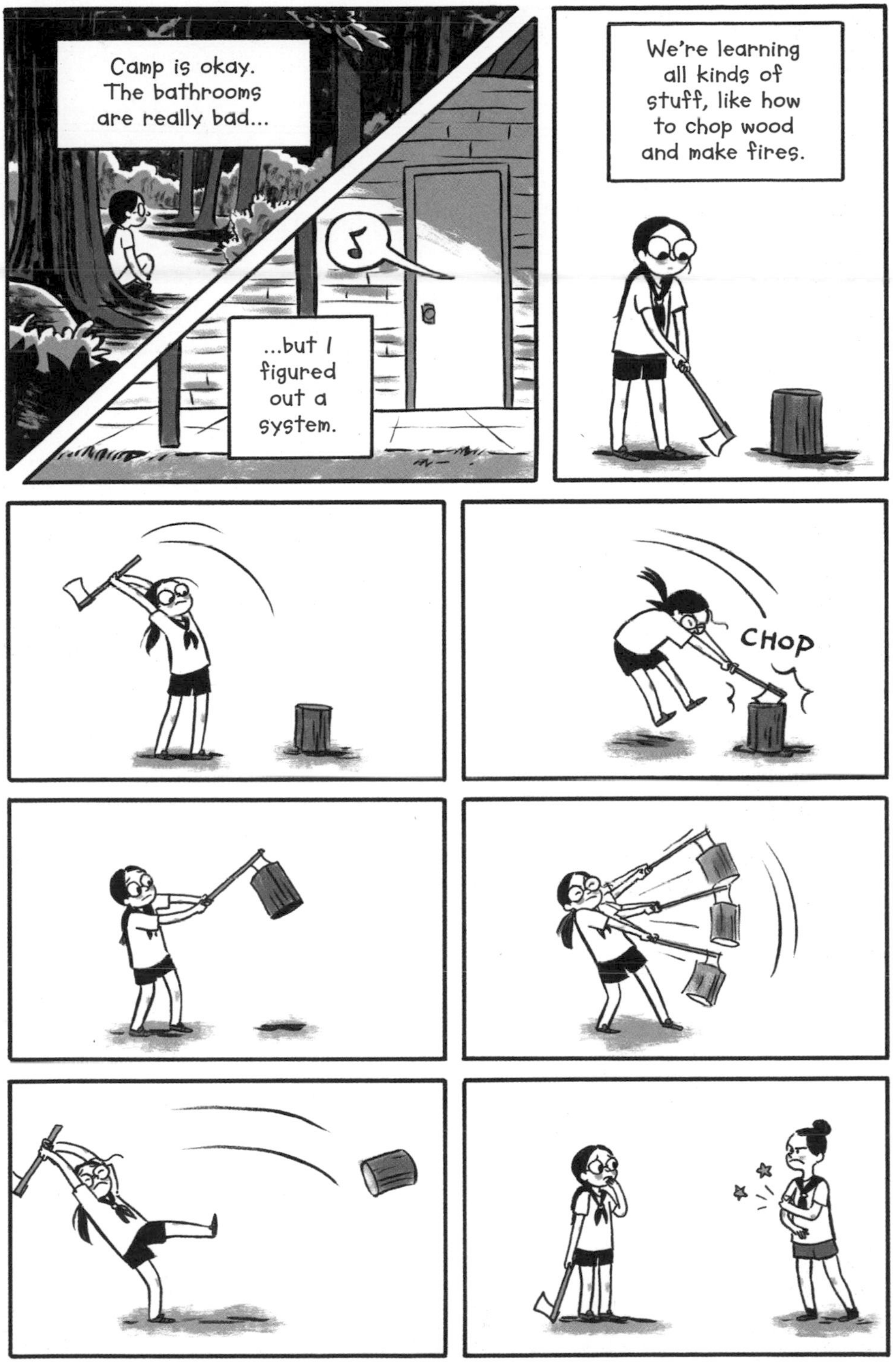

Camp is okay. The bathrooms are really bad...
♪
...but I figured out a system.
We're learning all kinds of stuff, like how to chop wood and make fires.
CHOP

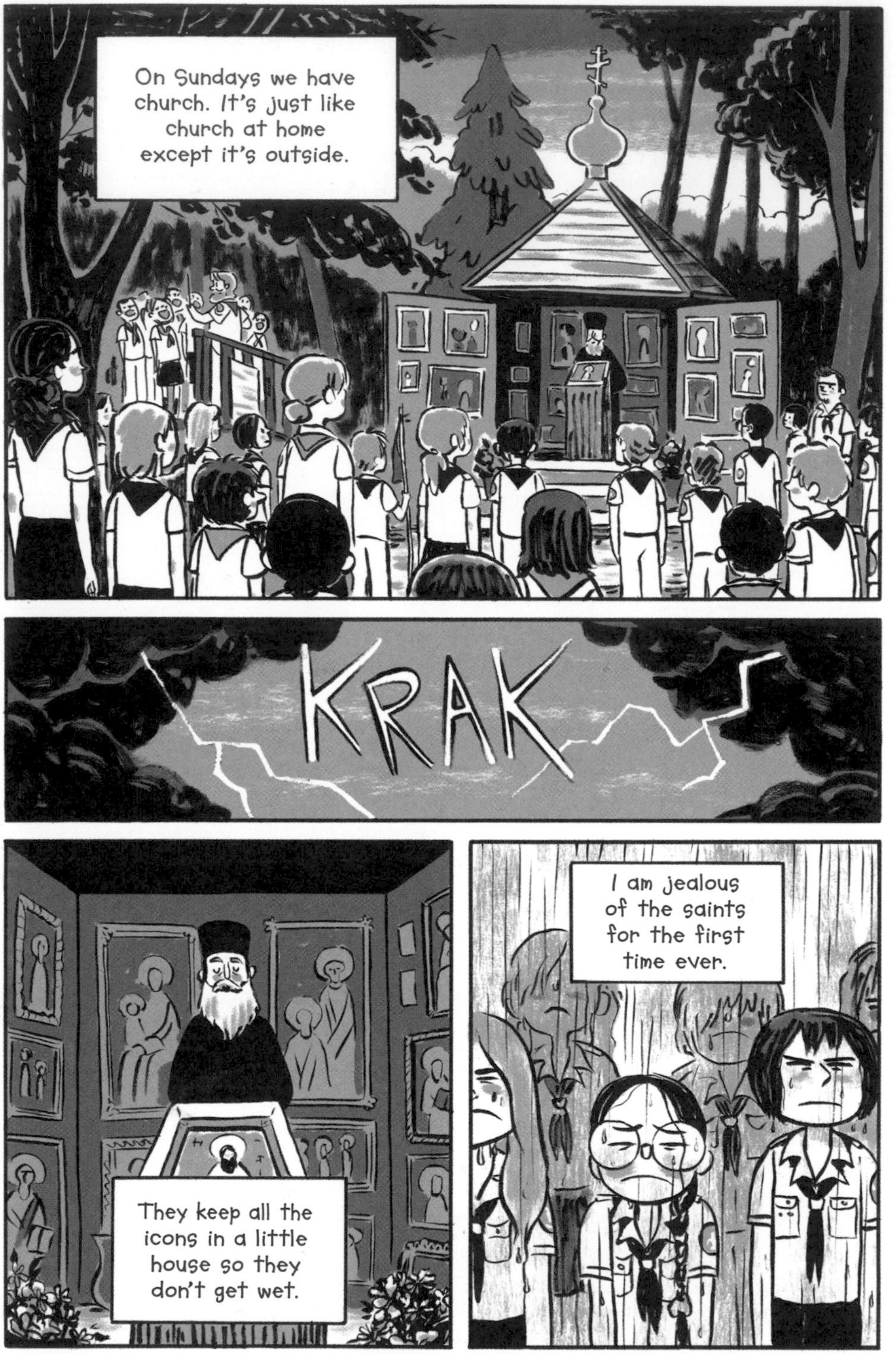
On Sundays we have church. It's just like church at home except it's outside.
KRAK
They keep all the icons in a little house so they don't get wet.
I am jealous of the saints for the first time ever.

Some mornings I have kitchen duty.

It means waking up at 6 a.m. and helping to prepare food for the campers.

My job is making bug juice. It's lots of different cans of juice mixed together.

DUMP

SWARM

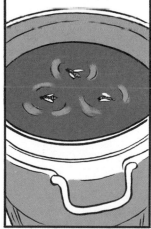

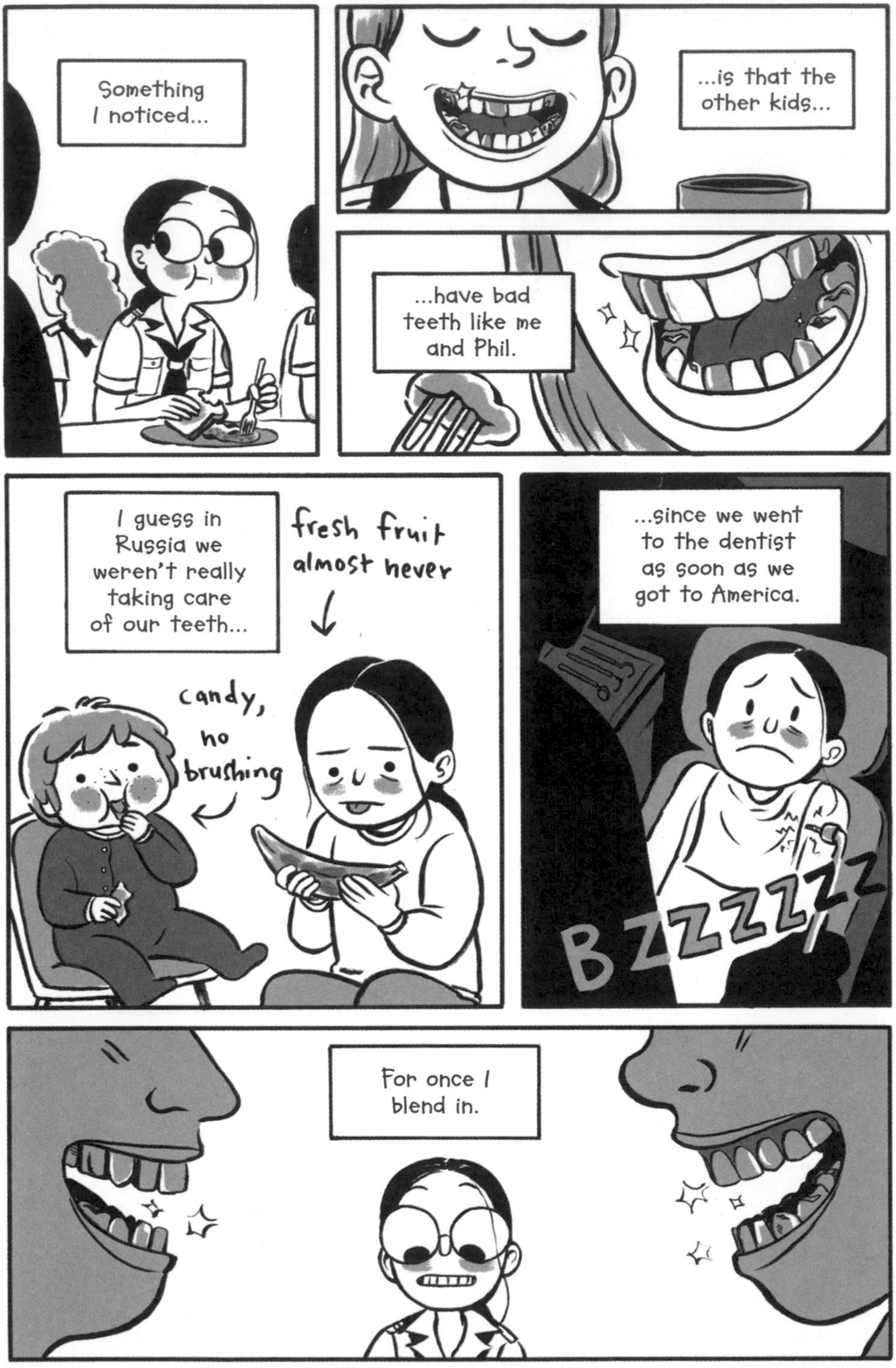
Something I noticed...
...is that the other kids...
...have bad teeth like me and Phil.
I guess in Russia we weren't really taking care of our teeth...
fresh fruit almost never
candy, no brushing
...since we went to the dentist as soon as we got to America.
BZZZZZZ
For once I blend in.

There are...

...lots of bugs.

Can you bring some bug spray?

The Culprits

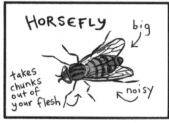

HORSEFLY

big

takes chunks out of your flesh

noisy

MOSQUITO

silent

you can't feel the sting

small

phew.

CINCH

AAAAAH!!!

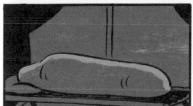

BZZZZ

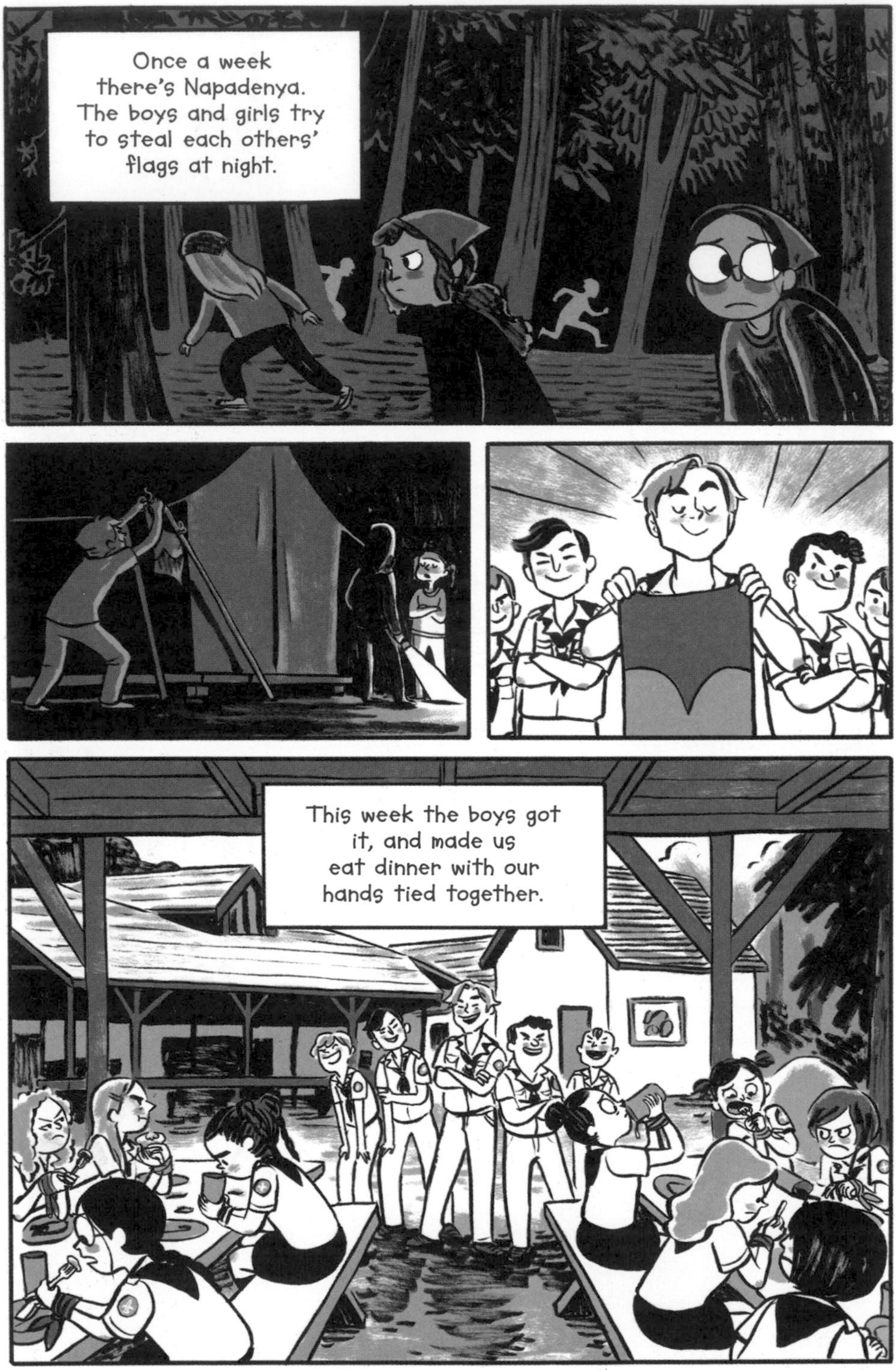
Once a week there's Napadenya. The boys and girls try to steal each others' flags at night.
This week the boys got it, and made us eat dinner with our hands tied together.

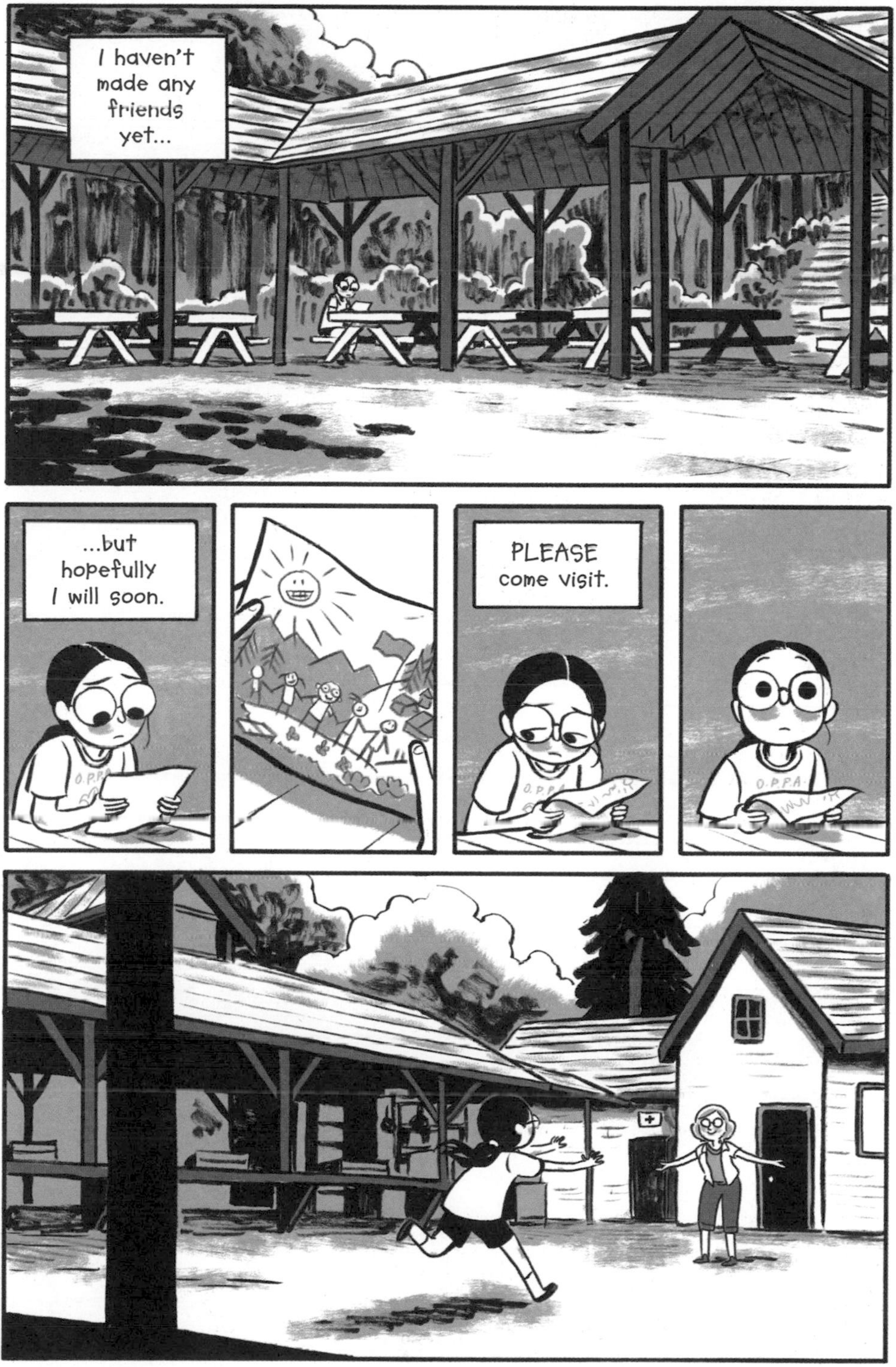
I haven't made any friends yet...
...but hopefully I will soon.
PLEASE come visit.

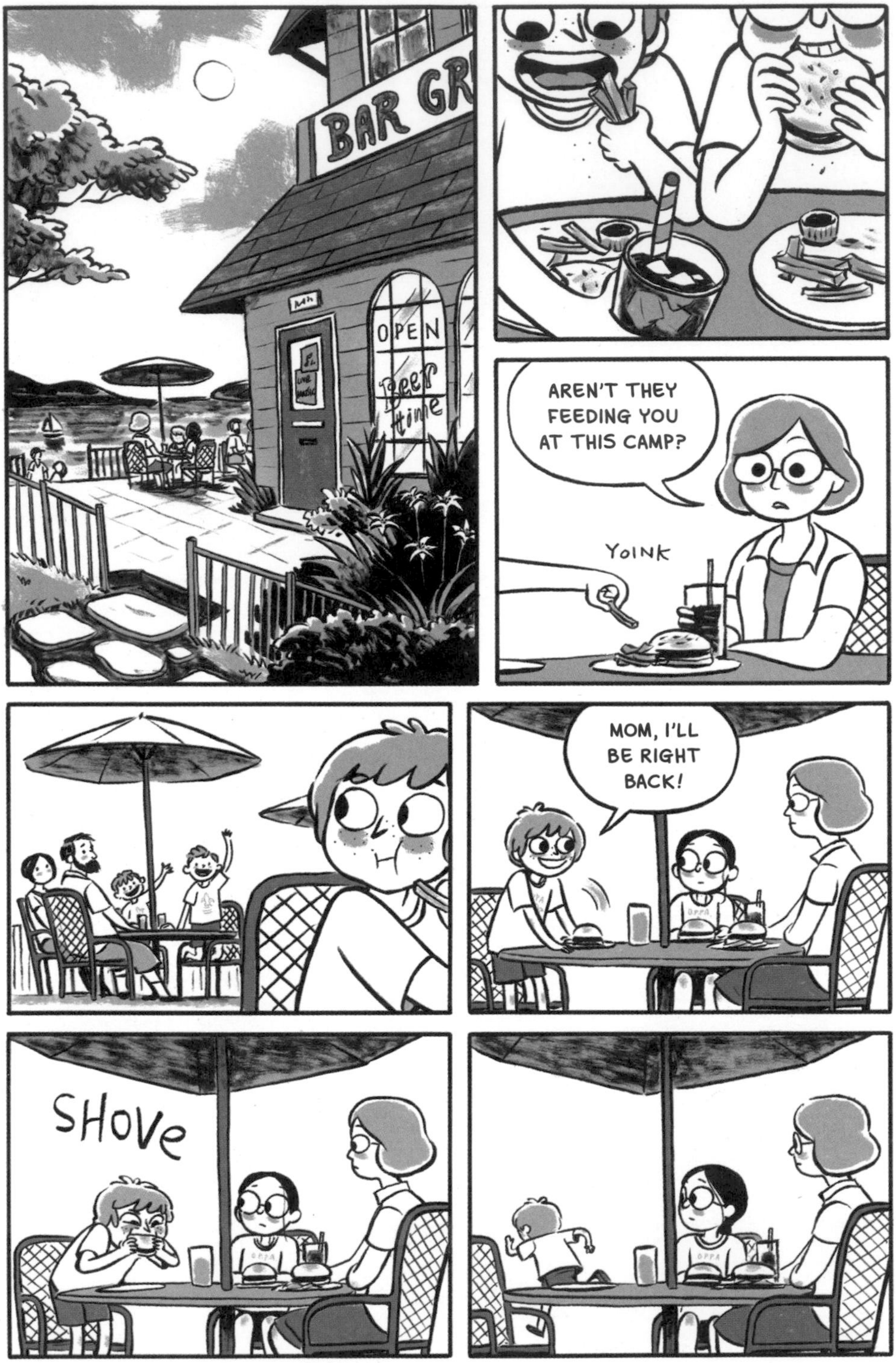
BAR GR
OPEN
Beer Time
AREN'T THEY FEEDING YOU AT THIS CAMP?
YOINK
MOM, I'LL BE RIGHT BACK!
SHOVE

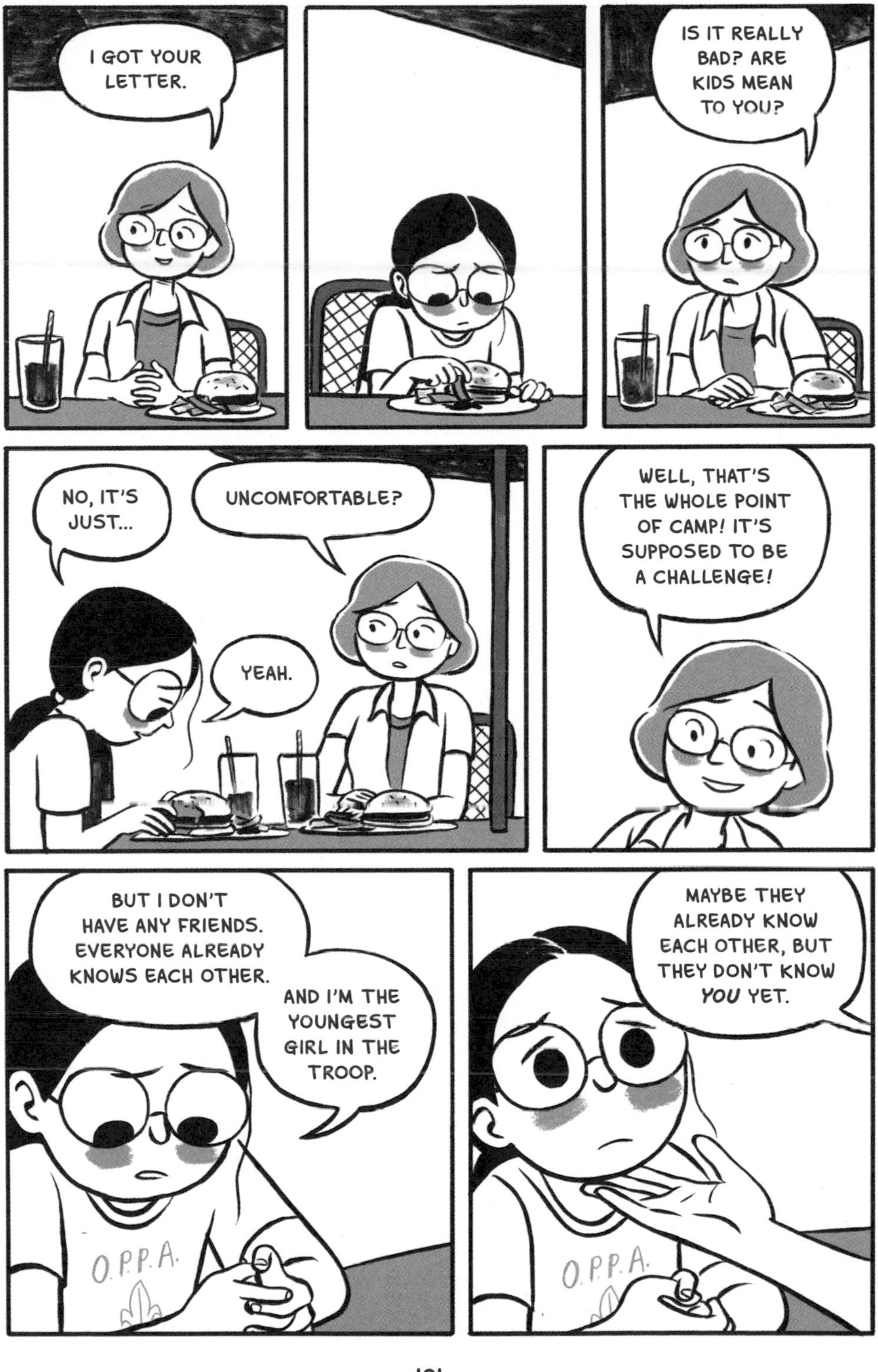
I GOT YOUR LETTER.
IS IT REALLY BAD? ARE KIDS MEAN TO YOU?
NO, IT'S JUST...
UNCOMFORTABLE?
YEAH.
WELL, THAT'S THE WHOLE POINT OF CAMP! IT'S SUPPOSED TO BE A CHALLENGE!
BUT I DON'T HAVE ANY FRIENDS. EVERYONE ALREADY KNOWS EACH OTHER.
AND I'M THE YOUNGEST GIRL IN THE TROOP.
O.P.P.A.
MAYBE THEY ALREADY KNOW EACH OTHER, BUT THEY DON'T KNOW *YOU* YET.
O.P.P.A.

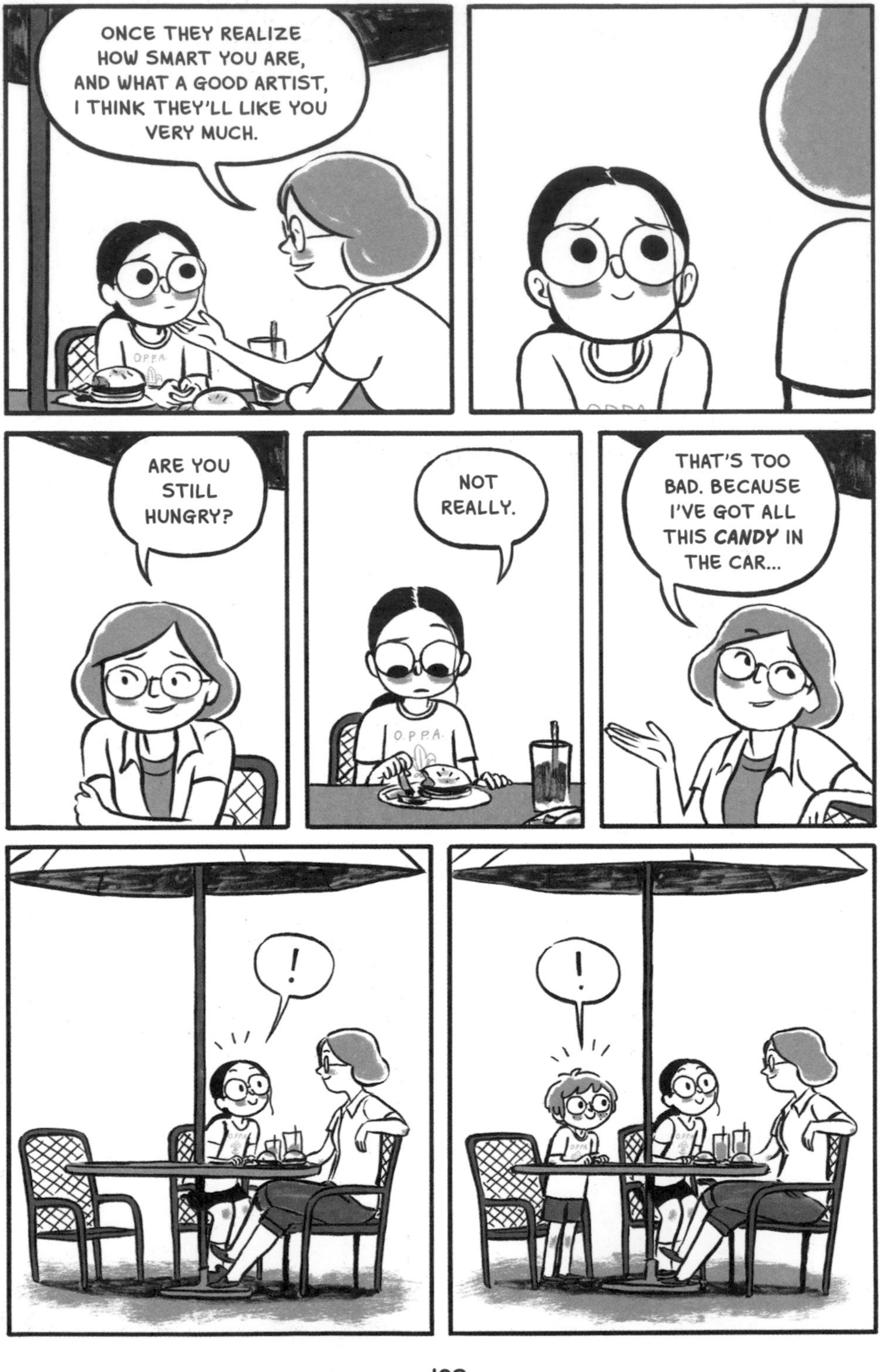
ONCE THEY REALIZE HOW SMART YOU ARE, AND WHAT A GOOD ARTIST, I THINK THEY'LL LIKE YOU VERY MUCH.
O.P.P.A.
ARE YOU STILL HUNGRY?
NOT REALLY.
O.P.P.A.
THAT'S TOO BAD. BECAUSE I'VE GOT ALL THIS **CANDY** IN THE CAR...
!
!

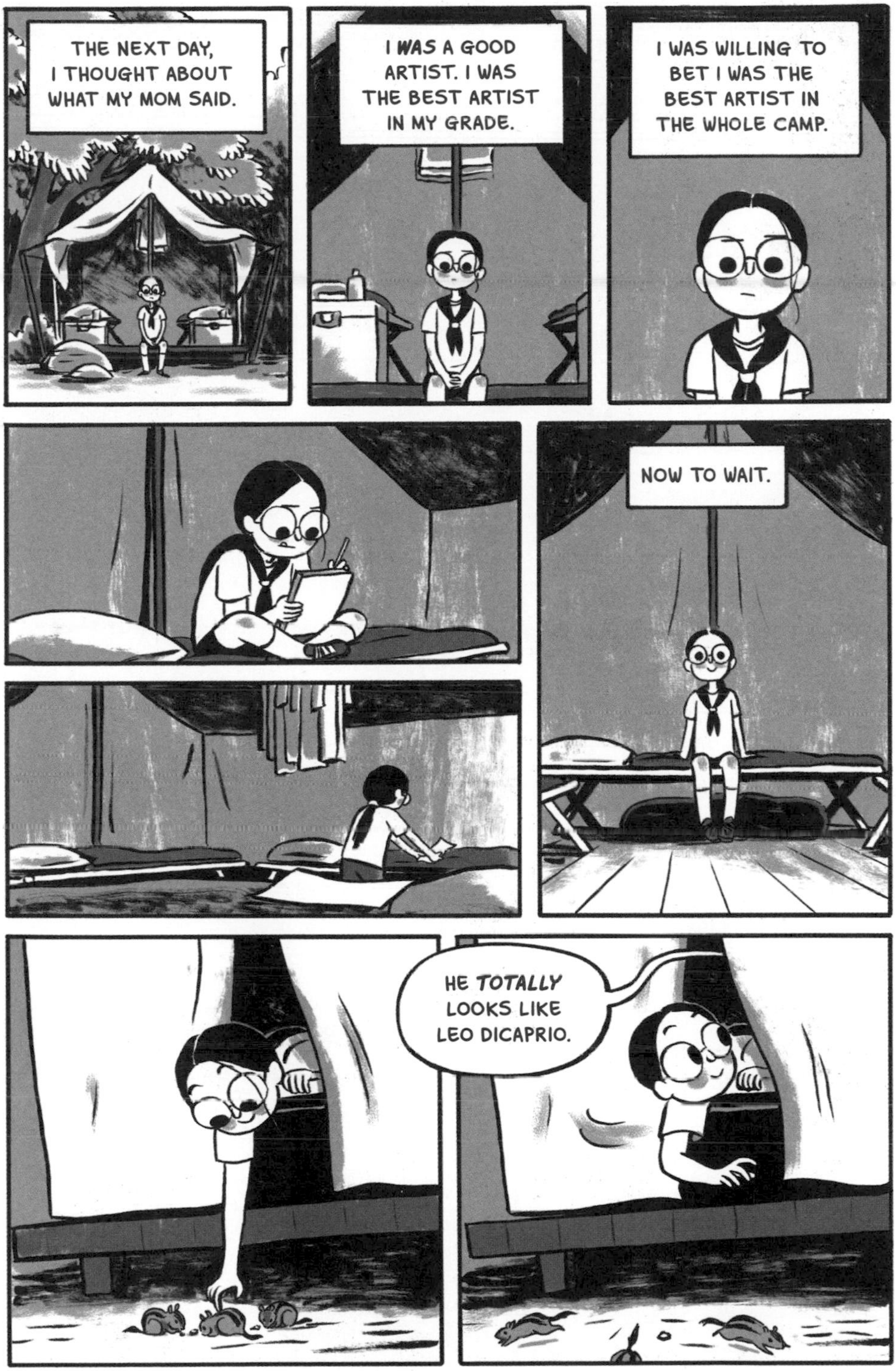
THE NEXT DAY, I THOUGHT ABOUT WHAT MY MOM SAID.
I *WAS* A GOOD ARTIST. I WAS THE BEST ARTIST IN MY GRADE.
I WAS WILLING TO BET I WAS THE BEST ARTIST IN THE WHOLE CAMP.
NOW TO WAIT.
HE *TOTALLY* LOOKS LIKE LEO DICAPRIO.

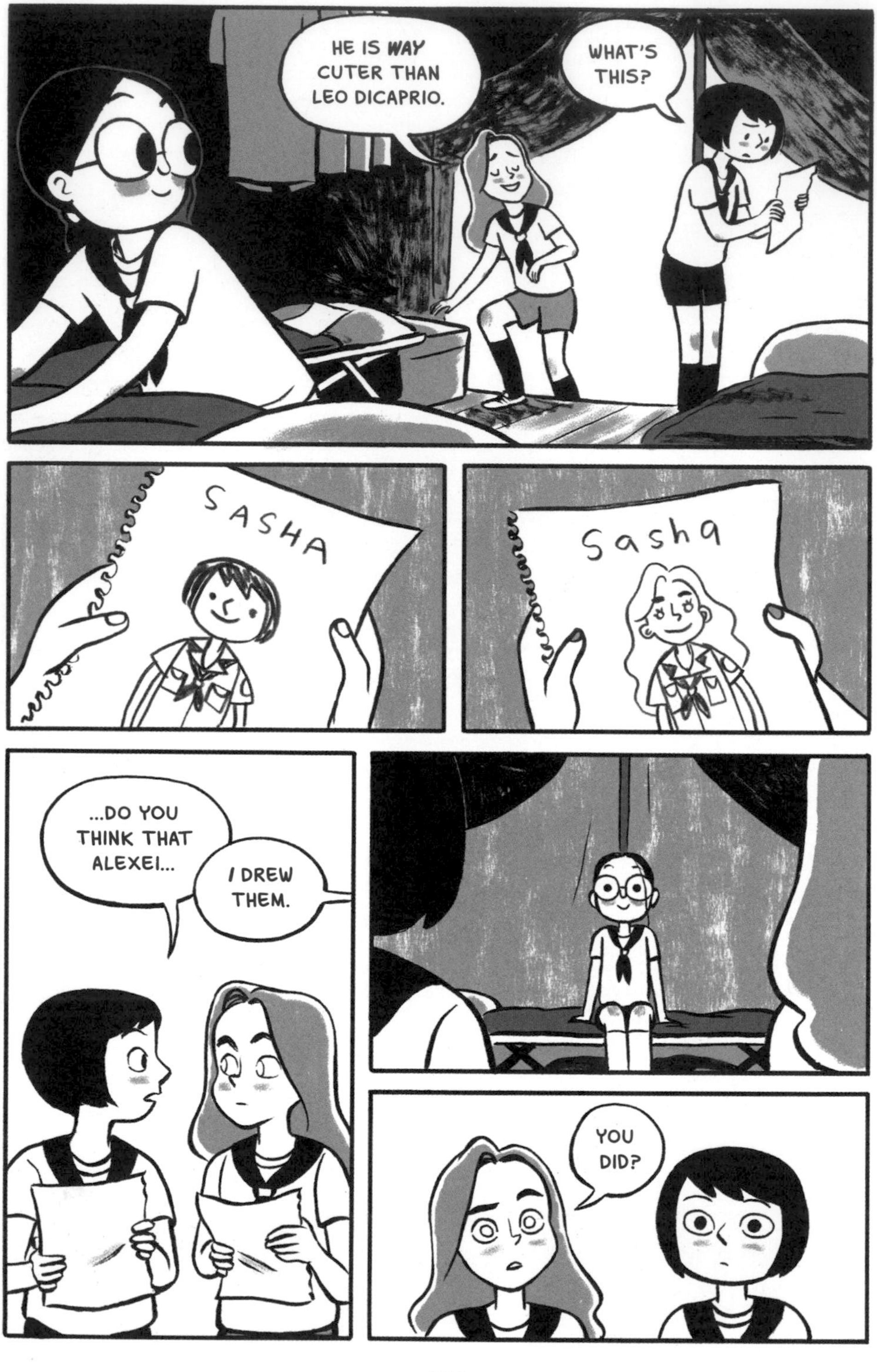
HE IS *WAY* CUTER THAN LEO DICAPRIO.
WHAT'S THIS?
SASHA
Sasha
...DO YOU THINK THAT ALEXEI...
I DREW THEM.
YOU DID?

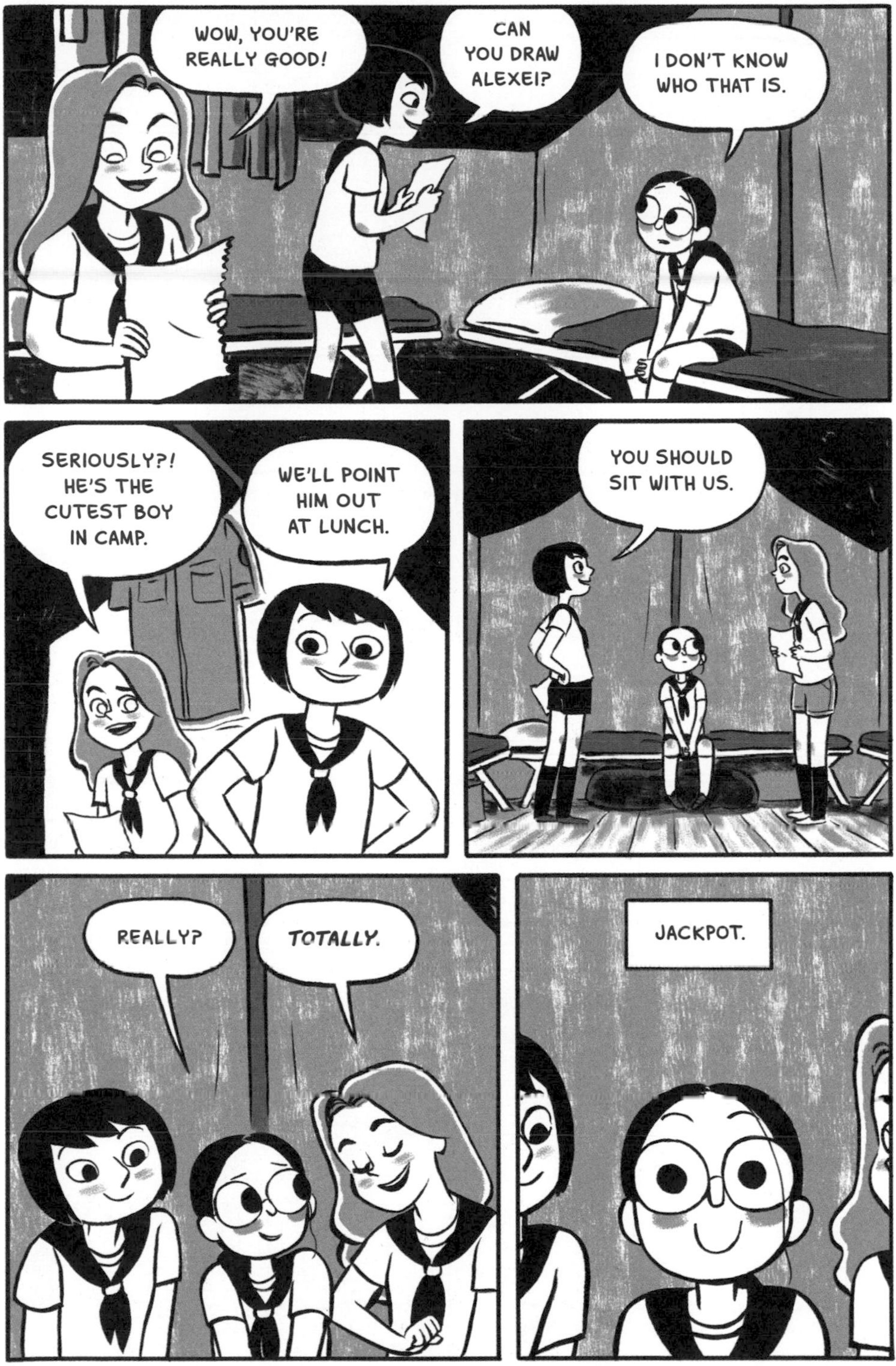
WOW, YOU'RE REALLY GOOD!
CAN YOU DRAW ALEXEI?
I DON'T KNOW WHO THAT IS.
SERIOUSLY?! HE'S THE CUTEST BOY IN CAMP.
WE'LL POINT HIM OUT AT LUNCH.
YOU SHOULD SIT WITH US.
REALLY?
TOTALLY.
JACKPOT.

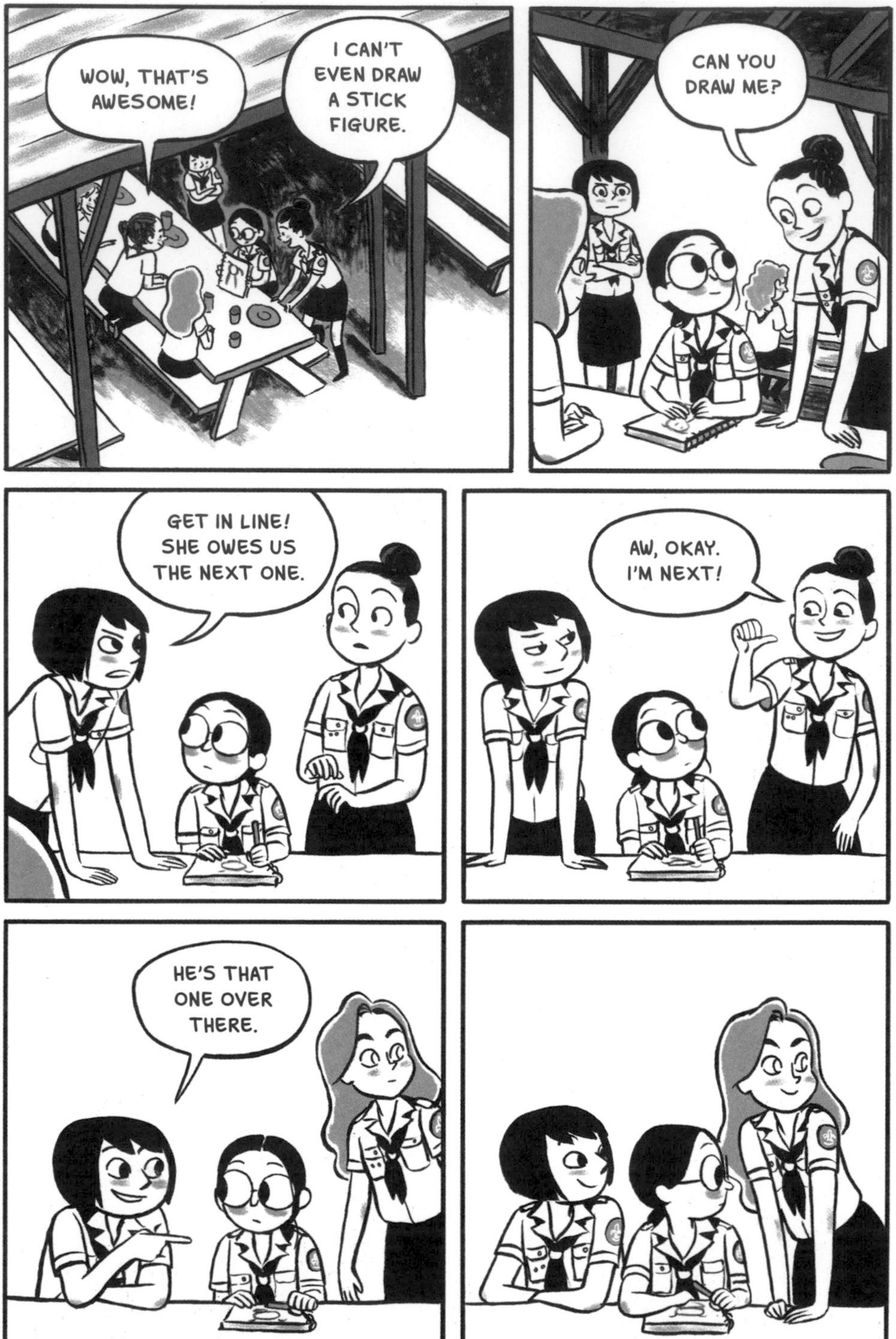
WOW, THAT'S AWESOME!
I CAN'T EVEN DRAW A STICK FIGURE.
CAN YOU DRAW ME?
GET IN LINE! SHE OWES US THE NEXT ONE.
AW, OKAY. I'M NEXT!
HE'S THAT ONE OVER THERE.

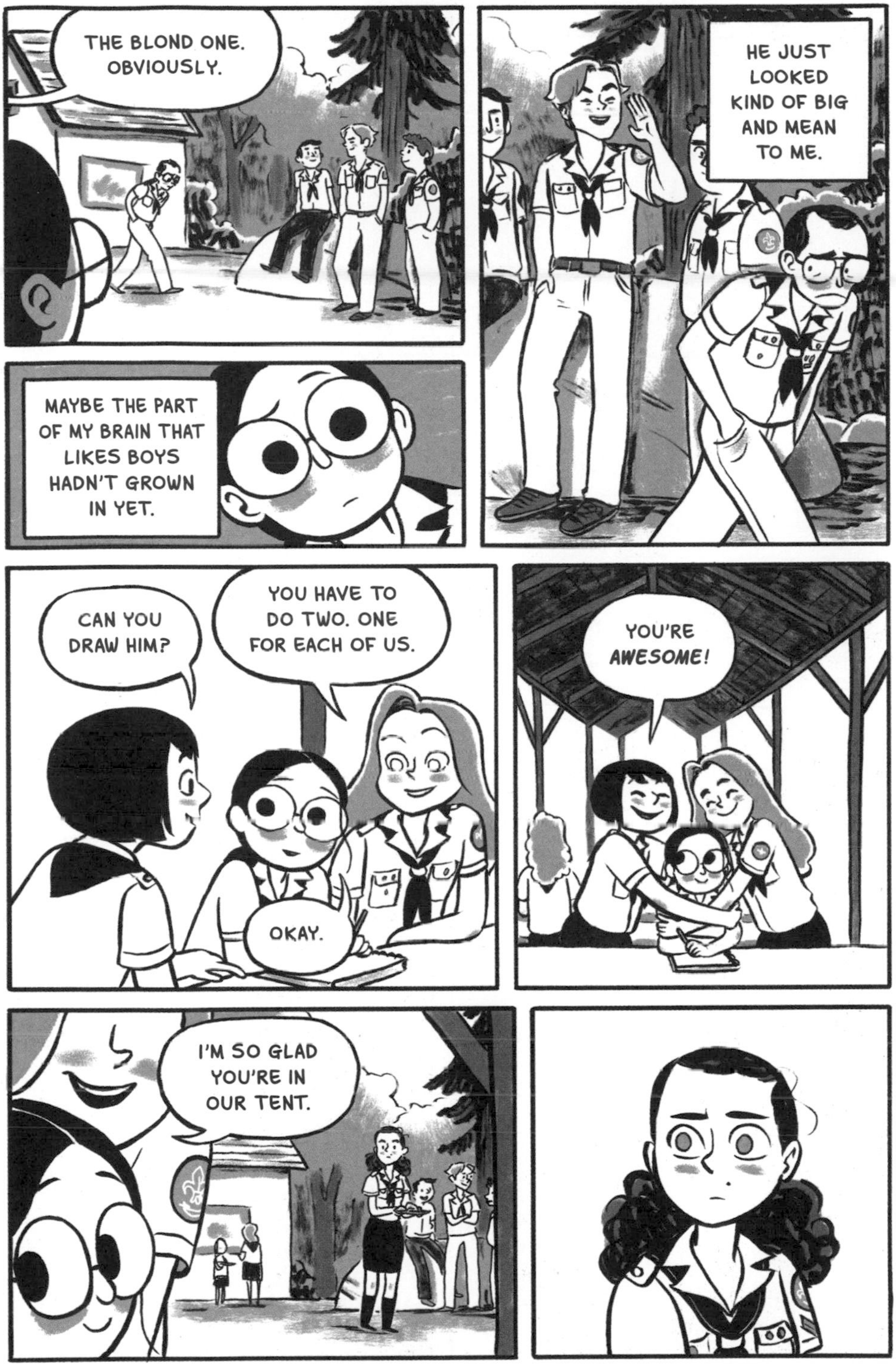
THE BLOND ONE. OBVIOUSLY.
HE JUST LOOKED KIND OF BIG AND MEAN TO ME.
MAYBE THE PART OF MY BRAIN THAT LIKES BOYS HADN'T GROWN IN YET.
CAN YOU DRAW HIM?
YOU HAVE TO DO TWO. ONE FOR EACH OF US.
OKAY.
YOU'RE AWESOME!
I'M SO GLAD YOU'RE IN OUR TENT.

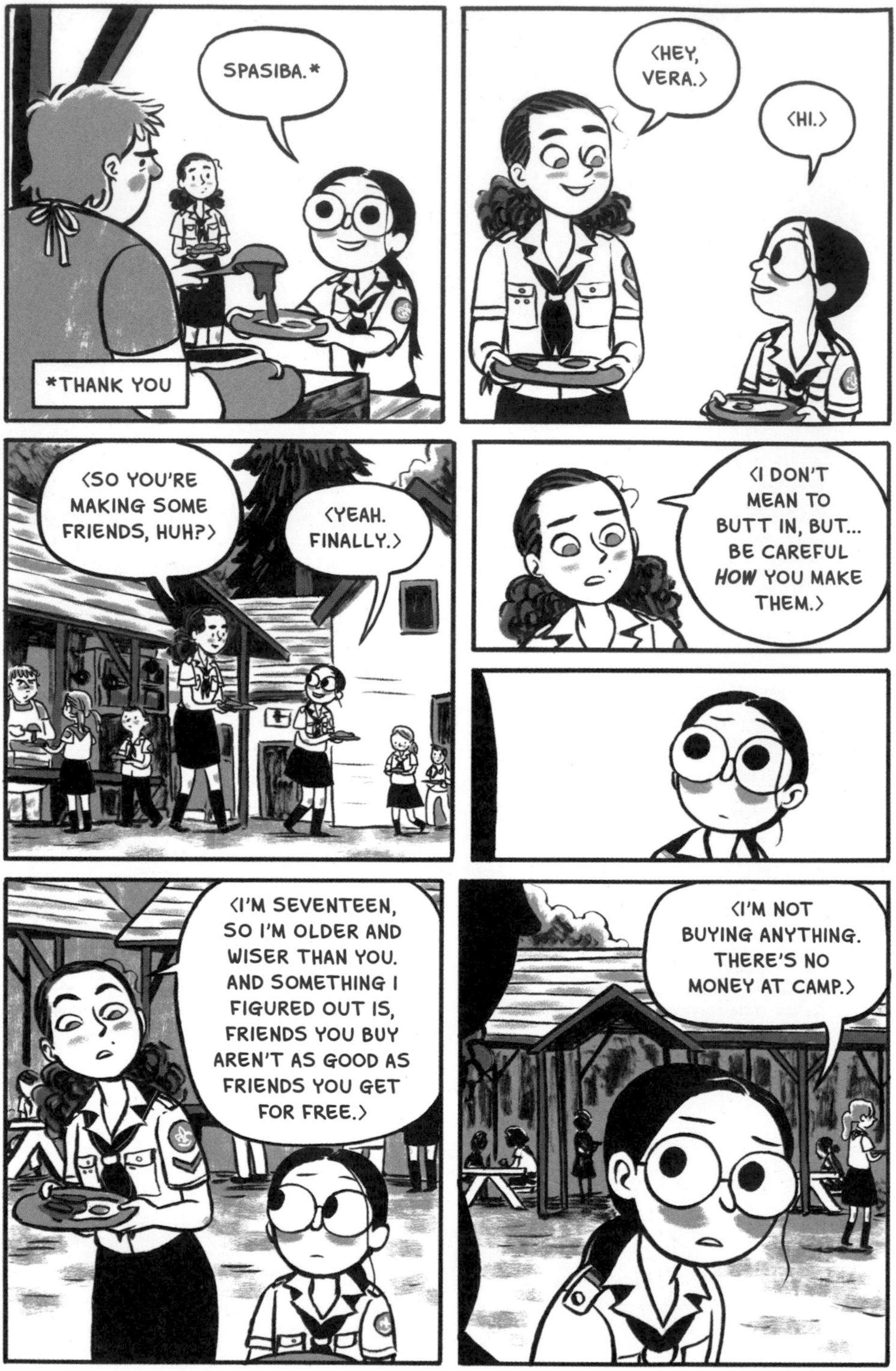
SPASIBA.*
*THANK YOU
<HEY, VERA.>
<HI.>
<SO YOU'RE MAKING SOME FRIENDS, HUH?>
<YEAH. FINALLY.>
<I DON'T MEAN TO BUTT IN, BUT... BE CAREFUL HOW YOU MAKE THEM.>
<I'M SEVENTEEN, SO I'M OLDER AND WISER THAN YOU. AND SOMETHING I FIGURED OUT IS, FRIENDS YOU BUY AREN'T AS GOOD AS FRIENDS YOU GET FOR FREE.>
<I'M NOT BUYING ANYTHING. THERE'S NO MONEY AT CAMP.>

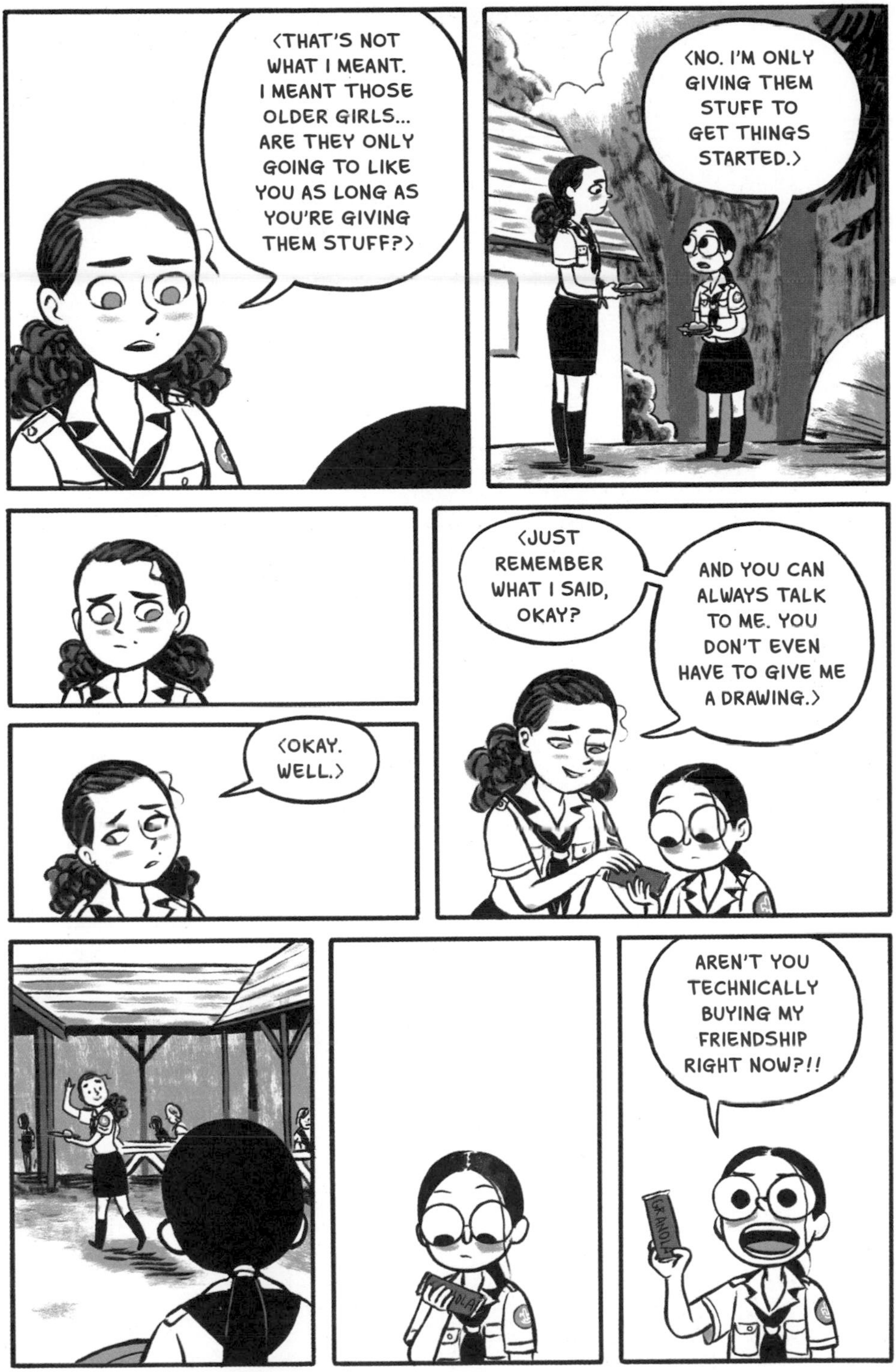
<THAT'S NOT WHAT I MEANT. I MEANT THOSE OLDER GIRLS... ARE THEY ONLY GOING TO LIKE YOU AS LONG AS YOU'RE GIVING THEM STUFF?>
<NO. I'M ONLY GIVING THEM STUFF TO GET THINGS STARTED.>
<OKAY. WELL.>
<JUST REMEMBER WHAT I SAID, OKAY?
AND YOU CAN ALWAYS TALK TO ME. YOU DON'T EVEN HAVE TO GIVE ME A DRAWING.>
AREN'T YOU TECHNICALLY BUYING MY FRIENDSHIP RIGHT NOW?!!

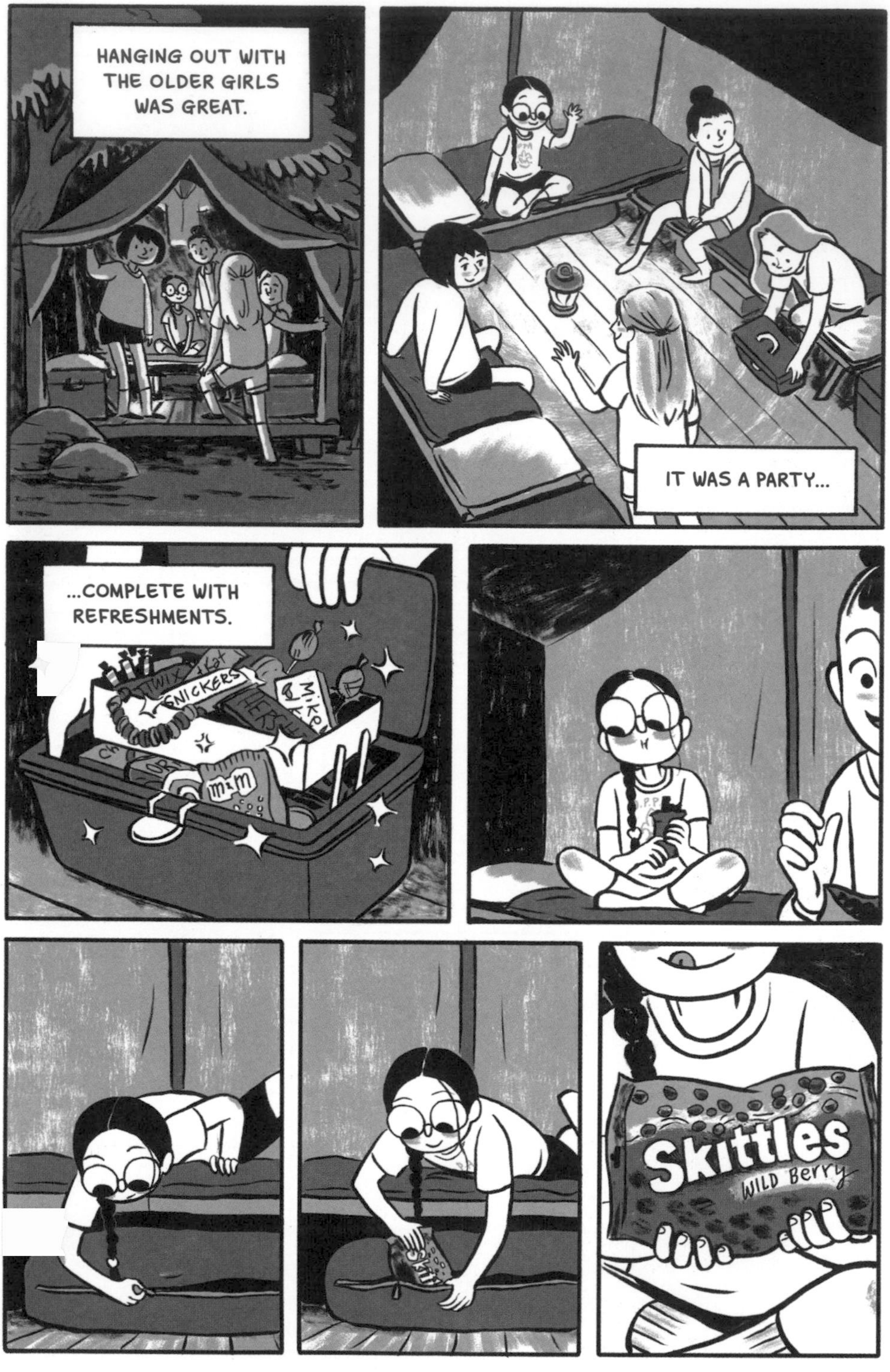
HANGING OUT WITH THE OLDER GIRLS WAS GREAT.
IT WAS A PARTY...
...COMPLETE WITH REFRESHMENTS.
TWIX
SNICKERS
m&m
Skittles
WILD Berry

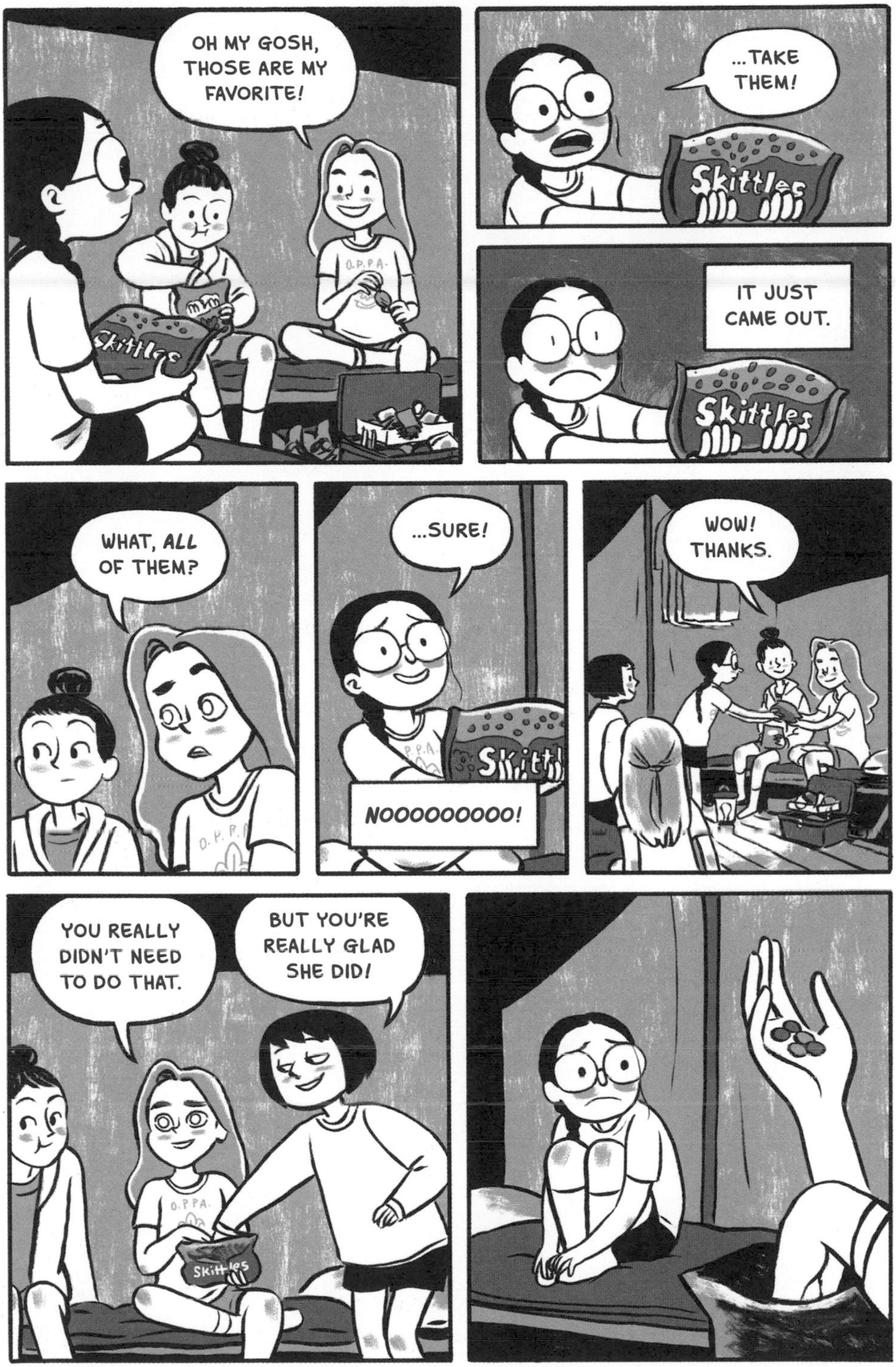
OH MY GOSH, THOSE ARE MY FAVORITE!
Skittles
m&m
O.P.P.A.
...TAKE THEM!
Skittles
IT JUST CAME OUT.
Skittles
WHAT, ALL OF THEM?
O.P.P.A.
...SURE!
NOOOOOOOOO!
WOW! THANKS.
YOU REALLY DIDN'T NEED TO DO THAT.
BUT YOU'RE REALLY GLAD SHE DID!
O.P.P.A.
Skittles

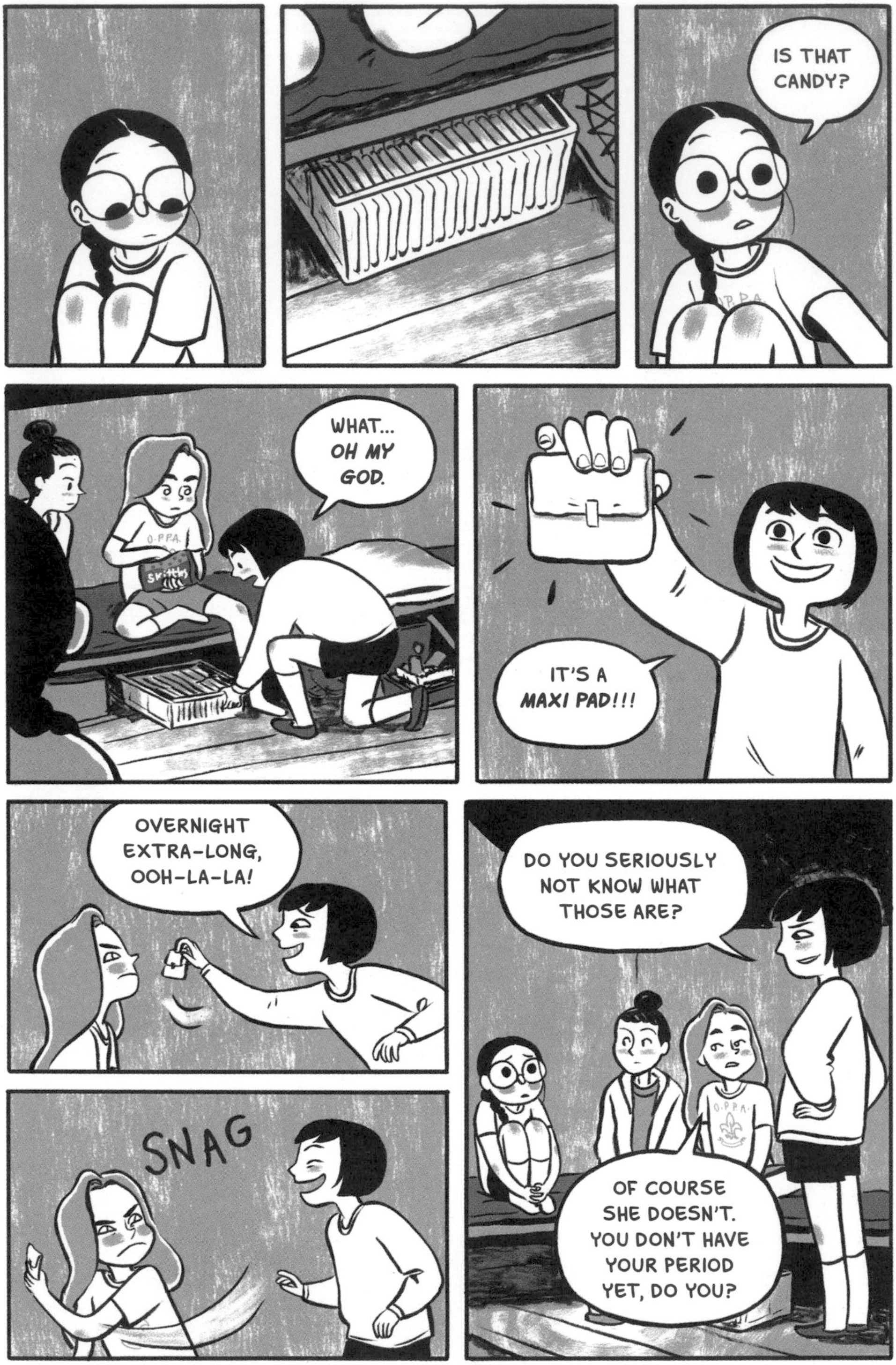
IS THAT CANDY?
Skittles
WHAT... OH MY GOD.
IT'S A MAXI PAD!!!
OVERNIGHT EXTRA-LONG, OOH-LA-LA!
DO YOU SERIOUSLY NOT KNOW WHAT THOSE ARE?
SNAG
OF COURSE SHE DOESN'T. YOU DON'T HAVE YOUR PERIOD YET, DO YOU?

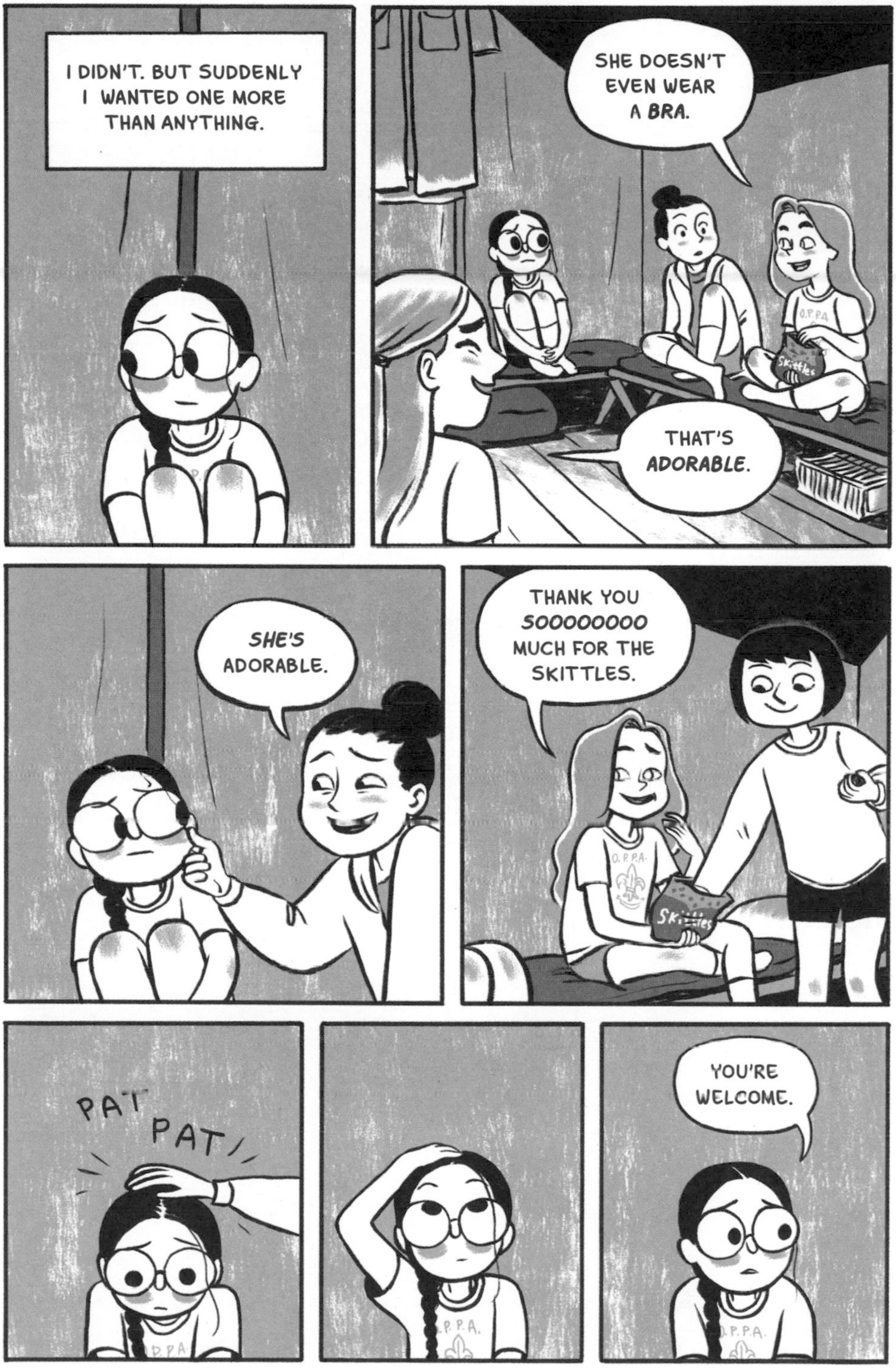
I DIDN'T. BUT SUDDENLY I WANTED ONE MORE THAN ANYTHING.
SHE DOESN'T EVEN WEAR A BRA.
THAT'S ADORABLE.
SHE'S ADORABLE.
THANK YOU SOOOOOOOO MUCH FOR THE SKITTLES.
PAT PAT
YOU'RE WELCOME.

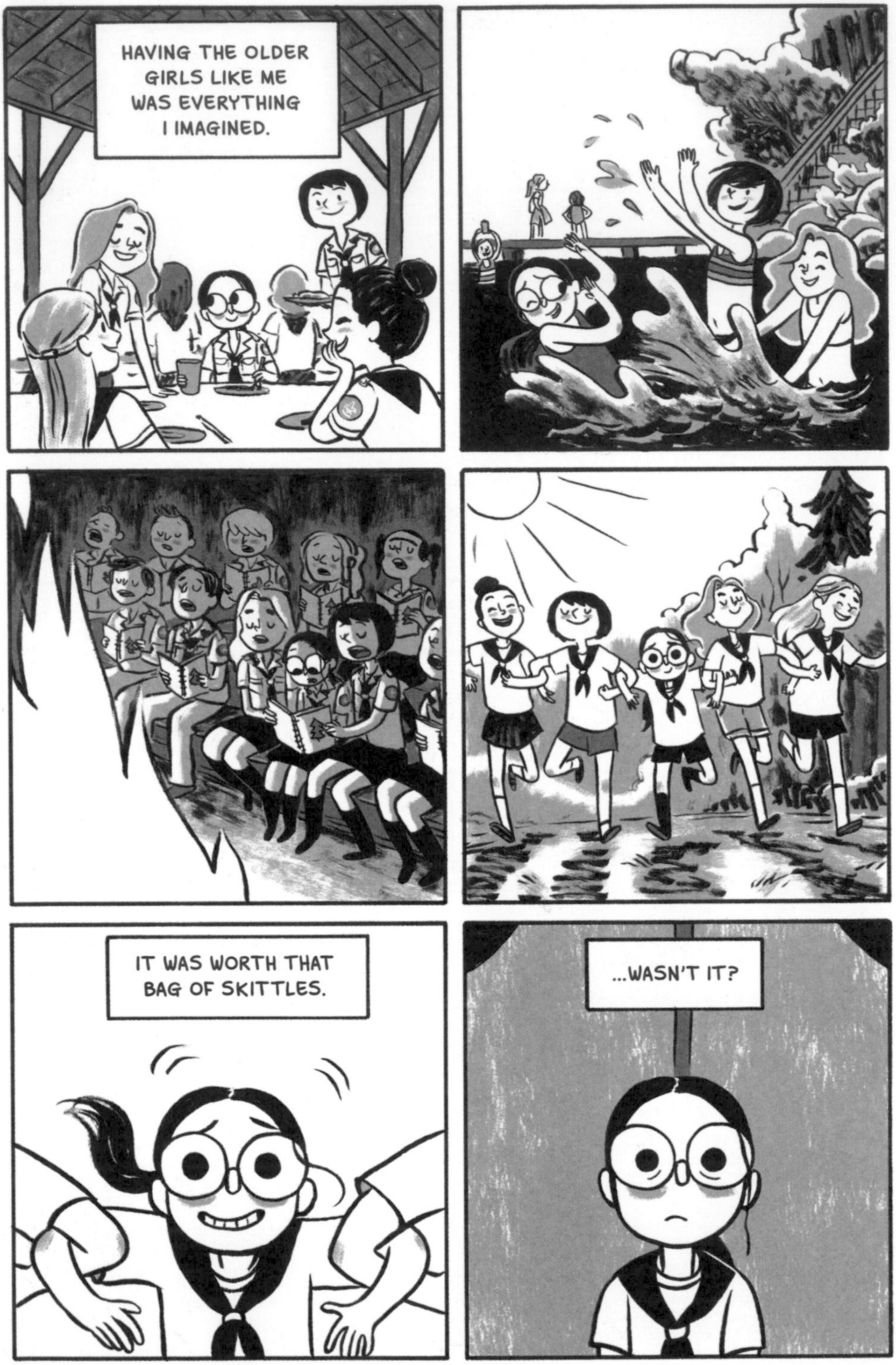
HAVING THE OLDER GIRLS LIKE ME WAS EVERYTHING I IMAGINED.
IT WAS WORTH THAT BAG OF SKITTLES.
...WASN'T IT?

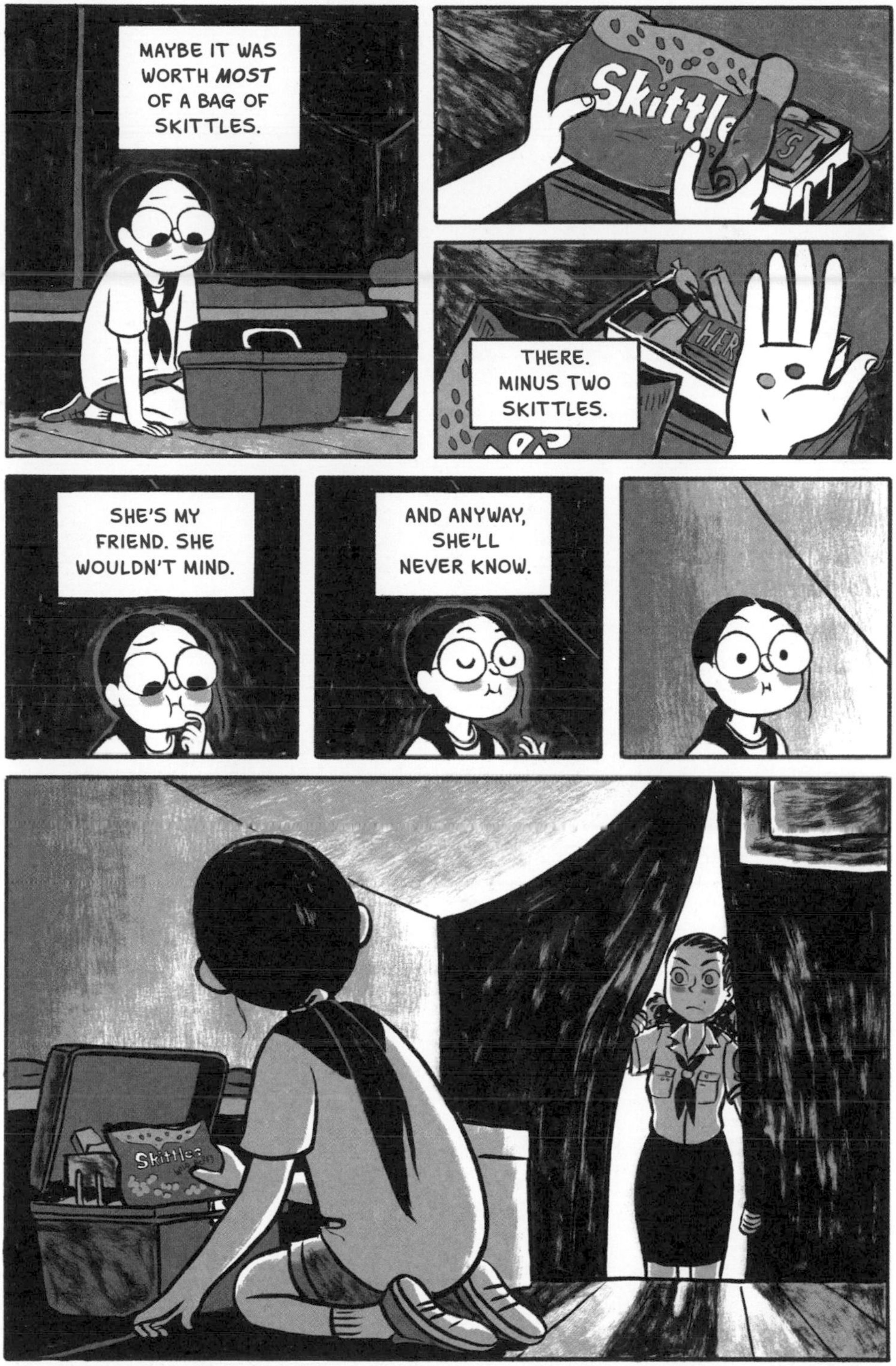
MAYBE IT WAS WORTH *MOST* OF A BAG OF SKITTLES.
Skittles
THERE. MINUS TWO SKITTLES.
SHE'S MY FRIEND. SHE WOULDN'T MIND.
AND ANYWAY, SHE'LL NEVER KNOW.
Skittles

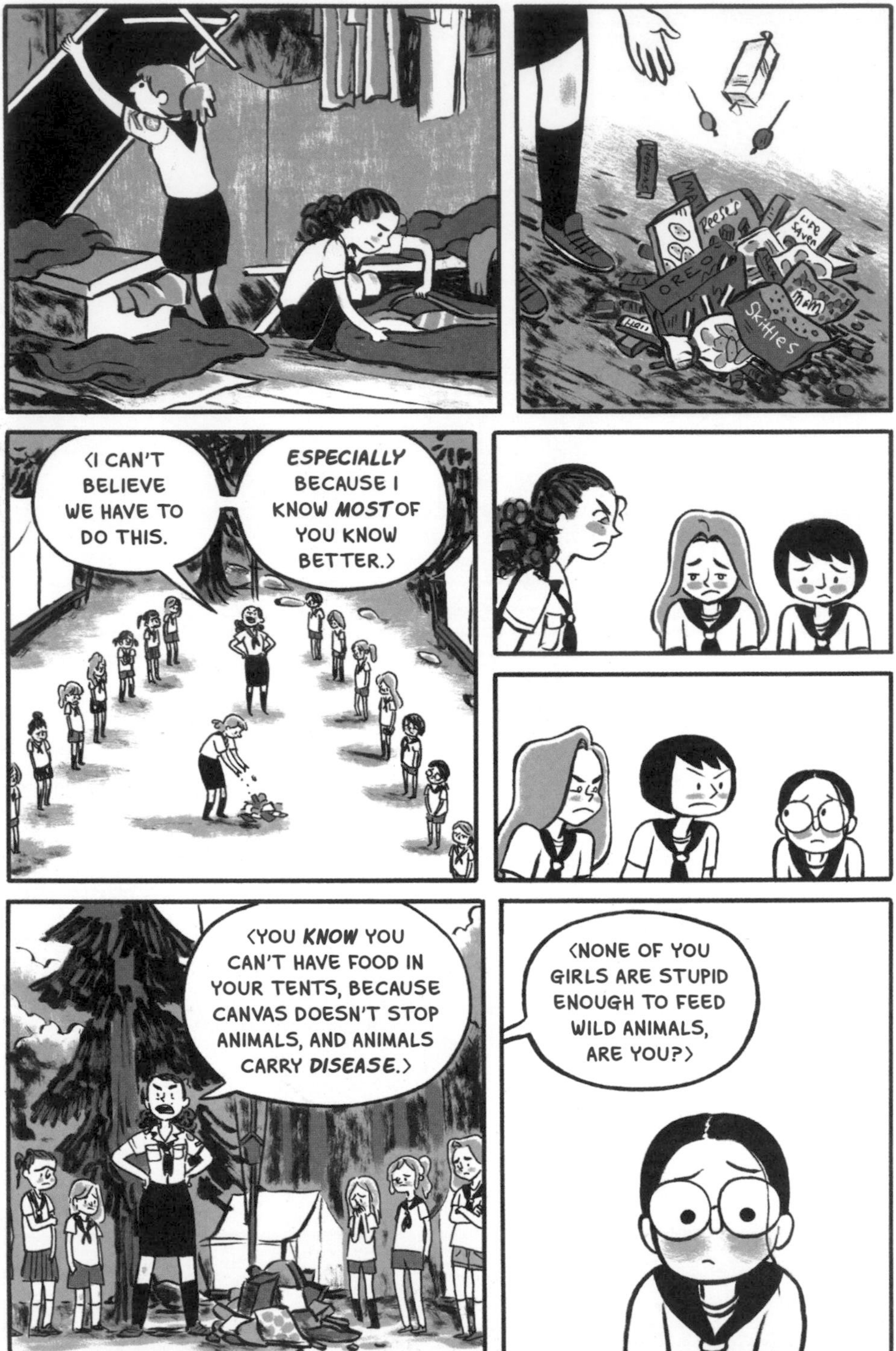
Reese's
Life Savers
OREO
M&M
Skittles
‹I CAN'T BELIEVE WE HAVE TO DO THIS.
ESPECIALLY BECAUSE I KNOW MOST OF YOU KNOW BETTER.›
‹YOU KNOW YOU CAN'T HAVE FOOD IN YOUR TENTS, BECAUSE CANVAS DOESN'T STOP ANIMALS, AND ANIMALS CARRY DISEASE.›
‹NONE OF YOU GIRLS ARE STUPID ENOUGH TO FEED WILD ANIMALS, ARE YOU?›

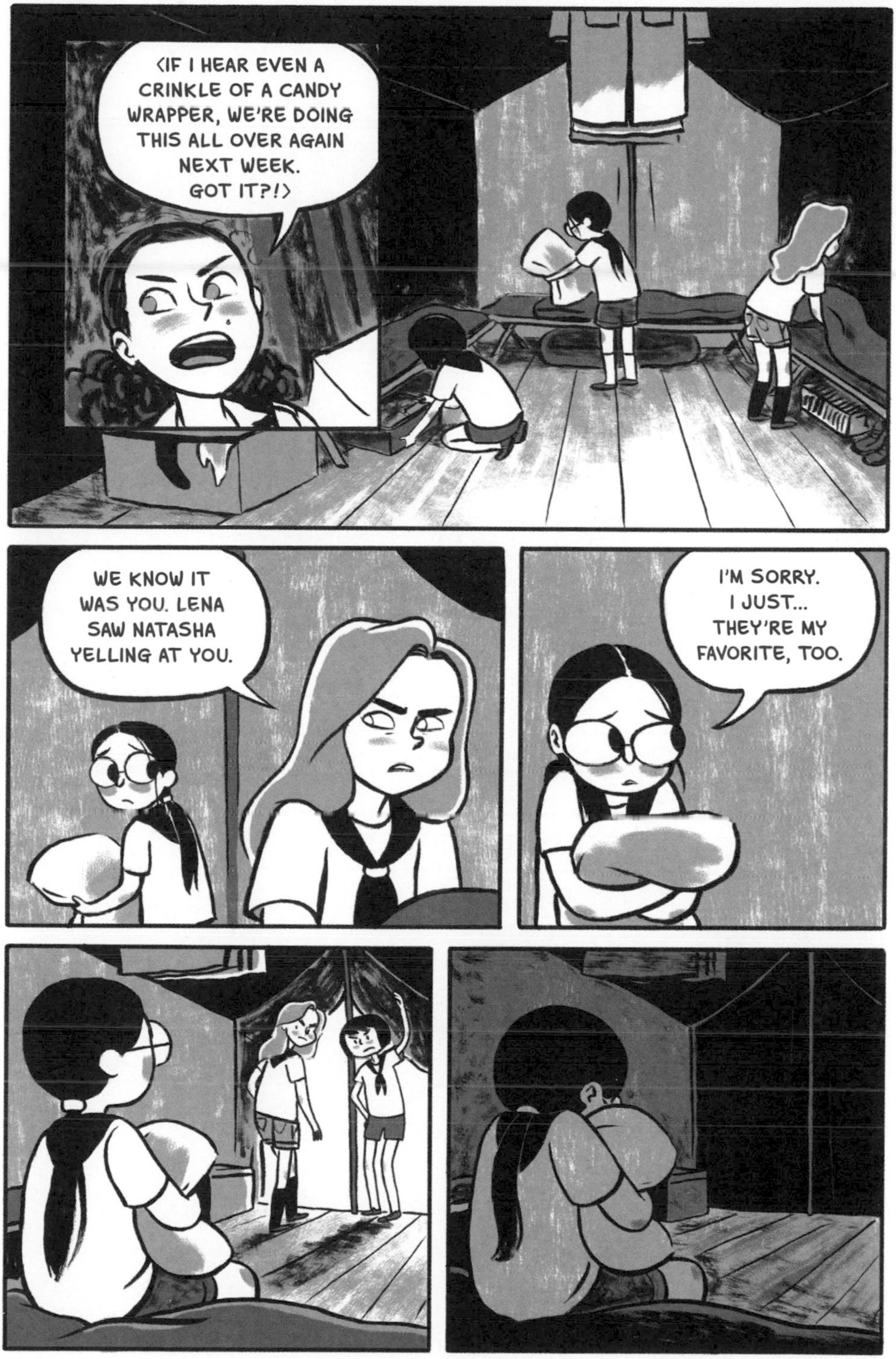

<IF I HEAR EVEN A CRINKLE OF A CANDY WRAPPER, WE'RE DOING THIS ALL OVER AGAIN NEXT WEEK. GOT IT?!>
WE KNOW IT WAS YOU. LENA SAW NATASHA YELLING AT YOU.
I'M SORRY. I JUST... THEY'RE MY FAVORITE, TOO.

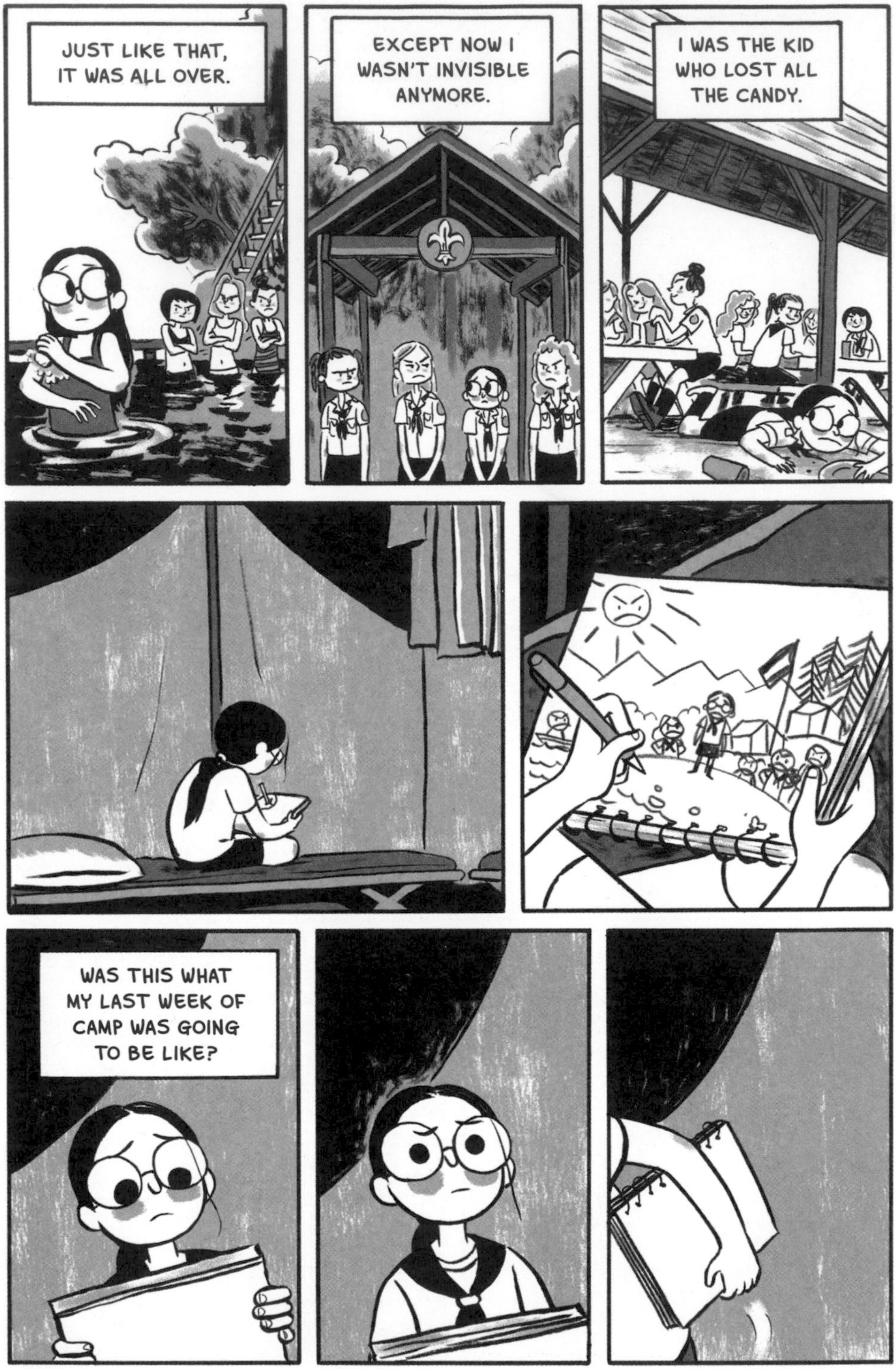
JUST LIKE THAT, IT WAS ALL OVER.
EXCEPT NOW I WASN'T INVISIBLE ANYMORE.
I WAS THE KID WHO LOST ALL THE CANDY.
WAS THIS WHAT MY LAST WEEK OF CAMP WAS GOING TO BE LIKE?

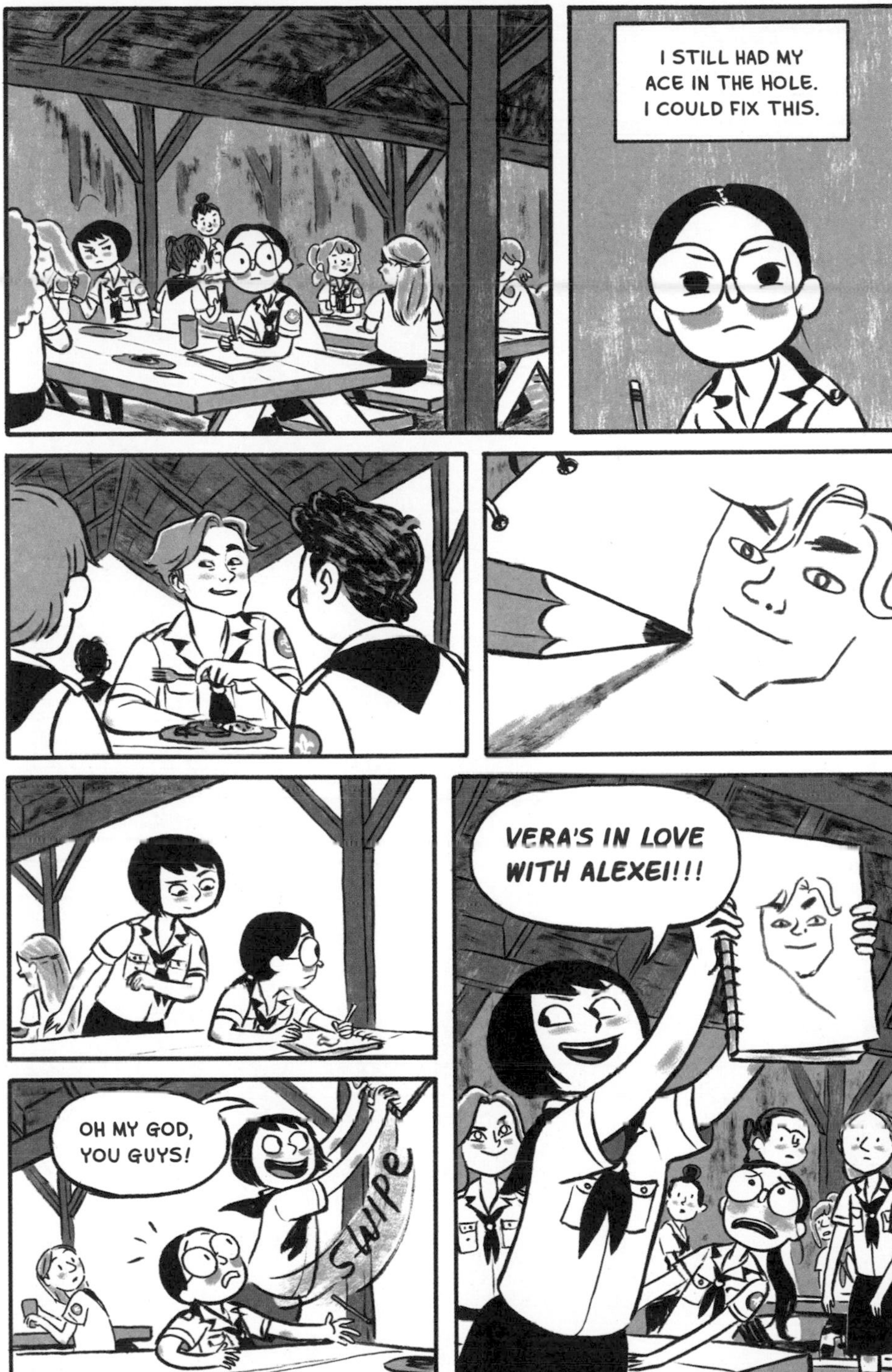
I STILL HAD MY ACE IN THE HOLE. I COULD FIX THIS.
VERA'S IN LOVE WITH ALEXEI!!!
OH MY GOD, YOU GUYS!
SWIPE

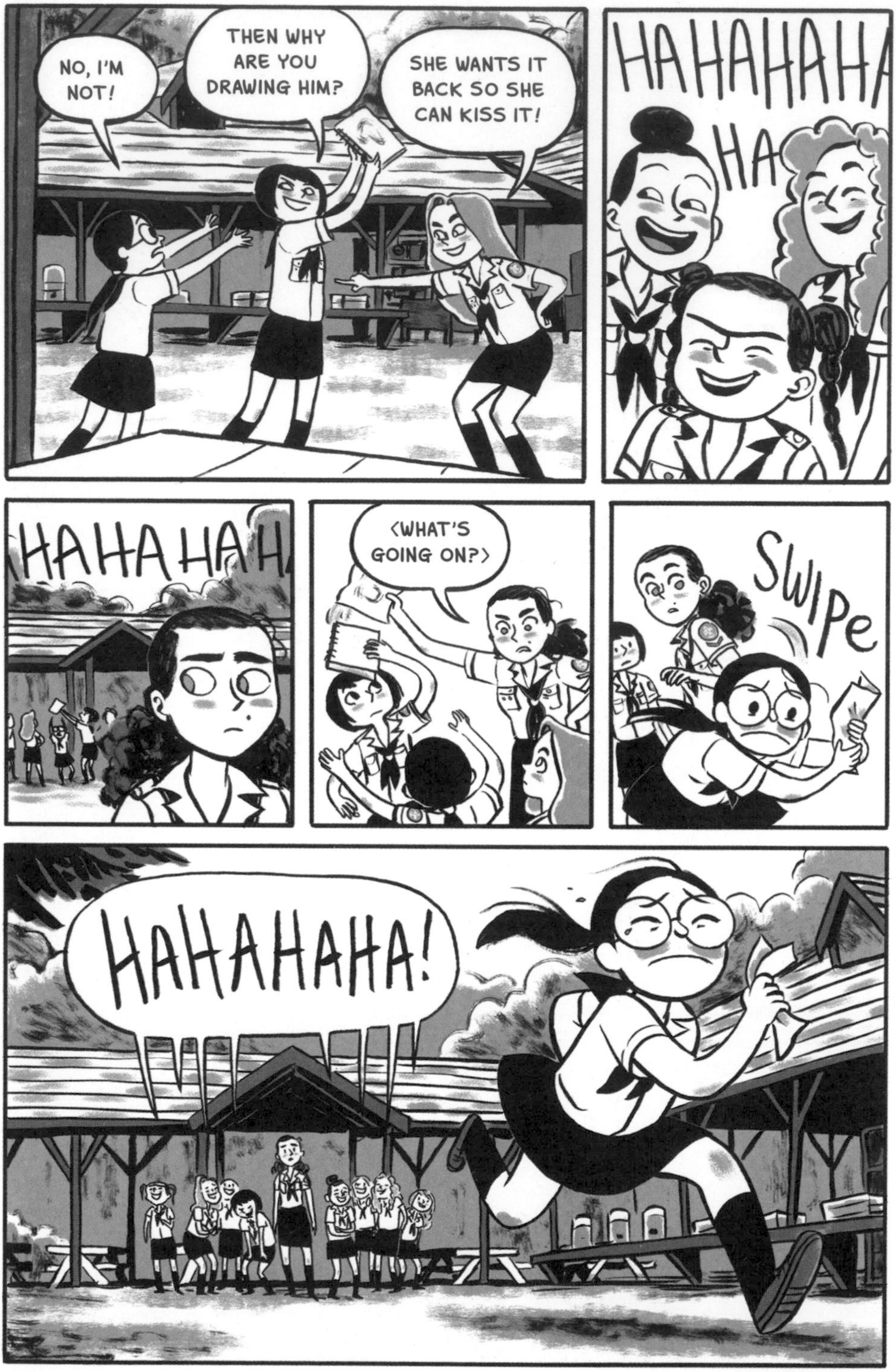
NO, I'M NOT!
THEN WHY ARE YOU DRAWING HIM?
SHE WANTS IT BACK SO SHE CAN KISS IT!
HAHAHAHA
HA
HAHAHA
<WHAT'S GOING ON?>
SWIPE
HAHAHAHA!

SNIFF

CRUMPLE

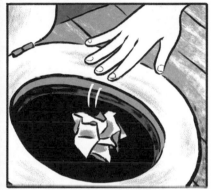

I WAS DONE TRYING TO MAKE PEOPLE LIKE ME. NATASHA WAS RIGHT, FRIENDS LIKE THAT WEREN'T WORTH HAVING.

I DIDN'T NEED THEM. I DIDN'T NEED ANYBODY.

I WAS GOING TO SPEND THIS WEEK HAVING A GREAT TIME ON MY OWN.

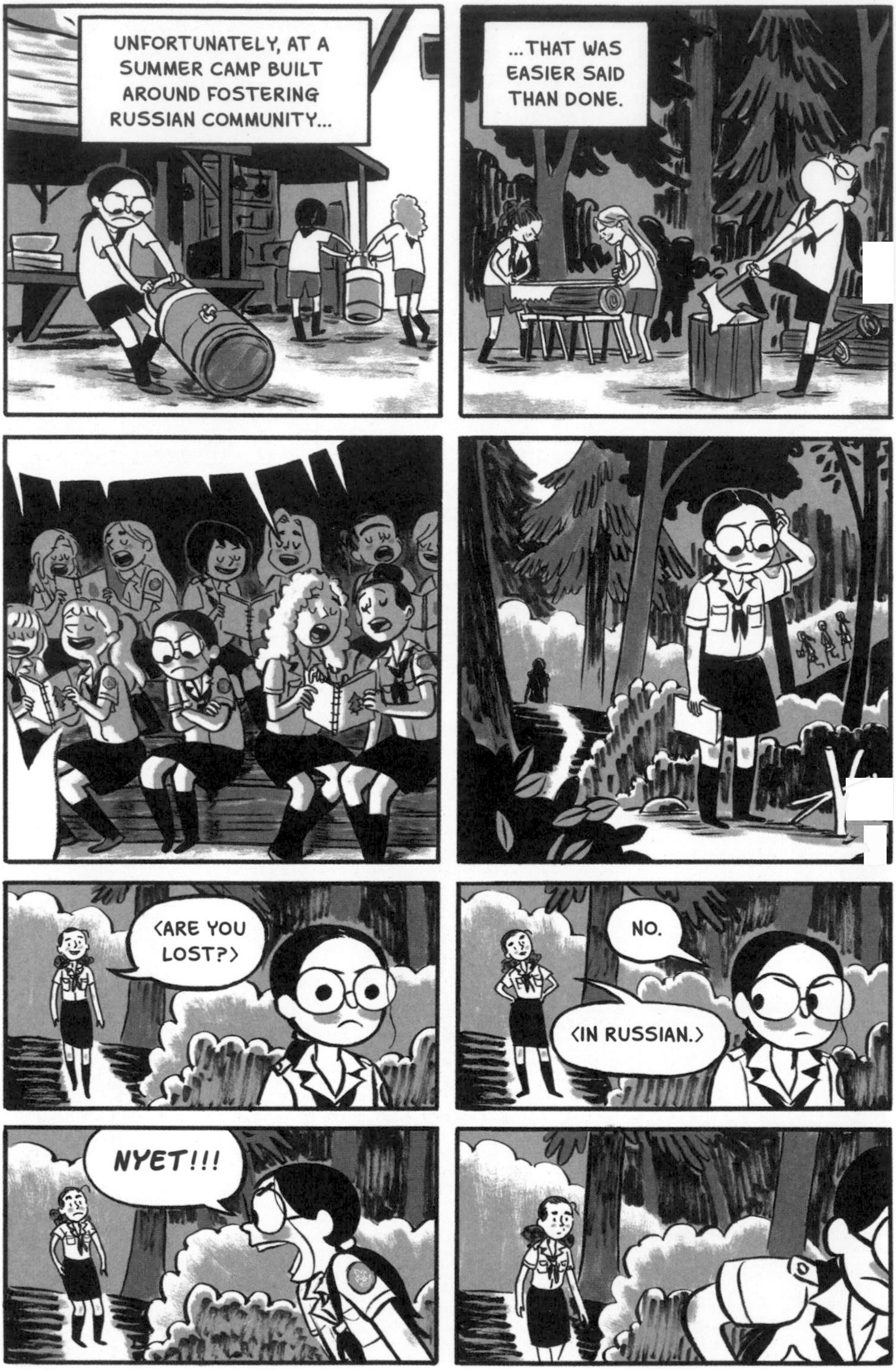
UNFORTUNATELY, AT A SUMMER CAMP BUILT AROUND FOSTERING RUSSIAN COMMUNITY...
...THAT WAS EASIER SAID THAN DONE.
<ARE YOU LOST?>
NO.
<IN RUSSIAN.>
NYET!!!

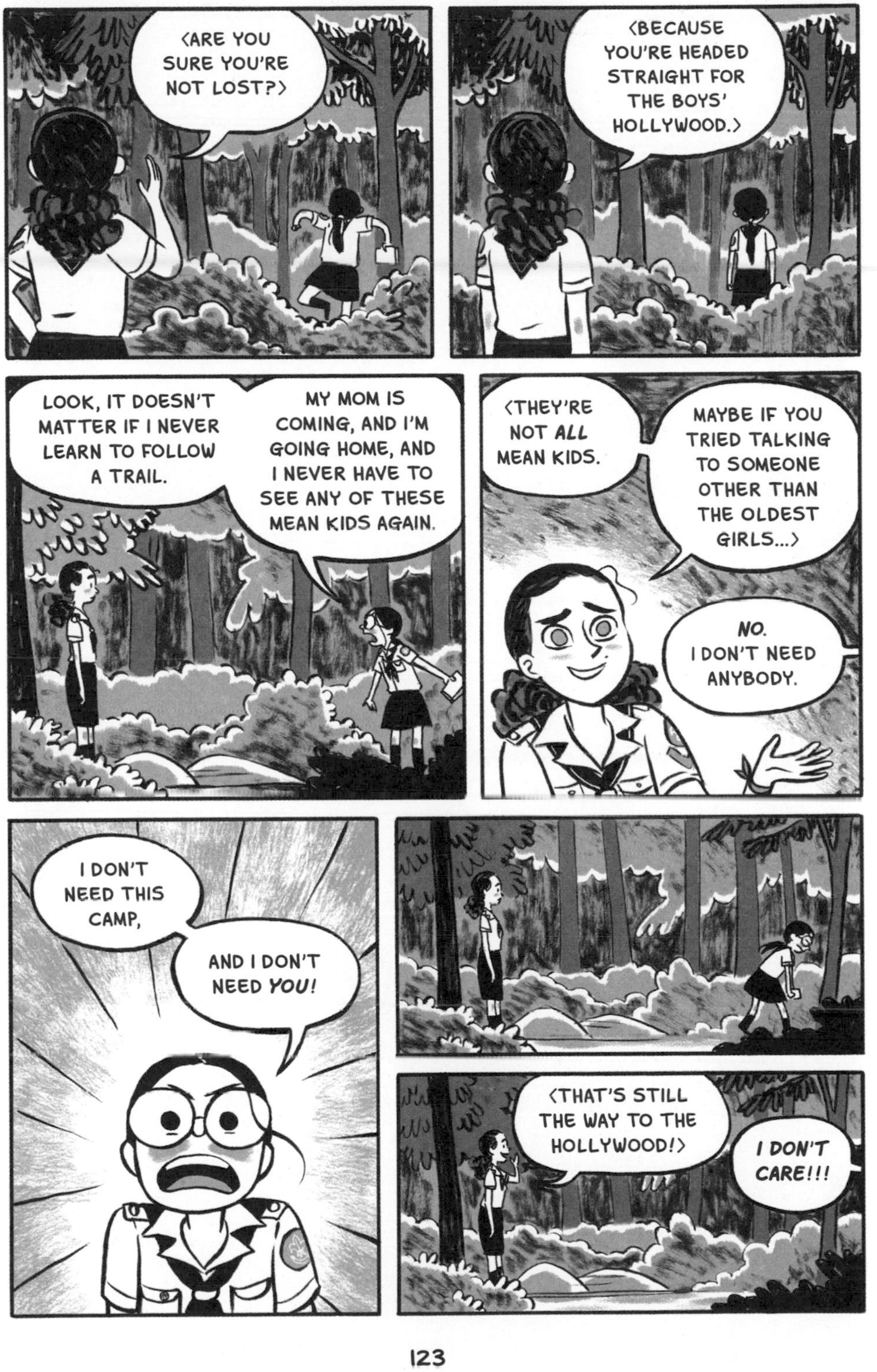
<ARE YOU SURE YOU'RE NOT LOST?>
<BECAUSE YOU'RE HEADED STRAIGHT FOR THE BOYS' HOLLYWOOD.>
LOOK, IT DOESN'T MATTER IF I NEVER LEARN TO FOLLOW A TRAIL.
MY MOM IS COMING, AND I'M GOING HOME, AND I NEVER HAVE TO SEE ANY OF THESE MEAN KIDS AGAIN.
<THEY'RE NOT *ALL* MEAN KIDS.
MAYBE IF YOU TRIED TALKING TO SOMEONE OTHER THAN THE OLDEST GIRLS...>
NO. I DON'T NEED ANYBODY.
I DON'T NEED THIS CAMP,
AND I DON'T NEED *YOU*!
<THAT'S STILL THE WAY TO THE HOLLYWOOD!>
I DON'T CARE!!!

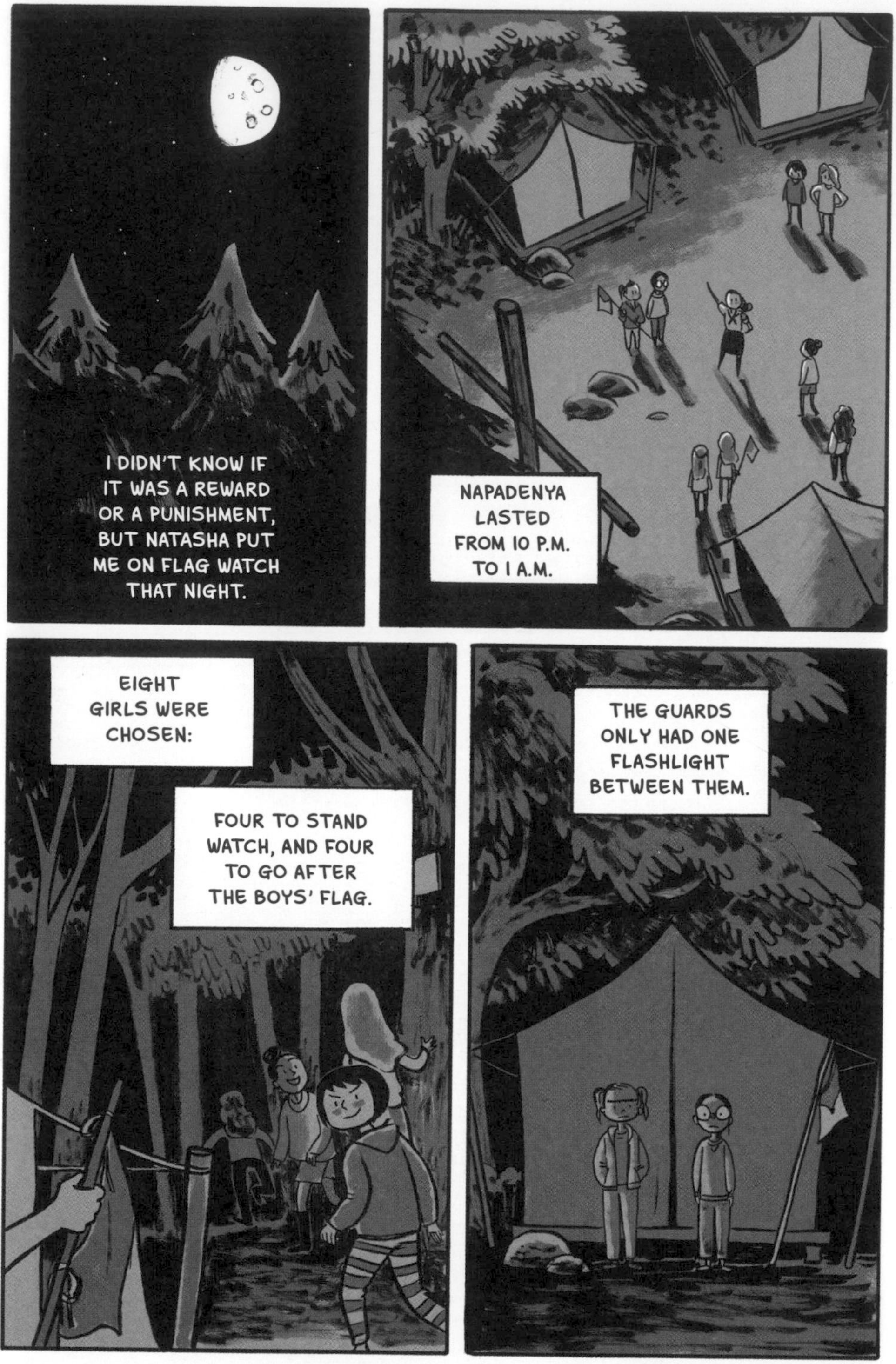
I DIDN'T KNOW IF IT WAS A REWARD OR A PUNISHMENT, BUT NATASHA PUT ME ON FLAG WATCH THAT NIGHT.
NAPADENYA LASTED FROM 10 P.M. TO 1 A.M.
EIGHT GIRLS WERE CHOSEN:
FOUR TO STAND WATCH, AND FOUR TO GO AFTER THE BOYS' FLAG.
THE GUARDS ONLY HAD ONE FLASHLIGHT BETWEEN THEM.

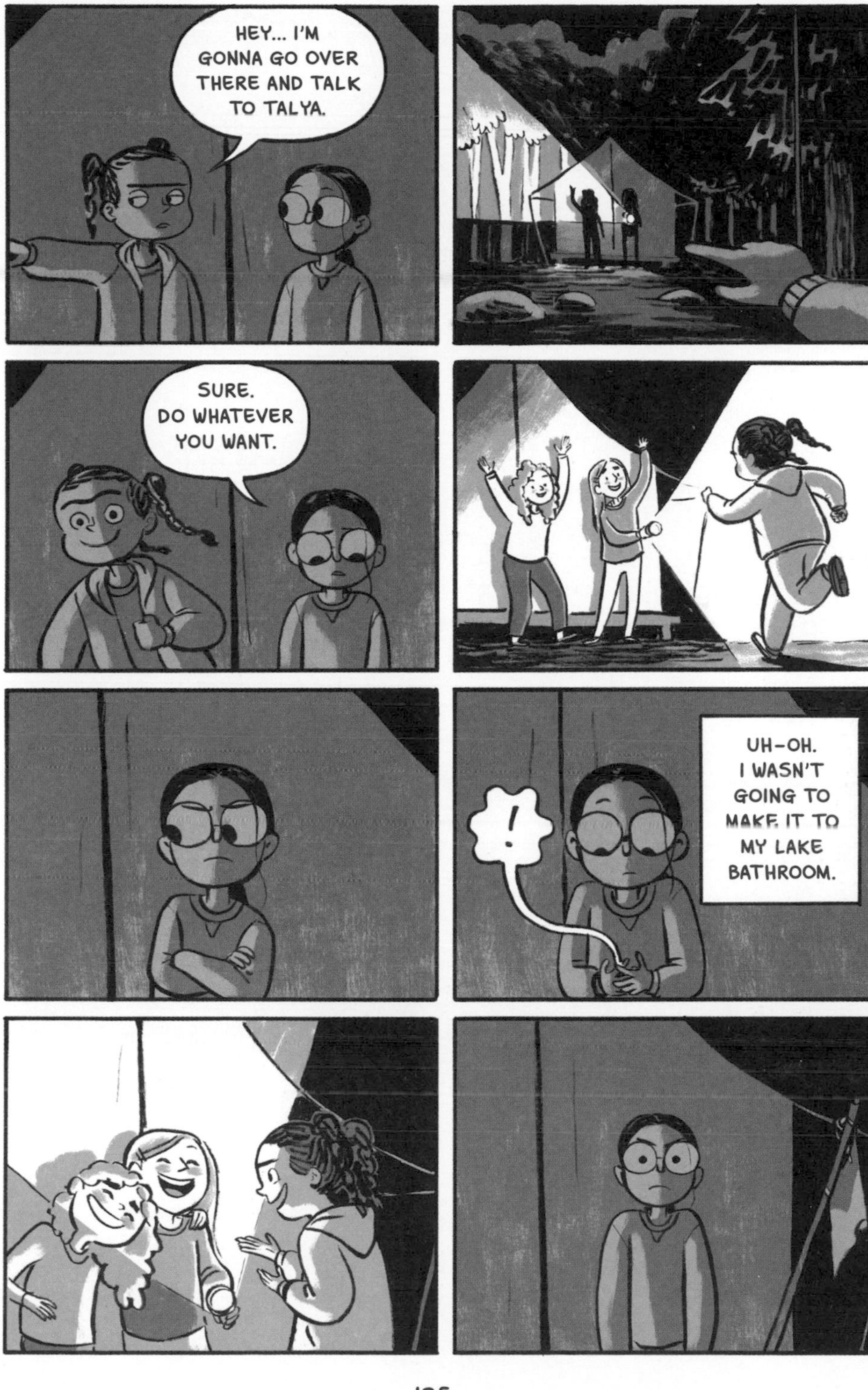
HEY... I'M GONNA GO OVER THERE AND TALK TO TALYA.
SURE. DO WHATEVER YOU WANT.
!
UH-OH. I WASN'T GOING TO MAKE IT TO MY LAKE BATHROOM.

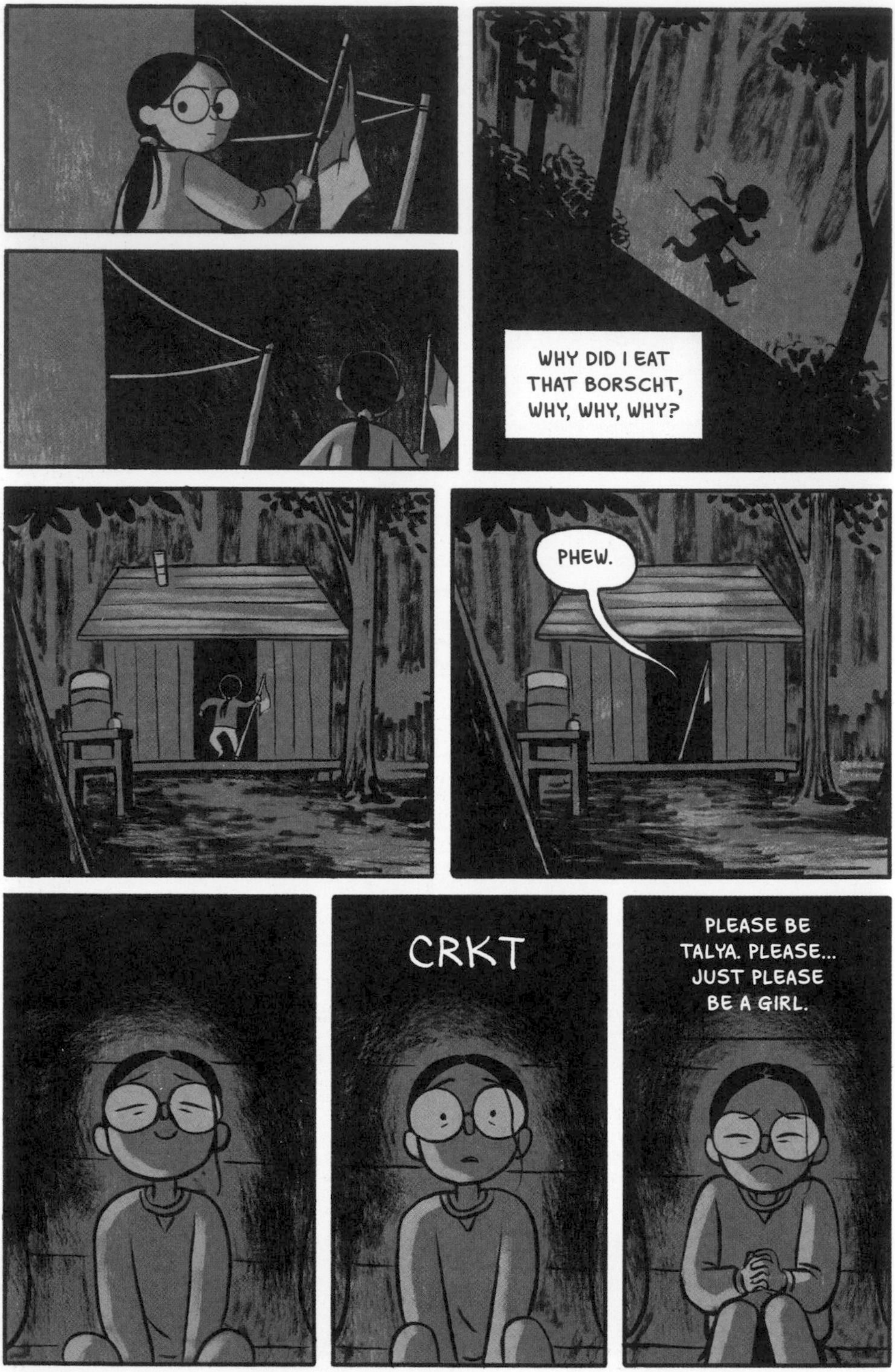
WHY DID I EAT THAT BORSCHT, WHY, WHY, WHY?
PHEW.
CRKT
PLEASE BE TALYA. PLEASE... JUST PLEASE BE A GIRL.

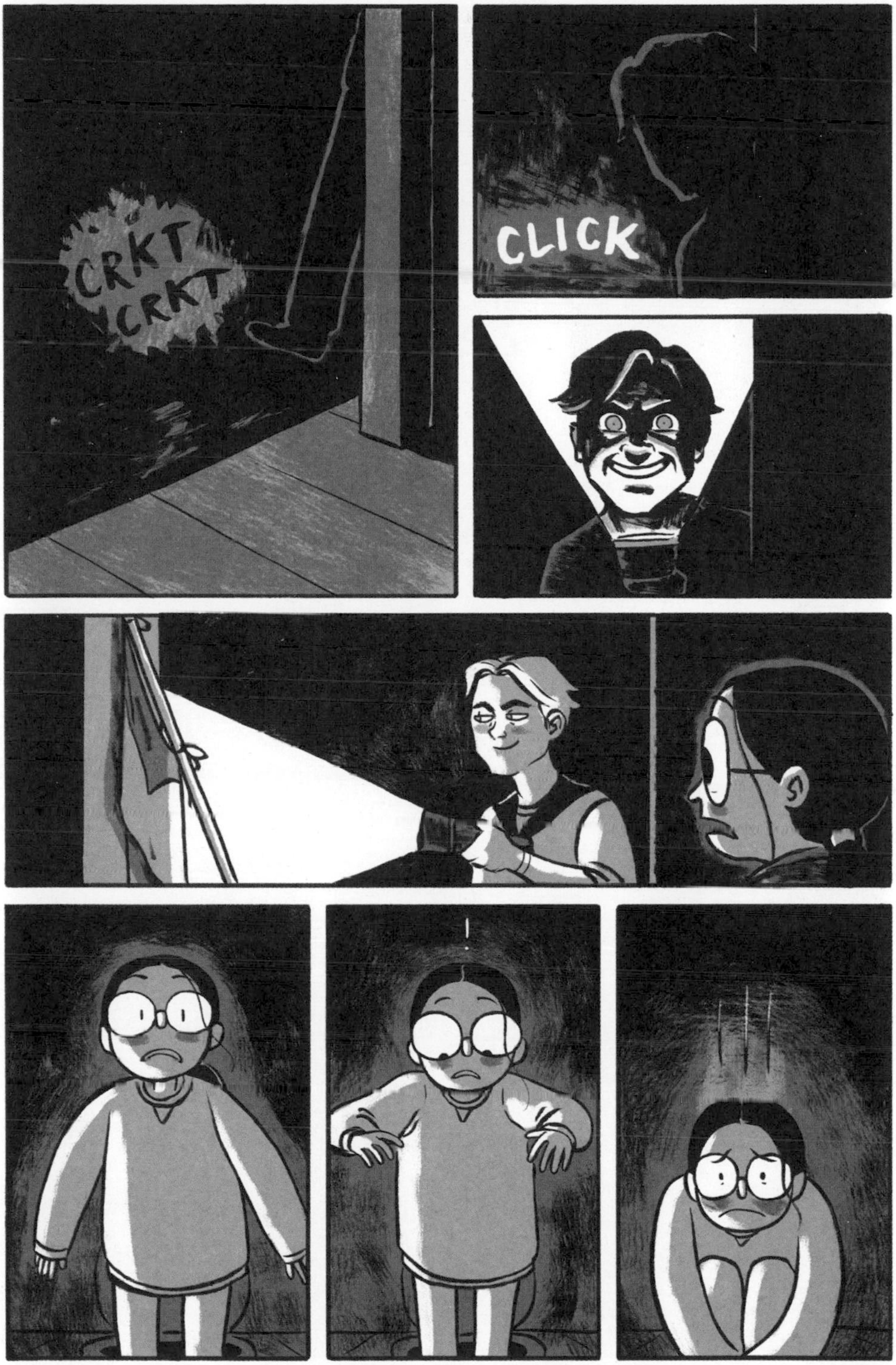
CRKT
CRKT
CLICK
!

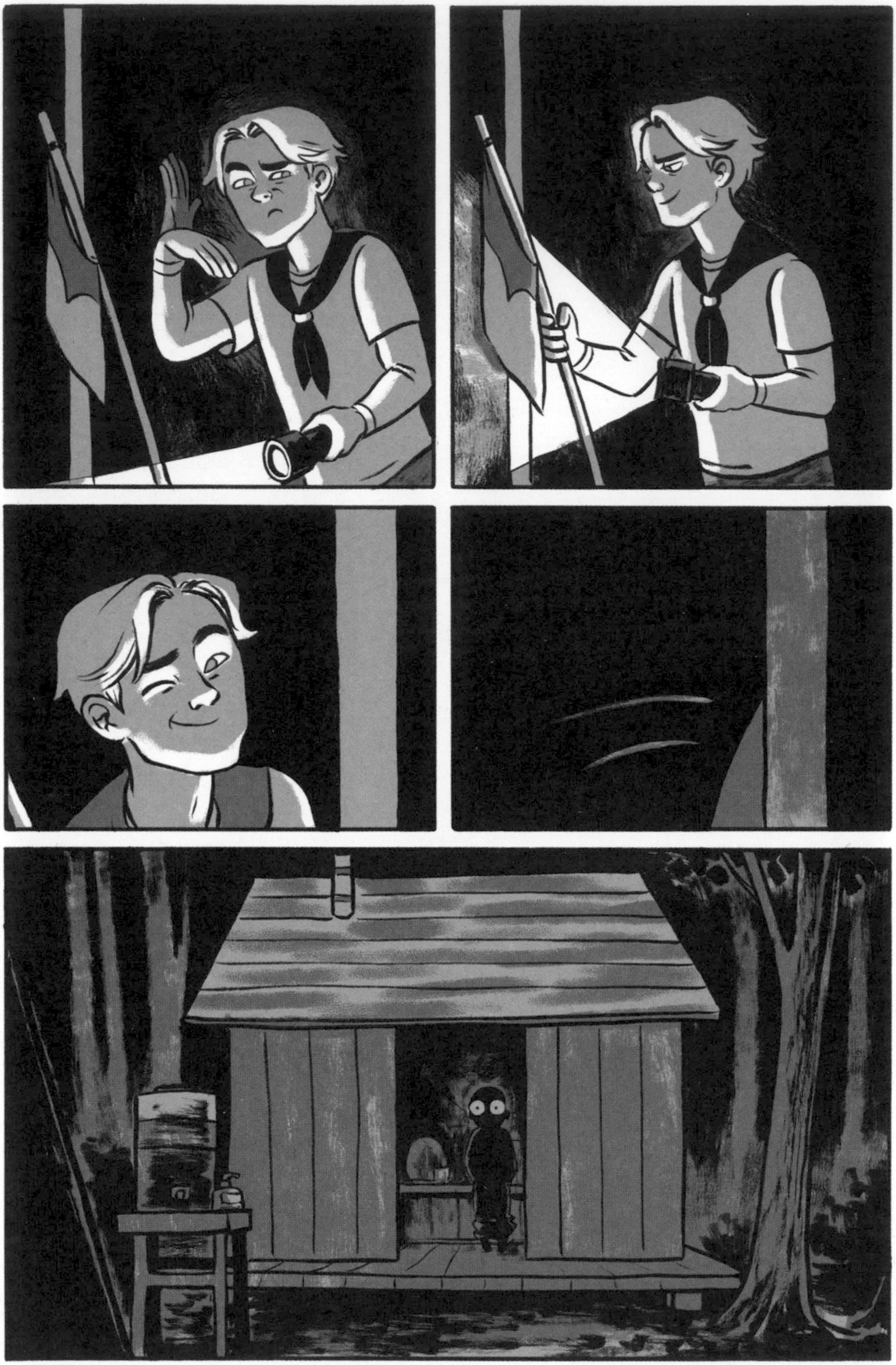

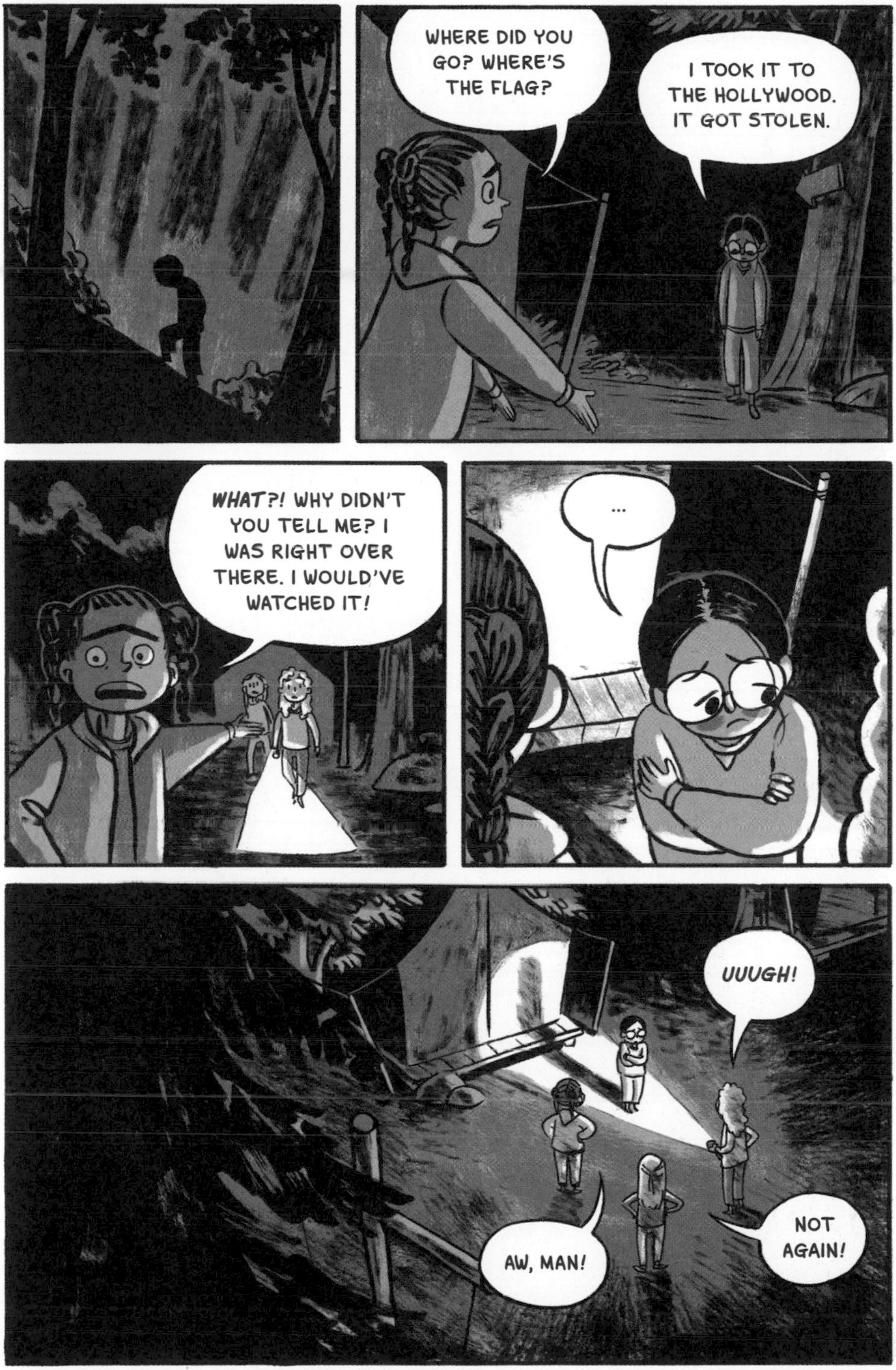
WHERE DID YOU GO? WHERE'S THE FLAG?
I TOOK IT TO THE HOLLYWOOD. IT GOT STOLEN.
WHAT?! WHY DIDN'T YOU TELL ME? I WAS RIGHT OVER THERE. I WOULD'VE WATCHED IT!
...
UUUGH!
AW, MAN!
NOT AGAIN!

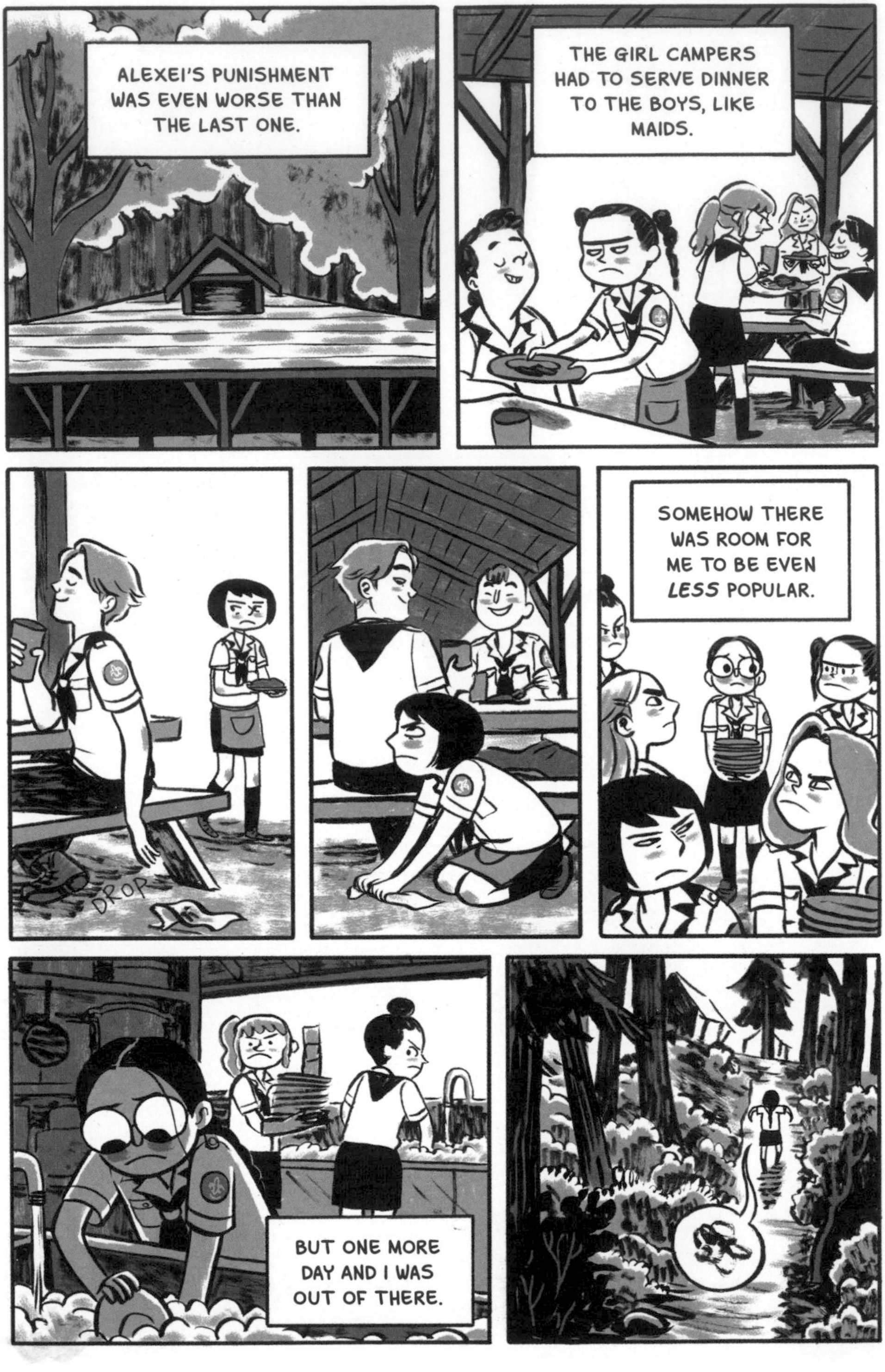
ALEXEI'S PUNISHMENT WAS EVEN WORSE THAN THE LAST ONE.
THE GIRL CAMPERS HAD TO SERVE DINNER TO THE BOYS, LIKE MAIDS.
DROP
SOMEHOW THERE WAS ROOM FOR ME TO BE EVEN *LESS* POPULAR.
BUT ONE MORE DAY AND I WAS OUT OF THERE.

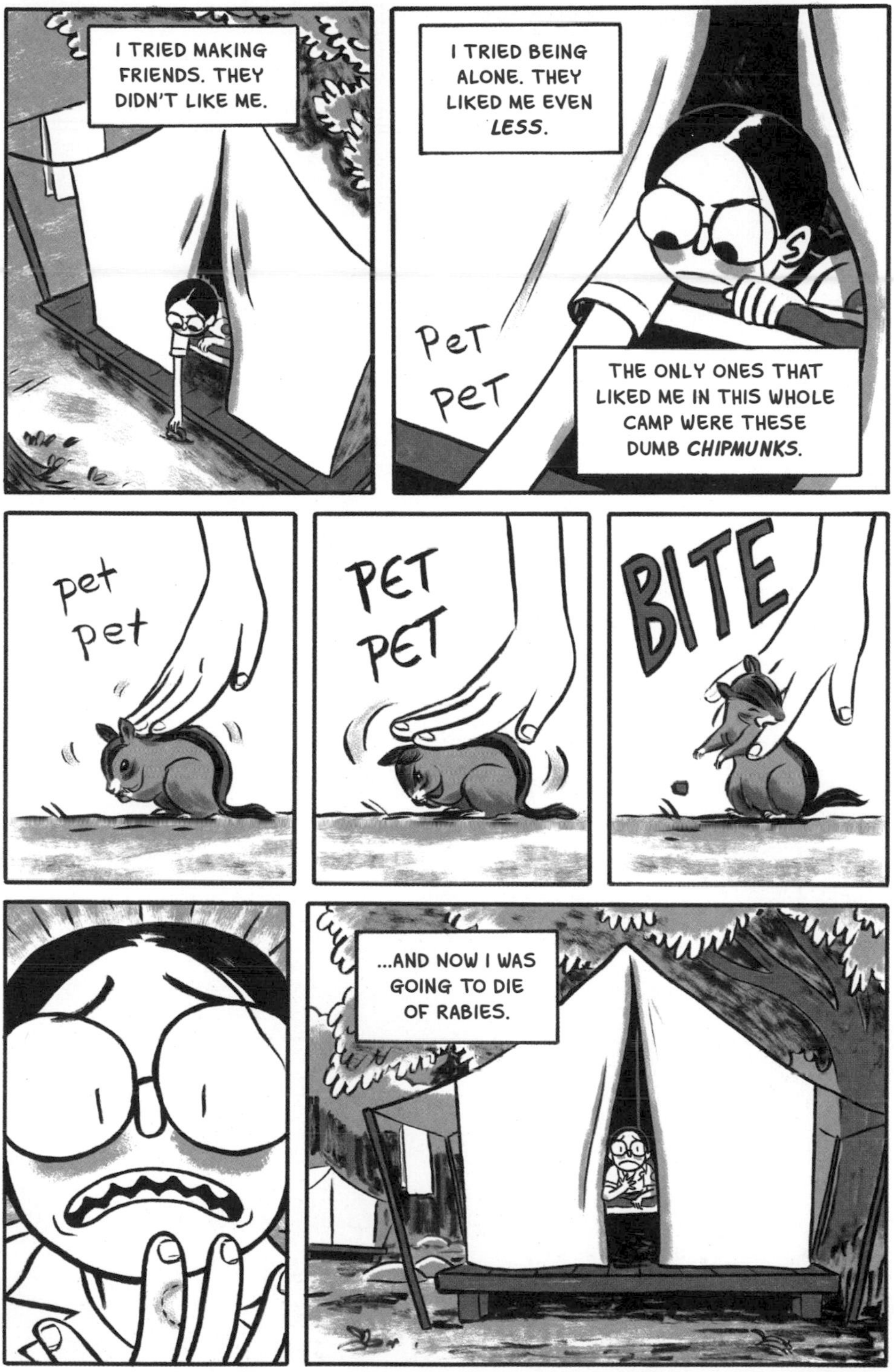
I TRIED MAKING FRIENDS. THEY DIDN'T LIKE ME.
I TRIED BEING ALONE. THEY LIKED ME EVEN LESS.
Pet Pet
THE ONLY ONES THAT LIKED ME IN THIS WHOLE CAMP WERE THESE DUMB CHIPMUNKS.
pet pet
PET PET
BITE
...AND NOW I WAS GOING TO DIE OF RABIES.

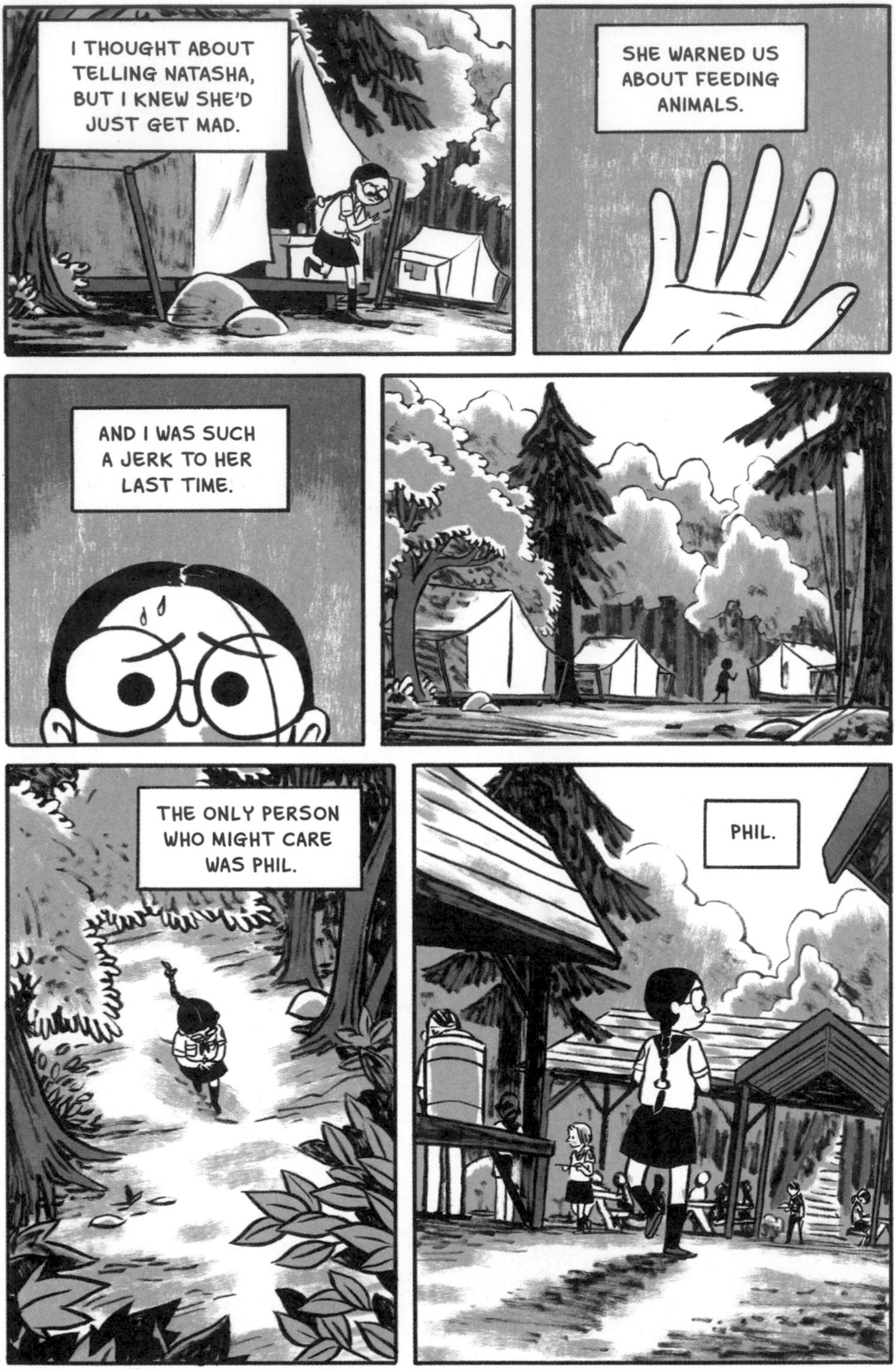
I THOUGHT ABOUT TELLING NATASHA, BUT I KNEW SHE'D JUST GET MAD.
SHE WARNED US ABOUT FEEDING ANIMALS.
AND I WAS SUCH A JERK TO HER LAST TIME.
THE ONLY PERSON WHO MIGHT CARE WAS PHIL.
PHIL.

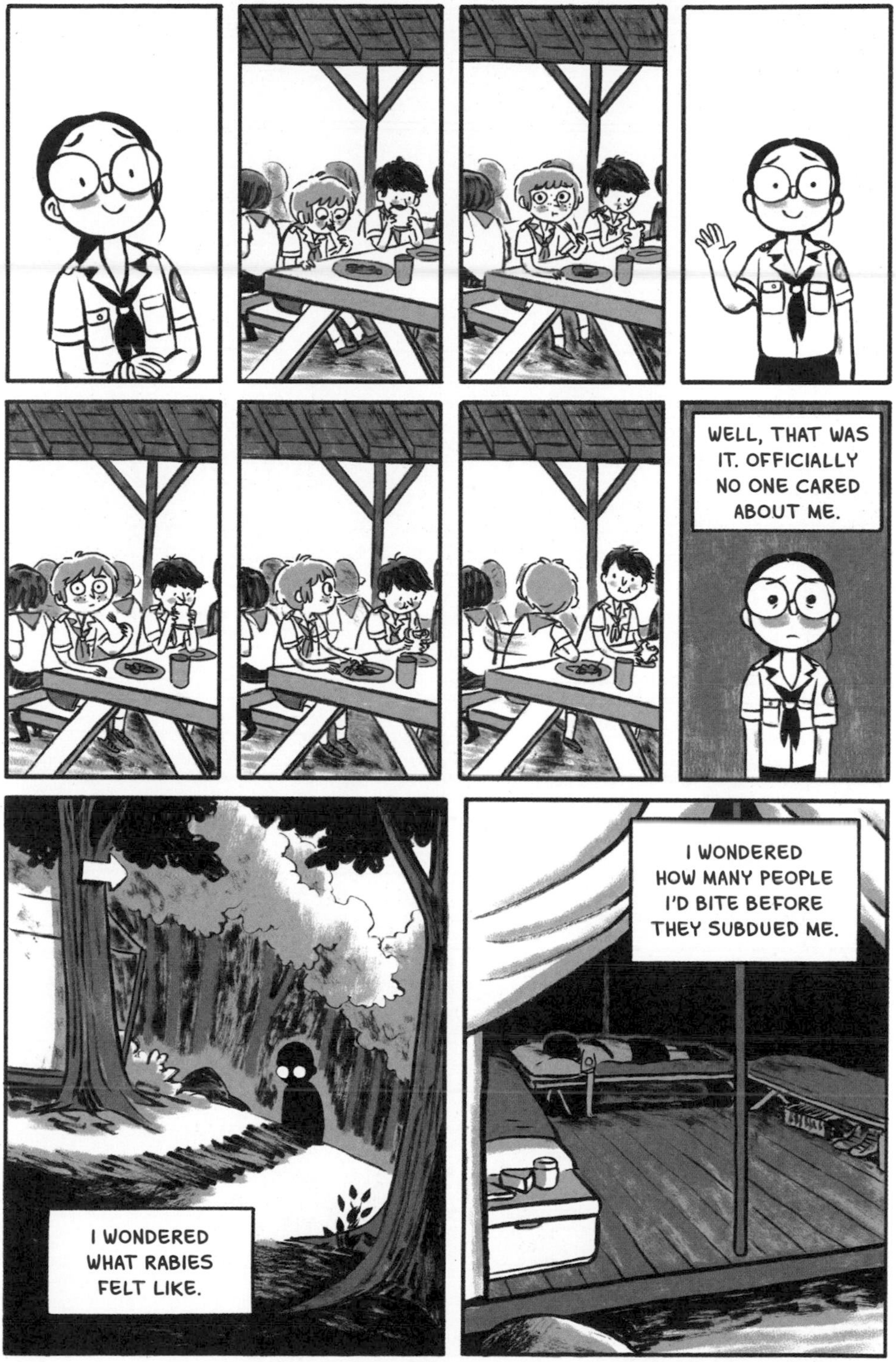
WELL, THAT WAS IT. OFFICIALLY NO ONE CARED ABOUT ME.
I WONDERED WHAT RABIES FELT LIKE.
I WONDERED HOW MANY PEOPLE I'D BITE BEFORE THEY SUBDUED ME.

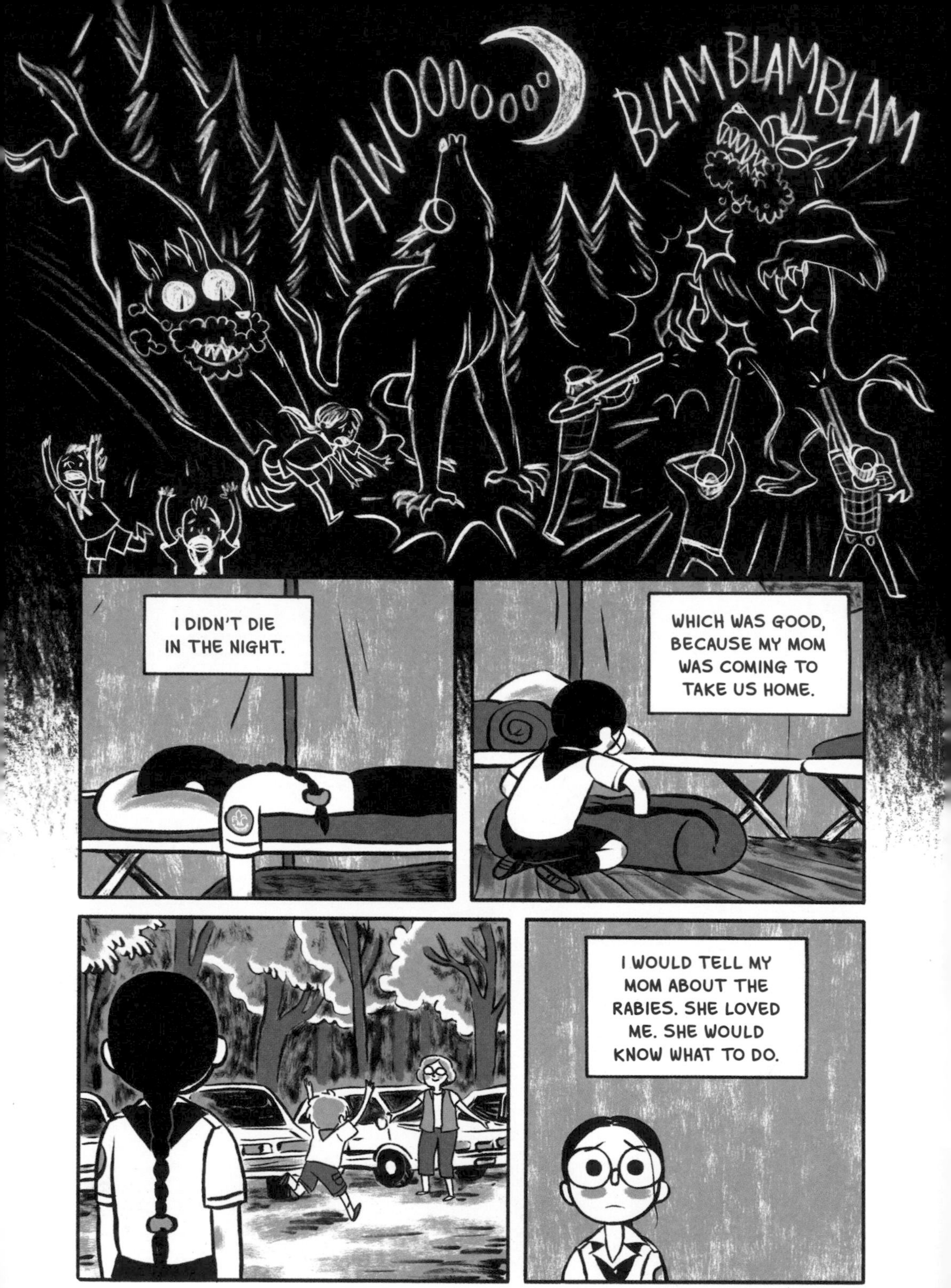
AWOOOoooo
BLAMBLAMBLAMBLAM
I DIDN'T DIE IN THE NIGHT.
WHICH WAS GOOD, BECAUSE MY MOM WAS COMING TO TAKE US HOME.
I WOULD TELL MY MOM ABOUT THE RABIES. SHE LOVED ME. SHE WOULD KNOW WHAT TO DO.

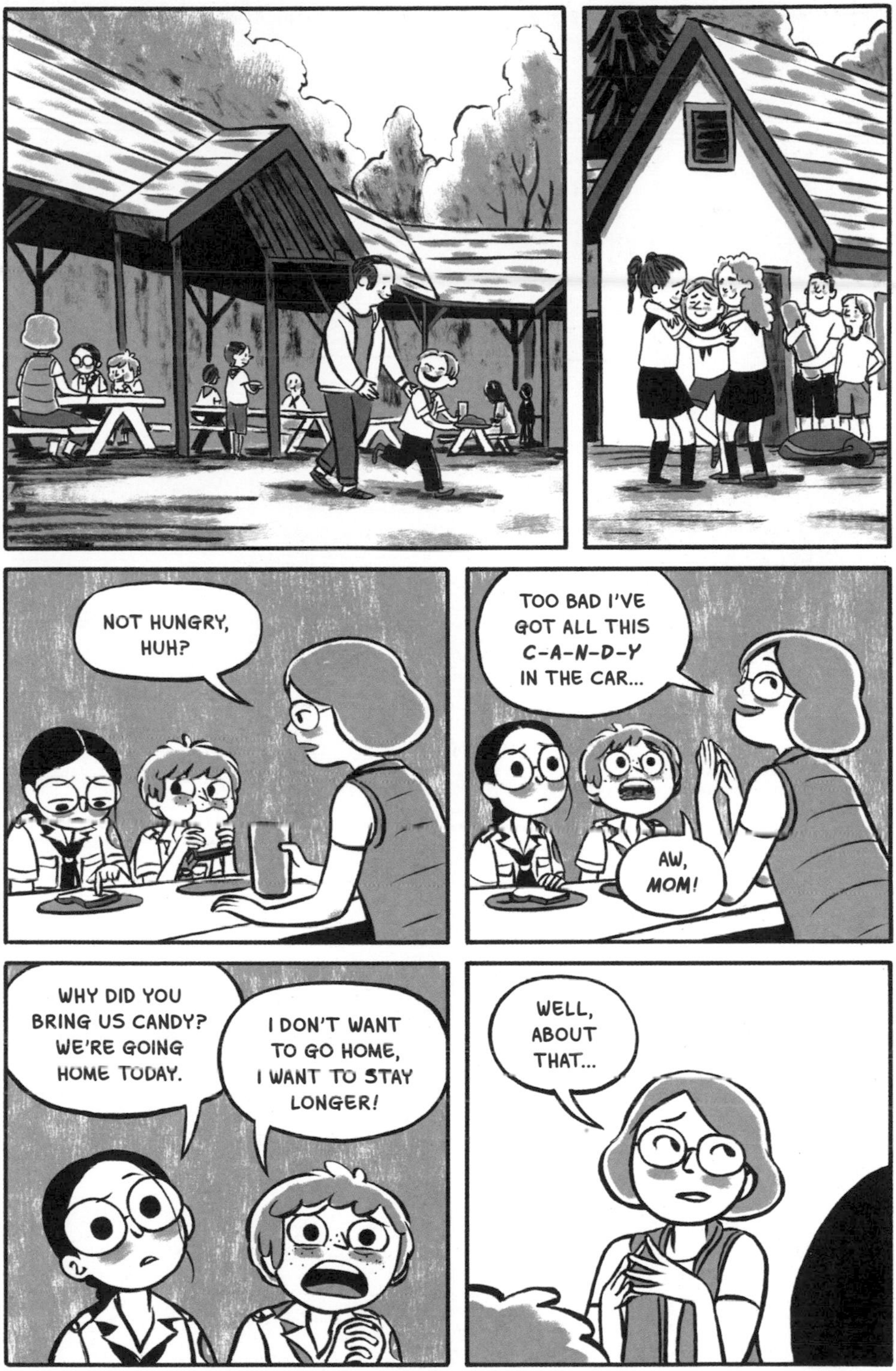
NOT HUNGRY, HUH?
TOO BAD I'VE GOT ALL THIS C-A-N-D-Y IN THE CAR...
AW, MOM!
WHY DID YOU BRING US CANDY? WE'RE GOING HOME TODAY.
I DON'T WANT TO GO HOME, I WANT TO STAY LONGER!
WELL, ABOUT THAT...

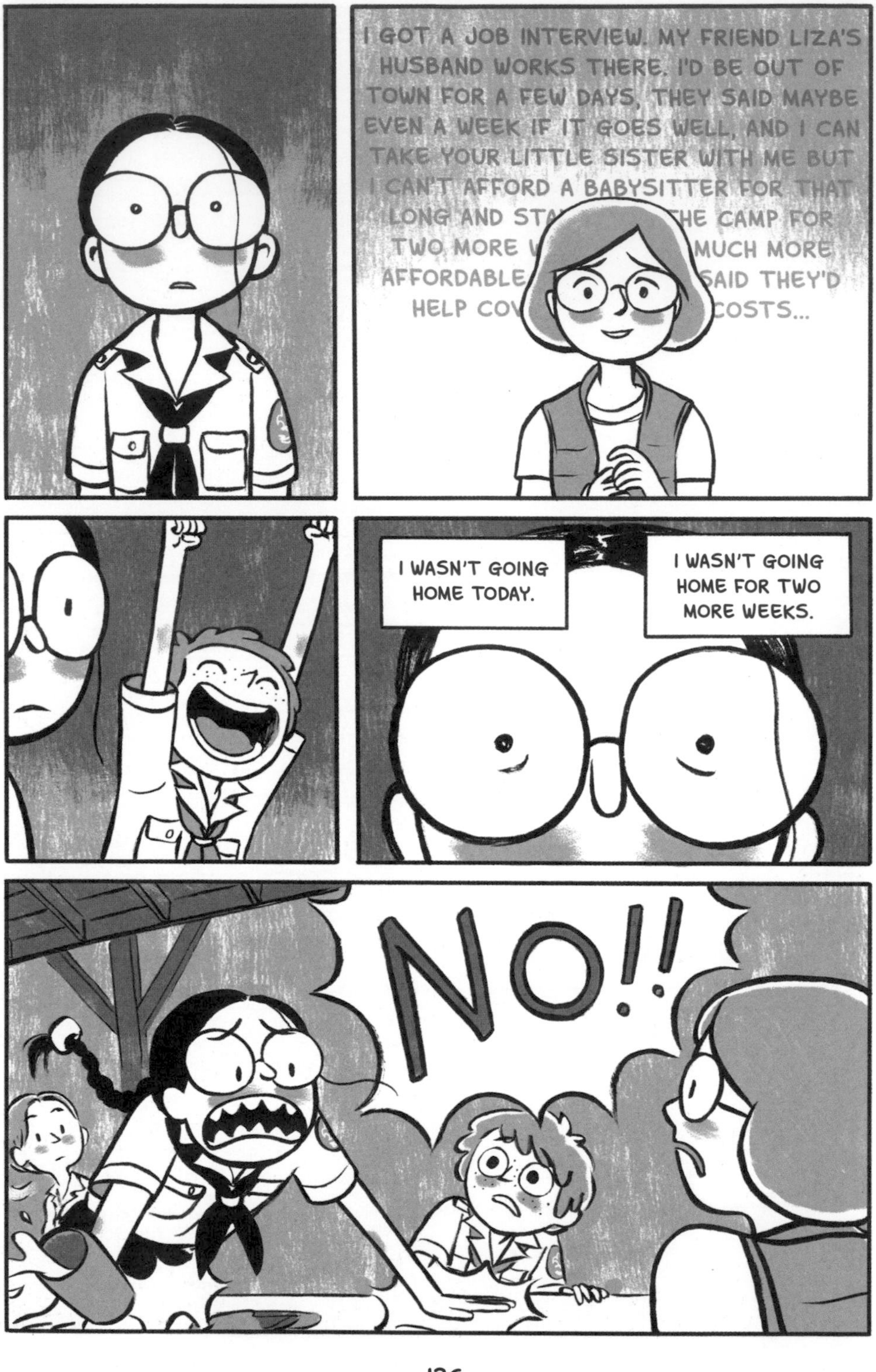

I GOT A JOB INTERVIEW. MY FRIEND LIZA'S HUSBAND WORKS THERE. I'D BE OUT OF TOWN FOR A FEW DAYS, THEY SAID MAYBE EVEN A WEEK IF IT GOES WELL, AND I CAN TAKE YOUR LITTLE SISTER WITH ME BUT I CAN'T AFFORD A BABYSITTER FOR THAT LONG AND STA
THE CAMP FOR TWO MORE
MUCH MORE AFFORDABLE
SAID THEY'D HELP COV
COSTS...
I WASN'T GOING HOME TODAY.
I WASN'T GOING HOME FOR TWO MORE WEEKS.
NO!!

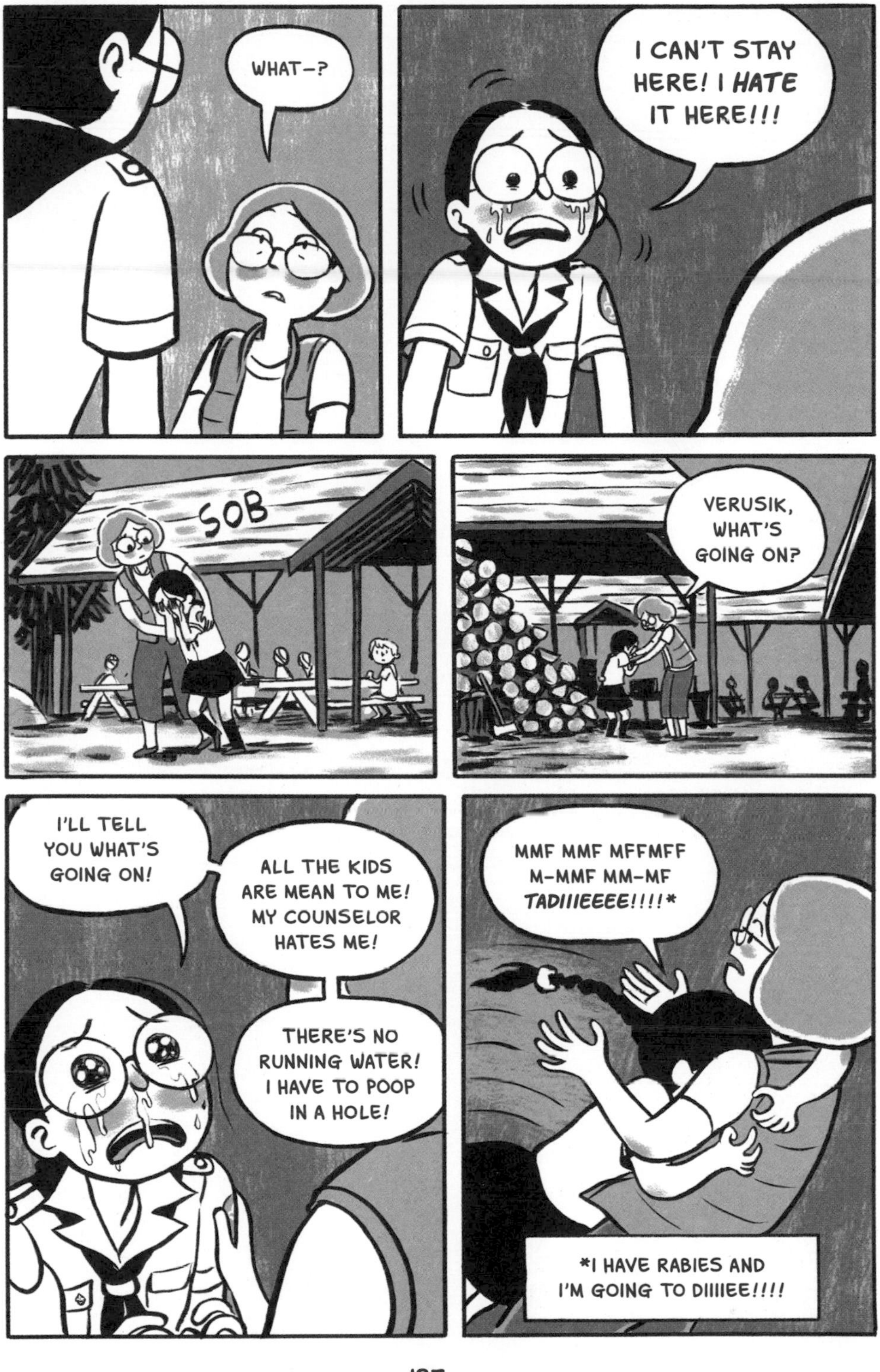
WHAT–?
I CAN'T STAY HERE! I HATE IT HERE!!!
SOB
VERUSIK, WHAT'S GOING ON?
I'LL TELL YOU WHAT'S GOING ON!
ALL THE KIDS ARE MEAN TO ME! MY COUNSELOR HATES ME!
THERE'S NO RUNNING WATER! I HAVE TO POOP IN A HOLE!
MMF MMF MFFMFF M–MMF MM–MF TADIIIEEEE!!!!*
*I HAVE RABIES AND I'M GOING TO DIIIIEE!!!!

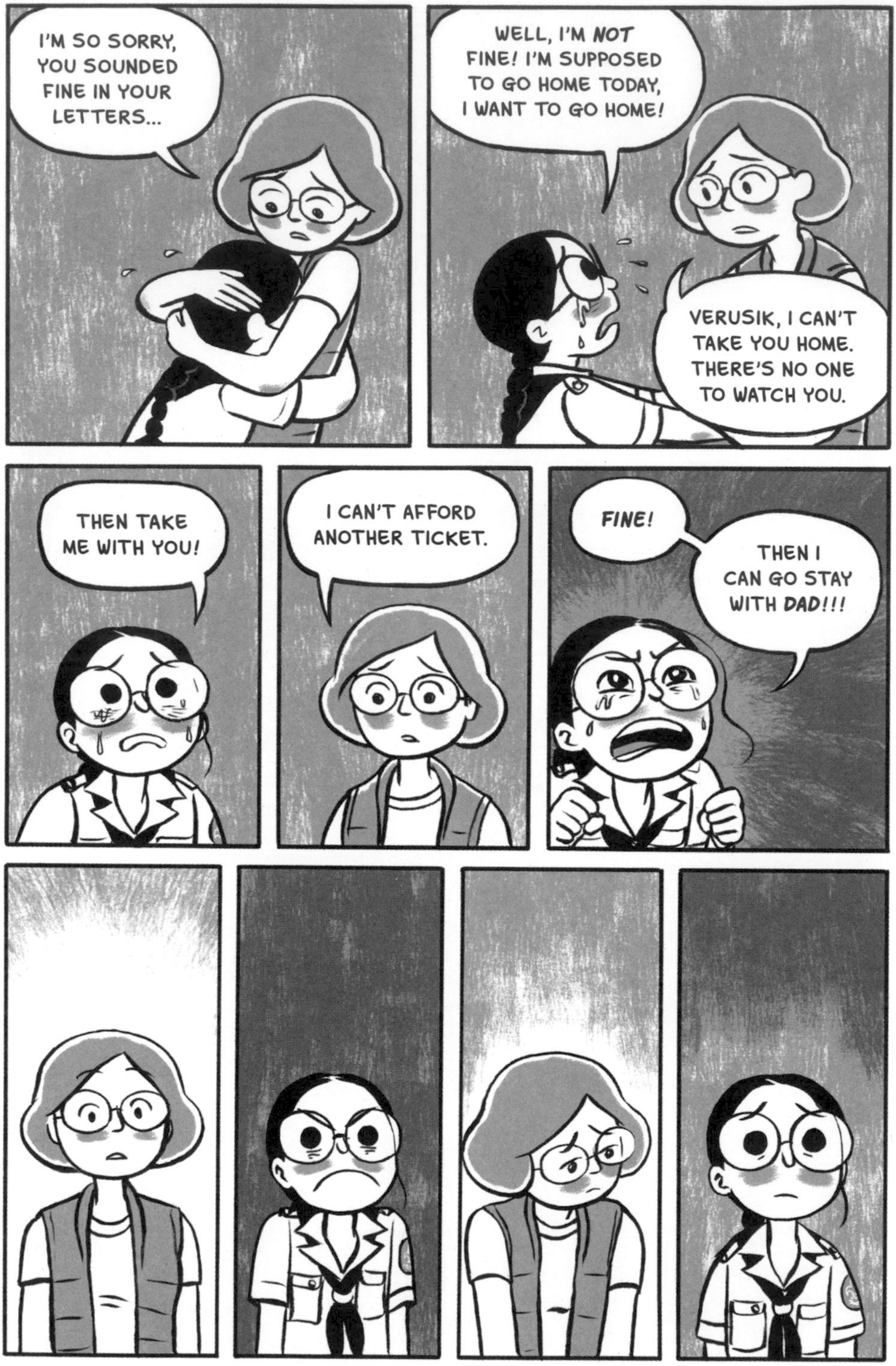
I'M SO SORRY, YOU SOUNDED FINE IN YOUR LETTERS...
WELL, I'M NOT FINE! I'M SUPPOSED TO GO HOME TODAY, I WANT TO GO HOME!
VERUSIK, I CAN'T TAKE YOU HOME. THERE'S NO ONE TO WATCH YOU.
THEN TAKE ME WITH YOU!
I CAN'T AFFORD ANOTHER TICKET.
FINE!
THEN I CAN GO STAY WITH DAD!!!

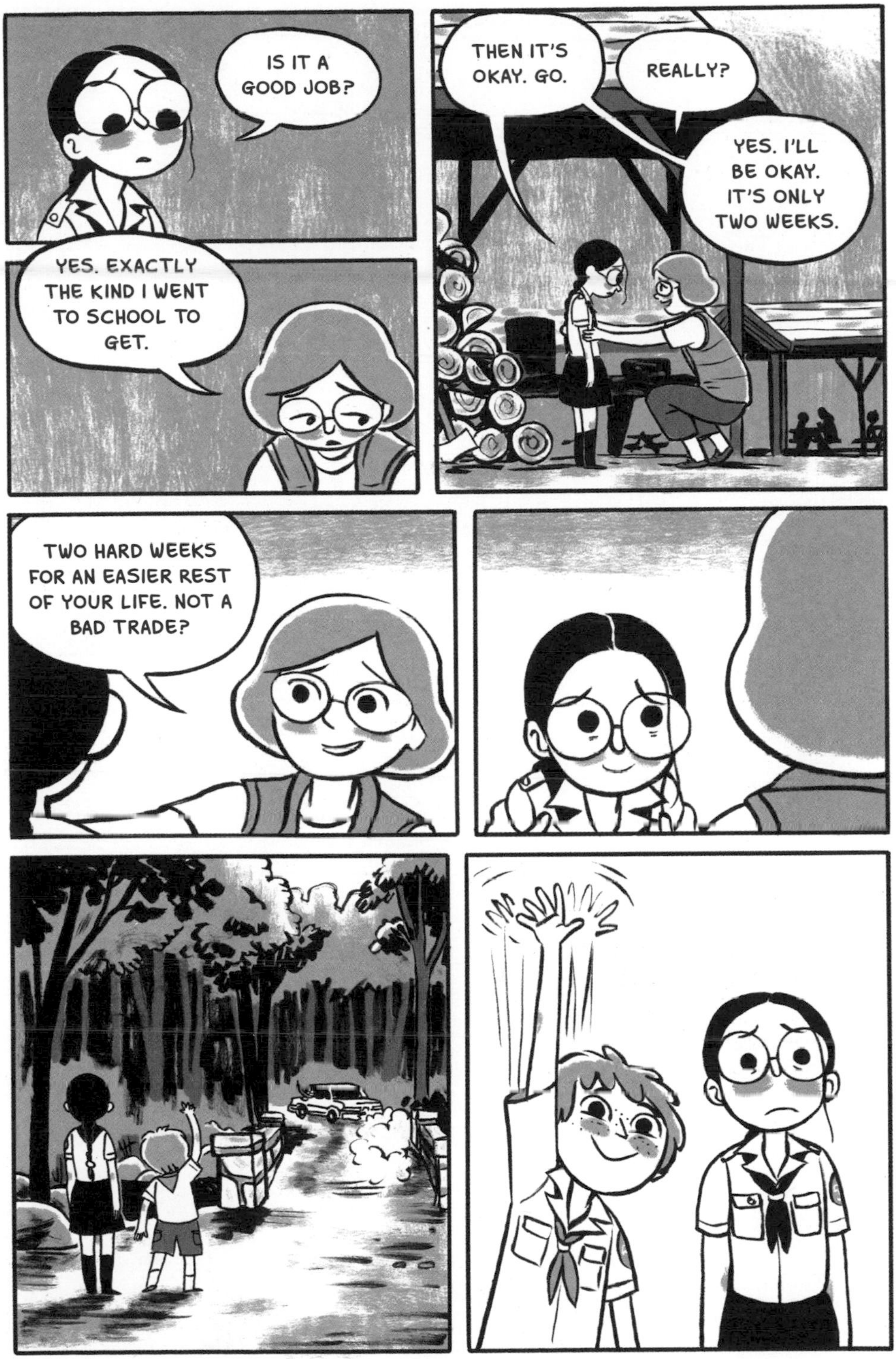
IS IT A GOOD JOB?
THEN IT'S OKAY. GO.
REALLY?
YES. I'LL BE OKAY. IT'S ONLY TWO WEEKS.
YES. EXACTLY THE KIND I WENT TO SCHOOL TO GET.
TWO HARD WEEKS FOR AN EASIER REST OF YOUR LIFE. NOT A BAD TRADE?

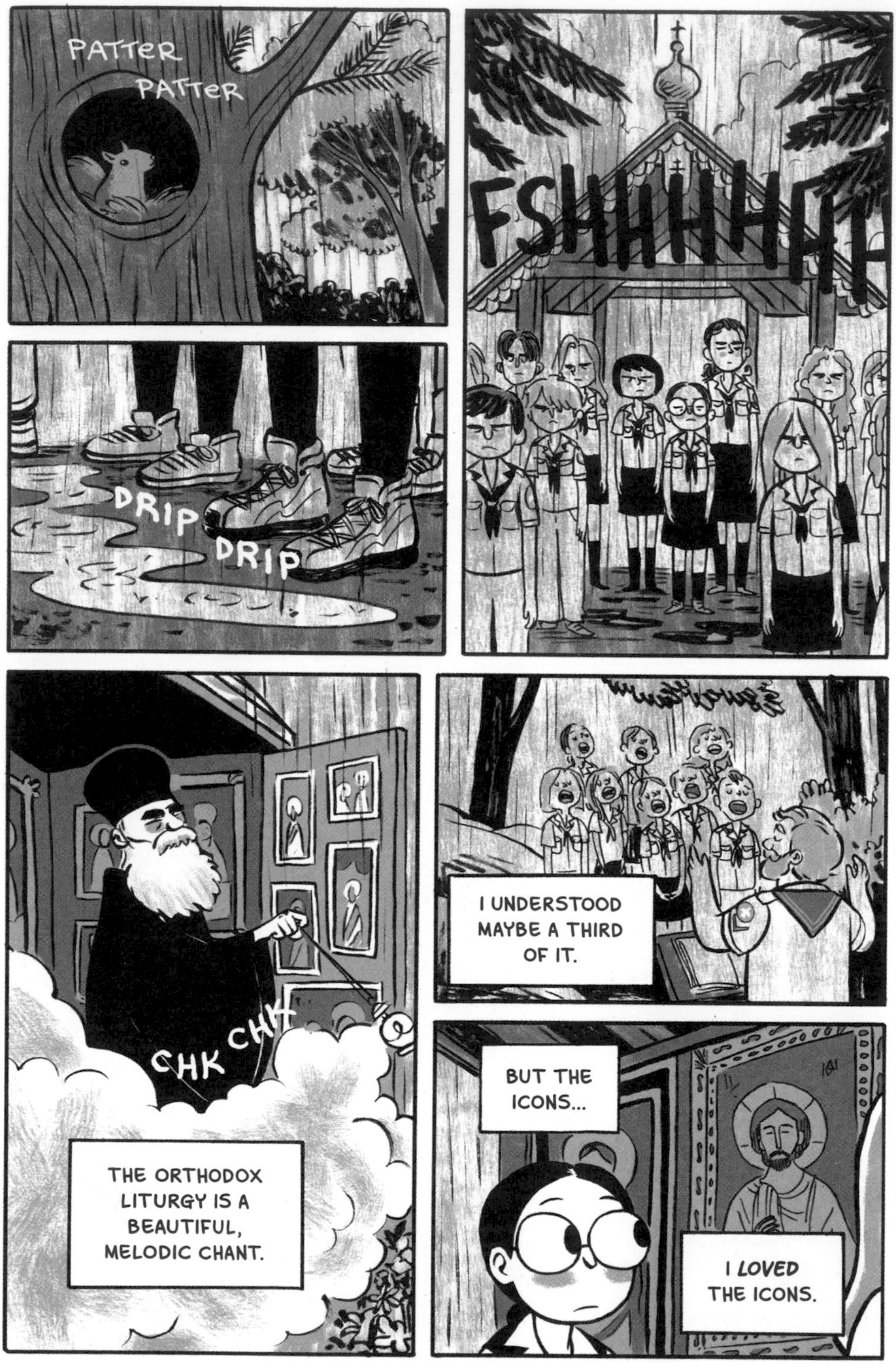
PATTER
PATTER
FSHHHHHH
DRIP
DRIP
CHK CHK
THE ORTHODOX LITURGY IS A BEAUTIFUL, MELODIC CHANT.
I UNDERSTOOD MAYBE A THIRD OF IT.
BUT THE ICONS...
I *LOVED* THE ICONS.

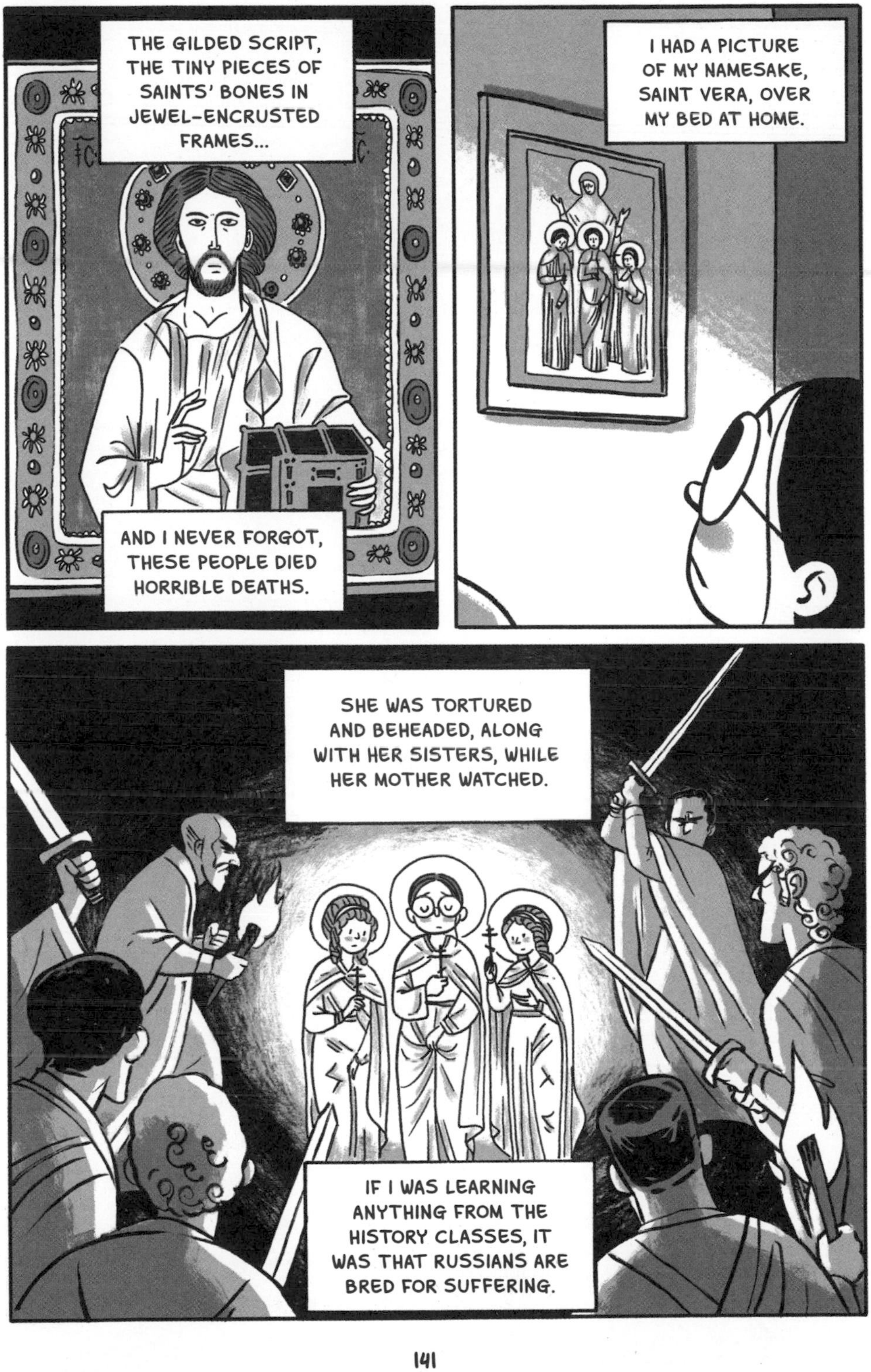
THE GILDED SCRIPT, THE TINY PIECES OF SAINTS' BONES IN JEWEL-ENCRUSTED FRAMES...
AND I NEVER FORGOT, THESE PEOPLE DIED HORRIBLE DEATHS.
I HAD A PICTURE OF MY NAMESAKE, SAINT VERA, OVER MY BED AT HOME.
SHE WAS TORTURED AND BEHEADED, ALONG WITH HER SISTERS, WHILE HER MOTHER WATCHED.
IF I WAS LEARNING ANYTHING FROM THE HISTORY CLASSES, IT WAS THAT RUSSIANS ARE BRED FOR SUFFERING.

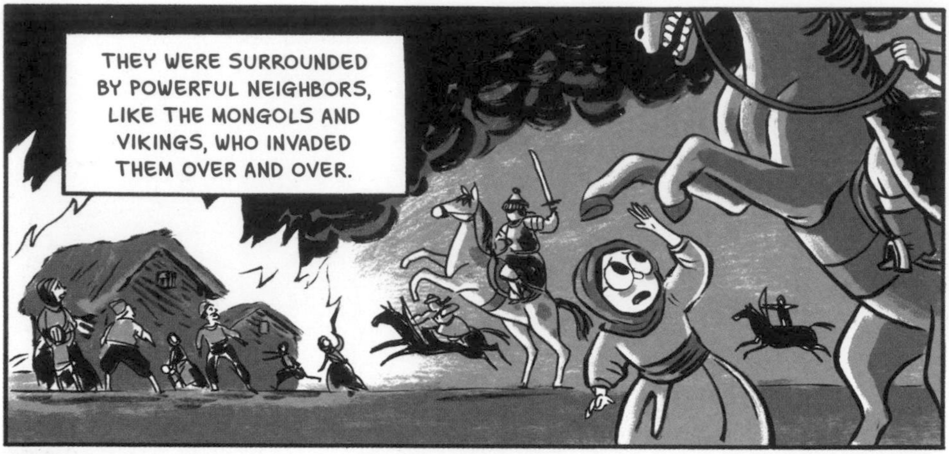
THEY WERE SURROUNDED BY POWERFUL NEIGHBORS, LIKE THE MONGOLS AND VIKINGS, WHO INVADED THEM OVER AND OVER.

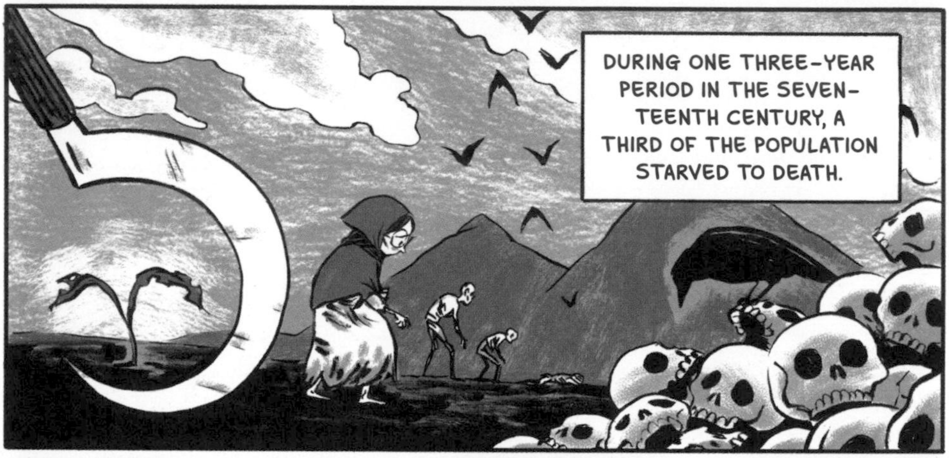
DURING ONE THREE-YEAR PERIOD IN THE SEVENTEENTH CENTURY, A THIRD OF THE POPULATION STARVED TO DEATH.

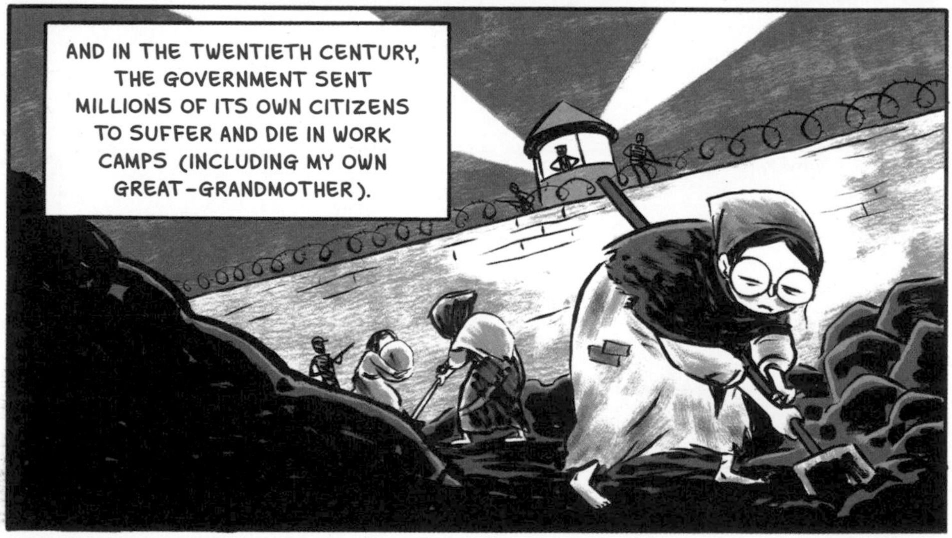
AND IN THE TWENTIETH CENTURY, THE GOVERNMENT SENT MILLIONS OF ITS OWN CITIZENS TO SUFFER AND DIE IN WORK CAMPS (INCLUDING MY OWN GREAT-GRANDMOTHER).

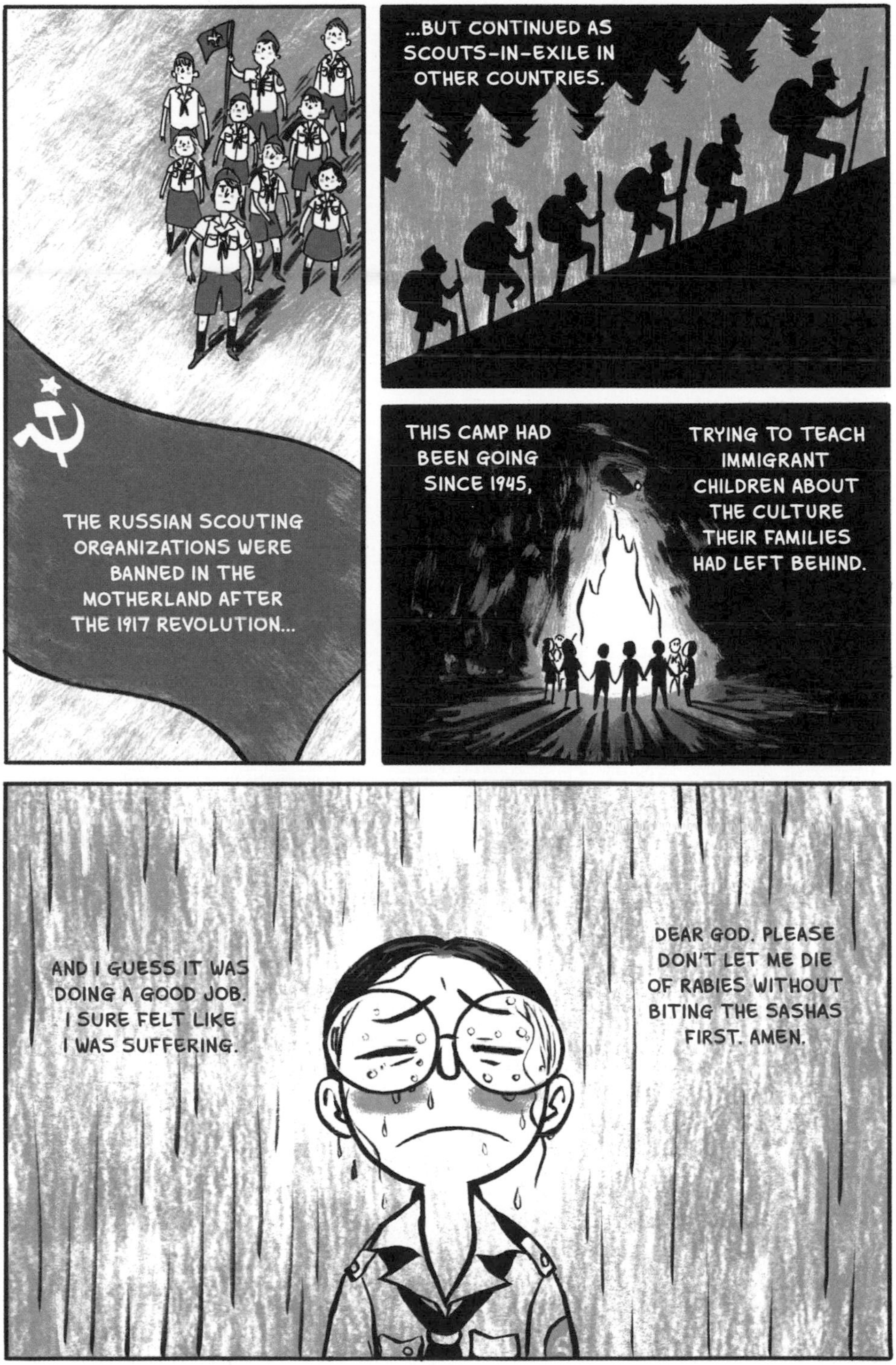
THE RUSSIAN SCOUTING ORGANIZATIONS WERE BANNED IN THE MOTHERLAND AFTER THE 1917 REVOLUTION...
...BUT CONTINUED AS SCOUTS-IN-EXILE IN OTHER COUNTRIES.
THIS CAMP HAD BEEN GOING SINCE 1945,
TRYING TO TEACH IMMIGRANT CHILDREN ABOUT THE CULTURE THEIR FAMILIES HAD LEFT BEHIND.
AND I GUESS IT WAS DOING A GOOD JOB. I SURE FELT LIKE I WAS SUFFERING.
DEAR GOD. PLEASE DON'T LET ME DIE OF RABIES WITHOUT BITING THE SASHAS FIRST. AMEN.

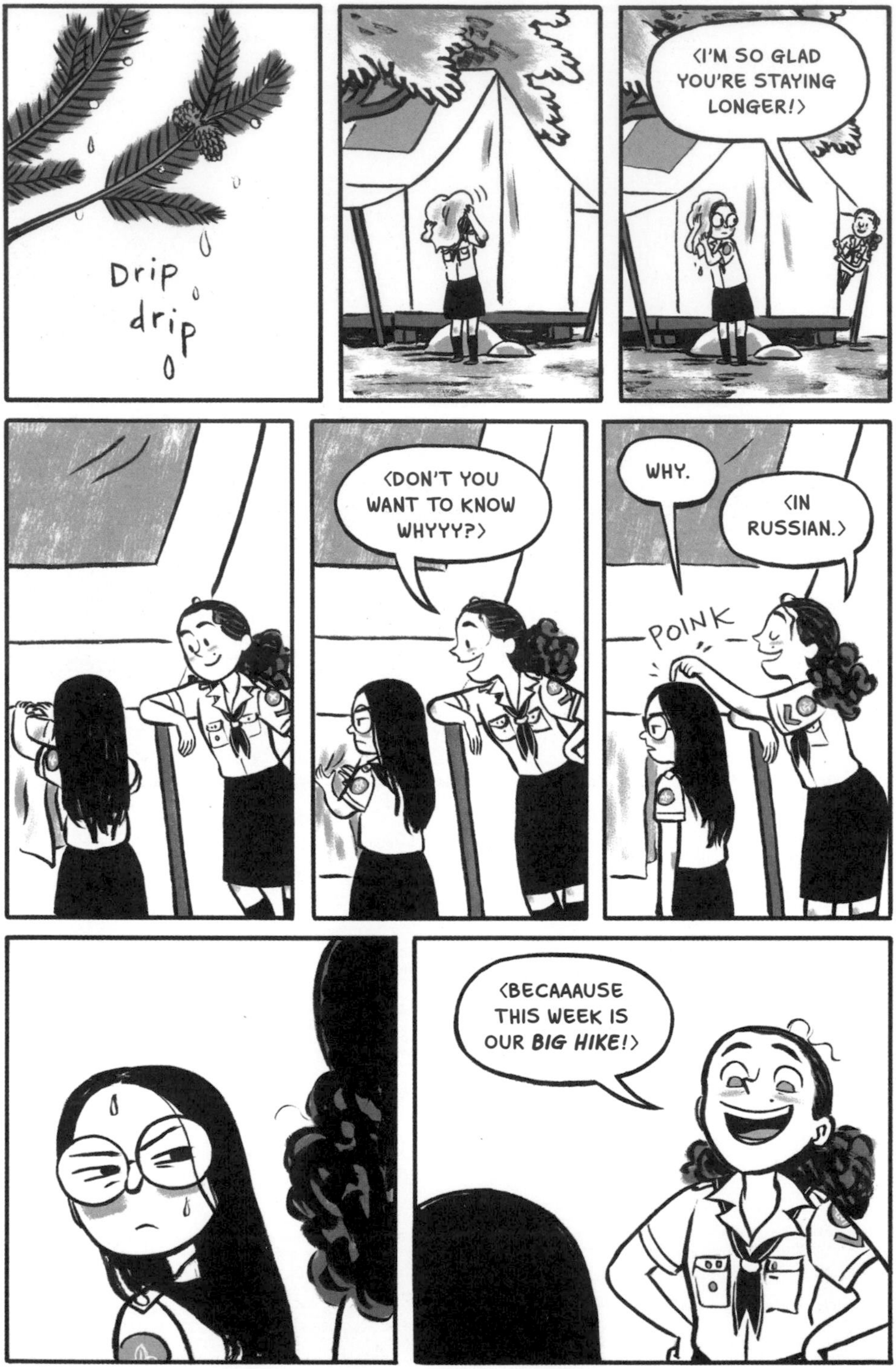
Drip
drip
<I'M SO GLAD YOU'RE STAYING LONGER!>
<DON'T YOU WANT TO KNOW WHYYY?>
WHY.
<IN RUSSIAN.>
POINK
<BECAAAUSE THIS WEEK IS OUR **BIG HIKE!**>

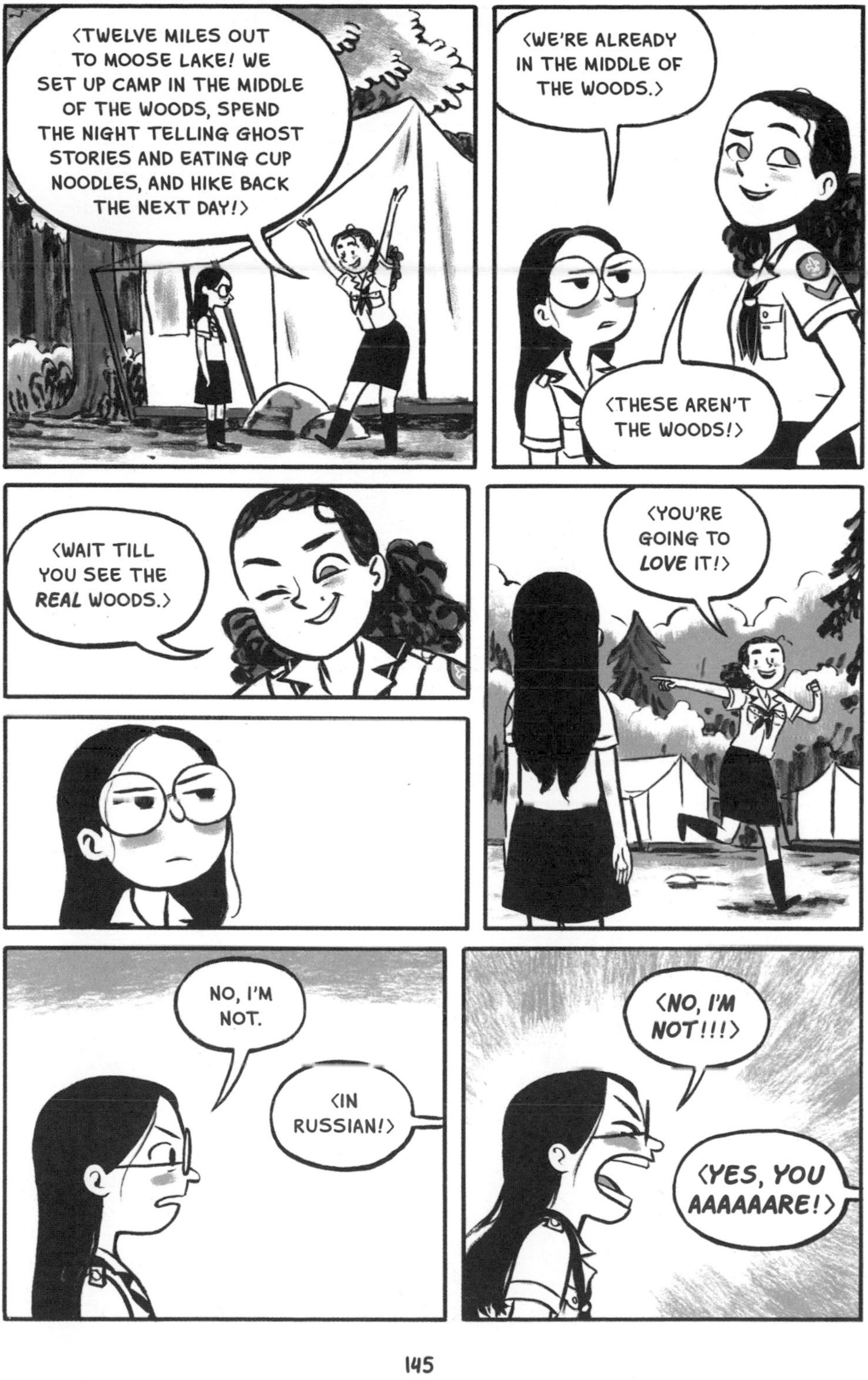
<TWELVE MILES OUT TO MOOSE LAKE! WE SET UP CAMP IN THE MIDDLE OF THE WOODS, SPEND THE NIGHT TELLING GHOST STORIES AND EATING CUP NOODLES, AND HIKE BACK THE NEXT DAY!>
<WE'RE ALREADY IN THE MIDDLE OF THE WOODS.>
<THESE AREN'T THE WOODS!>
<WAIT TILL YOU SEE THE *REAL* WOODS.>
<YOU'RE GOING TO *LOVE* IT!>
NO, I'M NOT.
<IN RUSSIAN!>
<NO, I'M NOT!!!>
<YES, YOU AAAAAARE!>

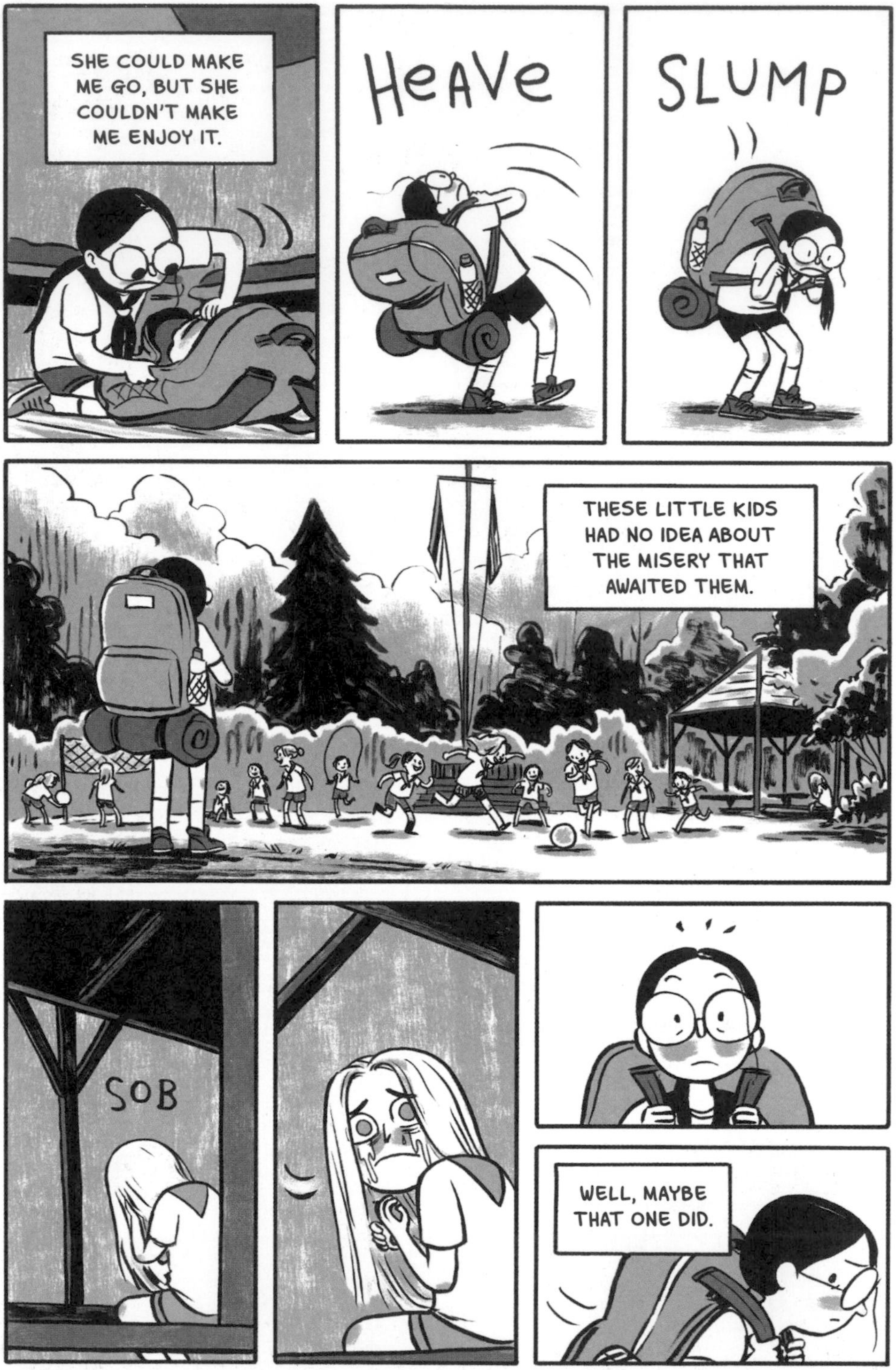
SHE COULD MAKE ME GO, BUT SHE COULDN'T MAKE ME ENJOY IT.
HEAVE
SLUMP
THESE LITTLE KIDS HAD NO IDEA ABOUT THE MISERY THAT AWAITED THEM.
SOB
WELL, MAYBE THAT ONE DID.

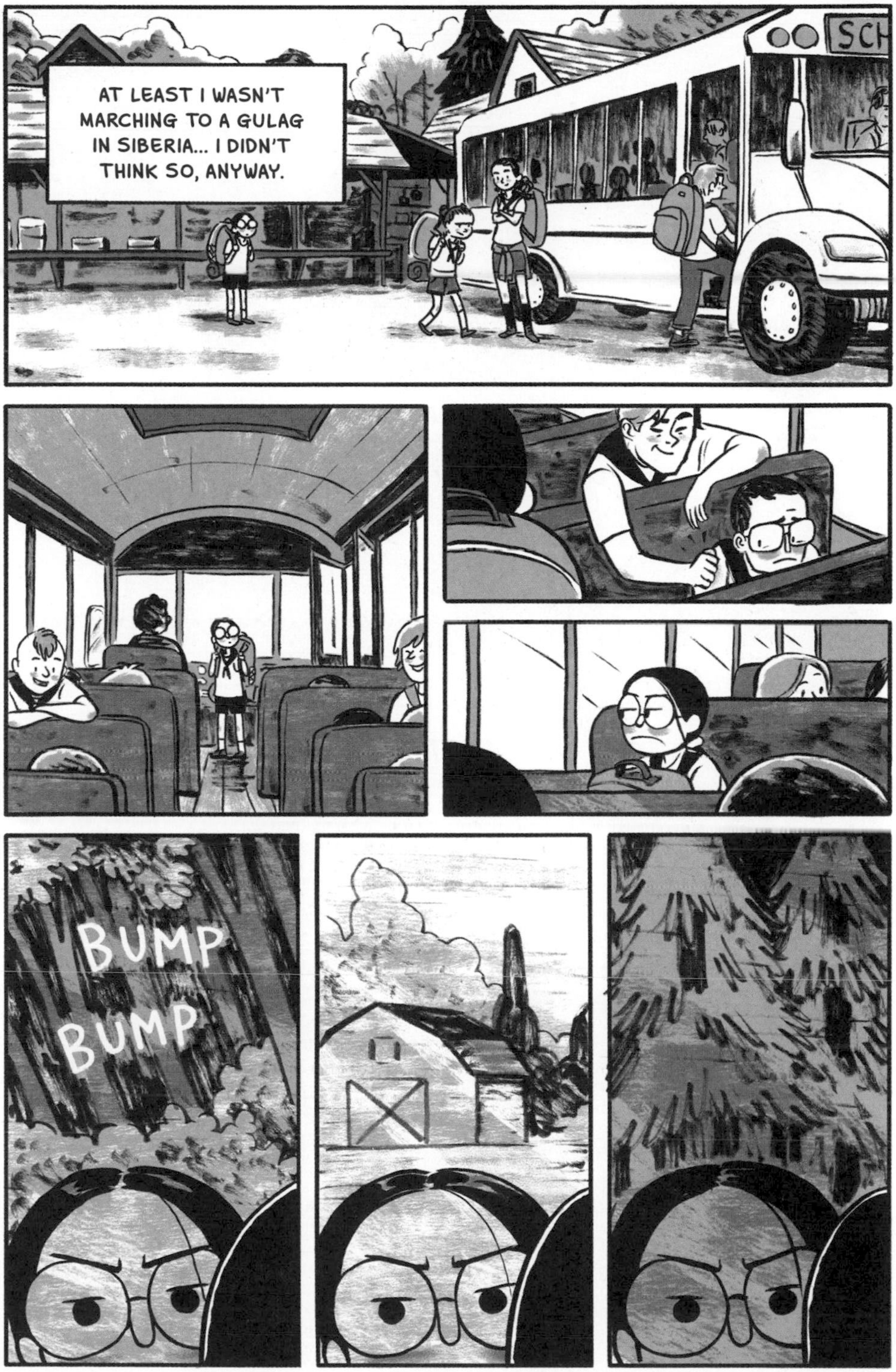
AT LEAST I WASN'T MARCHING TO A GULAG IN SIBERIA... I DIDN'T THINK SO, ANYWAY.
SCH
BUMP
BUMP

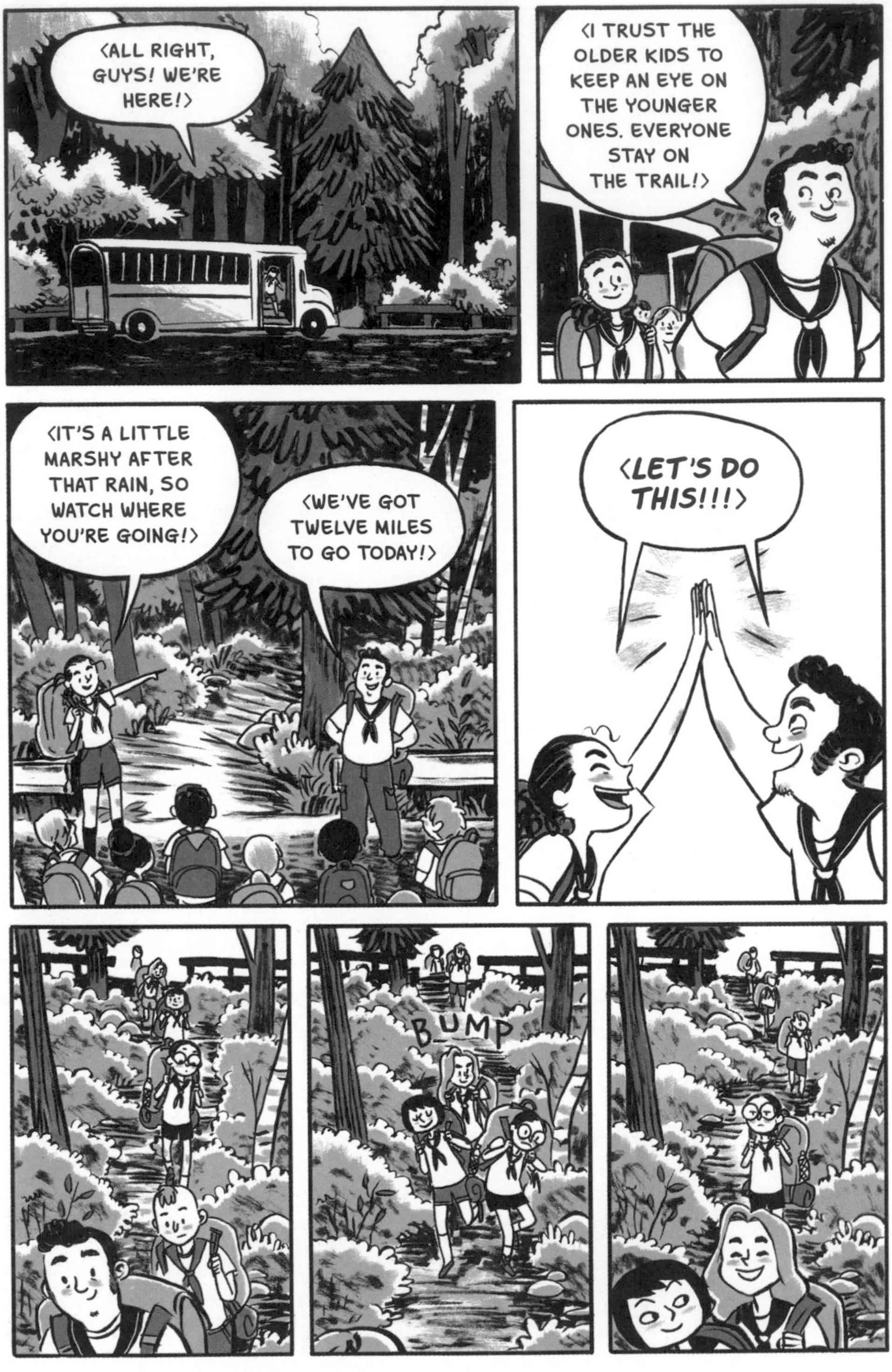

<ALL RIGHT, GUYS! WE'RE HERE!>
<I TRUST THE OLDER KIDS TO KEEP AN EYE ON THE YOUNGER ONES. EVERYONE STAY ON THE TRAIL!>
<IT'S A LITTLE MARSHY AFTER THAT RAIN, SO WATCH WHERE YOU'RE GOING!>
<WE'VE GOT TWELVE MILES TO GO TODAY!>
<LET'S DO THIS!!!>
BUMP

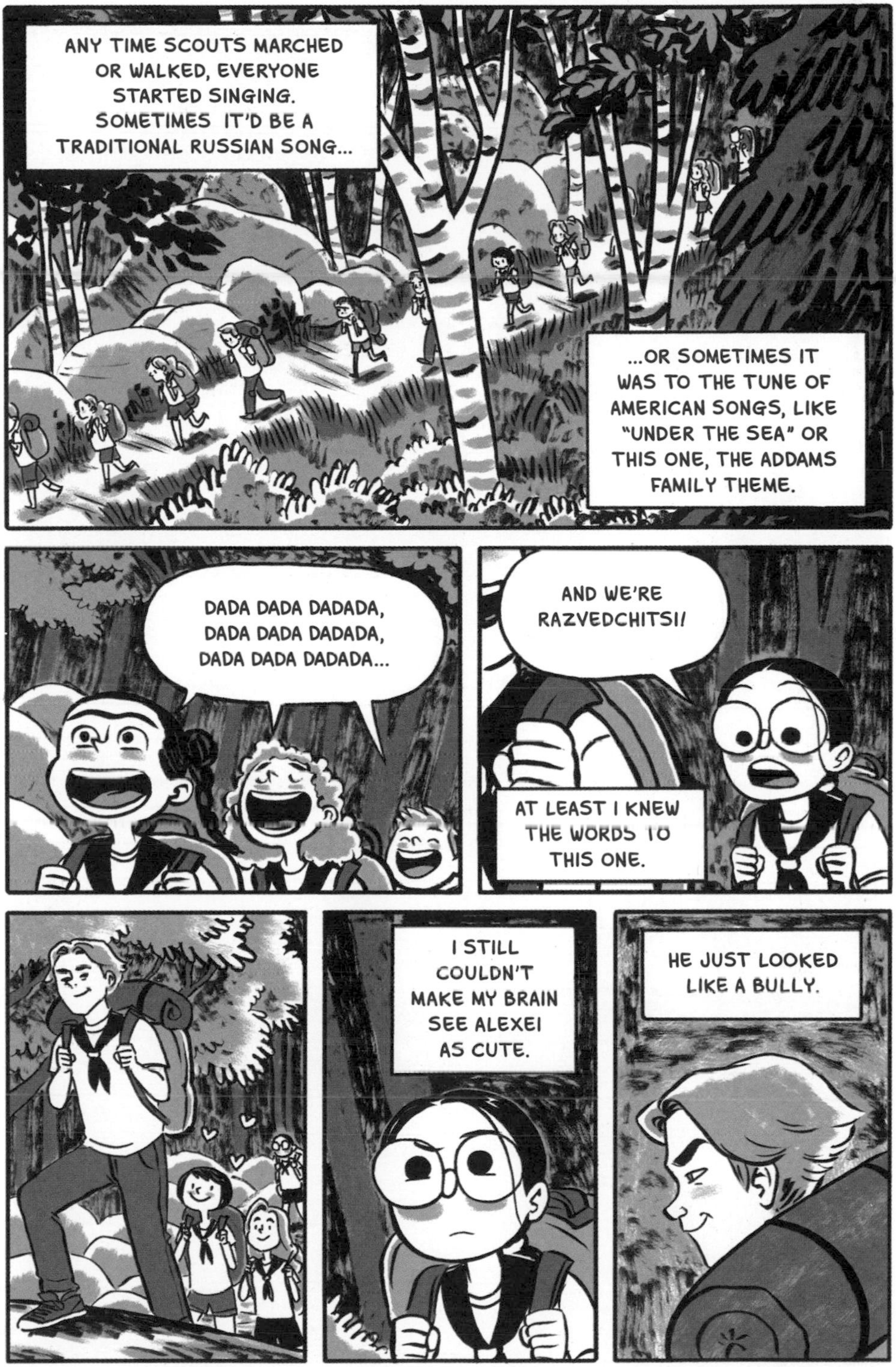
ANY TIME SCOUTS MARCHED OR WALKED, EVERYONE STARTED SINGING. SOMETIMES IT'D BE A TRADITIONAL RUSSIAN SONG...
...OR SOMETIMES IT WAS TO THE TUNE OF AMERICAN SONGS, LIKE "UNDER THE SEA" OR THIS ONE, THE ADDAMS FAMILY THEME.
DADA DADA DADADA, DADA DADA DADADA, DADA DADA DADADA...
AND WE'RE RAZVEDCHITSI!
AT LEAST I KNEW THE WORDS TO THIS ONE.
I STILL COULDN'T MAKE MY BRAIN SEE ALEXEI AS CUTE.
HE JUST LOOKED LIKE A BULLY.

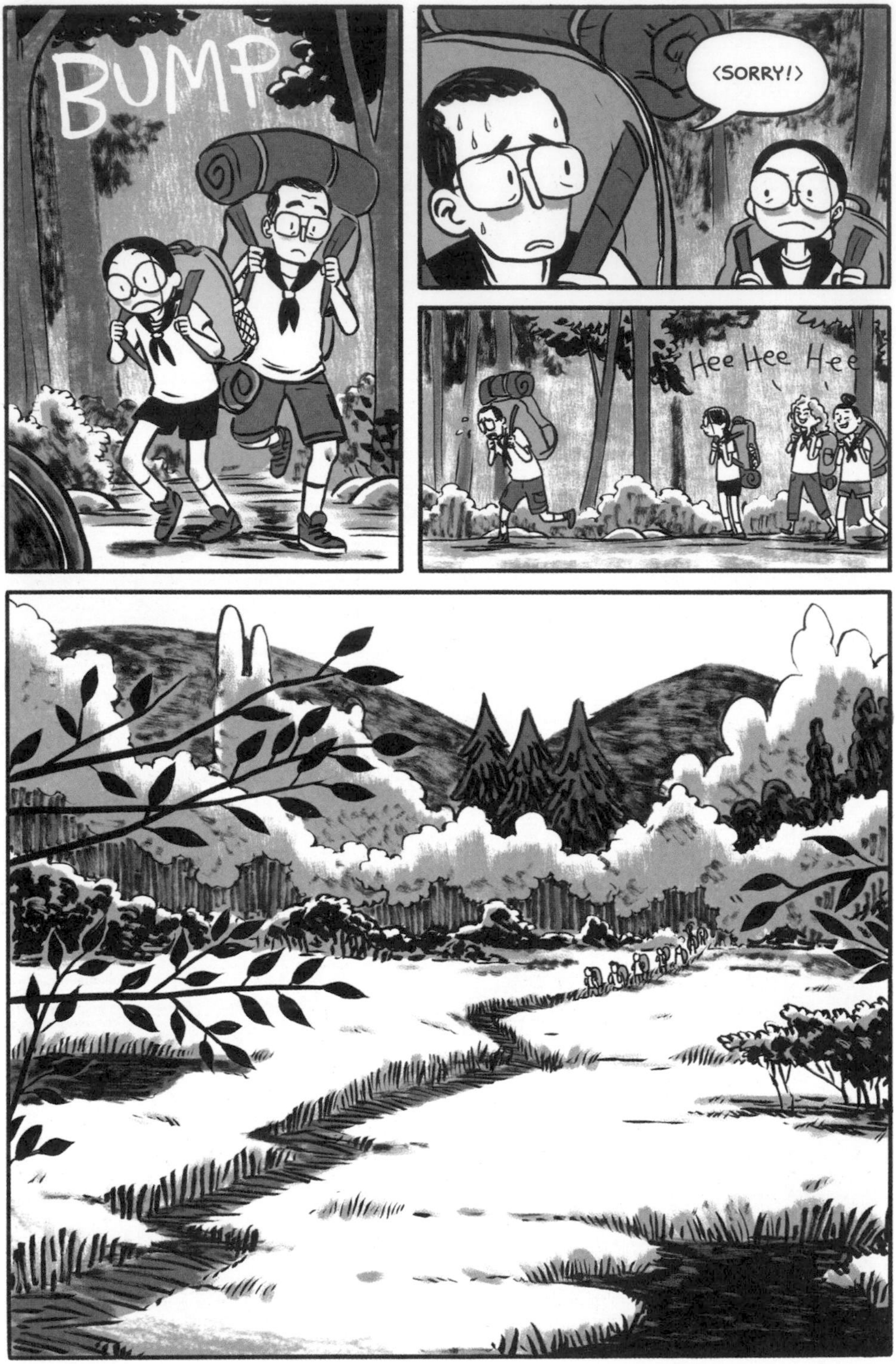
BUMP
⟨SORRY!⟩
Hee Hee Hee

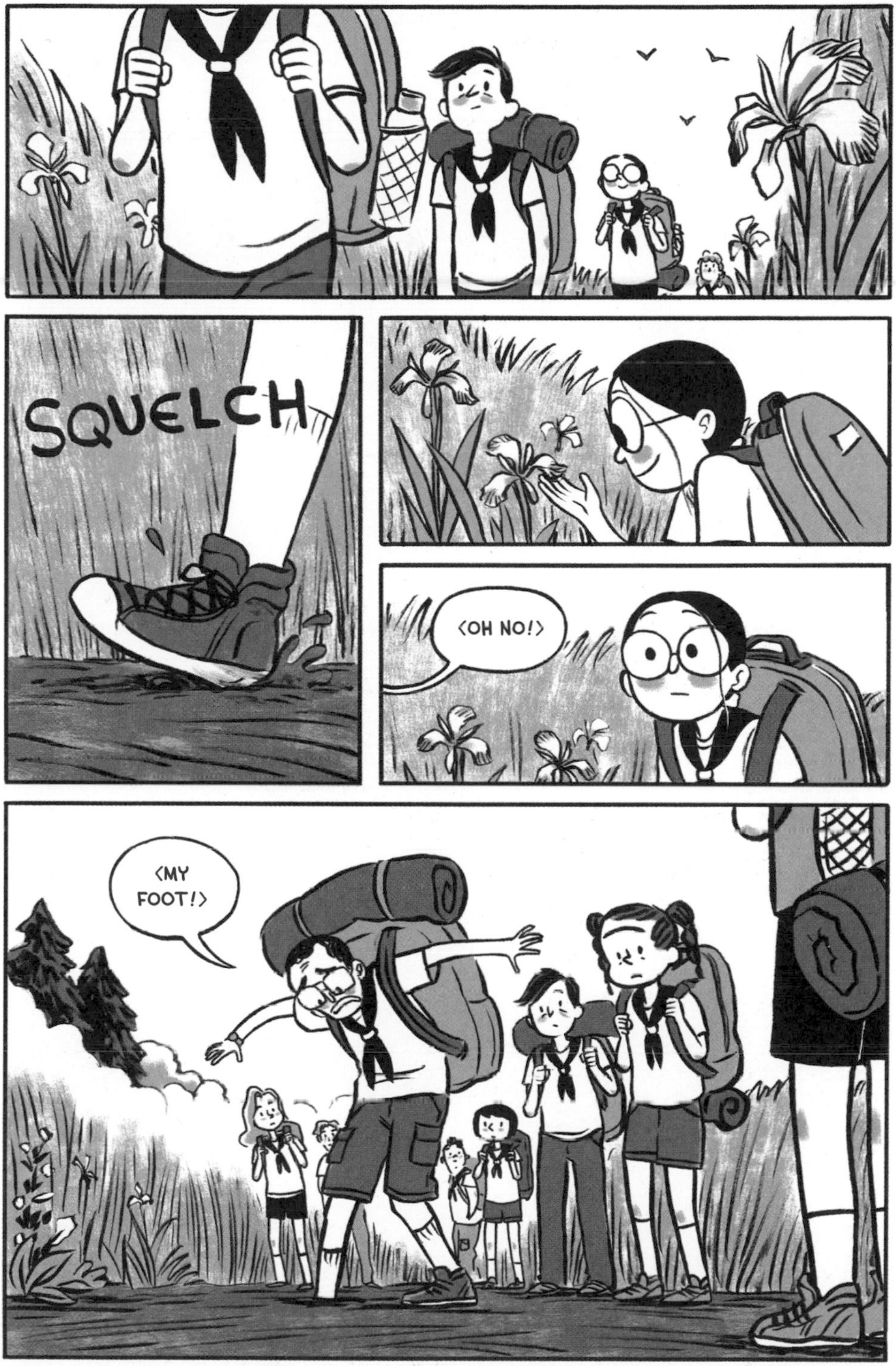
SQUELCH
<OH NO!>
<MY FOOT!>

⟨COME ON, GREGOR, PULL!⟩

NNGH!

SSSUCK

GLOOP

HAHAHH

HAHAHA

WE WERE ALREADY SEVEN MILES IN, SO IT WAS DECIDED THAT EVERYONE WOULD JUST HAVE TO KEEP GOING.

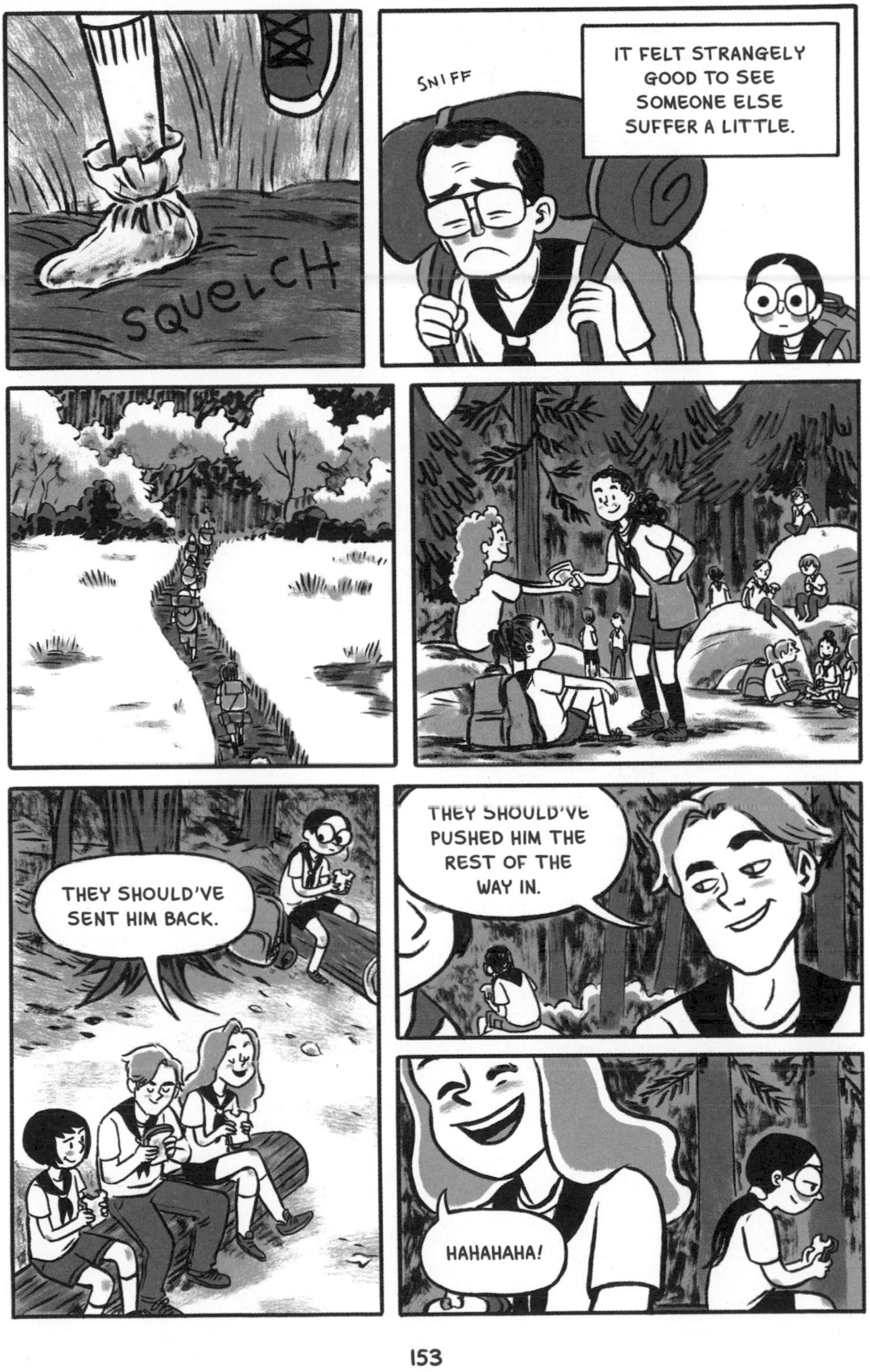
SQUELCH
SNIFF
IT FELT STRANGELY GOOD TO SEE SOMEONE ELSE SUFFER A LITTLE.
THEY SHOULD'VE SENT HIM BACK.
THEY SHOULD'VE PUSHED HIM THE REST OF THE WAY IN.
HAHAHAHA!

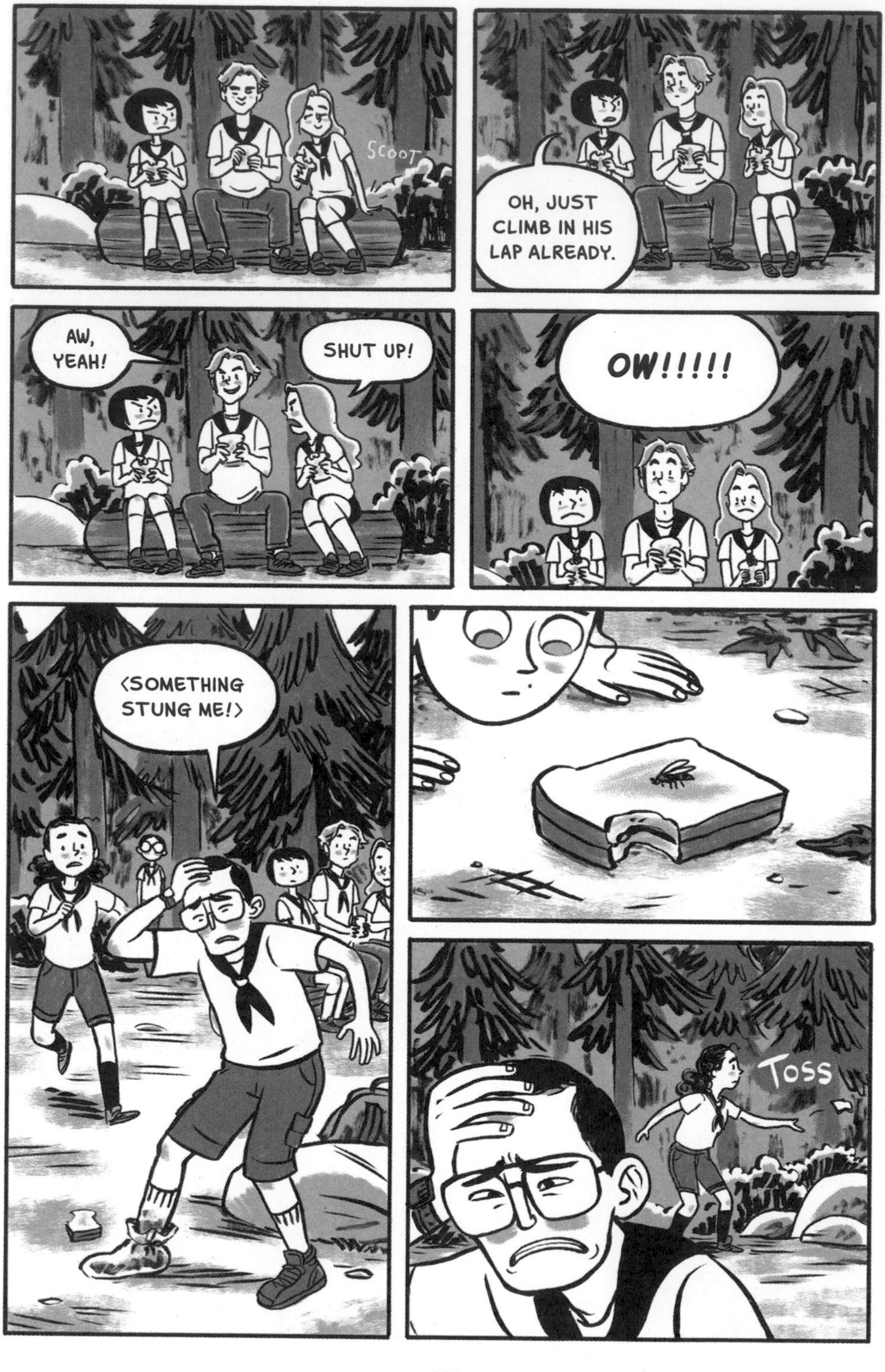
SCOOT
OH, JUST CLIMB IN HIS LAP ALREADY.
AW, YEAH!
SHUT UP!
OW!!!!!
⟨SOMETHING STUNG ME!⟩
TOSS

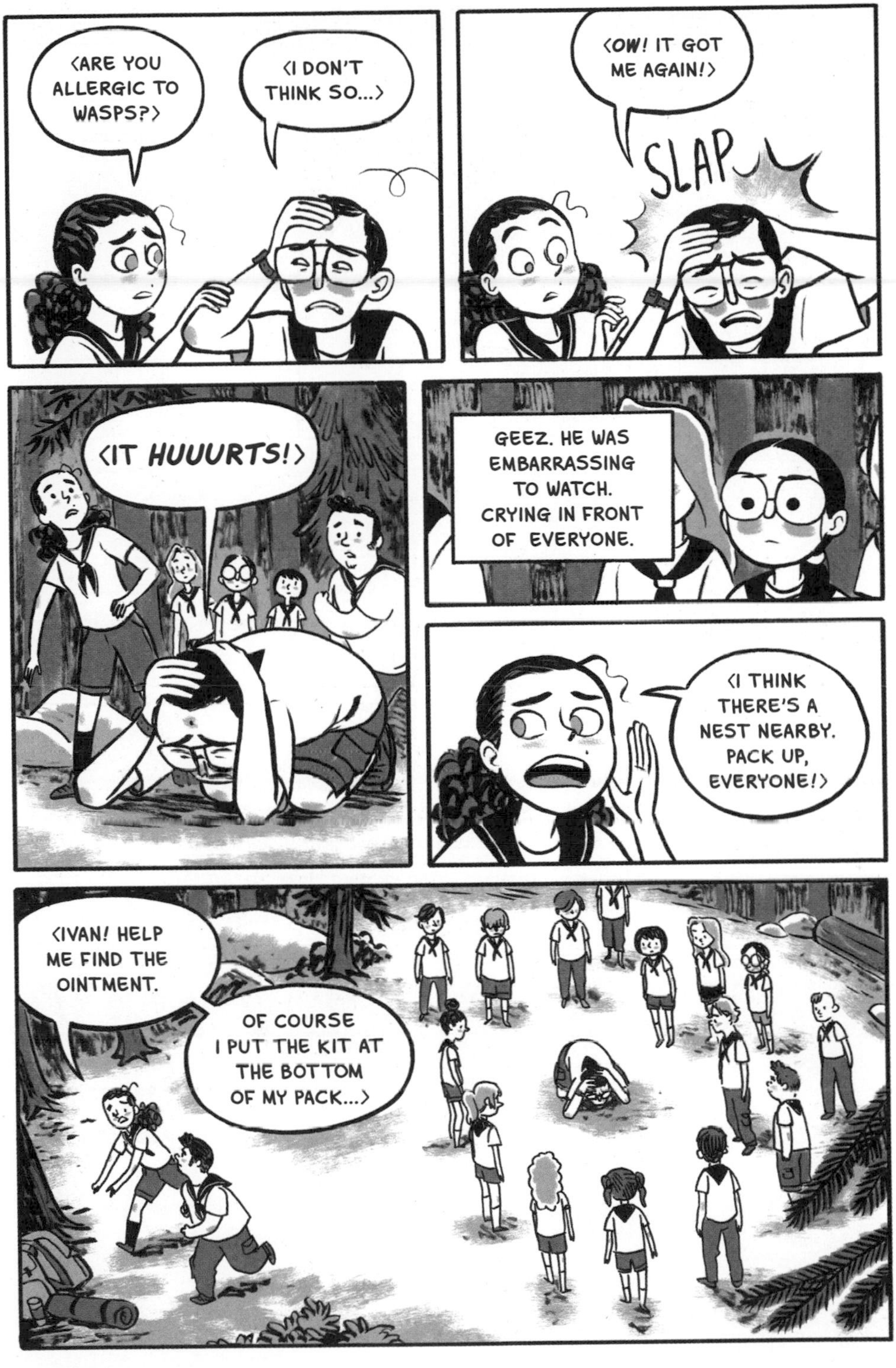
<ARE YOU ALLERGIC TO WASPS?>
<I DON'T THINK SO...>
<OW! IT GOT ME AGAIN!>
SLAP
<IT HUUURTS!>
GEEZ. HE WAS EMBARRASSING TO WATCH. CRYING IN FRONT OF EVERYONE.
<I THINK THERE'S A NEST NEARBY. PACK UP, EVERYONE!>
<IVAN! HELP ME FIND THE OINTMENT.
OF COURSE I PUT THE KIT AT THE BOTTOM OF MY PACK...>

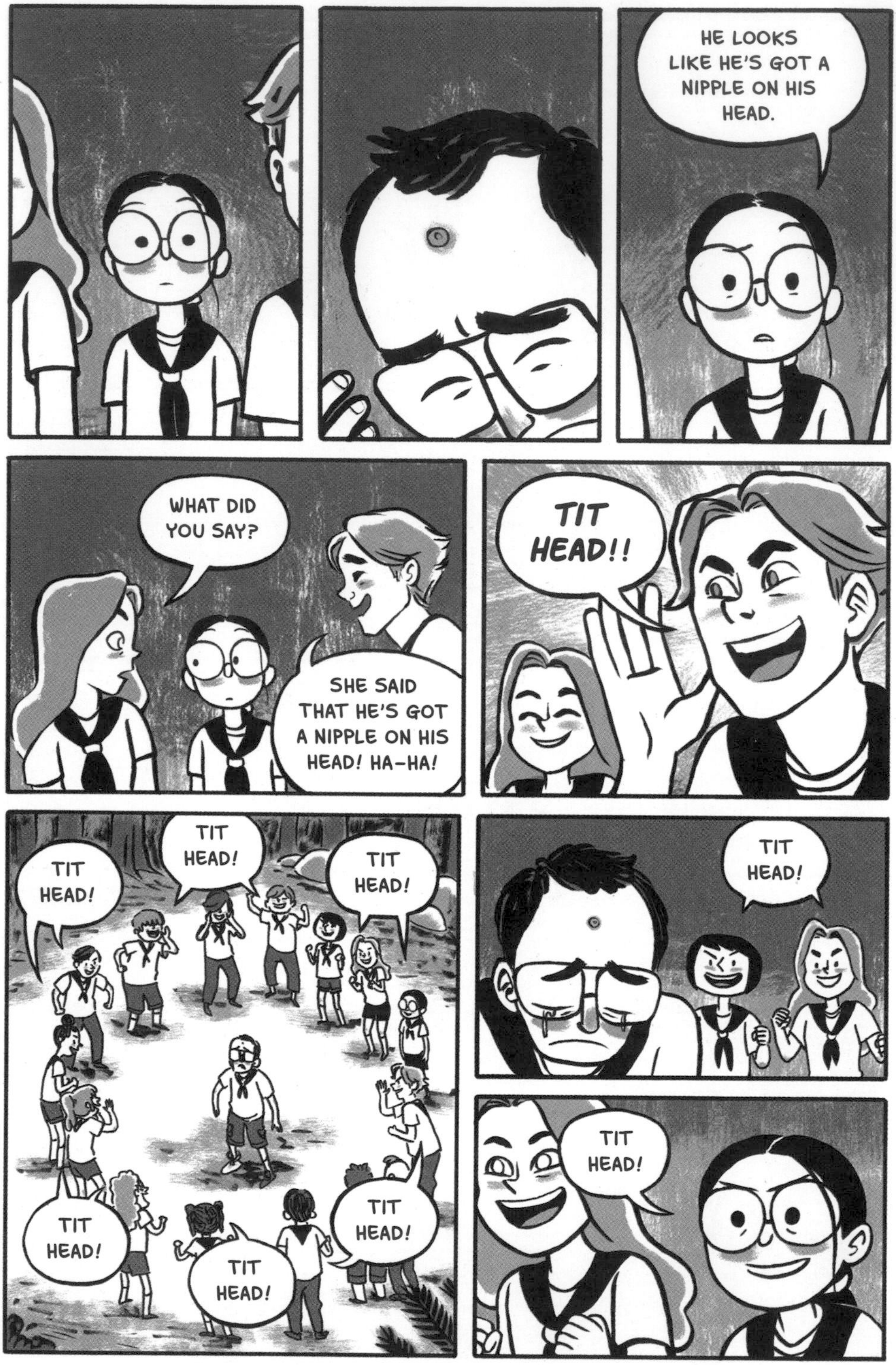
HE LOOKS LIKE HE'S GOT A NIPPLE ON HIS HEAD.
WHAT DID YOU SAY?
SHE SAID THAT HE'S GOT A NIPPLE ON HIS HEAD! HA-HA!
TIT HEAD!!
TIT HEAD!
TIT HEAD!
TIT HEAD!
TIT HEAD!
TIT HEAD!
TIT HEAD!
TIT HEAD!
TIT HEAD!

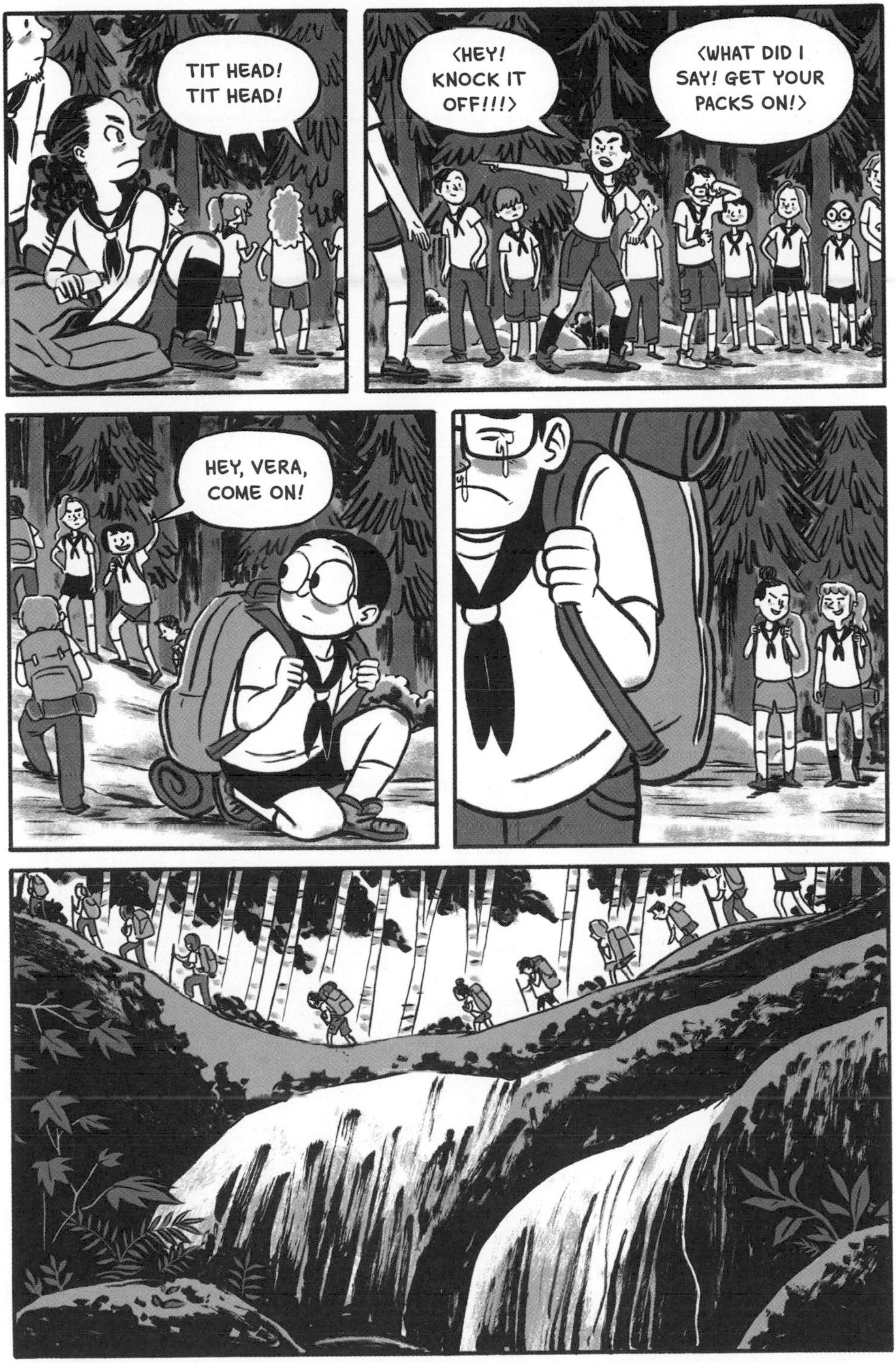
TIT HEAD!
TIT HEAD!
<HEY! KNOCK IT OFF!!!>
<WHAT DID I SAY! GET YOUR PACKS ON!>
HEY, VERA, COME ON!

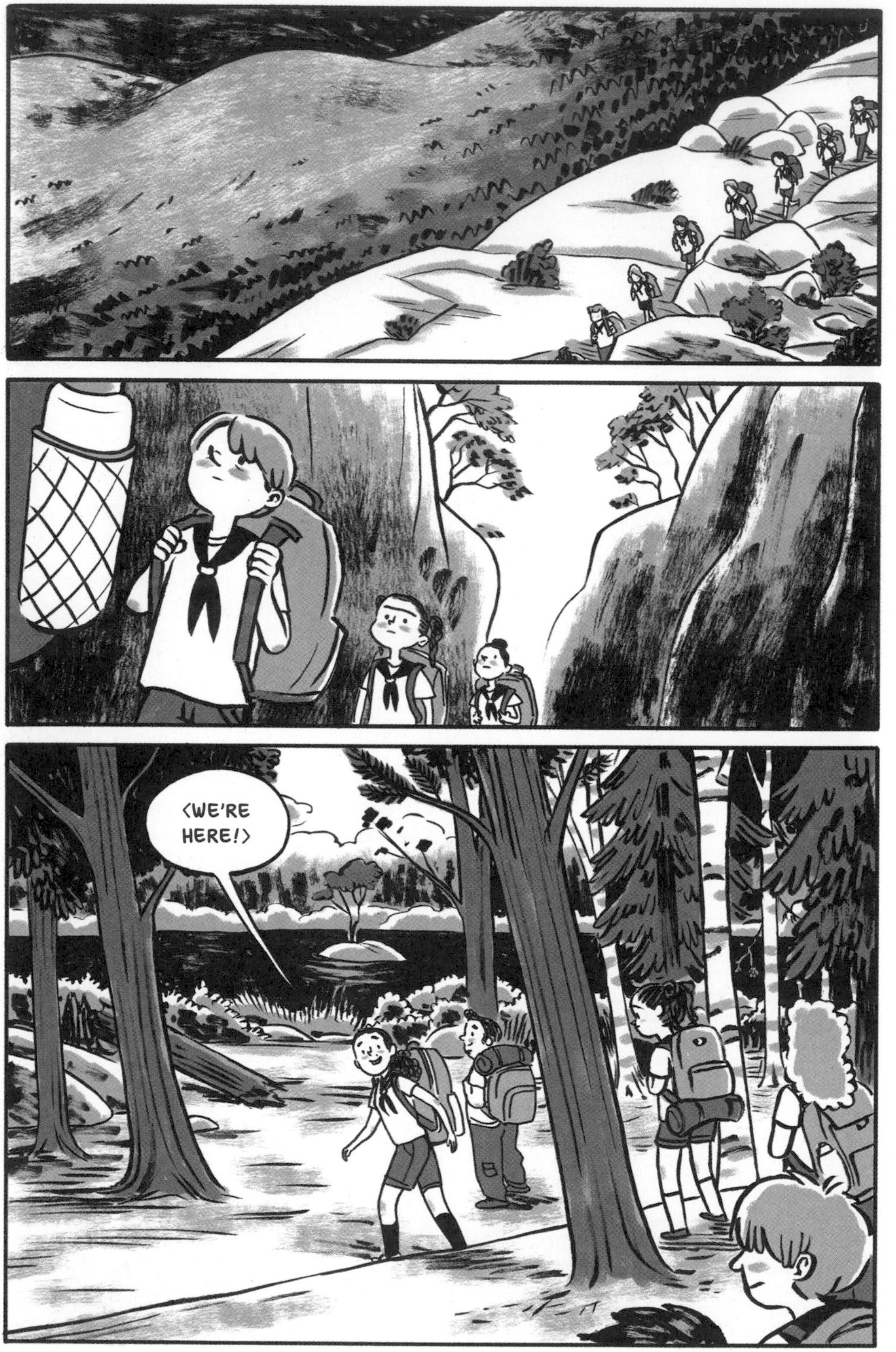
<WE'RE HERE!>

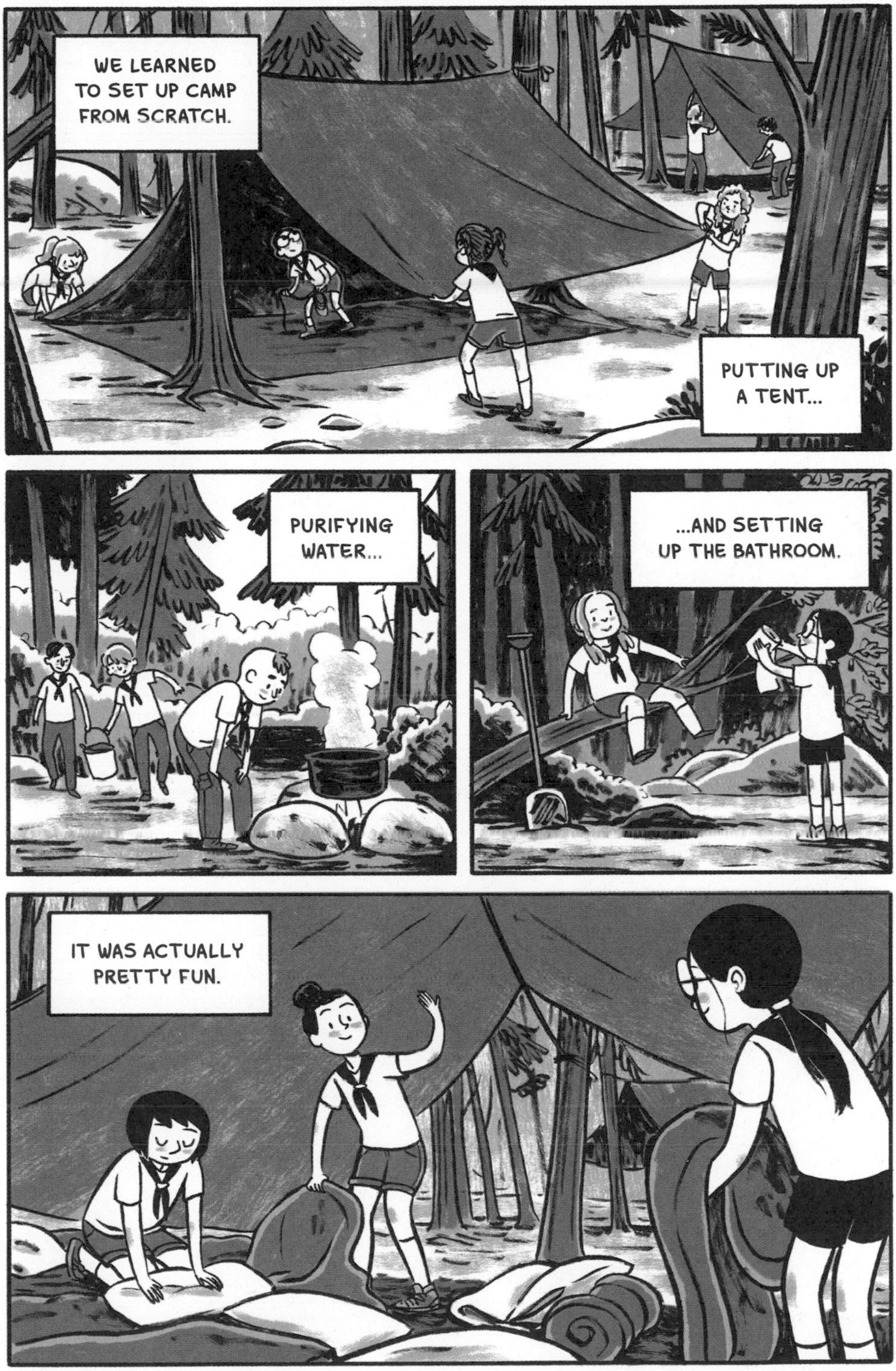
WE LEARNED TO SET UP CAMP FROM SCRATCH.
PUTTING UP A TENT...
PURIFYING WATER...
...AND SETTING UP THE BATHROOM.
IT WAS ACTUALLY PRETTY FUN.

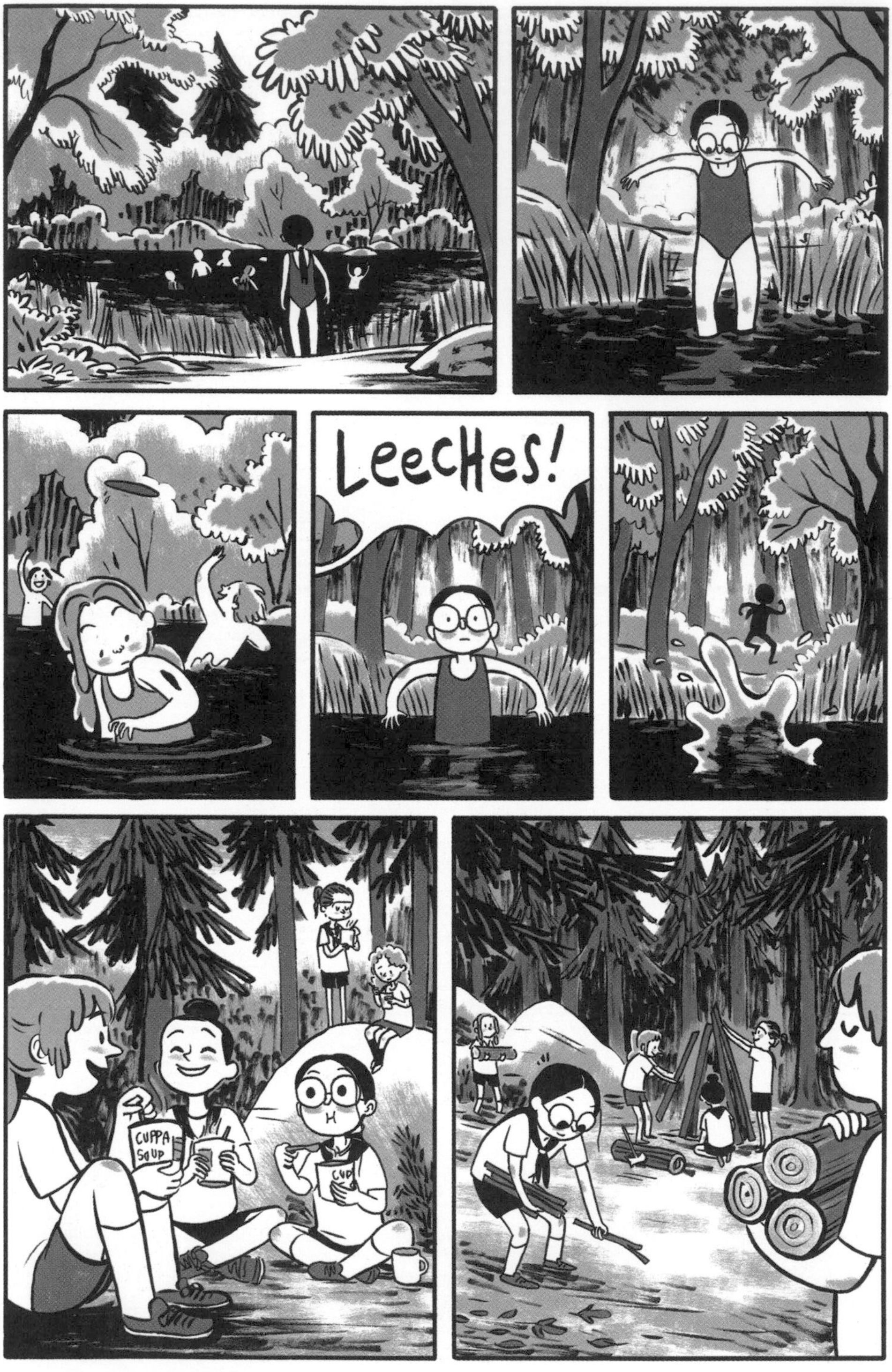
Leeches!
CUPPA SOUP
CUP

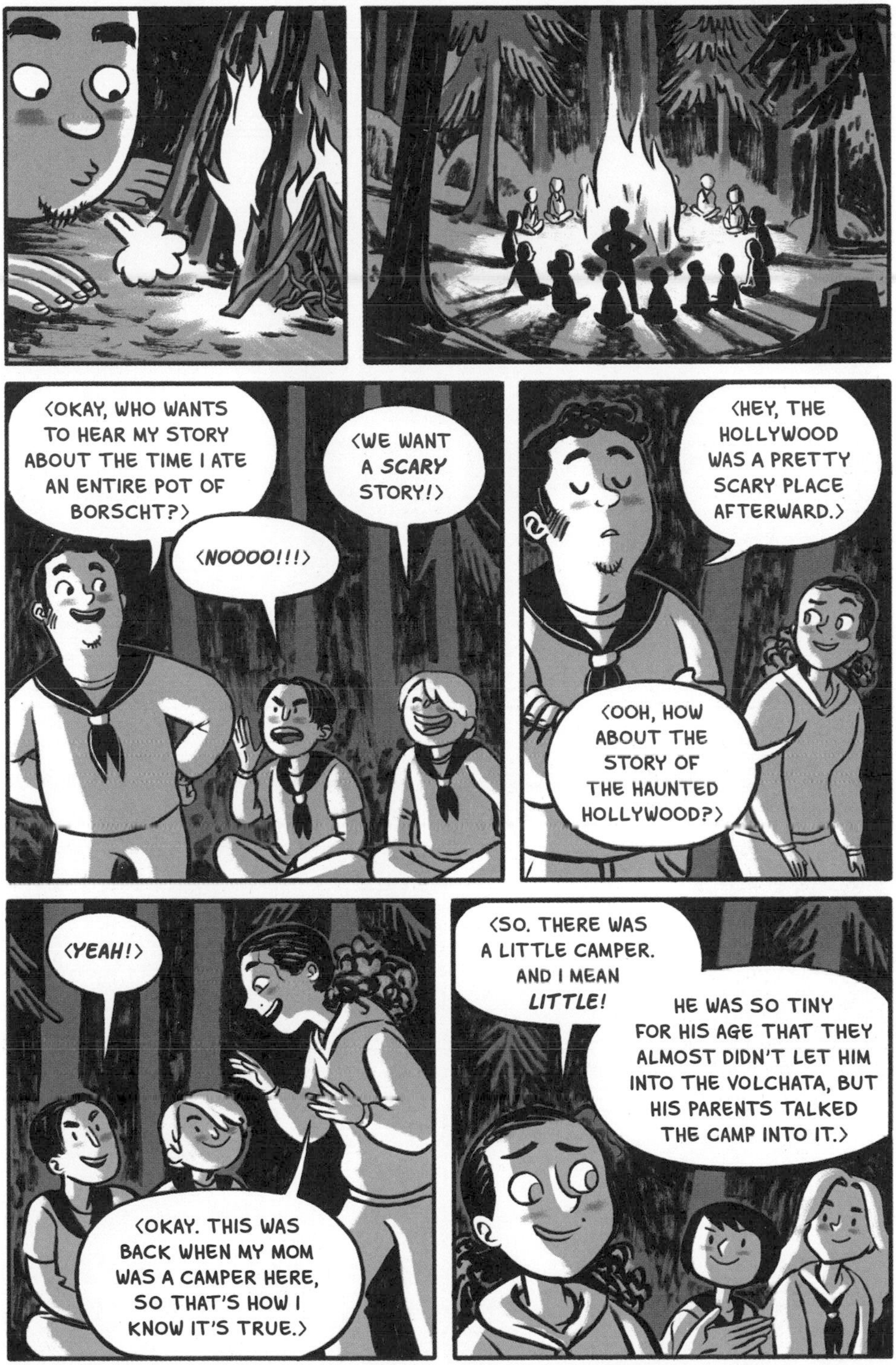

<OKAY, WHO WANTS TO HEAR MY STORY ABOUT THE TIME I ATE AN ENTIRE POT OF BORSCHT?>
<NOOOO!!!>
<WE WANT A *SCARY* STORY!>
<HEY, THE HOLLYWOOD WAS A PRETTY SCARY PLACE AFTERWARD.>
<OOH, HOW ABOUT THE STORY OF THE HAUNTED HOLLYWOOD?>
<*YEAH!*>
<OKAY. THIS WAS BACK WHEN MY MOM WAS A CAMPER HERE, SO THAT'S HOW I KNOW IT'S TRUE.>
<SO. THERE WAS A LITTLE CAMPER. AND I MEAN *LITTLE!*
HE WAS SO TINY FOR HIS AGE THAT THEY ALMOST DIDN'T LET HIM INTO THE VOLCHATA, BUT HIS PARENTS TALKED THE CAMP INTO IT.>

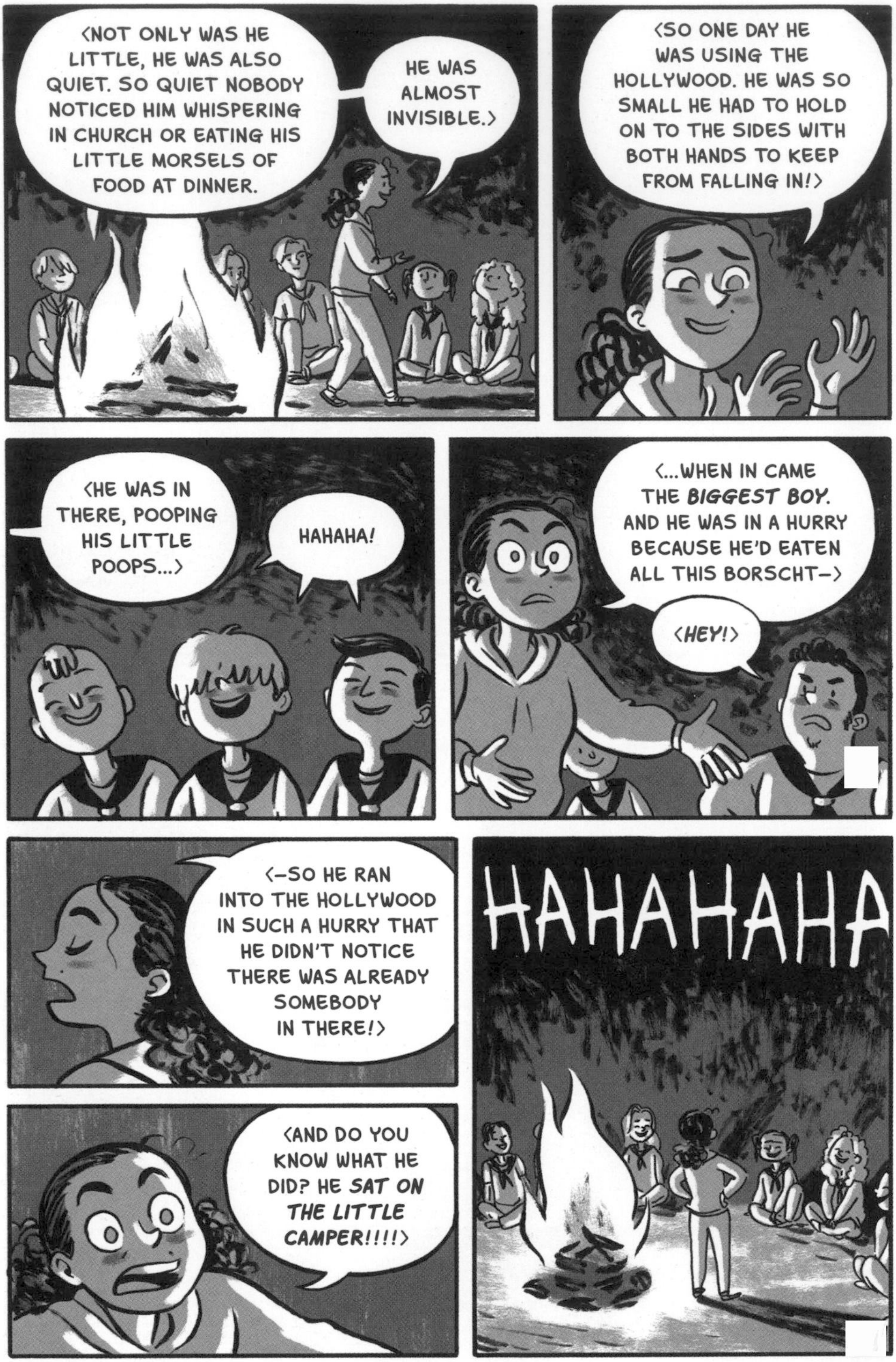

<NOT ONLY WAS HE LITTLE, HE WAS ALSO QUIET. SO QUIET NOBODY NOTICED HIM WHISPERING IN CHURCH OR EATING HIS LITTLE MORSELS OF FOOD AT DINNER.
HE WAS ALMOST INVISIBLE.>
<SO ONE DAY HE WAS USING THE HOLLYWOOD. HE WAS SO SMALL HE HAD TO HOLD ON TO THE SIDES WITH BOTH HANDS TO KEEP FROM FALLING IN!>
<HE WAS IN THERE, POOPING HIS LITTLE POOPS...>
HAHAHA!
<...WHEN IN CAME THE *BIGGEST BOY*. AND HE WAS IN A HURRY BECAUSE HE'D EATEN ALL THIS BORSCHT—>
<*HEY!*>
<—SO HE RAN INTO THE HOLLYWOOD IN SUCH A HURRY THAT HE DIDN'T NOTICE THERE WAS ALREADY SOMEBODY IN THERE!>
<AND DO YOU KNOW WHAT HE DID? HE *SAT ON THE LITTLE CAMPER!!!!*>
HAHAHAHA

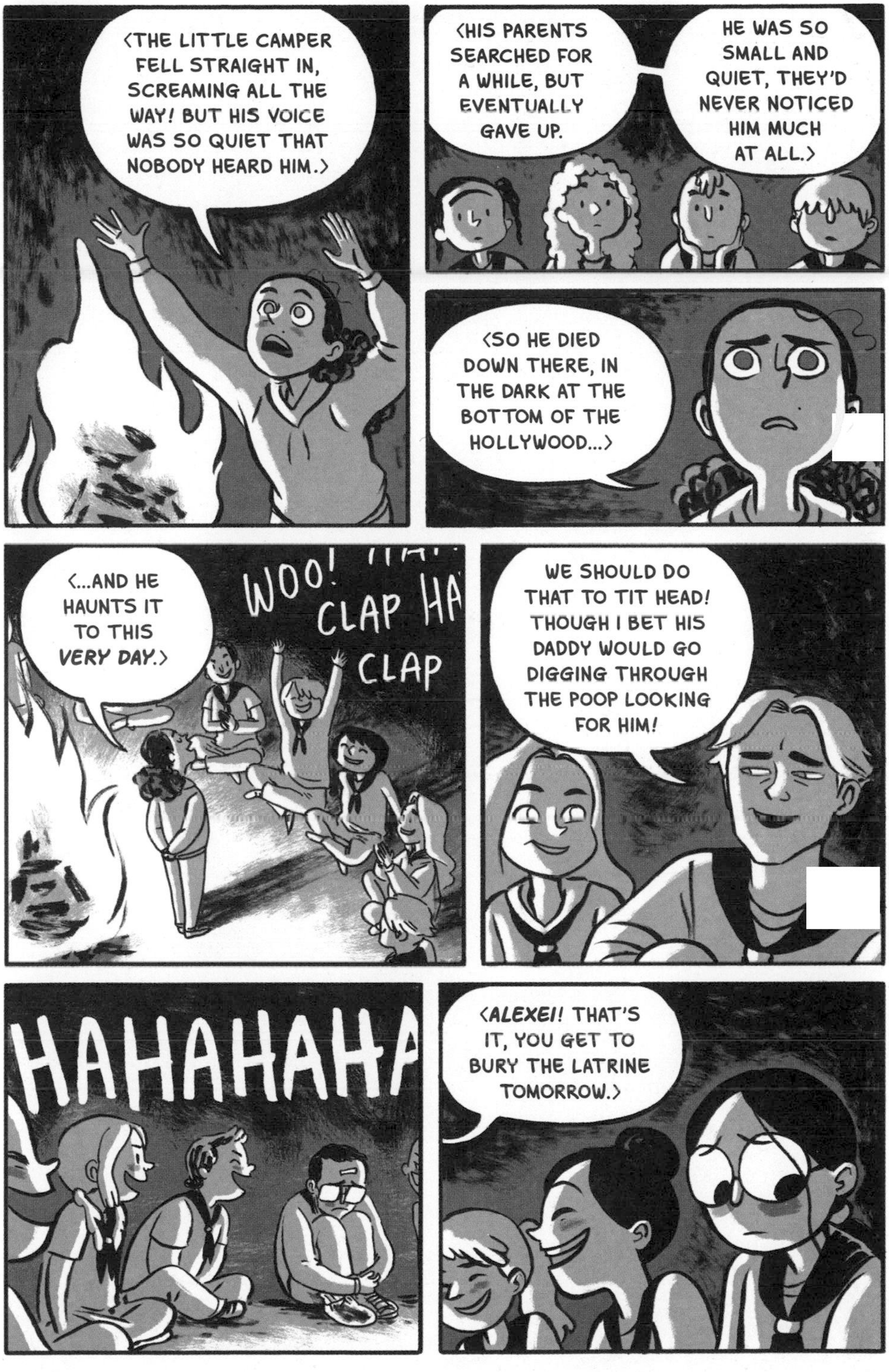
<THE LITTLE CAMPER FELL STRAIGHT IN, SCREAMING ALL THE WAY! BUT HIS VOICE WAS SO QUIET THAT NOBODY HEARD HIM.>
<HIS PARENTS SEARCHED FOR A WHILE, BUT EVENTUALLY GAVE UP.
HE WAS SO SMALL AND QUIET, THEY'D NEVER NOTICED HIM MUCH AT ALL.>
<SO HE DIED DOWN THERE, IN THE DARK AT THE BOTTOM OF THE HOLLYWOOD...>
<...AND HE HAUNTS IT TO THIS *VERY DAY*.>
WOO!
CLAP
CLAP
WE SHOULD DO THAT TO TIT HEAD! THOUGH I BET HIS DADDY WOULD GO DIGGING THROUGH THE POOP LOOKING FOR HIM!
HAHAHAHA
<*ALEXEI!* THAT'S IT, YOU GET TO BURY THE LATRINE TOMORROW.>

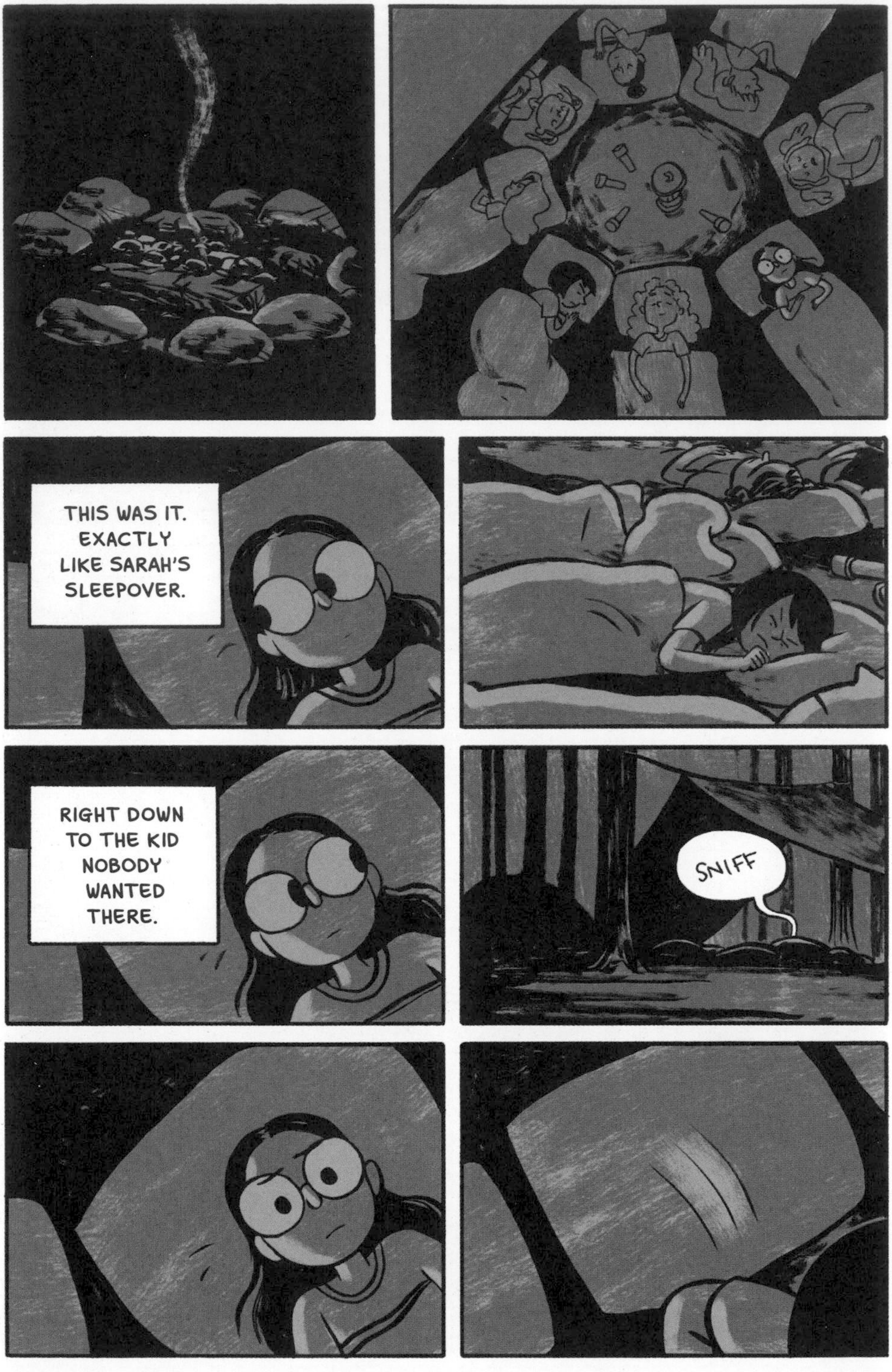
THIS WAS IT. EXACTLY LIKE SARAH'S SLEEPOVER.
RIGHT DOWN TO THE KID NOBODY WANTED THERE.
SNIFF

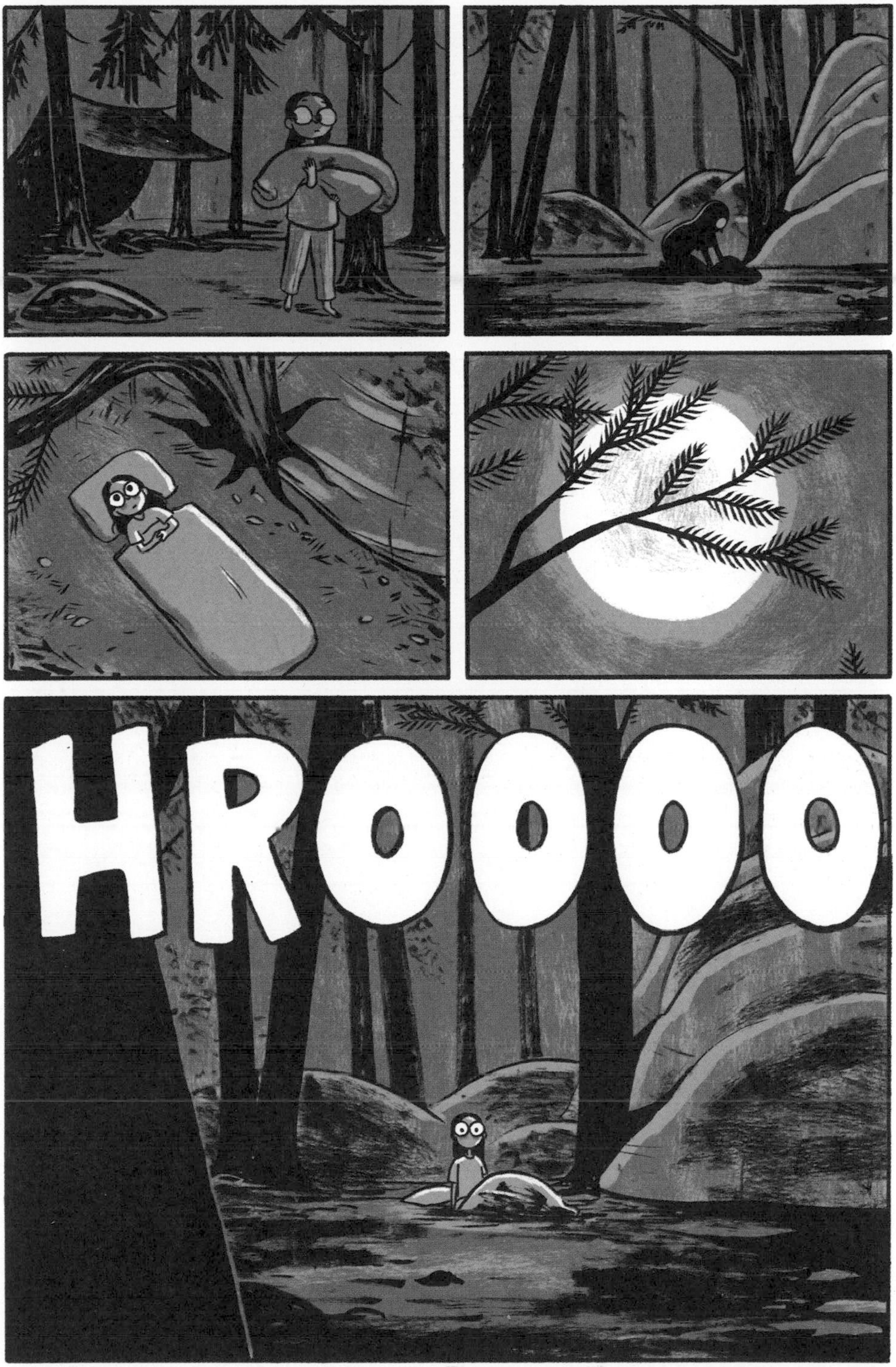
HROOOO

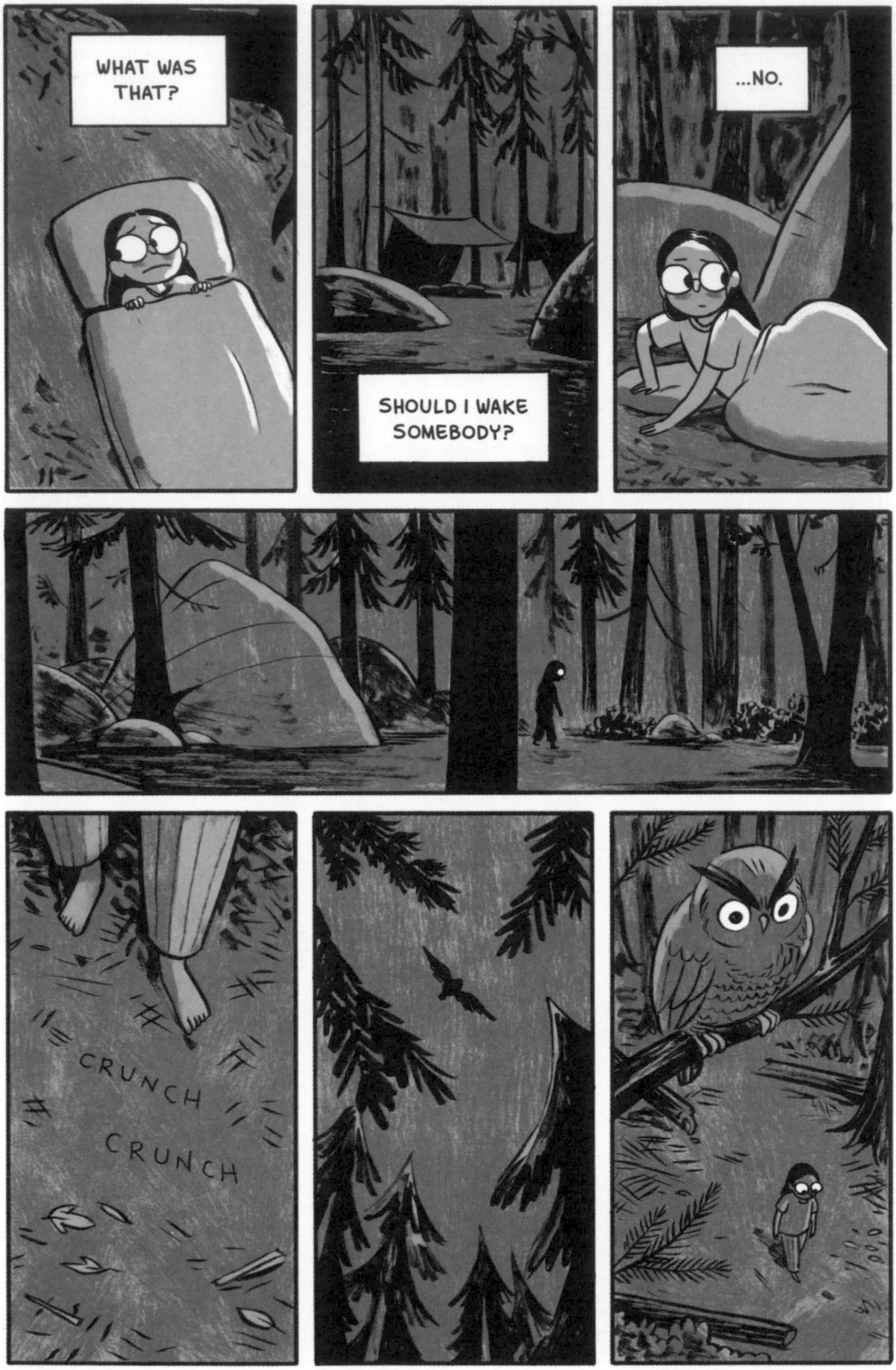
WHAT WAS THAT?
SHOULD I WAKE SOMEBODY?
...NO.
CRUNCH
CRUNCH

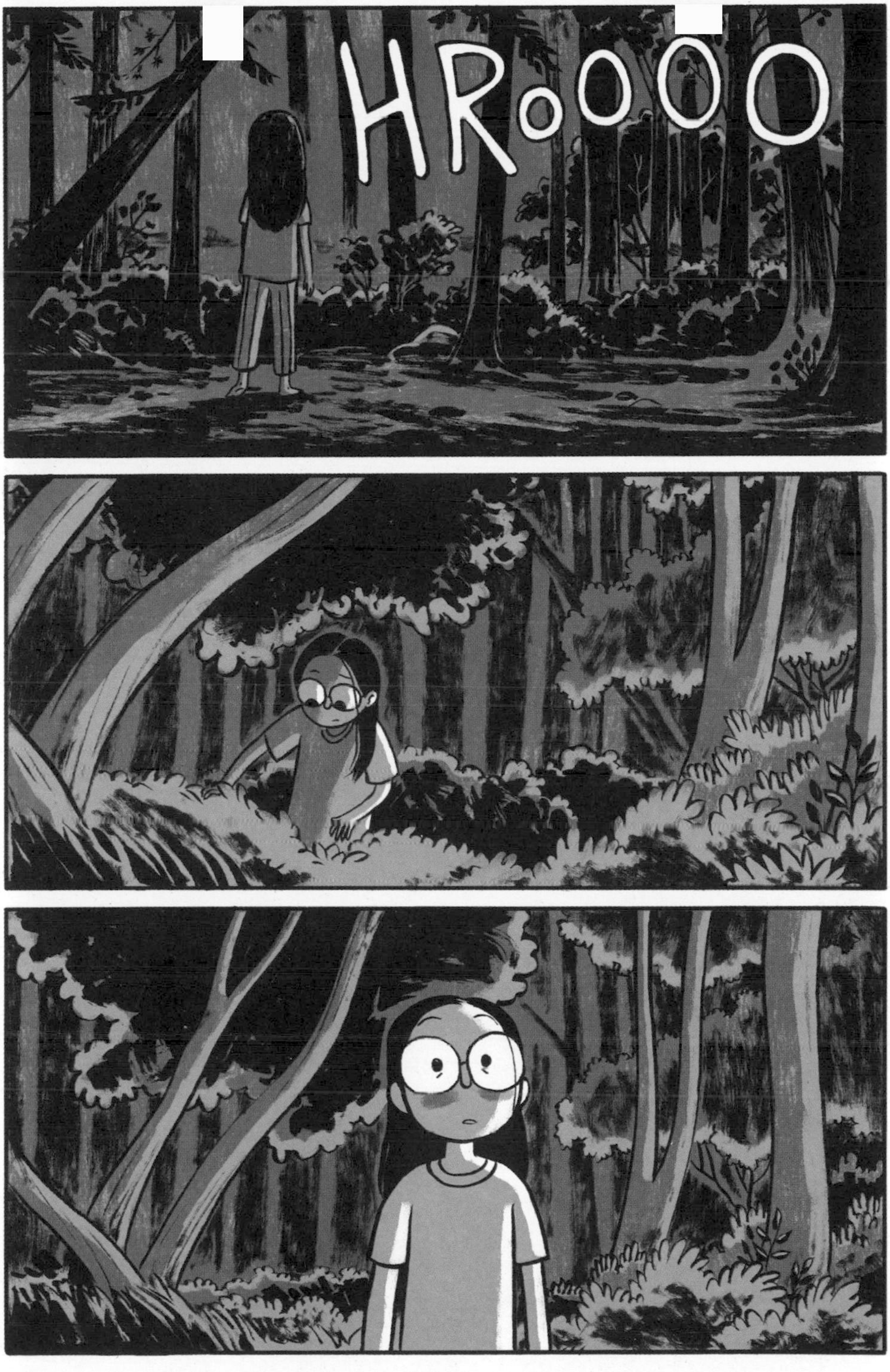
HRoOOO

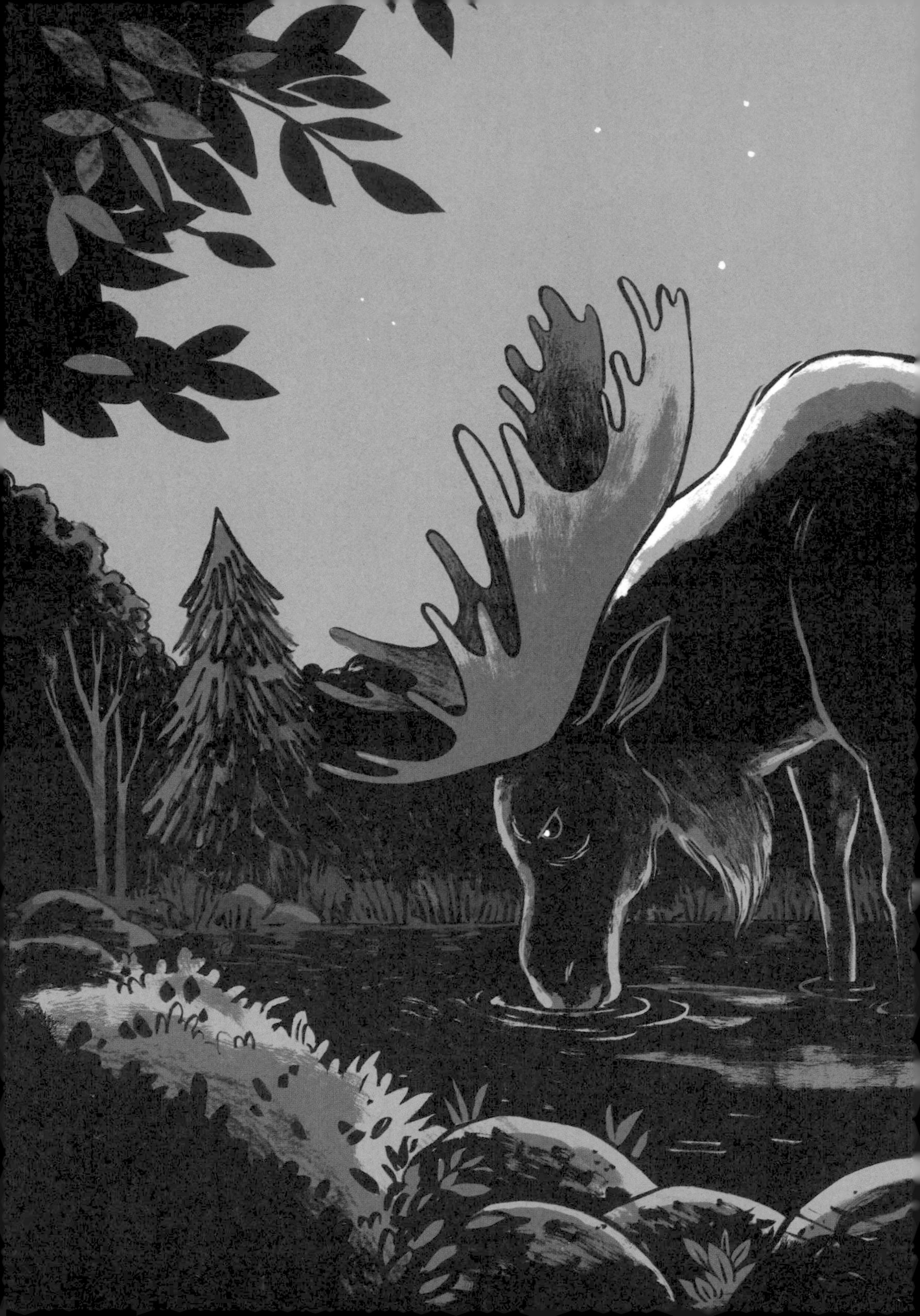

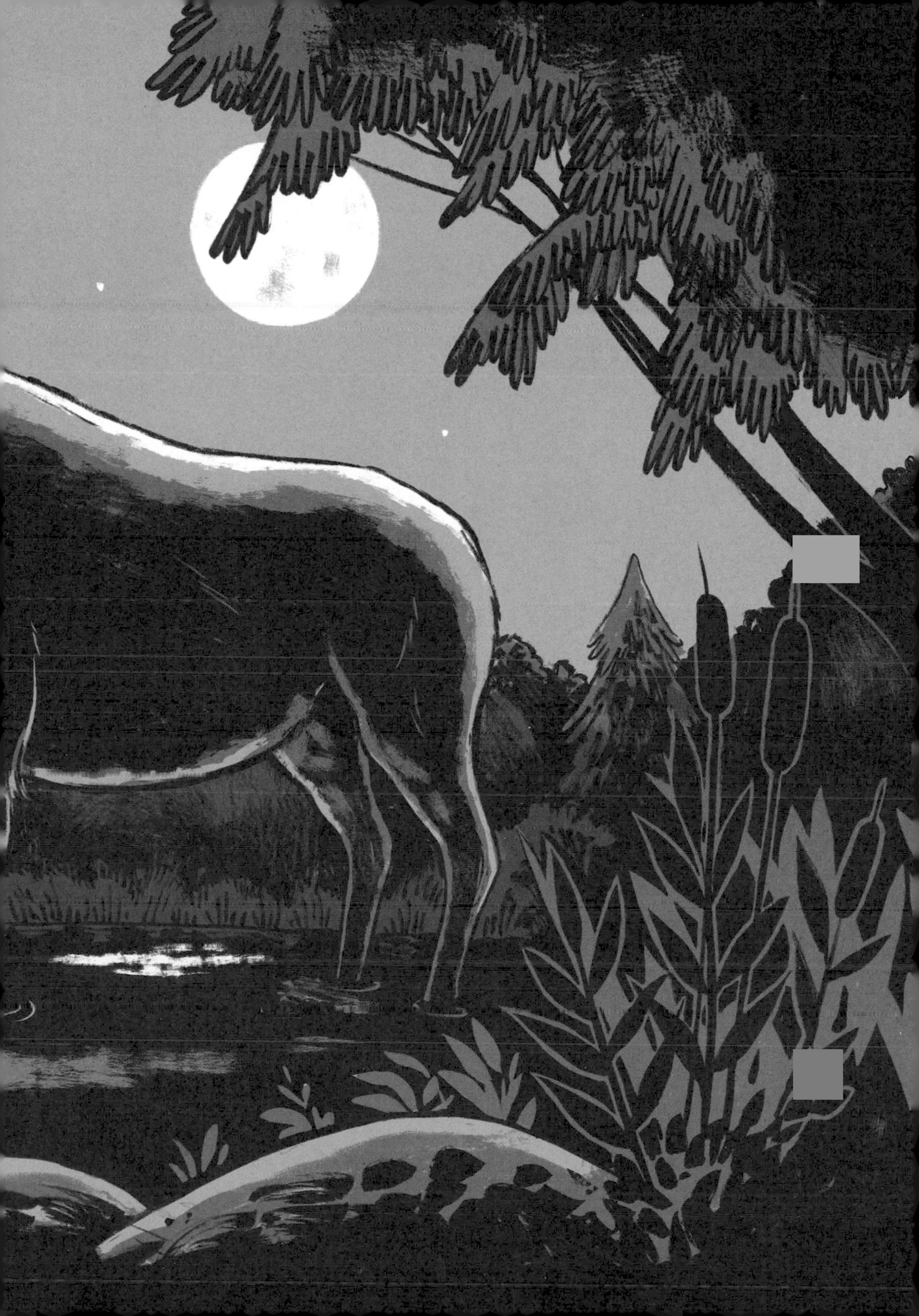

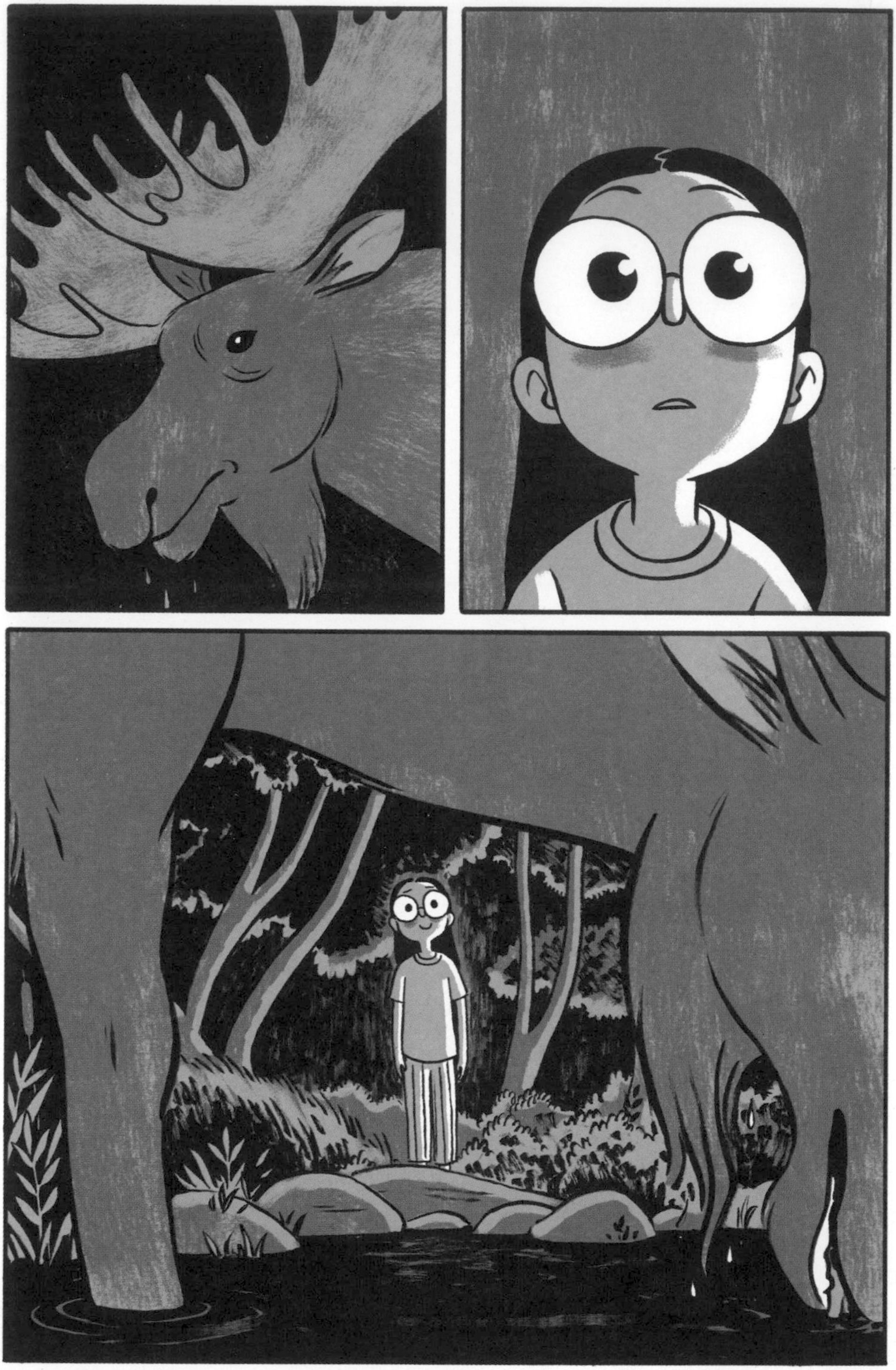

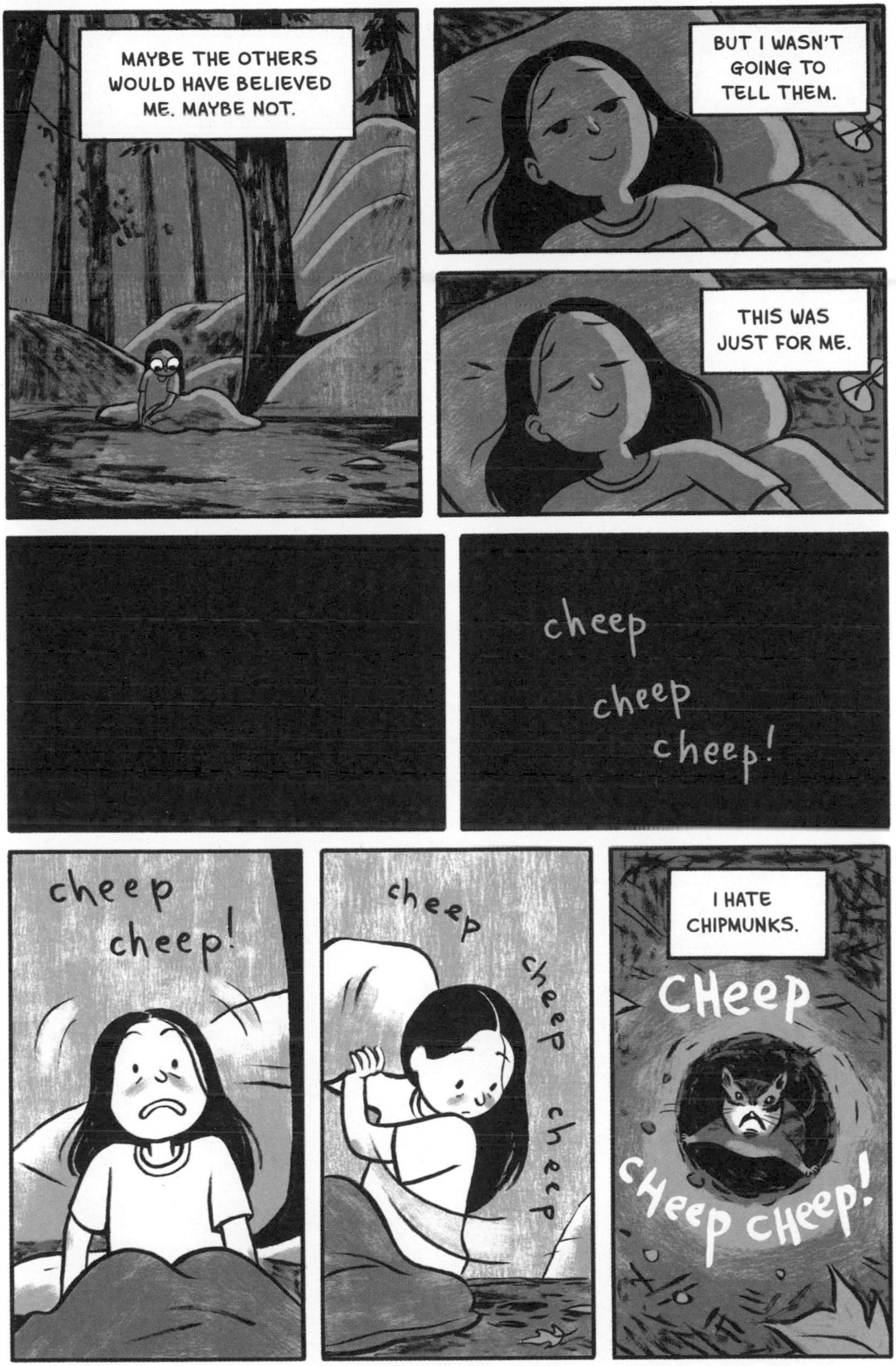
MAYBE THE OTHERS WOULD HAVE BELIEVED ME. MAYBE NOT.
BUT I WASN'T GOING TO TELL THEM.
THIS WAS JUST FOR ME.
cheep
cheep
cheep!
cheep
cheep!
cheep
cheep
cheep
cheep
I HATE CHIPMUNKS.
CHEEP
CHEEP CHEEP!

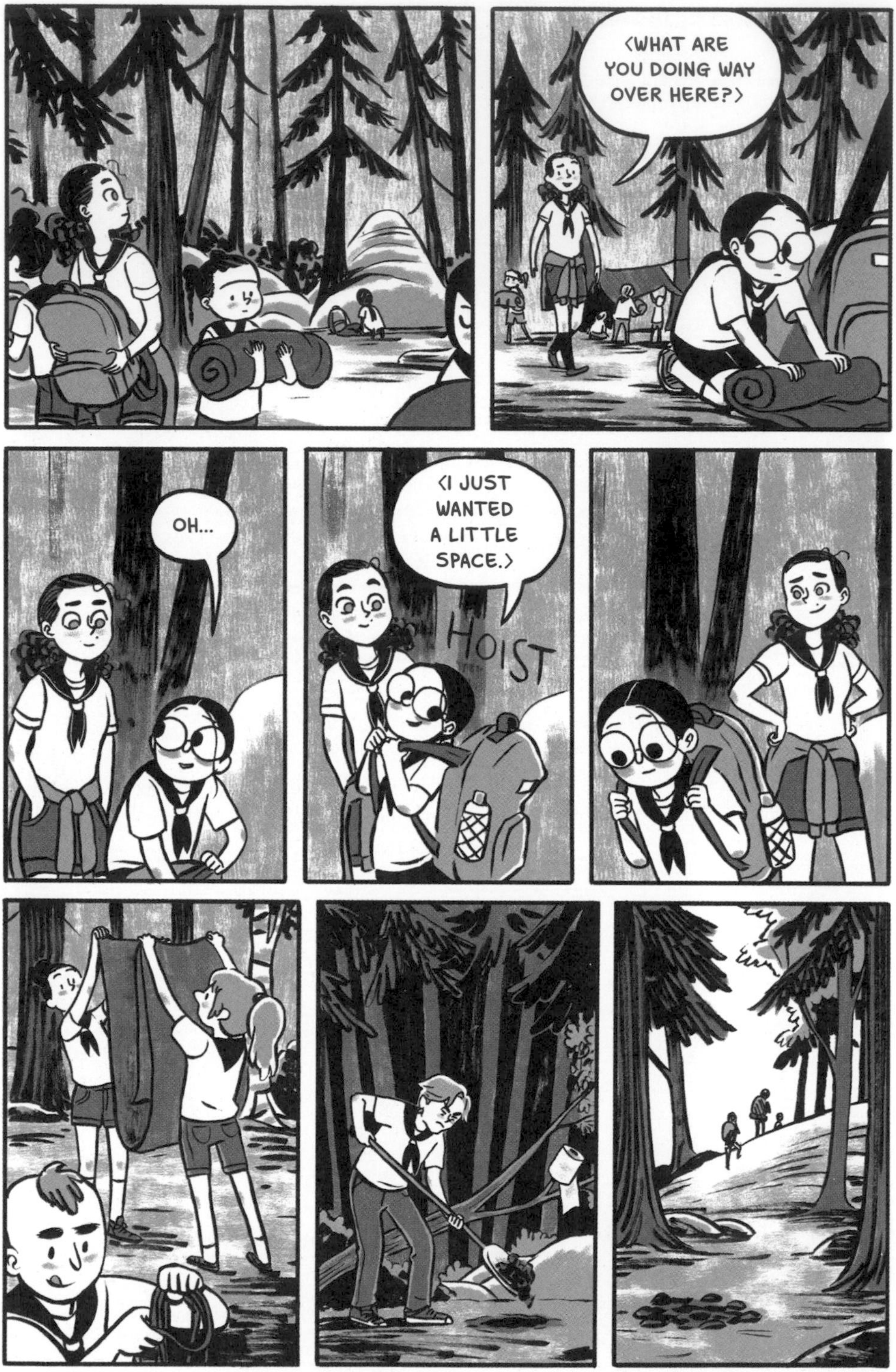
<WHAT ARE YOU DOING WAY OVER HERE?>
OH...
<I JUST WANTED A LITTLE SPACE.>
HOIST

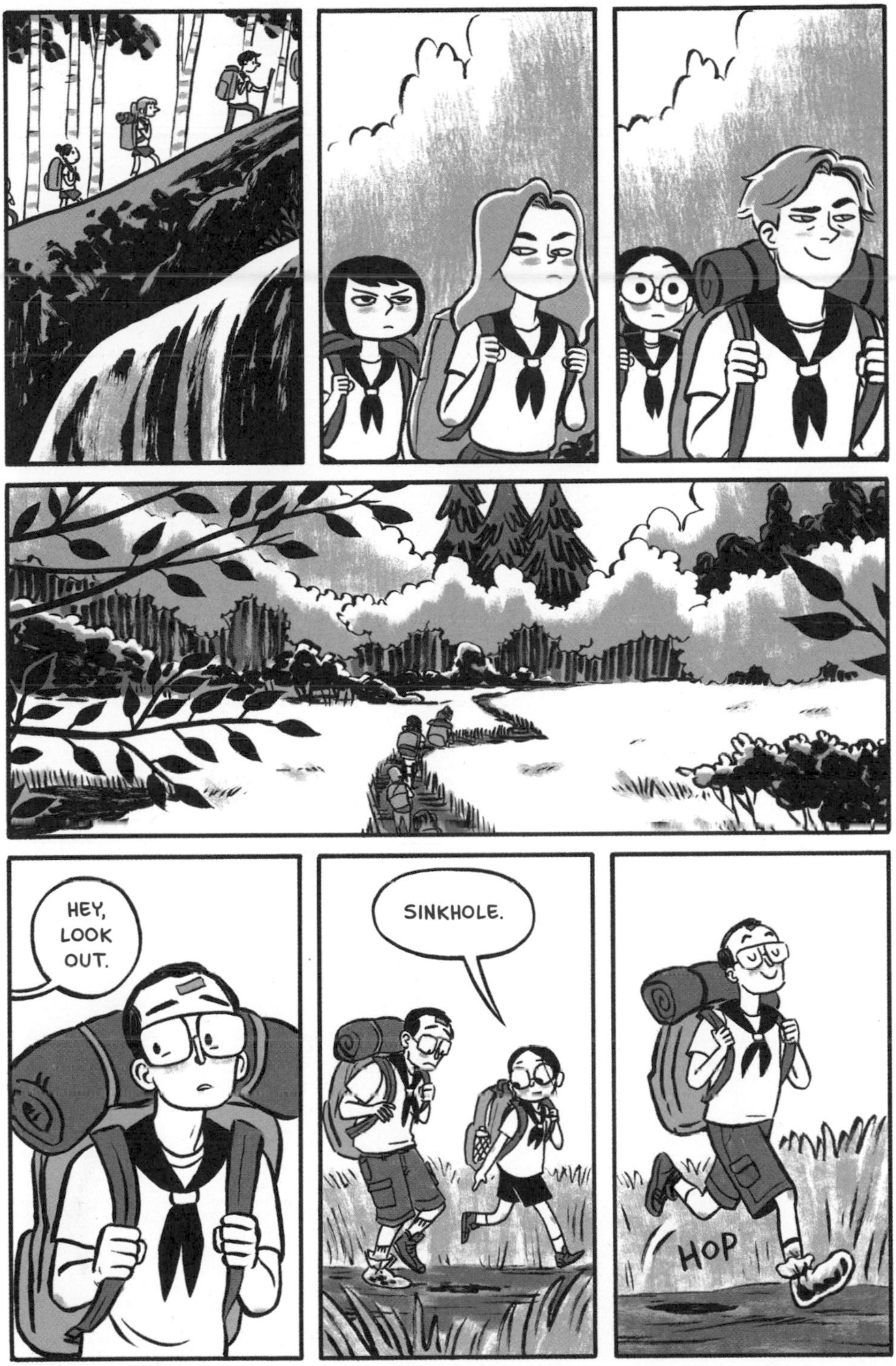
HEY, LOOK OUT.
SINKHOLE.
HOP

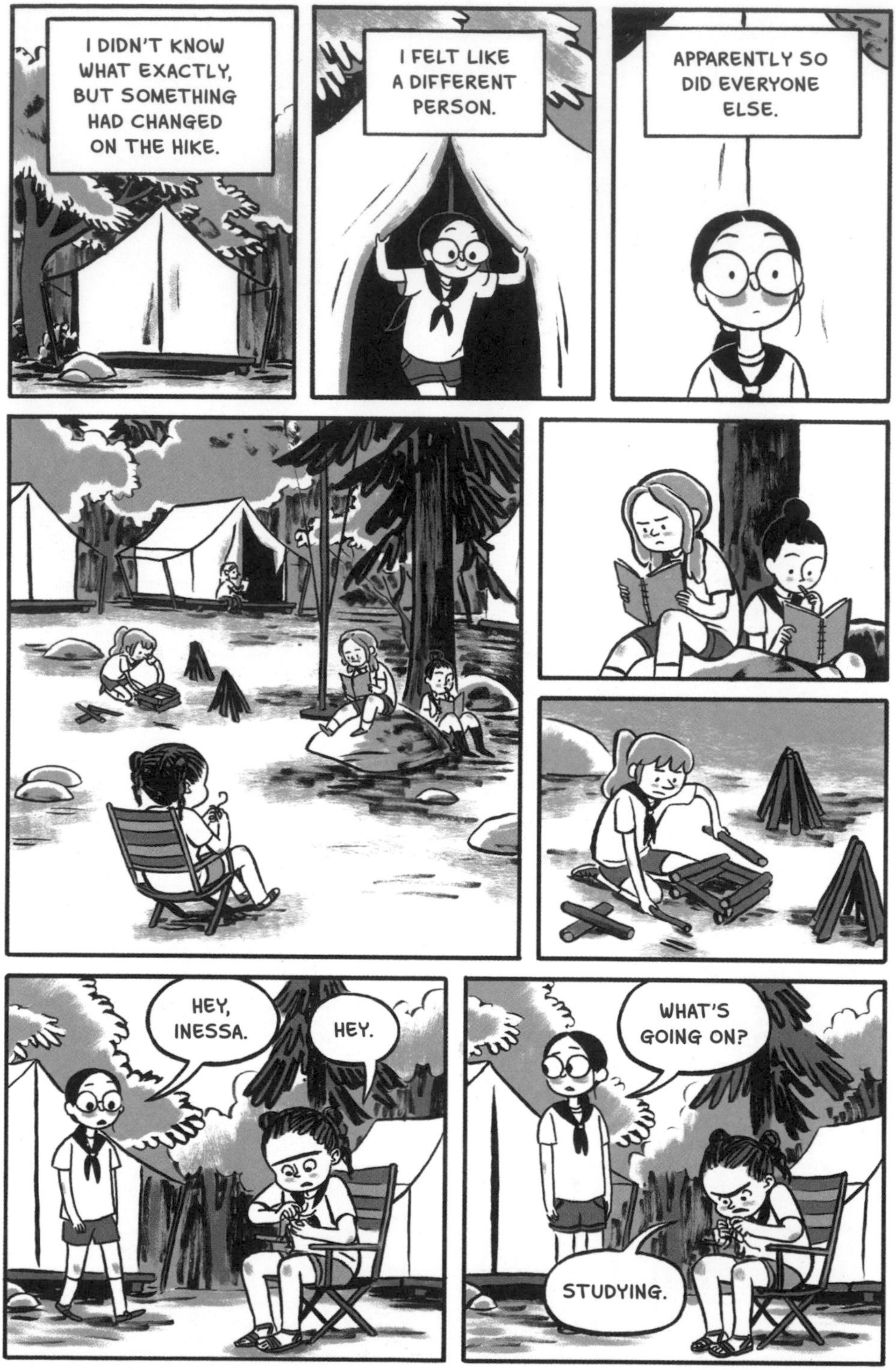
I DIDN'T KNOW WHAT EXACTLY, BUT SOMETHING HAD CHANGED ON THE HIKE.
I FELT LIKE A DIFFERENT PERSON.
APPARENTLY SO DID EVERYONE ELSE.
HEY, INESSA.
HEY.
WHAT'S GOING ON?
STUDYING.

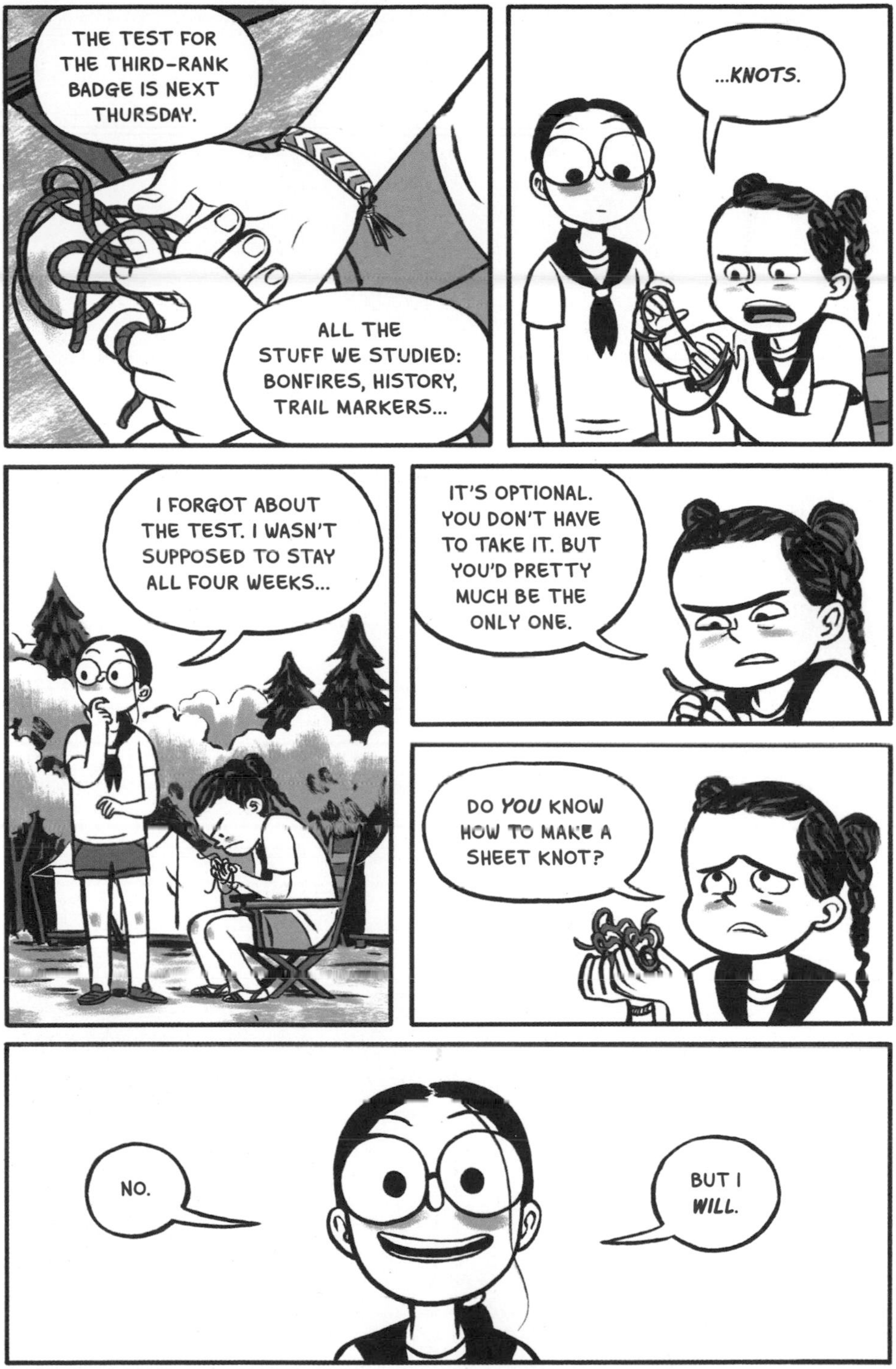
THE TEST FOR THE THIRD-RANK BADGE IS NEXT THURSDAY.
ALL THE STUFF WE STUDIED: BONFIRES, HISTORY, TRAIL MARKERS...
...KNOTS.
I FORGOT ABOUT THE TEST. I WASN'T SUPPOSED TO STAY ALL FOUR WEEKS...
IT'S OPTIONAL. YOU DON'T HAVE TO TAKE IT. BUT YOU'D PRETTY MUCH BE THE ONLY ONE.
DO *YOU* KNOW HOW TO MAKE A SHEET KNOT?
NO.
BUT I *WILL*.

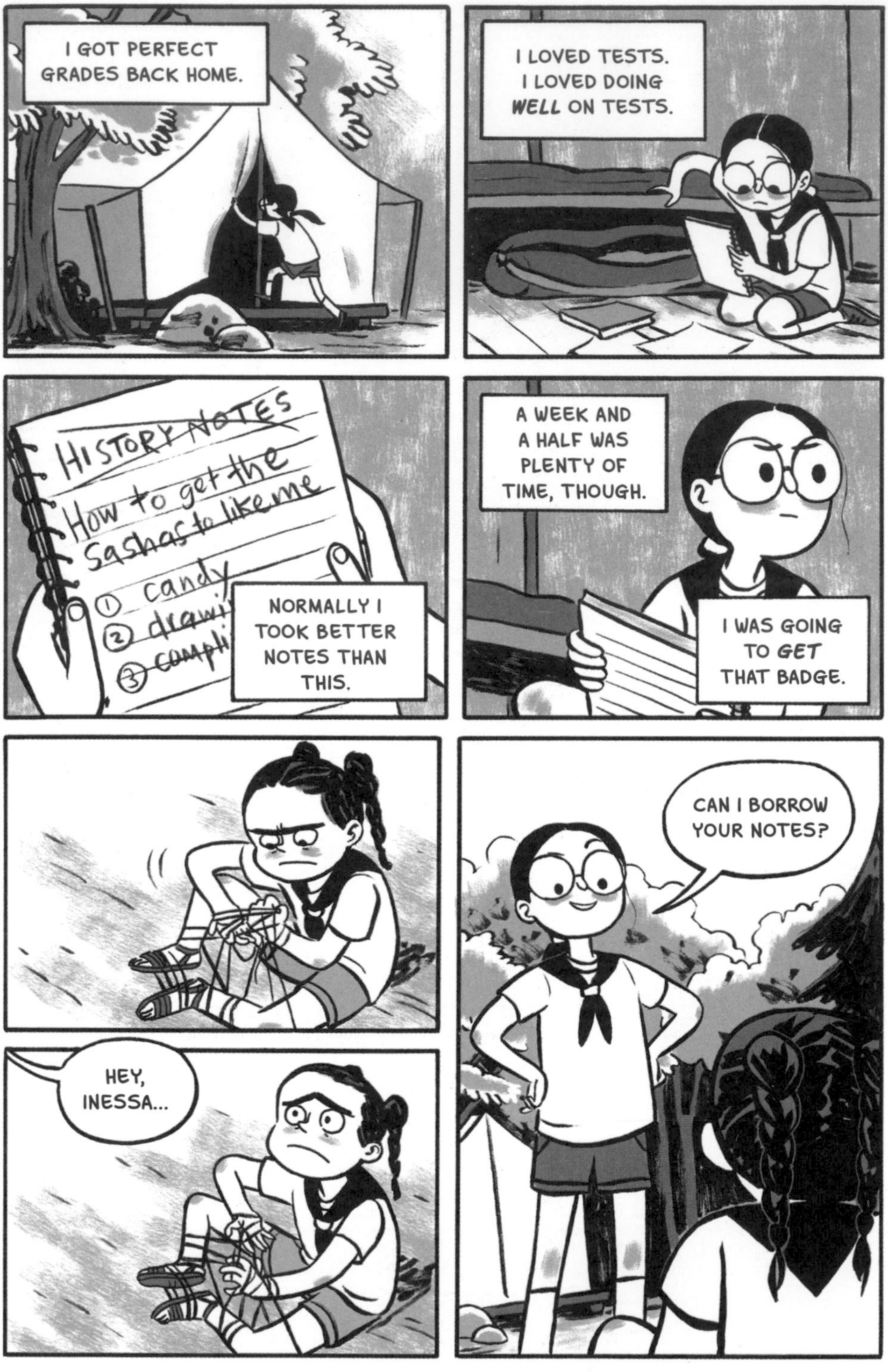
I GOT PERFECT GRADES BACK HOME.
I LOVED TESTS. I LOVED DOING WELL ON TESTS.
HISTORY NOTES
How to get the Sashas to like me
① candy
② drawi
③ compli
NORMALLY I TOOK BETTER NOTES THAN THIS.
A WEEK AND A HALF WAS PLENTY OF TIME, THOUGH.
I WAS GOING TO GET THAT BADGE.
HEY, INESSA...
CAN I BORROW YOUR NOTES?

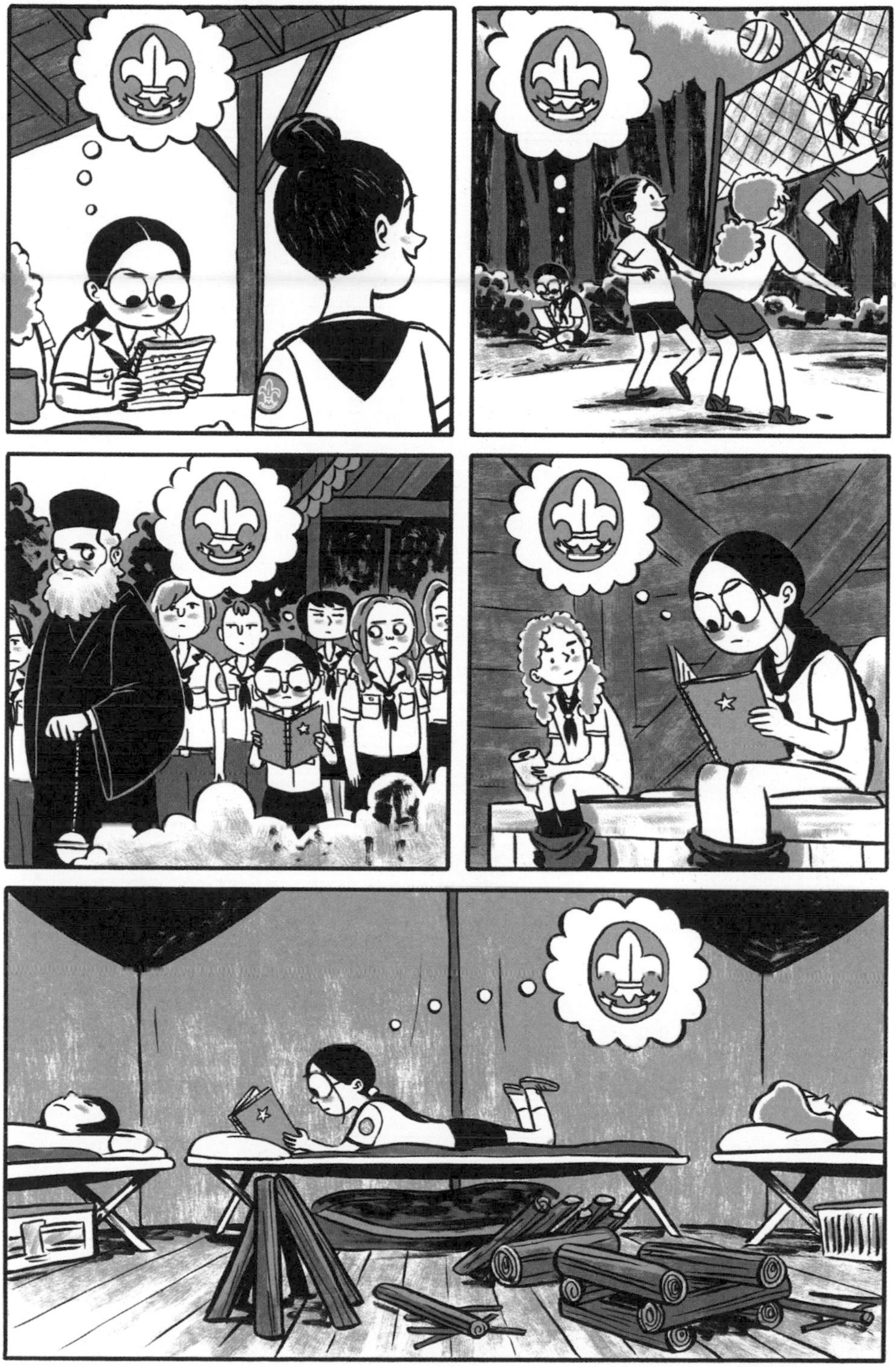

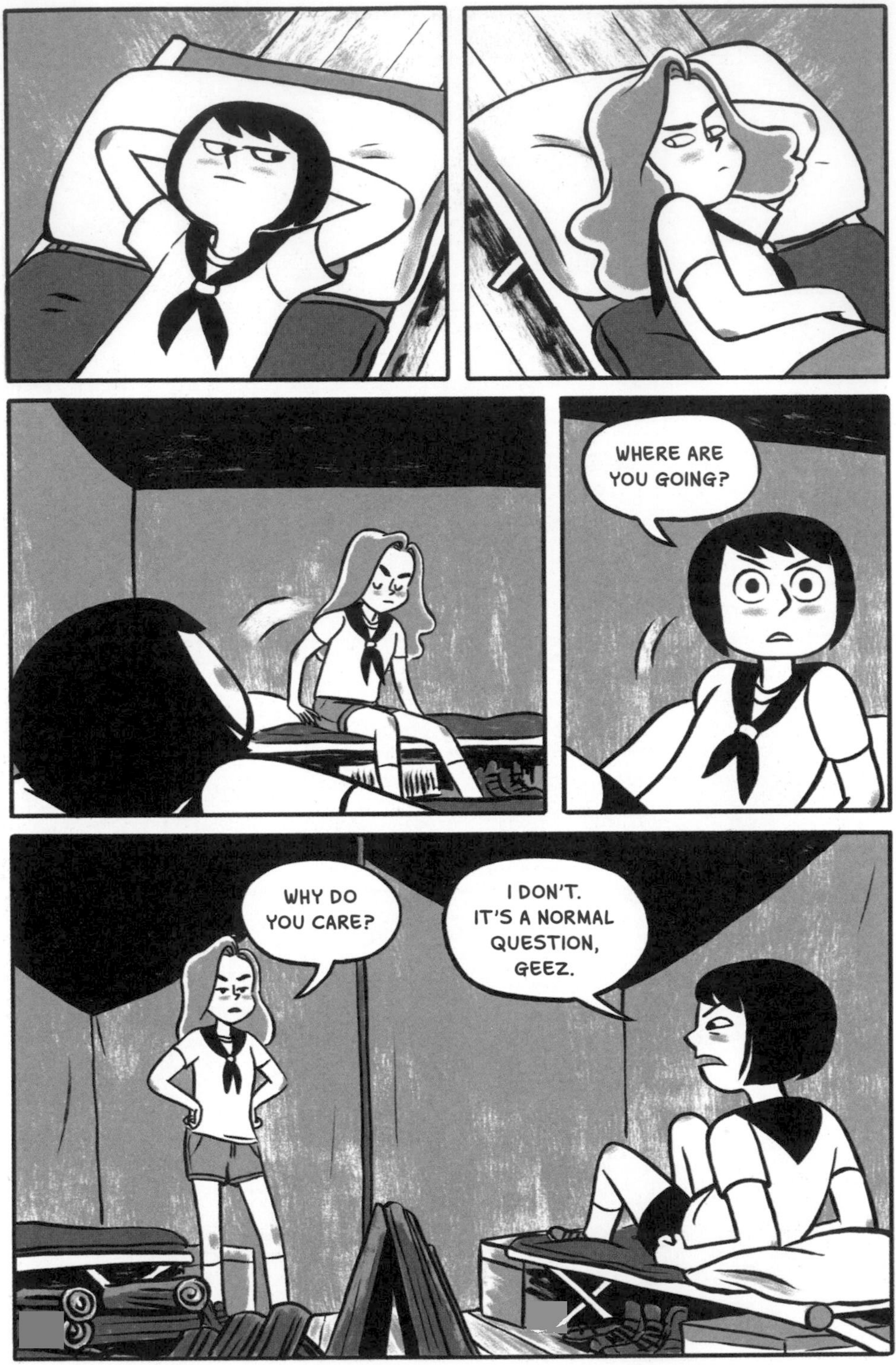
WHERE ARE YOU GOING?
WHY DO YOU CARE?
I DON'T. IT'S A NORMAL QUESTION, GEEZ.

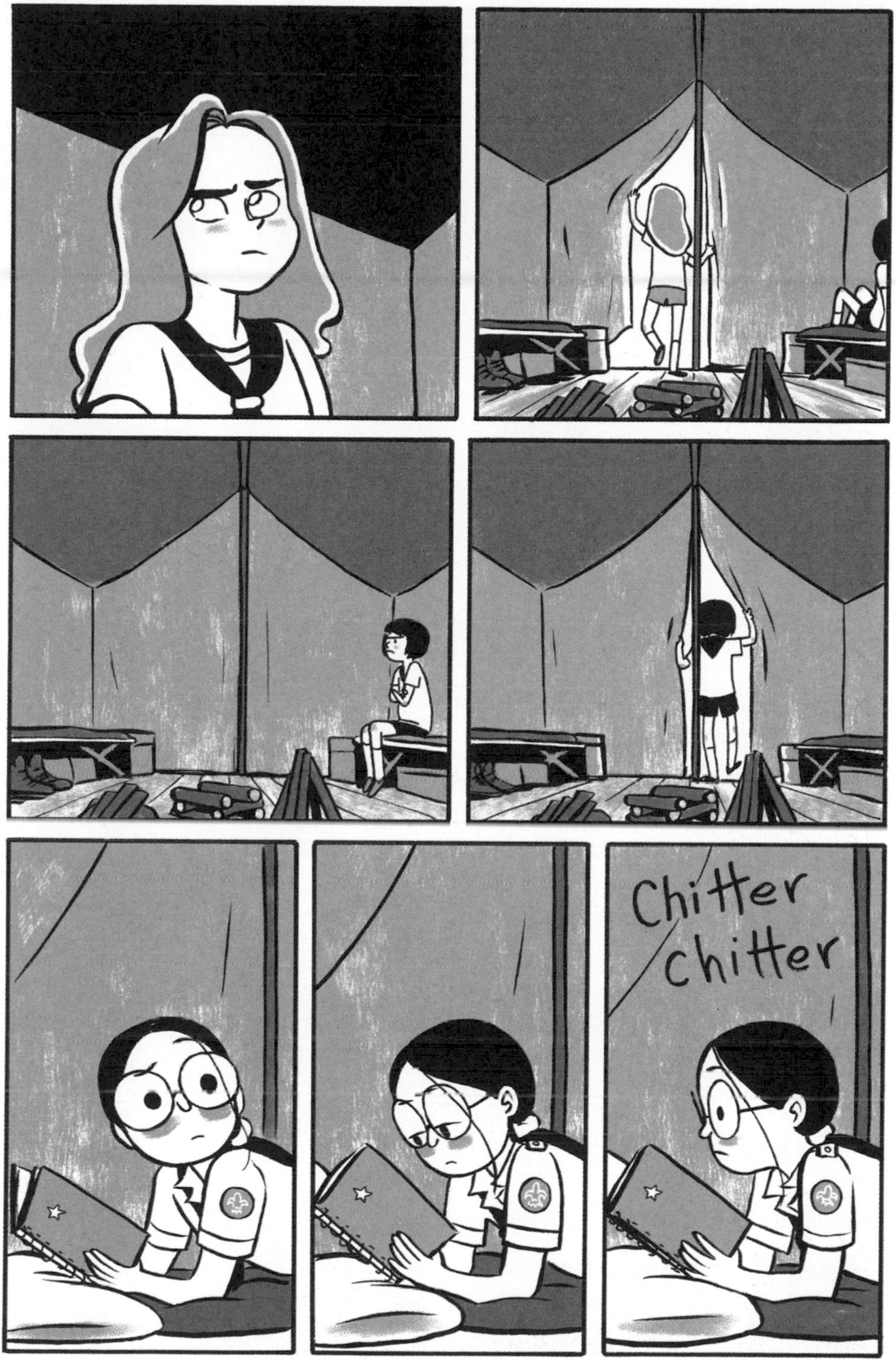
Chitter
Chitter

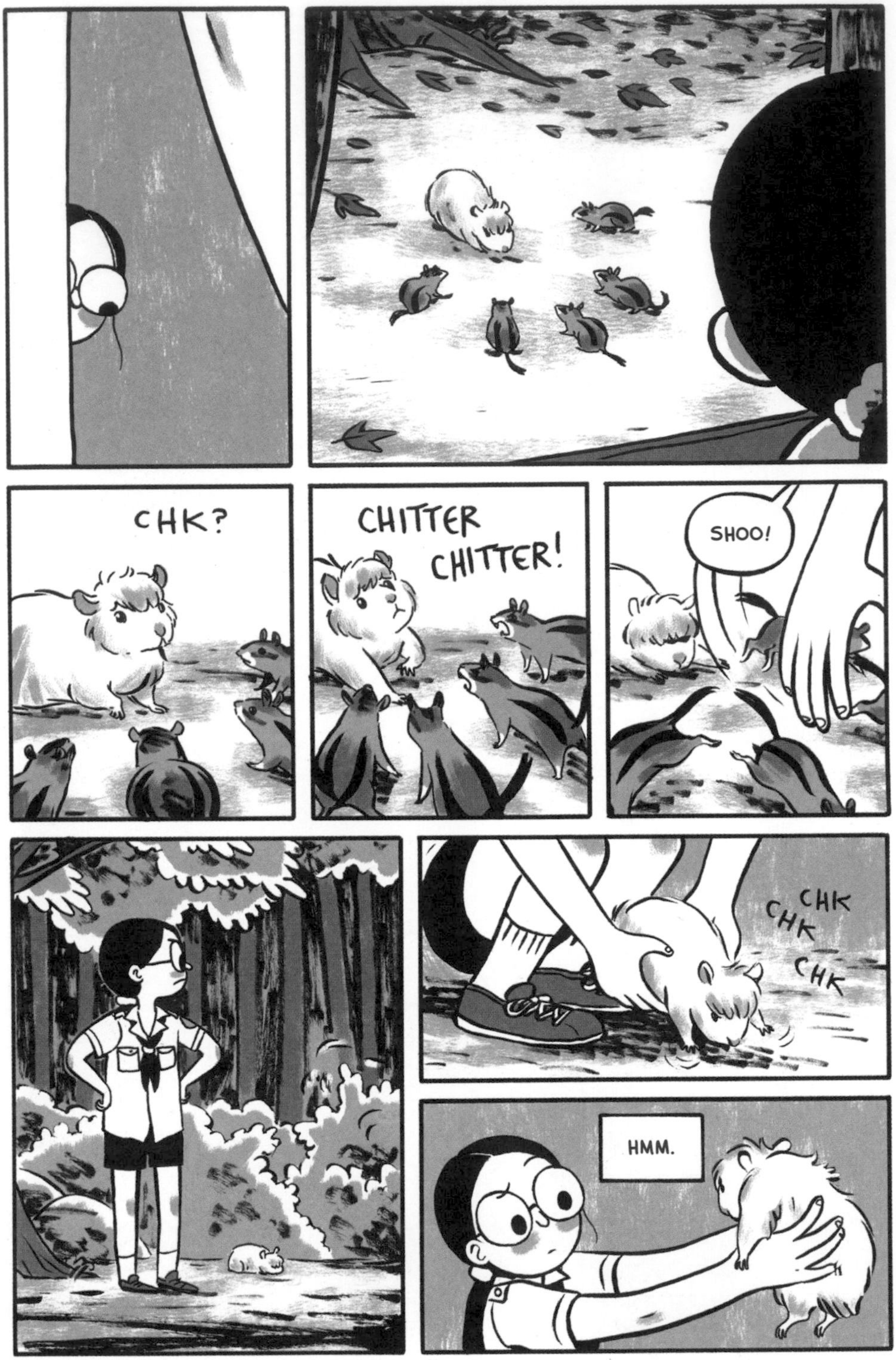
CHK?
CHITTER CHITTER!
SHOO!
CHK CHK CHK CHK
HMM.

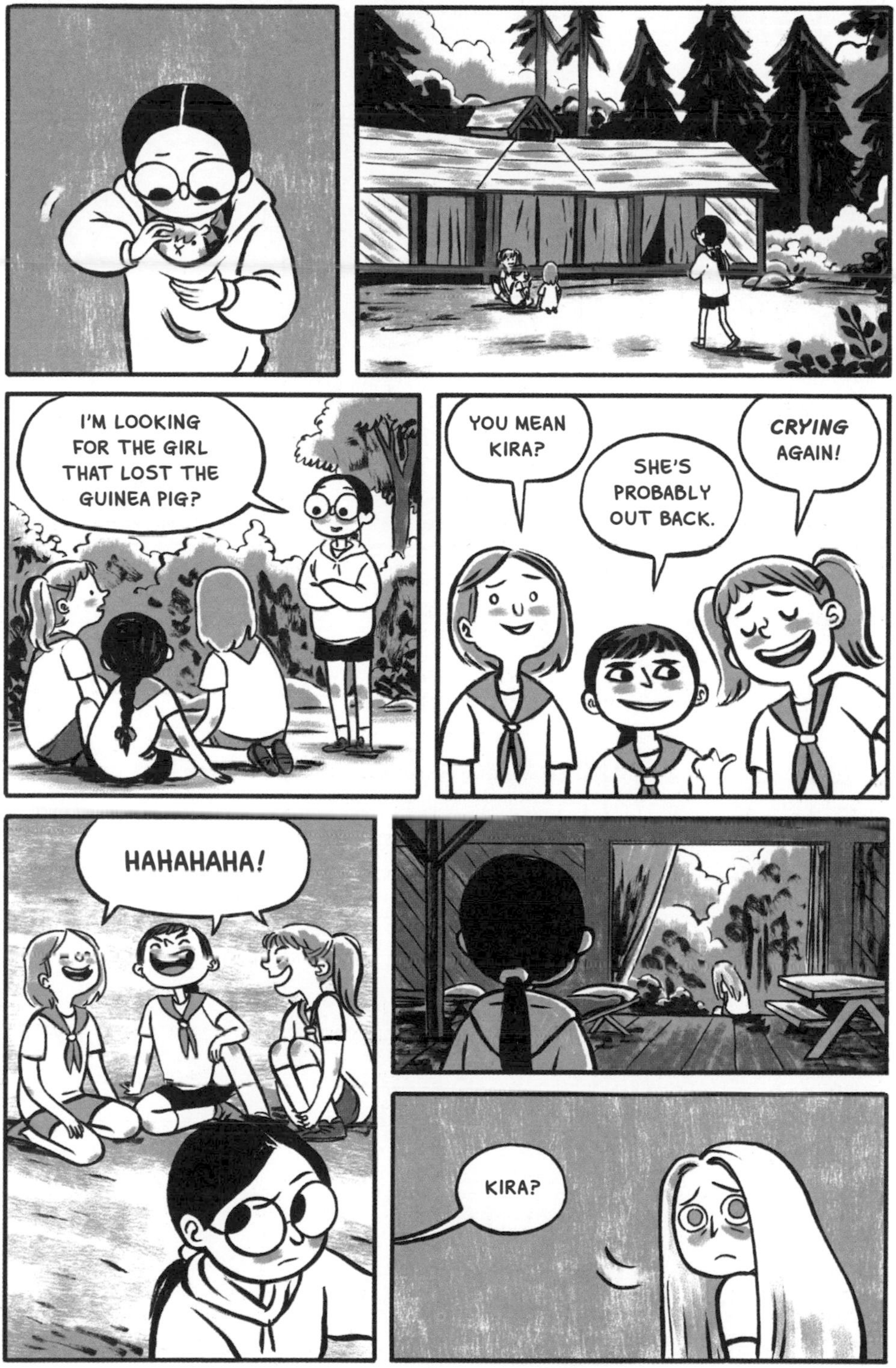
I'M LOOKING FOR THE GIRL THAT LOST THE GUINEA PIG?
YOU MEAN KIRA?
SHE'S PROBABLY OUT BACK.
CRYING AGAIN!
HAHAHAHA!
KIRA?

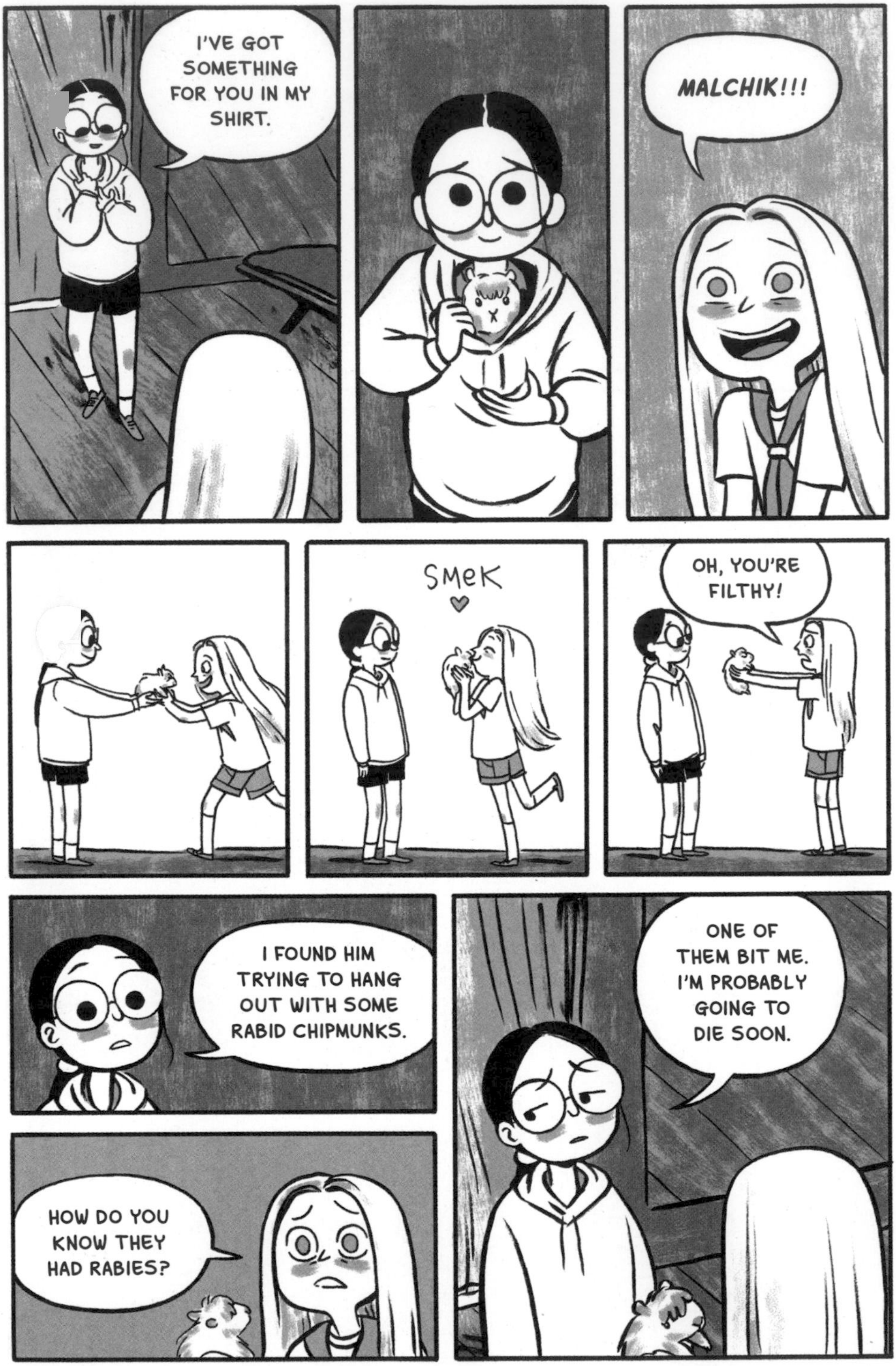
I'VE GOT SOMETHING FOR YOU IN MY SHIRT.
MALCHIK!!!
SMEK
OH, YOU'RE FILTHY!
I FOUND HIM TRYING TO HANG OUT WITH SOME RABID CHIPMUNKS.
HOW DO YOU KNOW THEY HAD RABIES?
ONE OF THEM BIT ME. I'M PROBABLY GOING TO DIE SOON.

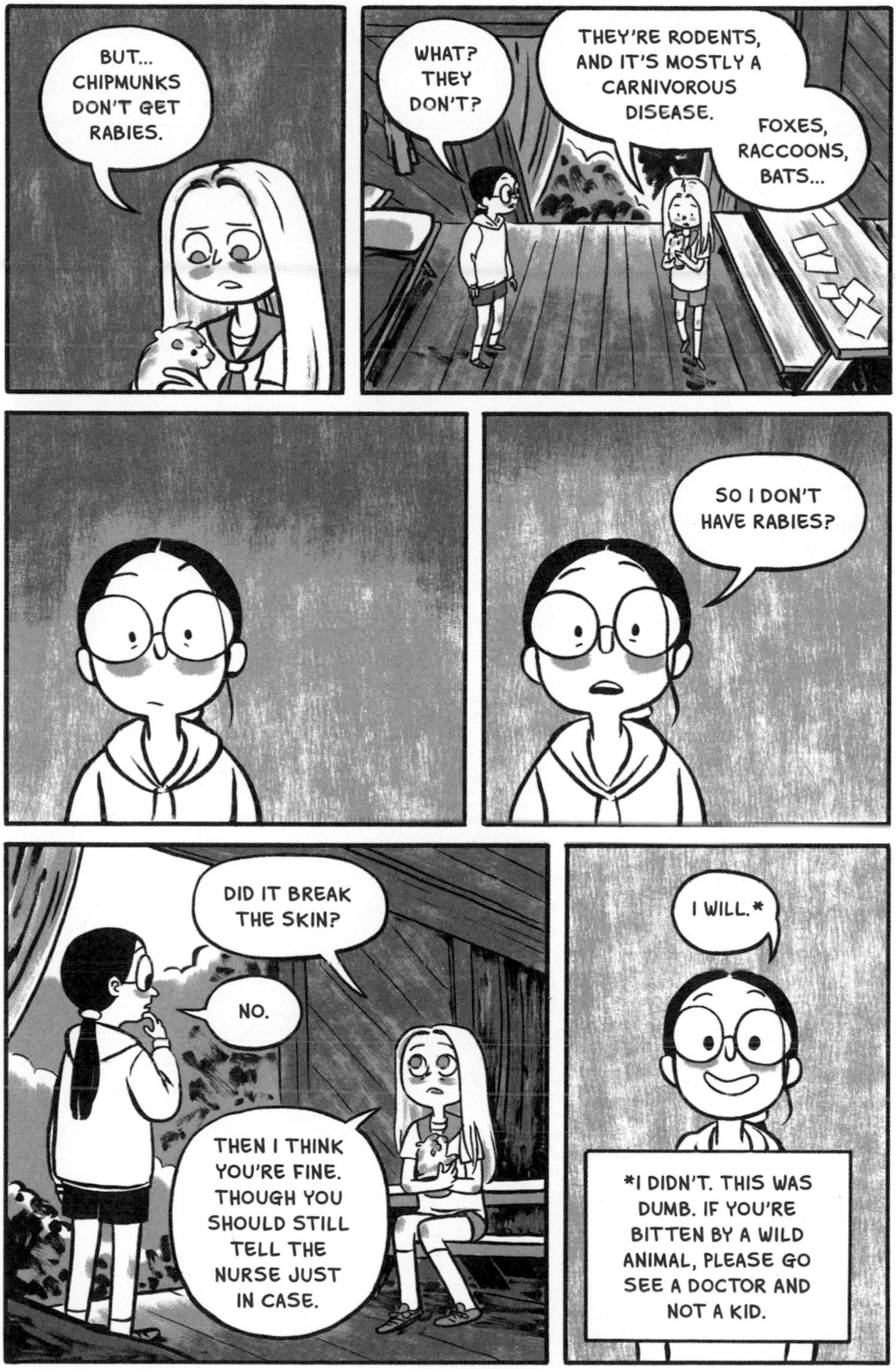
BUT... CHIPMUNKS DON'T GET RABIES.
WHAT? THEY DON'T?
THEY'RE RODENTS, AND IT'S MOSTLY A CARNIVOROUS DISEASE.
FOXES, RACCOONS, BATS...
SO I DON'T HAVE RABIES?
DID IT BREAK THE SKIN?
NO.
THEN I THINK YOU'RE FINE. THOUGH YOU SHOULD STILL TELL THE NURSE JUST IN CASE.
I WILL.*
*I DIDN'T. THIS WAS DUMB. IF YOU'RE BITTEN BY A WILD ANIMAL, PLEASE GO SEE A DOCTOR AND NOT A KID.

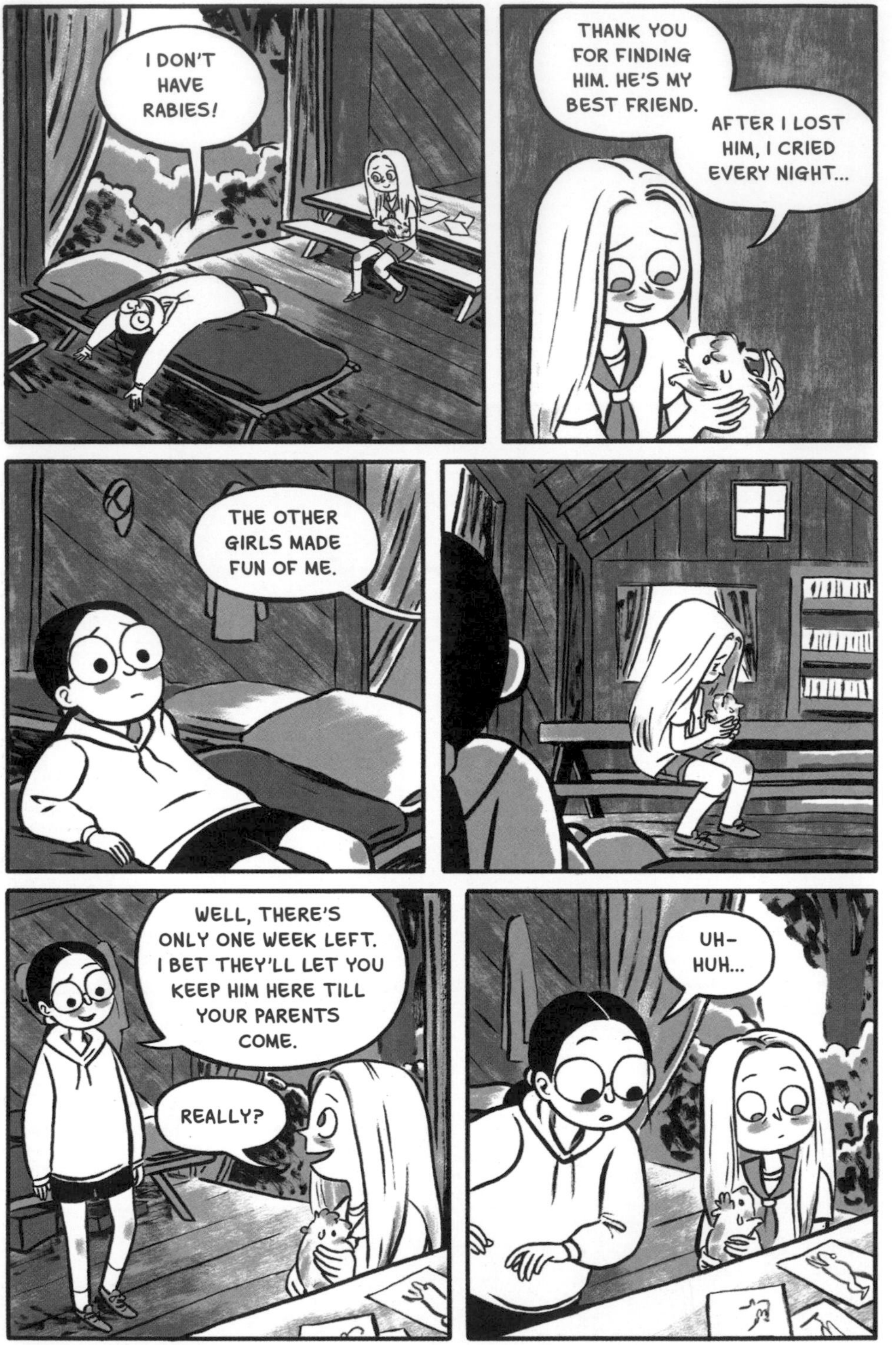
I DON'T HAVE RABIES!
THANK YOU FOR FINDING HIM. HE'S MY BEST FRIEND.
AFTER I LOST HIM, I CRIED EVERY NIGHT...
THE OTHER GIRLS MADE FUN OF ME.
WELL, THERE'S ONLY ONE WEEK LEFT. I BET THEY'LL LET YOU KEEP HIM HERE TILL YOUR PARENTS COME.
REALLY?
UH-HUH...

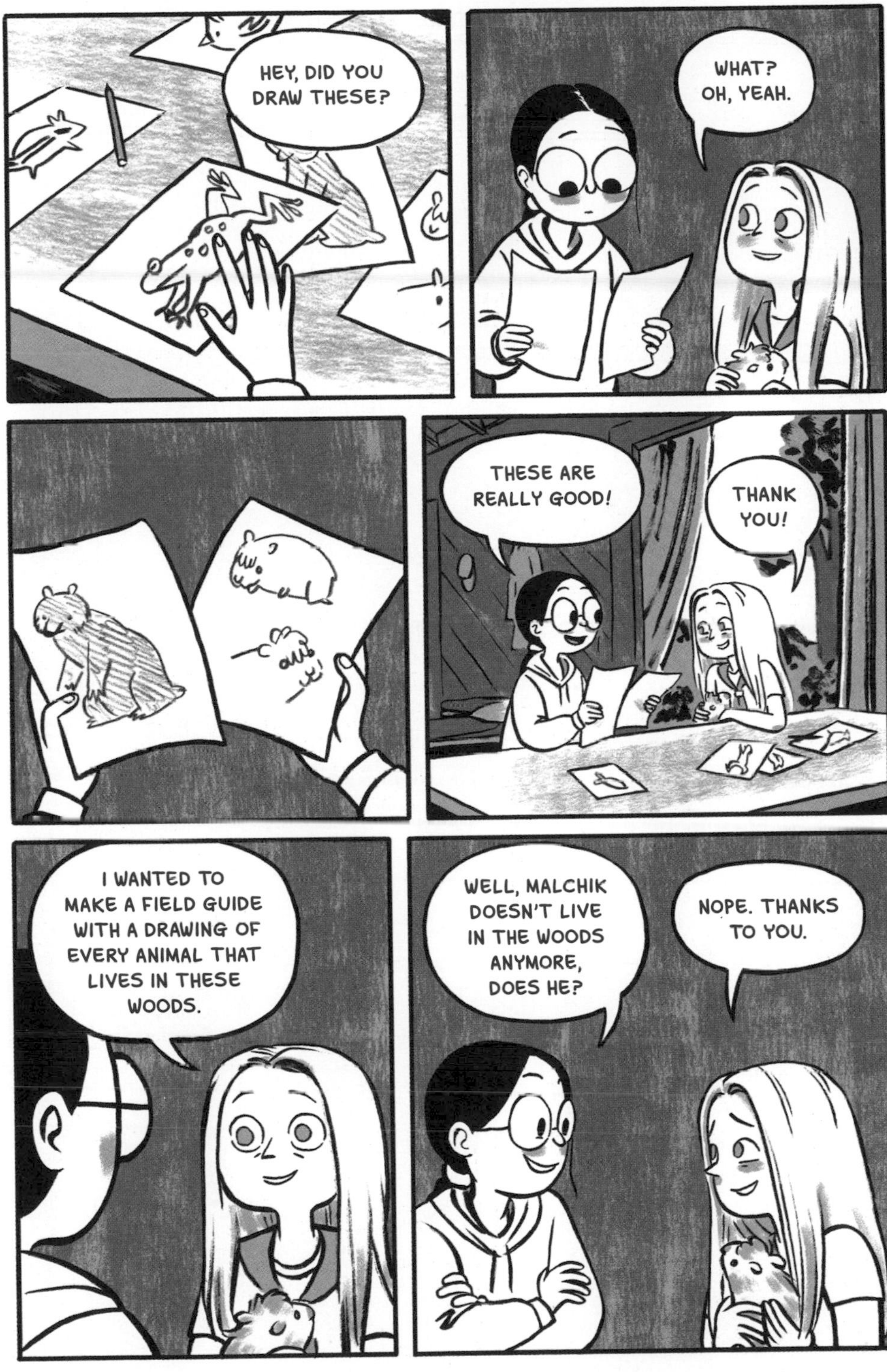
HEY, DID YOU DRAW THESE?
WHAT? OH, YEAH.
THESE ARE REALLY GOOD!
THANK YOU!
I WANTED TO MAKE A FIELD GUIDE WITH A DRAWING OF EVERY ANIMAL THAT LIVES IN THESE WOODS.
WELL, MALCHIK DOESN'T LIVE IN THE WOODS ANYMORE, DOES HE?
NOPE. THANKS TO YOU.

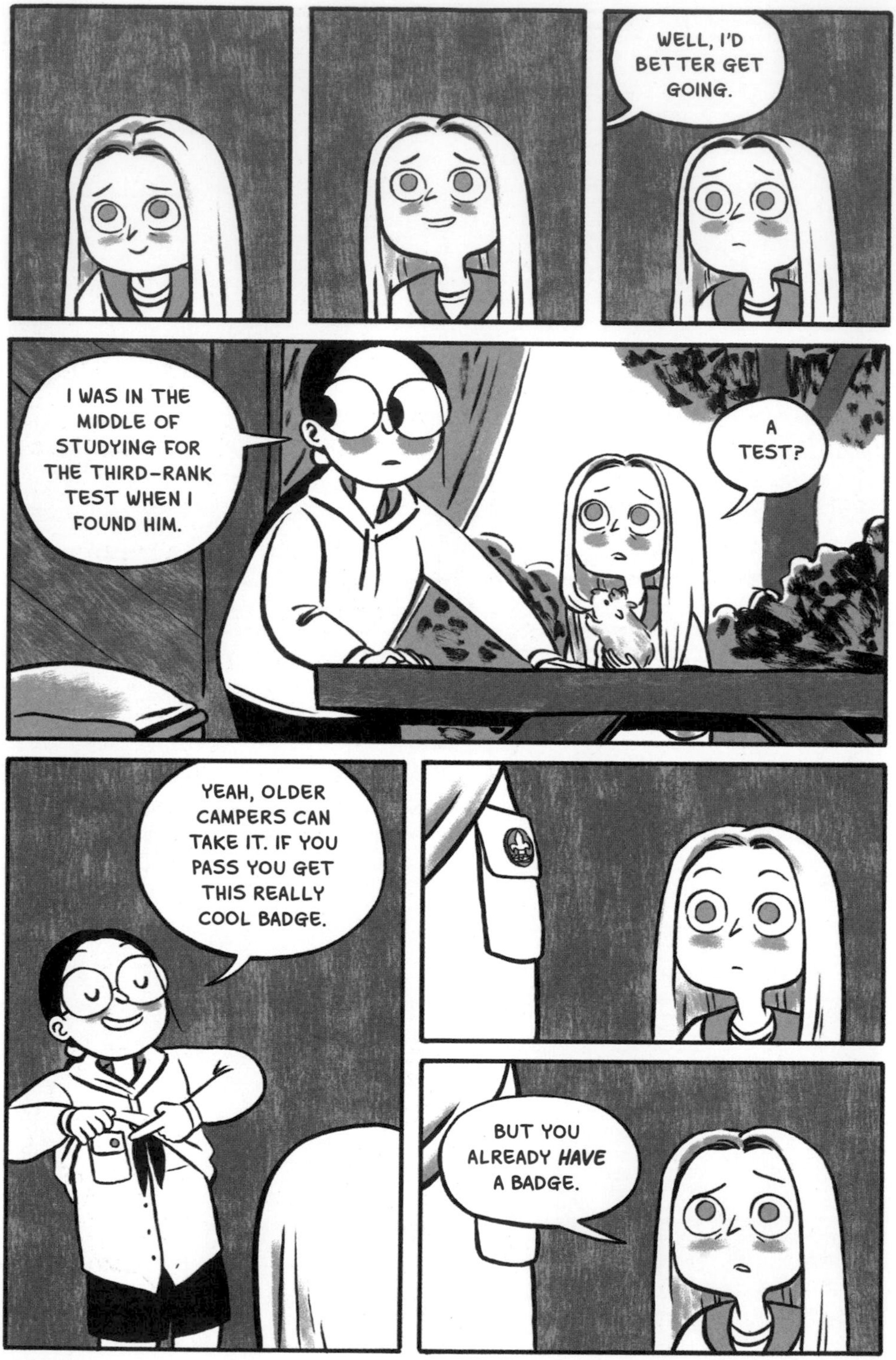
WELL, I'D BETTER GET GOING.
I WAS IN THE MIDDLE OF STUDYING FOR THE THIRD-RANK TEST WHEN I FOUND HIM.
A TEST?
YEAH, OLDER CAMPERS CAN TAKE IT. IF YOU PASS YOU GET THIS REALLY COOL BADGE.
BUT YOU ALREADY *HAVE* A BADGE.

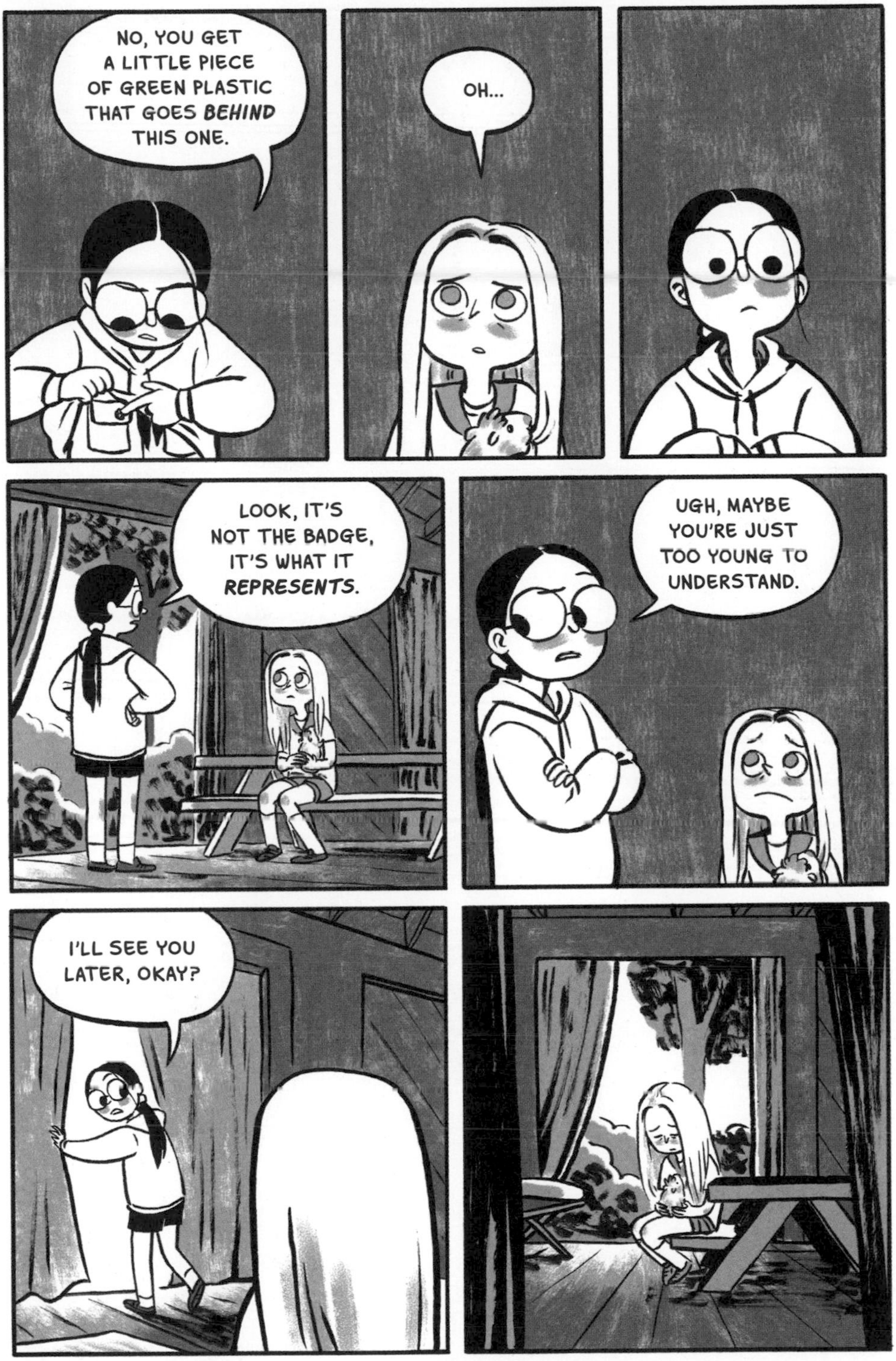
NO, YOU GET A LITTLE PIECE OF GREEN PLASTIC THAT GOES BEHIND THIS ONE.
OH...
LOOK, IT'S NOT THE BADGE, IT'S WHAT IT REPRESENTS.
UGH, MAYBE YOU'RE JUST TOO YOUNG TO UNDERSTAND.
I'LL SEE YOU LATER, OKAY?

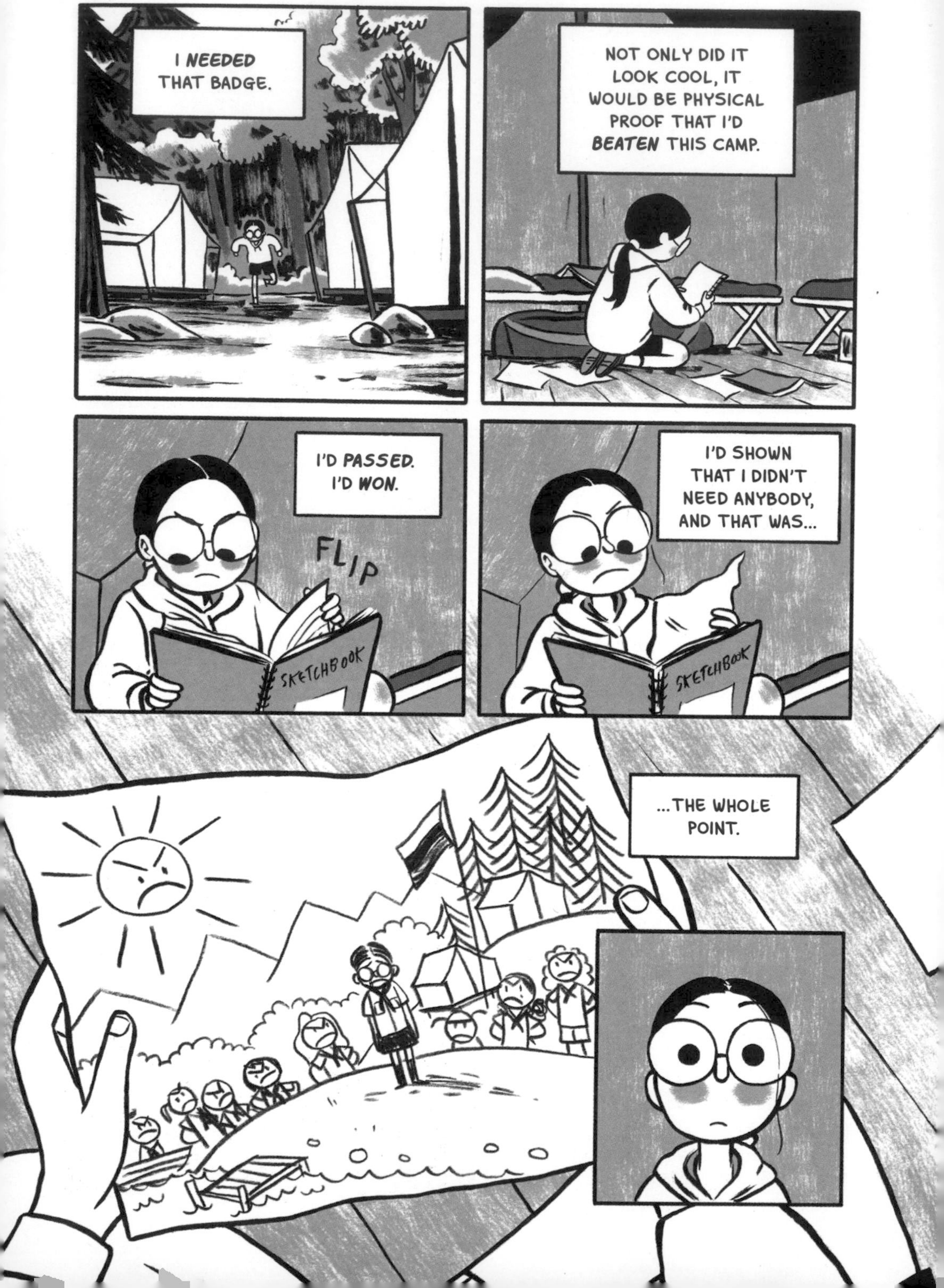
I NEEDED THAT BADGE.
NOT ONLY DID IT LOOK COOL, IT WOULD BE PHYSICAL PROOF THAT I'D BEATEN THIS CAMP.
I'D PASSED. I'D WON.
FLIP
SKETCHBOOK
I'D SHOWN THAT I DIDN'T NEED ANYBODY, AND THAT WAS...
SKETCHBOOK
...THE WHOLE POINT.

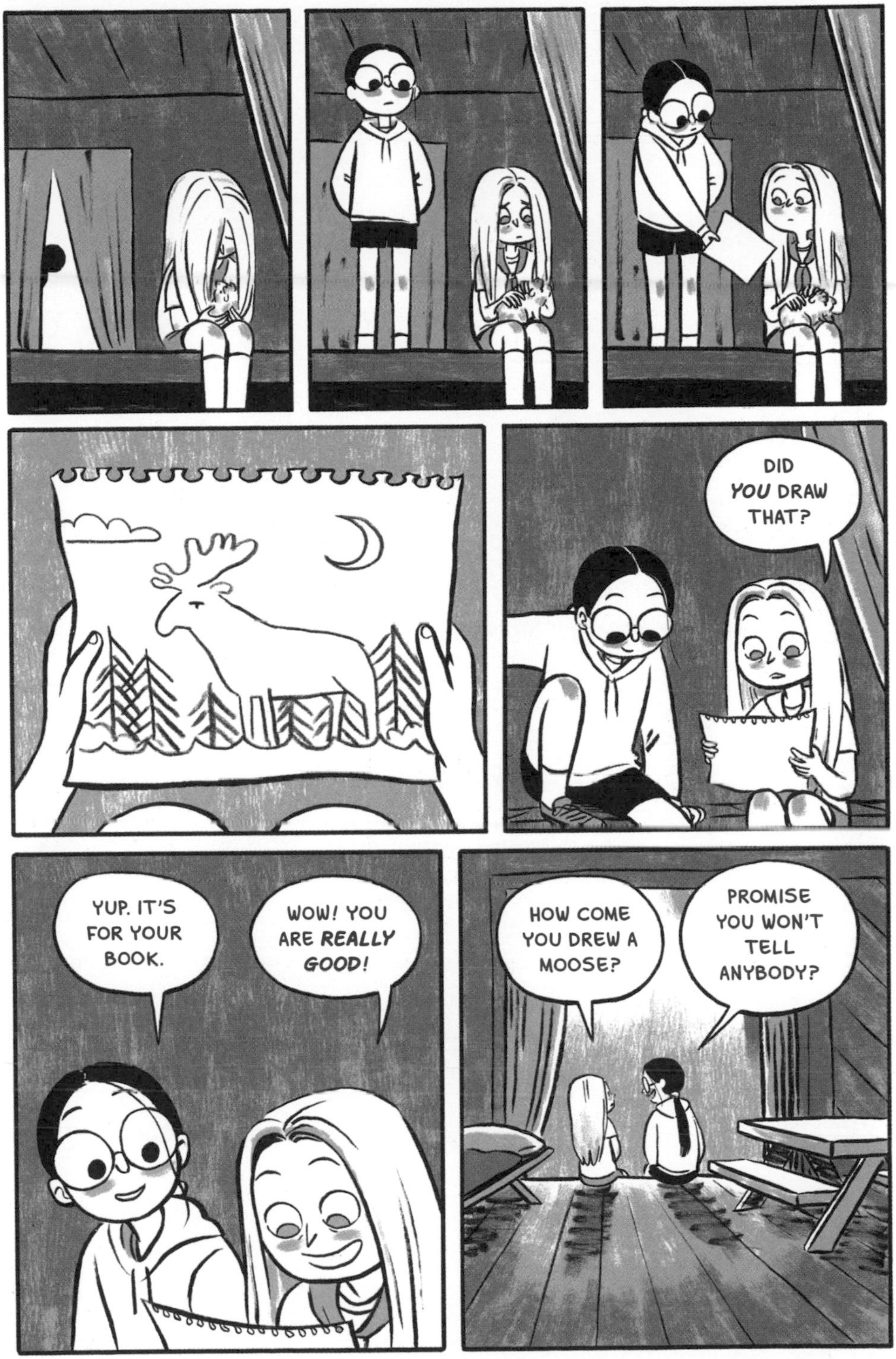
DID *YOU* DRAW THAT?
YUP. IT'S FOR YOUR BOOK.
WOW! YOU ARE ***REALLY GOOD!***
HOW COME YOU DREW A MOOSE?
PROMISE YOU WON'T TELL ANYBODY?

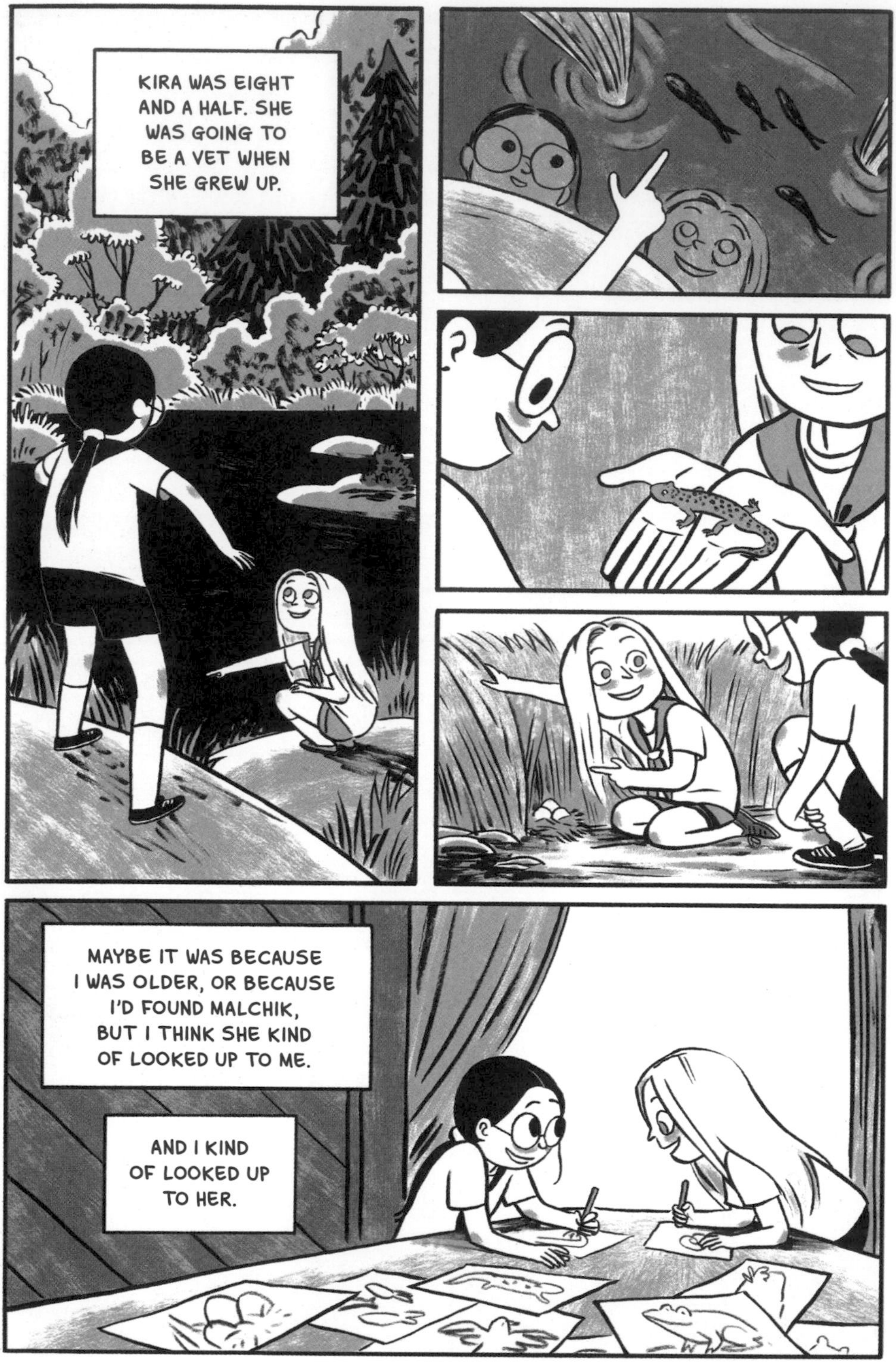
KIRA WAS EIGHT AND A HALF. SHE WAS GOING TO BE A VET WHEN SHE GREW UP.
MAYBE IT WAS BECAUSE I WAS OLDER, OR BECAUSE I'D FOUND MALCHIK, BUT I THINK SHE KIND OF LOOKED UP TO ME.
AND I KIND OF LOOKED UP TO HER.

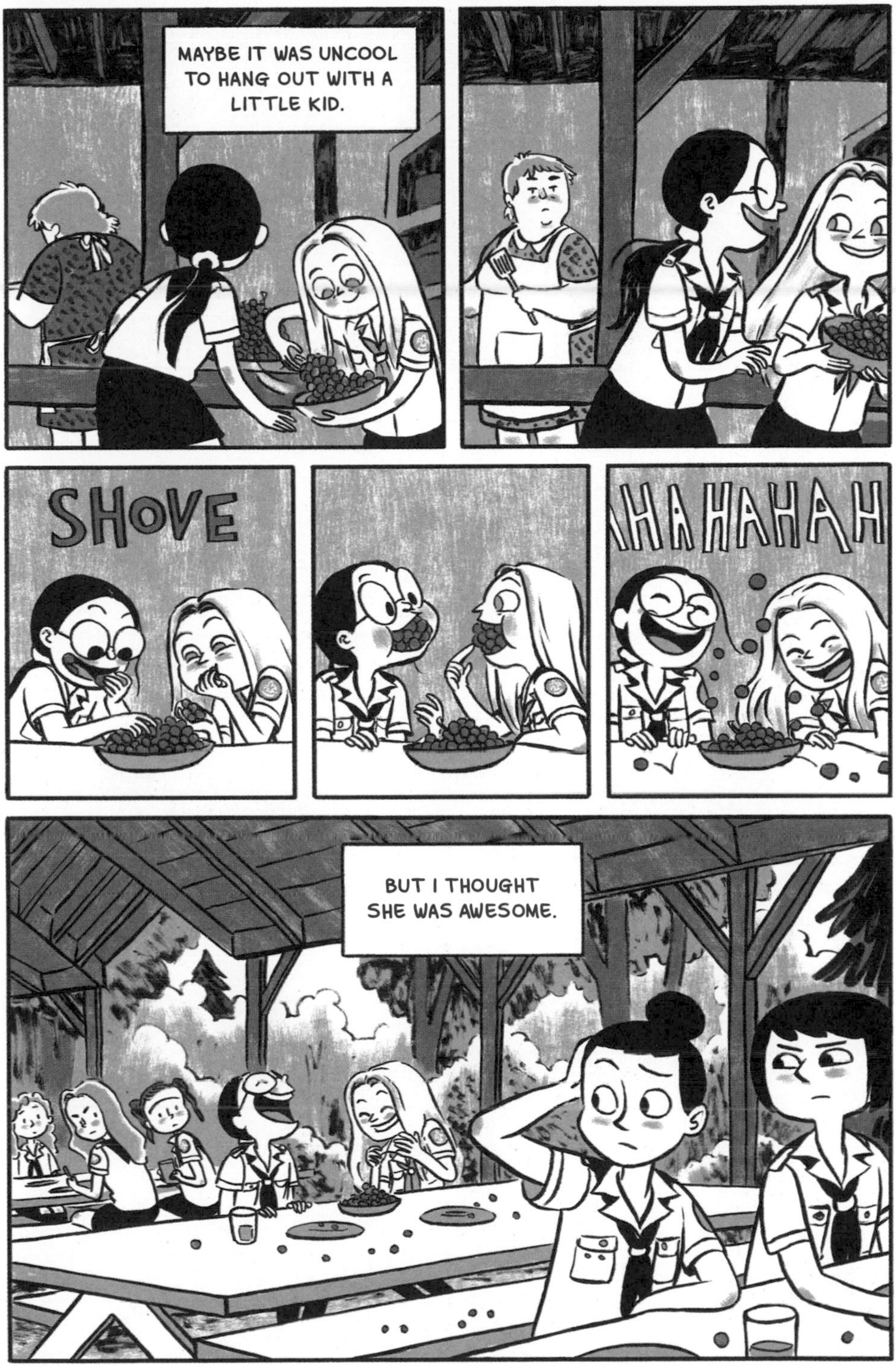
MAYBE IT WAS UNCOOL TO HANG OUT WITH A LITTLE KID.
SHOVE
HAHAHAH
BUT I THOUGHT SHE WAS AWESOME.

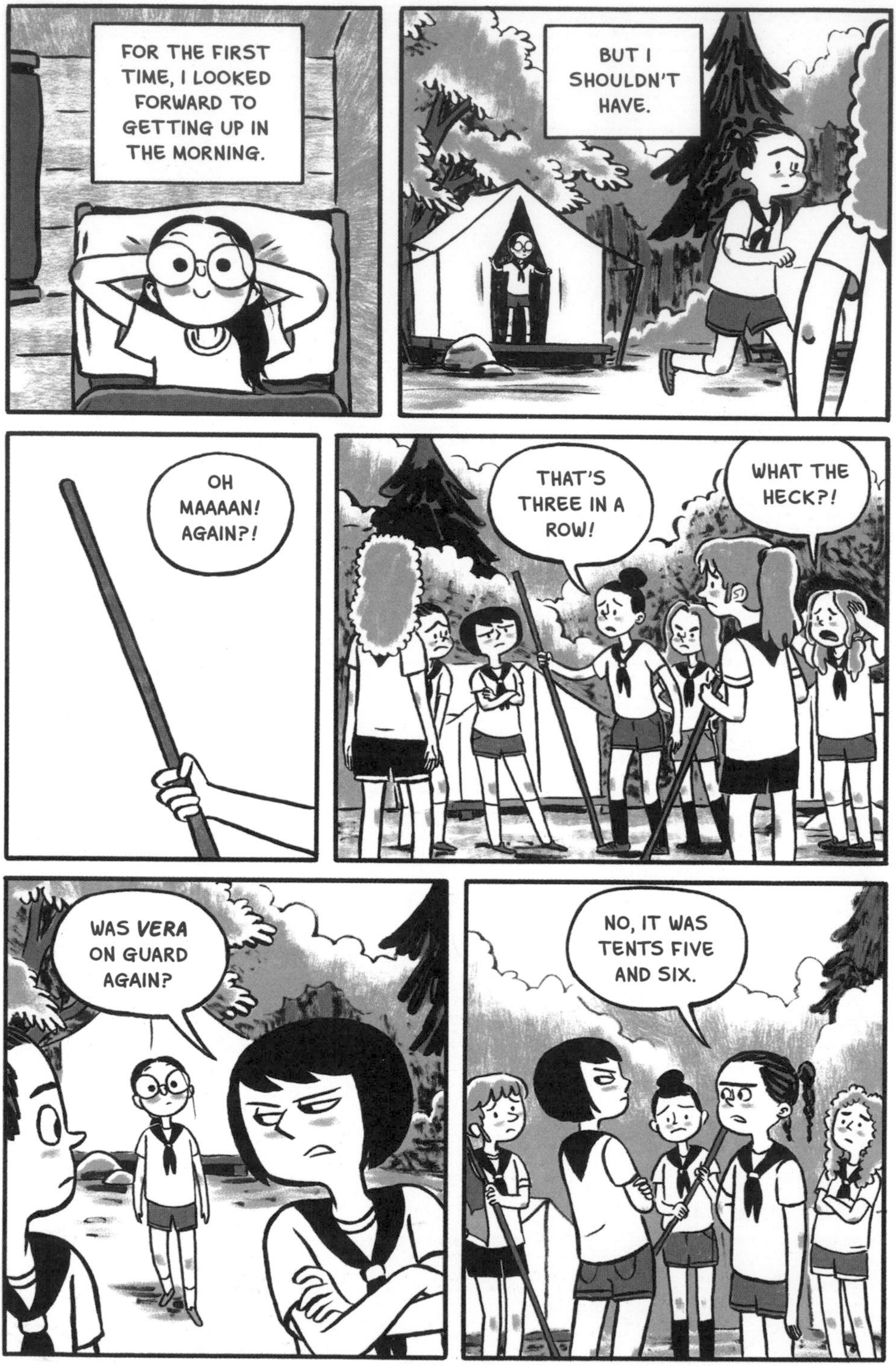
FOR THE FIRST TIME, I LOOKED FORWARD TO GETTING UP IN THE MORNING.
BUT I SHOULDN'T HAVE.
OH MAAAAN! AGAIN?!
THAT'S THREE IN A ROW!
WHAT THE HECK?!
WAS *VERA* ON GUARD AGAIN?
NO, IT WAS TENTS FIVE AND SIX.

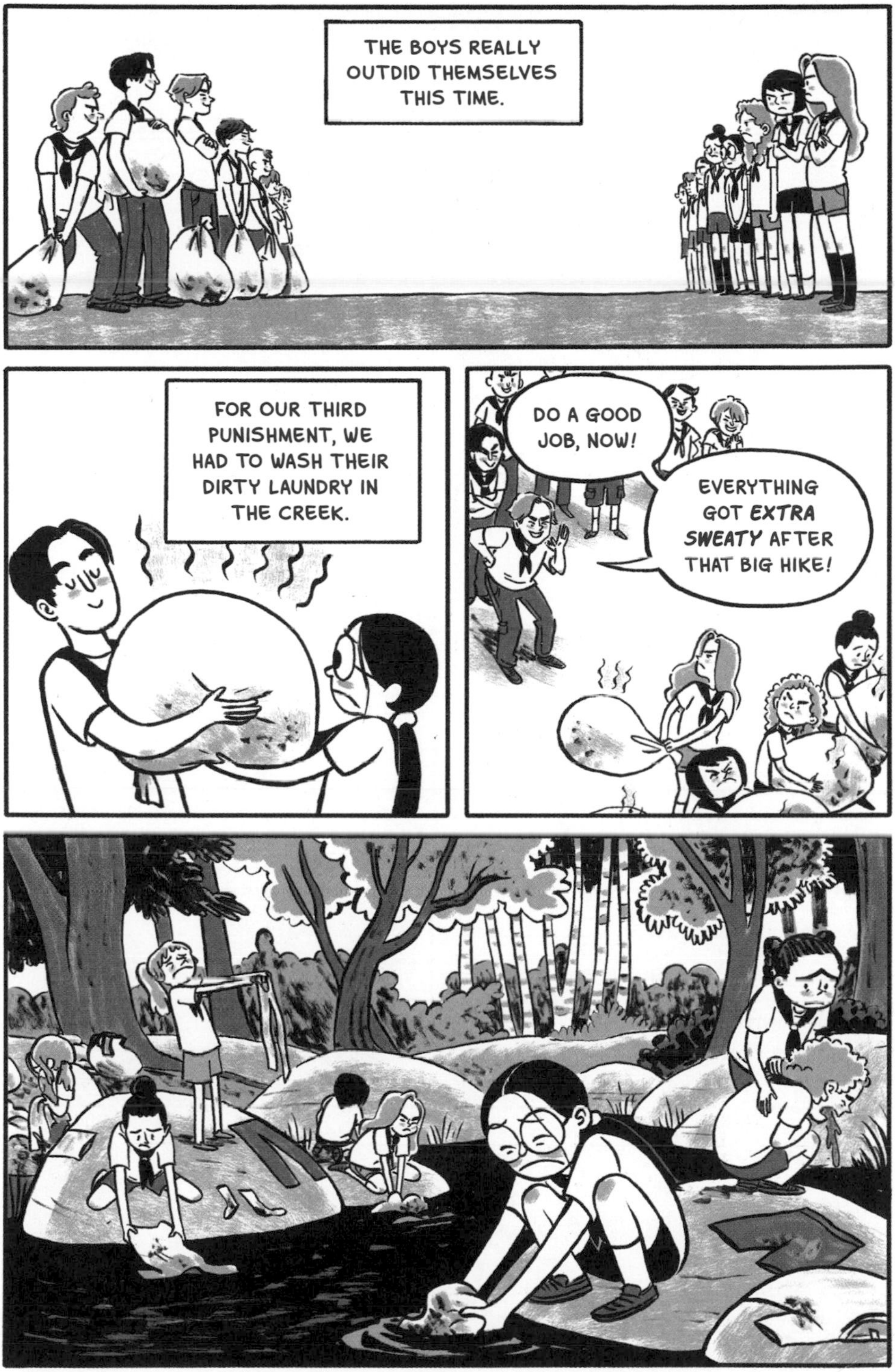
THE BOYS REALLY OUTDID THEMSELVES THIS TIME.
FOR OUR THIRD PUNISHMENT, WE HAD TO WASH THEIR DIRTY LAUNDRY IN THE CREEK.
DO A GOOD JOB, NOW!
EVERYTHING GOT **EXTRA SWEATY** AFTER THAT BIG HIKE!

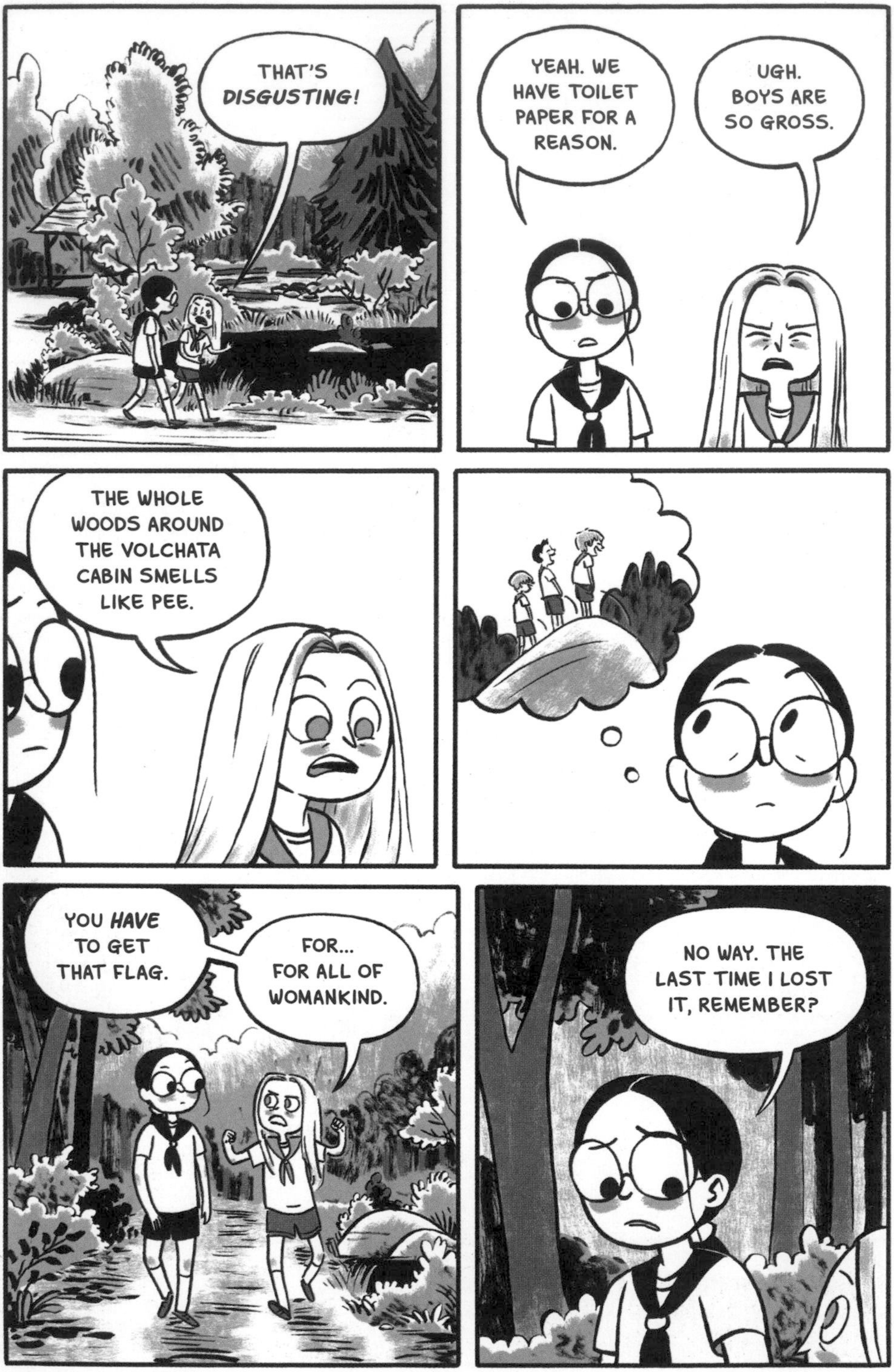
THAT'S *DISGUSTING*!
YEAH. WE HAVE TOILET PAPER FOR A REASON.
UGH. BOYS ARE SO GROSS.
THE WHOLE WOODS AROUND THE VOLCHATA CABIN SMELLS LIKE PEE.
YOU *HAVE* TO GET THAT FLAG.
FOR... FOR ALL OF WOMANKIND.
NO WAY. THE LAST TIME I LOST IT, REMEMBER?

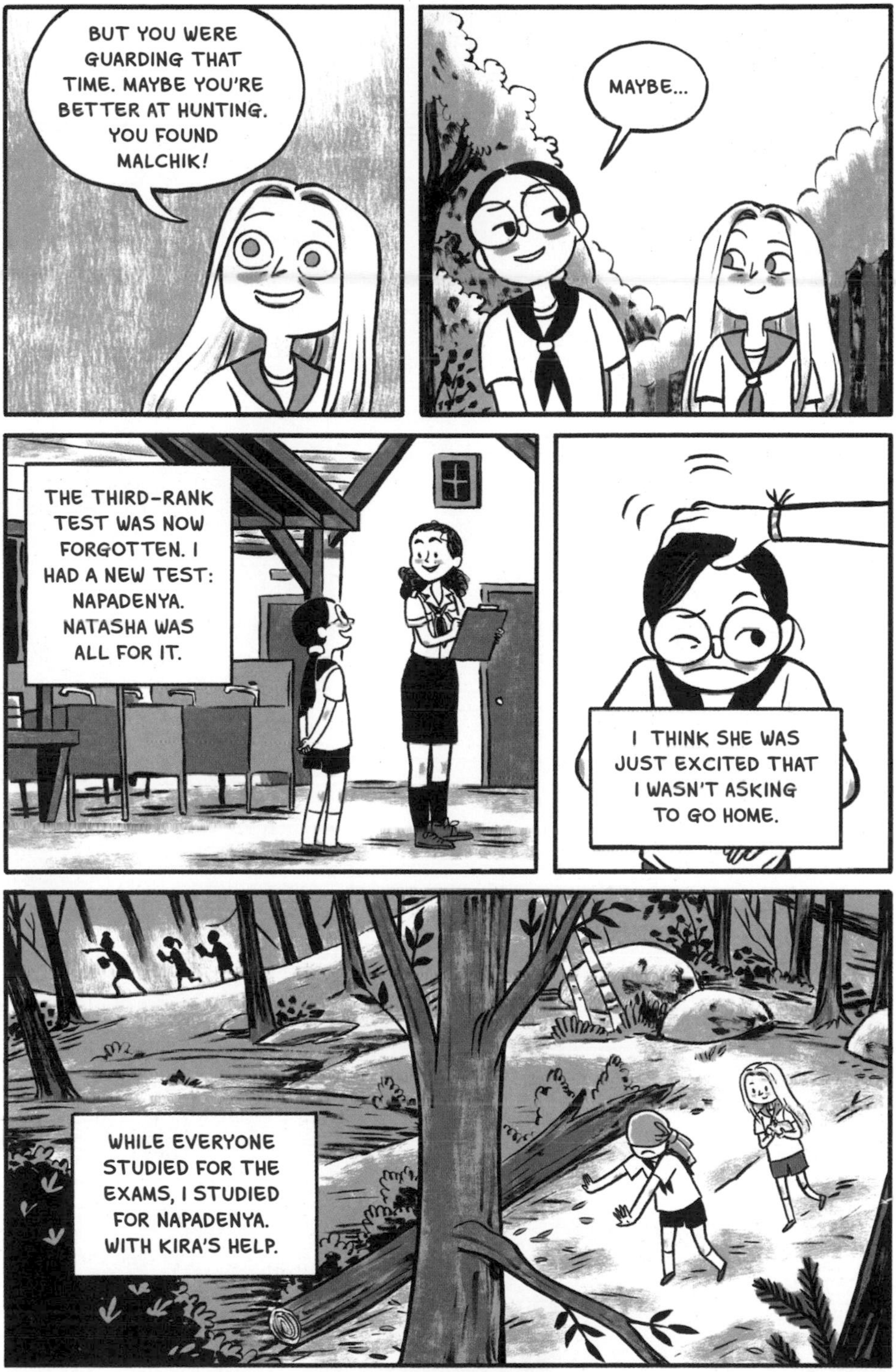
BUT YOU WERE GUARDING THAT TIME. MAYBE YOU'RE BETTER AT HUNTING. YOU FOUND MALCHIK!
MAYBE...
THE THIRD-RANK TEST WAS NOW FORGOTTEN. I HAD A NEW TEST: NAPADENYA. NATASHA WAS ALL FOR IT.
I THINK SHE WAS JUST EXCITED THAT I WASN'T ASKING TO GO HOME.
WHILE EVERYONE STUDIED FOR THE EXAMS, I STUDIED FOR NAPADENYA. WITH KIRA'S HELP.

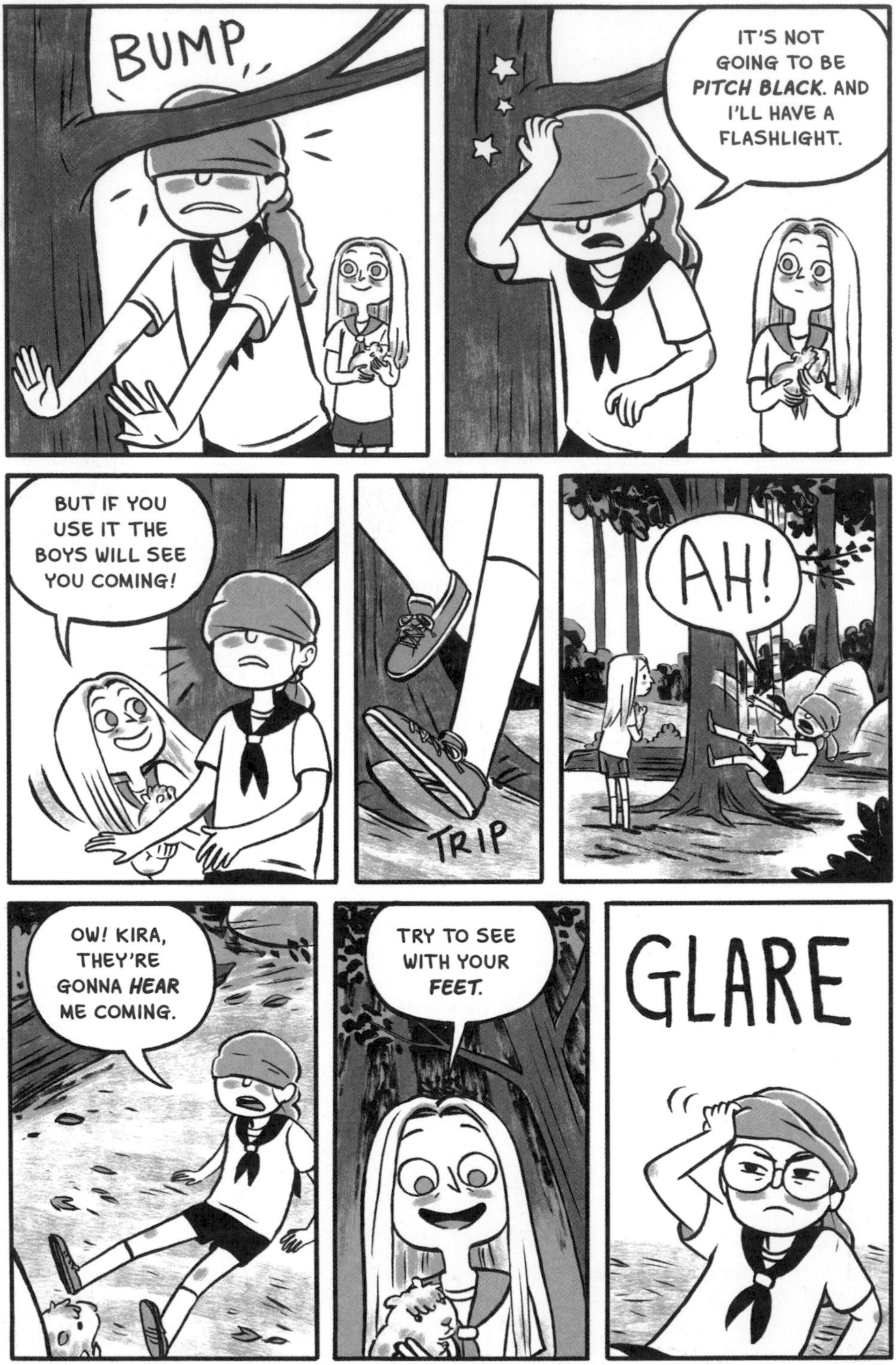
BUMP
IT'S NOT GOING TO BE PITCH BLACK. AND I'LL HAVE A FLASHLIGHT.
BUT IF YOU USE IT THE BOYS WILL SEE YOU COMING!
TRIP
AH!
OW! KIRA, THEY'RE GONNA HEAR ME COMING.
TRY TO SEE WITH YOUR FEET.
GLARE

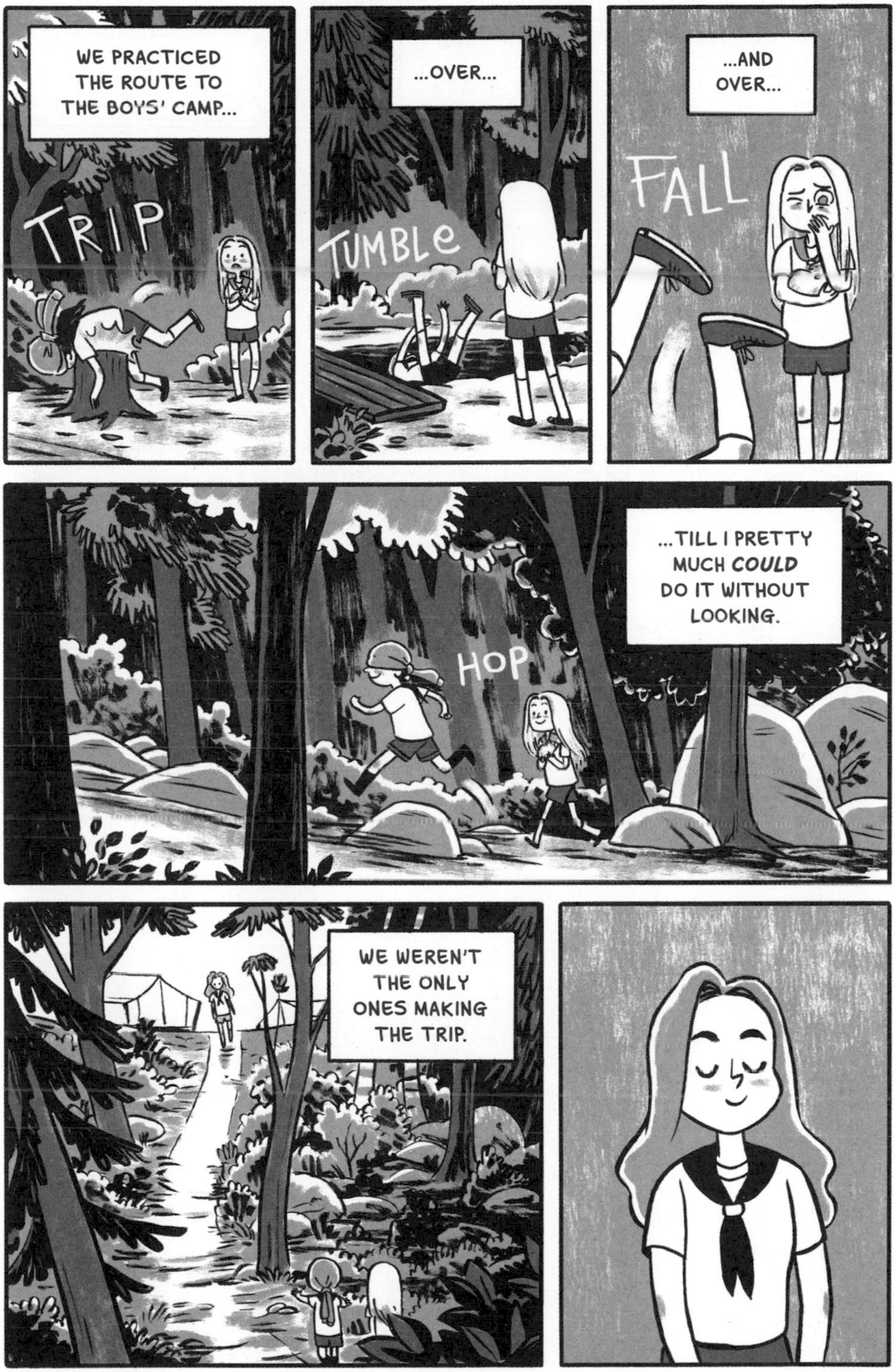
WE PRACTICED THE ROUTE TO THE BOYS' CAMP...
TRIP
...OVER...
TUMBLE
...AND OVER...
FALL
...TILL I PRETTY MUCH COULD DO IT WITHOUT LOOKING.
HOP
WE WEREN'T THE ONLY ONES MAKING THE TRIP.

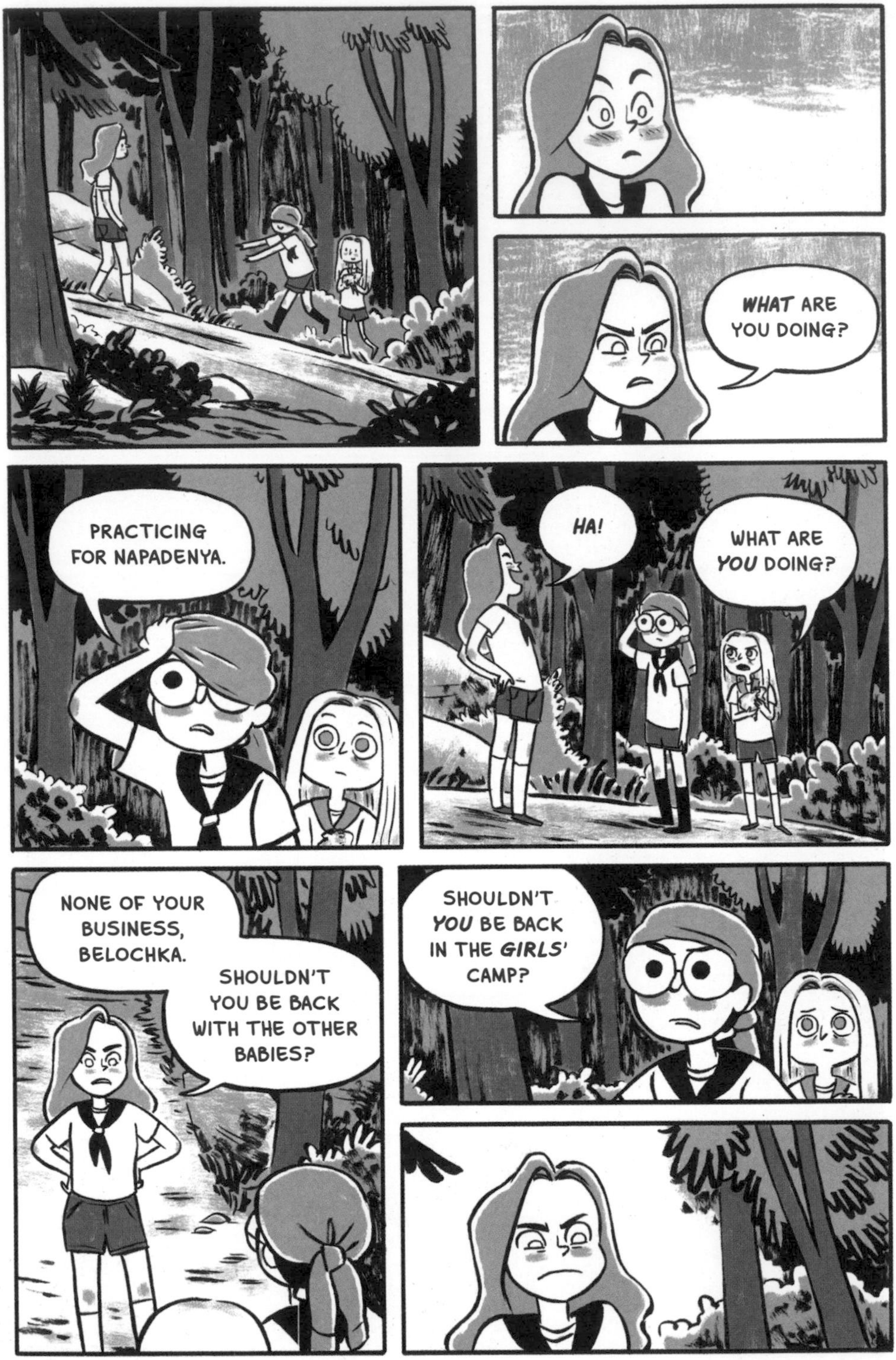
WHAT ARE YOU DOING?
PRACTICING FOR NAPADENYA.
HA!
WHAT ARE YOU DOING?
NONE OF YOUR BUSINESS, BELOCHKA.
SHOULDN'T YOU BE BACK WITH THE OTHER BABIES?
SHOULDN'T YOU BE BACK IN THE GIRLS' CAMP?

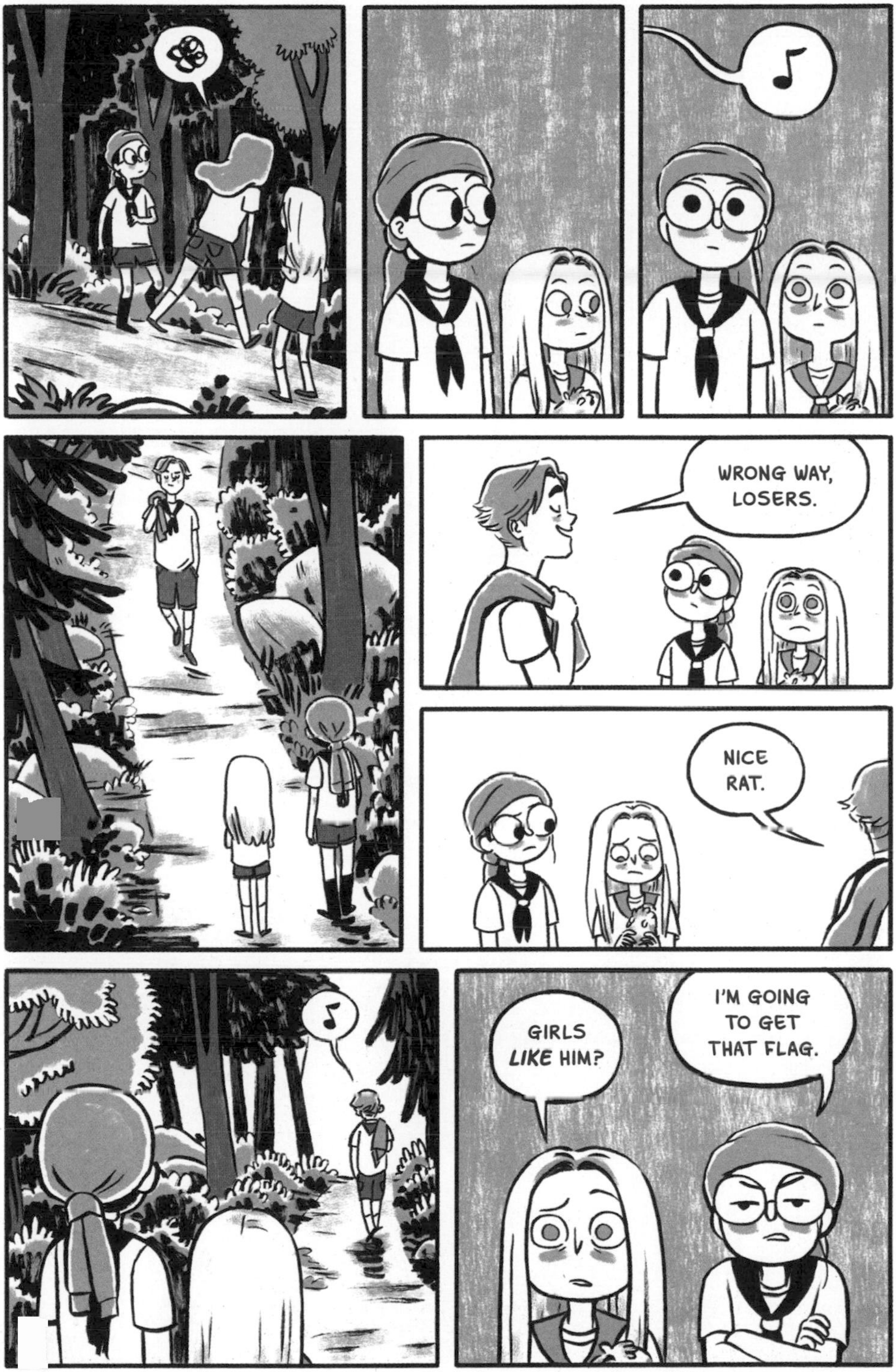
WRONG WAY, LOSERS.
NICE RAT.
GIRLS *LIKE* HIM?
I'M GOING TO GET THAT FLAG.

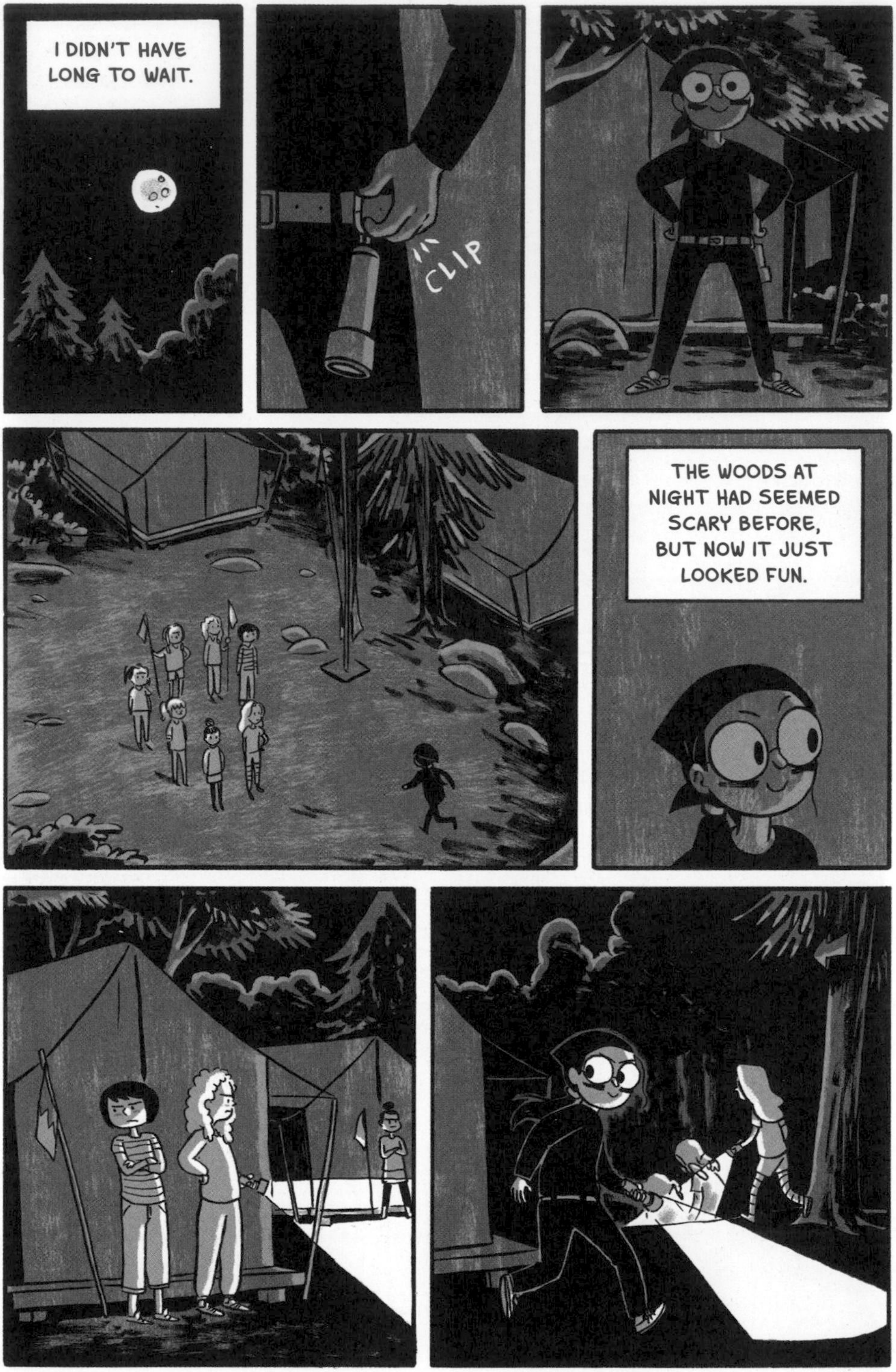
I DIDN'T HAVE LONG TO WAIT.
CLIP
THE WOODS AT NIGHT HAD SEEMED SCARY BEFORE, BUT NOW IT JUST LOOKED FUN.

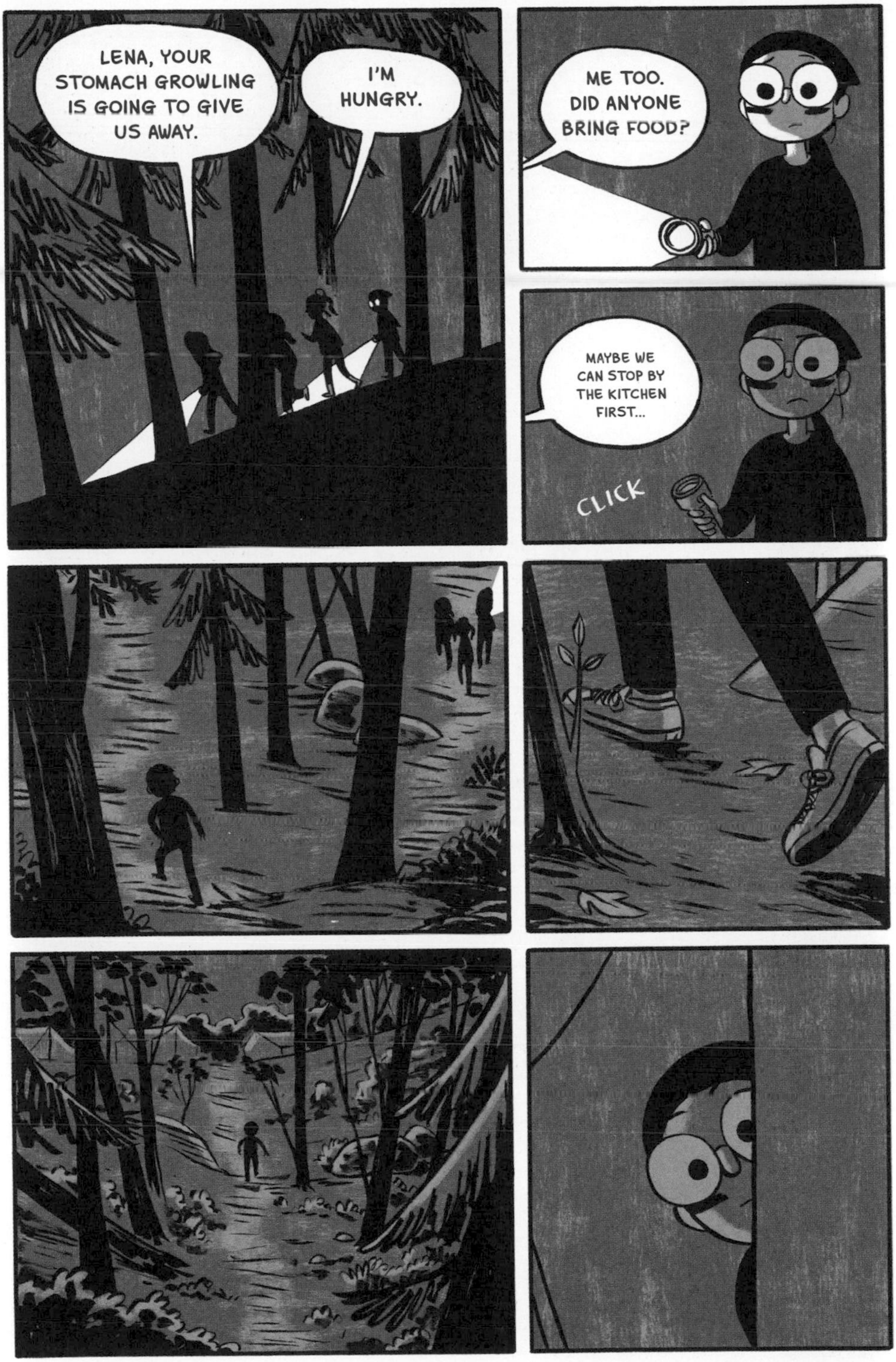
LENA, YOUR STOMACH GROWLING IS GOING TO GIVE US AWAY.
I'M HUNGRY.
ME TOO. DID ANYONE BRING FOOD?
MAYBE WE CAN STOP BY THE KITCHEN FIRST...
CLICK

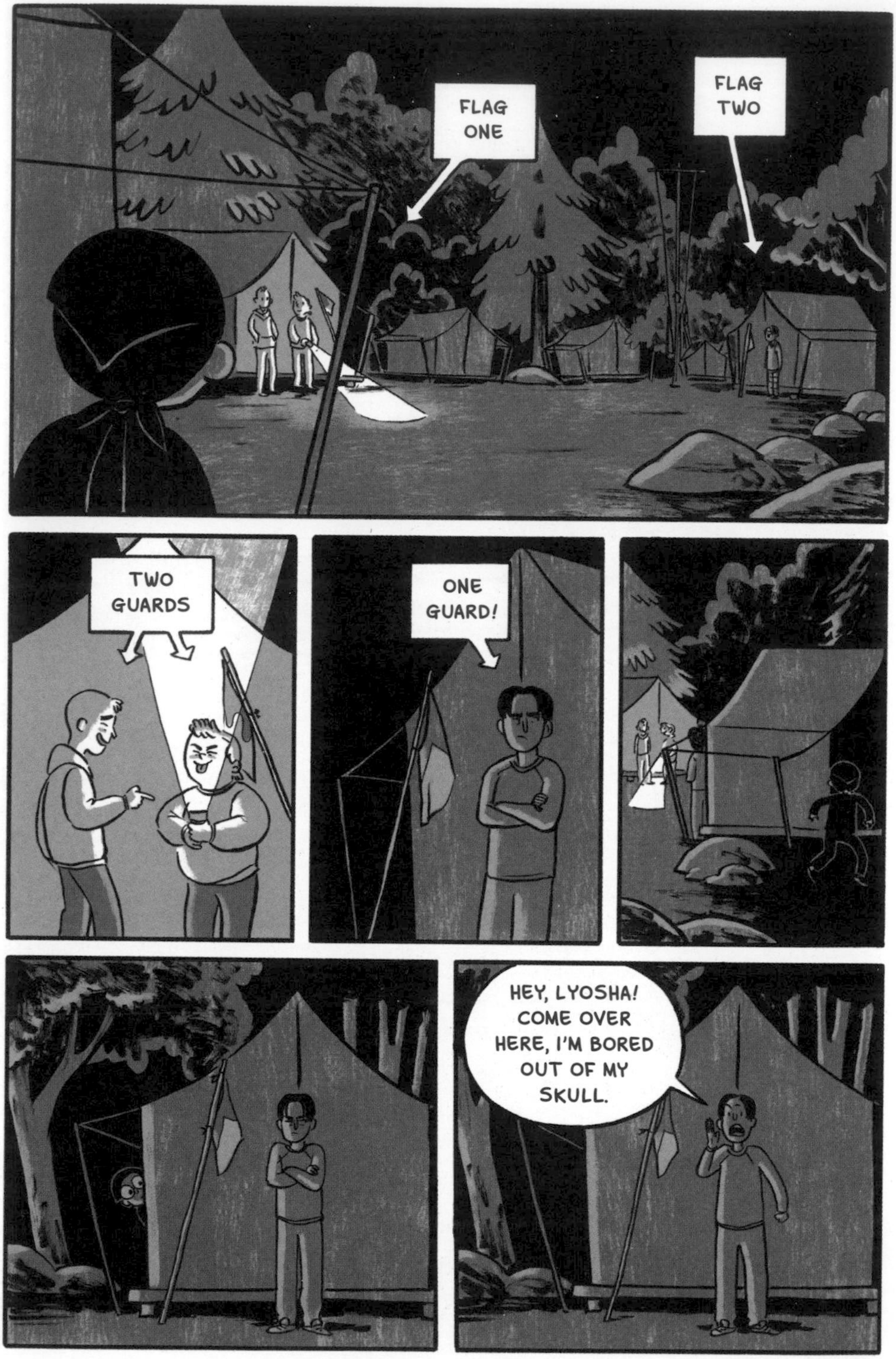
FLAG ONE
FLAG TWO
TWO GUARDS
ONE GUARD!
HEY, LYOSHA! COME OVER HERE, I'M BORED OUT OF MY SKULL.

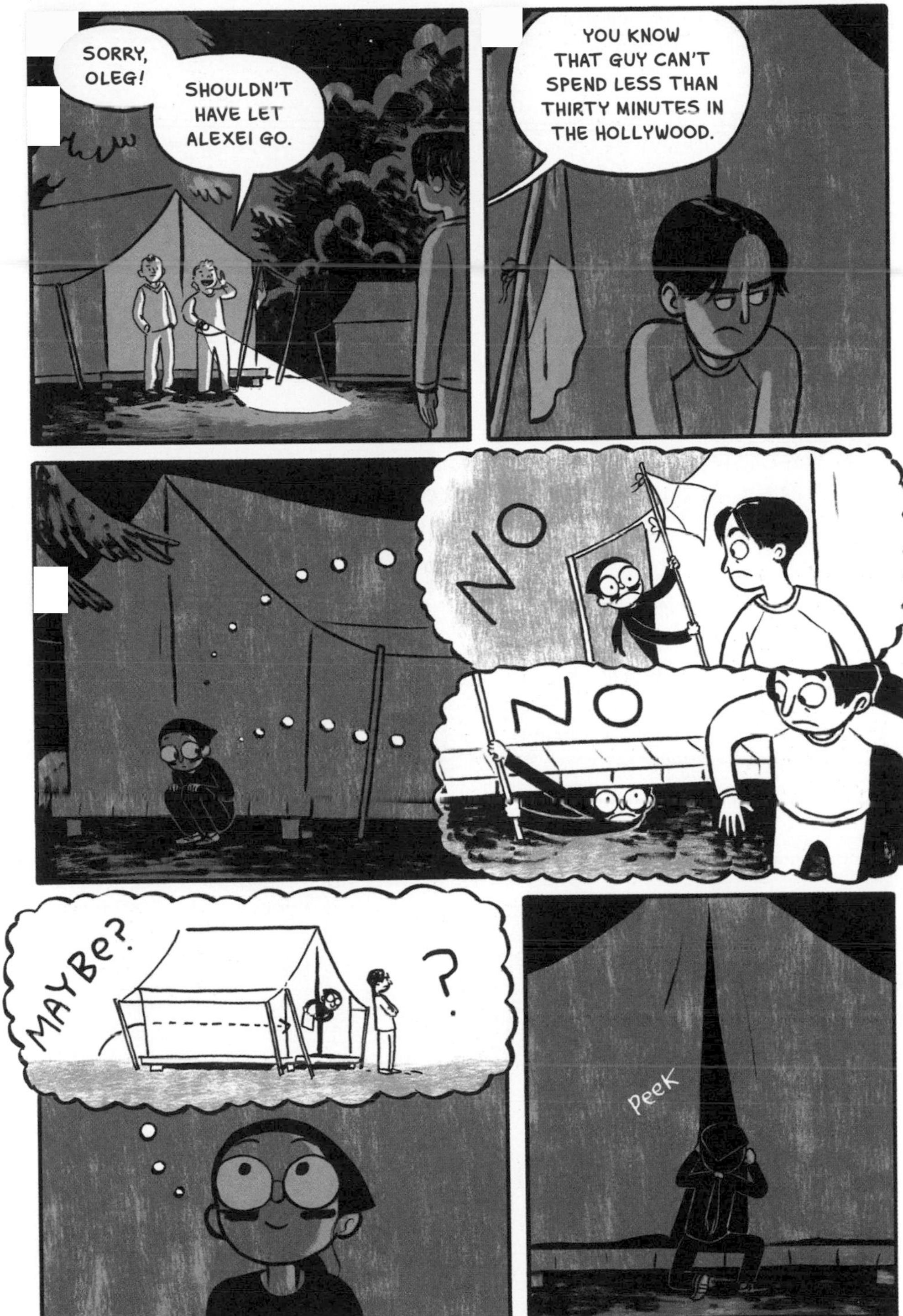
SORRY, OLEG!
SHOULDN'T HAVE LET ALEXEI GO.
YOU KNOW THAT GUY CAN'T SPEND LESS THAN THIRTY MINUTES IN THE HOLLYWOOD.
NO
NO
MAYBE?
?
PEEK

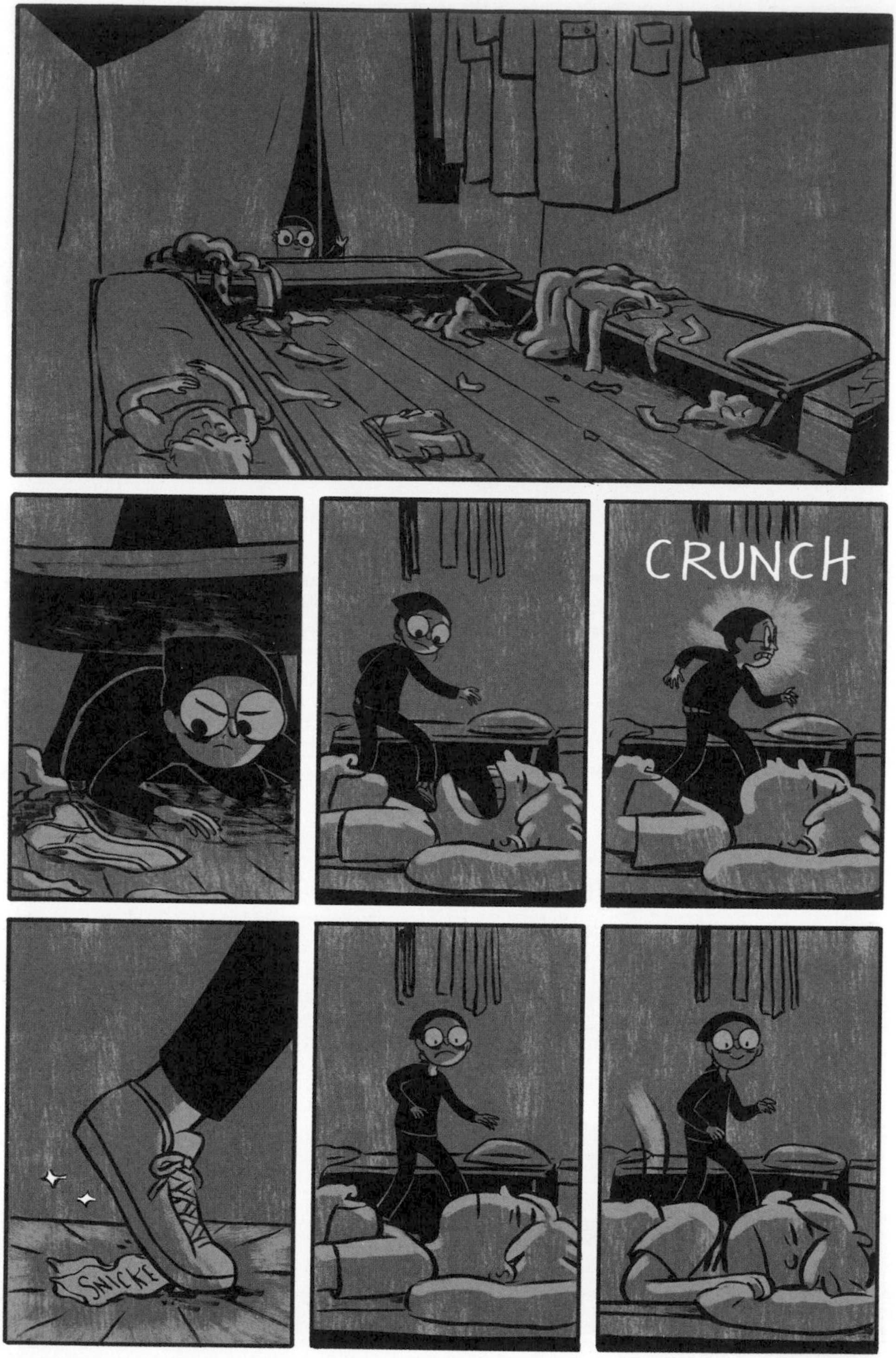
CRUNCH
SNICKE

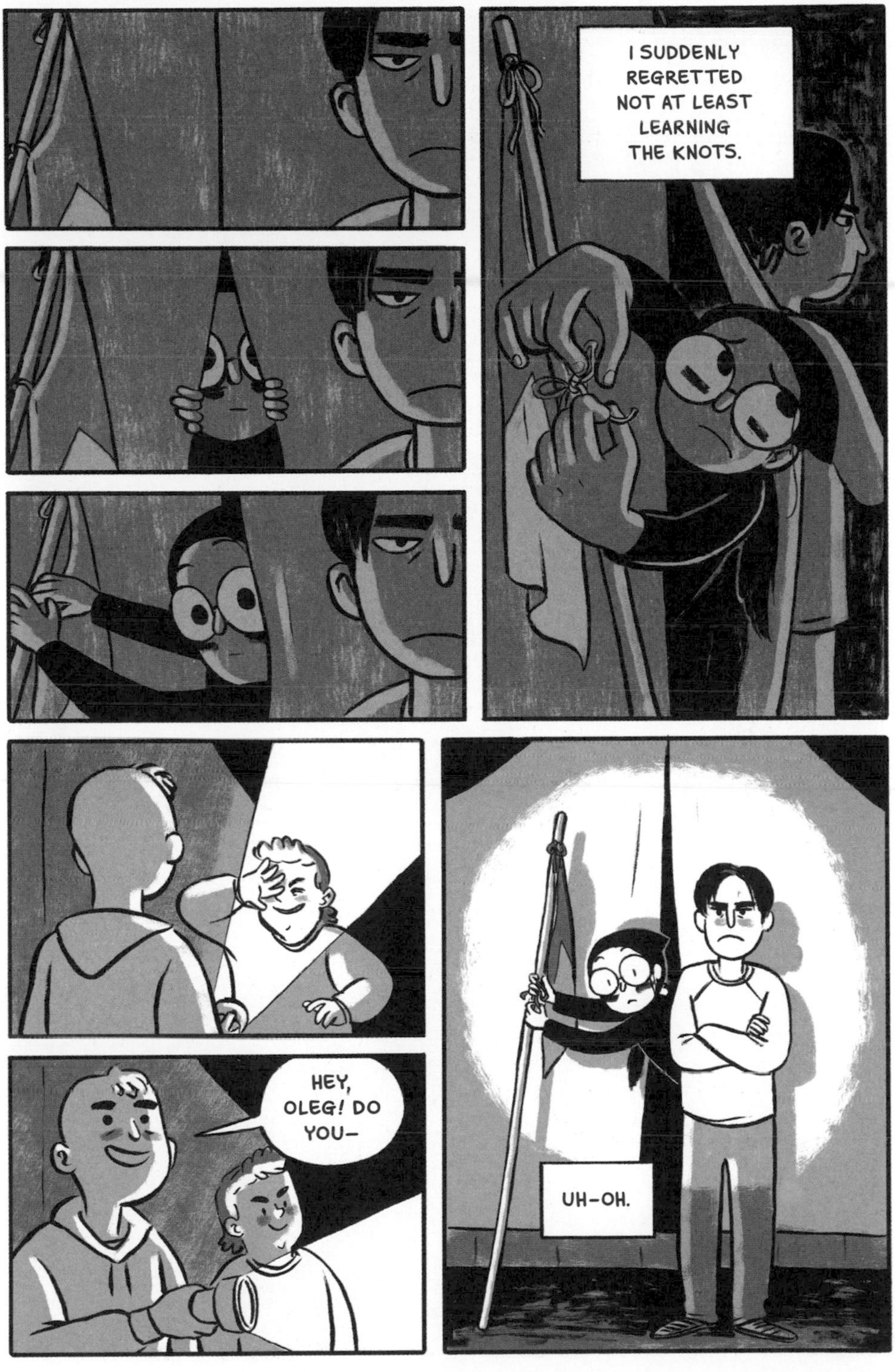
I SUDDENLY REGRETTED NOT AT LEAST LEARNING THE KNOTS.
HEY, OLEG! DO YOU–
UH-OH.

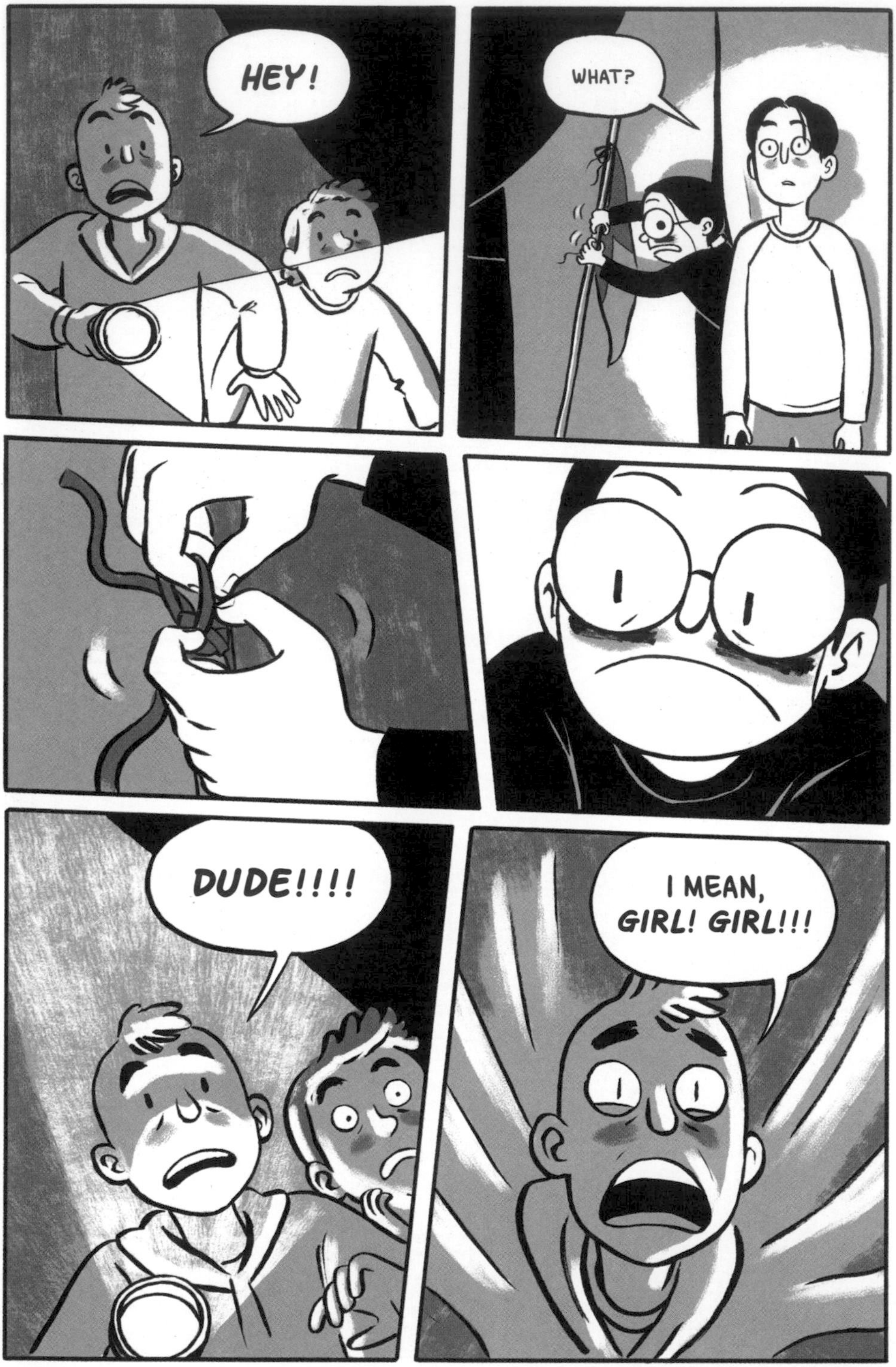
HEY!
WHAT?
DUDE!!!!
I MEAN, GIRL! GIRL!!!

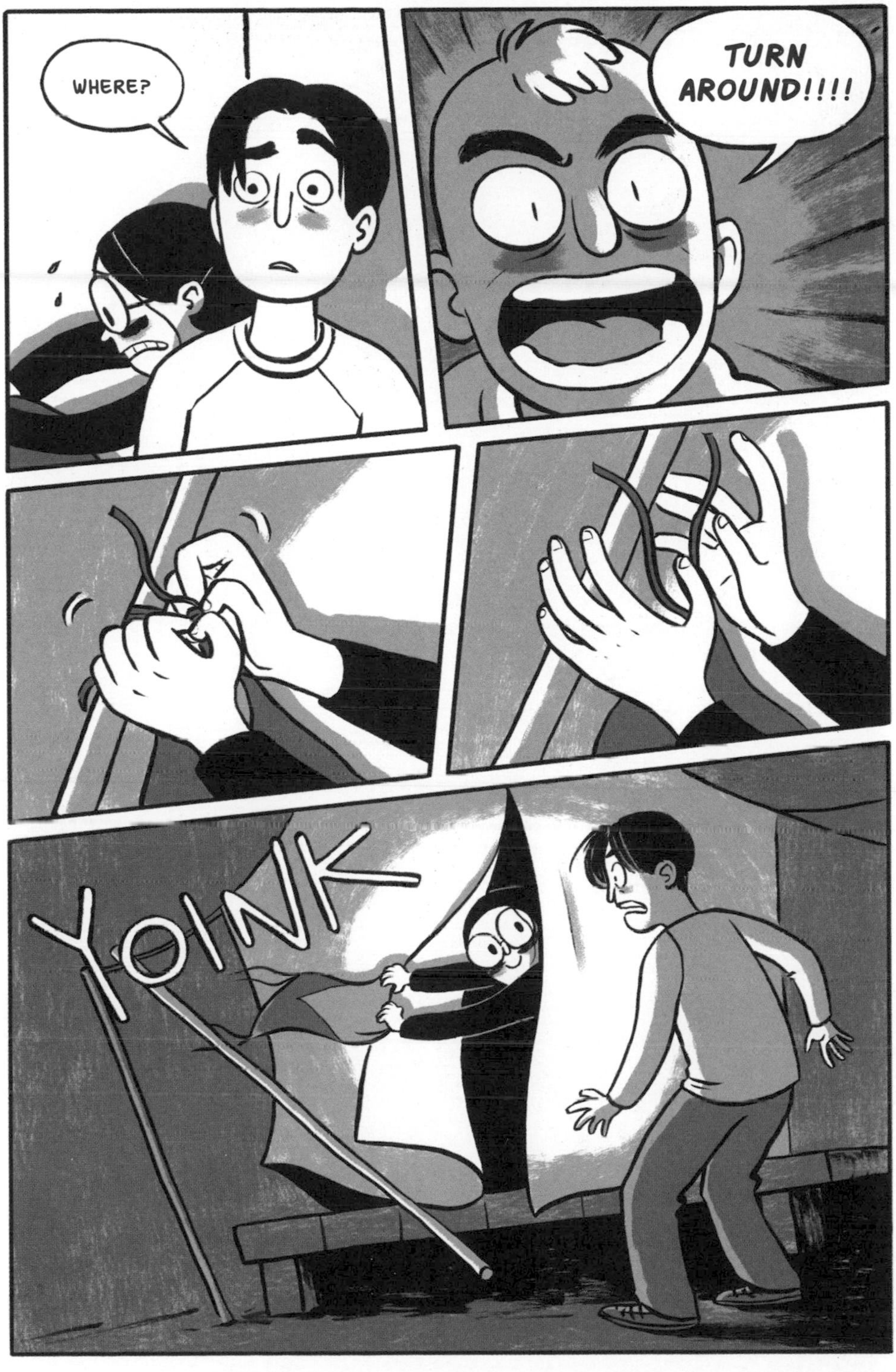
WHERE?
TURN AROUND!!!!
YOINK

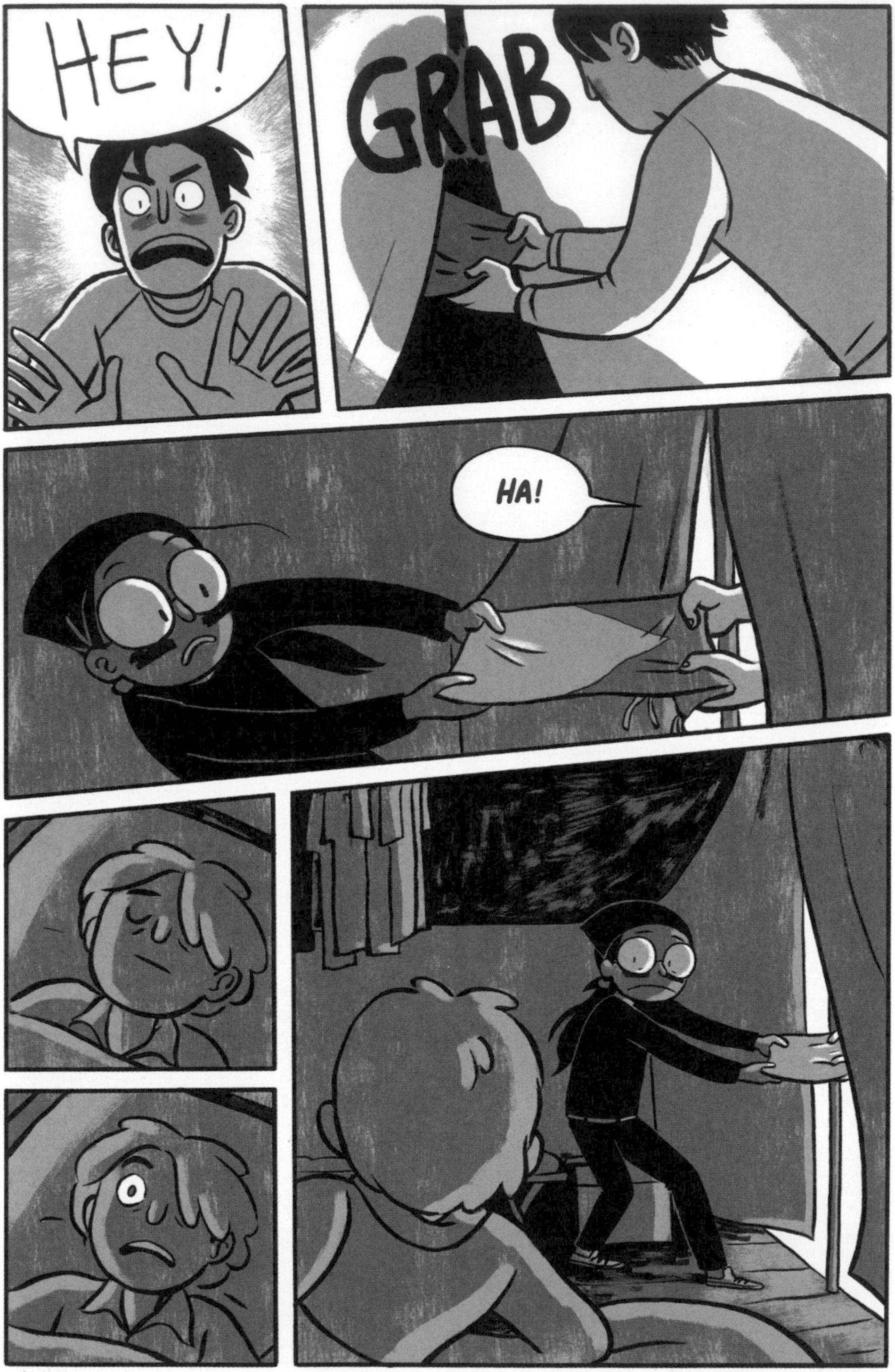
HEY!
GRAB
HA!

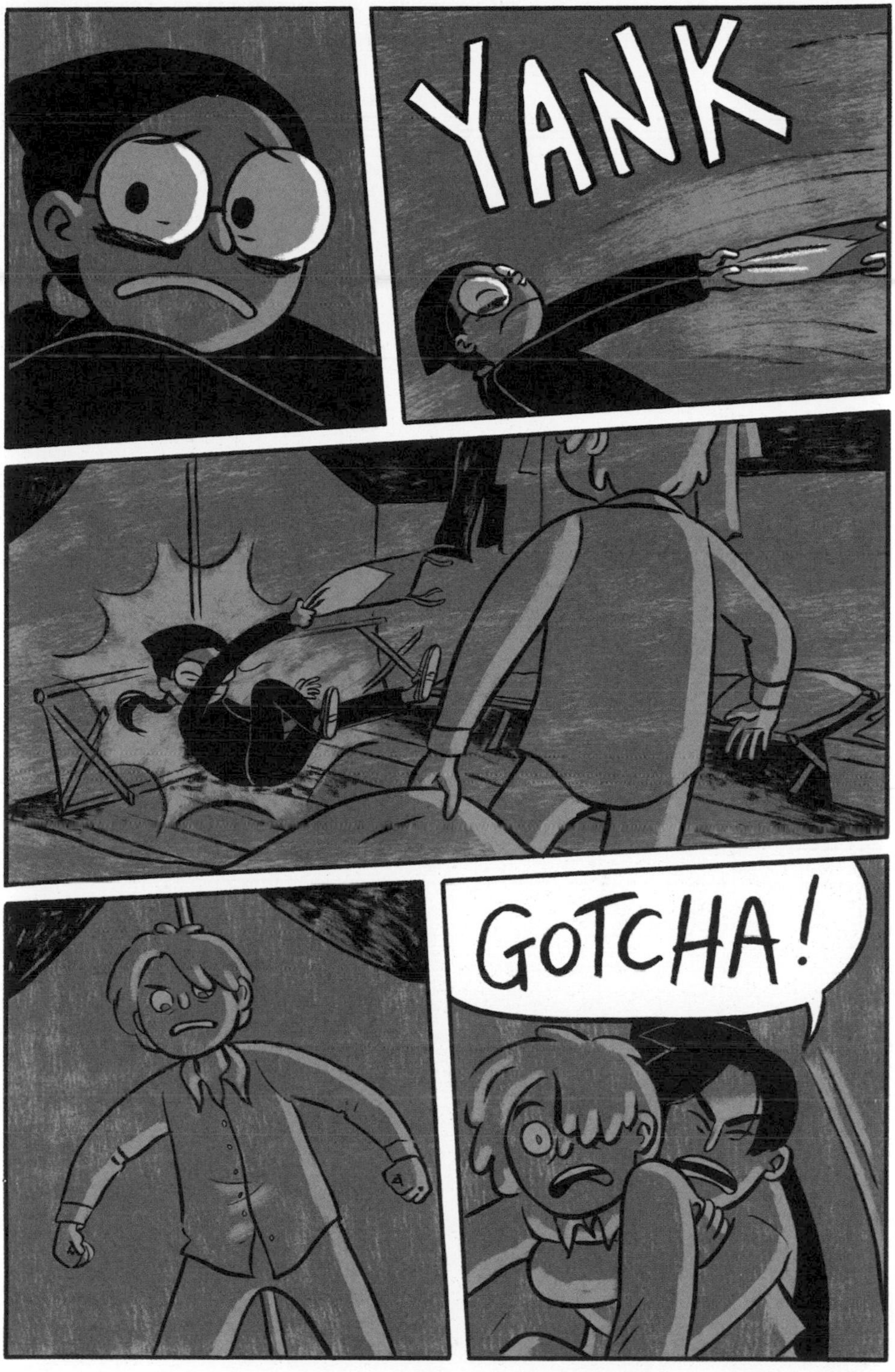
YANK
GOTCHA!

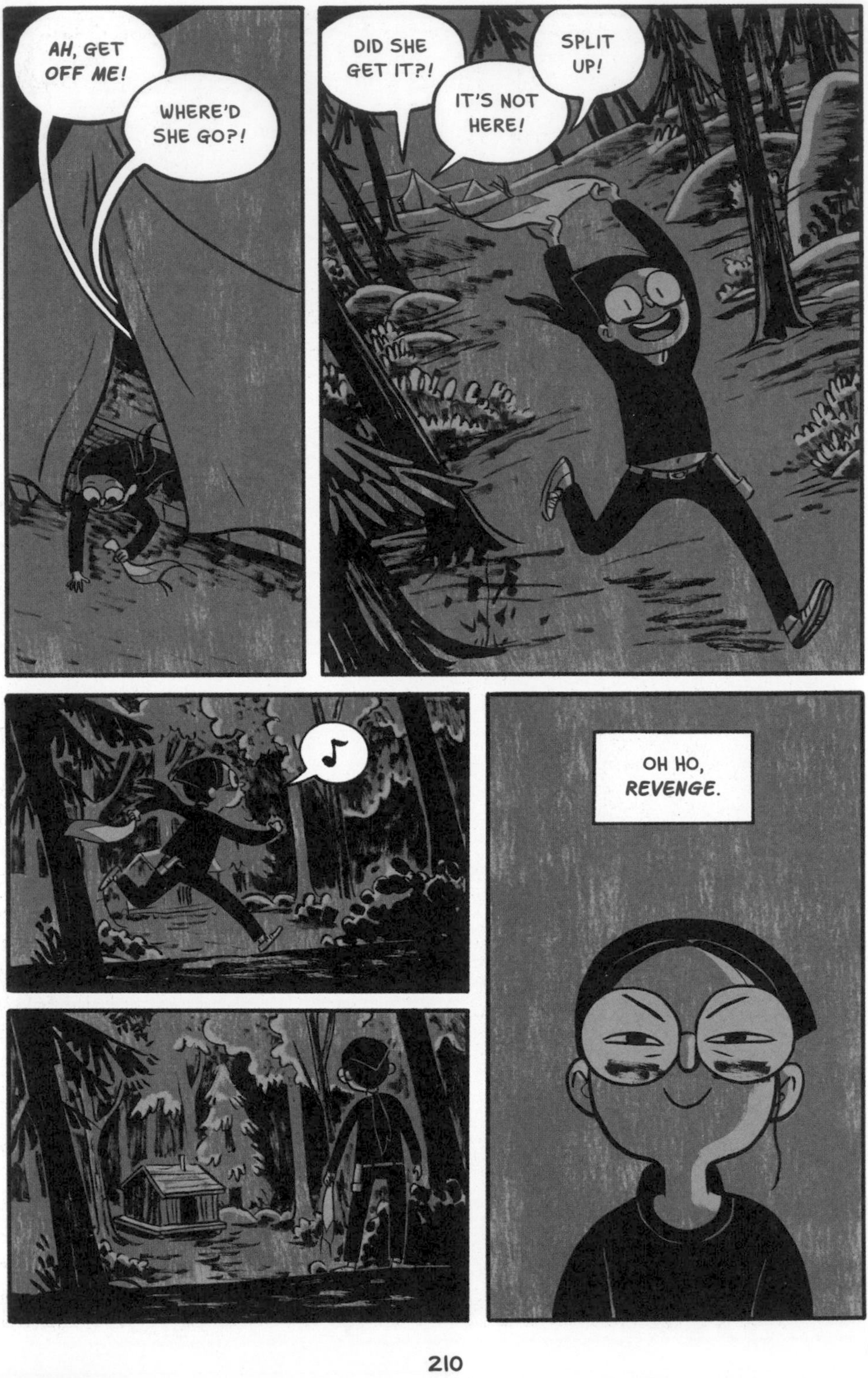
AH, GET OFF ME!
WHERE'D SHE GO?!
DID SHE GET IT?!
IT'S NOT HERE!
SPLIT UP!
♪
OH HO, REVENGE.

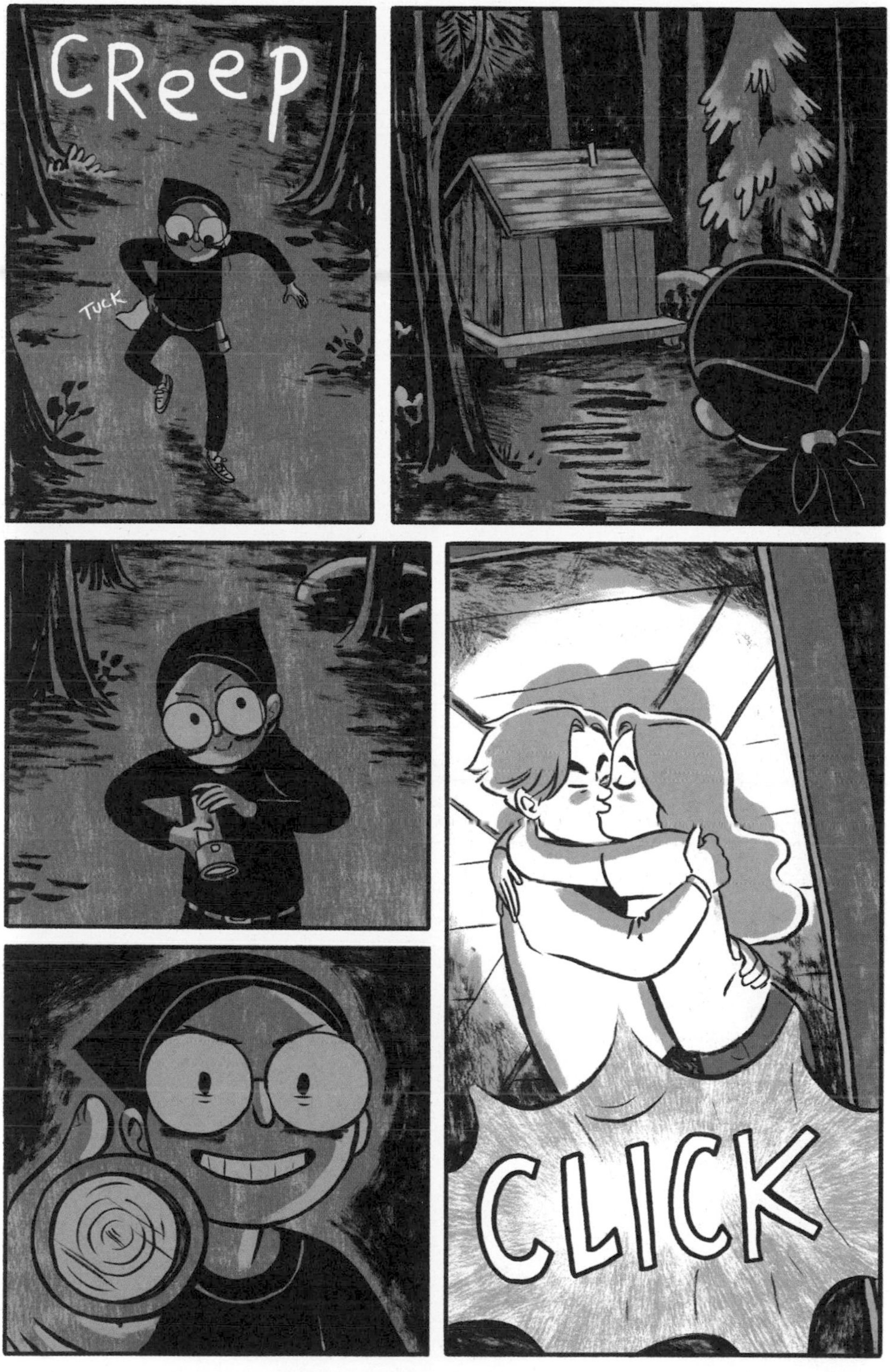
CReep
TUCK
CLICK

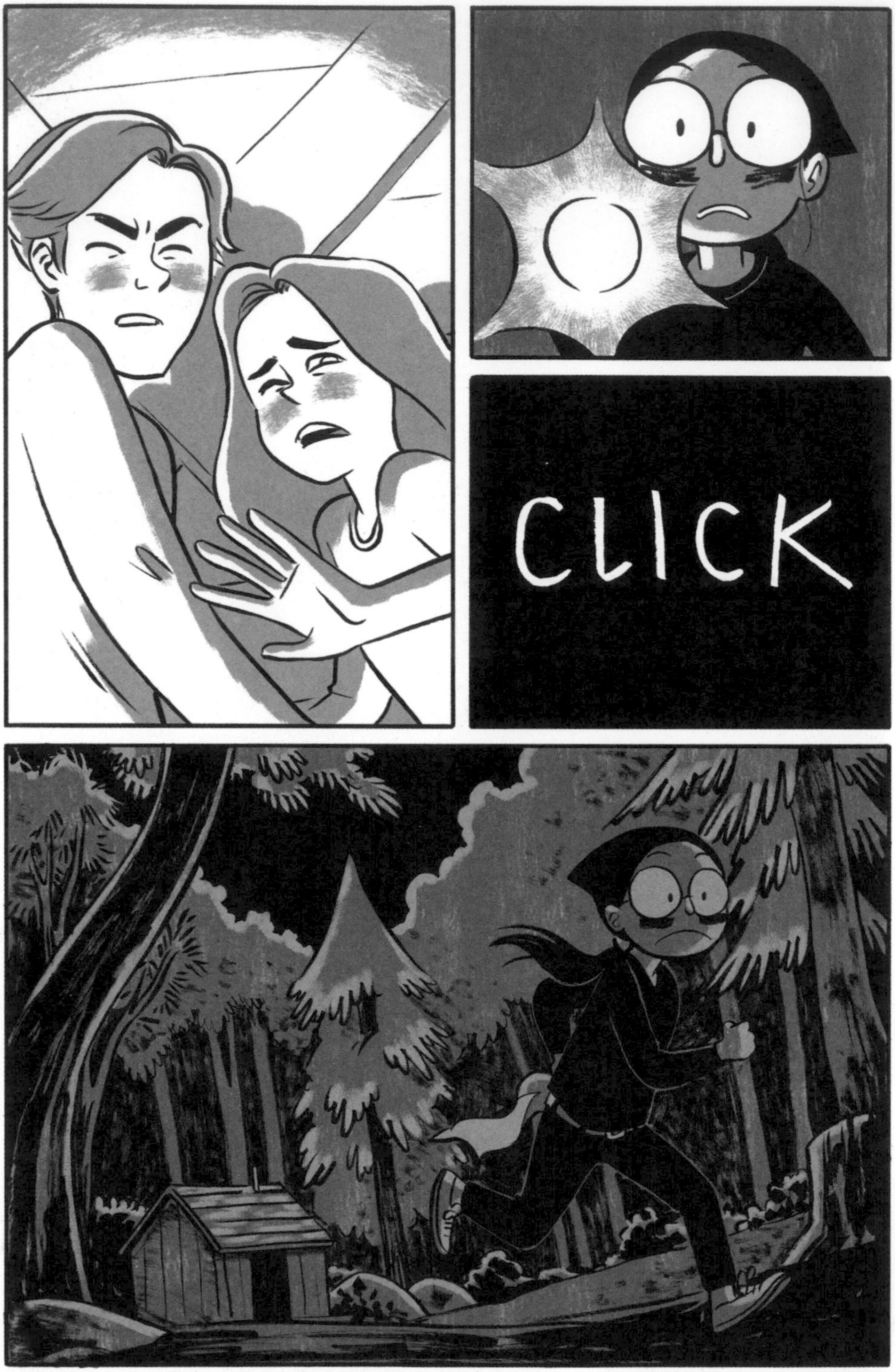
CLICK

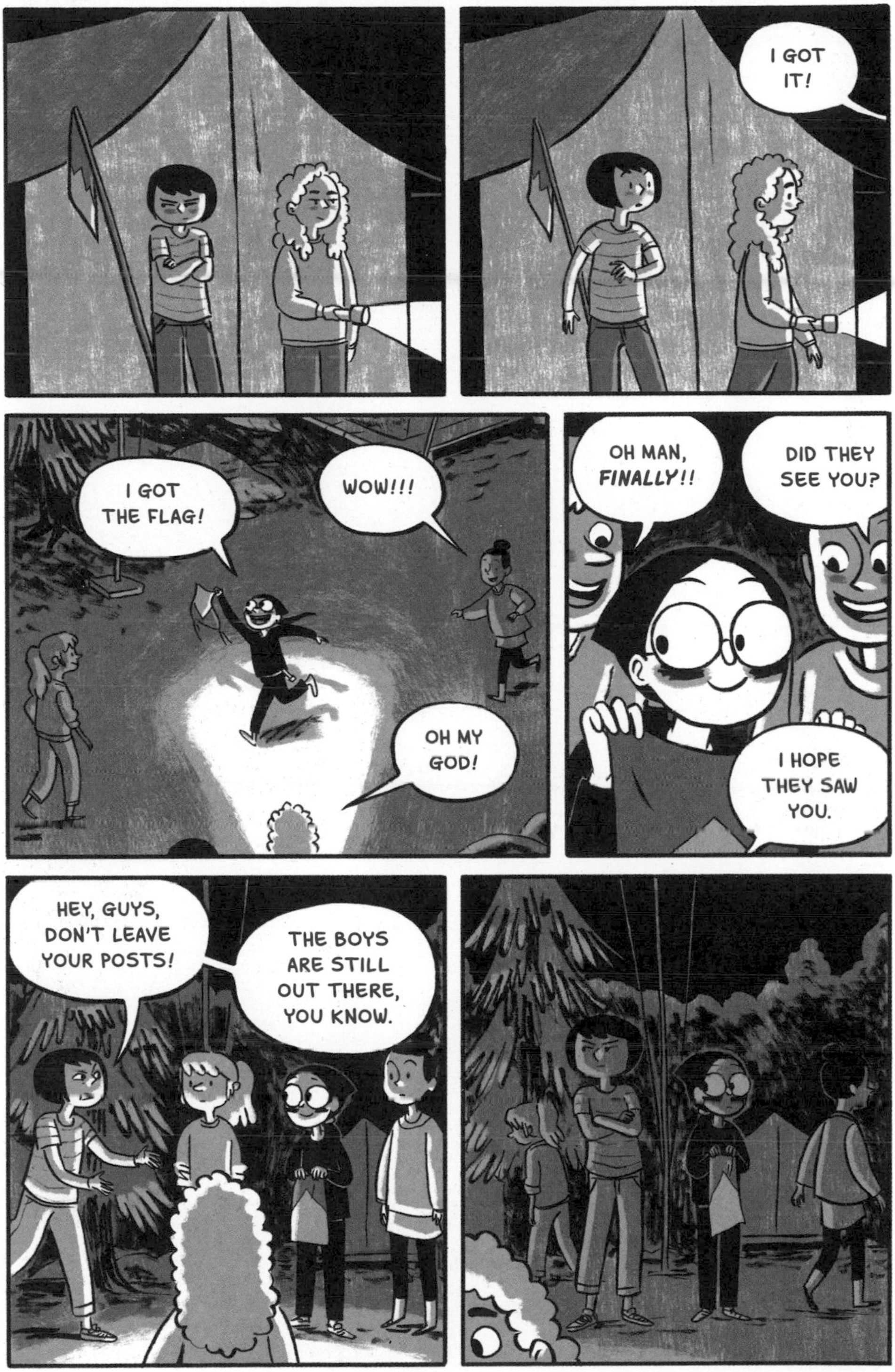

I GOT IT!
I GOT THE FLAG!
WOW!!!
OH MY GOD!
OH MAN, FINALLY!!
DID THEY SEE YOU?
I HOPE THEY SAW YOU.
HEY, GUYS, DON'T LEAVE YOUR POSTS!
THE BOYS ARE STILL OUT THERE, YOU KNOW.

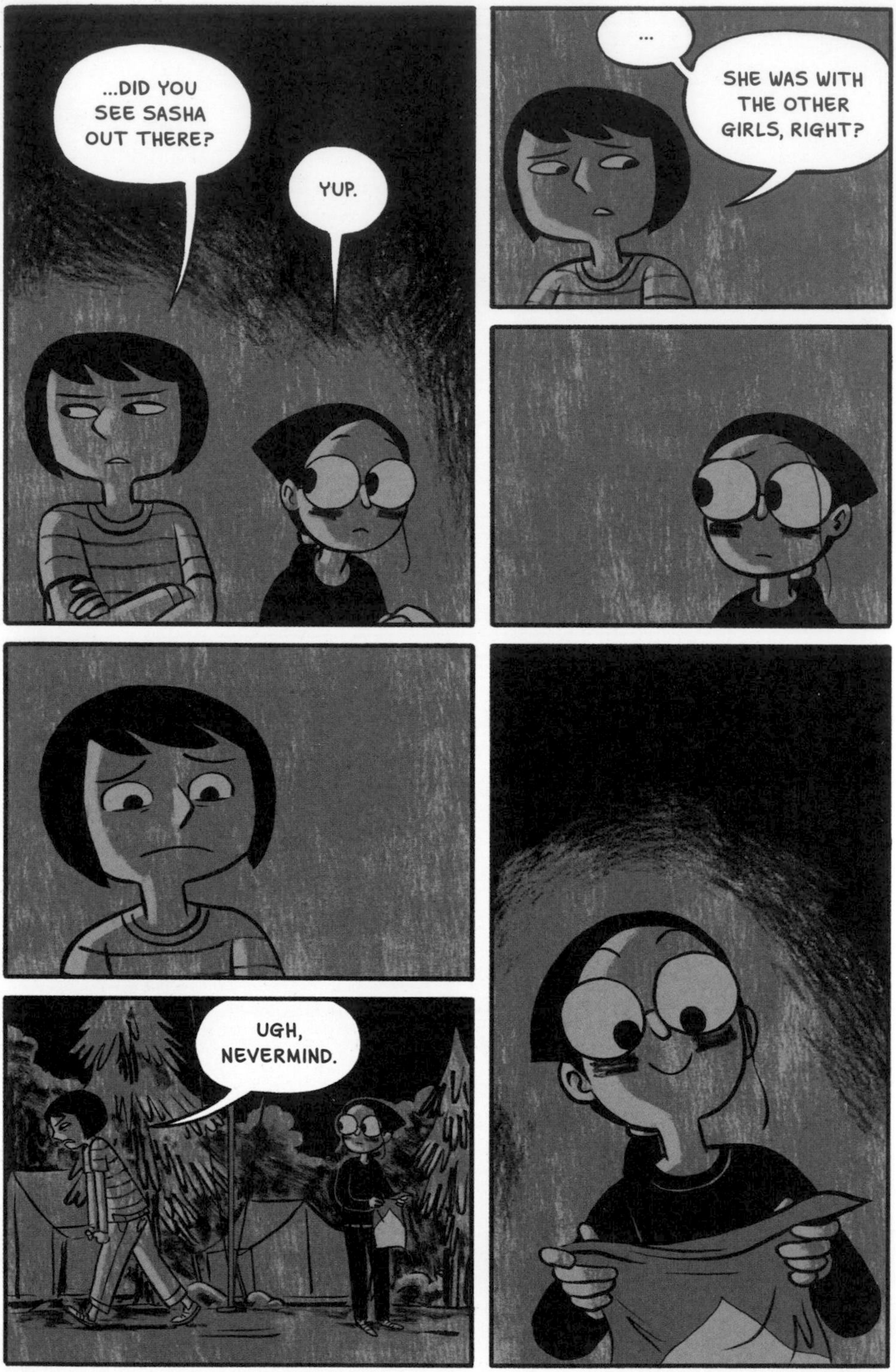
...DID YOU SEE SASHA OUT THERE?
YUP.
...
SHE WAS WITH THE OTHER GIRLS, RIGHT?
UGH, NEVERMIND.

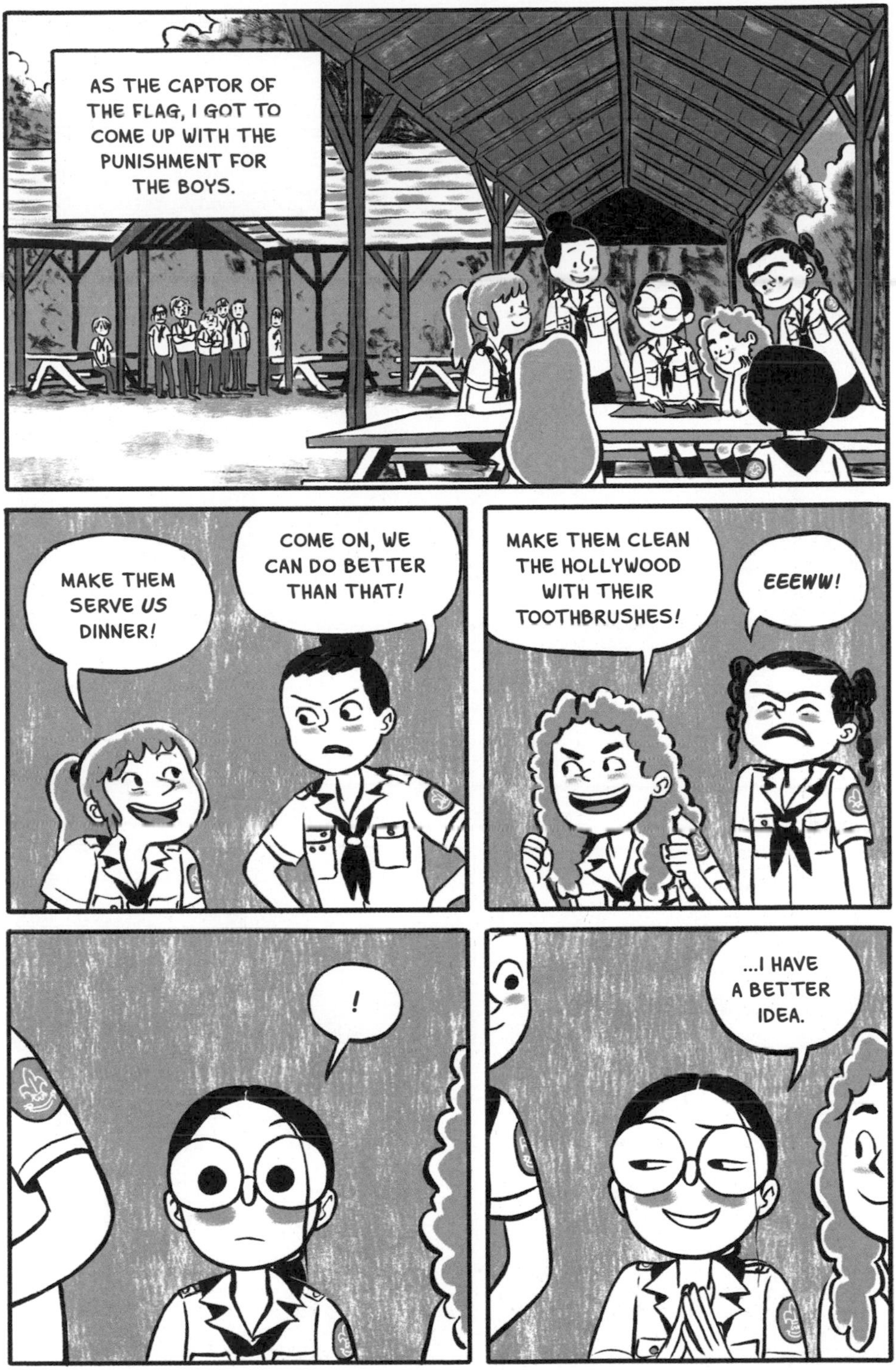
AS THE CAPTOR OF THE FLAG, I GOT TO COME UP WITH THE PUNISHMENT FOR THE BOYS.
MAKE THEM SERVE *US* DINNER!
COME ON, WE CAN DO BETTER THAN THAT!
MAKE THEM CLEAN THE HOLLYWOOD WITH THEIR TOOTHBRUSHES!
EEEWW!
!
...I HAVE A BETTER IDEA.

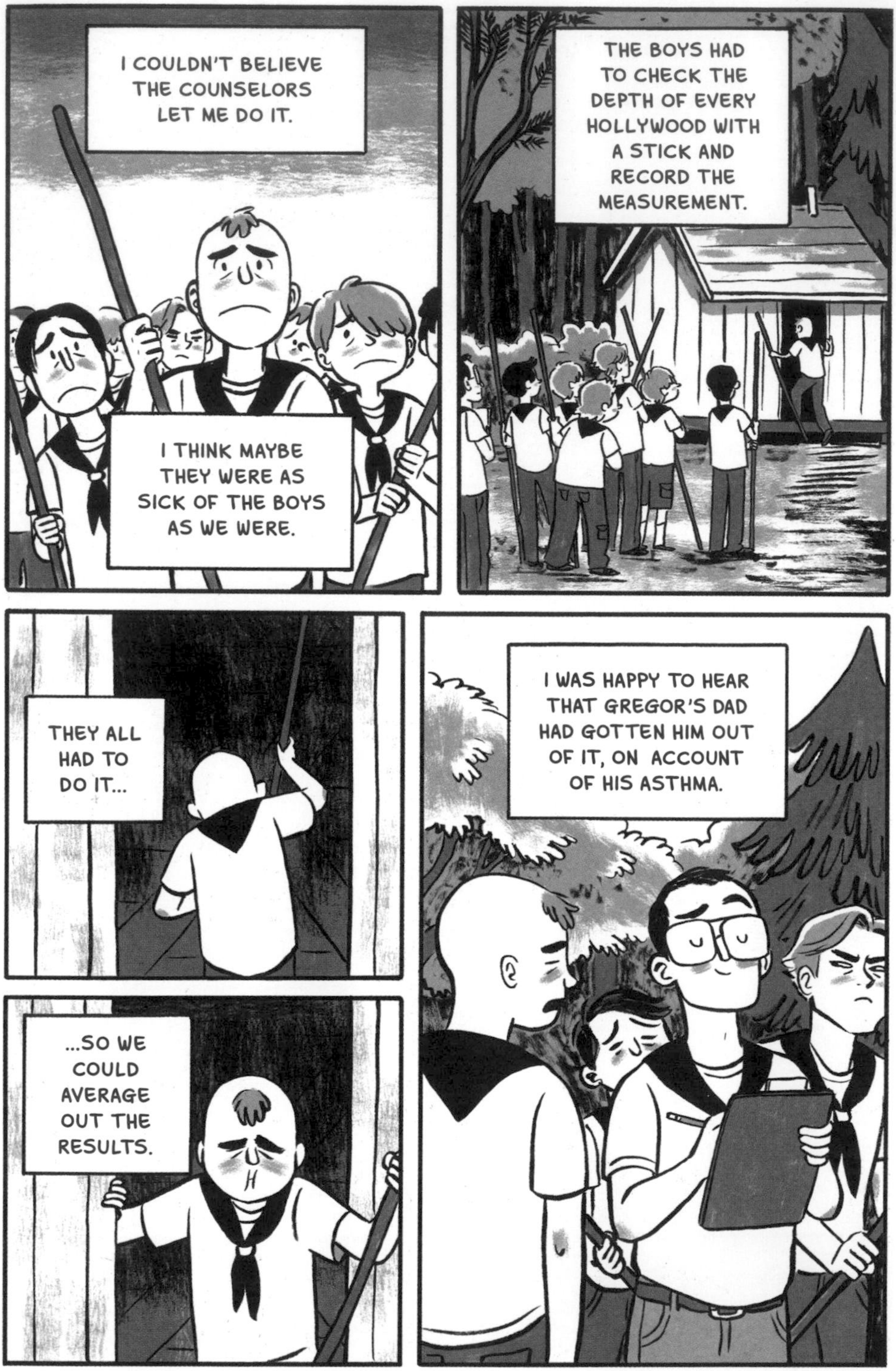
I COULDN'T BELIEVE THE COUNSELORS LET ME DO IT.
I THINK MAYBE THEY WERE AS SICK OF THE BOYS AS WE WERE.
THE BOYS HAD TO CHECK THE DEPTH OF EVERY HOLLYWOOD WITH A STICK AND RECORD THE MEASUREMENT.
THEY ALL HAD TO DO IT...
...SO WE COULD AVERAGE OUT THE RESULTS.
I WAS HAPPY TO HEAR THAT GREGOR'S DAD HAD GOTTEN HIM OUT OF IT, ON ACCOUNT OF HIS ASTHMA.

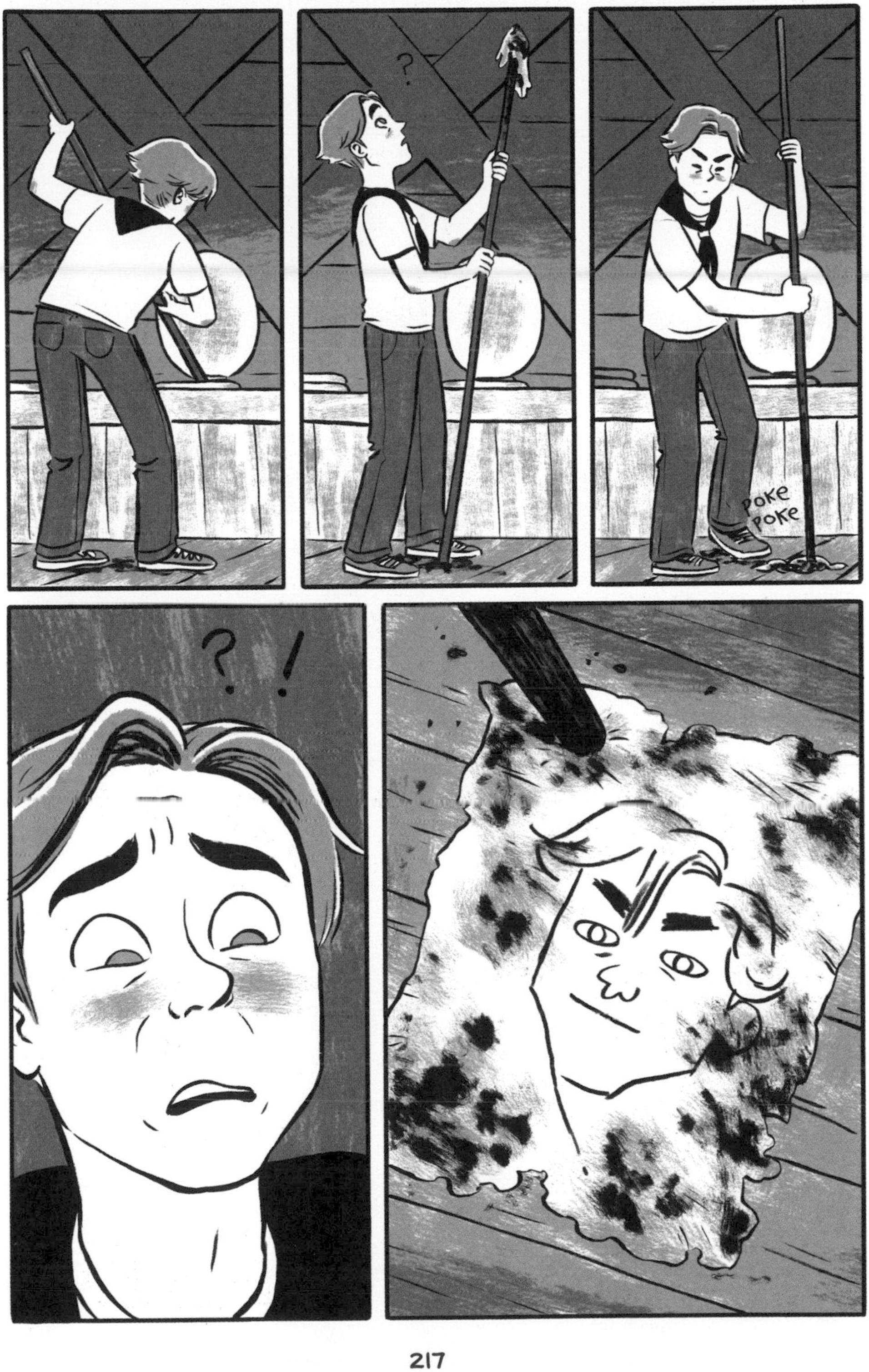
?
POKE
POKE
?!

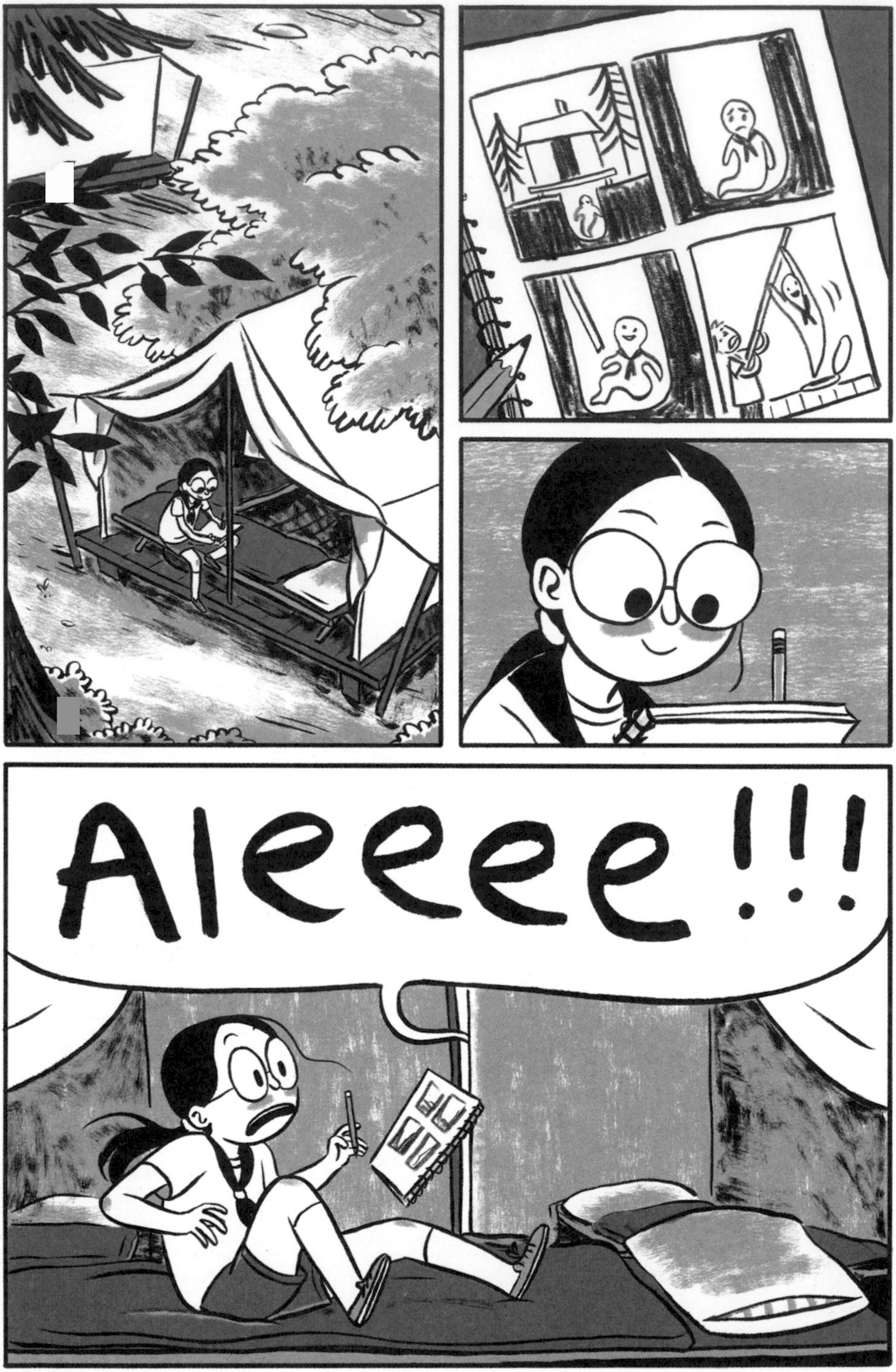
AIeeee!!!

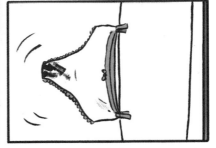

WHAT IS WRONG WITH YOU?!

ME?

I DON'T KNOW WHAT YOU'RE TALKING ABOUT.

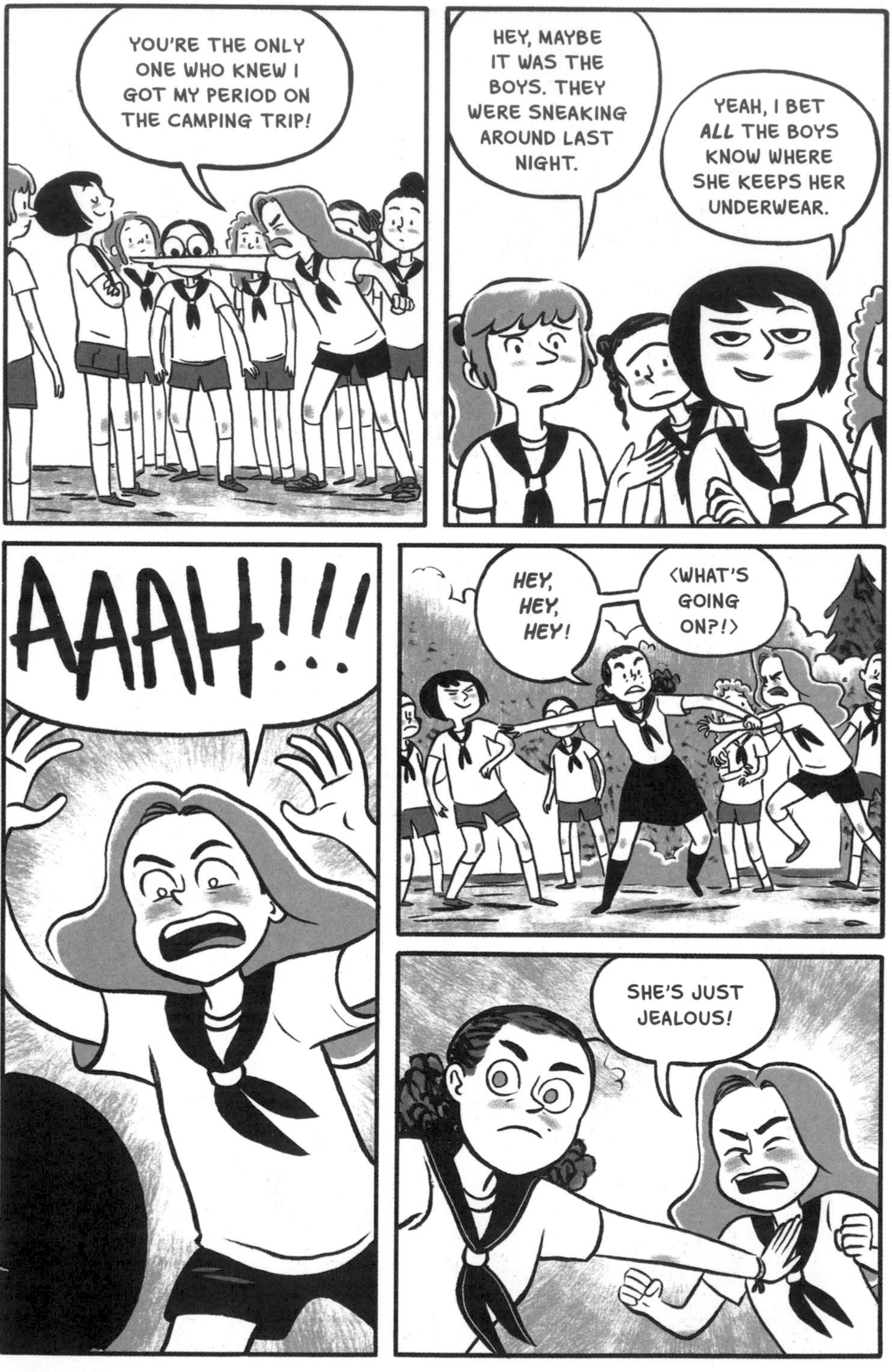
YOU'RE THE ONLY ONE WHO KNEW I GOT MY PERIOD ON THE CAMPING TRIP!
HEY, MAYBE IT WAS THE BOYS. THEY WERE SNEAKING AROUND LAST NIGHT.
YEAH, I BET ALL THE BOYS KNOW WHERE SHE KEEPS HER UNDERWEAR.
AAAH!!!
HEY, HEY, HEY!
<WHAT'S GOING ON?!>
SHE'S JUST JEALOUS!

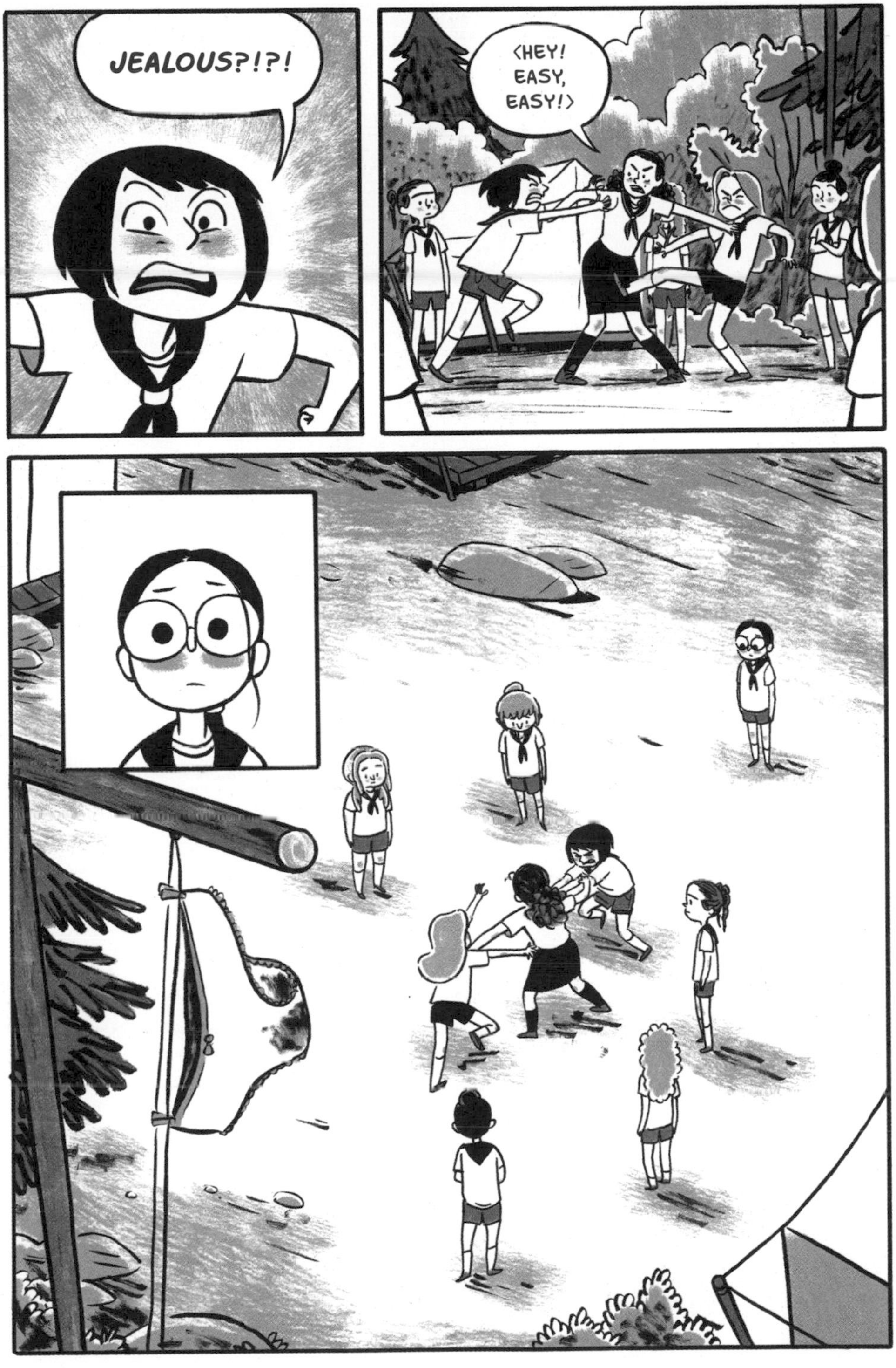
JEALOUS?!?!
‹HEY! EASY, EASY!›

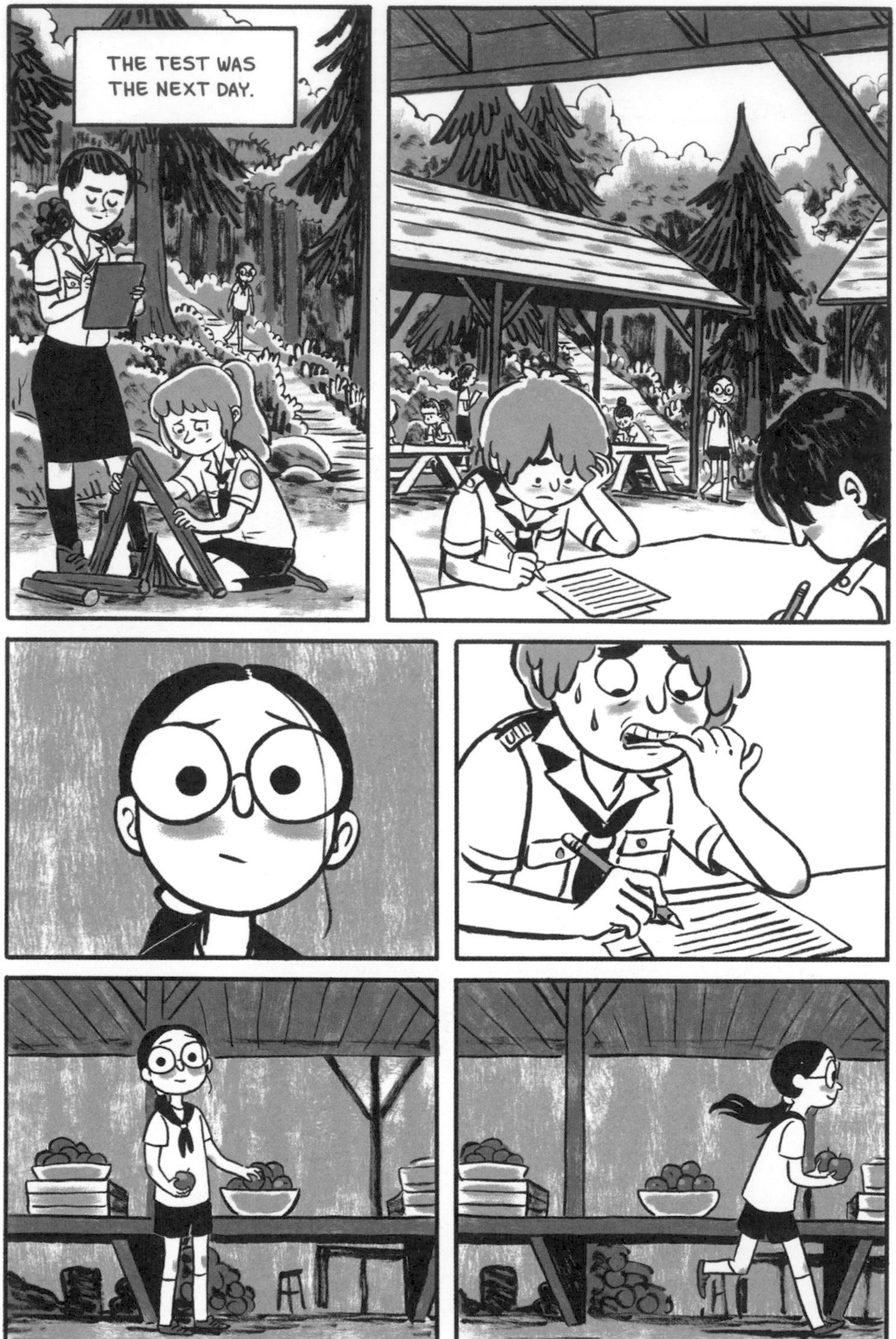
THE TEST WAS THE NEXT DAY.

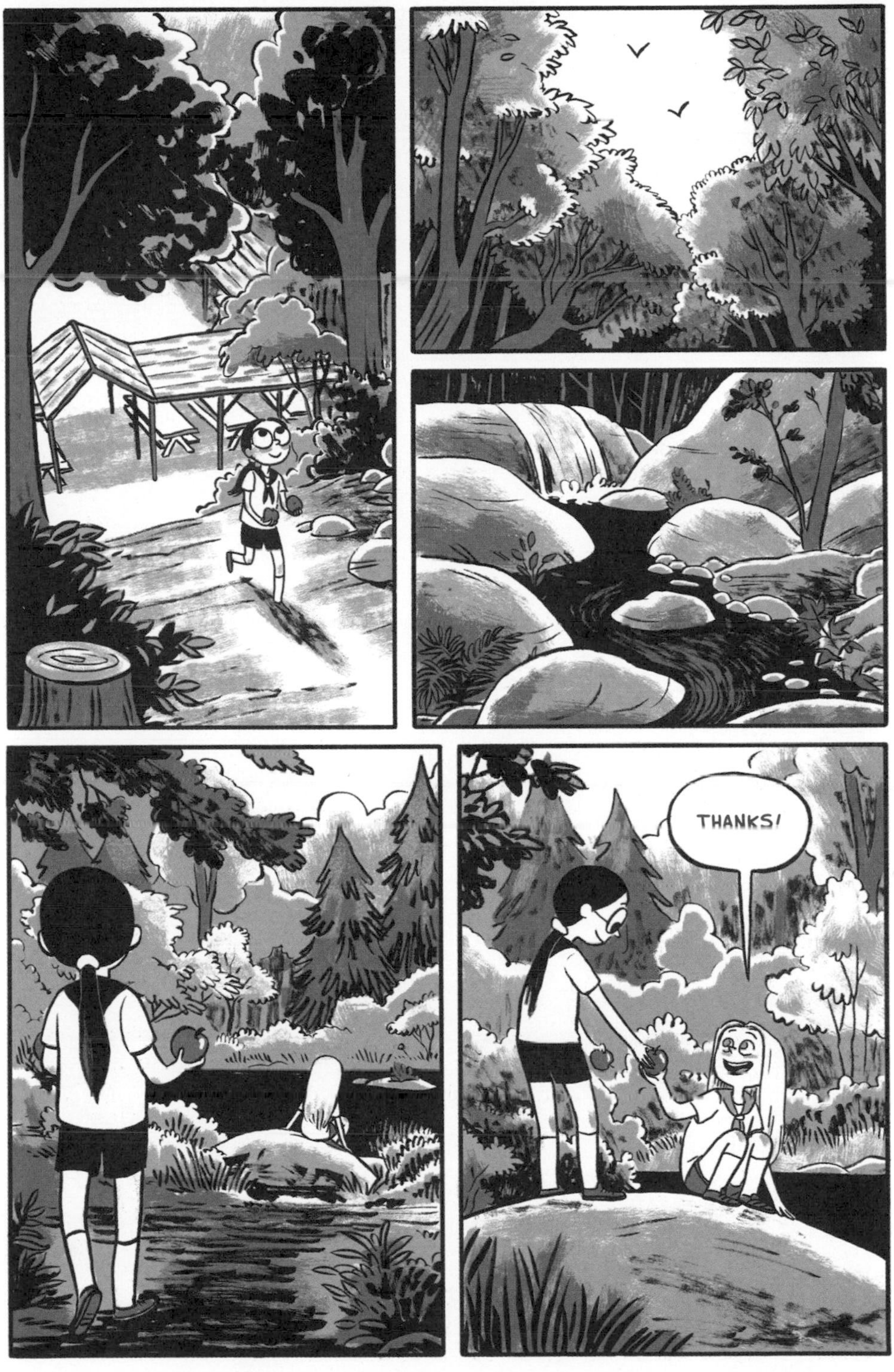
THANKS!

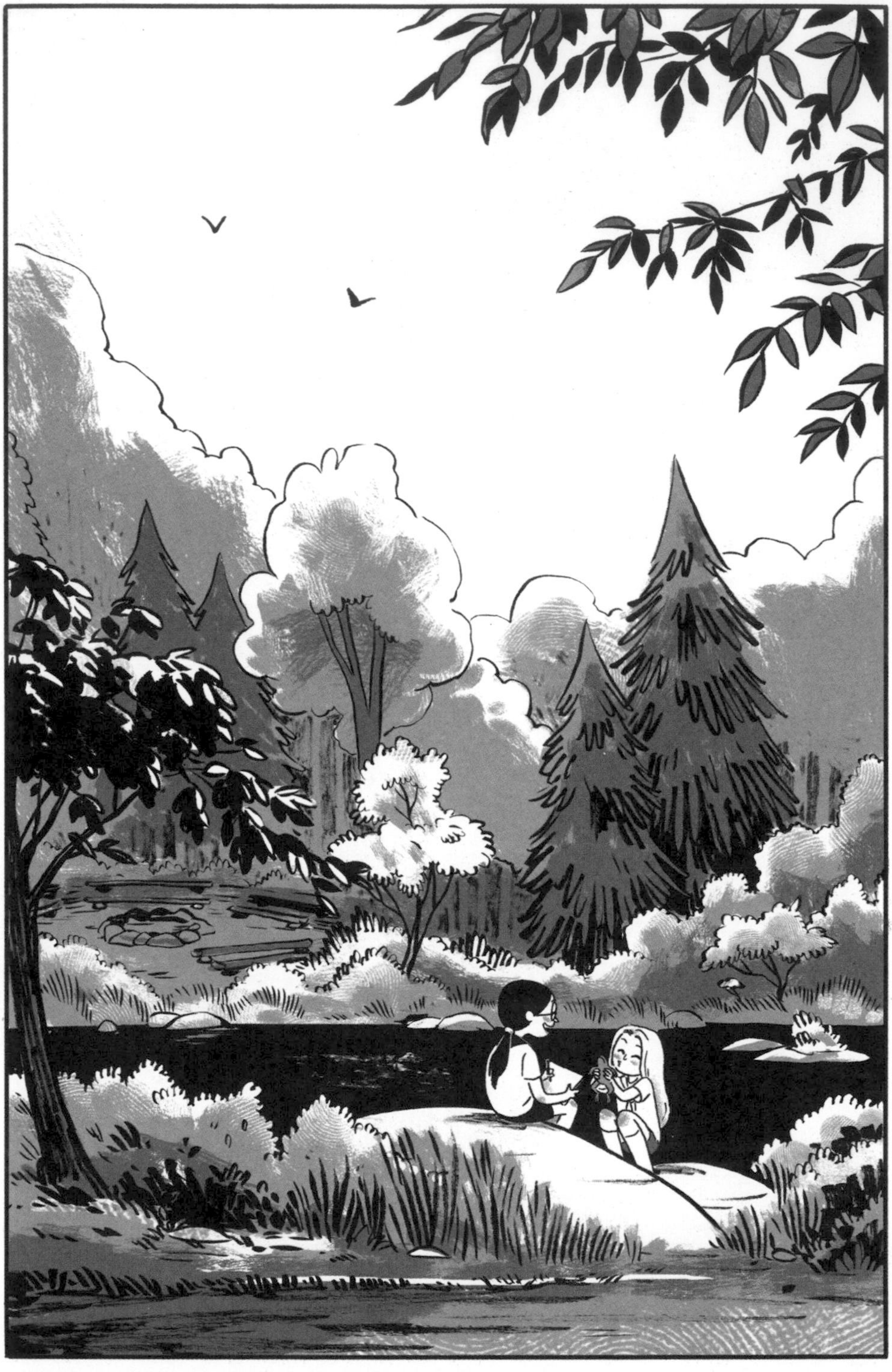

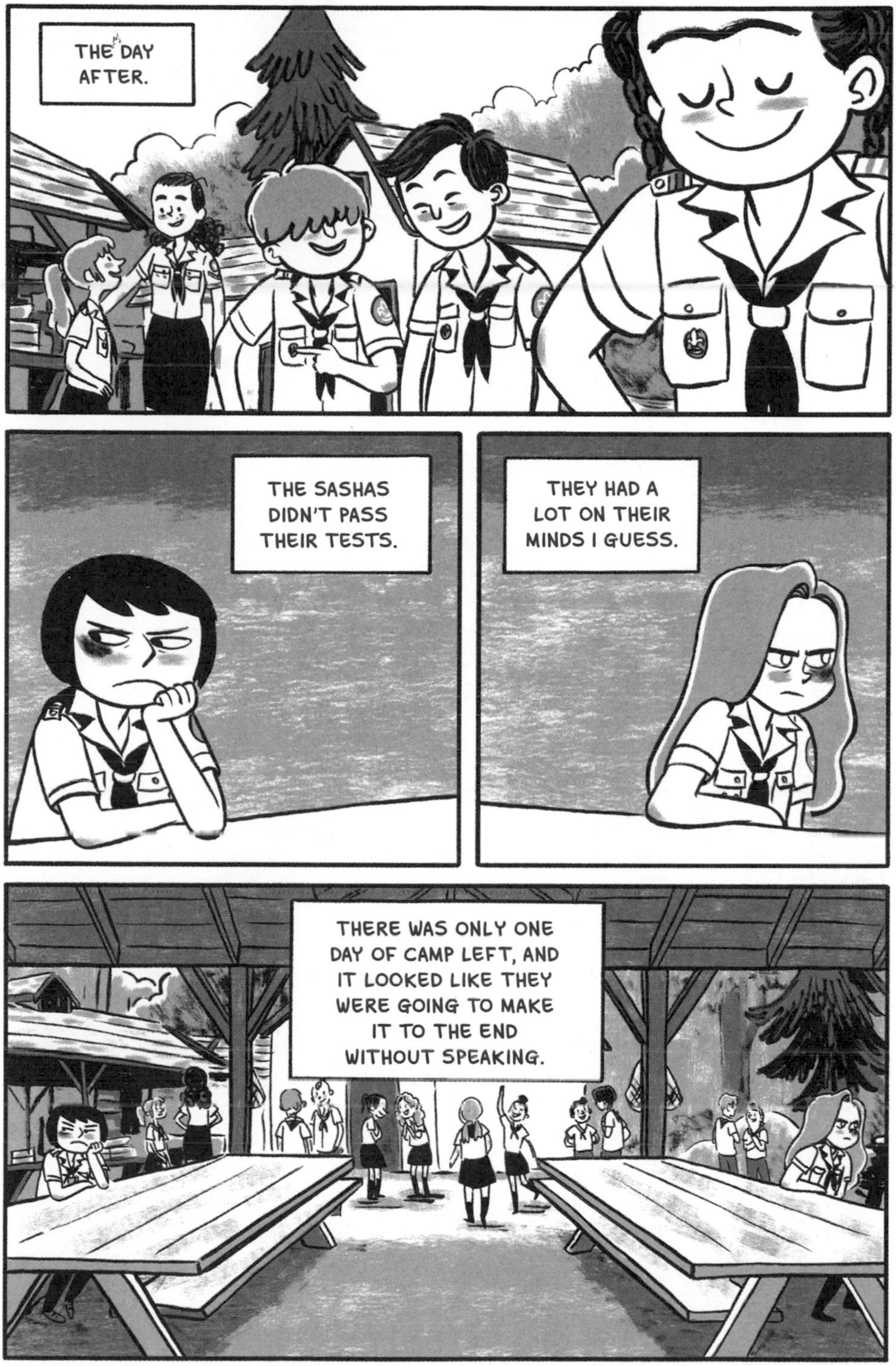
THE DAY AFTER.
THE SASHAS DIDN'T PASS THEIR TESTS.
THEY HAD A LOT ON THEIR MINDS I GUESS.
THERE WAS ONLY ONE DAY OF CAMP LEFT, AND IT LOOKED LIKE THEY WERE GOING TO MAKE IT TO THE END WITHOUT SPEAKING.

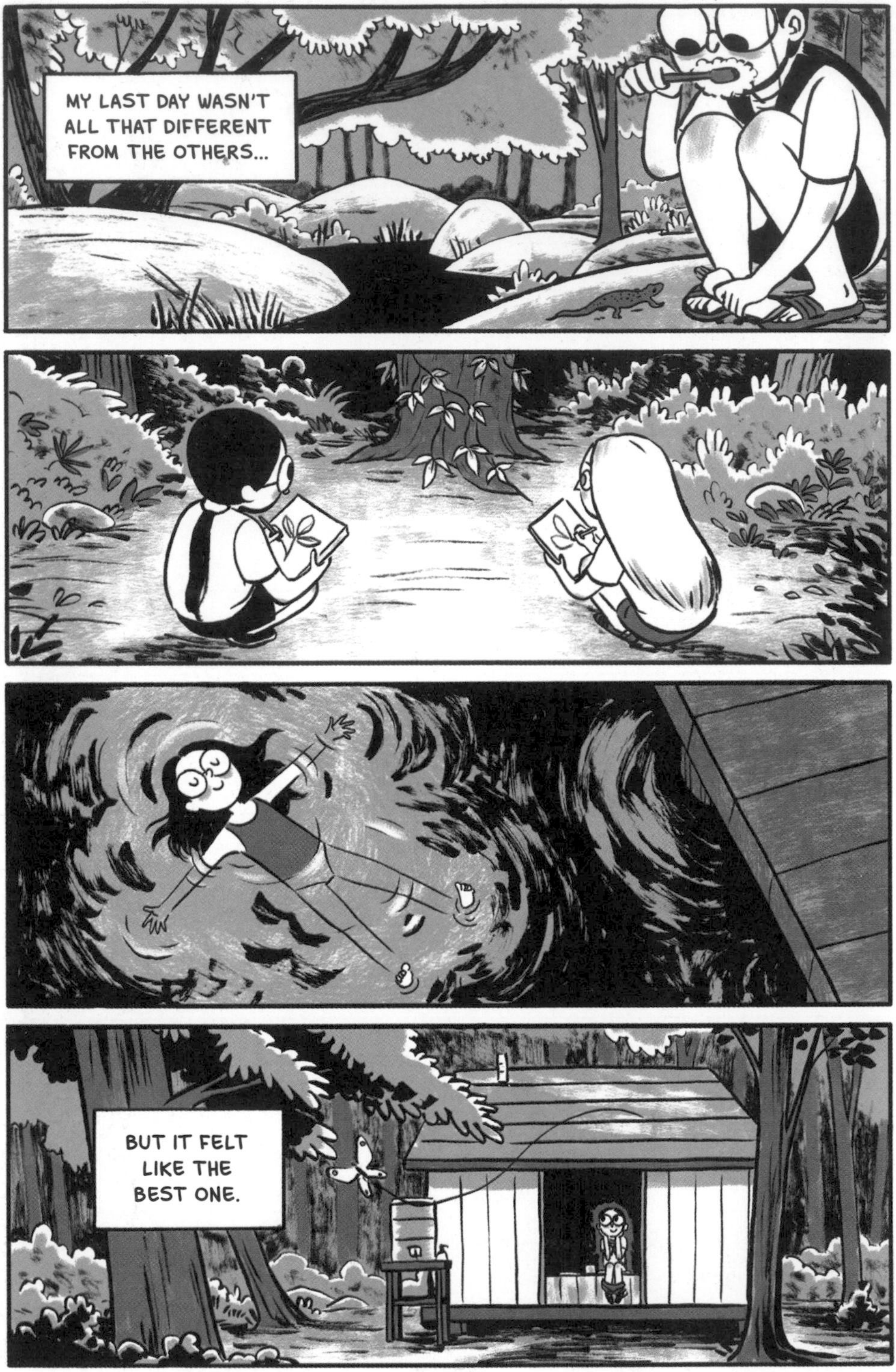
MY LAST DAY WASN'T ALL THAT DIFFERENT FROM THE OTHERS...
BUT IT FELT LIKE THE BEST ONE.

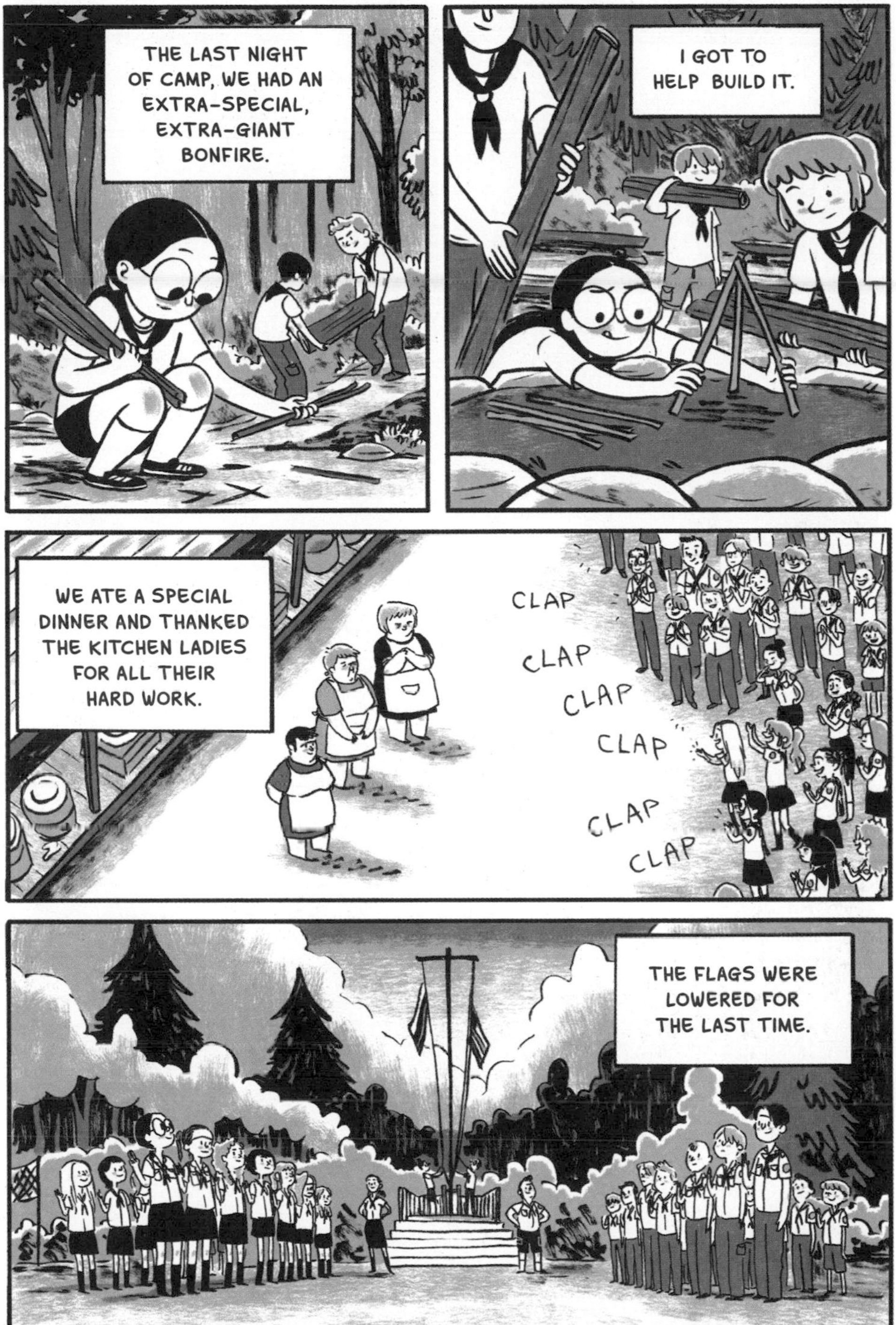
THE LAST NIGHT OF CAMP, WE HAD AN EXTRA-SPECIAL, EXTRA-GIANT BONFIRE.
I GOT TO HELP BUILD IT.
WE ATE A SPECIAL DINNER AND THANKED THE KITCHEN LADIES FOR ALL THEIR HARD WORK.
CLAP
CLAP
CLAP
CLAP
CLAP
CLAP
THE FLAGS WERE LOWERED FOR THE LAST TIME.

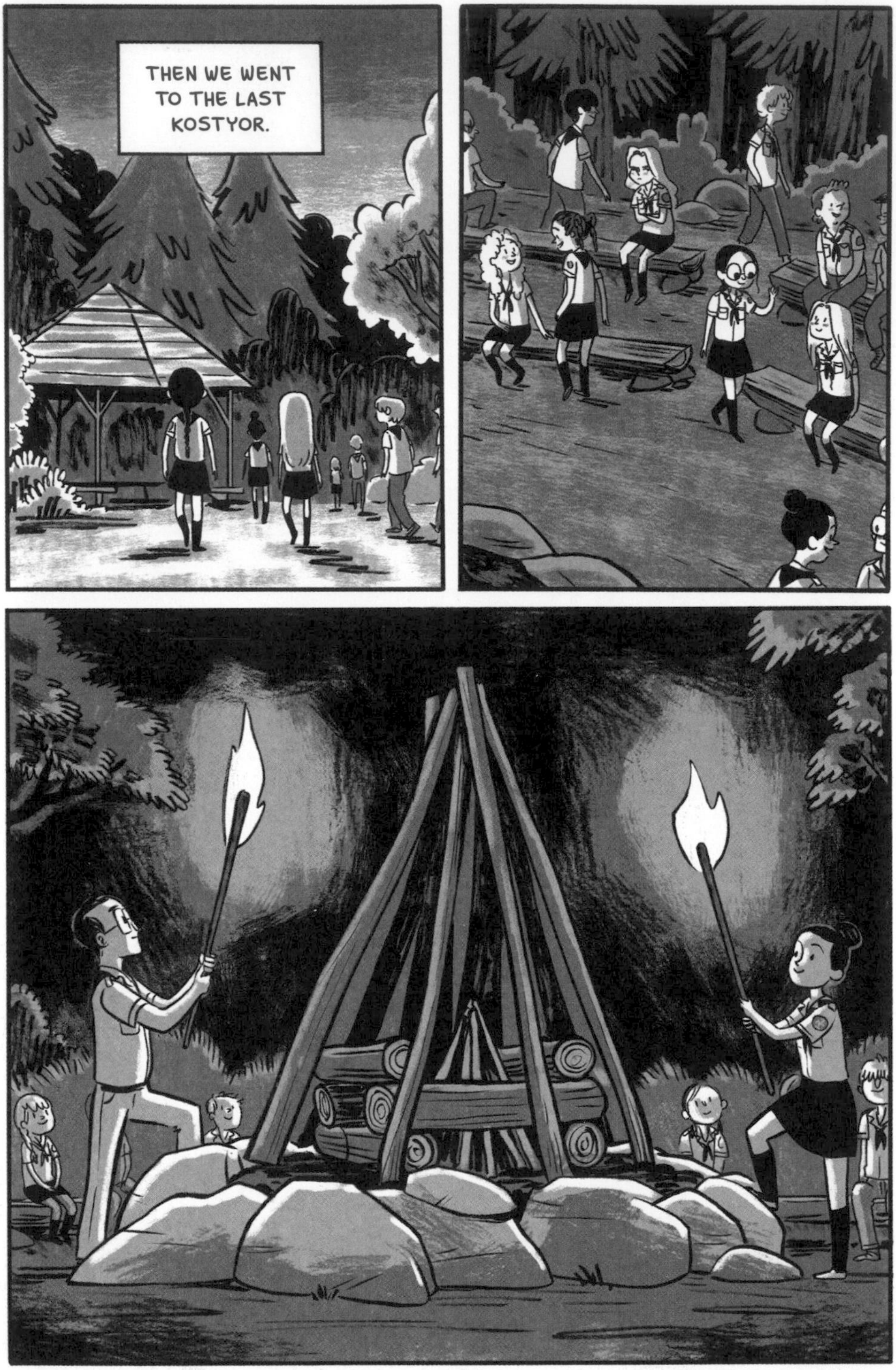
THEN WE WENT TO THE LAST KOSTYOR.

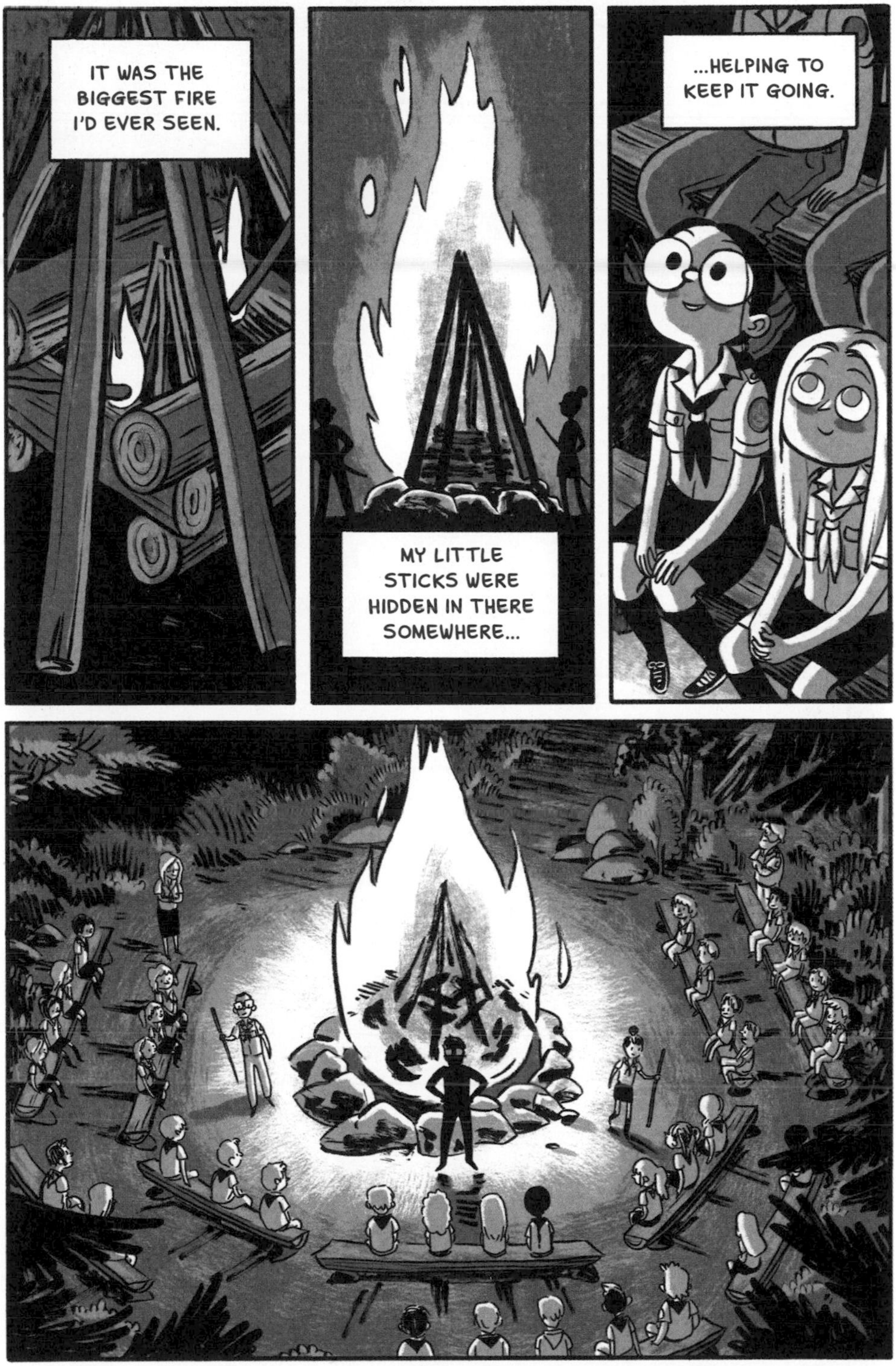
IT WAS THE BIGGEST FIRE I'D EVER SEEN.
MY LITTLE STICKS WERE HIDDEN IN THERE SOMEWHERE...
...HELPING TO KEEP IT GOING.

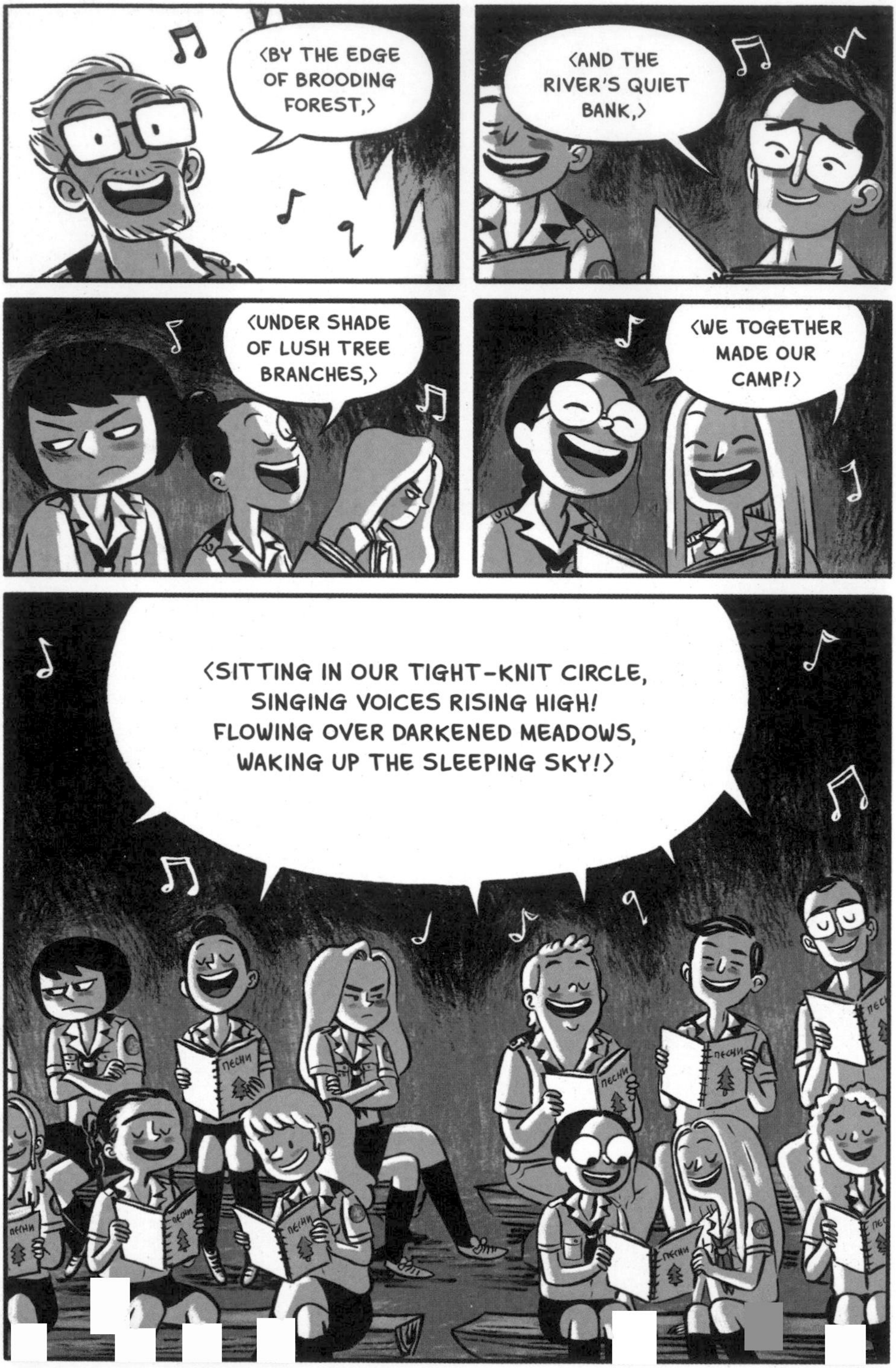

<BY THE EDGE OF BROODING FOREST,>
<AND THE RIVER'S QUIET BANK,>
<UNDER SHADE OF LUSH TREE BRANCHES,>
<WE TOGETHER MADE OUR CAMP!>
<SITTING IN OUR TIGHT-KNIT CIRCLE,
SINGING VOICES RISING HIGH!
FLOWING OVER DARKENED MEADOWS,
WAKING UP THE SLEEPING SKY!>
ПЕСНИ

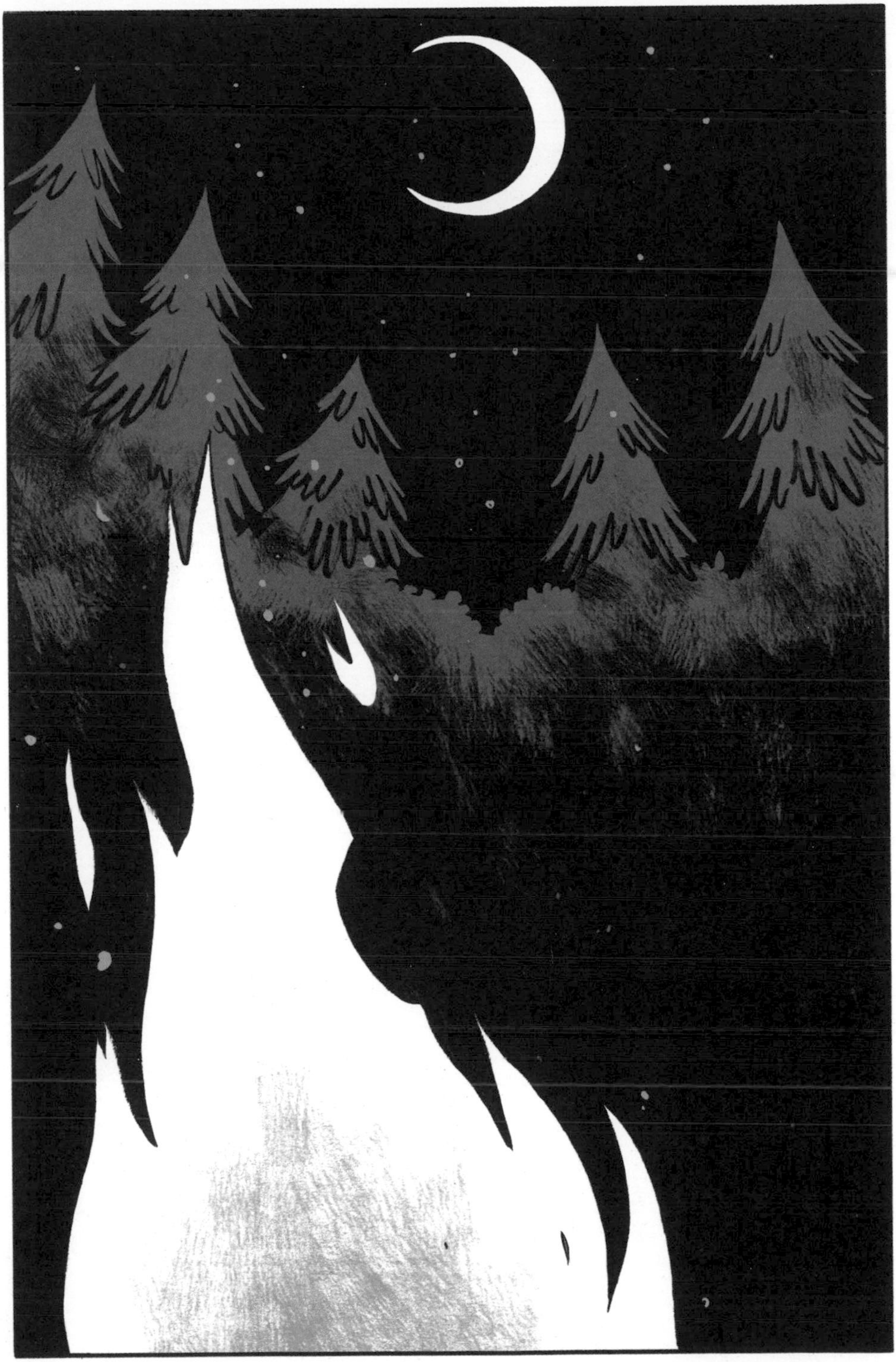

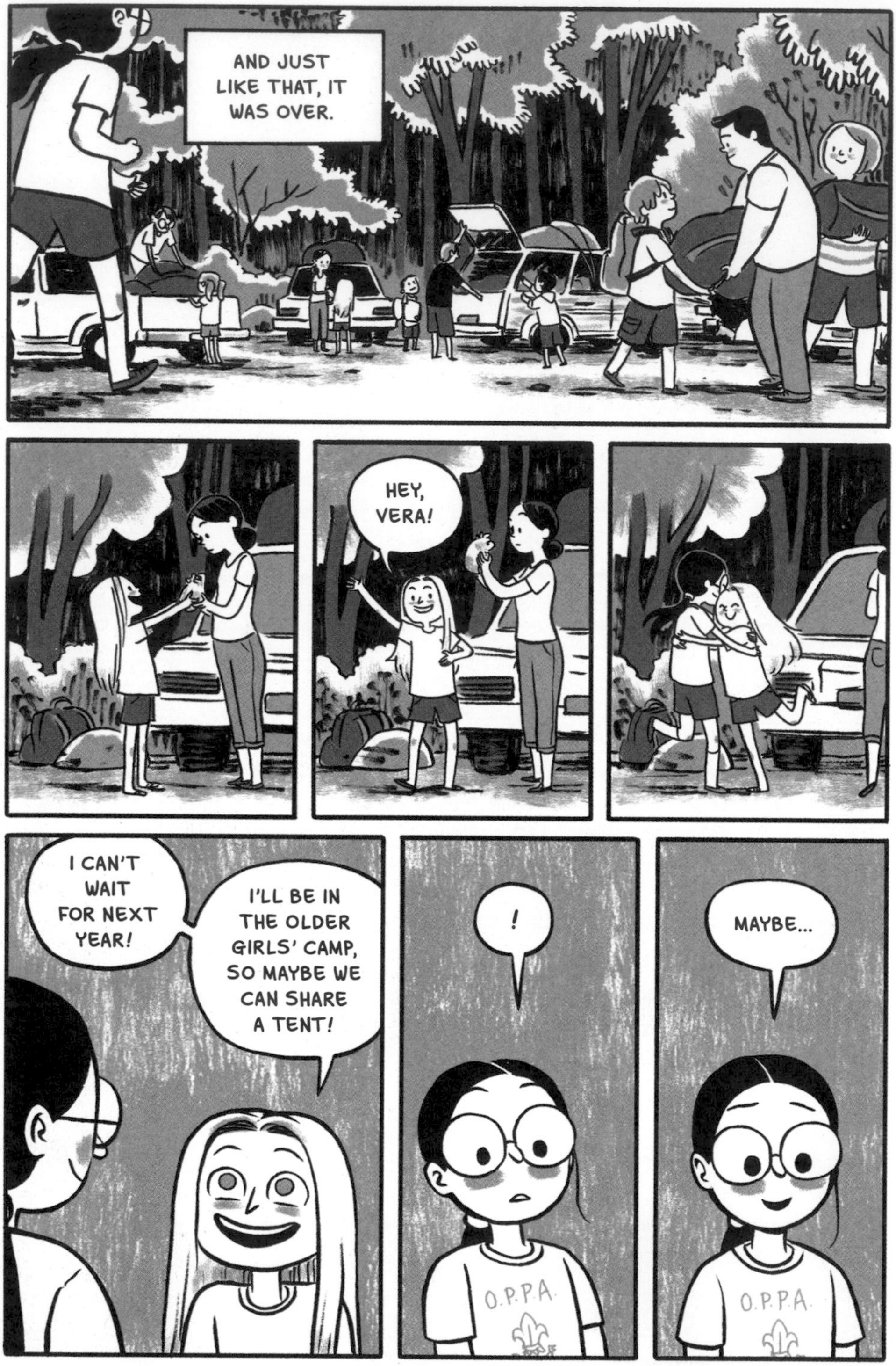
AND JUST LIKE THAT, IT WAS OVER.
HEY, VERA!
I CAN'T WAIT FOR NEXT YEAR!
I'LL BE IN THE OLDER GIRLS' CAMP, SO MAYBE WE CAN SHARE A TENT!
!
MAYBE...
O.P.P.A.
O.P.P.A.

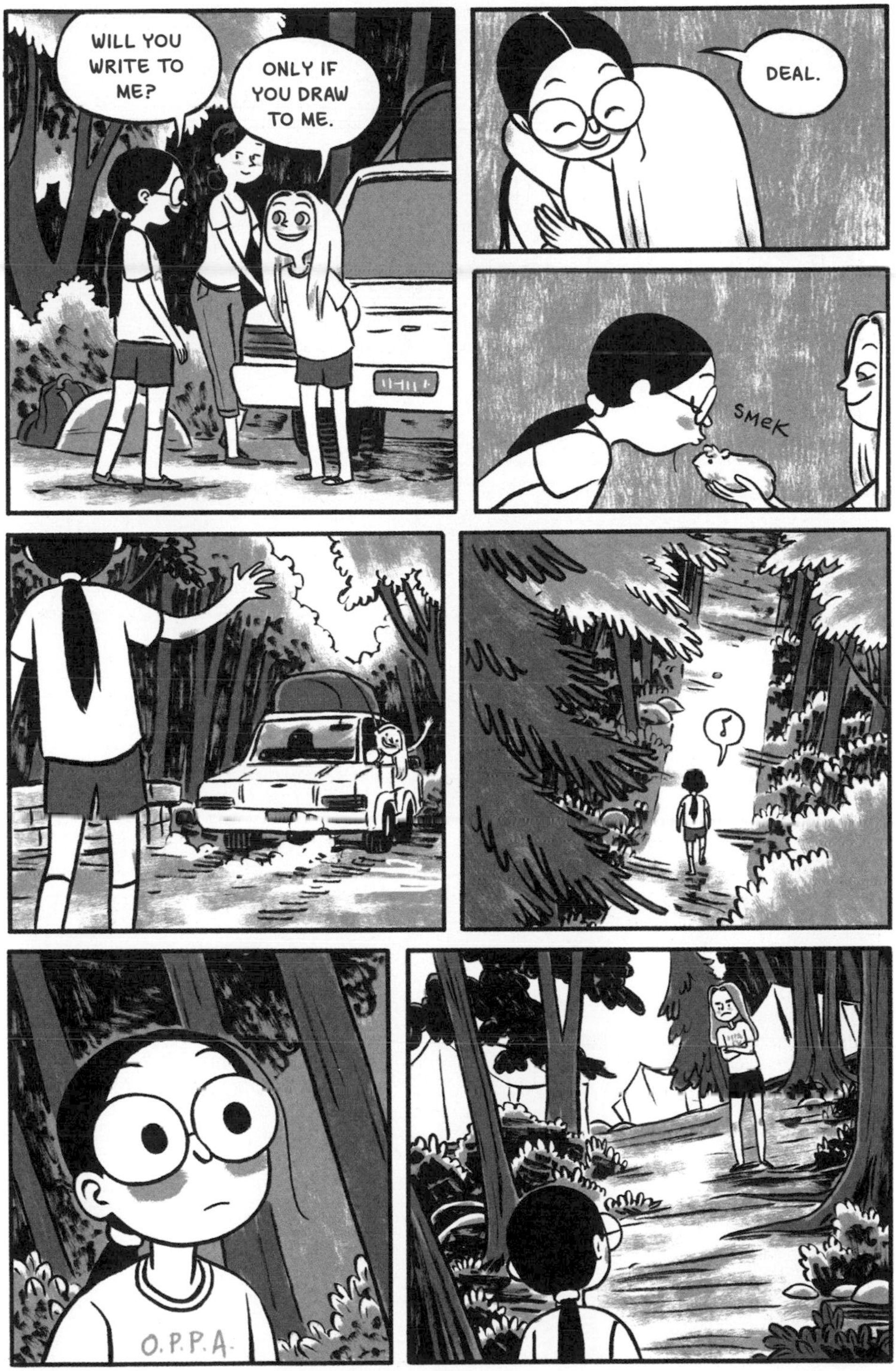
WILL YOU WRITE TO ME?
ONLY IF YOU DRAW TO ME.
DEAL.
SMEK
O.P.P.A.

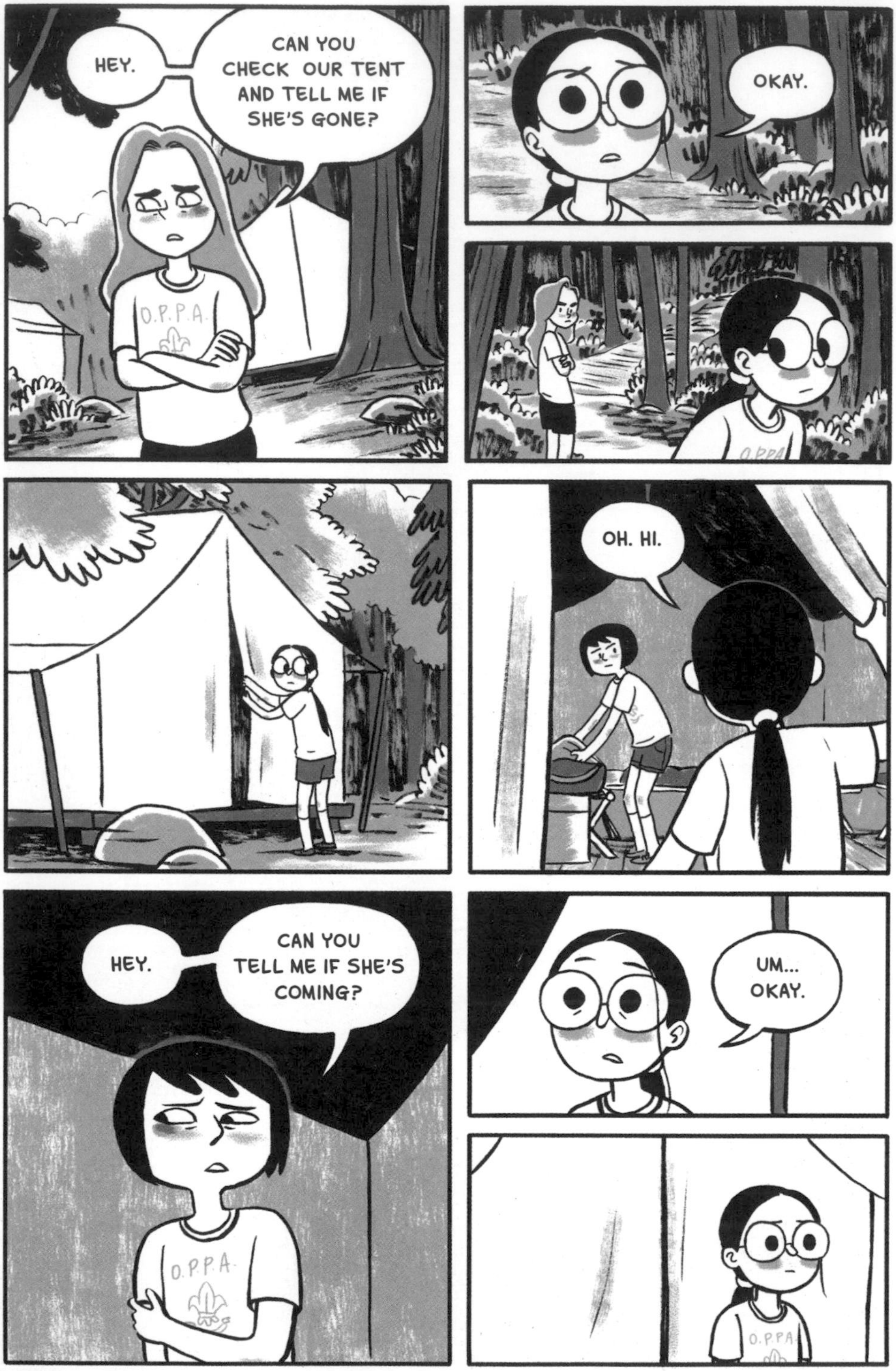
HEY.
CAN YOU CHECK OUR TENT AND TELL ME IF SHE'S GONE?
OKAY.
OH. HI.
HEY.
CAN YOU TELL ME IF SHE'S COMING?
UM... OKAY.
O.P.P.A.

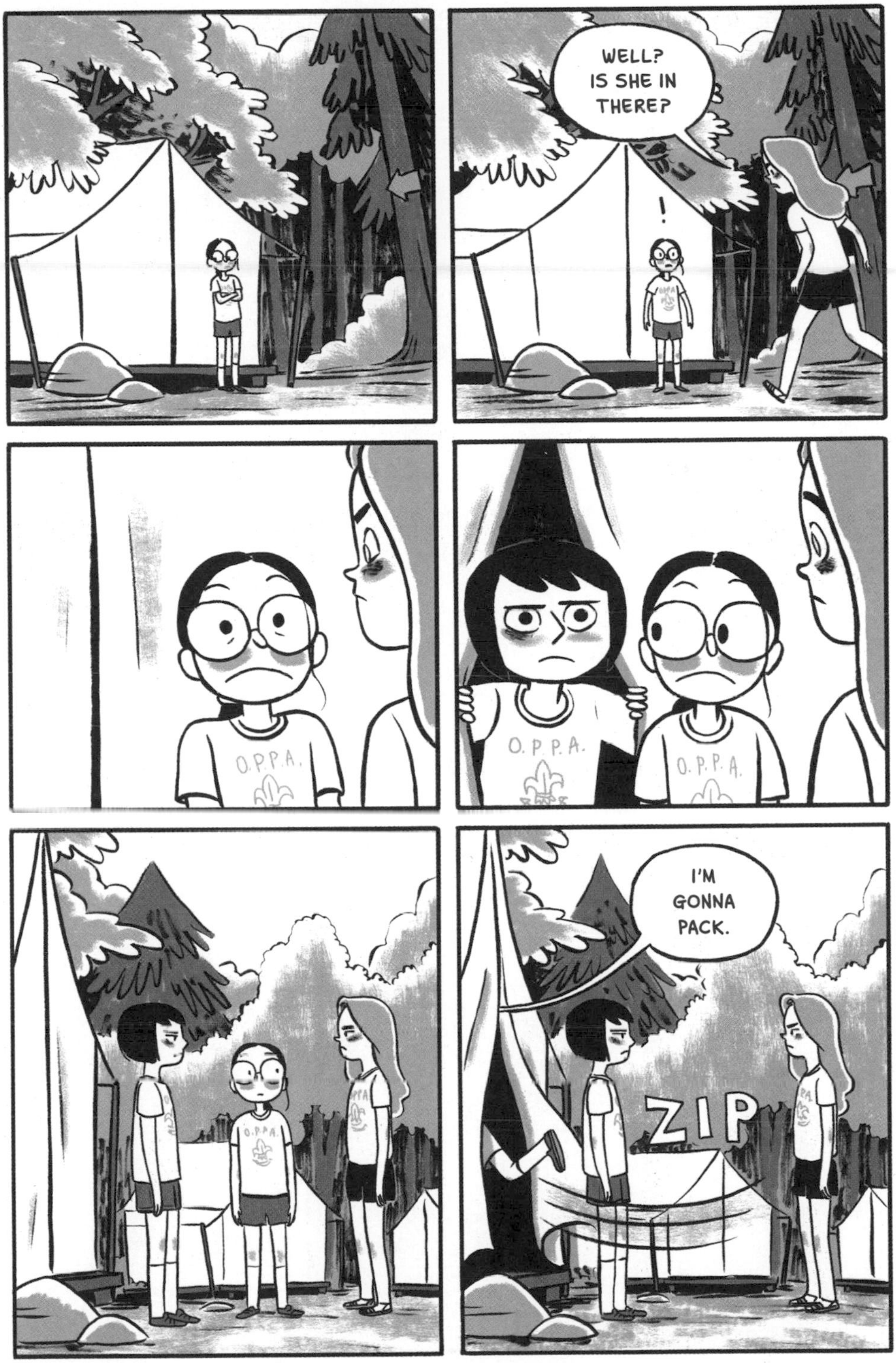
WELL? IS SHE IN THERE?
!
O.P.P.A.
O.P.P.A.
O.P.P.A.
O.P.P.A.
I'M GONNA PACK.
ZIP

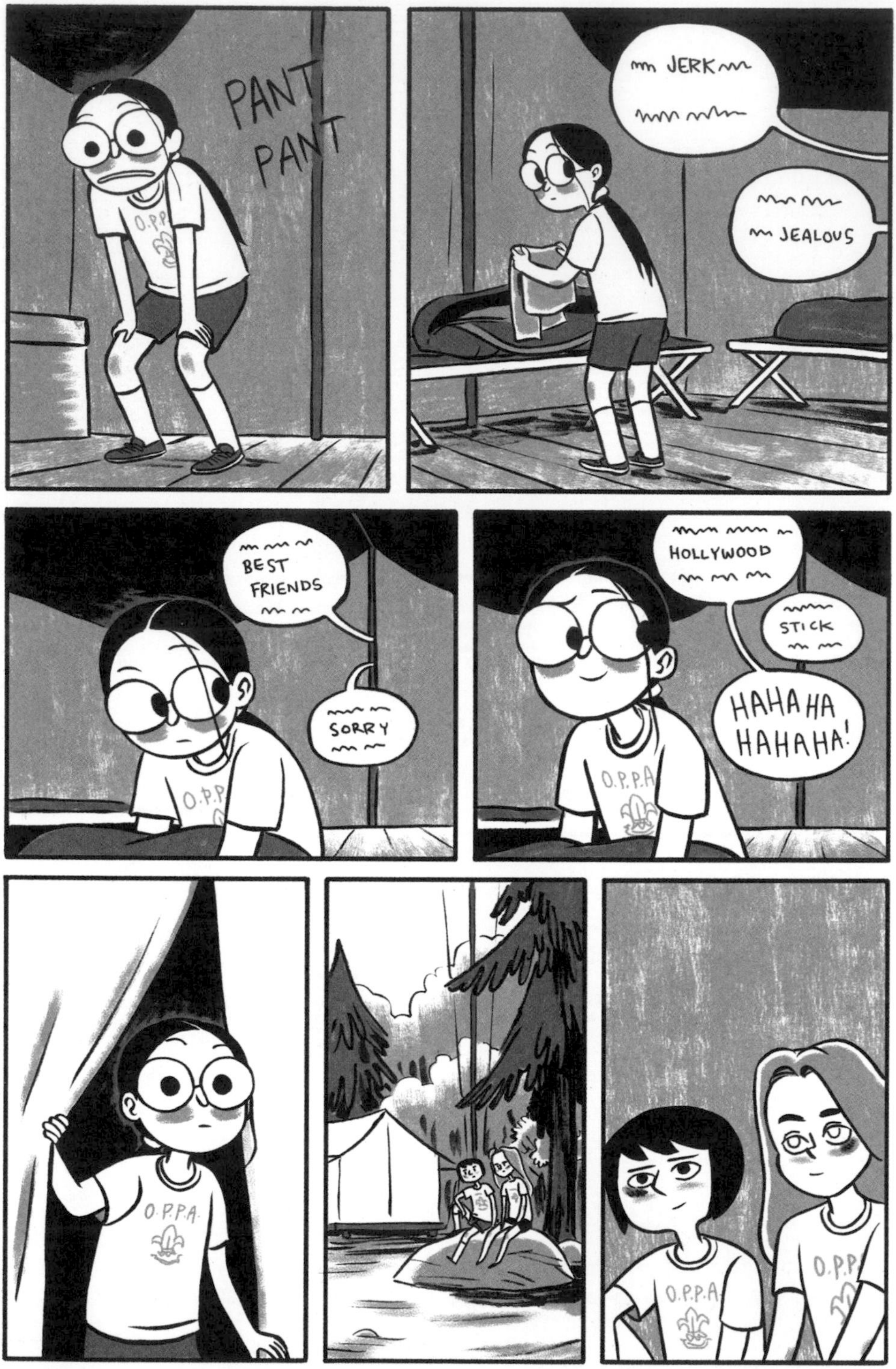
PANT
PANT
JERK
JEALOUS
BEST FRIENDS
SORRY
HOLLYWOOD
STICK
HAHAHA HAHAHA!
O.P.P.A.

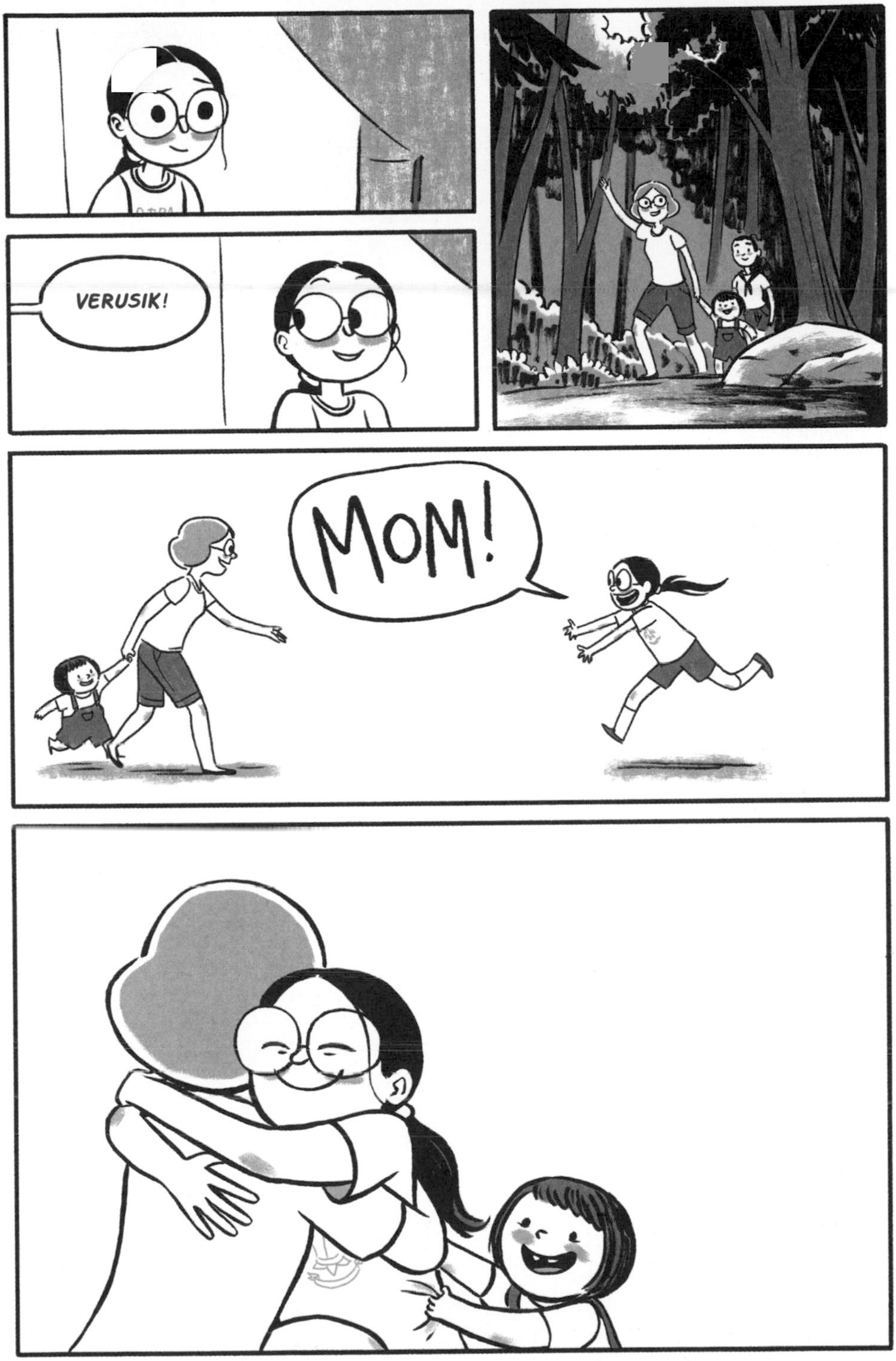
VERUSIK!
MOM!

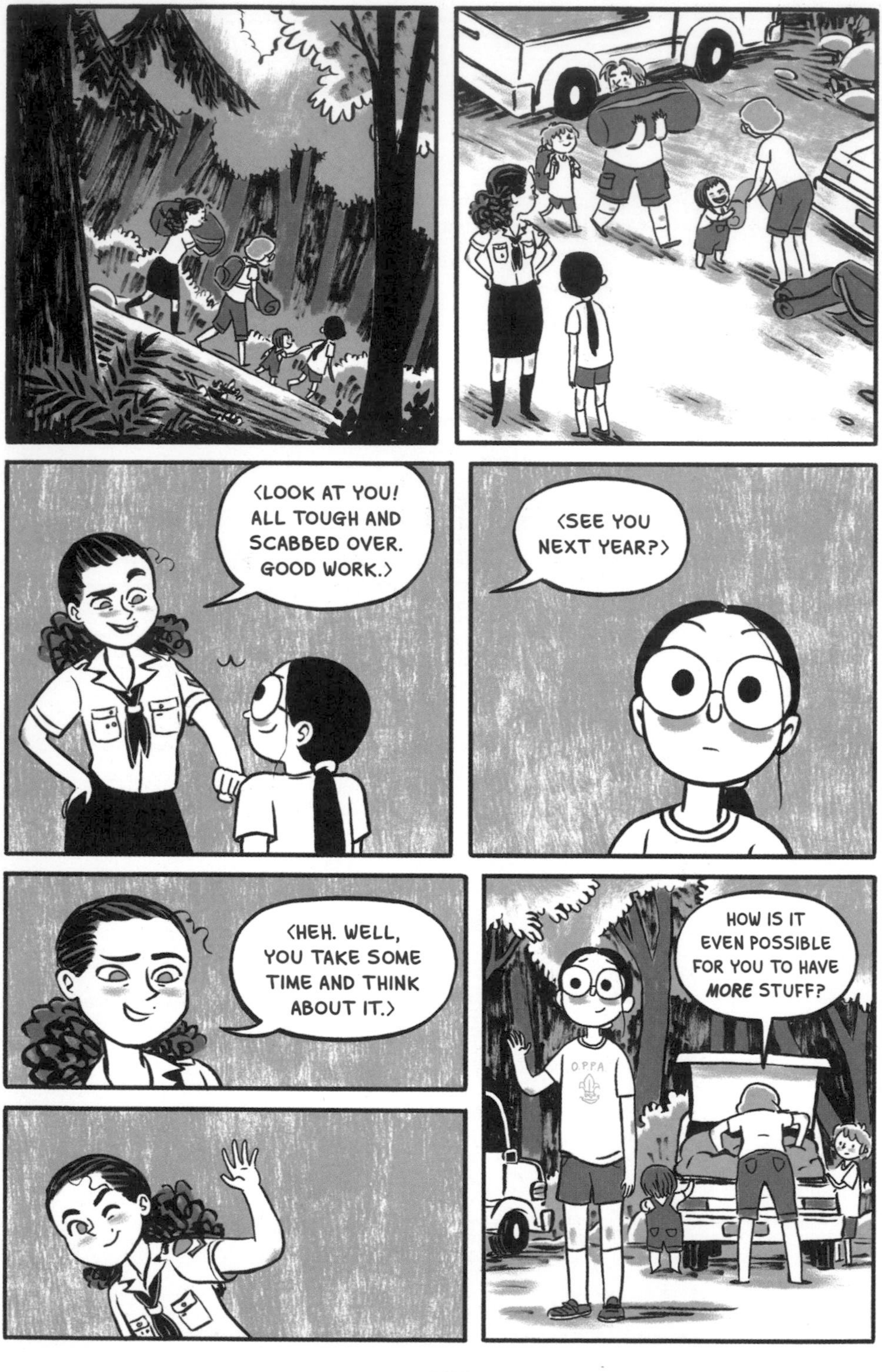

⟨LOOK AT YOU! ALL TOUGH AND SCABBED OVER. GOOD WORK.⟩
⟨SEE YOU NEXT YEAR?⟩
⟨HEH. WELL, YOU TAKE SOME TIME AND THINK ABOUT IT.⟩
HOW IS IT EVEN POSSIBLE FOR YOU TO HAVE *MORE* STUFF?
O.P.P.A

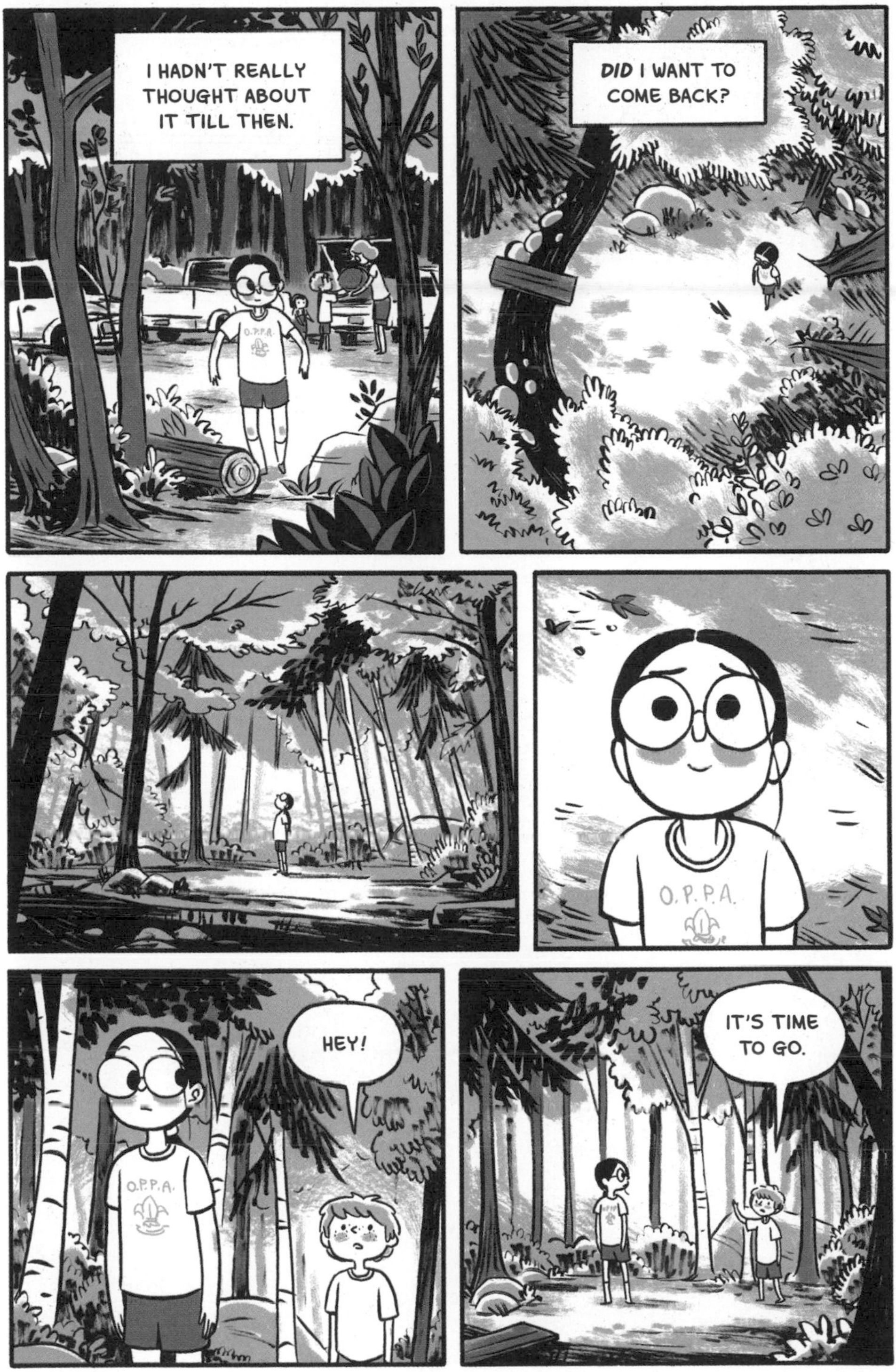
I HADN'T REALLY THOUGHT ABOUT IT TILL THEN.
DID I WANT TO COME BACK?
O.P.P.A.
HEY!
IT'S TIME TO GO.

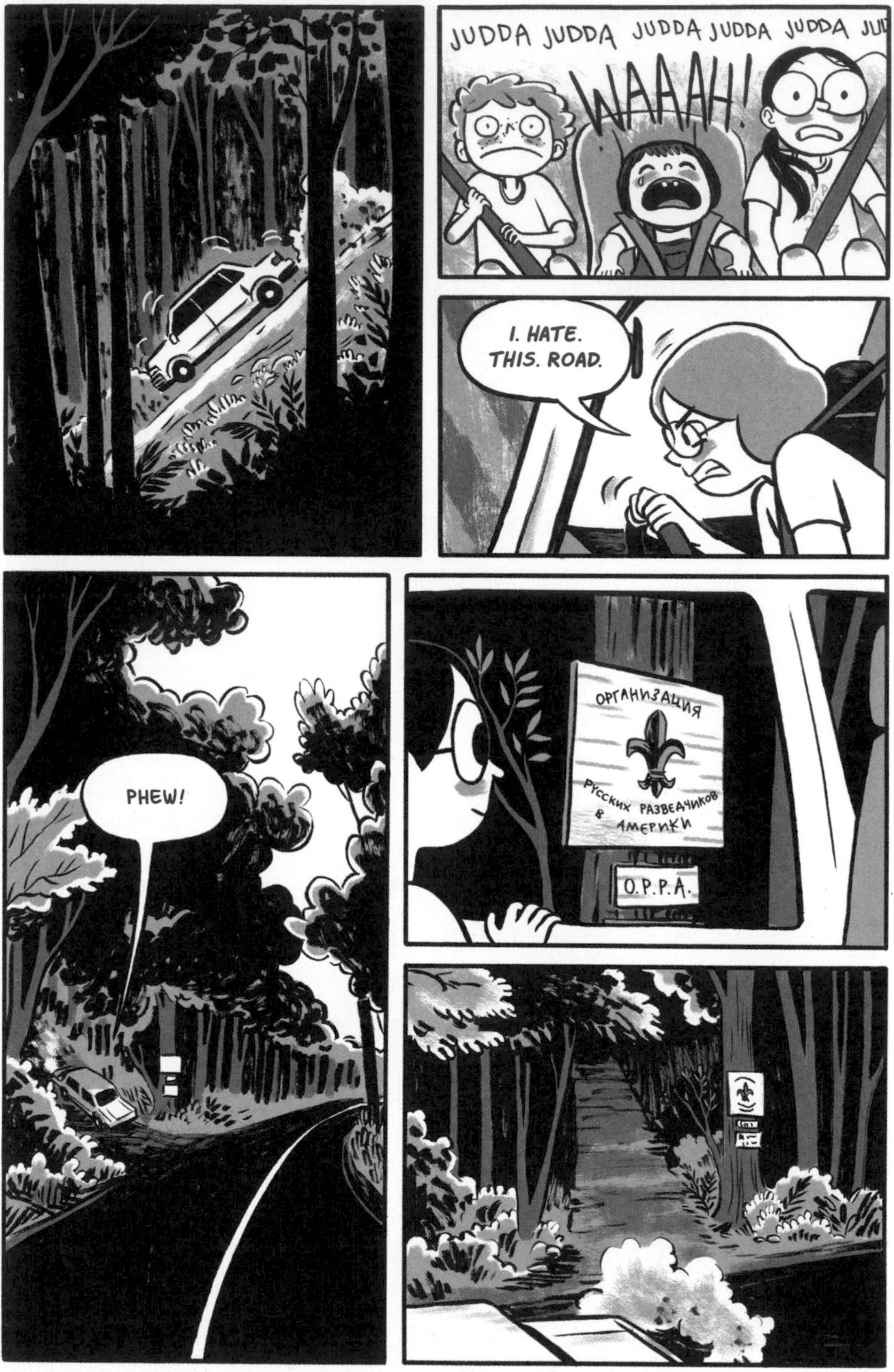
JUDDA JUDDA JUDDA JUDDA JUDDA
WAAAH!
I. HATE. THIS. ROAD.
PHEW!
ОРГАНИЗАЦИЯ
РУССКИХ РАЗВЕДЧИКОВ В АМЕРИКИ
О.Р.Р.А.

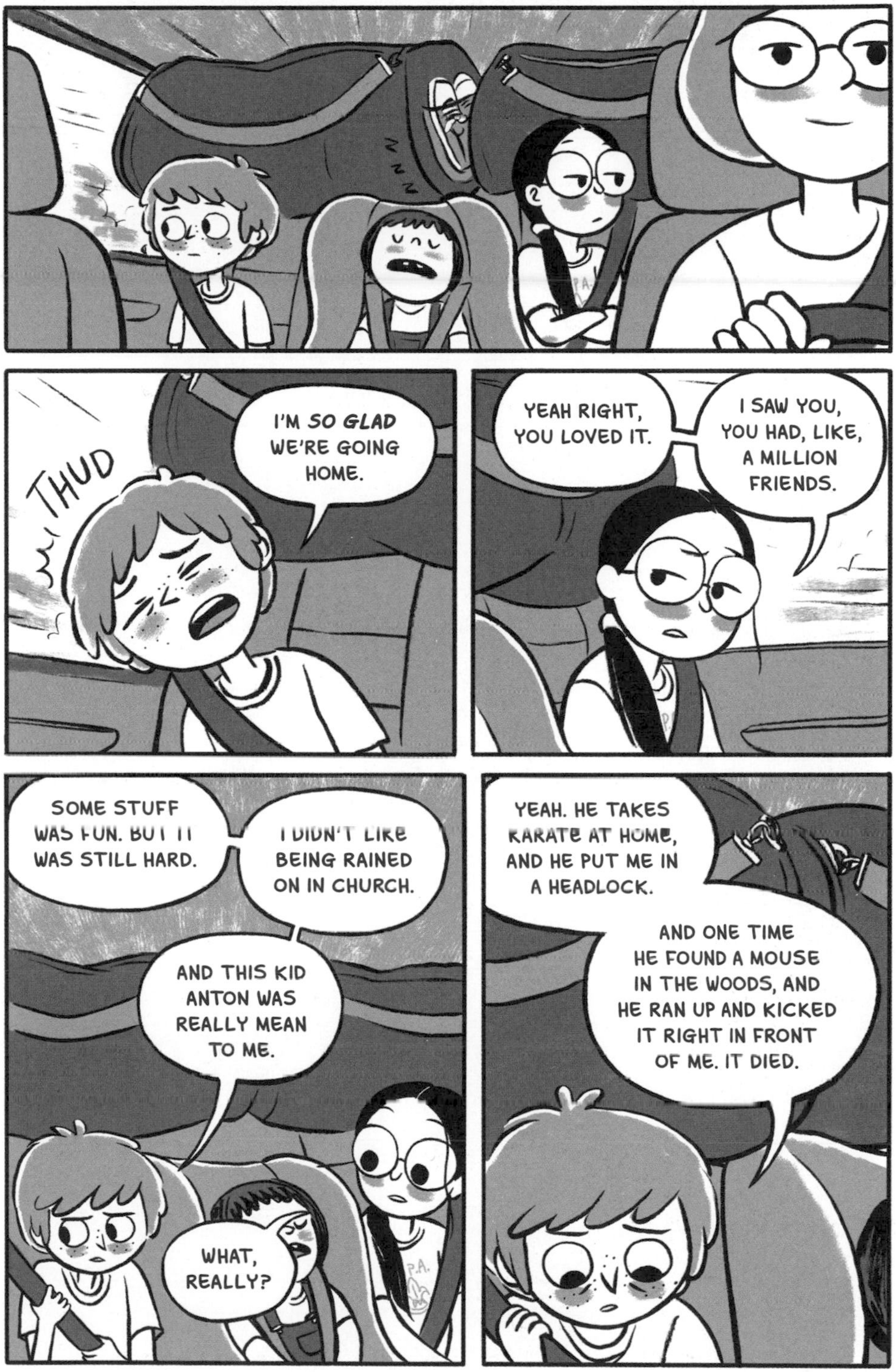
THUD
I'M SO GLAD WE'RE GOING HOME.
YEAH RIGHT, YOU LOVED IT.
I SAW YOU, YOU HAD, LIKE, A MILLION FRIENDS.
SOME STUFF WAS FUN. BUT IT WAS STILL HARD.
I DIDN'T LIKE BEING RAINED ON IN CHURCH.
AND THIS KID ANTON WAS REALLY MEAN TO ME.
WHAT, REALLY?
YEAH. HE TAKES KARATE AT HOME, AND HE PUT ME IN A HEADLOCK.
AND ONE TIME HE FOUND A MOUSE IN THE WOODS, AND HE RAN UP AND KICKED IT RIGHT IN FRONT OF ME. IT DIED.

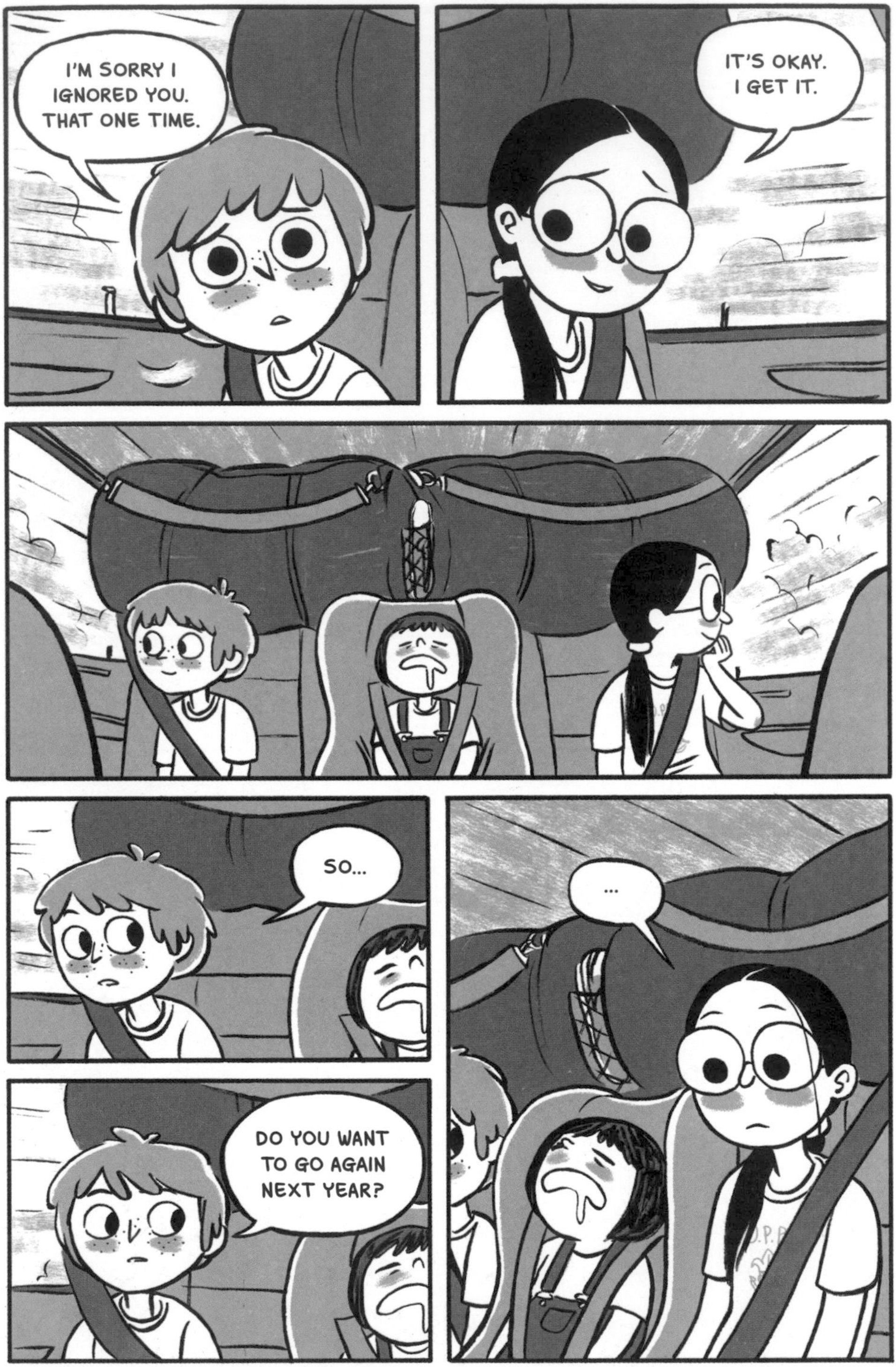

I'M SORRY I IGNORED YOU. THAT ONE TIME.
IT'S OKAY. I GET IT.
SO...
DO YOU WANT TO GO AGAIN NEXT YEAR?
...

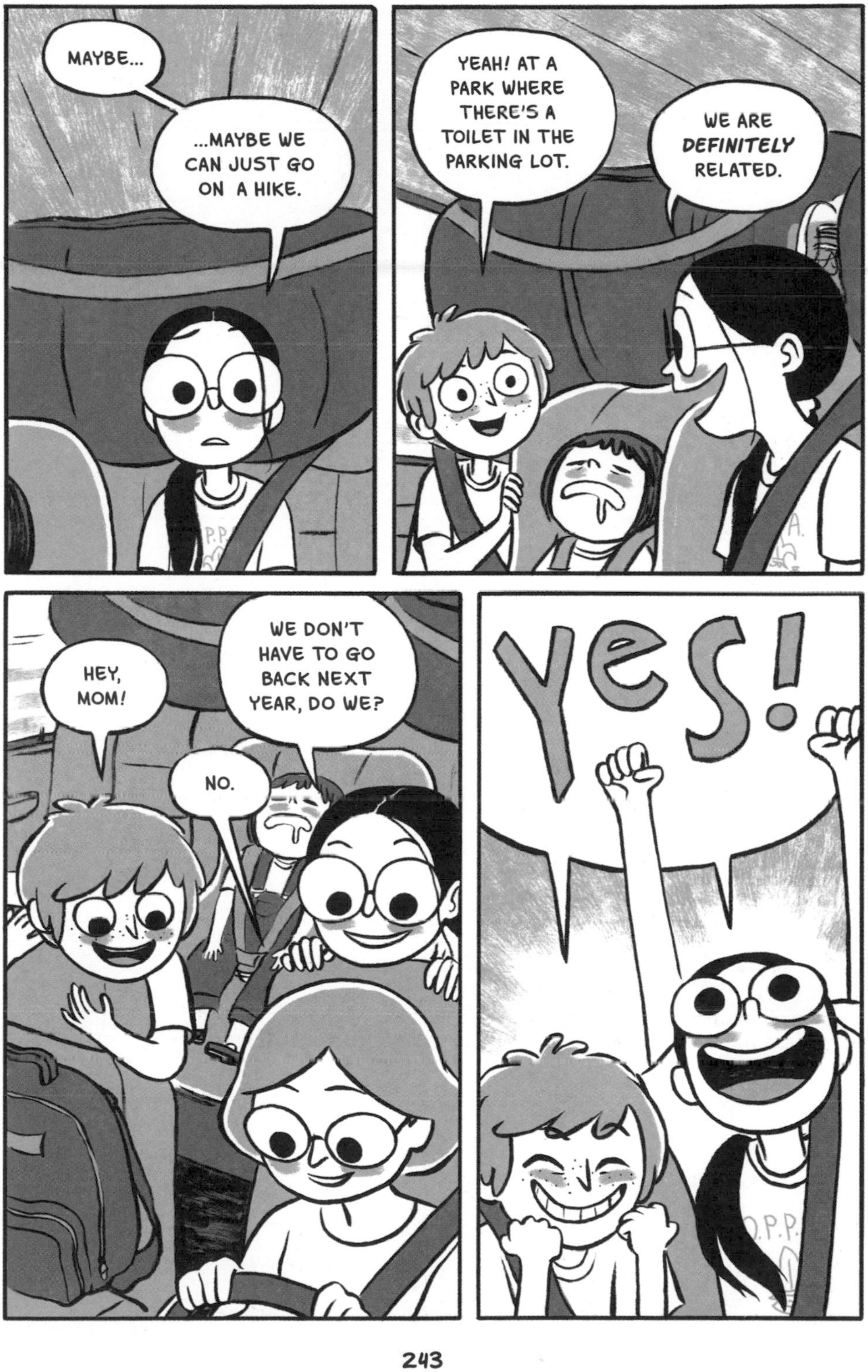
MAYBE...
...MAYBE WE CAN JUST GO ON A HIKE.
YEAH! AT A PARK WHERE THERE'S A TOILET IN THE PARKING LOT.
WE ARE DEFINITELY RELATED.
HEY, MOM!
WE DON'T HAVE TO GO BACK NEXT YEAR, DO WE?
NO.
YES!

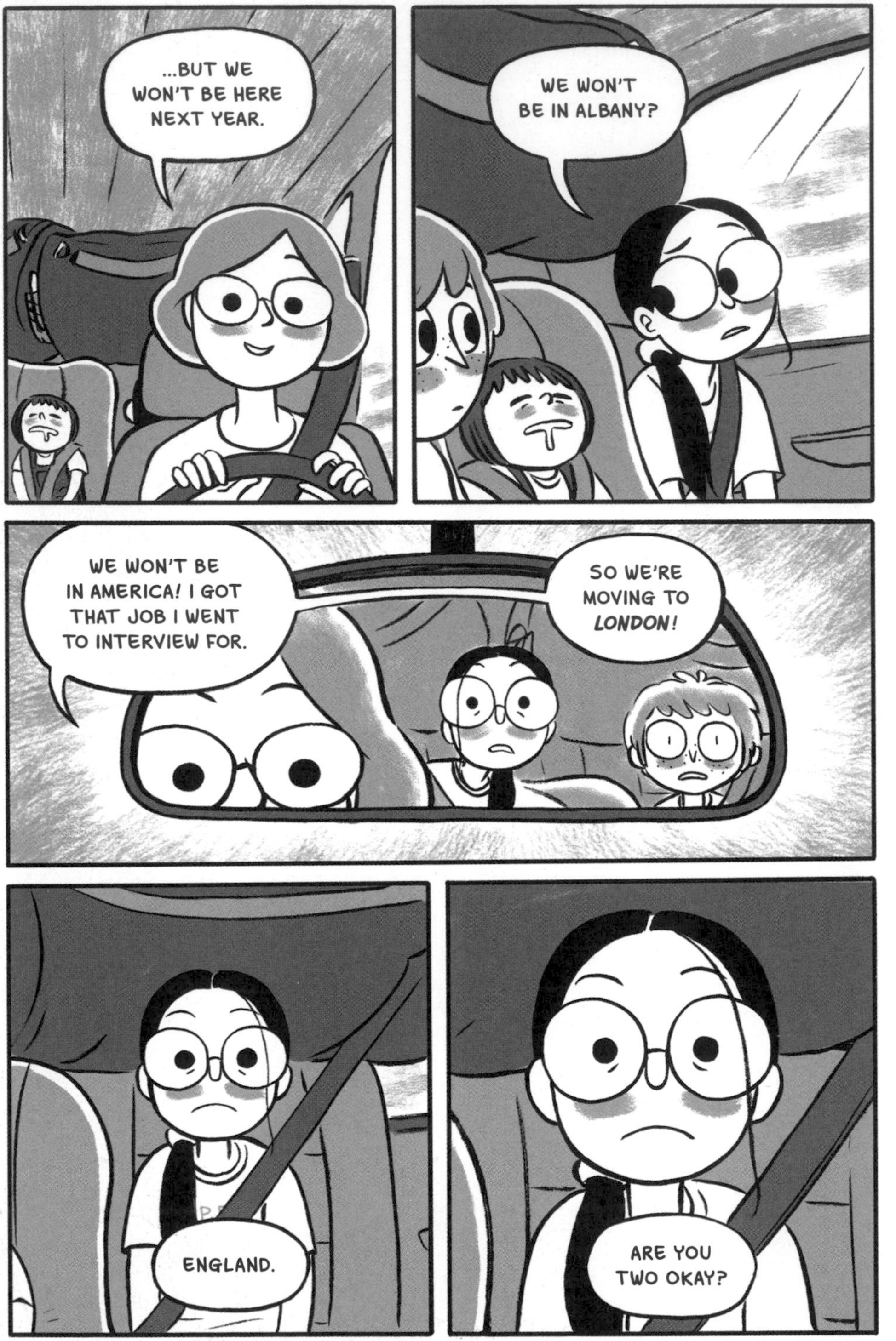
...BUT WE WON'T BE HERE NEXT YEAR.
WE WON'T BE IN ALBANY?
WE WON'T BE IN AMERICA! I GOT THAT JOB I WENT TO INTERVIEW FOR.
SO WE'RE MOVING TO *LONDON*!
ENGLAND.
ARE YOU TWO OKAY?

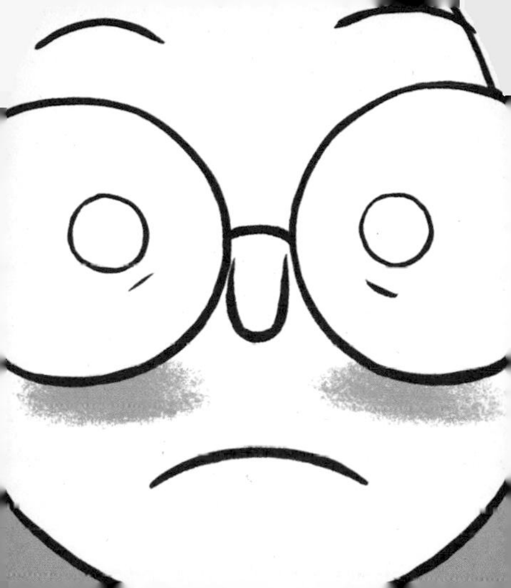

ПРИМЕЧАНИЯ АВТОРА*

*author's note

This book is a true story. And also made up.

Even if you could remember everything that happened during one month over twenty years ago, chances are it wouldn't make the best story. Days go by where nothing interesting happens. Then too much happens, but to the wrong people. Characters don't get their just desserts. It would be a bad book.

I actually spent two summers at camp (urgh), but consolidated the experience into one very eventful one. I wrote down all my memories in a big list, then grilled my siblings for THEIR memories. My mom dug up old letters and photos. I also interviewed Natasha, a former counselor who has been at camp much more recently than me. I even went to the camp myself, sneaking in during an open house to sketch and take photos. It was exactly as I remembered it, though they had added a door to the Hollywood and the campers were no longer washing their hair in the lake. (Thanks, Clean Water Act.)

I arranged those memories into what felt like a good story, changing names and locations to protect people's privacy and making up new characters. I really did have that awful sleepover party, and get bitten by a chipmunk. I didn't have an awesome counselor like Natasha, but I did have a great friend like Kira. I really did go off alone and hear a moose, but I never laid eyes on it. Gregor lost his boot in a mudhole, but I don't think he ever got justice. Books can be nicer than life sometimes.

Though some details changed a bit for dramatic purposes, the feelings are 100 percent true. I set out to write about a hard, lonely summer I had when I was a kid. It always took me a long time to make friends, and being dropped into a strange environment with older kids and giant horseflies didn't play to my strengths. Plenty of people love summer camp and look forward to it every year. Hooray for them, but I was not one of those people. I know I'm not alone in that experience, and this book will hopefully make some kids feel less alone, too.

Or you can just laugh at what a weenie I was.

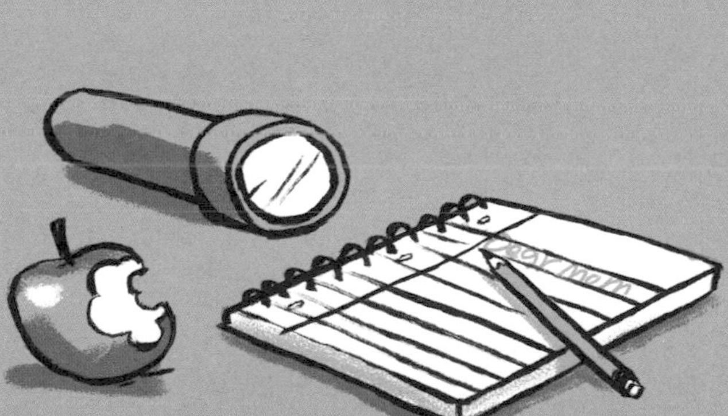
Dear mom

Dear Mom,

Hi. Camp is OK, but I really want to go home. For the first time, I hate camp. All the people here are mean to me. Everyone has candy and they eat it in front of me. It is so hard to make a call because there is a line. There is <u>no</u> running water in the whole camp, I swear. I cry almost every night. The people here are snobby and call me names. Last night at the КОСТЁР a girl called me the F-word because I stumbled in Russian, but had no accent or anything. When I told her I couldn't help it, she called me a liar. I almost cried in front of 45 people. I held it in? But at an overnight in the woods, I burst. I do it at night. We just had a fire drill. It sucked. I got a cramp...

had for dinner was 2 spoo...

and cheese with garlic in it...

a crappy camp game...

wake you up in the middle...

and go to the boy's camp. Th...

me up at 11:30 last night, ...

of sleep, and made me stand...

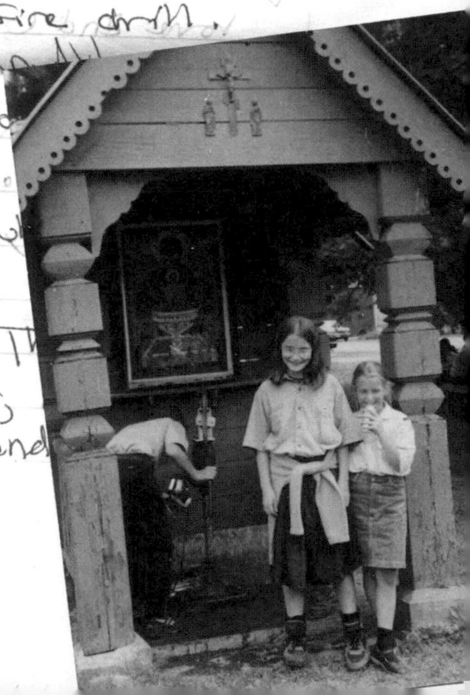

THIS IS AN ACTUAL LETTER I WROTE TO MY MOM FROM CAMP. THE ONE AT THE VERY BEGINNING OF THE BOOK WAS WRITTEN BY MY BROTHER, WHO IT TURNED OUT WASN'T ENJOYING HIMSELF AS MUCH AS I THOUGHT.

of camp without a flashlight. I didn't
have enough batteries. The people
here are nasty. I'm allmost crying right now.
I did something terrible, too. I played
a "joke", but I got into so much trouble.
Can you please stop those darn installments?
I really want to go home. I lost the
automatic pencil, but I have one friend. She
oil paints and draws too! Her name is KMPA.
She's nice. Everyone here is mean. They
have junk food and eat it without sharing.
So, if I don't go home early, can you bring
me a big bag of Skittles and one of Starbursts M&M'S?
pleeez? I know you probably won't but
at least take me home. I hate it here.
Say hi to Masha. I send her my 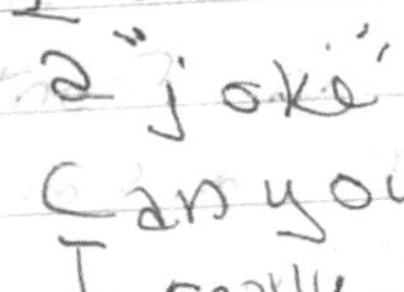
love and Geoffrey and his family, too.

Love,
(And homesick &crying)
Vera

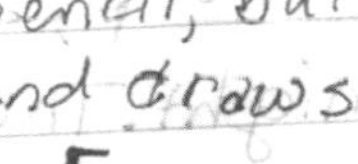

P.S. My stomach
hurts every night. It does right now, too.

СЛОВО БЛАГОДАРНОСТИ*

*words of thanks

Thanks to Mark Siegel and Judy Hansen for their wisdom, enthusiasm, and ferocious cheerleading. The invaluable eyes of the Story Trust made the book better each time they read it—thanks to Gene Luen Yang, Sam Bosma, Shelli Paroline, and Braden Lamb. Natasha Peavy was instrumental in helping refresh my memory of what camp was like twenty-two years ago, and even sent me photos of her uniform.

Alec Longstreth knocked it out of the park with his coloring, and I will owe him forever. The team at First Second put the book together with their customary aplomb.

Thanks to excellent buds Raina Telgemeier, Graham Annable, Tony Stacchi, Julian Nariño, and Brian Ormiston for their eyeballs, and to the gang on S.T. for their commiseration. Jeremy Spake loved this project from day one and wouldn't let me get down on it even for a second. Extra-special thanks to my family—Lyudmila, Philipp, and Masha—for merging their patchy recollections with mine and being such good sports. We all survived to tell the tale.

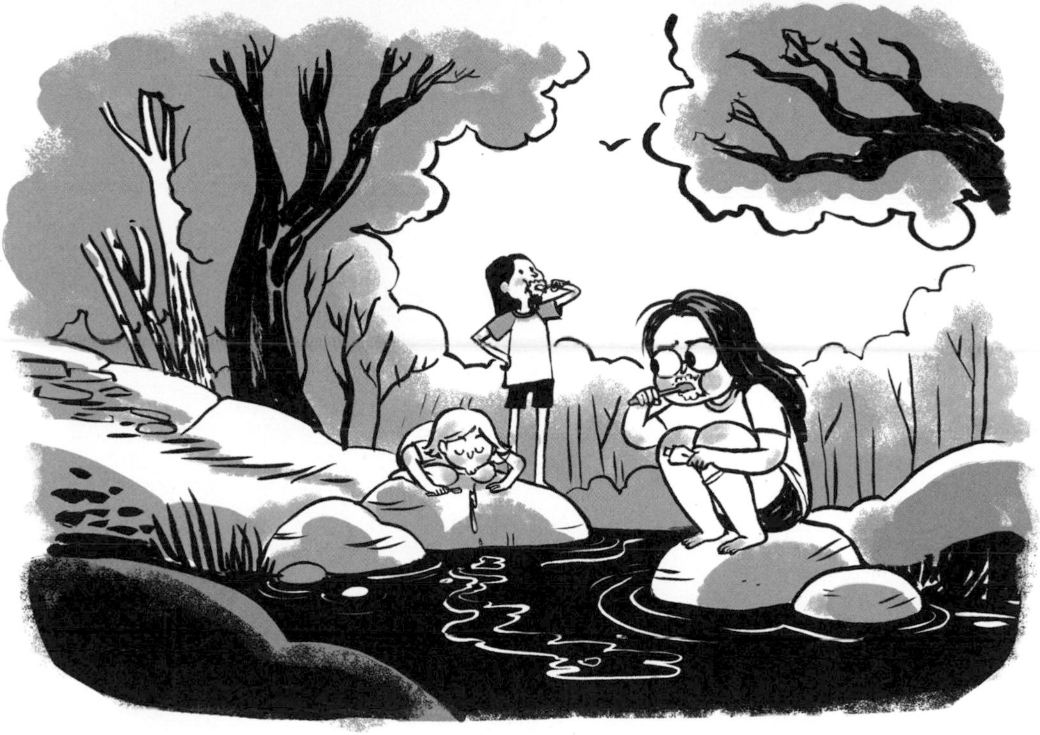

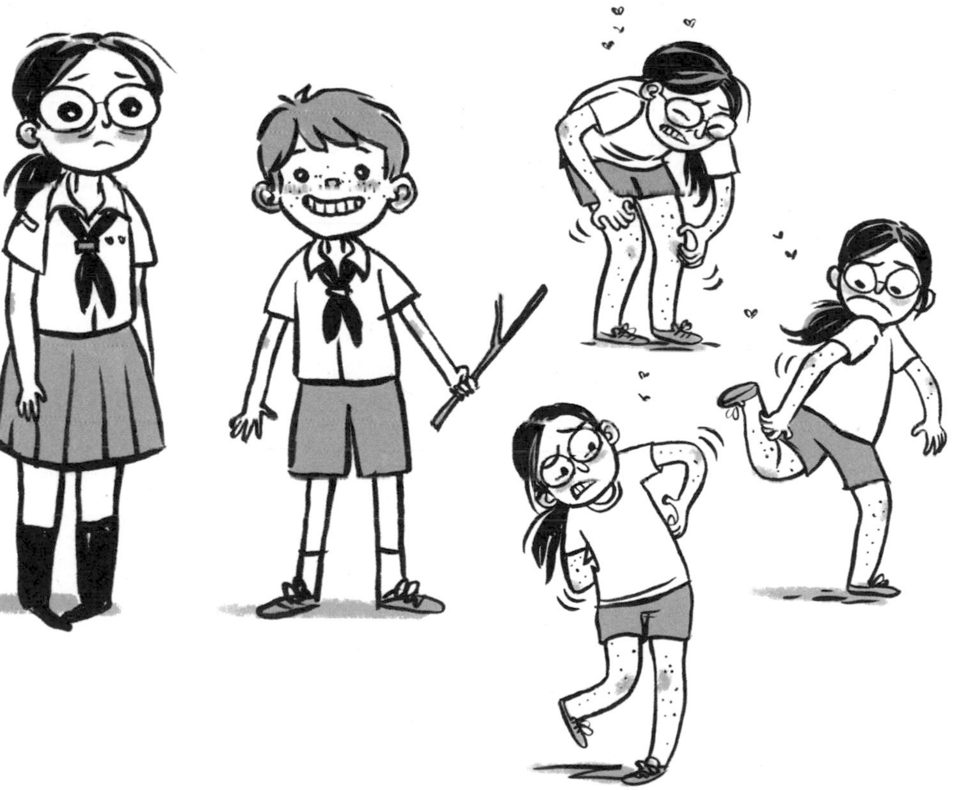

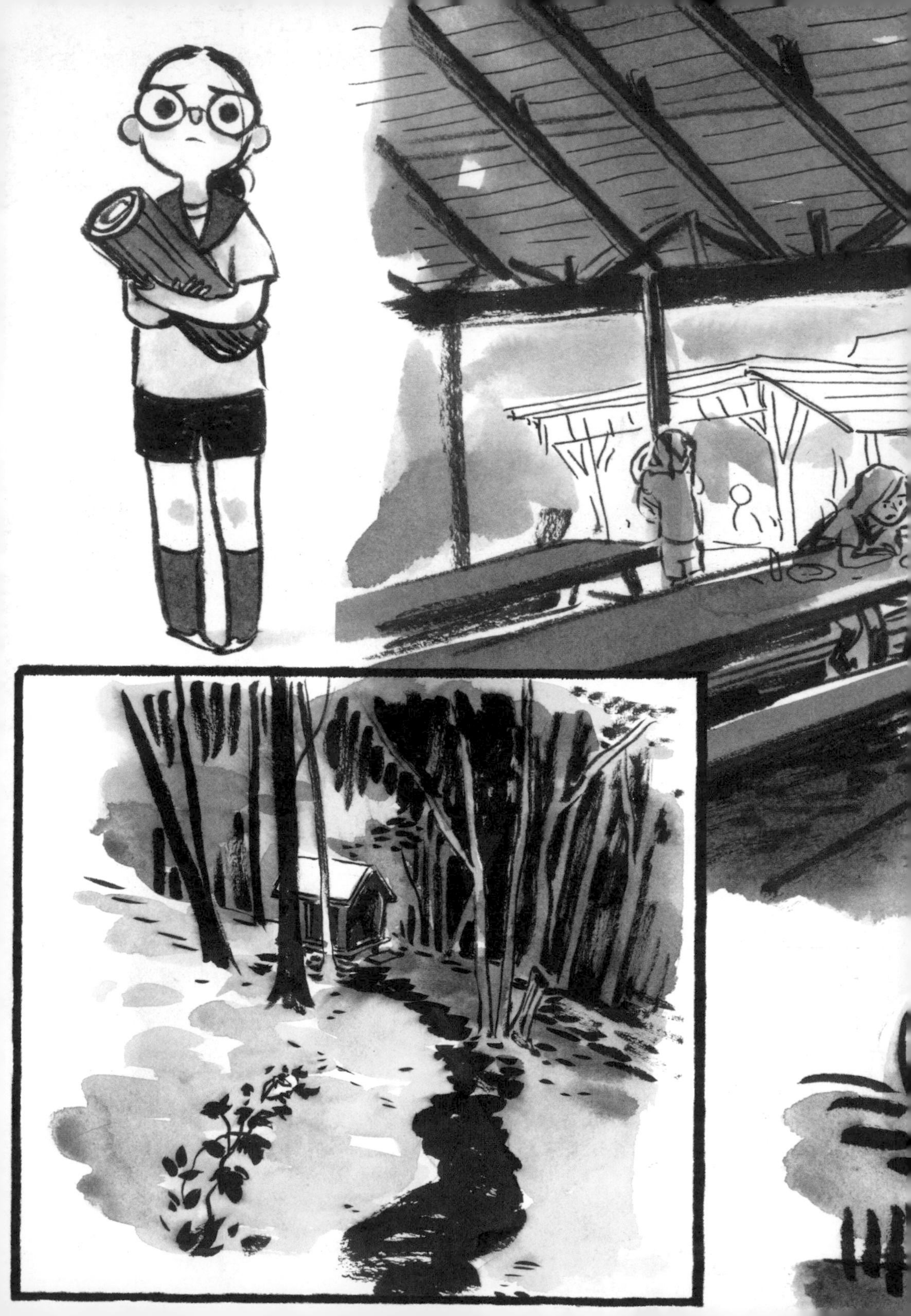

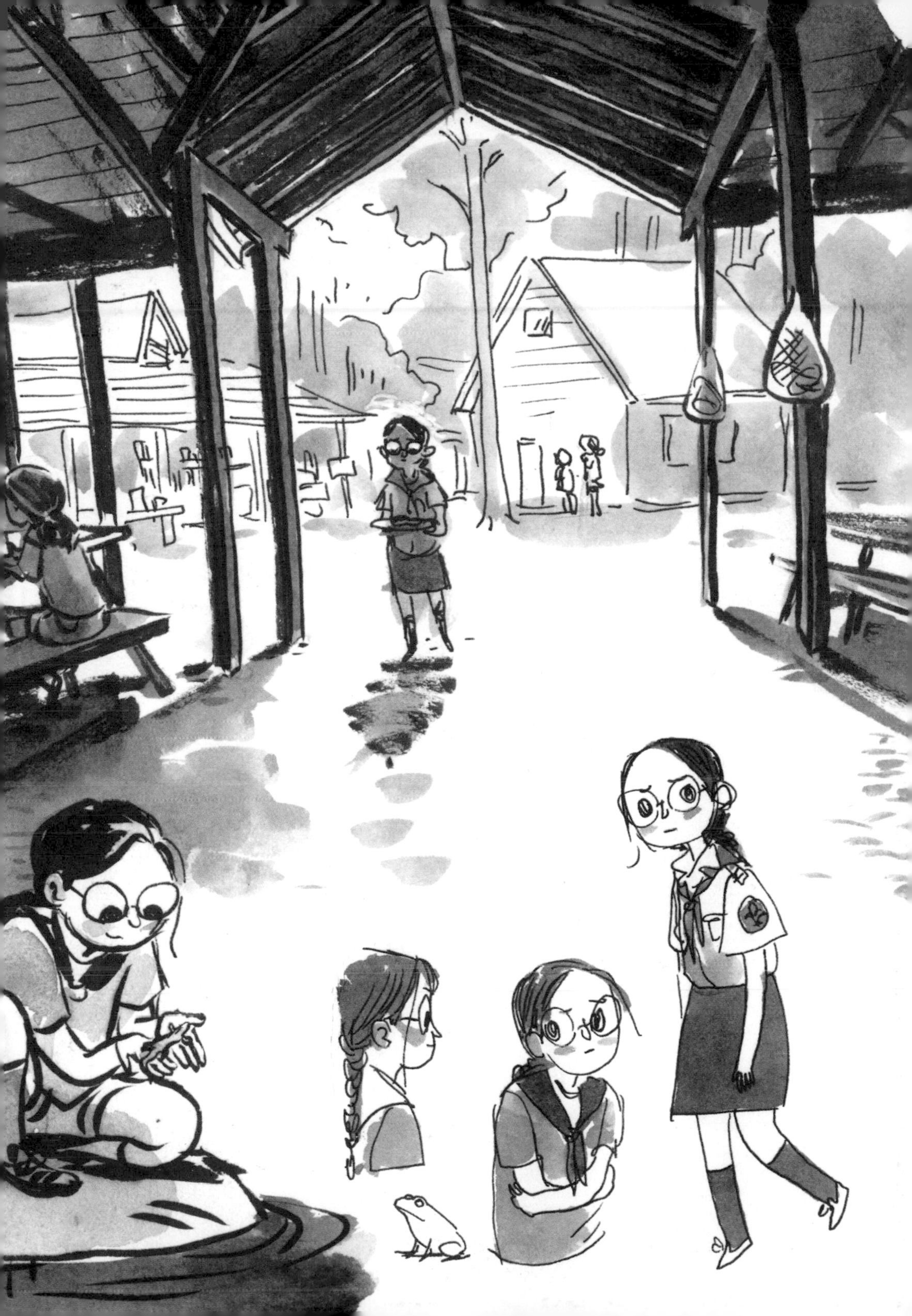

:01 First Second

PUBLISHED BY FIRST SECOND
FIRST SECOND IS AN IMPRINT OF ROARING BROOK PRESS, A DIVISION
OF HOLTZBRINCK PUBLISHING HOLDINGS LIMITED PARTNERSHIP
175 FIFTH AVENUE, NEW YORK, NY 10010

LIBRARY OF CONGRESS CONTROL NUMBER: 2017946145

HARDCOVER ISBN: 978-1-62672-444-0
PAPERBACK ISBN: 978-1-62672-445-7

OUR BOOKS MAY BE PURCHASED IN BULK FOR PROMOTIONAL, EDUCATIONAL, OR BUSINESS USE. PLEASE CONTACT YOUR LOCAL BOOKSELLER OR THE MACMILLAN CORPORATE AND PREMIUM SALES DEPARTMENT AT (800) 221-7945 EXT. 5442 OR BY E-MAIL AT MACMILLANSPECIALMARKETS@MACMILLAN.COM.

FIRST EDITION

FIRST EDITION, 2018
BOOK DESIGN BY DANIELLE CECCOLINI AND ROB STEEN
COLORS BY ALEC LONGSTRETH

PRINTED IN CHINA BY 1010 PRINTING INTERNATIONAL LIMITED, NORTH POINT, HONG KONG

PENCILLED DIGITALLY IN CLIP STUDIO PAINT. INKED WITH A BRUSH-PEN ON BRISTOL BOARD AND COLORED DIGITALLY IN PHOTOSHOP.

PAPERBACK: 7 9 10 8
HARDBACK: 3 5 7 9 10 8 6 4 2

BY ART WE LIVE

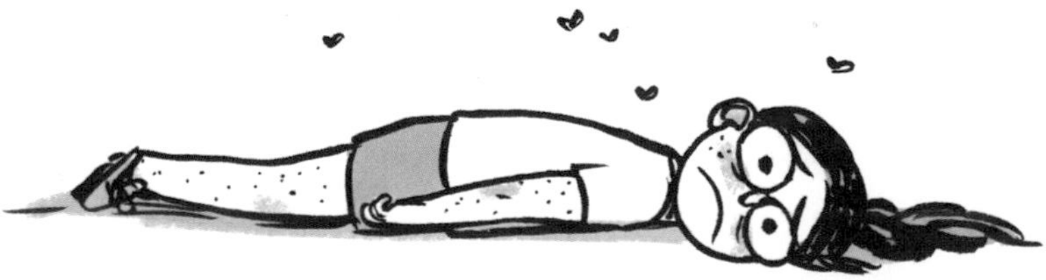